INNOCENTS OF OPPRESSION

DEAF OR NOT, YOU ARE NOT ALONE

Nick Sturley

Action Deafness Books
The Peepul Centre
Leicester LE4 6DP
Email: adbooks@actiondeafnessbooks.co.uk
Website: www.actiondeafnessbooks.co.uk

Published by Action Deafness Books 2012

Cover designed by Euan Carter www.euancarter.com

Original front cover photograph by Velychko

ISBN 978 0 9570822 67

British Library Cataloguing-in-Publication Data. A catalogue record for this book is available from the British Library.

Printed in the UK by Henry Ling, Dorchester, Dorset

About the Author

Nick Sturley was born in Basingstoke, Hants in 1967, but spent much of his childhood in Cornwall. He went to Burwood Park School and College in Surrey before returning to the South West to study Art & Design at Plymouth College of Art.

He moved up to Newcastle to undertake training in film and television production before setting up a short–lived production company in early 1992, Deaf Owl, with four other Deaf graduates from the course. After completing a successful four–year Usher in the Deaf Community Project with British Deaf Association and Sense, he moved to London as the Multimedia Information Officer for the BDA until 1999.

In 2003, he wrote his first award–winning novel, MILAN. He also wrote an ebook series for Deaf children, wrote articles for Deaf magazines and online blogs. He wrote scripts and directed two short comedy films for British Sign Language Broadcasting Trust's BSL Zone, which were broadcast on television, the internet and shown at many film festivals around the world.

Innocents of Oppression is his second major novel.

He is Deaf, uses BSL, and has Usher, which is a visual condition. He currently lives in Surrey.

Photograph by iantreherne.co.uk

Contents

For our innocent children who have suffered and/ or died from many years of oppression; banned from using their own sign language.

For my mother, Sue, with love.

PART I
BEGINNINGS

1

Death Remembers

"Signs are to eyes what words are to ears."
– KEN GLICKMAN; Deaf Proverbs.

The wheels of a black Mercedes bumped over the moss at the side of the road.

Switching off the engine, Chris Matthaus opened the driver's door and stepped out, gazing at something up ahead. He breathed in the pleasant late morning air with the autumn sun breaking through scattered clouds.

Chris walked over to a rotting wooden fence which was near his hire car and stopped by it. He saw something lying in the tall grass behind the fence, a large wooden board or something that he couldn't see at first because it was partly concealed by the grass. He leaned slightly over the fence to have a better look, his small paunch touching the top of the fence, and saw that it was a wooden sign. The large piece of wood no longer had its varnished gleam; it had suffered a good few years of neglect, rotted by rain, bird droppings and fungal mould. Either it had been vandalised, or the two supporting wooden stilts had given away due to decay or strong wind, he thought.

The wooden sign had a green and gold coloured crest with an image of a white stag with short antlers. The animal stood to the right, with its right front leg raised at an angle, as if it was walking proudly. A black outline around the animal made it stand out against the brown oak background, despite the faded colours.

Below the crest were the remains of large, rough words, painted in gold with a black outline: WELCOME TO EWING HILL PARK SCHOOL AND COLLEGE.

Chris felt a moment of sadness towards the dilapidated sign and wondered why they hadn't taken it when the school closed down. He straightened up and gazed over to his right at what he had come to see. After walking down a long, winding rough tarmac driveway for a minute or so, he stopped midway to take a better, closer, look, although he was still some distance away.

In front of a vast, unkempt field, there stood an imposingly large and empty three–storey Georgian mansion with dark brown walls. The centre of the building had three wide stone steps that led up to double front doors, with a window in the top half of each. A white painted stone porch rested above these steps, supported by a white stone pillar on either side.

On either side of the entrance were four huge double framed windows, decorated by crisscrossed black lines. Chris thought he could see a few broken glass sections in some of the windows, but couldn't be sure from this distance.

His gaze then shifted from the ground floor to the next floor up, which had six similar, but smaller and narrower, windows across the front. The top floor had the same window formations as the first floor. He half smiled to himself, remembering what the rooms behind these windows used to be for. The roof jutted inwards on all sides, having various flat surfaces with black or dark grey slates. Several unused stacks of single and twin chimneys stood lifelessly around it.

In front of the building was a large patch of tarmac, which was occupied by several building contractors' vehicles, a cement mixer and three large skips. Chris could see scaffolding around the corner at the west side of the building. A few workmen wearing yellow hard hats walked over the tarmac, carrying their tools and materials to and fro through the entrance. One was having a smoke, chatting into a mobile in his other hand.

Chris' eyes wandered across the east of the building and saw a half demolished, high ceilinged building; some of its dark grey concrete and red bricks were still waiting to be knocked down by the steel wrecking ball that was hanging idly nearby. Amongst the rubble was another skip that was filled with red bricks, large broken up chunks of the flat grey slabs that used to be the roof, white splintered wooden window frames, shards of glass and wooden flooring planks. Another large skip stood by, filled with what Chris believed were some chairs, a few large decagon shaped tables, some old kitchen hardware, some bits from the counter and a few other things that he couldn't make out. He knew what the building used to be. He felt sure another big building – the gym – round the rear would follow suit, if it hadn't already done. They were pulling down anything that had nothing to do with the original design of the mansion.

Chris had been told that they were converting the building back to its original form: a proper eighteenth century mansion for a wealthy family. The school had closed down about three years before and had been empty for about two years, until a local property developer finally acquired it on the cheap after a long legal wrangle over the ownership. It was then sold to a wealthy family; Chris didn't know who; for a reasonable profit, on top of being contracted to do the renovation work.

Chris then looked to the left, across the huge overgrown field that was in front of the building and the tarmacked area. He remembered that it used to be the playing fields, big enough to accommodate two or three football pitches, a cricket pitch and an impromptu athletics track.

He looked around at the array of oak, chestnut and yew trees surrounding the building and the field in front of it. Not much had changed in those trees after so many years; Chris tried to remember. He turned to the Mercedes behind him, which was parked just by the entrance of the winding driveway. The straight, mile–long private road that Chris had just driven down had clusters of different types of trees on either side. It stretched from an entrance point through the private park to the other end, and was used as a shortcut. The end of the private road met, through an open wooden gate, the main road, which led to the nearest town, Waltbridge, about a mile and a half away.

Chris returned to his car and tapped on his car remote, locking the vehicle. He then walked up the road for another two hundred yards, passing the mansion behind some trees on his left. Scanning the surroundings, Chris remembered and appreciated the beauty of the small and secluded park that surrounded him, which mainly consisted of forestry, some clearings, a lake, a few ponds and the road he was walking along. There were no other buildings apart from the mansion and the one that he was going to see. It was virtually an island; the main roads surrounded it in a kind of a pentagon, with the private road slitting through the middle.

He turned left, into a small footpath that was enclosed by a tunnel of trees, and strolled down it, soon coming upon a tiny, derelict one bedroomed cottage, surrounded by trees, in a small clearing. The rear of the mansion was almost visible in the distance, appearing through the trees behind the house. Chris could now clearly see that the gym building that used to be at the rear was nothing but rubble, consisting of several mountainous piles of debris. There was also other debris around the back, seemingly from smaller buildings or extensions that he did not recognise; he presumed they were later additions.

The dark brown bricks of the cottage were covered with old moss and ivy. It had small windows that were dirty from many years of neglect; some were broken; the dark wooden front door was shut, and the roof had some holes and several slates missing. The garden around it was overgrown with weeds, fallen branches, twigs and dead autumn leaves. The cottage had an enchanted feeling about it as he walked around to the back and came upon the biggest of the small windows that overlooked the main garden and the mansion beyond. He leaned forward, his eyes squinting through the dusty glass to try to see inside, but because of the dirt on both sides, he could only manage to see the empty floor–to–ceiling wooden shelves around the walls. He leaned back and sighed wearily, feeling momentarily sad about the whole thing: the memory of this little house that he had been inside one fateful Friday afternoon, as a fifteen–year old boy, had stayed with him for the last thirty–two years.

Chris returned to his car. He took one last look at his old school before pulling his loose black tie tightly into his white shirt collar and checking his black suit to be sure that he was looking decent. He smoothed down his crew cut; dark with some grey strands. Then stared at the knuckles of his right hand for a long moment: they had several small dried–blood cuts that were still healing. Tucking his hand into his inside suit pocket, took out his iPhone, clicked on the circular button and checked the time: 11:58. Two hours to go before the service, he mused, so there was plenty of time to pay a visit to someone special first.

Chris arrived at the large wooden doors under the arched stone porch at the base of the curved turret fronting the sixteenth century double–spired church. A small wooden sign on one side of the archway welcomed him to St. Peter's Church of England, Waltbridge.

He knew he was a bit late for the service, as it was now after two o'clock. The visit had flown by. He paused, briefly feeling a sense of trepidation about going in. Grasping the large metal knob, he slowly pushed one of the doors slightly ajar, creating a small gap just wide enough for him to squeeze through.

The sombrely lit nave was completely packed; figures clad in black filled the rows of pews. Chris glanced around the vast surroundings, not really taking in the interior stone architecture; it was already familiar to him. He looked for somewhere to sit amongst the congregation who were watching the proceedings at the front. He looked up ahead and saw that a female vicar, wearing a black cassock and an ornate white surplice, was ascending the short flight of steps towards a pulpit on the left side of the platform. A man in a black suit was already standing waiting beside the pulpit. In the centre, beside the man, a coffin stood on a decorative stone slab, adorned by wreaths. A huge decorative arched window boasted an image of Christ, arms outstretched. It had hundreds of tiny coloured glass panels, nestled together by lead frames. The sun barely shone through the coloured panes, adding to the interior's slight bleakness, though the bearded figure on the window seemed to radiate warmly.

The vicar spoke to the congregation, welcoming them: 'Good afternoon, ladies and gentlemen. We are gathered here to remember Donald Thomas Langston …'

The man standing by the pulpit began to move his hands in time with the vicar's spoken words. Because Chris was a considerable distance away at the back, he could only just manage to follow what the man, who he thought must be in his late forties like himself, was signing.

'He was born on the fifteenth of June 1927,' the vicar continued, 'and leaves his wife, Frances, his two sons, Damien and Marcus, and a daughter, Shaleen. He also leaves five grandchildren …'

Standing in the aisle between the centre and the left sections of pews, Chris searched for a seat; he soon found a small gap in the second row from the back of the centre section, to his right. There was barely enough room for him to sit down, but it would have to do. He discreetly squeezed himself in, asking the man who was sitting next to him to move up a bit. The man grumbled and begrudgingly moved a little to his right to make room for Chris to sit; it was a tight squeeze between the man and the end of the pew. Chris looked ahead, craning his neck a bit to watch the man – the sign language interpreter – as he continued to convey the spoken proceedings into British Sign Language.

'As you all know, Donald Langston was the second headmaster of Ewing Hill Park School, working there for seventeen years, from September 1975 until he retired in 1992 …'

Chris watched, but his mind began to drift away.

'Let us pray,' the female vicar said. 'Could everyone please stand?'

Everyone stood obediently; Chris too. As the vicar began the prayers, Chris closed his eyes, shutting out the interpretation.

Not because he did not want to pray.

He wanted to remember.

2

The Arrival

"What matters deafness of the ear when the mind hears? The true deafness, the incurable deafness, is deafness of the mind."
– VICTOR HUGO, 1845

Sunday, September 12, 1977.
'Aaron, we're here!'

The excited voice echoed around in the interior of the Austin Maxi. Geraldine had just turned her head round to look at the seat behind her; her huge, orange triangular earrings swaying, complementing the thick flow of feathered blond hair that ran down to her shoulders.

She tapped her index finger at the left end of her lips to make her announcement; as though she wanted to make sure she was making herself understood by having her lips properly read.

Aaron perked up in the back seat, having just seen his mother talking. He looked through the windscreen to see a long, straight road with clusters of trees passing them on either side. He could see a tiny brown building looming in the far distance between the trees and widened his eyes to register it.

'About bloody time!' a boy's voice echoed. Geraldine turned to the back seat again, dismayed. 'Jamie!'

Jamie, who was sitting next to his younger brother, folded his arms, taking some pleasure at his latest outburst. He rested his hands on the tape recorder and headsets that were resting on his lap, along with a batch of Elvis cassettes; he had been somewhat stroppy throughout the long drive along the M4 from the West of England. He turned to Aaron and reached out to pull a cord that was hanging from his right ear, forcing an earpiece to fall out of Aaron's ear. Aaron yelped and tried to catch the tumbling earpiece, but only managed to grab the cord.

'At least,' said Jamie, 'they'll make you hear and speak better by making you wear this in the evenings and at weekends, Bra Boy ...' He mockingly gestured the outline of a woman's bra. '. . . and improve your shit brain, butthead.'

'Jamie!' bellowed an annoyed male voice. Jamie turned to look at the back of the thick black hair that belonged to the driver, his eyes still on the road. 'Leave your brother alone. And don't swear.'

'Sorry, Dad,' Jamie smirked.

Aaron replaced his earmould. The cord was attached to one of two metallic boxes that were each slightly larger than a pack of playing cards. The other was for his left ear. The top of each acoustic had an on/off switch, controls for volume and a small microphone grille.

The Oticons were tucked and clipped inside a blue support harness that was wrapped around his deep–collared white Adidas tee shirt and held in place by Velcro. It was made from nylon by Aaron's mother, who had lovingly spent days stitching it together with her sewing machine. The one that he was wearing was the third new "bra" – as Jamie liked to call it – in the last five years, Aaron smiled as he remembered. The last two had been "accidentally" damaged: he cut one up with a pair of scissors and the other was torn up by the family's now deceased pet Alsatian, Bram. Aaron and Jamie had filled the two pockets in the harness with Pedigree Chum and broken up bits of Dairy Milk; the brothers watched excitedly as the large dog tore the nylon fabric to shreds trying to get to the delicacy. After the third one was made, their exasperated parents had sternly warned the boys that another "accident" would result in their being grounded after school for a month and having their pocket money halved for six months.

Aaron had always hated wearing those hearing aids, which were uncomfortable and embarrassing. The hard amber–coloured plastic earmoulds, which were moulded into his ears by his audiologist, had often made his ears itch and go red with a rash. The weight of the aids on his chest made him feel as though he had heavy girls' breasts. Come to think of it, he wondered to himself, how did teenage girls with growing breasts manage to wear these aids and harnesses on top of their shirt–covered bras? He shuddered at the thought and thanked God that he had been born a boy.

At home, in his Westbury–on–Trym neighbourhood, everyone would stare at him each time he went about with his mother; to the shops, to the playground in the park, to the two cinemas in town, and to neighbours' houses. They would lean over and coo at him as if he was a baby, or shout into the microphones on his aids to see if he could hear what they were saying, but the sounds they made were always shrill and often made his eardrums tingle.

Some of the hearing children in the neighbourhood were the worst; they would call him "Chimp" or "Dumbo", pull the cords and sometimes beat him up. Fortunately for Aaron, he had a protector: his older brother, Jamie, who had always stood by him and picked fights with the tormentors, even if some of them were bigger than he was. Aaron recalled one occasion the year before when Jamie had come home from his Henbury Court Comprehensive, his shirt torn and bloodied. He had a broken nose, a fractured right wrist and a huge grin on his face. He had won a serious fight with Trevor Smudgewell, the school's bully, who was bigger and older than he was. All because Trevor had taunted Jamie about his "poor deaf–and–dumb bionic little brother."

Aaron would discard his aids as soon as he came home from Elmfield School for the Deaf. He saw no point in wearing them since he could hear nothing with them anyway. His mother had tried to make him wear them, but in vain. Not even his dad's bribe of extra pocket money and sweets tempted Aaron to wear them in the evenings and at weekends.

Aaron turned to his brother, who was twenty months older than him. He poked both of his hands into Jamie's stomach in revenge, causing him to yell and push him away. Aaron then quickly turned his attention to something he had seen outside.

Peering through the side window as the car approached the long, winding driveway; Aaron had spotted the wooden sign standing proudly on a couple of wood stilts behind the low wooden fence. He saw the white stag crest, which gleamed with varnish, and the golden words below it that welcomed him to Ewing Hill Park School for Deaf Boys.

The sign whizzed past his eye line and Aaron looked at his mother. He had never felt so nervous in his whole life. He was even more nervous than he had been when he had visited the school for the first time last March, with his family, to look around and undertake the entrance exams. The exams had involved written English and Maths, observation and speech tests. The English and Maths tests had been the easiest ones for him. He did well with the observation test, which involved identifying items such as a cup, models, toy animals and other items on a table – about twenty of them, he thought – and then, when they were covered by a sheet, he had to say the name each of item, from memory and had managed to name nearly all of them. It was the speech aspect that he had struggled with – he had wondered if the two teachers had actually understood him at all.

Finally, Aaron had been given a sheet of the Lord's Prayer to recite for a tall, thickly spectacled teacher who looked rather goofy, and had become unnerved halfway through when he saw that the teacher, who sat opposite him listening, had a skewed look on his face. He knew that his speech was rubbish and did not think he would be granted a place at the school. Besides, he did not really understand why he was going there anyway. He had really liked Elmfield School, but now, at the age of eleven, he had to move to another school to further his education. That was fine with him, but this school, of all places in the world, was almost two hundred miles away from his home. When he was told he had won a privileged place at Ewing Hill Park School, it surprised him completely.

'It's exciting, isn't it?' bellowed Geraldine, with her index finger tapping her lips to ensure that her deaf son was reading them. Aaron broke off from the memory of the entrance exams. He looked at his mother and the school that loomed through the windscreen. Oh, how he wished his mother would stop that stupid habit of pointing at her mouth: he could read her extremely clear and expressive lips a mile away, he thought.

'Isn't it, John?' Geraldine turned to her husband at the wheel. His eyes still on the winding driveway, John sported thick, parted black hair and sideburns that reached down to his jaw.

'Yeah, Geraldine, it is,' said John. He quickly glanced behind him, keeping his mind's eye on the driveway. 'Don't worry, Aaron, you'll be fine.'

As soon as Aaron's father returned his attention to the driveway, his mother turned her head back to him; again pointing at her mouth, 'It's the best school we've heard of,' she exclaimed. 'You will make new friends!'

Now, Aaron was even more nervous than before.

The tarmacked area at the front of the school was a scene of commotion. Several cars of various types were parked side by side at one end of the car park, in front of a well–maintained playing field. There were white lines around a large part of the field, complete with goal posts at either end. A second football pitch was next to it.

Boys from the ages of eleven to sixteen scurried around the car park; some playing, some using sign language to chat about what they had done during the summer holiday, some lugging their large box trunks from their parents' cars to the school and some bidding their parents goodbye.

The white Austin Maxi slowly drove through the commotion, taking care not to hit anyone. Aaron had already moved over to Jamie's side and was peering at the school through the window, wide–eyed in wonderment and trepidation.

Scores of boys, their parents and teachers walked in both directions through the entrance.

Chris Matthaus walked out through the doors and stopped at the top of the three wide stone steps, scratching an itch under his thick, unkempt dark hair. He descended the steps, his head panning around in search of someone; he found him.

Chris strolled over to Steven Clarke, a boy with long sandy hair, who was sitting on the ledge of the large double–framed ground floor window, and sat down next to him. Fiddling with one of the two Amplivoxes mounted on his harness, Steven acknowledged Chris' presence. They began to use their hands to communicate in sign.

'Good summer?' asked Steven, gesturing a thumbs up and sliding his cupped hand across his face.

Chris shrugged, 'It was okay. I'm glad to be back here though. Second Form now!''

'Yeah, Second Form now! Our turn to pick on the new boys!' He pointed wildly ahead, referring to some of the new boys who were loitering nervously with their parents in the car park. 'Oh, by the way, happy birthday.'

Chris signed, 'Thirteen today and on the first day back to school; the perfect birthday present!'

Steven regarded Chris with affection and respect. They had been good friends since they had first arrived at the school. When Steven had first met Chris, he had found him difficult to be friendly with, for Chris could barely sign. He was like a wild cat lost amongst a school full of house cats, and the teachers had struggled to tame him. However, as soon as Chris demonstrated what he did best – and that was football, which he was extremely good at – he eventually began to make friends with the boys in his Form and with some others. Steven was his best friend, for he also loved football and they both played constantly in their free time.

In spite of his tough, broodingly handsome and strong physique, Chris had matured rapidly into a well–respected boy who took no shit from anyone, nor disrespected anyone. Well, except for Basher, of course.

Steven taught Chris sign language, which he'd picked up very quickly, although he still struggled to read and understand English; sometimes Steven had to explain in sign what he understood from a written or printed text. Chris preferred to look at pictures in magazines, especially his favourite football rag, Match, which he always borrowed from Steven. Steven had always wondered how and why the school had accepted Chris in the first place, as he hadn't taken the entrance exams that he, Steven, had had to take in order to get a place there. Chris had repeatedly maintained that he didn't know why, and refused to talk about his own family or his past.

'I'll be thirteen this November,' said Steven, coming back from his reminiscing. 'Anyway, Liverpool will win the European Cup again next year! They were brilliant last May. 3–1! Against Boru ...'

Chris sighed. He had heard this same old story from the Liverpool fanatic many times. He couldn't blame Steven, who was from Merseyside after all, but he loved to see him struggle to fingerspell that long German name. He knew that Steven had Borussia Moenchengladbach at the back of his mind and so did Chris, but they still couldn't convey the letters in fingerspelling.

'Moe ... something,' the Liverpool fan gave up. 'Shit, I can never spell that stupid foreign club! Emlyn Hughes was the first Liverpool captain to lift the cup!'

'Arsenal will win Division One!' exclaimed Chris.

'Up the Kops!'

'Up the Gunners!'

They both raised clenched fists, reaffirming their support for their respective clubs. In doing so, Chris accidentally caught the cord of his only hearing aid, which was tucked in the top left pocket of his blue tee shirt, causing his mould to fly out of his ear. 'Oh, not again,' he cursed to himself.

'I hate them!' he whined as he tucked his mould back into his left ear. 'Why do we have to wear them? I can't hear a bloody thing with it.'

Steven shrugged and watched Chris replace his mould. Chris was one of the few boys in the school who only had one hearing aid and did not wear the harness. He couldn't wear one in his right ear because it gave him a really nasty rash. Steven had often wished this was the case for him, too, so that he could get rid of that bloody bra, as everyone in school liked to call them.

'Did you see that new James Bond film, The Spy Who Loved Me, during summer?' Steven asked, changing the subject.

'Nope. It looked like a shit film,' Chris shrugged; he wasn't really into James Bond.

'Shit film?' Steven exploded at his friend. 'It was awesome! Best James Bond film I've ever seen. Roger Moore was brilliant! Oh, that cool white car …'

Chris' eyes drifted away from Steven's ramblings; not because he was not interested in knowing more about it, but because he had spotted something rather unusual in the car park. A London black cab had just pulled up.

'Where did that come from?' Chris looked at it in surprise.

'What?' Steven asked, trailing off and looking at the vehicle that Chris was now pointing at. He frowned, surprised as well.

'There are no black cabs around here,' said Chris. He knew that the area only had private taxis of various types; those London black cabs were very rarely, if ever, seen around here. He beckoned to Steven to follow him. 'Come on!'

Chris and Steven scooted over to the cab just as a smartly–dressed black man hopped out, followed by a black boy with tightly curled Afro hair and then a black woman. The man leaned over to the driver's window and handed him a large wad of banknotes.

Chris peered through the open window at the other side, looking at the fare meter that was resting on the dashboard, and saw that their journey had cost thirty–four pounds. He gasped; Steven peered through beside him and saw the fare too.

'Bloody hell!' cried Chris. 'They must be rich!'

'Blimey. Where did it come from?' asked Steven.

'From one of those big London stations!' replied Chris. 'Must have been over an hour's drive here!'

The cab driver, having put the cash into a box beside him, waved the peering boys away. They did as they were told and the cab drove away. The black family looked at their surroundings with some anxiety. The woman tidied a small short–feathered black hat over her thick black hair. Like every other boy in this school, Ian Snyman wore the body aids; albeit that the beige–coloured moulds looked quite out of place in his dark ears.

'Right,' the father said to his son, 'let's go inside, Ian, and see if your trunk has arrived by special delivery.' They moved on inside.

Having parked his car in the middle of the line of parked cars by the field at the front, John looked down at the large trunk on the ground. Geraldine put her compact mirror and lipstick back into her handbag. Jamie picked his nose and Aaron looked around.

'Mr and Mrs Stephens?' a voice came from behind them. Geraldine and John both turned to see a formidable, thickly bespectacled man of average height; his naturally white hair seems to make him look older than his fifty years. He beamed warmly at the parents.

'Hello, Mr Langston,' greeted John, extending his hand to the older man, who returned the shake. He then looked down at Aaron.

'Hello Aaron, remember me?' said Mr Langston, smiling. 'I am Mr Langston. La–ng–ston. The headmaster. We met here at your entrance exams last March.'

Aaron nodded, remembering Mr Langston very well, as he had been one of those two in the observation test. He was quite easy to lipread at close range.

Haloooo, Pr Lazy.

Mr Langston shook his head and smiled, knowing that the boy had just tried to say "Hello, Mr Langston." He ruffled his thick blond hair, knowing the boy's speech was beyond his control. He turned to the parents.

'Don't worry, we'll work on his speech,' said the headmaster.

Mr Langston then looked at the red clipboard that he was holding. He looked around the car park for someone, and waved his clipboard at him when he found him.

'Christopher Matthaus!' Mr Langston yelled, although he knew that this would literally fall on deaf ears. Fortunately, Steven spotted him and indicated to his friend to direct his attention to the headmaster. 'Come over here.'

Chris ran over to the headmaster and the Stephens.

'Christopher,' the headmaster introduced him to Aaron; 'this is Aaron Stephens. You will be looking after him.'

Chris already knew who he was going to be looking after, having seen the list on the school noticeboard. It was the school's practice for boys in the Second Form to each look after one of the new First Form boys for a month, to help them get through the many induction processes; explain the school rules and show them how to make their beds properly; help them to be on time for morning roll call; go into Waltbridge town centre with them on Saturday afternoons and do anything else necessary to help them settle down at the school.

Chris and Aaron acknowledged each other. For a brief moment, something seemed to pass between them, a mutual sense of unity, though it was not evident to either of them.

'Hi,' Chris introduced himself and fingerspelled his name. 'I'm Chris Matthaus.'

Aaron fingerspelled his own name back, smiling at him.

3

Dorm One

"Quiet does not make the silence. Being deaf makes the silence."
– PRINCESS BEATRICE, one of Queen Victoria's granddaughters (who was deaf).

'Your speech is very good, David!'

Mr Whittle looked down with pride, his hands resting on his hips. He smiled through his beard, thick with ginger hair.

Having read his lips, David Wheeley smiled back in appreciation at the young, lean teacher of English. David tucked his hands into the pockets of his baggy flares. He was a plump eleven–year–old with parted dark hair that ran down to his collar. He wore thick rounded spectacles.

Mr Whittle glanced down again at fairly large beige hearing aid resting on the boy's chest. Straps round his upper body and over both shoulders supported it. Two cords ran from one insertion point on the aid to the moulds in both ears. The Phonak insignia was imprinted on the front.

It must be the new SuperFront hearing aid with the highest amplification yet – the first digital sound; he had heard it would be coming out next year. Seeing it for the first time, Mr Whittle wondered if David was testing it for the company.

Mrs Wheeley, a short, plump woman, hugged her son, pleased as punch. 'Did you hear what Mr Whittle said, darling?'

'We're very proud of you!' added an even larger Mr Wheeley, who was standing next to his wife; the boy was the spitting image of his father, but without the sideburns which ran across his jaw. Mr Wheeley leaned over, stretching his tight suit to its limits, and ruffled his son's hair. 'Say "Thank you" to Mr Whittle,' he instructed.

'Thank you, sir,' said David, in flawless speech.

Mr Whittle smiled, encouraged. 'He will be a fine example to the boys here, Mr and Mrs Wheeley. Hopefully they can learn from him.'

'Oh that's marvellous!' David's mother clasped her podgy hands together proudly and looked down at David. 'You will be *very* popular here!'

David smiled nervously and stared at a scruffy looking boy with jet–black hair and puffy cheeks standing next to him. Andrew Brener rolled his eyes and chewed on his bubblegum. *Oh why, why, why was I picked to look after that fat boy for a month?* he silently cursed to himself. One week, tops; that was it for him.

'If it wasn't for his meningitis when he was seven,' said Mrs Wheeley, flapping her hand on her chest, 'he wouldn't have gone deaf … Oh; I don't want to even think about it. It was such a terrible time for him!'

Not really understanding Mrs Wheeley's chat with the English teacher, Andrew blew a fairly large pink bubble. The teacher looked down at him in disgust and pointed at it.

'Andrew Brener!' barked the teacher. 'Throw that away now!' He pointed at a metal bin next to the boy.

Reluctantly, the Second Former chewed the gum back into his mouth. Cocking his head down towards the bin, he spat the squashed pink substance directly into it. It hit the inside side of the bin and stuck.

Mr Whittle shook his head, disgusted. That neurotic boy from Sheffield had been quite a handful ever since he first came last year, he silently mused, and his speech – he spared a thought for poor old Jonathan, giving him speech lessons.

Andrew turned his head away from the teacher and the Wheeleys to see a tall man in a black suit enter Dorm One with a boy with brown hair, carrying the large box trunk between them. A blonde boy and his mother followed them, with Chris just behind. Miss Hogarth ushered them towards one of the ten beds, the one which used to be Andrew's.

With Jamie's help, John heaved the large trunk onto the bed; it bounced slightly and the bed creaked under the weight. Aaron scanned his surroundings. The high–ceilinged dormitory was a large room. A long, narrow double–framed window with crisscrossed panes overlooked the front field on one side of the light blue painted wall; there was another in the adjacent wall. Both windows had long navy blue curtains. Five metal beds were neatly laid out along the wooden floorboards by the wall with the front window, and another five beds along the wall opposite. Each bed was neatly made with a pillow propped up against a wooden headboard and a green and black patterned blanket covering a white sheet. The top end of the blanket was partly covered by the sheet, which was neatly folded over. The blanket and sheet were immaculately tucked in between the mattress and metal bed frame. Low–level birch wardrobes rested between the beds; each comprised of one hanging compartment, two top drawers and a bottom cupboard. Aaron looked up at the high ceiling, which was painted white and had four fluorescent tubes stretching across the length of the rectangular room. A couple of framed landscapes hung on the wall above the five beds and there was another one next to the door on the adjacent wall. Aaron sniffed; a kind of stale smell wafted faintly in the air.

Chris briefly explained to Aaron that this room, Dorm One, was for the First Formers and there were three dormitories on the top floor, one for each Form. Dorm Two, where Chris slept, was next door. He explained that Dorms Four and Five, for the Fourth and Fifth Formers respectively, along with some private rooms for the residing teachers and Mr Langston's large apartment, were on the floor below. Chris pointed to another door opposite Dorm One and said it was the washroom. It had three toilet cubicles and ten washbasins that would be shared by the thirty boys on the floor. It also had a small room with a bath and two showers that were rarely used; the boys often used the large shower rooms in the gym building at the rear of the school after their sports lessons. He then explained that there was another smaller, but similar, washroom on the floor below, for the seniors. He directed Aaron to a white towel with a green and gold stripe at either end that was hanging over a bar on the side of Aaron's wardrobe; it was his to use in the washroom and showers. He went on to say that the matron, Miss Hogarth, and the assistant matron, Miss Turner, also had their own rooms next to their office, on the same floor.

Miss Hogarth, a tall, burly woman with her hair scraped into a tight bun, was wearing large round spectacles and dark brown attire that ran down to her knees. 'If you have any questions,' she said to the Stephens, 'ask for my assistant, Miss Turner, or me; I'm Miss Hogarth, the matron here.' She then turned to Aaron and fingerspelled her name. 'I can sign a little bit, Aaron.'

Aaron nodded in acknowledgement. The large woman smiled, turned and left the room. Aaron looked at Chris, who was sitting on the bed next to his. Chris smiled back, knowing how the new boy was feeling on his first day.

'A bit like the barracks in the Army, isn't it?' commented John as he observed the surroundings, reminiscing on his three–year stint in National Service.

Geraldine turned to the wardrobe next to Aaron's bed, ignoring her husband's remarks, and opened the hanging compartment door to peer inside. 'A bit dusty in there,' she said to herself, before closing it and turning to Aaron. 'Don't worry; I know it isn't like your bedroom at home, but you'll be all right here.'

Chris mentioned that he could put his own clothes into the wardrobe, but not his school uniform or his underwear; this would be explained to him and the others in his Form during the week. He then glanced to his right at a woman approaching Aaron's mother from behind, her face lit up with surprise.

'Geraldine Taylor?' called the woman, from behind Geraldine. She whipped round to see a freckled woman with ginger hair, similar in age to herself. Her eyes widened when she recognised her.

'It is *you*, Blabbermouth!' exclaimed the woman.

'Specky?' yelled Geraldine. 'What are you doing here?!'

Geraldine and Specky threw their arms round each other and hugged. John, Aaron, Jamie and Chris watched the excited women curiously. The women broke off their hug.

'This is Doreen "Specky" Simpson,' introduced Geraldine. 'We were in the same class at school in Swansea!'

'It's Doreen Hardcastle now,' corrected Specky. She showed off a diamond encrusted wedding ring.

'Stephens now!' Geraldine followed up, showing off her own gold band. She then introduced her family: 'This is my husband, John, my son Jamie, and Aaron, who's the new boy here.'

'*My* son, Michael, is starting today too.' Specky said. She pointed to a skinny boy with thick curly in the same colour as his mother's, standing by his bed next to David Wheeley in the far corner of the room. He saw his mother pointing at him and continued unpacking the trunk that was on the bed.

'Where's your husband?' Geraldine asked.

'He couldn't come. He travels all over the world. He's a senior manager in a company working on an oil rig. He's in …' she tried to remember. 'Oh yes. Argentina.'

'Oh, that's marvellous!' exclaimed Geraldine. 'What an amazing coincidence: we both went to the same school and now our sons are in the same school. Same class too. What a small world!'

Geraldine and Specky laughed out loud.

4

Goodbyes

"It requires wisdom to understand wisdom; the music is nothing if the audience is deaf."
– Walter Lippmann (1889–1974)

It was time for tearful goodbyes.

The large, wide front hall was full of commotion as parents said their goodbyes to their deaf sons. Some boys clung tightly to their parents. Other boys' mothers pecked on their cheeks while their fathers stoically shook their hands or patted their backs. Some boys were more than happy enough to see the back of their parents as they walked out through the entrance doors.

It was usually the new boys and their parents that had the most emotional farewells.

'Sssshhh, my baby,' said Mrs Wheeley, her soft voice breaking down. 'Everything will be all right. Oh, my baby!' She pulled in and cradled a tearful David tightly again.

David's arms wrapped halfway round her plump body, trying to squeeze as hard as he could. His spectacles nudged up from his tiny nose as he pushed against his mother's body, tears flowing down his cheeks. 'Mummy, I don't want to stay here ...' David trailed off.

'I know, I know, my dear.' She silently cursed at Hugo for walking away to the car without even saying goodbye to their only son. She'll have a right go at him on the journey back to Shropshire, she thought to herself. She heard loud running noises above and looked up at the grand staircase she and David were standing beside. She saw a boy with blond curls whom she recognised as one of the new boys: she had seen him in Dorm One and his bed was next to David's.

Duncan Nielson ran down one of the two flights of polished wooden stairs from the first floor and reached the landing at the top of the wide grand staircase that led down to the lobby. He stood there, his face agitated, his mouth wide open, exposing his long front teeth, his eyes desperately searching the ground below. He hurried to his left, leaning over the banister to see the ground below. There was a wide corridor directly opposite the side of the grand staircase that he knew led to a maze of corridors, some of the classrooms, the library and other areas he had yet to explore in the east of the building. He saw some boys and their parents in the area between the staircase and the corridor, but could not find the two people he was looking for. He darted to his right; craning his head over to scan the ground below. Like the other side, it also had a wide corridor with a similar ground plan. But still he could not find who he was looking for.

He slowly sidestepped towards the middle, his eyes gazing down still, realisation sinking in. Then he shifted his attention ahead to the front hall, visible through the wide open doorway between two white pillars. The front hall was larger and longer than the lobby he was in. It had a circular oak table in the centre; the walls were painted cream above wooden panelling and the floor covered by hard–worn dark gold carpet. Eyes searching amongst the boys and parents in there, he still couldn't find them.

Mrs Munnings, a burly woman, hurried down the stairs to meet Duncan on the landing, slightly out of breath. She wiped away a light sheen of perspiration on her forehead, beneath her heavy short–styled black hair, with the patterned silk scarf that was wrapped around her neck. She gently touched the boy's shoulder to bring him round to her. She fluttered her fake eyelashes, exhaled again and slowly spoke with thick lips that were laden with glossy red lipstick. 'I have already told you that your parents have gone home, Duncan,' she said, not without sympathy. She cursed at having to be the one to break the news to him in the dorm. 'They wanted to leave quietly.'

Duncan pounded down the staircase, his arms waving in agitation. Mrs Munnings sighed. She quickly descended the stairs, her right hand resting on the smoothly curved wooden handrail to stop her high–heeled shoes slipping across the surface. She saw that Duncan had already reached the entrance doors. She reached at the bottom and made her way towards the wide–open doorway into the front hall. She hurried past a man and his son standing beside the school's wooden post box that had a slit at the top and a padlocked door. A shelf on the wall next to it had a few letters piled on it. The man averted his eyes from the shelf, now realising it was where the boys collected their letters from home, and returned his attention to his son. The eleven–year–old was wearing a green and white striped top but no body aids.

'You understand? Sign it!' urged the father, putting his tartan cap back on his head.

'I'm Derek Ferguson and I'm proud of Scotland!' followed the boy.

His father laughed and ruffled Derek's short curly dark hair; he was so proud of him, a chip off the all–deaf family block. He looked round and saw a balding man filming his son's goodbyes with a cine camera as he walked backwards towards the entrance doors. What a *glaikit* man, he thought to himself.

Shaun Knight wept as he waved at his camera–toting father. Someone jostled him, passing on his left and he turned, with the cine camera still pointing at his waving son, to see a burly woman rushing past. He recognised her as one of the teachers, though her name escaped him.

'Sorry, excuse me!' Mrs Munnings apologised, as she darted through the open glass doors.

'No harm done,' Mr Knight said to her, but she was already well gone. He sniffed at the strong scent that the woman had left in her wake. 'Chanel number 5.'

'Opium,' came a reply. Mr Knight turned to his wife, who was holding a handkerchief. 'By Yves Saint Laurent; it's just come out.'

Whatever, he thought to himself. He returned his attention to his son and began to wave with his free hand while still filming. 'Goodbye, Shaun, see you at half term!' he heard Patricia say as she leaned over to whisper in his ear, 'Alan, there's a black family over there.'

With his other eye, he squinted across the front hall to see a tall black man leaning over the circular table and picking up a newspaper. His wife and son stood close by.

The man read the front page as the headline had caught his eye. He had not had time to buy the newspaper at Birmingham New Street station earlier that day; they managed to catch the train just in time and then took the cab straight from Euston to the school. *STEVE BIKO DEAD.*

'*The bastards!*' he cursed. 'They murdered him!'

'Clement!' his wife said back, keeping her voice low. She looked around her to make sure that no one had heard the outburst. 'Not here, not on Ian's first day.'

Clement Snyman nodded apologetically to Talasia. He closed his eyes for a short moment to silently pray for the young black activist that he had been following in the news. There had been an uprising in Soweto in June of last year, with mass protests against the government's policy of enforcing education in Afrikaans rather than English. The police had opened fire on ten thousand or so marching black students in Orlando West. Biko had been quite prominent in the news and Clement had hoped that the world would condemn the police for their brutality, but no, they simply stood back and did nothing. Now, with his death, Stephen Biko had become a martyr.

He opened his eyes, rolled up the newspaper and tucked it into the inside pocket of his long black overcoat. He looked around and considered how he hadn't seen another black boy in the school: Ian must be the first. The father bent his knees to be level with Ian and pointed at his own lips. 'Be careful with yourself here, Ian. OK?' he said slowly. 'Show them what we blacks can do and be proud of it. Do well here, my boy.'

Ian nodded. His father smiled and hugged him.

Aaron turned away from the black boy and his father. He knew the boy was Ian Snyman, after having already met him in Dorm One. He was the first boy in his new Form to introduce himself. It was the first time Aaron had ever seen a deaf black boy in his life, but he thought nothing of it.

He squirmed when his mother suddenly kissed him. Geraldine then straightened while Aaron wiped his moist cheek with his hand. His father ruffled his thick blond hair with pride.

'Be a good boy!' said Geraldine. 'Work hard, especially on your speech.'

'See you next month,' said John. 'We'll have an early birthday party for you!'

Aaron smiled at the prospect of having his twelfth birthday party two weeks early, during the October half term. Jamie gently punched his younger brother's arm to bring him round. 'See you soon, butthead.' Jamie said. He had a knowing twinkle in his eye. He switched off his voice so that his parents wouldn't hear him and began to sign fluently. 'I know where you hid them. You think I'm blind?'

Aaron winced; he knew what his brother was talking about.

'Action Man? Thunderbirds 2 and 4? Bionic Man? James Bond's Aston Martin? Formula One Top Trumps cards? All mine!' exclaimed Jamie.

Aaron cursed himself; he had hidden them under his bed. The toys were his, but Jamie always played with them. As much as he loved his thirteen–year–old brother, he was sometimes a bloody pain in the ass. Like most brothers, they sometimes argued and always called each other names, but from brotherly love rather than sibling rivalry – they were very close. Jamie was learning sign language from Aaron and he absolutely loved it. Any new signs Aaron picked up, Jamie demanded to know. They used to love watching the Vision On! television programme for deaf and hearing children. Presented by Pat Keysell, it was the only kids programme with sign language in. Pat told stories and signed for Tony Hart who was amazing at creating art. Jamie would listen to her and pick up the signs at the same time.

They both loved to sign each other at dinner, which sometimes infuriated their parents, who understood very little of their silent communication. Their mother would urge Jamie to repeat himself using his voice, but he cheerfully refused.

The boys shared a keen interest in science fiction films and television, and Jamie always signed for Aaron during their favourite Friday and Saturday evening television shows such as Tom Baker's Doctor Who, Six Million Dollar Man, Planet of the Apes and Thunderbirds; Jamie sometimes liked to tease Aaron about trying to lipread the yapping wooden mouths. He sometimes did the news too, when something big or important happened. Also, there was Mrs Moreliver. Jamie didn't really mind doing that for Aaron, but there was always a price tag attached to it.

'Goodbye, my love,' Geraldine said weakly. She dabbed at her eyes with a tissue. She and John then walked towards the entrance doors, not wanting to look back. Jamie hugged Aaron fondly and then followed his parents.

Aaron silently watched them walk away.

For the first time in his whole life, he felt truly alone.

5

Silent Nightmare

"Historians are like deaf people who go on answering questions that no one has asked them."
– Leo Nikolaevich (1828–1910)

He ran in slow motion through the long, narrow corridor, which was lined with wood panels from top to bottom on either side. Overhead, the fluorescent light tubes, which ran along the entire length of the ceiling, were flickering furiously as though trying in desperation to switch on, which added to the unsettling and claustrophobic creepiness of the interior.

It felt as though the walls were closing in on him as he ran onwards, approaching the double doors at the end of the corridor. A feeling of oppressiveness was crushing his body and yet nothing was physically touching him.

He felt an overwhelming need to get out. He reached out his hands towards the doors.

They swung open without difficulty.

He ran out into a large, empty field; it was pitch dark, with only the moonlight shining down faintly from above.

He froze.

Suddenly, bright light shone from behind him, stretching a dark shadow of his own across the grass in front. He spun round to face the doors, but now they belonged to a blue box which he recognised instantly. A man stood between the open doors, silhouetted against the brightness of the white interior. The four walls were patterned with several illuminated circles and in the centre stood a hexagonal console with a large glass cylinder mounted on top. The man's arms were outstretched to reach across the entire doorway. He wore a floppy hat, a dark brown overcoat and a long, striped wool scarf that ran down to his knees.

Despite the darkness, he could tell that this man was not the one with the thick, curly hair whom he had idolised as a child, but someone else he recognised; Mr Langston.

The school's headmaster gave him a familiar smile as he pulled the doors inwards to close them, plunging the field into foreboding darkness once again. The little blue light atop the blue box, which had the illuminated POLICE sign on the front, began to flash. The iconic object began to dematerialise and then it was gone.

He turned full circle, trying to make sense of the unusual yet strange surroundings, but he could see nothing but the cold, dense blackness of the field, which went on as far as his eye could see. The oppressive feeling he had felt just now as he ran through the corridor was fading and he could breathe easily again. But where was he? What was he doing in this field in the dead of night? He wanted to get out of this nightmare.

He felt a sudden heaviness on his chest, a familiar feeling to him, and he looked down, unsurprised to see that he was wearing the blue harness holding his two hearing aids with the cords leading up to the moulds in his ears.

Upon seeing the rest of his body, though, he realised that he was completely naked, except for the harness on his chest. He felt something at his wrists and raised his hands, finding them bound by a rope. He shuddered at the strangeness of his situation. He tried to wrestle his hands free, but to no avail.

He jumped as the field was suddenly filled with figures sprawling around him, stretched out as far as he could see. Children – thousands of them. They all wore different types of clothing and from what he had seen on television and read in books, he judged their clothing style as being from the last one hundred or so years. Some were clearly from the Victorian era, others from the First and Second World Wars, some from the Sixties. Others clothed in things he had never seen before … *are they from the future?*

He shivered, aware that he was the only naked one amongst the younger people. He saw however that, like him, they all had ropes tying their hands, and that they too were also trying to break free. They stumbled in all directions around him, their faces frozen and dazed; their mouths moved and yet no sound came out. He could see the despair in their faces and wanted to help them undo the ropes, but he was frozen to the spot.

Suddenly, something throbbed into his mind, like icy fingers pressing against his forehead. Someone … or something … was trying to tell him something, but it was vague. He closed his eyes to concentrate.

One … eight … eight … nought …

He opened his eyes, puzzled at the cryptic nature of the numbers.

A girl, wearing an old school dress that he could not identify, though he suspected it was from the last decade or so, came up to him. She was wearing headphones of some kind and carrying two large brown boxes, one strapped over each shoulder. The headphones were attached to one of them with a thick cable.

He recognised the contraption as one of the older, heavier Brownie hearing aids that he had seen in a photograph at his old school. The other box must be the battery pack. Pleading, she raised her tied hands to him.

. . . help us ...

Suddenly, the girl and every other child on the field burst into trillions of tiny, brilliantly sparkling pieces, yet their hands, every pair, remained and plummeted to the grass. The green field had become a field of dismembered hands with blood flowing freely from their severed bits. Soon enough, the field was no longer green, but a mixture of flesh and scarlet.

He screamed at the abominable sight, but no sound came out of his mouth. He looked up towards the night sky and saw that there were no stars ... and no moon either – they were all gone, yet moonlight still shone down on him. The night sky seemed peppered with tiny black holes ... no, wait, they weren't black holes! They were constantly moving as though they were speaking ... *they weren't black holes, but mouths!*

His eyes gazed in wonder at the daunting sight of those dark honeycombed moving shapes. Were they speaking ... or crying? He couldn't tell because they were too far away above. He turned round, still looking upwards. They were everywhere and he could clearly tell now that there were *millions of them.*

Soon enough, a wind began to howl fiercely around him. It was no ordinary wind though, for it came at him from all directions at once.

It was coming from the dark holes above, as though they were blowing at him. And it was getting stronger and stronger.

His thick blond hair fluttered furiously as he tried to keep his balance against the gusts. The crimson sea rippled and small waves began to form, causing the severed hands to float to and fro against the small tides. Streaks of crimson liquid began to splash onto his naked flesh. He raised his still–tied hands to his terrified face in a futile effort to hide himself from this tumultuous experience.

Suddenly, he felt a gentle prod on his back; he quickly turned to see the head of an animal that he couldn't identify at first. Taking a couple of steps back, his feet splashing in the sea of blood, he saw that it was a deer – no, not just a deer, he corrected himself; a stag. Its body was completely white; it had long, curved grey antlers with three points on each, and its long white tail swayed furiously in the wind. He gazed at the animal, wide–eyed and awestruck; he had never seen such a beautiful, pure and innocent animal before. Its whiteness shone brightly in the total darkness around them, its black eyes seeming to stare at him. Slowly, it trotted towards him, its head nodding and its hooves splashing through the crimson ripples, but strangely, its four lean legs remained spotlessly clean and free from blood. He slowly lifted his hands, tempted to stroke its head. When he did, though, he found he was touching the head of his older brother Jamie, who was standing there, smiling chillingly at him, his thick brown hair blowing furiously in the strong gusts. He was also covered in blood, but his own rather than that from the ground, and his bloodstained white school shirt flapped in the wind – he recognised the shirt as the one Jamie had worn when he fought with Trevor Smudgewell a year ago.

With outstretched index fingers, Jamie pointed at his own ears.

. . . no hear ...

He then pointed at his own mouth.

. . . no speak ...

Jaime then thrust his hands between the cords and the neck of his younger brother, pushing outwards, causing the moulds to fly out. He took his hands and easily removed the rope from his wrists as though it was never properly tied. Then joyfully, he smiled.

. . . yes, sign ...

Jamie cocked his head upwards and stretched out his arms as if he were on a crucifix. Raising his arms up as though to embrace the night sky, he closed his eyes and grinned broadly. His body began to shimmer radiantly, swirling into a ball of blinding whiteness.

Almost instantly, the brilliant white light swept away from him across the field and Jamie was gone. The grass was green once again; the grotesque manifestations no longer there. The wind had died down and the night sky was once again filled with stars and the shining moon.

He checked his naked body, finding it blessedly free from splattered blood. He breathed a sigh of relief, despite himself, for he was still in the surreal world that he so desperately wanted to get out of.

He felt a hand resting on his left shoulder and whirled round to see his mother standing there. Acutely aware of his own nakedness, he cupped his hands over himself out of natural shyness; even though he knew he was dreaming. Geraldine, wearing a pink sweatshirt and trousers, picked up the moulds that were hanging down by their cords and replaced them in his ears, tapping on her own lips.

. . . work hard ...

Suddenly she morphed into two items of clothing, which fell to the ground. He recognised them as his own navy blue pyjamas. Quickly bending down, he picked up the bottoms and shoved his legs into them, covering himself finally and finding some comfort in that. He discovered that he was no longer wearing the body aids on his chest. He put on the top and was beginning to button it up when lights suddenly appeared in front of him. It was Ewing Hill Park School with all of its windows blazing with light; a dazzling sight in the night.

A fat boy came into view, his arms outstretched as he ran round in slow motion like an aeroplane. He recognised him as David Wheeley. He was wearing his school uniform, but without the green blazer. A strange–looking tie hung round his neck and over his white shirt, but it was not a school tie ... it was a rope. Its crude knot, the end of it dangling down to his paunch, made it look like a noose.

David ran a circle round his new form mate, as though flying in slow motion, compelling him to follow by turning his body round. Circle completed, he was back facing the school building again and David was suddenly sitting on the grass, legs crossed, elbows resting on his knees, face buried in his hands, crying. He was no longer wearing his school uniform and the rope tie, but his red pyjamas.

As he bent down to comfort David, he suddenly became aware that something wet was touching his lips, as though he was being kissed. He retreated, wiping his mouth with the back of his hand, to discover his new friend Chris grinning at him, wearing the school uniform.

. . . friends ...

Chris raised his hand to shake his and he instinctively returned the gesture, but the hand he grasped was not a boy's hand anymore, but a man's.

He looked up to see a tall man, still wearing the same uniform, which had grown to accommodate his bigger size. Though he had never seen this man before in his life, he was familiar – it was Chris as his older self. The man smiled.

. . . are we friends again? ...

Before he could answer the strange question, the man disappeared.

Rain began to fall. Thunder roared and lightning flared in the night sky, even though there were no clouds at all. Rain fell anyway, and it was getting heavier.

He looked up, the raindrops splattering on his face and soaking his pyjamas, and shivered. He turned to face the school and discovered that David was no longer sitting on the grass.

Something was forming above the school ... a massive dark shape that grew quickly in the darkness beyond. Dull white structures appeared, lining the top and bottom of the massive opening, now bigger than the school itself.

It was a mouth.

And it was laughing manically.

He stepped back a little, frightened of this terrifying but awesome sight.

As he gaped, an enormous hand slowly emerged through the huge hole, furiously changing colour from blue to red to yellow. Once fully extended, the end of its bare forearm pushing up against the teeth, its fingers began to clench and it turned ninety degrees in a mechanical fashion.

It rose upwards, then thrust down towards the school below, slamming it with incredible force. The school exploded thunderously, the debris flying out as though the bricks were made of plaster, the wood made of cardboard and the glass of thin plastic.

The impact of the destruction shook the ground. He wobbled, trying to keep his balance, and screamed in terror at the magnitude of what he was witnessing.

The clenched hand rose again and then slammed into the shattered building once more, razing it to the ground. Lightning flashed and the rain poured down like never before.

He turned to discover that the children he had seen earlier had returned. Thousands of them. Their hands were no longer tied, but clamped to their ears as though to shield them from the incredible smashing noise, despite already being deaf. They all were standing motionless, watching the destruction, their eyes frozen and their mouths wide open.

The loud thumping noise came again, shaking the ground once more and he almost lost his balance. With the deaf children still in a trance behind him, he turned to face the school – what was left of it now – and screamed loudly.

The fist continued to slam down.

Lightning continued to flash.

6

The First Day

"This daily struggle is like having to do a mental crossword without pen and paper, and requires having to calculate all the time, rather than just listening naturally as hearing people do. Although many deaf people make it look easy, it is actually a massive feat, which can take a lifetime to improve."

– DEAF EX–MAINSTREAMERS GROUP; *Deaf Toolkit: Best Value Review of Deaf Children in Education From Users' Perspectives* (on the myth of deaf children 'listening' through hearing aids, cochlear implants or acoustic equipment in the classroom), 2004

Aaron's eyes snapped open.

One of the four overhead lighting tubes he was looking up at flickered into life. He still felt the stomping around him, the consciousness of his vivid dream fading away. He stared at the white ceiling, expecting it to come crashing down onto him.

He slid his sleepy eyes down to see Miss Hogarth's feet clomping on the wooden floorboards as she walked across the room, clapping her hands hard.

'Wake up, boys!' she bellowed and signed at the same time. 'Get up!'

Michael Hardcastle shot up in bed, wide–eyed. Shaun Knight begrudgingly sat up and began to unbutton his pyjama top. The matron went over to the still sleeping David Wheeley and shook him, but he didn't move. She tried again, this time harder, pulling away the bedding until David came round. Satisfied, the big woman went over to the window and drew open the curtains; the early morning sunlight shone through.

Aaron blinked at the bright sun and looked at the watch that he was still wearing on his left wrist: half past seven. He groaned: it had been a rough first night. David and Jonah Kaisermann who slept next to Aaron, had both been crying because they were homesick. The two matrons had had to come in several times to comfort them and had needed to turn on the lights so that the boys could see them clearly, something which had at times infuriated the others in the dorm, who were trying to sleep. Aaron closed his eyes again, wanting to go back to sleep.

The tarmacked car park at the front of the school was filled with four long, straight rows of green and black–clad boys, lined up, facing the brown building. Aaron had already observed that his form's row of ten boys stood the furthest left, while the next row on their right was the Second Form. The following two rows contained the Third and Fourth Formers respectively. Each row began with the shortest boy at the front; the line ascended to the tallest at the back; Aaron was fifth in his line. He fiddled with his tie. Black with diagonal green and gold stripes, it was draped over his body aids, which were strapped over his white shirt. He idly checked his new dark green wool blazer; there were thick gold strips along the edge of the lapels, another strip at the top of the left breast pocket and more on the ends of each sleeve. With his hand, he brushed the white stag crested badge sewn to the breast pocket. He looked down at his black trousers and shiny black shoes. He felt a bit strange wearing a school uniform for the first time in his life; at his former school he had always worn his own clothes.

Aaron glanced to his right to see Chris in the next row; he stood third from the back of the line, his hands behind him. Chris glanced back at him. Aaron turned to see the Fifth Formers loitering in front of the four rows of boys, keeping a watchful eye. They were all wearing a different type of tie: it was dark green with a small, embroidered white stag logo – they were the prefects. The head boy hovered around his form mates, taking pride in his first day as a man of authority. Earlier, on their way down from their dormitories, Chris had strenuously advised Aaron that the head boy, Theodore Elliott, had all the power he wanted and every boy had to obey him; he added that Theodore was really a good lad, but his authority should never be challenged. The prefects were like his soldiers, keeping control of the boys, although they sometimes tended to cause trouble themselves. Chris moved on to say that every boy had to be outside for the daily roll call at precisely ten to eight each morning, except for on Sundays, when roll call was at eight o'clock. If a boy should be a minute late, one of the prefects would tell him to run a lap of the entire car park. Two minutes late; two laps. Three minutes; three laps, and so forth. Sometimes they would tell the latecomer to run round the entire field, even if was ankle deep with snow. Aaron quietly chuckled as one of the Third Form boys – he didn't know his name yet – ran round the car park.

Along with the others, Chris and Aaron strode through the connecting corridor towards a large modern extension, set on the east side of the school. They soon arrived at a small square foyer with two sets of swinging double doors; the left one led to the dining room where they were heading, and the other to the large Assembly Hall. Aaron had already seen from outside the stark contrast between these two buildings; the school had magnificent Georgian architecture while the other was a large, bland, dark grey concrete block with a flat roof and white wooden window frames.

As they walked, Chris explained that the extension, which housed the Assembly Hall, dining room and kitchens, had been built about three years ago under the former headmaster, Mr Williams, after the school received a generous donation from the wealthy family of Jacques Magnat, a former pupil. Chris wasn't quite sure why they had made such a gesture, though rumour had it that they were very pleased with Jacques' improved speech, and so made the donation as a token of their gratitude. The building was called Magnat House, named after the French family; Chris showed Aaron its humorous name sign, *magnetic*, by touching his left palm with the tips of his three right–hand fingers, depicting an *M*, as if they were magnetic. Aaron wondered where the old dining room was and where the morning assembly used to be held.

They entered the dining room and Aaron looked around again – he had been there before for lunch during the entrance exams earlier that year and for supper yesterday. It was a large room with a high ceiling and enough room to seat at least one hundred people. All of the three brick walls were painted cream; the ceiling was white and had six fluorescent lighting tubes. Further down at the other side – or at the back, from their point of view – opposite the doors, were three floor–to–ceiling windows that overlooked the small field and the forest beyond it. Each of the windows, as far as Aaron could make out, was about five feet wide and ten feet apart. A canteen counter with an open plan kitchen behind it occupied about two thirds of the space on the left; three dinner ladies were working there. The rest of the space led to another room that was hidden from view; Aaron presumed that it was for the kitchen staff only. On the right, opposite the canteen, was a floor–to–ceiling white partition wall that divided the dining room and the Assembly Hall. The dining room had five large decagonal shaped tables, each with ten chairs. Four of the tables were strategically positioned; two across by the counter and the other two by the partition wall opposite. The fifth one was positioned centrally by the three windows at the back. A long rectangular table, with chairs only facing out into the room, was positioned at the front left, between the doors and the counter; Aaron already knew it was for the staff.

Soon enough, at the counter, one of the three dinner ladies served Aaron with a bowl of cereal, a plate of hot breakfast, a glass of orange juice and an empty cup for his tray. He was too preoccupied with Chris' explanations of the general rules about eating in the dining room to properly notice the food. Chris guided him to the table that was closest to the staff table and the counter and they sat. Chris said that this table was for the First Form, and that he was sitting with him on the first day to help teach him how to keep the table tidy, how to clear up afterwards and how to behave properly. The same went for his form mates; the Second Form table today acted as an overspill for both forms, but from tomorrow onwards, the table would be for First Formers only. The Second Form table, where Chris would usually sit, was by the partition wall in front of the staff table and the doors. The Third Form table was next to the First Form table along the counter, while the Fourth Form table was next to the Second Form table along the partition wall. The Fifth Form table, of course, was by the three windows at the back. The head boy always sat on the chair facing the room with the middle window behind him.

Aaron glanced round the table at the mixture of First and Second Formers, the latter keeping a watchful eye on the former. Watched by a repulsed Andrew, David was digging into his breakfast as if he had not eaten for a week. Ian cautiously dipped his spoon into his milk–filled cereal bowl as if he was checking that it was safe to eat, and a Second Former with chestnut hair – Aaron didn't know his name yet, but knew he was from Belfast – watched him with a smirk on his face. Duncan was practically cutting through his ceramic plate with a knife and fork, trying to cut a burnt piece of streaky bacon. Michael struggled to lift an oversized metallic teapot from the centre of the table with his skinny arms and wobbled it over his cup. The hot brown liquid began to pour slowly; however, the tea had also trickled from the base of the spout as if it was not properly soldered to the body, and dribbled onto his half–eaten breakfast. He cursed and dipped up the pot to stop the trickle.

Aaron looked down at his tray in disbelief. It consisted of a bowl containing one soggy Weetabix with milk, a sparse plate of "English breakfast", namely one small, burnt piece of streaky bacon; a squishy boiled tomato that he hated on sight; one small, stiff–looking sausage; some bubble and squeak that looked as if it had been cooked in radioactive waste and two thin slices of white bread. Aaron turned to his right to see a smirking Chris who seemed to know how he felt.

'Eat!' Chris said with a broad grin, waving his spoon at him as though instructing him. He then tucked into his own cereal.

Aaron picked up his spoon, his eyes staring warily down at the cereal.

Back in the dorm, Aaron weakly fluffed his pillow and rested it against the wooden headboard, then feebly tucked the blanket between the mattress and bed frame, leaving some loose bits hanging down. He then patted down the top sheet, which was already folded over the blanket, and stood back, satisfied with his bed–making skills. Chris, who had been watching him, shook his head impatiently at the bed that was not made properly. He yanked out the top blanket, then the sheet, and flipped away the pillow. Aaron watched in bewilderment, catching sight of other Second Form boys doing exactly the same around the dormitory, watched by the astonished new boys. This made for a comical sight.

Chris smoothed down the base sheet and then neatly tucked it around the mattress. He flapped the second sheet down on top and made sure its sides ran in perfect parallel with the frames. He then flapped down the blanket, again making sure that the sides were exactly in line with the sheet underneath, and gently tucked them both in, folding the two loose bits at the bottom end of the bed into each corner, then folding the top end of the sheet over the blanket and tucking it in too. Finally, he picked up the pillow, fluffed it and carefully put it against the headrest. 'You must do it like this *every* day.' Chris said, stepping back and pointing at the immaculately made bed. 'Or you'll get into trouble.'

After they had brushed their teeth in the washroom, Chris and Aaron returned to Magnat House for morning assembly. The hall was similar to the dining room behind the partition wall, but much larger, with five of the same floor–to–ceiling windows. Aaron took in the surroundings. There was a stage that stood at the far right – or at the front as they called it – next to the wall with the windows. About a metre high and three or four metres deep, it spread across the entire breadth of the rectangular hall. Short steps led up to the stage on the right. With Chris' guidance, Aaron arrived at the front row of ten chairs, which were about ten feet away from the stage. He observed that there were five rows of ten chairs: one for each Form, each with enough legroom. Another row of chairs stood against the partition wall at the back. Aaron presumed these were for the staff; some adults were lingering there, chatting to one another. The hall was already filled with boys seated, chatting to each other in sign language.

Chris explained that assembly started at nine o'clock every day, except at weekends; all boys had to be on time for it. He also said that all boys had to stand up when the headmaster came in, and sit down when he got to his lectern on the stage. Chris sat on an empty chair at the end of the second row while Aaron sat on the second one in the front row. He sat between Bradley Watts, whom he knew came from Ipswich, and the Scot, Derek Ferguson. Soon enough, he felt a tap on his shoulder and saw that Chris was standing up, along with everyone else. He and his form mates rose to their feet. Behind Chris, he saw Mr Langston enter the hall at the back, and watched him walk along the aisle on the right, towards the stage. He was carrying a dark blue ring binder. The headmaster walked past Aaron, climbed the short staircase and arrived at the lectern. Aaron quickly glanced back to check that everyone was sitting down; he sat too. He returned his attention to the stage; the headmaster was putting a black strap around his neck; a small silver cylinder hung from it, resting on his chest. Aaron knew this was a microphone; a long, thin black cable ran from its bottom to an amplification box mounted on the lower part of the wall on the far right of the stage. The headmaster muttered something into the microphone and tapped it, testing it. He then addressed the gathering.

Aaron frowned and squinted. He could see the headmaster's mouth moving, but he was too far away to lipread him. Out of habit, he glanced down to his harness to check that the hearing aids were switched on. They were, though he knew very well that he could never hear anything with them. He looked back up at the still speaking headmaster, his mouth like a tiny black moving dot. He quickly glanced back at Chris, confused. Chris raised his eyebrows and told Aaron to turn and watch, but Aaron shook his head quietly. So, Chris discreetly pointed to his left, telling him to take a look at someone else. Aaron slowly turned to see the Second Form boy, Mark Cameron; he knew his name from Chris, also that he was from Birmingham. The boy had thick mousy hair and a face that always seemed to be cheerful. He was sitting near the middle of his row, secretly moving his hands, his eyes fixed on the man on the stage. Aaron saw that the rest of the boys in the row were discreetly glancing at Mark from either side. Aaron began to pick up the gist from the moving hands:

Good morning boys …

Mark paused, his smile growing as he listened for the reply with anticipation. He chuckled when it came and signed it:

God boring, Pr Lazy!

'Always the same old rubbish speech every time!' Mark told Aaron. He waved him away to watch the headmaster. Reluctantly, Aaron did so. He glanced to his left along his own row and saw that David seemed to be quite content with what was being said on the stage, smiling and nodding his head at every word or two. The rest of the row just stared at the stage with blank faces.

When assembly was finished, the boys streamed out into the passageway. For the whole fifteen minutes, Aaron had not been able to follow the headmaster, despite trying his damnedest to lipread. He kept glancing back to Mark to pick up some of what was being said; he wondered how Mark had managed it. Most of the time, he hadn't understood anything the headmaster was talking about, except for when he once pointed at the front row; Aaron knew he was welcoming the new boys. And then there was The Lord's Prayer that everyone had to recite in unison, reading from the sheet provided. Aaron had mumbled his way through, not knowing whether he was in sync with the others or not, but wondering if they did either.

'I couldn't understand what Mr Langston said,' Aaron said to Chris, pointing back at the hall as they walked side by side through the connecting corridor towards the main building.

'Most of us can't,' agreed Chris. 'He's too far away for us to lipread. He thinks we all have magic eyes! You just pretend to understand.'

'But he might say something important and we won't know what.'

'We use the phone–good.' Chris gestured a telephone and followed it with a thumbs up.

'Phone–good?'

'Mark Cameron is one of them,' Chris answered, smiling. 'Like him, a few boys here can speak and lipread very well – there are always one or two in each Form. They're not one hundred percent deaf like most of the boys; like you and me. They can use the telephone to phone home. They sign in secret during the assembly for us to understand Mr Langston. Sometimes, they'll tell us more afterwards, or you can just read the notes Mr Langston always puts on the school noticeboard after assembly. Your Form should have a phone–good.'

Aaron already had a pretty good idea who that might be.

When Aaron looked at his Form's timetable for the first day, he was pleased to find that English was the first lesson of the day; it was his best subject. He observed from the timetable that each day of the week had six fifty–minute lessons – the first started at half past nine, the second at twenty past ten, followed by a twenty–minute break at ten past eleven before resuming with the third lesson at half past eleven. Lunch was at half past twelve and the fourth and fifth lessons resumed at two o'clock and ten to three respectively. The twenty–minute afternoon break was at twenty to four, followed with the sixth and final lesson of the day. He noted that the fifth and sixth lessons were for sports, alternately juniors and seniors. Teatime was at five o'clock, while homework – or prep, as it was called – started at six o'clock for an hour. After that, the boys were free to do as they chose with their time. Chris had already told Aaron that the First Formers had to be in their dorm at quarter to nine for lights out thirty minutes later. The Second Form had to be in their dorm at nine o'clock; the Third Formers had to be in at quarter past and the Fourth Formers at half past. The Fifth Formers, however, were free to go into their dorm any time after ten, although, their lights had to be out by eleven. Each day and evening, the school had a Duty Teacher, working on a rota system.

Aaron was most interested to learn from the timetable that each subject was taught by a different teacher in a different classroom; he had never had that kind of thing at his old school; everything had simply been taught by one teacher in one classroom.

During his first class, Aaron sat in the middle of a semicircular formation of ten wooden desks, facing the teacher's desk and the blackboard. He looked round the English Room as it was called: it was a fairly large classroom with a high ceiling and two large double–framed windows on one side. The classroom was one of several classrooms located along the east and west sides of the school; Aaron had already seen that each had its own sign on the door – Maths Room, Geography/History Room, Religious Studies Room, Physics Room, Art Room and Speech Room. Craftwork was located outside in a small workshop next door to Magnat House. There were more rooms Aaron that had yet to explore.

Aaron examined the wooden desk in front of him. Its white top featured a collection of scribbles and doodles done by other boys. He raised his eyebrows at one, which read in small yet bold handwriting, *English is boring!* He glanced up at Mr Whittle who was writing *Welcome!* on the blackboard, wondering if the teacher had actually seen this comment. He then looked at the right side of his desk, which had a vertical amplification unit with three knobs – on/off, volume control and right/left ear balance. At the bottom was a pair of cumbersome–looking headphones that hung on a metal hook. He picked it up and felt its weight. With his other hand, he wound down the black rubber cording, which was attached to the bulky right muff and the amplification unit, around the curved steel headstrap. As he continued unwinding, a long, curved mouthpiece, which was also attached to the right muff, flapped up and down. He then saw that his form mates were doing the same.

Mr Whittle turned to face the boys after having finished writing his name on the blackboard, under *Welcome!,* and waited as the new boys began to put on the headphones. Aaron handled his steel muffs with both hands; each had a thick red plastic padded ring and a small grate on the inside. As he began to put them on, he quickly remembered that he was still wearing his moulds, so he yanked both of their cords and they fell limply from his ears. He then put the headphones on, soon realising that they were quite uncomfortable, sitting lopsidedly on his head. He pushed them to try to level them out, but struggled in doing so. Mr Whittle rounded his desk, briskly walked over to Aaron and leaned over to adjust the headphones. Aaron whimpered at the warm, tight, rubbing on his ears in opposite directions. Once he was done, the English teacher gently patted the muffs with his hands, smiling through his thick beard as he returned to his position.

Aaron felt as though his head was suddenly twice as heavy. The red padding was already hurting his ears and the heavy, curved steel strap was bearing down on top of his head. He bent his head down, taking the weight of the headphones with him, and tentatively turned the on/off knob. Suddenly, a loud blare shot through his ears, making his eardrums tingle. Aaron jumped from his chair in shock and quickly looked down at the control panel to discover that the volume knob was at the maximum setting of six. He turned it to one and his still–ringing ears embraced the complete silence. He began to hate them already.

Mr Whittle put a strap over his own head, tapped on the microphone and spoke to the boys.

The boys stared at him, wondering what he'd just said. Aaron could only *feel* the short, but quiet vibrations of the teacher's voice in the headphones. He tried to work out what the teacher had said, as his beard was in the way of his lips, but couldn't figure it out. He turned to his right to see David, who was sitting at the end of the desk formation, his hand up.

'I can, sir!' said David. Aaron and the others frowned; what was the question?

'Good,' the English teacher nodded, gesturing a thumbs up. Aaron managed to lipread that one all right. Mr Whittle then pointed at the blackboard behind him. 'Welcome! My name is Mr Whittle …'

Aaron rested his elbows on the desk, his eyes squinting hard at the small gaping black hole in the man's thick, ginger facial hair.

Aaron sniffed once again.

The classroom was like a perfume shop, he thought. He carefully watched the thick, bright red moving lips of Mrs Munnings as she finished writing *Geography and History* on the blackboard, holding the microphone in her hand.

'I'm Mrs Munn …' she introduced herself. 'I teachoo geographee and hiss try. I … sure you … enjoooy them!'

Aaron managed to read most of what she had said, so she was alright, but he still couldn't hear her voice through the headphones, despite the volume control being set at five. He only could feel some vibrations on his ears; that was about it. Mrs Munnings – *Fluttereyes* was her sign name because of her long eyelashes – seemed to have good, almost clear lips, as long as she kept her head still.

The Geography/History Room had a similar set up to the English Room, except that it only had one window and its back wall was covered with several maps of the world, pictures of famous landmarks from around the world and some historical material at which Aaron didn't have the chance to take a look. Along another wall, opposite the window, was a small bookcase filled with a variety of geography and history literature.

'Let's … introoo OUR–selves, shaaall weee?' Mrs Munnings announced, picking up the nominal roll and raising the microphone to her mouth. 'WATCH my lips for yooour … name and when I SAY it, PUT … your hand UP. Okay, boooeees?'

Aaron had managed to lipread each boy's name in turn – he knew most of them so far – as the teacher wrote their names on the blackboard, though he did wonder how she managed to follow their deaf speech. Except for David, of course. He noted their names – Bradley Watts, David Wheeley, Derek Ferguson – who dared to fingerspell his name instead of speaking it; the teacher told him to use his voice, though Aaron knew he couldn't – Duncan Nielson, Jonah Kaisermann, Ian Snyman, Michael Hardcastle, Shaun Knight and Andy Farmleigh.

Following what Derek had tried to do, Mrs Munnings said firmly that signing was not allowed in the classroom, although they were allowed to do that outside their lessons.

Aaron folded his arms, the weight of the headphones pressing down on his head.

A large right hand slapped thunderously on a Bible that was resting on the teacher's desk. The First Formers shuddered. Not because of the thunderous noise, which they barely heard, but because of the way Mr Arkwright went about it.

Aaron already knew the tall teacher; he was the one who had watched him recite The Lord's Prayer at the entrance exams. Strands of long dark hair were immaculately combed around his head, held together by Brylcreem that glistened under the fluorescent lighting above them. The man – who was close to fifty, Aaron figured – wore dark brown thick–rimmed spectacles which somehow complemented his weathered cheeks, neck and the thick, rubber–like lips that seemed to stretch from side to side. The teacher also had a distinctive personality, camp and affected as if he had been born in a theatre. He wore a theatrical, brown wool suit and black baggy trousers, which, for some strange reason, seemed to form a natural part of his personality.

Mr Arkwright clasped his hands together with the microphone sandwiched between them. 'My name is Mr Arkwright,' he said, before turning round, picking up the chalk from the wooden groove at the base of the blackboard and quickly writing his name across the board. He then turned back to face the boys again and he repeated slowly: 'Ark–wrig–ht. I teach religious studies and speech.'

The teacher panned his head around the semicircular formation of desks, waiting for a response or acknowledgement, but all he saw was a set of blank eyes staring at him. He quickly noticed the curved mouthpiece on the headphones that Duncan was wearing was awkwardly positioned upright. He walked round the teacher's desk towards Duncan and pulled the stick down with his big hand, levelling it with Duncan's mouth. 'You must always position this by your mouth, so that you can hear your own voice when you speak. Is that understood?'

Duncan nodded. Aaron thought the teacher's lips were quite explicitly and expressively clear – well, with that kind of big mouth, it was not that hard. He looked down, saw that his own mouthpiece was positioned slightly low and lifted it up a bit.

The Physics Room was located at the back of the east side of the school. After lunch, the First Formers took a short stroll through a few corridors – one of which led to the connecting passageway to Magnat House – through the lobby to reach the classroom. Aaron observed the medium sized square room with two smaller windows. Magnat House was in view close by, which reduced the amount of natural light that streamed into the classroom. The classroom was of a different type: the desk set–up consisted of three rows of high, polished wooden tables, with three or four high stools at each, a teacher's desk at the front, with the blackboard and a pull–down projection screen next to the door which the boys had just come in. The teacher's desk had an overhead projector with a raised mirror head. On one side, opposite the windows, was a long bench with gas taps and burners attached to it. The wall at the back had several shelves of science books. The boys loitered around the three rows of desks, and then sat on the high stools. Aaron made himself comfortable at a desk and sighed when he saw those headphones hanging underneath it. He hated them already; his ears were a bit sore. He rested his forearms on the desk and idly let his eyes wander around the room, excited – he loved science and wanted to learn as much as he could.

Suddenly, the door swung open and a young lady hurried in, carrying a stack of notebooks which she placed on her desk. 'I'm sorry I'm late!' she addressed the new boys.

Aaron looked at her with wide eyes. She was beautiful! Her face was nicely shaped, with rosy cheeks below her deep brown eyes which were complemented by a delectable pout. Her long blond hair was styled round her head like a beehive and held in place by a blue headband. She wore a tight pink jumper and a cream skirt in stripes. Aaron could easily see the rounded shape of her breasts. She turned her slim figure to the blackboard and Aaron saw her peachy bottom, which was flaunted just above the desk. She wrote her name on the blackboard, but Aaron did not pay attention to it, for he was still gazing at her backside. He thought she resembled Lady Penelope from Thunderbirds, minus the wooden appearance, and she must be in her mid–twenties. The physics and biology teacher turned back to face the boys, pointing at the blackboard. 'Hello, I'm Miss Stephenson, your physics and biology teacher.'

Oh, her lips moved smoothly, Aaron told himself; she was quite easy to lipread. He was going to enjoy his physics and biology lessons for the next five years. He soon became aware that he wasn't the only boy in the room who was gazing wildly at the pretty teacher.

Aaron and his form mates entered the Art Room, which was adjacent to the Physics Room, for their fifth lesson of the day. A man was at the teacher's desk, his back to them. He had short black hair and wore a navy polo–necked jumper and black flares. The man wheeled round to see the new boys streaming in and waved at them to take their seats before turning back again. As they walked to their desks, Aaron looked round; the set–up was similar to that of the Physics Room, except that it was much larger and the three rows of desks were lower; they looked brand new and had tops that could be tilted up to become drawing or painting boards. Several easels were mounted idly across the right side of the room, while the back wall was filled with various painted and sketched pictures that the boys had done. The left side of the room had three small windows; Magnat House, once again, obscured the view.

Aaron took his seat in the centre of the middle row. Having already developed a new habit, Aaron and his form mates leaned down to pick up their headphones, but to his surprise, there were none in sight, not even any amplification units. He looked around and saw that the other boys had the same reaction as him.

After he had finished sorting out some items on his desk, the art teacher turned back to the boys. He was a young and fairly handsome man, in his late twenties or early thirties, Aaron thought, and he had a fresher and more cheerful personality about him than the other teachers he had met so far. Like Aaron, the man had blue eyes. He had short sideburns that ran down from his black hair to his jawline, and a smile that could light up a room. Aaron directed his eyes to the man's mouth for another strained round of lipreading.

The teacher rolled up his sleeves, exposing his forearms, then rubbed his hands. He began to move his fingers; 'Hello boys, I'm M–R M–C–S–H–A–N–E,' he signed and fingerspelled his name.

Aaron's jaw dropped as Mr McShane cheerfully folded his arms, observing the boys' silent reaction.

'I know you're a little surprised,' the smiling Mr McShane went on, signing fluently as if he was deaf himself. 'I can sign. I come from a deaf family. My parents, my two brothers and my sister are all deaf. I'm the only hearing child – I grew up around deaf people and sign language.' He rested his bottom on the edge of his desk and indicated to the absent headphones. 'Those headphones don't work for most of you; Art is visual – like sign language!'

The boys cheered and whooped; they liked him already.

Sitting on his bed, Aaron twiddled his thumbs and looked at the wall clock: quarter past four now. He scanned around Dorm One; six of his form mates were also sitting on their beds, either signing to one another or waiting idly. They had been told earlier that they had to skip the last lesson because a school doctor was coming to check their health. Each boy had to go in on his own; four had already gone in and Aaron knew it was his turn next because he was the fifth oldest boy in his form and they had started with Duncan, who was the oldest. Andy, the youngest, would be last.

Derek came through the door and everyone turned to him. He pointed at Aaron to tell him it was his turn next. Aaron rose and walked towards the door while Derek backed away from the doorway. He gave Aaron a wry smile, before turning to the corridor behind him and trudging on his way. Aaron wondered why Derek had smiled like that, but shrugged it off and headed towards the matron's office at the other end of the foyer.

He entered a small, square room next door to the matron's office, which had a worktop and cupboards on the left; he assumed they contained medical supplies. A small frosted window was on the adjacent wall. A man was sitting in the centre of the room; he was almost bald, with some greying hair round the sides of his head, and he was looking downwards, writing on a sheet of paper on a clipboard. Aaron presumed that the doctor was still writing notes on his previous examination with Derek. His dark brown suit matched his thickly rimmed spectacles.

Miss Hogarth was standing between the worktop and the doctor. She smiled warmly at Aaron. 'It won't be too long, Aaron,' she said.

The doctor finished his notes, swapping them with the next sheet, which he clipped down. He then looked up at Aaron. 'Hello!' he greeted him. 'You must be Aaron Stephens then.'

Aaron nodded. He was fairly easy to lipread. The doctor waved him forward. He then placed his thumbs just below Aaron's eyes and pulled them down slightly, checking his eyes. He nodded, mumbling to himself, and let go. He then took an auriscope from his breast pocket, switching it on. Aaron immediately knew what the cylindrical instrument with the metal cone was; he took out both of his moulds. The doctor checked Aaron's right ear first. Aaron shivered a little, feeling the coldness in his ear. After a brief moment, the doctor then proceeded to the left ear. Aaron gazed to his left to see the man mumbling to himself again. Once he was finished, he replaced the instrument in his breast pocket.

'Open your mouth please,' the doctor instructed, pointing at his own open mouth. Aaron did so; the doctor inserted a lollipop stick into his open mouth and pressed it down on his tongue. Aaron's stomach churned in uneasiness. The doctor nodded, mumbling to himself and withdrew the stick.

Right, Aaron thought, *he's finished with me now.* He began to put his groping moulds back in.

'Pull down your trousers and your pants please,' the doctor told him.

Aaron froze. He quickly turned to Miss Hogarth, bewildered.

'It's all right, Aaron,' she said, signing some of what she was saying. 'He needs to check your testicles to make sure that you are in good health. I'll turn my back if you like.'

Aaron turned to the smiling doctor who nodded for him to get on with it. He looked back at the matron again, expressing his apprehension.

'It won't take too long.' she said reassuringly. 'He won't touch your penis; he'll only feel around it, that's all. I can promise you that.'

Reluctantly, Aaron opened his trousers and allowed them to slide down to his knees. Miss Hogarth, as she had promised, turned away. The doctor waited impatiently as Aaron began to pull down his blue and white Y–fronts. The top of his underwear stopped at the top of his penis, still concealing it from the prying man's eyes. The doctor leaned forward and pulled down the underwear, exposing his modesty. Aaron stood like a statue. The doctor placed his thumbs around the lower part of Aaron's bladder, pressing it firmly. Aaron flinched when the doctor moved down to check the testicles, groping them. Aaron coughed when he felt the pressure. It only took him about fifteen seconds to complete the examination, but for Aaron, it felt like minutes. As soon as the doctor was finished, Aaron pulled up his underwear, and then his trousers, in a flash. He gave the man a hard stare.

'Thank you, Aaron,' the doctor said, then bowed his head to write his notes again. Miss Hogarth turned back to Aaron, picked up her sheet from the worktop, read the list and told Aaron to send David in next.

Aaron caught up with Chris afterwards in the front hall and told him about what the doctor had done.

'He did that to me last year,' Chris said, smiling. 'I hated it as well. Dirty old man! Dean Hopkirk punched him.'

'Really?' gawked Aaron.

'Yeah, really,' replied Chris. 'Broke his nose, blood everywhere! He was the first boy in my Form to get detention.'

7

The Ghost

"Facts do not cease to exist because they are ignored."
– ALDOUS HUXLEY (1894–1963)

That evening, Aaron suddenly felt a sense of déjà vu as he and his form mates walked along a long, narrow corridor, lined with wooden panels. Wood–panelled double doors were at the end and fluorescent lighting tubes ran the length of the ceiling.

Aaron shrugged off this eerie feeling as he followed the group, which was led by Chris, Andrew and an older boy with long, dark hair and spectacles; Aaron had yet to learn his name, although he knew the boy was a Fourth Former. This boy pushed one of the heavy looking doors inwards and held it open to allow the rest in; they entered the school's big library. Aaron took in his surroundings. The library was impressive and well–structured, tucked away in the back corner of the ground floor on the west side of the building. Floor–to–ceiling shelves, some built in, covered each of the four walls; they were filled with books, magazines and documents of all types, sizes, some pretty old, some fairly new. Two tall, wide double–framed windows were on one side, opposite the wall where the double doors – the only centrally positioned entrance – were. The windows with crisscrossed panes were between three sections of shelf which otherwise filled the entire wall. A similar window was in the middle of the adjacent wall. Aaron looked away from the window on his right and noted that, like all the windows in the school, it could be opened by unbolting a latch between the upper and lower frames; then, either the lower frame could be pushed up or the upper frame down. All of the windows had thick, dark green curtains; at the top of each window, a decorative wooden pelmet concealed the top part of the curtains.

Aaron saw that there were a number of oil paintings between the shelves; mostly landscapes and nature scenes, as well as two portraits. One was of an authoritative–looking man in his early sixties – Aaron didn't know who – in a dark, pinstriped suit. The other, the largest of the paintings in the library, hung in the centre of the wall on Aaron's left, opposite the wall with the solitary window.

It was of a young woman in a Regency gown.

In the centre of the large room stood an exquisite, large rectangular oak table with deep curves in each corner. High–backed decorative oak chairs stood elegantly around the table and Aaron quickly counted them as twelve. He also saw that there were a number of cushioned black metal chairs were also scattered around the thick dark green and gold patterned carpet.

He gazed up at the high ornate ceiling, impressive with decorative carvings and deep, curved plaster cornice running around the tops of the walls. Four large dark green painted square medallions with gold trim took up the entire ceiling. In the centre of the squares was a huge crystal chandelier hanging over the large table.

When the boys had finished digesting their surroundings, Chris waved at them to get their attention. 'This is the library,' he announced. 'It's the biggest room in the school. There's plenty to read!'

Andrew stepped in and pointed at one particular shelf, which had a line of yellow spines across it. The boys looked at what Andrew was pointing at and turned back to him. 'They're the National Geographic magazines.' he said; 'You can see plenty of pictures of naked–'

Chris gently whacked Andrew's head with the palm of his head to cut him short, shaking his head. He pointed at the older boy, who was quite eager to get on with things. 'This is Justin Pope,' Chris introduced, signing his name to depict a cross. 'He is the Library Officer. He'll explain about the library and its rules.'

Justin then proceeded to talk about the library, the variety of literature that they could take out. He also explained how each boy had to use the logbook to record the title and reference number (that was printed on the inside page of the cover), their own name and the dates of borrowing and returning books that they wanted to take out. He added that certain books could not leave the library, and implored that the books were returned to their exact places. Justin finished his talk by inviting the new boys to have a look around.

Aaron wandered around, browsing from one shelf to another, while noting several books that he would like to read. One caught his eye and he took it down; it was a thin book about the history of the mansion which now housed the school, and the surrounding park. He replaced it, promising himself that he would read it later.

He then came upon the large painting of the woman that he had seen earlier. David joined him and they both looked at it. The beautiful young woman had immaculately styled dark hair; her face was perfectly formed and she had ravishing, pouted lips. She stood in a proud but firm pose; her light blue gown reached to the floor and her hands were clasped in front of her waist. In spite of her beauty, there was something about her eyes: they were piercingly sad and it was as though she were *watching*. Aaron shivered a little under her intense gaze. He looked down at a bronze nameplate at the bottom of the carved gold–painted wood frame to note that she was Lady Rodrigues, the painting dated 1780.

The library doors slowly opened, as if someone was making a grand entrance. Everybody turned to see three Third Form boys entering. Aaron quickly recognised the beefy one in the middle as Brian Thompson – Basher, he was nicknamed – who Chris had warned him about earlier.

The beefy fourteen–year–old stopped in the doorway while the other two each held one of the heavy doors open. He had chubby cheeks, a small mouth and wavy black hair, which covered both of his ears, concealing the moulds in them. The cords ran discreetly down the back of his neck towards the aids that were in a hidden harness, tucked under his white shirt with rolled up sleeves. He glanced menacingly around the silently watching crowd.

Aaron also knew from Chris who Basher's form mates on either side of him were: Gary Portmore and Timothy "Spook" Hutchinson. Gary was the tallest of the three; he was quite lanky, with long, parted fair hair. According to Chris, Gary was one of the phone–goods – he was born half deaf, so he could hear reasonably well and had perfect speech. His sign name, was *oral*; this consisted of bent index and middle fingers circling the mouth. Timothy had unusually mournful eyes, framed by arched black eyebrows; one could almost believe that he had risen from the grave, hence his nickname. He was slightly shorter than Gary, but taller than Basher; and thin, but not as lanky as Gary. The boy with black hair was well known for his wicked sense of humour.

Basher slowly strolled into the library with a self–confident swagger, scanning the room. He glared at Chris, regarding him with some scrutiny. Chris returned the same hard stare, silently gritting his teeth, showing little regard for his adversary. Their rivalry started when Chris had first arrived at the school the previous year. He was one of the very few who would stand up to the school bully and Basher had always resented him for that.

Chris broke off from the intense, lingering glare and dipped his hands into his pockets. Basher strolled purposely over to where Aaron and David were, and pointed at the painting.

'Do you know who she is?' Basher asked.

'It says Lady Rodrigues,' Aaron replied, pointing at the nameplate.

Basher nodded. 'Do you know what happened to her?' he followed up, with a knowing twinkle in his eye. Aaron and David shook their heads. 'She was murdered,' he said. 'By her jealous sister, over a man they both loved. It's true. There's a book here that you can read about the history of this place.'

Aaron quickly remembered the book he had seen a moment ago and looked at David, who said nothing. Gary wheeled in beside Basher, smiling eerily.

'Her ghost haunts this school,' he announced.

Chris began to move forward to stop the charade, but Andrew placed his hand on Chris' chest, stopping him. 'Let them, he said. 'It happens with the new boys every year. Remember last year?'

Chris sighed, folding his arms and thinking about it. It had always been the school's tradition, first started as a joke by a former teacher shortly after the school was first opened, aiming to spook the new boys with a ghost story, using the murdered woman as a source. Over the years, it became a tradition and each year, the haunting was increasingly creative. Chris smirked when he remembered the "ghostly" incident that his Form had experienced last year. He and his form mates had been taken to the gym, which they were told was haunted by Lady Rodrigues because she had been murdered on that very spot less than two hundred years before. They were warned that if they felt a chill down their backs, it was her; she would sometimes move things in the gym. Chris and some of his form mates knew it was all rubbish, but Jamon Cranley believed it. Their attention was directed to the line of six climbing ropes, which hung from the high ceiling; one of them moved creepily to and fro as if it had a mind of its own. Jamon suddenly burst into tears, ran for the moving rope and grappled it. The rope went limp as though it had died from strangulation, much to the surprise and amusement of others. It turned out that one of the Brannigan twins – Paul or Peter, it was impossible to tell them apart – was hiding behind a stack of blue floor mats at the back of the gym, pulling a fishing line that was tied to the rope. The line had snapped when Jamon wrestled with the rope. Chris brushed away the memory and wondered how Basher and his two accomplices would top that tonight.

Timothy stood on his toes, arms raised high with droopy hands, hovering over Aaron and David to invoke fear in them. 'Boo–hoo!' He then lowered his arms and leaned menacingly over them. 'She was murdered … where?' he asked, smiling ghoulishly. David shook his head. 'In Dorm One! That's where her ghost haunts. Boo–hoo!'

Timothy raised his arms again and hovered away towards the new boys, running round them like a demented ghost. Basher leaned down slightly, coming eye level with Aaron and David, widening his eyes to throw fear into them.

'Be afraid … be *very afraid*.' Basher said.

He straightened back up, satisfied with what he and his friends had done, then they left the library. Chris walked over to a bewildered Aaron and shrugged. David, on the other hand, trembled.

'I want my mummy!' he cried out.

'Goodnight, boys,' said Miss Hogarth, giving them a thumbs up before swiping her flattened hands down by her face. She then reached for the light switch by the door and flicked it off. Dorm One was plunged into almost complete darkness, with only the light from the foyer outside shining in. The matron heard strangely quiet, yet terrified, gasps from some of the boys, but thought nothing of it. As she turned to leave, she heard a voice calling out to her.

'Can you ... please leave the door open?' asked David.

The big woman turned, directing her eyes at David's bed at the far end of the darkened room. She nodded, pulling the door in halfway as she walked out, disappearing from view. The First Formers looked around the room wide–eyed. Aaron's eyes searched for the slightest glimpse of whatever it might be. He jumped slightly when a shadow moved across the wall on his right and his eyes darted to the partially open door, only to see Dean in the foyer, heading for Dorm Two next door. Get a grip; Aaron thought to himself, *it isn't real!* He had had been watching too many children's programmes about ghosts and scary stuff. *Children of the Stones* sprang into mind: that seven–parter children's show that he had seen last January was unbelievably *scary*. Jamie had signed much of the dialogue, the spooky atmospheric sounds and creepy music. He would sometimes go a bit overboard just to scare him even more, especially the terrifying climax in which people had turned into stones just like the ones at Stonehenge. He raised his head and glanced at David's bed further down, wondering if he was all right. He hadn't stopped crying for quite a bit that evening; they had told him Basher was only joking, but he believed the story. Many old buildings had ghosts, he said. Aaron rested his head on his pillow, thinking about the good point David had made and praying that he would fall asleep before anything happened.

David couldn't stop staring at the half open door, taking some comfort from the light from the foyer. His hands grasped his top sheet and he closed his eyes to try to sleep, but each time he did so, the image of that woman's ghostly form came into view. Resignedly, he opened them again, looking once more at the door. Without his spectacles, his vision was blurred, but at least he could still take solace in the light.

It went out suddenly.

Aaron gasped when the dorm was plunged into pitch–black darkness. David froze, his blurry eyes still staring at the now darkened foyer through the half open door. Even without his hearing aids, he heard gasps from some of the other beds. Especially his left ear; had a mind of its own – one minute he could not even hear a loud clatter, the next he could almost hear a pin drop. He listened carefully for any kind of noise, but there was none, and although he thought he could almost hear a soft pattering of feet, he could not see anything, for he had had a problem with seeing in the dark ever since becoming deaf at the age of seven.

Ian held his breath; he was sure he could see something crawling on the floor towards the middle of the room. Like his father, he was good at seeing in the dark, but it was difficult to tell what was on the floor. He could almost make out three dark forms, like moving black boulders. He was tempted to jump out of his bed, run across the room and switch on the lights, but was far too scared to do so. Derek saw them as well; his bed was closest to the door and he had already seen them crawling through it. He was itching to go for the light switch, but decided not to, as he wanted to see what would happen next, just for the fun of it. Sitting on his bed, he folded his arms, waiting with glee.

Aaron jumped when a loud thud rocked the floorboards. Bradley grasped his bedsheets. Duncan squinted into the darkness, trying to make sense of what was happening. Jonah gritted his teeth. Shaun, who was already sitting up on his bed, folded his arms, waiting with anticipation. David then heard creaking sounds coming from the centre of the room.

'Who's … there?' David quietly asked, trembling.

Suddenly, something white shot up like a water geyser, illuminated by lights from below. It was a white clad figure of no identifiable form; it had three humps on top, the middle one being the largest. The other two moved around wildly as though striking out in fear. The rest of the white form flowed like sails against the swaying illuminations from below, which gave the white shape a terrifying presence.

David went to hysterics. He heard screams and laughter, with the loudest coming from the apparition. He recognised the unmistakable voice:

Hoo–boo–hoo!

Derek laughed out loud. The young Scot then jumped out of his bed and flicked on the lights. There, before everyone's eyes, were Basher and Gary crouching on the floor, each holding a large metal torch. A figure stood between them, covered by the white bed sheet. A hand reached out from underneath the sheet and pulled it away to reveal Timothy. They were all laughing. Basher and Gary rose to their feet and they all walked briskly out of the dormitory, having successfully upheld the tradition for another year.

Just as they left the room, the lights in the foyer came on to reveal several Second and Third Formers, who had been standing there waiting while the prank went on.

Aaron slumped back onto his bed, relieved and laughing.

8

Football and the Church

"Thou shall not curse the deaf, nor put a stumbling block before the blind, but shall fear thy God: I am the LORD."
– LEVITICUS 19.

Aaron looked down at his new Puma football boots, feeling their comfort and the tightness from the long black laces wrapped round each boot and tied at the top. He checked the underside of one to inspect the moulded plastic studs. It was the first time he had ever worn them and he remembered again the trip he had made to Sportsfair in Bristol city centre with his dad during the summer, to buy the boots and a new pair of plimsolls to replace the old ones that he had used for gym lessons at Elmfield.

His dad used to play football at school and had been quite good at it, so he said. He had played for his local team on Sunday mornings until he retired about few years back. He sometimes talked about how he idolised the legendary Stanley Matthews, who had continued to play football into his late forties. Apparently, he had twice watched him play when he was a boy.

There was an incident in the shop that had helped him decide on the Puma. As he had lifted down a pair of Umbro boots from the shelves that were filled with different brands, examining them, he had suddenly felt a presence behind him. Turning round, he came face to face with a boy of about fourteen who was trying to speak to him from behind and couldn't understand why Aaron hadn't responded. John spoke to the boy and Aaron knew he was explaining that he was deaf. He wasn't wearing his body aids out shopping. It turned out that the boy was trying to advise him to choose the Puma on the top shelf instead of the ones that Aaron was looking at. Aaron followed this, but was soon was left floundering when his dad and the boy had a brief exchange of words, which he couldn't understand. Suddenly, Aaron's dad became annoyed with the boy and shooed him off. The boy cast a final stare at Aaron, as though he had grown another head, before leaving the shop. Aaron looked up at his dad quizzically for an explanation. John, speaking slowly and writing on the notepad that he always carried to communicate with his deaf son, explained that the boy, who had introduced himself as Ian from Cadbury Heath, was a very good footballer who would go professional after school. Apparently he was still trying to decide whether to play for City or Rovers and John had bluntly told him to go for Rovers; a team he supported. Ian said that his dad had told him the same thing and then he had remarked out of the blue that he hoped his own children would not be deaf and dumb, as he was of the opinion that they would never be good at football, let alone able to join a professional club. This had riled John, who had retorted that if he had deaf children himself, his view would definitely change. He also told the boy that he didn't like the term "dumb" because it implied stupidity.

Aaron glanced up from his boots and looked around to see his form mates and the Second Form gathered in a semicircle on the playing field in front of the school. They were watching a short, pigeon–chested man in his late forties, Aaron assumed, who had a huge conk of a nose. His short hair was parted and he had pig–like eyes and plump cheeks. He was waving his index finger in all directions as he rambled on, without even stopping between words. Aaron concentrated hard on the sports teacher's lips; no easy task, given his constantly moving head.

'Rememberlookseepasskick,' he spoke rapidly. 'Donotlookdownatyourball anddribblealltheway!' he gave a demonstration by looking down and moving his feet with such frenzy as though he was dancing on hot coals. With the back of his left hand, he pushed his own chin up and swayed his head from side to side as if to tell them to look around.

Aaron gave up trying to follow the man's fast–moving lips and thought about the sports lessons they had to do every afternoon. According to Chris, Mondays were usually for cross–country running, Tuesdays, Thursdays and Saturday mornings for football or rugby from September to April, replaced by cricket and athletics from May to July. Wednesdays were for other sports such as tennis, badminton and squash – the latter being at the Leisure Centre in Waltbridge, as the school didn't have a squash court. Fridays were swimming at the local baths. P.E. lessons were usually in the mornings during the week: each Form on a different day. Chris told Aaron that Mr Norris used to be a sergeant major in the Army and that he had also been a semi–professional boxer, so he was *not* to box with him during P.E. lessons. He told Aaron of an amusing incident that had happened earlier the year when Chris had been in Form One. Mr Norris had caught Mark Cameron bullying another boy and had challenged him to a boxing match, using real boxing gloves, at their next P.E. lesson. Mark had been floored by every punch, even the slightest pokes, and he'd even got a bloody nose.

'Comeon!' the sports teacher clapped his hands and waved them. 'Playmoveon!' He turned and briskly marched away.

Aaron tugged at his new green and gold checked long–sleeved jersey, trying to make himself feel comfortable in it. He smoothed his hands round his black shorts. The school provided all the boys with sportswear. Aaron was already a little wet from the slight drizzle. He folded his arms, shivering a bit.

Chris and the captain of the opposing team, Dean Hopkirk, moved to stand in front of the group. Chris waved at them. 'Forget him. He doesn't know anything about football – he always talks crap!' He pointed to the lanky boy with dark hair on his left, sliding his other hand down his chest as though Dean was rich, for his name sign, 'Dean Hopkirk and I are captains and we'll both pick our teams.'

Chris and Dean took turns to select their players, starting with the best. The captains asked the new boys whether they were any good at football. Derek, Ian, Michael, Shaun, Jonah and Bradley put their hands up to say they were. Aaron had considered putting his hand up, but decided not to; he had never played football properly, only kick–abouts in the back garden with Jamie at home.

'Can you play football?' Chris asked Aaron. Aaron shrugged in response. Chris beckoned for him to join the team anyway. 'You'll be defence.' He motioned for Dean to take his turn.

'Matthew Burke,' Dean pointed at his best friend, signing as if a pair of horse blinkers were on his face and beckoning for the boy who had a soft, round body with black hair to join him. 'Goalkeeper.'

Yeah, Matthew mused to himself as he trotted over; he already knew that. The safest thing was to stick him between the goalposts to stop the opposition from scoring with his hands instead of his feet, he thought; he used to play right back – and he'd been very good at it – but he was having some problems with his sight and he couldn't understand why. He kept bumping into other boys and always gave bad tackles. Mr Norris had often told him not to look down at the ball when dribbling, but it was *impossible* for him not to do that. Every time he tried that, the ball would disappear from view, so he needed to *look down* to see it. The opposing players easily took it from his feet, from either side, despite the fact that he should've easily seen them. It was as if he had some kind of invisible cone on his face with a hole at the end. Because of this, he now had the name sign *horse blinkers,* which he hated. He had been asking his parents about this problem since he first came to the school, when he realised he was different from the other boys, but they never gave him straight answers. It wasn't just a football problem though.

Matthew stood next to Sammy Maguire with freckles and chestnut hair, who was hopping on the grass to warm himself up. He remembered the first time he realised that there was something wrong with his eyes: it was last November when they were in the craftwork lesson. Mr Bronte was teaching the class how to hammer the red–hot end of an iron bar on the anvil, while holding it with a pair of tongs. Once done, the bar had to be dunked into water for cooling. Each boy took his turn and when it was Matthew's turn, he swung the bar towards the bucket, only for the red–hot end to hit Sammy's upper shirtsleeve, causing a small burn hole and scorching his arm. The teacher was furious with him. Dean said that he should easily have seen Sammy standing right there, but Matthew claimed that he didn't and was adamant that Sammy must have stepped forward and got struck, though the others said he didn't move an inch.

Matthew quietly chuckled at the memory; Sammy's shocked face had been a picture. Sammy saw him chucking. 'What are you laughing for?' he asked.

'Nothing,' Matthew answered smugly, looking away. The boy from Belfast resumed his warm–up exercises.

The next thing Matthew remembered was during teatime in the dining room a few weeks later. He was busy eating his dinner, not paying any attention to what was going on around the table, when he noticed that all his form mates were looking at him and laughing. Steven gestured with his butter knife to tell Matthew to look to his right. He did and jerked his head backwards on seeing Sammy waving a fork close to his right eye. Lester Morrison told him that Sammy had been doing it for about two minutes, but he hadn't seen it when he should have. Matthew felt hurt and embarrassed. There had been other things too, such as other boys trying to wave at him to get his attention, then, when they couldn't, assuming he was ignoring them on purpose. Sometimes he bumped into people or tripped over things when they should have been clearly visible, or dropped things that he then couldn't find. He'd also discovered that he could not see well in the dark; after lights out in the dorm his form mates could communicate in sign using torches, but he couldn't. The park outside was worse; it was like wearing a blanket over his head because the area was almost pitch black, with very little lighting. He just had to follow the other boys as best as he could, using his finger sometimes to sneakily touch another boy's back from behind to help guide him. He struggled, too, to read the blackboard from his desk, particularly Mr Arkwright's handwriting, which was often elaborate and was particularly difficult for him to read. Miss Stephenson sometimes used the new overhead projector in physics and biology lessons and that was a lot worse: he could barely read anything against the bright screen. She used a black pen for much of the time, which was bad enough, but other colours such as red, green or blue were virtually impossible to read. He sometimes had to lean over another boy's notes to copy down what was being written on the transparent sheet on the projector.

Mr Bronte would sometimes mock him by offering up his own thick–rimmed spectacles during craftwork lessons, when he struggled to see the scratched markings on the copperplate. Every time the teacher did this, he would wave the glasses close to Matthew's eyes, almost poking them. The last time he did so, Matthew grabbed them and smashed them on the floor under his foot, much to the amusement of his form mates. He'd been given three detentions from the fuming old man for it, though.

Lipreading the teachers was always a challenge for him because they always stood so far away from the desks. Their lips often seemed blurred and indecipherable: it was like lipreading the fishes' small mouths swimming around in a tank. The headphones didn't work either – they never did for him anyway, it was the same for most of the other boys – no intelligible sounds or words came through; he only felt vibrations and blares. So he, and the others, always just pretended to understand. The only thing he was good in classes was speaking, as he had fairly good speech. His parents taught him how to speak properly when he was growing up in Cardiff and that was fine with him.

The other boys took advantage of his woes; they teased him. One would tap his shoulder from behind, then cower as Matthew wheeled round, seeing no one, even though the culprit was below him. Sometimes, he would blame the wrong boy and end up in bickering arguments. Occasionally someone would throw something at him, crumbled paper or the like, and he would never find out who'd done it because he couldn't see on either side. Another would mockingly wave his hand on either side for a long time and he wouldn't even notice it – not even close by.

Sports had been particularly difficult for him. He was a sporty lad, but sometimes struggled to do well, particularly at cricket, badminton and squash. He couldn't understand why he had such trouble seeing the cricket ball approaching fast or why he always missed it. The ball only came into view when it was a few feet away from him, but by then it was too late for him to whack it and he was always being bowled out. When fielding, he could barely see the ball that flew up in the air and he always missed catching it, even when he was able to see it, because he was frightened it might hit his head. Some boys had taken to – aptly – saying he was blind as a bat. Badminton was all right, although when he missed the shuttlecock he always struggled to find it on the floor, even when someone would point it out. Sometimes he struck lucky and found it; sometimes a disgruntled boy would come over to pick it up and slam it into his hand, causing him to flush with hurt and embarrassment. Playing doubles was even tougher for him because he had trouble seeing his partner. Sometimes the boy would suddenly come into view and whack the shuttlecock back over the high net with his racket just as he was about to do it himself. Once, he accidentally whacked his own wooden racket on Chris' face and broke it. Chris ended up with a big bruise on his cheek, although he wasn't angry with Matthew at all because he felt it was his fault for coming up from behind. Still, it made him feel bad and angry with himself. Squash was the worst of all; trying to focus on the fast bouncing little ball as it darted around the confined space of the court. He always tried to watch the ball being hit by his opponent to work out where it was going; watching the wall ahead of him as he was supposed to was useless as he couldn't see the ball. Mr Norris had often barked at him *not* to watch the bloody ball, but the wall, but this proved impossible.

He had always dismissed his eye problems, assuming that he needed glasses or that he was simply stupid and clumsy. His problems weren't just at the school but at home too. Once, he ran out of the back door and tripped over his younger sister's bicycle, which had been left lying in full view. He sometimes knocked things over at the dinner table, sometimes bumped into lampposts along the street and people in shops, and he frequently tripped over the family's pet Labrador, Sonny, sometimes treading on his tail.

Shortly after the incident with the fork at teatime, he wrote home to say that there was something wrong with his eyes. He told his parents about his problems at school and his mother immediately wrote back to say that he simply had a "little problem" with his eyes and that she and his Dad would talk to him about it during the Christmas break. They never did though, in spite of him asking them several times. Perhaps they either didn't want to explain to him out of fear, or they didn't fully understand the problem.

The final straw came towards the end of his first year at Ewing Hill Park when, at the end of an art lesson, he accidentally knocked over a tray of small paint tins that he was going to take back to one of the shelves. Mr McShane was very understanding and, with Dean, helped him clean up the mess. The art teacher said that he had already noticed Matthew's eyesight problem and offered to listen if he wanted to talk about it. When the rest of his Form – except for Dean, with whom he had become friends – left the room, Matthew broke down in tears and poured his heart out to the art teacher. The sympathetic Mr McShane was the first and *only* staff member in the entire school who was able to understand him as he was fluent in sign language. Much to his surprise, Mr McShane said that he knew a few deaf people back home in Manchester who might also have the same problem. Mr McShane had been around deaf people all his life, but even he did not really understand what exactly the problem was, except that the people he knew had poor peripheral vision. McShane also mentioned that Jeffrey Gibbs, the head boy, seemed to have a similar problem, though he couldn't be sure. He pointed out that Matthew may not be alone and strongly advised him to talk to his parents again about it during the summer holiday. Matthew said that it was very difficult because they did not sign and only spoke to him. Although Matthew had fairly good speech, it was easier for him to express himself in sign language, but he agreed he would try, nevertheless. Mr McShane promised he would ask Mr Langston to have a word with Matthew's parents when they came to collect him at the end of term.

He had asked his parents again during the summer, but they'd either changed the subject or avoided it altogether, although his mother did say that she and his dad had known about the problem for about three years. She briefly explained that when he was ten, she'd taken him to the local opticians in Cardiff city centre to get his eyes tested because of the problems he was having at home. The optician had found something unusual in his eyes through his ophthalmoscope and referred him to the eye unit at the local hospital. She reminded him of his visits there and the several tests that had been done on his eyes. The doctors hadn't really explained the problem clearly to her and his dad because there was very little information available about this condition, however, she did promise she would try to find out more. Matthew decided to leave it at that for now.

Matthew brushed away his reflections and took out the new goalkeeping gloves he had tucked into the back of his black shorts. He put his hands into the gloves and wriggled his fingers to get them comfortable. He saw that the team selection by Chris and Dean had finished; it was now time to play football.

Aaron stood in the pitch, the centre line in front of him and the penalty area behind, arms folded, shivering in the drizzle. For the last twenty minutes or so, he had hardly moved an inch from his position, let alone kicked a ball. More of a spectator than a player, he watched the action in the other half of the pitch. He had so far observed that "football practice" involved simply chasing after the ball and fighting for it by any means necessary. The best players often competed against others on their team to score the most goals. Compared to the strategically organised football he sometimes saw on his dad's favourite Match of the Day show on Saturday nights, presented by Jimmy Hill, this was a shambles. So far, it was 7 – 6 to Chris' side, with Chris having already scored twice on his own. The best players always refused to let go of the ball, not even passing it to a team mate; they always dribbled all the way to the goal. Sometimes they scored; sometimes they missed. Both teams seemed to like to crowd round the ball and run together as though they were magnetically attached to it, trying to win the ball from one another and then break away with it towards the goal – it was every boy for himself.

Aaron saw that Chris was really good with the ball, showing fantastic dribbling skills. Dean wasn't bad, although he tended to be quite aggressive in taking back the ball. Matthew seemed to be a good goalkeeper, in spite of having conceded seven goals in the last twenty minutes, (to be fair, three of them were penalties). As for his form mates, Ian was an amazingly fast runner and seemed comfortable with the ball when he had it. Shaun was also good, but slow at times. Bradley had said earlier that he was good, but it turned out that he wasn't and he eventually faded away, ending up trailing around after the pack, waiting for the opportunity to come to him. Derek played like a man possessed. He made lunging tackles to get the ball and always ended up hitting the calves and ankles instead. Once, his boots flew right into Matthew's back when he caught the ball on the grass and Matthew was furious with him for almost breaking his back. Chris scolded him for his dirty tactics. The rest were reasonably good, save David, Andy and Aaron himself; they were absolutely rubbish. David spun round, arms outstretched, like an aeroplane. Andy sat on the grass and picked his nose, standing up when the "crowd" came towards him only to move away from it. Aaron looked to his right at the car park and saw that Mr Parsons was stood next to Mr Norris, watching the match. He thought about the maths teacher they had first met that morning.

The Maths Room was the smallest of the classrooms in the school. It was so small that either end of the semicircular formation of ten desks almost touched the walls and there was a claustrophobic feel to the room. The boys had to literally squeeze through the gaps on either end to get to their desks. The back of the wall was right up against their backs; so little space that there was barely room for them to pull up a chair. The teacher's desk was up close to the desks, although, because of the formation, there was ample space in the middle. As usual, each boy's desk had the amplification unit and headphones.

The room was not the only thing that was rather unusual: Mr Parsons himself was a bit of a character. The balding, white–haired man, in his mid–fifties, Aaron guessed, was a health and fitness nut. When the boys walked in, the maths teacher was doing quick push–ups on his chair and, instead of introducing the basics of numeracy; he gave a short lecture about how to stay fit and healthy. At least, that was what they thought he was saying; he wasn't easy to lipread at all.

Aaron quickly swept away his thoughts as he suddenly saw Steven running towards him with the ball, with a pack of boys behind him. Aaron gasped and was momentarily paralysed at the fast approaching line of advancing bodies; he held his breath. Steven swerved effortlessly round Aaron, who was shoved to the wet grass by the force of the wall that followed as the other boys ran past him. He glanced back through the gaps between the boys and saw Steven running towards the goal and smashing the ball past a diving Andrew, straight between the net–less goalposts. Seven all.

Picking himself up, Aaron saw Chris coming towards him, visibly annoyed.

'Why didn't you stop him?' Aaron shrugged; he simply didn't know how. Chris shook his head and waved at Andrew to throw him the ball, then walked back to the centre line, but not before turning back to Aaron. 'Next time, try to stop the ball!'

Aaron tucked his towel round his waist as he looked around the large changing room. He could see other boys taking off their sportswear and then their swimming trunks – the boys were not allowed to wear ordinary underwear during sports lessons – and wrapping their towels round their waists before heading into one of the two communal showers.

He sat on the wooden bench, his hands resting on his covered thighs, and stared blankly at the door leading into the showers. His heart pounded; he had never been in a shower room with other naked boys before. Chris had shown him the communal showers yesterday and said everyone had to shower after playing football or other sports. Aaron saw that he wasn't the only one with cold feet: David and Jonah were sitting on another bench, also with towels round their waists, staring at the two doors. His other form mates had already gone in, although he had noticed Duncan's trepidation on entering. Aaron's stomach churned. He knew he *had* to go in. He rose to his feet, his eyes fixed on the door, and slowly approached it. His heart pounded rapidly as he drew nearer. Suddenly, the door opened and he jumped as Sammy came out with a towel draped round his neck as he dried his wet hair. He held the door open for Aaron to enter. Aaron walked through and the door closed behind him.

He froze.

He felt a sudden rush of nausea at what he was seeing. Naked, fleshy bodies standing along the row of six white ceramic bases, hot water spraying down on each from wall nozzles, steam rising and billowing around the rectangular room and escaping through the small window, open high up on the wall at the far end. Some boys faced the wall as they washed with soap and shampoo. Others faced forward, either washing or signing to the waiting boys who stood in front of them. Those waiting stood along the opposite wall where several towels hung on hooks. Aaron couldn't help but take sweeping curious glances at their penises, and it unnerved him, for he knew that he was going to have to expose himself to everyone too, a first for him. He glimpsed Chris at the far end. Chris turned, showing his naked body, and saw Aaron, waving at him to come on over, but Aaron lunged for the door instead, his face now red with embarrassment.

A few minutes later, Chris came out with a towel wrapped round his waist and saw Aaron sitting quietly on the bench. He came over and sat next to him. 'You'd better hurry up and go in,' he said. 'You mustn't be late for tea.'

Aaron shrugged his shoulders. Chris frowned. 'What's wrong?' Aaron gazed at the shower room door and Chris followed his gaze and then realised. He smiled reassuringly. 'We all get nervous the first time,' Chris said. 'Me too, last year. You get used to it.'

Chris briefly thought about his first time being amongst the naked boys. He bet that Aaron would go straight to one of the shower units, face the wall with his back to everyone, his head bowed, soap his body and shampoo his hair quickly and be out in a flash without even looking at anyone. That was what Chris had done last year, only he was forced to turn round to face everyone when Basher had whipped his bare bottom with the wet towel. Chris resented that and their intense rivalry started from that day.

Chris held on Aaron's bare shoulder to get his attention and smiled. 'Don't ever look at Andrew Brener's prick or you'll turn to stone!'

Aaron laughed. He knew Chris was only joking, but at least it relaxed him. 'Come on,' he commanded, gently pushing Aaron to his feet and they both walked to the door. He saw David and Jonah still sitting on the bench and waved at them. 'Come on, both of you, get in there now!'

Chris wasn't surprised when Aaron went straight to one of the vacant shower units, facing the wall. Chris contemplated whipping Aaron's bottom with his towel to force him round so that he could have a proper look at him, but he thought better of it. Instead, his gaze lingered on the back of Aaron's naked body before David and Jonah interrupted him by gingerly walking in.

Eight o'clock. Aaron yawned. It wasn't out of tiredness; he'd had a good night's sleep and felt quite fresh for a Sunday morning, although he would have preferred to stay in bed a little bit longer, as he usually did at home. Putting on his black blazer – the boys had to wear those every Sunday morning instead of the usual dark green ones – he reflected on how the rest of the week had flown by so quickly. His head was crammed with so many new things learned during that week. When Saturday came, they had played football in the morning – he had become used to the showers by now – and in the afternoon, Chris had taken him into Waltbridge, about a mile and half away, for a bit of shopping, spending their pocket money and hanging out. Aaron had been happy and relieved to be wearing his own clothes for the first time in almost a week: he missed wearing his favourite red Adidas tee shirt with deep collars and navy flares. He was also free from wearing his body aids; the boys were given the choice of whether or not to wear them in their free time during the weekends, so like most others, Aaron was happy enough to consign them to his wardrobe. Initially, he couldn't understand why they were given this choice, but Chris explained that in the past boys had been targeted by local hearing lads who had sometimes damaged their hearing aids. The aids were also a disadvantage in that the boys had difficulty defending themselves because the harness often got in the way. It was safer just wearing them within the school grounds. When Mr Langston had become headmaster, two years before, he'd initiated the policy. He'd also laid out two new rules; the first being that the boys had to fill in an "Out Of School" slip, stating their names, the date and time of leaving, their intended time of return and their destination. This had to be signed off first by the duty teacher before the boy was allowed to leave. Returning boys had to report back directly to the duty teacher and return the slip. They automatically got three detentions if they did not comply with the rule. The second rule was that the boys were not allowed to go anywhere outside the school grounds alone: they had to stay in pairs or in groups for protection from strangers they had been warned about. These rules were explained to Aaron and his Form during their induction earlier that week.

Chris also told him that shopping on Saturday afternoons was one of the boys' favourite pastimes. They loved spending their pocket money on confectionery, fizzy drinks and comics. As they'd walked towards town, Chris had explained that each boy was allowed no more than one pound a week from the school bank, for fear of them spending too much on sweets, or on contraband such as cigarettes and alcohol. The boys' pocket money was sent directly to the school by their parents, to be apportioned by staff. Every Friday after lunch, the boys would queue up to collect their pocket money, and each amount was meticulously logged in the Pocket Money Ledger. Some boys would only get fifty pence, or seventy–five pence; they would only get a pound note if they were lucky. The green pound note was cherished because it was easily enough to buy plenty of sweets, chocolates and a can or two of fizzy drinks. Chris also said that some boys were lucky enough to receive secret backhanders, usually from their grandparents, without their parents knowing. Sometimes it was five pounds, sometimes ten, but they would always keep this bonus hidden from the school.

Waltbridge was, Aaron had observed, a typical town with high street shops, including his favourite W.H.Smith & Sons. Other amenities included Safeway, Woolworths, one of the new Kentucky Fried Chicken outlets that had just started popping up all over the country, and, much to Aaron's delight, a one–screen Plaza cinema. He saw a promotional poster for the new *Star Wars* film and prayed that he would see after it had been released in London though he wasn't sure when it would be shown in his home town. They browsed the shops and bought what they wanted. As they walked back, they stopped by the St Peter's church. Aaron knew that the boys would be going there the next morning.

Aaron yawned again, brushing away the memory of the previous day. He looked around for the third time in about ten minutes to see that the nave was now packed; the congregation's attention was directed at the vicar on the pulpit at the front. Sitting on the third pew, Aaron observed the gloomy interior once more and glanced back above the heads and shoulders to see the back of the church where the double doors they had entered through were. He then panned his head across the vast nave towards the front to see the stalls where the singing choir was. In the sanctuary rested an altar and behind it stood the Cross with a seven–branched candelabrum. The morning sun shone through the enormous arch window with decorative panes depicting the image of Jesus Christ on the crucifix. It gleamed radiantly behind the Cross. Organ music echoed, though Aaron could feel only the quiet, sombre vibrations through the wood bench in front of him. He tried to listen through his aids but nothing penetrated the complete silence. He tried increasing the volume, but it made no difference, the microphone on both aids wasn't picking up anything. Besides, even if his aids could pick up something, he still wouldn't get it anyway.

He looked left across his own pew to discover that he wasn't the only boy who was bored. Andrew was writing something on the hymns books. Michael picked his nose. Duncan was reading a rolled up comic. Some boys were dozing off. Some were looking up at the arched ceiling high up, lost in their own private thoughts. Some were discreetly signing to each other. Aaron learnt for the first time today that not every boy from Ewing Hill Park was at the church; there were a handful of Roman Catholics who had to go to their own church on the other side of town. Only one boy, Jonah Kaisermann, got to stay back in school because he was Jewish and he wasn't allowed in either of the two churches. Instead, he had to do an hour's prep on his own. Aaron quietly chuckled when he saw the Third Former, Carl Dunn, sneakily tapping Matthew's left shoulder from behind and letting Sammy take the blame for it. Aaron then scanned the pew in front, seeing more bored and restless boys. Mr Arkwright, who sat at the end of the pew, gently slapped Derek's head back to the vicar.

Aaron thought that he would try to do the same, and, directing his eyes over the rows of heads, he stretched his neck up a little to see above them to the Reverend on the pulpit. The servant of God preached in vain. His mouth was a tiny black, blurred dot. Aaron squinted in an attempt to lipread, but he couldn't: the vicar was too far away. He mused to himself that even if he sat at the front, he probably still would not understand because the vicar would be saying things that would be very difficult, if not impossible, given the subject matter. He and the other boys were condemned to sit through an hour or so every Sunday morning in complete silence and utter boredom, Aaron thought. He wondered what the point was. He turned to his right to see Chris, who was sitting next to him, staring blankly at something ahead. His mouth was silently moving and Aaron watched his lips.. . . *23 … 24 … 25 … 26 …*

Aaron followed Chris' gaze but he couldn't see anything that he could be counting. He gently poked Chris' left arm to bring him round, but Chris ignored him as he continued counting.

. . . 32 … 33 … 34 …

Aaron slapped his arm. This time, Chris stopped counting and turned to Aaron, scowling at him.

'What are you doing?' Aaron asked.

'See that window?' said Chris, pointing to the decorative window at the front. Aaron looked at it, acknowledged it, and turned back to Chris. 'I've been trying to count how many of those little coloured panes ever since I first came here last year, but I always fail. It's better than being bored shitless.'

'Why do we have to come here every Sunday? I can't follow or understand him.' Aaron pointed at the vicar.

'I don't know,' replied Chris, shrugging. 'Want to try it?' Chris pointed at the window, encouraging Aaron to start counting.

Aaron turned to the window, starting from the top of the arch …

1 … 2 … 3 … 4 … 5 …

He lost count almost immediately. Chris smiled. 'Not easy!'

As though they had read each other's minds, they both turned to the window and began to count again.

9

First Awakening

"The White Stag has a message for you. Hunters of old pursued the miraculous stag, not because they expected to kill it, but because it led them in the joy of the chase to new and fresh adventures, and so to capture happiness. You may look on the White Stag as the true spirit of Scouting, springing forward and upward, ever leading you onward to leap over difficulties, to face new adventures in your active pursuit of the higher aims of Scouting.

– ROBERT BADEN–POWELL;
on symbolism of the white stag, which also represents purity, 1933

Aaron turned the last page and shut the ancient–looking book. He sat back, resting against the velvet padding of the straight–backed chair, and placed the book on the oak table in front of him. He looked at his watch: half past seven. It had been another long Monday and he couldn't believe that he was already in his third week at the school.

He looked around the library and saw that there were about five or six boys, busy either reading or signing to one another. Roy Kirue, a Fifth Form prefect, was flipping through a copy of the National Geographic with some interest; Aaron knew what he was looking for and it wasn't images of a scientific or geological nature. He glanced back at the book he had just finished reading and thought about it; it was about the history of the mansion and the estate the school was on that he had promised himself two weeks before that he would read. It was a very thin, but quite interesting, book. Pushing the chair back, he picked it up and headed towards the shelf where it should be returned. As he strolled round the long oak table, he thought about what he had read.

It wasn't of much historical interest, as the details were quite sporadic and the book had been published a year before the First World War, so there was very little to read. The building of the mansion was completed in 1750 for the wealthy Rodrigues family. The father, Comie de JeFnimesan–Pierre Rodrigues, came from Avignon in France and had married an Englishwoman from an aristocrat family, Jane Stokes. They had a son and two daughters. It was true that Lady

Rachel Rodrigues – the woman in the picture – did stab her older sister, Bella, to death over a footman they both loved in 1780, though the book did not clearly say where the crime had taken place. To avoid bringing scandal and shame to the family, they sold the place and moved to France. The book did not explain what became of Rachel; whether she had been arrested, imprisoned, executed or had gone to France with her family.

The mansion passed from one family to another, and its estate grew larger as each family clan bought more acres over the years. Several trees were planted over a period of one hundred and fifty years to form the forest around the mansion, which stretched for about a mile from north to south and a mile and a half from east to west. Open countryside surrounded the small park island, along with Waltbridge and other towns, villages and roads, including the motorway. Apart from Magnat House, the gym building and the workshop, the mansion itself and the tiny cottage close by behind it were the only buildings in the vicinity. The book also mentioned that the estate had deer, which explained the school's crest, although he wondered about the significance of the white stag.

The book stopped a year before the First World War. Aaron assumed that the author must have been involved in the war in some way because the mansion became empty after the war and there was no further information about that, although Justin Pope said that the place became one of the regional headquarters for the D–Day invasion in 1944. He said there was an album in the library that contained some old photographs of army vehicles, tanks and soldiers occupying the building and the park. The Army had built the mile–long road – One Mile Road, it was named – that crossed from one end of the park to the other, as well as the winding driveway to the school. They'd also built some roads around the park for vehicle access. The mansion stood empty once again for about four years after the war, until Benjamin Williams, the man in the other portrait in the library and the school's first headmaster, acquired it with the help of funding from his wealthy close friend, Lord Ewing–Boyd Hill, to form Ewing Hill Park Boarding School for Deaf Boys in 1950. Aaron was already aware from Chris that a sister school, Boyd Hill Grammar School in the next county, had also opened in the same year; it was a mixed boarding school for deaf children. Lord Ewing–Boyd Hill had deaf children who were also twins; Alex and Rose, who were two of the first pupils at Ewing Hill Park and Boyd Hill Grammar respectively. Mr Williams was the headmaster for twenty–five years until he retired two years ago and Mr Langston had taken over.

Aaron slotted the thin book between two others on the shelf. He stood there for a short moment, scanning the vast array of books, wondering what he would read next. He decided he would leave it at that for now and turned round. He stopped suddenly.

Basher stood there right in front of him, smiling in apparent glee. Aaron shuddered. Did he just creep up from behind or had he been standing there the whole time that Aaron was thinking about the book? The Third Form bully looked down at Aaron with a knowing look on his face and smiled menacingly. Aaron began to move around him, but Basher raised his arm like a barrier to block him. Suddenly, with his other hand, he poked his index finger between Aaron's neck and shirt collar. Aaron looked down, quickly realised what Basher was about to do, and began to grab his forearm in an effort to push it away. Basher pulled away sharply, with his finger still tucked inside; the collar button broke away and flew out. Before Aaron could react, Basher inserted both hands between the two cords on either side of Aaron and pushed them outwards, causing Aaron's moulds to fly out of his ears. Aaron watched them swing down and glared up at the school bully with contempt.

'You know the rules,' Basher said, grinning. 'All shirts must be fully buttoned up.' He turned away and headed for the double doors.

Aaron soon became aware that everybody in the library was watching him. They seemed to be expressing sympathy in silence at him being the latest victim of Basher's collar button extraction mission. Aaron knew that he was neither the first nor last; David had been got during the first week. Shaun, Andy, Duncan and Ian soon followed the week after and now it was Aaron's turn, in the third week.

He looked down at the patterned carpet to search for the white button and found it. He knelt and picked it up, his moulds swinging to and fro from their cords. When he was on his feet, he replaced the moulds, making sure they were comfortable in his ears. He then looked at the button in the palm of his hand and made his way towards the doors.

Aaron strolled down the corridor; Tom Quillot turned the corner at the other end, making his way towards the library. Aaron knew that the tall white–haired Third Former was from Lincoln and was timid; he always liked to talk nonsense about everything and was unintentionally hilarious. He was rocking his head as he walked, as though he was listening to music. The two boys met midway and Aaron expressed his curiosity at Tom's peculiar behaviour.

'I'm listening to music!' exclaimed Tom, as he pointed at his own body aids and then his moulds with a knowing sense of humour. 'Funny! Ha, ha!' Tom moved past Aaron, chuckling to himself.

Aaron shook his head, bemused, and continued walking towards the end of the corridor.

He stopped at the end, seeing two corridors, the left a short one leading to the emergency exit, which in turn led to the rear of the school. It could only be opened from the inside, by a push bar. Aaron quickly remembered one night the previous week when his Form had had a rude awakening at eleven o'clock by the two matrons who'd told them that there was a fire. Following the matrons' instructions, the boys had quickly put on their dressing gowns and slippers before leaving their dormitory in an orderly manner, along with those from Dorms Two and Three, to go down the small emergency stairwell and then through one of the emergency exit doors on the east side of the building. All boys had to line up for roll call in the dead of night to make sure that everybody was accounted for. It soon turned out to be one of the fire drills that helped to ensure that if there was real fire, they would know what to do without any panic. Chris had told Aaron that they'd had to practise the drill about six or seven times last year; three drills were false alarms as some boy had smashed the glass on the fire alarm box. No one ever knew who the culprit was, although many fingers always pointed at one or both of the mischievous Brannigan twins from Belfast.

Aaron turned right to enter a wider corridor that led to the lobby, stopping at a door on his right that was ajar. There was a wooden *Speech Room* sign on it. Odd that it was open, he thought, since it was always closed and locked in the evenings and at weekends. Mr Arkwright, who taught speech, was quite strict about this, so he must be still in the room, or perhaps he had forgotten to lock the door. Aaron decided to investigate and peeked with caution through the opening, slowly pushing the door inwards to make room for his head. The light was still on, but there was no one inside. He took a quick glance around the small, cramped, windowless room, which had a table at the back; its ends almost touching the walls on either side. A pair of chairs stood by the table, which had equipment on it. Aaron knew what it was.

During the second week, Mr Arkwright first showed Aaron the room, saying that speech instruction was a very important part of his education. Aaron sat by the table and groaned inwardly at having to wear the same old headphones again. The tall teacher reached over to a microphone rod that was resting on a small metal tripod on the table and moved it between the teacher and the pupil. He then reached for a fairly large wooden box with three metal knobs, an on/off switch and two small, curved windows that looked like meter readings. *Amplivox Speech Trainer* was imprinted on the top. The teacher flicked on the metal switch at the bottom, then twisted one of the three knobs to the right. He turned to reach up to a shelf that was on the wall above him, retrieving a blue file and placing it on the table. Aaron saw *Speech for Beginners* on the spine, just as the teacher flipped the file open. The letters of the alphabet were on the first page. Aaron's eyes darted to the teacher's mouth to lipread.

'We will start your first speech lesson by saying each letter from A to Z,' he said, his finger moving briskly across each letter. 'So I will know which letters you're able to say or not. Do you understand?'

Aaron nodded. Mr Arkwright moved the file over to him. Aaron knew that he would not be able to utter most of the letters perfectly; especially *K, N, B, P* or *T*. Mr Arkwright then placed the microphone on his own mouth and uttered something to test it.

'Can you hear me, Aaron?' he asked.

Aaron thought about that for a moment; he was absolutely certain that he couldn't, he was too deaf. There was simply nothing but silence. He shook his head.

'Goddamned thing!' Mr Arkwright gently thumped the top of the microphone and then banged the palm of his hand on the top of the box in frustration. 'This blasted thing is old and keeps breaking down!'

He motioned for Aaron to go ahead anyway. Aaron read aloud each letter as best as he could, sometimes stopping to glance at the teacher's look of concentration. Once he was finished, the teacher asked Aaron to say *N* again. When he did so, Mr Arkwright placed his index finger on the side of his own nose and beckoned for the boy to do the same: 'Hold your finger on your nose and blow down your nose a bit, but use your voice at the same time. *N*. Do it.'

Aaron did as he was told.

NNNNN.

'That is very good!' exclaimed Mr Arkwright, his big hand patting Aaron's right shoulder. 'Well done!'

Aaron half smiled at the memory. He took another look at the empty shoebox of a room before flicking the light switch, plunging it into total darkness, save for the partial light from the corridor outside. He closed the door and moved on.

Aaron walked into the lobby and suddenly remembered the collar button that he was still holding: he had forgotten about it for a moment. He made his way towards the grand staircase, but stopped when he saw two of his form mates, Shaun and Duncan, signing to each other in excitement. Shaun was holding a large hand–held device which Aaron recognised as Kobena 321: the school's 8mm film camera. Shaun had recently discovered that the school had a film club and told Aaron about it as he showed him the camera.

'My dad,' Shaun said to Duncan, using his free hand to sign and acknowledging Aaron's presence, 'he's thinking of buying a new JVC VHS camera: the new big red one, you know?'

'V–H–S?' queried Duncan, fingerspelling the three letters. 'I've never heard of it. What does it mean?'

'Video Home System,' replied Shaun. 'It's new. JVC invented it, my dad said.

I think there'll be VHS machines in our homes soon, so that we can watch films on television.'

Aaron moved closer, becoming interested. The idea of watching films that could be played back repeatedly on television at home sounded too good to him. 'Does this mean we can watch films like *Jaws* on VHS?' asked Aaron, hopefully. He had caught the rerun of the film at the ABC in Bristol over the summer, even though it was rated AA; restricted to people over the age of fifteen. His dad had managed to get him and Jamie inside to see it. Oh, the film had scared the flipping hell out of him; he smiled to himself. He wanted to see it again – he liked the young director, Steven Spielberg, and hoped to see more of his films.

'Yeah, that's what my dad thinks,' replied Shaun.

'How much is that JVC camera your dad's going to buy?' Duncan cut in.

'£2,500, I think!' Shaun beamed.

Aaron and Duncan exchanged surprised glances. His family must either be rich or crazy, Aaron thought.

The three boys soon became aware of a presence close to them. They turned to see Mr Bronte, who was holding a straight pipe with used tobacco still in its pot. He was quite short with balding grey hair and his drab face was heavily wrinkled. He wore thick pair of black–rimmed spectacles, which further gave him a grotesque, old–fashioned appearance as if he had been stuck in time since the last World War. The boys had likened him to Winston Churchill, but with the pipe rather than Churchill's trademark cigar. Aaron's Form had first met the craftwork teacher in the workshop next to Magnat House on their second day, two weeks back. He taught metalwork and woodwork. In the centre of the workshop there was a forge, an anvil and workbenches with vices, with others around the room. When they started their first lesson, it quickly became evident to them that Mr Bronte was *impossible* to lipread. Aaron tried, but it was like watching frozen lips; nothing came out at all. Even David struggled to understand him because his short, whispering mouth movements were impossible for David's Phonak to pick up. He had often asked the old man to speak up a bit, in vain. Chris told Aaron afterwards that Mr Bronte was the worst teacher in the school and should have retired by now. Aaron was astonished to learn that the teacher had been at the school for eighteen years.

Mr Bronte waved the mouth end of his pipe, gesturing the form of a "2" and pointing it at each of the three boys, like a gun. He then pointed it at his own mouth to imply speaking and quickly gestured a cross. Mumbling something, he moved on, pleased as punch. Aaron stared blankly at the departing duty teacher.

Aaron and Shaun turned to Duncan, seeking his comment. After David, Duncan was the next best in his Form at reading lips. 'I *think* he gave us two bad points each for signing, not talking,' Duncan said grimly.

Aaron groaned: his first–ever bad points. The school had a strict disciplinary system to ensure good achievement and prevent bad behaviour. During the first week, Mrs Munnings had explained – writing clearly on the blackboard – about the system that had been in existence since the school first opened. The staff had the power to give good and bad points – or marks as they were sometimes called – to the boys. Good points were given for excellent school and prep work, for achieving something positive, or for good behaviour. A pleased teacher would log these in a little Good Points Book that was held by each boy; they were usually given between 1 to 10 points; then the reason was noted, signed and dated. Bad points were given to any boy who misbehaved, broke the school rules, damaged something (by accident or not), signed in class, or did anything that was out of the ordinary. The staff also had the power to issue detentions for more serious bad behaviour or for boys who had five bad points in total, which meant automatic detention. Ten bad points resulted in two automatic detentions, and so forth. The boys' names were logged in both the Bad Points and Detention books, which were kept locked in the drawer of the headmaster's desk. Aaron's Form was told that there would be a House Meeting on the last Friday of each month, at which they would learn more about how the system worked.

'But we're allowed to sign in our free time!' protested Shaun.

Duncan shrugged. Aaron sighed and excused himself from his form mates. He strode up the grand staircase two steps at a time and arrived at the landing. He stopped for a moment to decide which way to go, left or right, for the next flight of stairs that led up to the first floor. He turned left and ascended, again taking two steps at a time. He stopped midway and leaned over the wooden handrail on his left to view the lobby below, and saw that Shaun and Duncan were gone. He then caught sight of Dwight Greenland, a Third Former with long brown hair and thick lips, trotting across the hall, who then disappeared out of Aaron's view. Chris had told Aaron earlier that Dwight was a bit of a sissy and had the *limp hand* name sign, but that he was a very friendly lad all the same and many liked him. Aaron resumed his way up towards the first floor. Arriving, he headed for the double doors opposite. Idly flipping the button in the palm of his hand, he pushed one of the two heavy doors inwards.

Aaron found himself inside a gloomily lit foyer. Dorms Four and Five were next to each other on the right. As he walked past Dorm Five, he stopped for a moment and peeked through its half open door to see Gary Portmore and Kevin Kelvedon, a burly Fifth Former with straggly black hair who was a bit of a bully, signing to each other. Kevin took a small black box from his blazer pocket and passed it to Gary, followed by an even smaller box. Aaron thought it looked like they had a pack of JPS cigarettes and a box of Swan matches, but he couldn't be sure. When the boys saw Aaron peering through the door, they angrily waved him away. Aaron soon made off, suddenly thinking about Gary's speech reading session during morning assembly last week; he had told a story about Noah's Ark. However, in spite of his excellent speech, not many – in fact, almost none – of the boys understood him. Aaron struggled to lipread Gary because not only was he reading from a book with his head down, but also because of the distance between the stage and the sitting boys. Fortunately for him and the rest of his Form, David was one of the phone–goods and was able to sign some of what Gary said, as well as the assembly proceedings, although he took care not to attract the headmaster's attention, for they were sitting in the front row.

Aaron took a quick glance at Dorm Four next door, which was dark and empty, before turning left to the short, narrow corridor that led to another flight of stairs to the top floor. As he passed through it, two figures suddenly ran down the stairs, taking two or three steps at a time. Aaron paused, moved away and pressed his back against the wall to make way for the Brannigan twins who were running in his direction. Peter and Paul were identical, although their blond hairstyles were distinctively different; Paul's hair was somewhat shorter than his twin brother's and Peter had a small patch of acne on his jawline. Otherwise, they were indistinguishable and were the first ever deaf twins the school had had. Aaron knew that the Fourth Form twins – dubbed the Terror Twins of Ewing Hill Park – were troublemakers, but fortunately they had not done anything to him yet. They rushed past him, but Paul – or was it Peter? – stopped to greet Aaron.

'Aaron Stephens, isn't it?' he asked.

'Yeah.'

'You're in bad shit!' he said, pointing at Aaron's open collar. 'Basher, right?'

Aaron nodded.

'Don't bigmouth to Miss Hogarth.' He put his clawed hand on top of his own head, signifying her *hair bun* name sign. 'Or you'll get into *more* shit!' he warned.

Aaron already knew that he wasn't going to do that. Peter or Paul gestured a thumbs up and turned away, beckoning his twin to move on. 'Let's go to the recreation room and play snooker!'

They disappeared round the corner. Aaron sighed, resting the back of his head against the wall. He thought for a moment about the recreation room, which was centrally located. It was a large room with a table tennis table, a half–sized snooker table and two dartboards. The slightly smaller TV room, with its small window, was next door, with a new Philips colour television on a high mount. Many boys often crowded in with chairs; the Fifth Formers had the privilege to sit at the front, while the First Formers had to sit at the back. Aaron turned to the stairs again and made his way towards them.

He pulled open the door at the top of the stairs, entered the corridor and began to walk towards the foyer. His pace then increased to a jog; his legs were still aching from the cross–country run earlier that afternoon. Mr Norris and Mr Parsons, who sometimes came along, accompanied the juniors through the country for about an hour. Each Second Former had to be with their assigned First Former during the first month, to guide them so that they would learn the route and not get lost. As his guide, Chris accompanied Aaron; both were quite competent runners and Aaron liked it very much; it was far better than playing football. Aaron ceased jogging towards the end of the corridor and bent down to feel his toned thighs. He chuckled when he remembered how David had come last in their first run last week. Everyone had thought it was because he was fat, but it turned out he'd got lost in the forest because he'd apparently lost his guide, Andrew. David complained that Andrew ran on ahead and turned a bend, then suddenly disappeared. David was unable to find him and couldn't find his way back to school, so had walked back the same way he and the others had come. Andrew accused David of being slow and wandering off somewhere. Mr Norris reprimanded him for this and warned him that he would get detention if it happened again. From what Chris told Aaron in confidence, it turned out that Andrew had jumped into a bush and hid from David for a prank.

Aaron quietly shook his head, amused by the memory. He made his way towards the Matron's office, which was at the end of the foyer, passing Dorm One on his left. He then passed by Dorm Two next to it, but stopped when he saw a piece of folded paper lying on the lino. He bent down to pick it up, then studied it. There was nothing written on it, so some boy must have dropped it, he thought. He placed it close to his mouth and barked at it.

Blaaaccc!

The paper flapped once from the force coming from his mouth. He reflected on the English lesson his Form had had last week. Mr Whittle tested the boys by holding a piece of paper over his mouth, the microphone in between; the boys had to listen through their headphones to each word he said. With the headphones still weighing down on his head, Aaron and the rest of his Form concentrated hard, trying to pick out the next word by carefully watching the top part of the teacher's face in order to determine what he would say – it was always down to guesswork. When he uttered each word, his cheeks moved above the top of the paper and followed by with a brief equivocal blast through the headphones. Aaron had attempted to listen with the volume on full, to try to pick up clues based on the strength and composure of the vibrations he felt on his ears. He failed at every word he tried to guess. Like the others, he hated that stupid test. Did he say

Bar? *Pu*–something? The first letter was definitely either *B* or *P*, judging by the force of the sharp vibration on his ears; Mr Whittle's cheeks above the paper had suggested that too. Was there a kind of click at the end of the word? Was it either *K* or *T*? He had just started learning to say those letters in his last speech lesson, clicking his vocal chords and tongue. No, he figured, it wasn't one of those letters. Or was he wrong? Was it *place*? He made a final guess that this might be the word, so put his hand up.

Plaaassseee?

Mr Whittle lowered the paper from his mouth and frowned, trying to figure out what Aaron had just said. Was it *please* or *place*? He shook his head. 'That's not correct, Aaron. Anyone?'

David glanced round the semicircular formation of desks and gingerly put his hand up. The teacher beckoned for him to go ahead, smiling through his ginger beard.

'Black, sir.'

'Right again, David!' exclaimed the English teacher. 'He is very good at it, isn't he? Why can't the rest of you do it? *Listen harder!*'

Aaron got what he said. He was getting better at lipreading the teacher, although he still struggled to understand most of what he said. Mr Whittle turned to write the word on the blackboard, which already had a row of single words chalked on it. "DW" followed after each word. With the English teacher's back still to the boys, Derek, riled, chucked a crumpled piece of paper at David. 'Show off!'

Aaron rolled the paper and carefully tucked it into the left pocket of his blazer; he thought it might be of some use. He approached the matron's office.

Once inside, he looked around the office, which was much more of a workshop with a long table in the centre, two sewing machines with clothes nearby. A workbench was at the back of the room. On his right, he saw three washing machines and two tumble dryers along the side. He looked to his left and saw an ironing board with the iron resting on its end, still plugged in. Aaron could feel the heat still from the iron plate and noted how there was one white shirt not done on the board. Miss Hogarth and Miss Turner were nowhere to be seen. Aaron turned his attention to another door by the ironing board, which led to the clothes store. The door to it was half open and he could see slight shadowy movements coming from inside, so he made his way there.

He thought about the clothes store, which he had been inside a few times before. All the boys' school wear was stored in the small room. Fifty large pigeon holes were on one side, one each boy, five rows of ten boxes, placed in the order of the five forms. All clothing had a cotton label sewn on it, with the owner's name printed in red letters. Aaron's mother had spent days and nights sewing labels on all of his shirts, underwear, socks, trousers and all of his casual clothes. In order to ensure the boys wore clean clothes, the matrons had a strict clean and dirty clothing exchange system. Every night at bedtime, a basket of clean clothes was placed in each dormitory for the boys to exchange for their dirty ones. Clean socks were provided every night; underwear every two days, bundled together with socks; shirts every three days, again bundled together with socks and sometimes underwear that fell on the same rota day; with clean trousers, pullovers and pyjamas at the end of each week. At bedtime every Sunday, they had to dispose of their dirty sportswear and casuals. Every Monday morning, they had to change their bedding, replacing the dirty linen with clean ones.

Aaron reached the door left ajar and peered through the gap to see if the matrons were in there. He gasped in speechless astonishment at what he saw.

Miss Hogarth's back was pressed against the storage wall, her burly body hunching down. Some hair straggled from her tight hair bun as her head, bowed, moved furiously. Her large round spectacles were askew on the bridge of her nose and her eyes were closed. Her beefy arms were wrapped round the smaller assistant matron, hands stroking her curly dark hair and her clothed back. Miss Turner squirmed at the pleasurable stroke. The matrons' mouths were pressed hard against each other, their lips and cheeks moving wildly. The assistant matron pushed her larger colleague against the wall; her left hand was already inside Miss Hogarth's partially unbuttoned attire, caressing her left breast. Her right hand slowly moved down between the legs of the larger woman and rubbed hard over the fabric. Miss Hogarth moaned pleasurably in response and clasped her assistant's bottom.

Aaron was mesmerised by what he saw; he had never seen anything like that before. He wondered why they were doing this; he had always thought that only a man could do it with a woman, but women? Was it allowed? Were they lovers? Having a bit of fun? Brushing away the questions in his head, he looked at the matrons again, who were still at it and hadn't noticed him. He had an urge to burst in and shock the hell out of the women, but thought better of it. He quietly stepped back and looked round, thinking for a moment. He looked at his watch: almost eight o'clock, forty–five minutes before bedtime. He looked at the button in his hand and then at the hot iron on the ironing board. Reaching for the cord, he pulled it, stepping back just as the iron toppled over. It plummeted to the floor and crashed with a loud thud that Aaron felt with his feet. The iron bounced once towards Aaron and he stepped back again, away from the danger. Although he could not hear them, he imagined the startled screams that were coming from the clothes store. Within seconds, the door swung open and Miss Turner darted out, looking almost as out of breath as if she had run a mile. She came to a halt when she saw Aaron.

'Oh, it's you, Aaron!' said the assistant matron, trying to act normally. Miss Hogarth soon followed, her hands patting her hair bun, correcting its position with a hairpin. Aaron saw that she had already buttoned up her attire, but only just: one of the buttons was in the wrong hole.

'It's only Aaron,' Miss Turner called back. She saw the fallen iron, bent down to pick it up by its handle and placed it back on the board. 'He tripped over the cord.'

'We were just … stacking up in there, Miss Hogarth said limply, gesturing at the shelves. 'What's up, boy?'

Aaron opened his hand to show the button and warily pointed at his shirt collar.

'Oh no, not again!' screamed Miss Turner. Aaron silently watched as the assistant matron angrily mumbled a few words to herself; he couldn't pick them out, although he thought he saw her swearing under her breath. She then gestured at his shirt. 'Take off your shirt!'

The man smiled and waved before turning to mount his large motorised lawnmower, perching on the driver's seat. He turned the key and pressed the button; the machine roared into life, with the long, wide blades at the front rumbling forward. Grass was sucked under the sharp, rolling blades and a flurry of cut grass sprayed out. He then pressed on the clutch with his foot, his hands holding the steering wheel, and the monster trudged forward.

Sitting on the grass, Aaron idly pulled up some grass as he watched the long–haired, bespectacled, middle–aged man and his machine slowly advancing at a distance across the front field. Aaron only knew the school's gardener as Hubert and he had yet to properly meet him, though, from what he had been told, the man was a nice chap with an odd mind who enjoyed gardening, animals, and loved the boys like they were his own. No one knew much about his past, except that it was believed he came from somewhere in Eastern Europe and he had been working as the school's gardener ever since the school first opened – twenty–seven years now, Aaron figured. His job was not just gardening; he also did some odd jobs around the school, making repairs and keeping things in good condition.

Aaron crossed his legs and turned to his right to see Chris sitting next to him, reading Roy of the Rovers he had borrowed from Dean; he liked to read it at lunchtimes. Aaron couldn't stop thinking about what he had seen yesterday evening. He had almost told his form mates about it at bedtime, but decided not to, for he was still confused. He would try to ask Chris about it the next day first to see if he knew anything. Perhaps he knew about the women, or why they did that. It had only been three weeks since he'd first arrived, but Aaron's friendship with Chris was growing stronger by the day. He felt Chris was someone that he could talk to and trust. Chris' occasional broodiness had sometimes unnerved him, but that was probably his way of expressing things. Aaron had noticed that Chris was popular with many of the boys, but that did not seem to go to his head; he simply wanted to be himself and that made Aaron feel comfortable with him. Aaron waved at Chris, who looked away from the football comic and at him, raising his eyebrows for him to go ahead.

'Can, uh, can two women kiss each other?' Aaron asked.

Chris frowned at the question. 'You mean, like, a peck on the cheek?'

'No, I mean … like they're in love, you know?'

'Oh, right,' said Chris as he nodded, knowing what his friend meant. 'Yeah, I think so. Why?'

Aaron paused for a moment, seeing Chris' curious expression. 'I saw Miss Hogarth and Miss Turner kissing and hugging in the clothes store last night.'

'What?' Chris shrieked. 'They did that? You *saw* them? Honest?'

Aaron nodded. He mimicked what the matrons did, taking on the role of the assistant matron, exaggeratedly kissing and hugging an imaginary figure, even going as far as to caress an invisible breast with his left hand.

'Oh, brilliant!' Chris exclaimed wildly. 'FIRST PROOF! Oh, that's fucking brilliant!' He shot to his feet and turned to face the school. He glanced across the car park to see Andrew coming out of the entrance doors; he was about to descend the stone steps when he saw Chris waving furiously at him.

'Aaron saw Miss Hogarth and Miss Turner snogging last night!' Chris announced, pointing at his bewildered friend, still on the grass. 'It's true now! WILDFIRE SPREAD!'

Andrew whooped in excitement, almost tumbling over the step before regaining his balance. Even at that distance, Aaron could see Andrew's broad grin as he shot back inside, armed with the juicy gossip to tell the world.

Aaron laughed feebly as he watched Chris slump back on the grass, whooping and grinning. Chris turned to a bemused Aaron.

'We knew it!' Chris said. 'There've been rumours for a long time that they were in love with each other, but you've finally given us proof!'

'Oh,' Aaron said, with a half–smile. Curiosity flared in him as he thought for a moment. He waved at Chris, who was about to return to his comic. 'Can men do that as well? I mean, like, man kissing man, you know?'

'I dunno,' Chris replied, following with a sign, closed hand rocking sideways, his thumb and little finger protruding. 'Probably.'

For a short moment, Chris and Aaron's eyes met. A strange sensation passed between them, as though something was drawing them closer together. Aaron quickly broke away. Chris turned his attention back to the comic on the grass. Aaron glanced ahead to watch Hubert driving the lawnmower across the field.

10

Letters Home

"I've always wanted to write a book relating my experiences growing up as a deaf child in Chicago. Contrary to what people might think, it wasn't all about hearing aids and speech classes or frustrations."

– MARLEE MATLIN; Oscar winning actress of the 1986 film *Children of a Lesser God.*

Friday 30th September 1977.

Dear Mum, Dad and Jamie,

My first letter home!!! Sorry I did not wrote home before. Mrs Munnings, our Form Master, say said my Form we must writing home every week! The school is very good. I am enjoyed here very much. But I miss home!!! It is hard work at school! English is my best subject.

We ~~have~~ had our first House Meeting today. I ~~have~~ had 7 Good Points and 2 Bad Points! Mr ~~Brute Brot~~ Bronte (think right spelling!!!) gave me 2 Bad Points for signing!!! I am a Green. The other House is Gold. Green vs. Golden Staggers – 25 Green and 25 Golden boys. My friend, Chris ~~Matthews~~ Matthaus is a Green. He had no Good Points, but 3 Bad Points! I got 5 in total. 7 – 2 = 5. Green House won for ~~best most~~ Good Points total. If I got 25 Good Points and 5 Bad Points = 20 points. Less 20 (24 – 5 = 19, etc.), it is House Detention!!! 5 Bad Points = Detention. Chris got House Detention because he had –3 points. He do it tomorrow! (Saturday). He will clean the boy's toilets!

Chris Matthaus. You know him. You met him on my first day. He ~~was~~ is very nice. He help me a lot. Went ^to church. It is very boring!!!

Mr ~~Whistle~~ Whittle. Our English teacher. He said my English is very good. But I still learning!

Hope Jamie leave my toys alone!!! I know you play with them! Leave my F1 Top Trump cards alone! Don't steal them!!!

I must stop write because I have to go to swimming soon with Form 1 and Form 2. Mr Norris, the sports teacher, is take us. Last week, we all cram in an old minibus to go swimming. 20 of us!!!

Love from,

Aaron xxx

Saturday 15th October 1977.
Dear Mum, Dad and Jamie,
My last letter before half term next week! I can't wait to go home next Friday 21st! Will you and Dad come and pick me up?!? Is Jamie coming too? I hope not because he was bad mood when we ~~drived~~ drove here last month!!! Is he still upset about Elvis dead?!? Can't wait for my early 12th birthday party! What presents will I have?!? Will I get one from Aunt Barbara? I want 007 Lotus ~~Espert~~ Espirit white toy car. Saw it in Woolworths in Waltbridge last week. It cost £3.99. Remember, we all saw the 007 film last summer – THE SPY WHO LOVED ME. That car! You press a button and fin things pop out. Cool!!! I want it!

We will have Open Day next week. You and Dad can watch my Form and me in lessons. David Wheeley will stand on stage in Assembly Hall to read and speak from a story in front of everyone. Mr Arkwright picks a boy from each Form every year to do it. I hope he won't pick me!!! I will ^be ~~embass~~ embarrassed (is this right spelling?).

I did cross country run on Monday. I like it very much. Mr Norris said I was very good and he give me 5 Good Points!!! My friend, Chris, hate it. He wants to play football! I'm no good at football! David Wheeley, from my Form, always come last in cross country run. He is fat!!!

Please don't post me the 2000AD comic. Bring it with you next week. I read it on the way home. I really like this new comic very much. It is better than Battle comic!

I have to stop now. I am post this letter on the way to Waltbridge town. This is my last envelope and last stamp!

Love from,
Aaron xxx

Monday 14th November 1977.
Dear Mum, Dad and Jamie,
I have chickenpox!!! And it's my 12th birthday today! (I know you will laugh, Jamie!) I am in bed, writing this letter. Miss Hogarth will post it in the Postbox downstairs (it's made of wood. Hubert made it long time ago. He is the gardener. He is nice man but not clever. The boys post their letters into it and a staff take them to Waltbridge G.P.O.). I not allowed outside Dorm One. OK to the toilet. It is boring in bed! 15 other boys ~~had~~ ~~has~~ have chickenpox too!!! It ~~was~~ is like Black Death here! Miss Turner put on pink cream on my chest and face for the spots. Calium. Horrible smell!!! Have spots on my chest and my face! Did I have chickenpox before? I can't remember. I remember I had mumps before.

I showed my Form the 007 car Aunt Barbara got me for my birthday. They all like it. Derek Ferguson tried to put it in the bath! Stupid boy!!!

Please post me some more money. I know you gave me some when I came back here after half term, but I ~~has~~ have now almost run out! No, I did not buy too many Coca Colas or comics! Please be very kind. I need it until the end of this term. Please, please, please!

I must stop now. I am very tired and I go to sleep. I hope I will get better soon.

Love from,

Aaron xxx

Friday 9th December 1977.

Dear Mum, Dad and Jamie,

One more week to go before I go home for Christmas. Will Dad come and pick me up? I know you (Mum) can't come because you have to look after Jamie after his school. A big mummy's baby!!! (Jamie, no I am not mummy's boy! You!!!)

We will ~~had~~ have Christmas Party tomorrow (Saturday). We will have girls from other schools! I hope I can find a nice girl!!! We will have it in Assembly Hall. Form Five had been busy decorated it. We all exchanged Christmas cards. I have 20! David Wheeley only have 3 (I gave him mine). My friend, Chris, got 35!!!

Mr Parsons, our Maths Teacher, is mad! He is always keep fit. We saw him standing upside down on a chair and did push ups. Like press ups we did in P.E. but upside down on the chair. I tried it, but it was impossible! I keep falling down! He always come to cross country run with us. He does not have a car, only bicycle. Perhaps his heart will blow up one day because of too much ~~excrise~~ ~~eserice~~ exercise! (I am still learning good spelling!)

I found out STAR WARS will be ~~relae~~ released in London on 27th after Christmas. Can you find out if it will be at Odeon or ABC in Bristol too? I fed up with films always show first in London!

I have been learn how to play chess. It is interesting. I have joined Chess Club. I joined Film Club, Model Club, Typing Club (I am learning type on a typewriter. Not easy! My fingers always fall into gaps!) and Library Assistant. I work with Justin Pope (Form 4) who is Library Officer. I like reading books. You know me!!! The school has a newsletter every week called The Stag Press. Conrad Chargate (Form 4) is the Editor. I hope I will be Editor when I am Form 4!

Mr McShane, our Art Teacher, is brilliant!!! He can sign. He said his mum and dad and 2 brothers and 1 sister are all deaf. He is only hearing in his family. We all can understand him because he can sign. I wish all other teachers are the same as him. They are very hard to understand. Mr Bronte is the worst!!! Impossible to lipread! Mr Langston, our headmaster, is very easy to lipread if he is close to me. But not far away like in the Assembly every morning! Don't tell him please! I wish he can sign like Mr McShane!

I must stop now. Please don't post me my Warlord, Action and Lookin comics. Please bring them next week. Don't forget!!!

I can't wait to go home for Christmas! I hope lots, lots of presents!!!

Love from,
Aaron xxx

Tuesday 7th March 1978.
Dear Jamie,
HAPPY BIRTHDAY BUTTHEAD!!! 14 now! No, I not forgotten your birthday today! I am ~~write~~ writing my first letter to you only. Please don't show it to Mum and Dad. Keep it private. OK?!? I will write more to you in future, I promise! (if you promise to write back!).

Mum wrote in her last letter about you. You got into bad trouble at your school for fighting a boy. Was it Pongy? (Trevor Smudgewell). Good on you!!! I really hated him – he's a big wanker! Hope you are OK.

Chris is my best friend. He great. You will be his friend too. You will like him very much. He is 13 but will be 14 this September 12th. But I not know much about his family. He never talk about them. I only know he ~~don't~~ doesn't live with his mum or dad. Don't know who looks after him in school holidays. He is from ~~Islang~~ ~~Inlington~~ Islington in London (I check the underground map for spelling. I found Highbury & Islington station!) He supports Arsenal! You support Manchester United. (Both red!).

Chris is like you. Strong! Not like me! No, I'm not a wimp!!! He is always fighting with Basher. His real name is Brian Thompson, but we all call him Basher. Or Bastard because he has a sign name for it. Remember I told you all about the swear sign words at half term last October? You know the sign for bastard? That's the one for him!!! No one know why he got "Basher" name. He will not tell us! He is a bully. He is always bullying my other friend in my Form, David Wheeley. I know he is fat and wimpy, but I like him. I don't know why! He loves aeroplanes and always talk about them. He can hear and talk like a hearing boy. Basher is a thickhead. Like you!!! Anyway, Chris always stand~~ing~~ up to Basher. Not like everyone else. Lots of boys like Chris very much because he is always very brave. He is very popular. But I am his best friend!

One of my Form boys, Andy Farmleigh, saw STAR WARS at a cinema in London last Christmas. He lives in north London, lucky him! He said it was BRILLIANT and saw lots of things in the film he never seen before. He said Han Solo's ship, Mill … (can't spell it, but you know!) Falcon, is AMAZING! Can't wait to see it in Bristol this summer!!! Andy said there was a very, very long queue outside the cinema. Hope not for us!!! I borrowed his STAR WARS comic. Only issue number 1 out of 4. It is brilliant. It is done by Marvel Comics, so can you find out more? I did ask Mum about it, but she doesn't know where to find out!!!

Must stop writing now. Need to write to Mum and Dad now. I am on lunchtime break and cross country run (we didn't do it yesterday, don't know why!) soon and I have to change. I only got two stamps left, so will post both letters. I will see you on Friday next week (17th) for the Easter holiday. Hope we have lots of Easter Eggs!

Miss you, bro.

Aaron xxx

(P.S:– I will sellotape the back of the envelope. You know Mum can be very nosey!)

Tuesday 7th March 1978.

Dear Mum and Dad,

I've no money left. I've run out of pocket money in the school bank. Please send me £2. Be Kind! I need it to buy a new pen and sweets this weekend. Please send it tomorrow so that I can receive the money on Thursday or Friday. Don't forget it!!!

I was fourth in the junior cross country run ~~comept~~ competition in Weyton, near here on Sunday. Boys and girls from local schools ran too. I was fourth, but was first for my school. Mr Norris wrote down (I can't lipread him – he always talk too fast!) and told me that he and the school is very proud of me! Hope you and Dad are proud too!!!

~~I had my first detention last week. Don't be angry with me! It not my fault. I broke the headphones by accident (it was already broken!). But Mr Arkwright gave me detention!!! He thought I broke it because he know I hate them! Had Detention last Saturday evening. It was really easy! I had to write down a list of verbs, their present tense, past tense and past participation. Like "was" in past after "is", etc. It was really easy. Finished it in one hour (Detention is two hours) and helped improve my English! There were 7 other boys in Detention too and they all copied from me because they did not understand them. Don't tell Mr Arkwright please!~~

(Sorry for the crossing out above. I can't throw away this sheet because I have no more sheets left! The second last sheet was for my letter to Jamie.) I not write any more until the Easter holidays. Will Dad come and pick me up on the 21st? Hope Jamie gets my letter too. Don't pull out the sellotape and open the envelope! It's for Jamie only!!!

I read in the newspaper this morning that a new film called CLOSE ~~ENOCUTERS~~ ENCOUNTERS OF THE THIRD KIND will be in cinemas next week (13th). The same man who made JAWS made it. Steven Spielberg. It is about UFOs. Can we see it during Easter from 17th March? Please!!!

Must stop now. I've run out of space and I have my cross country run now (we didn't run yesterday). Don't forget the £2 please!

Love from,

Aaron xxx

Sunday 14th May 1978.

Dear Mum, Dad and Jamie,

My Form went to Science Museum in London on Wednesday. Miss Stephenson took us. It was brilliant! It had Apollo 11 rocket there. Not the real one – too big for the museum! A smaller one and it also had films of the first man on the moon. Neil Armstrong,

I think. Jamie will like it very much.

Miss Hogarth said I have grown up by almost two inches since I came to here. She measured me yesterday. 5 foot and 5 inches. How tall is Jamie? He is a little taller than me.

One boy in Form Three. ~~Basher~~ Brian Thompson's older brother (think his name is Adrian) died a few days ago. Mr Langston said it was cancer. Brian ^is now home in London for the ~~furnel~~ funeral. Many of us do not like him very much, but we all ~~feel~~ felt sad. We prayed for him in Assembly.

Yesterday, Mr Whittle gave me a "C" (and 5 Good Points) for writing a good essay about Charles Darwin. I was top of my Form (again!!!). But everyone in my Form had "E" and "F" (Failed) in their essays about him! It was very, very hard to lipread and understand Mr Whittle (his stupid beard!) about Charles Darwin. In Prep, my Form want^ed me explain more about him and the origin of species because I am brainy! I did not really understand much, so I ~~have~~ had to read the Ladybird book about it in the Library!!! It had really easy text and pictures and it helped me understand.

I am still playing chess! It is good but very hard game. I always lost, but will win one day!!!

We went to church again this morning. It is VERY BORING! Why do we go there every Sunday? Never mind!

I must stop now. I want to go and play Escape From Colditz board game with Andy Farmleigh and Jonah Kassier. It' is brilliant game!

Love from,
Aaron xxx

Friday 9th June 1978.
Dear Mum, Dad and Jamie,
The weather is very HOT here! 26ºC! I am sweat like a waterfall. Phew!

I forgot the stamps in my bedroom at home!!! I ~~leave~~ left them on my small desk last Sunday when I came back here with Dad after half term. I borrowed a stamp from Derek Ferguson. Please bring them next week (Sports Day). Thanks!

I wish Jamie ~~can could~~ can come to the Sports Day next week. Lucky him go to France with his school! Hope you (Jamie) eat LOTS of frog legs! Yuk!!! Are you both (Mum and Dad) staying at Aunt Barbara's next weekend? I am in Junior 100M and 200M. Mr Norris said (I think!!!) I was very good at fast running. Chris, my best friend, said I should try junior 1,500M. No way!!! I will be worn out half way! Mr Norris painted ~~alethics~~ athletics track ~~at~~ on front field. Like the ~~Oymp Olm~~ (you know five colour rings! Can't spell it!). White lines round the field.

We going swimming this afternoon. Can't wait!!! Cool down!

Love from,
Aaron xxx

Friday 7th July 1978.
Dear Mum, Dad and Jamie,
ONE MORE WEEK TO GO! SUMMER HOLIDAY!!!

Jamie wrote to me two weeks ago. He said STAR WARS will be at Odeon in Union St on 21st July! Please, PLEASE, can we go and see it? Many of my friends at school saw it! They said it was in London last December, then other cities in UK last January. But not Bristol!!! Not fair!!! They said LONG ~~qeues~~ ~~queus~~ queues (right spell?) wait outside cinemas! Jonah Kassier, from my Form, said he waited for TWO HOURS with his mum, dad, his brother and sister at The Dominion Theatre, Tottenham Court Road (in London) on 2nd January 1978. (He still have ticket. He showed it to me). He said a man tried sell to woman (behind Jonah) £2.20 ticket for £30!!! Police arrest^ed him! Jonah said STAR WARS is AMAZING. Can't wait!!!

I asked Chris if he was looking forward to summer holiday. He said no!!! I don't know why! He never talk about his family.

I am very, very excited to go away on holiday in Majorca for two weeks on 30th July! (We see STAR WARS first!!!). First time in a plane! I told you before that David Wheeley, from my Form, is mad about aeroplanes! He said my plane will crash into sea! Hope not!

Don't post my 2000AD comic and StarLord comic. Bring them next week. I will read them on the way home. Will you and Dad come pick me up? Or just Dad?

Love from,
Aaron xxx

Sunday 18th September 1978.
Dear Mum, Dad and Jamie,
One week gone at school already! Form Two now. I am guide for Hendrik Swart for 1 month. He is from South ~~Acrifa~~ Africa. He is white boy, not black boy. He is a very small boy! Ian Synman was his guide, but Mr Langston swapped us. I don't know why!

I told everyone that we saw STAR WARS last July. Twice!!! I told them Jamie MOANED about the long queue at the Odeon! Chris did not see it. He is the only boy at school who did not see it! David Wheeley brought STAR WARS board game. It is great! Can I have it for my 13th birthday this November?!? Please!!!

Last Monday (12th)) it was Chris' 14th birthday. Every boy punched his arm (we all always do that with boys on their birthdays). But he refused to let me punch his arm! We both ran around the school as I tried to punch his arm! I finally caught him and we fought (just playing, not real fight!) in his Dorm Three. I punched his arm and we both hugged. Chris is ^a brilliant best friend. You will like him.

Afterwards, some boys caught Chris and they bobbed (is this the right word, Mum?) him 14 times (same as his age) like he was a trampoline! My turn on November 14th. Gulp!!!

We have a new music teacher! Her name is Mrs Bonnington. She is an old lady. She is impossible to lipread! My Form ~~don't~~ doesn't know why we have to learn music. We are deaf! (Except for David Wheeley. He can hear music). In our first music lesson last Thursday, she played a record and she told us to sing along!!! I heard nothing! Stupid!!!

Have to go. Will write again soon.

Love from,

Aaron xxx

Friday 14th October 1978.

Dear Mum, Dad and Jamie,

My last sheet of writing paper now. Someone thieved some of them! I am not happy! I will buy ^new writing paper at half term. I know Dad is coming next Friday 21st for Open Day. You (Mum) can't come because you have an operation on your toe next Wednesday. Hope Jamie will look after you! Make him cook and wash up!!! (Jamie – I know you won't!).

Last week, Mr Whittle gave me a "B" and 10 Good Points for writing a very good short story with few mistakes with my English! My Form thought I was bighead because they all had "D" or "E" with lots of mistakes in their English. David Wheeley had "C". Mr Whittle said my English ^has improved very well in one year and he is very pleased with it.

You remember I told you about the music lessons? Chris told me that his Form went crazy with the musical ~~intrum~~ instruments! CRASH! BANG! WALLOP! The whole school heard them! Mrs Bonnington was furious with them and she refused to teach Chris' Form music again! Lucky them!!! I love playing with the ~~cmbyals~~ cymbals – you know the round ones? I love making her jump when I slam them together HARD! She told me off!

I am going swimming this afternoon. Weather is OK here.

Love from,

Aaron xxx

Wednesday 15th November 1978.

Dear Jamie,

Thanks for your birthday letter yesterday. I'm 13 now! Teenager at last!!! No, I'm not a BUTTHEAD. You are!

Sorry to hear that you had mumps last week. I wish I was with you. So that I can kick your butthead like a football! Ha, ha!!!

Don't tell Mum and Dad about this. Last Saturday many boys went to Waltbridge town centre and they thieved the Ever–Ready torches – you know the new small rectangle ones? I didn't steal one, but Chris stole two and gave one to me! In bedtime, after lights out, we ^all played with it from our beds! It was really funny. I think every boy has one.

I have bruises all over my arms! All boys punched them for my birthday. Basher (from

Form 4) tried to punch me very, very hard, but Chris punched him harder. On his face! Told him to leave me alone! I had 13 bobs this morning and my white shirt got ripped! Miss Turner ~~went~~ was MAD with me! Not my fault!!!

Weather outside is shit! Big heavy rain. We will play badminton in the gym this afternoon. I am not very good at it!

Will see you this Christmas!

Miss you, butthead!

Aaron xxx

Wednesday 7th March 1979.

Dear Jamie,

HAPPY 15TH BIRTHDAY, BUTTHEAD!!!

Aaron xxx

(Ha, ha, no letter!)

Sunday 13th May 1979.

Dear Mum, Dad and Jamie,

I did not write on Friday as I was not feeling very well. But I am fine now.

Yesterday was the F.A. Cup Final. Arsenal vs Manchester United. Arsenal won 3–2. Chris went mad!!! Very happy Arsenal won because Arsenal was 2–0 up, but Manchester United fought back 2–2 in last four minutes. Arsenal scored the winner ~~at~~ in last minute! The TV Room was full up with 50 boys! Chris never stopped talking about it. He's always ~~shouting~~ signing Arsenal! Arsenal! He kissed on my cheek! Eugh!

But I missed the first 30 minutes of the final because some boys and I watched a programme on BBC2 called SIGNS OF LIFE, which was at same time ^as kick–off. (Jamie; thanks for finding out about it in radio last week!). Did you all see it too? (I bet Mum and Dad argued over which to watch in our TV!). We watched it in the small black and white TV in Staff Room. We asked Mrs Munnings, who was on Duty yesterday, to watch it. She watched it with us. First time I have seen Deaf people signing on TV! A bearded deaf man started the show. He look^ed like a weird hippy! That woman – I think Dorothy – signed poetry. It was beautiful. First time I have seen signed poetry. There ~~is~~ was that bald man, he used fingerspelling all the time. It was hard ^to follow him. Another man said we must have signing in all deaf schools. I agree with that! I wish all staff here could sign. David Wheeley told me Mrs Munnings' face was like shocked!!! I don't know why! Afterwards, we all ran to TV Room and Arsenal was 1–0 up.

Mr Langston told all of us that we will not have more music lessons after half term. Hurrah! Mrs Bonnington ~~got~~ was fed up with us because we couldn't play music properly.

The church this morning was boring again. I fell asleep! Some boys had tried to get to the altar to eat bread and drink red wine, but the vicar only touched their heads.

Will be play^ing chess with Jonah soon, so will stop writing now.

Love from,

Aaron xxx

P.S. Hey, Jamie, I know you're not happy that Manchester United lost! Ha, ha!.

P.P.S. Mrs Margaret Thatcher, who became the first female Prime Minister two weeks ago, visited this school in 1973!

Friday 15th June 1979.

Dear Mum, Dad and Jamie,

This is a quick letter! You and Dad and Aunt Barbara will be coming to Sports Day next week (23rd). Jamie can't come again! He is going away for weekend in Cornwall for his school's camping trip. Lucky him! Hope you don't fall over Land's End, Jamie!!!

I will be doing Junior 100M, 200M and 400M. I hope I will be the first and beat Ian Synman! He is a very fast runner. I am ~~prasticing~~ practising Discus Throw and Long Jump too.

Do you remember Pat Keysell? The woman from VISION ON who could sign? She came to the school last week! She gave drama and mime lessons to each Form in Assembly Hall all day. She still can sign and we all understood her. Mr McShane said he knew a deaf friend who knew her and he asked her to come to the school. It was brilliant!!! I might be an actor one day!!! Chris told me he loved it too and he said Andrew Brener LOVED it and he said he wants to be an actor in future. I have an autograph of her!!! (Jamie, yes, I have one for you from her with plenty of xxxs!). Andy Farmleigh from my Form said he wants to be a magician when he grows up. He is good at magic – he has Paul Daniels magic toys. He told Pat Keysell about it and she told him he should go for it. She told us that we all must express ourselves in our way, so we all used signing to tell a short story each. Mr Arkwright came in to have a look and I don't think he was too happy!!!

Must stop now. It is very warm outside! We are going swimming soon.

Love from,

Aaron xxx

Friday 6th July 1979.

Dear Mum, Dad and Jamie,

ONE MORE WEEK TO GO BEFORE THE SUMMER HOLIDAY! Will Dad come and pick me up next week? Don't post my comics. Please bring them, thanks!

David Wheeley and a few other boys have new hearing aids. They are very small and fit behind the ears. David said they are called Behind The Ear Hearing Aids. He said they were better than the horrible old hearing aids. Mum, can you ask Miss Graham about them please? I promise I will wear them all day and evening and at weekends!!! I think many boys here will have them.

Jamie – I know Mum has told you about what happened to me at Sports Day. I know you laughed about it!!! It was not my fault! Mr Norris used a starter gun, but we can't hear it! I failed to run 100M because I couldn't SEE or HEAR the stupid gun! I was left standing at the starting line while everyone ran! Why couldn't he use a flag or a BIG DRUM?!? I am still angry about it!!! But I was more careful in 200M and came 2nd. 2nd in 400M too. Chris came 1st in all Junior Discus Throw, Javelin, Long Jump and Cricket Ball Throw. He's a very strong boy!

Must stop now, no more paper left! Don't forget the comics next week!!!

Love,

Aaron xxx

PART II
CHANGE

11

Chris' New Haircut

". . . there has always been a sufficient retention of manual methods to justify the oft–reiterated phrase "opposing camps", and the conflict, bitterness and extremism of the warring factions has been all too evident throughout the educational arena."
– G MCLOUGHLIN; on non–acceptance of the oral system in the UK, 1987

Monday September 10, 1979.
Aaron hurried down the short corridor towards Magnat House, his legs making great strides. He took a quick glance at his new digital watch with some pride; his dad had bought one each for him and Jamie during the summer, they were all the rage. The small rectangle LCD screen within the dark blue circular face inside a plastic flat–top dome told him it was now 09:02. Two minutes late, he cursed to himself.

When he entered the Assembly Hall, he was relieved to see that assembly had not yet started. Mr Langston was not present; the boys were still mingling, sitting and signing, and the staff were chattering away at the back. He took another look at his brand new school uniform with some relish. The school had completely changed the fabric of the blazer from wool to polyester nylon – he had memorised its spelling earlier – and they were much thinner and lighter than the previous ones, which was a huge relief because the woollen blazers had been quite hot and uncomfortable, especially during warm days. The new blazer was dark green, without all the golden stripes that were on the old style. The same white stag crest remained on the breast pocket though. The new blazer was also much more comfortable. When Aaron arrived earlier that morning, he was still wearing the old version, only to discover with surprise that everyone else was wearing the new one. His new blazer was hanging in his wardrobe, waiting for him, in Dorm Three. This was not the only new item: the school had also introduced a new school tie. The nylon tie was similar in design to the old cotton one, albeit more modern, with leaner green and gold stripes on black, along with a small embroidered white stag in the centre. He had new black trousers, too, which were also thinner and lighter. He had no time to inspect his new uniform though, as he was already late for the first assembly of the new term, so he hastily switched his old blazer and tie for the new ones and dashed out.

Aaron smoothed his new tie against his white shirt as he strode briskly down the right side of the hall, his eyes searching for someone amongst the rows of chairs on his left, feeling nothing between his tie and shirt. He felt a sense of lightness for the first time in his two years at the school – in his life as a whole. He was no longer wearing his body aids. Not for the first time, he put both of his hands behind his ears to inspect the small, curved plastic objects that were resting there. He and several other boys had learned of the new behind the ear hearing aids from David earlier that year, and he had pestered his parents about them during the summer holidays. It was not that he really *wanted* them, but they would be so much better than the body worn ones. With his thick blond hair covering his ears, he would be able to conceal the new aids and people would not stare at him as if he were an alien from outer space anymore; he would look like a hearing boy. He had promised his parents that he would wear them from the moment he woke up in the morning, just like a child would put on his glasses, and wear them all day and evening until bedtime, except for when he washed.

Eventually, his mother phoned the audiologist at the local hospital to find out more about it all and an appointment was made. Miss Graham, the audiologist, was initially reluctant to consider giving a profoundly deaf teenager like Aaron such new and sophisticated aids and suggested that he should continue wearing the body aids, for he would be able to hear better through the microphone in front of him rather than having them behind his ears. Jamie came along as well – he wanted to wind up his younger brother about the new aids – and was able to sign the conversation between their mother and the audiologist for Aaron.

Geraldine had pointed out to the woman that the body aids did not work for Aaron anyway, so the new aids would be no different, although she felt that Aaron would probably receive sounds better with them. She added that she had already given up making another new harness – the last one, her *fifth,* had been severely damaged by a boy just before the summer break.

'Basher! It was him!' Jamie suddenly blurted out in both voice and sign. Annoyed, Aaron jumped from his chair next to the audiologist's desk to silence his grinning older brother: he had confided in him with the story of what happened. Geraldine calmed them down and resumed her chat with Miss Graham.

'Besides,' she said, 'my son has always refused to wear them at home, so with the new aids being smaller and lighter, I'm sure he'll wear them all the time. Won't this help with his speech? It has improved steadily–'

'Steadily?' Jamie broke in, pausing as interpreter, but continuing to sign for Aaron's benefit. 'He still talks like R2–D2–'

'Be quiet, Jamie!' warned his mother.

'You're C3PO!' Aaron hit back, mimicking the droid with angled arms. 'A stupid tinpot!'

'At least, I'm smarter than you, butthead,' replied Jamie, his fist knocking on Aaron's forehead. 'I can speak six billion languages. No, no, no. I mean six billion *and one* languages. C3PO can't sign, but I can!'

'Be quiet, both of you!' their mother scowled, glancing back at Miss Graham, whose expression was one of strained patience. 'So, what do you think?'

Aaron scanned along the fourth row from the front and found him. He almost didn't recognise him at first. He found his way along the gap between the two rows of chairs, greeting Sammy, Dean and Mark along the way, before sitting down next to Chris, who was signing to Matthew next to him. Aaron saw that Matthew was now wearing glasses; perhaps this might help to improve his bad sight, he thought. Aaron rubbed Chris' head, feeling the soft short bristles. Chris swung round, smiling with delight at seeing his best friend again. Aaron gazed at him, studying his new look. Chris had had his hair sheared; much of the thick brown hair was gone, but he was not a complete skinhead. It was quite a sight compared to the other boys' various long, thick or straggly hairstyles.

'Hi!' Chris greeted him. 'Where have you been? You didn't come yesterday.'

'My dad's car broke down, so we had to wait until this morning. I had to get up at four o'clock!' Aaron half yawned as he reflected on the previous day. His parents, Jamie and him were all set to leave home and drive across the country when the engine had broken down because of a blown gasket. All garages were closed on Sundays, so John had had to call on a colleague who was a mechanic. By the time he was finished, it was too late to travel, so John took Aaron the next morning while Geraldine stayed at home to get Jamie to school. 'What happened to your hair? Fell under Hubert's lawnmower?' he pointed at Chris' hair.

'I just fancied a change,' he replied, remembering his recent trip to the barber's. There, he had seen another boy of his age wearing a green bomber jacket and boots, having his head shaved by the barber. The boy gave Chris a thumbs up to encourage him to do the same. Chris, however, had decided not to and had asked for a no.3 cut.

'Mr Langston won't like it,' said Aaron.

'So what? It's my hair, not his!' replied Chris, smiling wryly. 'Anyway, welcome to the halfway line.'

'Halfway line?'

'Third Form; you're halfway through your five years here.'

'Oh.'

Matthew rubbed his closed hand on Chris' head as though he was scrubbing it. 'Scrubhead! Should be brilliant for cleaning toilets. Hope you get some Ajax for your fifteenth birthday on Wednesday!'

'Piss off!' Chris snapped, pushing the hand away. Matthew scoffed and sat back. He blinked again. He put his finger between his right eye and his new glasses to rub away the wetness on his lower eyelash, and then straightened the silver–frames. He looked across the stage and the backs of the nodding and shaking heads in front of him, again checking for some kind of improvement in his vision, but apart from a somewhat enhanced clarity through the lens, he saw no difference. Looking ahead, he still couldn't see Chris on his right, Jamon on his left, the lighting tubes on the high ceiling above, nor his hands and thighs below him. The lectern on the stage a short distance away was just a blur to him. When Mr Langston was standing there for the morning assembly, he could never see his lips, which were like a tiny blurred speck; but then again, many boys couldn't, he mused. His mother thought having new glasses might help improve his vision in some way, so she had taken him to the opticians during the summer. He found the appointment very difficult; the optician had turned down the lights, making him read aloud the letters on a backlit board which was reflected on a mirror that he struggled to see because of the glare. Then, she shone her ophthalmoscope into his eyes, hurting them, and asked questions that he could barely lipread in the poor light. He repeatedly asked her to turn on the lights so that he could see her and his mother better, but it was all in vain. She and his mother had long conversations that he couldn't follow. The next thing he knew, and without warning, the lady was putting bifocal trial frames on his face. Again, she made him read the letter board on the mirror, while she changed the lenses to test his eyes by trial and error. He had struggled not only with his inability to read the letters, but also with how the optician kept changing the lens so quickly; the bright light coming from the instrument that she kept shining into his eyes did not help matters. Every time she turned to change around the lens in the lens box, she moved the light away and he was virtually blinded – everything became completely black. By the time his pupils slowly began to adjust – he had since discovered from other boys that his eyes were very slow at adjusting from dark to light and vice versa – the optician had inserted another new lens and shone the ophthalmoscope back into his eyes before he could adapt. He finally lost it, threw off the frames and stormed out. He was so angry and frustrated by what was happening to him and bluntly told his mother to tell the optician to 'fucking slow down!', much to her shock. Eventually, the optician did so, although Matthew sensed her impatience. A new pair of glasses was set, though he knew they still might not work for him.

They didn't. He lifted up his glasses and squinted at the empty stage, but it looked much the same to him as it did when he was wearing them. All they seemed to do was give him headaches, like the one he was having right now. He felt two short, sharp taps on his shoulder from behind. He ignored them, knowing it was the same old trick. He had learned not to rise to it, to avoid another round of bickering. He slid the glasses back down just as another tap came, this time harder, almost hurting the bone of his right shoulder. He wheeled round as fast as he could, hoping to catch the perpetrator red–handed, only to see Gary signing to Timothy next to him. They both looked innocently at him.

'What are you looking at?' Gary said, with a mischievous half–grin. Matthew hesitated, knowing that arguing with the new prefects would be pointless. He decided it wasn't worth it. He suddenly felt his legs being pressed against his chair and turned back see Andrew plodding through, waving at Aaron.

'You're on my chair,' Andrew said, pointing at the chair on which Aaron was sitting. He saw that Aaron was no longer wearing the body aids. 'You got them as well!' he pointed behind his own ears.

Aaron nodded. Chris pointed at his own ears too, to show that he also had the new aids. 'Me too! Can't hear anything though.'

'Everyone has them now,' said Andrew, swinging his hand around to indicate the others. 'I got them through the Blue Peter Key Note van. That blue van was great!'

'It's still around?' queried Aaron, recalling how the BBC children's television show, Blue Peter, had made an appeal for old keys and unwanted toy cars to help towards the cost of creating mobile classrooms for the deaf – or Blue Peter Key Note vans as they were known – to help deaf children in rural and isolated areas to get some education. They also sometimes provided free hearing aids; the body worn ones. He knew this because Jamie had signed for him what the three presenters – Peter Purves, John Noakes and Lesley Judd – were saying about the appeal. He had not come across the van yet, although some of the other boys had. They had told him stories about it during the last two years; none of the volunteers who drove the vans and provided the education could sign and some were very difficult to lipread. He was surprised to learn from Andrew that they were still around and now providing the new aids.

Everybody rose to their feet when Mr Langston entered the hall with Mr Arkwright following him. Aaron squeezed between two chairs in front of him; Ian Snyman sat on one and the other was empty. Andrew moved to his now vacant chair. Chris leant over, pressing against the back of Aaron's chair, and tapped his friend's shoulder. Aaron glanced back.

'Have you heard the news?' Chris asked.

'No. What news?'

'Mr Parsons is dead,' Chris announced. 'Heart attack during the summer, I think.'

'What?!' Aaron gasped in disbelief. How could a health and fitness freak like him die? All those lectures about healthy living and being fit, the cross–country runs and his trademark chair push–ups. He was still in his early fifties. 'He seemed so fit!'

'I know! Probably *too* fit and his heart went boom!' Chris gestured an exploding heart, with a hint of sarcasm.

Mr Arkwright paced down the back row of chairs where the staff members stood, greeting each one as he passed them and found an empty chair next to Mrs Munnings.

'Morning, Jonathan,' the geography and history teacher greeted him. 'Good summer?'

'Delightful, Elizabeth,' replied Mr Arkwright. 'Josephine and I went to Jerusalem again for our holiday. It's always such a magnificent city. You should go there one day.'

'I'll remember that,' she said. How many times had he been there, she wondered. She sensed that her colleague was about to launch into another of his travelogues about the Israeli capital and quickly changed the subject. 'Do you remember Dr Reuben Conrad?'

'I can't say I do,' Mr Arkwright queried. 'The name rings a bell, though.'

'He's from University of Oxford,' she explained. 'He carried out a five–year study on the lipreading skills of deaf children in oral education ... '

'Ah, I remember him now,' Mr Arkwright nodded. The professor had visited the school for a couple of days a few years back to observe the boys' education. He recalled how the man had attended two or three of his religious studies and speech lessons. He'd had to stand awkwardly, with his back against the door, behind the teacher and one of the boys, in the small and cramped Speech Room. He hoped he had impressed the professor; he was looking forward to reading the outcome of the study when it was published later in the year, hoping that it would offer further evidence that the oral approach to deaf education was more efficient than sign language. He had always strongly believed that once the boys mastered lipreading and speaking skills, they would be better served in their lives upon leaving school. 'I sincerely hope that he was quite satisfied with what he saw here.'

'Well, not exactly,' said Mrs Munnings carefully, knowing that Jonathan would react badly to the findings. She picked up a book that was lying on her chair. Her tall colleague leaned slightly to his left to see the thick, dark green book, entitled *The Deaf School Child* in gold; the author was Dr Reuben Conrad. 'It was published last June.' Mrs Munnings said. 'I brought it here to show Penny and I told her that it's such an interesting read that she must read it sometime–'

'Yes, yes,' Mr Arkwright interrupted, his Cumbrian accent impatient. He briefly glanced over the many standing figures in front of him to see Mr Langston reaching the stage. Mrs Munnings acknowledged her colleague's impatience. She flipped through the book to the page where the summary was.

'Here's the summary.' Mr Arkwright tuned back in and listened as she read. 'When deaf children leave school, half of them have a reading age of less than seven point six; half of them lipread worse than the average hearing child, untrained and inexperienced; seventy percent of them have speech which on the whole is too difficult to be understood, and only ten percent have speech which their own teachers considered fairly easy understood.'

Mr Arkwright furrowed his brows behind his thick–rimmed spectacles, wrinkle lines forming across his forehead as he tried to digest this statement.

She acknowledged her colleague's perplexed expression, closing the book and tucking it under her arm, her own private thoughts swirling within. Until she had first read the book, she had always believed that the oral approach was the best and only way of educating the deaf, in spite of her constant frustration at having to repeat the same things over and over again during her lessons in the last six years. She could never understand *why* this was always the case. She had always thought that she was failing as a teacher of the deaf. She tried to make herself understood in other ways, such as by writing almost everything on the blackboard, drawing things, showing pictures, occasionally shouting into the microphone, stretching her mouth to the limit, going from one boy's desk to another to check and correct their notes – or the lack of them – on what she taught, exploring alternatives and so forth, just to make the boys understand even the simplest things. Her eight–year–old hearing daughter, Elise, would have easily understood her first time round. She knew very well that the boys were not incompetent; they were quite intelligent in their own way. It was their inability to comprehend what was being said to them orally. Now, this book … *this book* made perfect sense to her: it wasn't her failure to teach the boys that was the problem; it was primarily the lack of an adequate method of communication other than the oral method. Would teaching through sign language work? This was something she was keen to explore; she must have a chat with Miles about it soon. She glanced back at the still waiting Mr Arkwright.

'Most deaf children are leaving school at sixteen with a reading age of less than eight years old because they've had problems understanding their teachers orally. Another interesting point is that Dr Rueben Conrad and his team also tested groups of hearing schoolchildren in the same way as they tested the deaf schoolchildren, so that they could compare the two groups. In one test, the hearing schoolchildren wore earmuffs during some of their lessons and tried to understand their teachers through lipreading, without hearing them. As it turned out, the tests showed that the hearing children fared better than the deaf children. Also, did you know that the minimum age standard set by the government for school leavers' literacy skills is nine? It seems that the majority of deaf children are one point four years below that. I feel–'

'Ridiculous!' the tall man remarked, keeping his voice low. 'The boys are doing fine here. We pride ourselves in very high standards.'

'Yes, I agree,' she nodded in spite of herself, 'but doesn't it make you think–'

'Preposterous!' A German–accented clipped male voice suddenly screeched through Mrs Munnings' left ear, cutting her short. Her head whipped round to the source. 'I agree with him. Hearing and speaking is superior!'

Mrs Munnings, momentarily unnerved, felt her spine turning into ice. She looked away from the man and saw that everybody was sitting down as the headmaster arrived at the lectern. She sat quietly, disliking the new maths teacher already.

Mr Langston tapped on the microphone that was resting on his chest, hung by a neck strap. 'Testing. Everyone hear me?' As usual, he received a muted response. He ignored it: the sound amplification had never worked properly anyway. 'Good morning, boys,' he greeted them warily.

God Boring, Pr Lazy!

He sighed, long resigned to the fact that the boys could never utter "Good morning, Mr Langston" clearly with their labyrinthine speech. He cleared his throat, ready to make the announcement. 'Right ... before we start our first assembly of the new term, I have some sad news to tell you ...'

'. . . sad news to tell us,' David signed in the third row with his hands low at his stomach, his eyes fixed on the headmaster and the hearing aid in his left ear picking up the best possible sound from the voice that echoed around the hall. The rest of his row were watching him furtively from either side, digesting the secret interpretation. He quickly glanced behind to see his fellow phone–good, Mark, finishing signing the sentence, and Gary doing likewise behind him. David turned back and quickly peeked over the Second Form row in front of him to see that Rowan Ince had just done his job. David wasn't too sure yet who would be the new First Formers' phone–good; doing the secret job visibly in front of the headmaster was very challenging and he believed that Mr Langston already knew the secret, but he did nothing about it for some strange reason. Bradley nudged David in discretion to tell him to carry on, as the headmaster was still speaking.

'. . . Mr Parsons, who was our maths teacher for seven years, died suddenly during the summer.' Mr Langston said, sombrely.

Johan Broadwater gently slapped the arm of his fellow new First Former, thin with olive skin and fair hair. What was his name again, he mumbled to himself. Conor Blackwell? No, that was the black one. Nicolo Perran? Yes, that was him; he finally remembered the chat he'd had with the boy from Italy in Dorm One yesterday. Nicolo turned to the black–haired boy, knowing the perplexed look on his face. 'What did he say? I can't understand him.'

Nicolo shrugged. 'Me neither!'

Watched by his form mates in the fifth row, Gary lazily signed the spoken proceedings as he listened through his aids. 'Before we pray for him. He would like to introduce us to the new maths teacher. They managed to find him in a very short time. Mr ...' Gary stalled, failing to pick up the name. He saw Mark glancing behind at him for clarity, but shook his head. 'It's a foreign name. German, I think,' he told him, placing an upright index finger on his head to signify the pointed top of a helmet.

He looked ahead to see that Mr Langston was beckoning for someone in the staff row behind him to come over to the stage and introduce himself. Gary glanced at the seated members of staff.

Miss Stephenson crossed her legs as she watched the new maths teacher rise to his feet and head across the hall. Her interest, though, was more in Mr Whittle, who was sitting next to her. She admired his new appearance. 'Charles, you look much younger without your beard.'

Mr Whittle turned to her, smiling appreciatively. He stroked his bare jawline to show it off. 'Yes, Penny, I decided to shave it all off last week. I think the boys were having trouble lipreading me because of my beard, so I thought perhaps if I shaved it off, they might understand me better. Still feels a bit cold though!'

'You'll get used to it,' Miss Stephenson said, a girlish chuckle in her voice. She couldn't stop noticing him. She had always detested bearded men, believing they looked older than they should. However, when she saw the young English teacher's new look, which also included a shorter hairstyle, she felt her heart flutter. She tenderly placed her hand on Mr Whittle's lap, smiling at him. 'You *do* look rather handsome, my dear.'

Aaron shook David's arm to bring him round, frowning: David didn't get the name properly. 'Fingerspell the name again.'

'It's a German name,' David responded. 'A long one. I couldn't get it, but I suppose we'll know later from Mr Langston's daily assembly notes on the noticeboard.'

Aaron nodded briefly and watched the new teacher passing his row. He turned back to David. 'How was your summer? Did you go to the Farnborough Air Day that your parents were taking you to?'

'It was fine,' David answered flatly. 'Just my mum took me.'

'Not your dad too?'

'He didn't come with us.'

'Why not? He's interested in aircraft like you.'

'Just leave it, okay?' David looked away.

Aaron decided to leave it, suspecting that something had happened during the summer. He looked ahead and saw that the new maths teacher was now standing next to the headmaster. Aaron shuddered at seeing the man clearly for the first time.

Heinrich Schneider stood proudly in front of the assembled. He was an extremely tall and solid figure; his broad shoulders lay strangely flat on either side of his sturdy neck and his hands looked menacingly large for his sturdy form; as though he could easily snap a person's neck with one swift move. From what he could see, Aaron estimated that the new maths teacher was about six foot seven, maybe a little more, and was in his early forties. He looked neither obese nor hulking; he was just monstrously built. Aaron deducted that the man was now the largest and tallest staff member in the school. Even Mr Langston looked like a dwarf next to him. He had a long, beaky nose, complemented by bony sparrow–like facial features, along with thick, moist lips that seemed to stretch from side to side in a permanent sneer. His eyes were intensely dark and piercing under furrowed brows. It was as if he had a fierce power to turn people into stone with one stare. To finish off his platitudinous Germanic appearance, his blonde hair was immaculately parted to the right, leaving quite a wide parting line on the left side. He wore a beige suit that seemed to fit him like a glove; made to measure, Aaron guessed, given his imposing size. The immense man graciously opened his arms to welcome his new pupils.

'Hello boys,' said Mr Schneider, closing his arms and clasping his hands with such casualness.

Aaron glanced around undecidedly; it felt as though Hell had just frozen over.

Mr Langston pinned the sheet of paper to the noticeboard. When he moved away, some of the boys, who were waiting behind him, quickly moved in and crowded round to read the morning assembly notes. The headmaster made his way from the lobby to the front hall, which was occupied by several scurrying boys as they prepared for their first lesson of the day. His eye caught Chris at the entrance doors and he sighed to himself. He went over and tapped the Fourth Former's shoulder. Chris turned to face the principal.

'What have you done with your hair, Christopher?' he asked, pointing at his crew cut; 'You're like a skinhead!'

Chris shrugged, smiling at him. Because of Chris' poor speech, Mr Langston knew that he would not give a verbal excuse, so he decided to leave it at that. With that, Chris headed away, leaving Mr Langston to ponder. Chris passed David, heading the opposite direction. Gary accosted David with intent.

'You know Basher's the head boy now?' said Gary.

'So?' David shrugged and began to move away, but the new prefect grabbed the lapel of his new blazer and pulled the fat boy back. 'He wants a slave to work for him,' he announced. 'Guess who he chose?'

Gary let David go, and then patted his head, making it obvious to him. He headed away, leaving him to whimper. Chris saw this, his thoughts spinning: why had the school chosen Basher as head boy? He was the worst bully in the school and the boys were scared of him. Chris wasn't, though. He thought Basher was totally brainless; he knew from others that he was absolutely hopeless at every subject except for art, at which he was extremely good. He was even rubbish at football. He fancied himself as a bit of a Bobby Moore, because Moore played for West Ham United, a club Basher supported, but in reality he was a gaping hole at the back. If Chris was the captain of the senior football team, he would have gladly dropped him in matches against the local hearing schools, but Gary Portmore was captain and he would always select Basher for the team, out of friendship.

Chris turned to his right to look up at a large wooden board on the wall, which listed all of the school's head boys since 1950. Each boy's name and year was painted in gold with a thin black outline. He soon became aware of a presence next to him and looked down to see a pint–sized boy with light brown hair, gazing up at the board as well. Chris knew he was one of the new boys; he was the shortest of all the boys, but he didn't know his name.

'What's your name?' Chris asked him.

'Toby Eriswell,' he replied, signing his name sign, with the index finger of his right hand pointing at his chest then becoming a thumbs up, and followed it with an infectious impish grin.

The surname rang a bell to Chris, who was caught up by the boy's smile. His eyes darted back to the board and spotted it: *1975–76: James Eriswell.* He turned back to Toby quizzically.

'He's my oldest brother,' he pointed at the name. 'My family are all deaf. I've got three brothers and two sisters. My younger brother, Casey, will come here next year, I hope! All my uncles, aunties and cousins are deaf too.'

'Wow!' Chris exclaimed. 'James was the head boy at the same time Mr

Langston became headmaster, right?'

'Yeah, right!' Toby nodded. 'They got on very well. They still write to each other sometimes, I think.'

Chris looked back at the board again to read down from James Eriswell's name. *1976–77: Jeffrey Gibbs. 1977–78: Theodore Elliott. 1978–79: Graham Hill.* Chris knew whose name would occupy the board the following year. Toby tapped Chris' arm to bring him round.

'Will you be head boy next year?' he asked.

Chris smiled back, liking the sound of that.

Carrying a thick ring file, Mr Schneider walked briskly towards the door of the Maths Room, checking his watch again: almost half past nine. He politely nodded at Hubert as he passed by, carrying a toolbox. The gardener slowed his pace when he glanced at the new maths teacher.

'Good morning,' Mr Schneider greeted. 'It's Hubert, isn't it?'

Hubert did not reply for a long moment as he sized the man up. He stared at the German teacher's face for a long while until he nodded. 'Yes, Hubert, me, yes.'

'Well, pleased to meet you,' Mr Schneider extended his hand. Hubert, however, did not return the gesture. Instead, he hurried away. Mr Schneider shrugged; Donald had told him that the school gardener was a reserved man, so not to take him too seriously. He twisted the handle to open the door.

He entered and paused for a moment to take in the confined surroundings. With his own abundant size, he felt quite claustrophobic and the four walls of the small room seemed to close in on him. He quickly shook off the uncertain feeling and made his way towards the teacher's desk right next to the door, directing his eyes at the Fourth Formers who were sitting at their desks, waiting. He placed his file on the desk and straightened up as he prepared for his debut maths lesson at the school. He soon noticed that some of the boys had smirks on their faces, and assumed that they were welcoming him.

'Good morning, boys,' he greeted them. 'I would like to make sure that you know my name properly. It is Mr Schneider. Sch–nei–der. I will write that on the blackboard for you.'

He turned to face the blackboard and began to pick up the chalk. He froze as he read what was written in large letters across the blackboard.

HEIL HITLER.

Mr Schneider heard muffled laughter from behind. He slowly turned to face his new pupils, grinning without humour. He took a deep breath and firmly clasped his hands. 'Very funny,' he said. 'So you know I'm from West Germany then.'

Chris raised his eyebrows in surprise; that man was quite easy to lipread with those big, wide lips. He folded his arms as he watched the giant walk round the teacher's desk.

'I have come here to teach you maths,' said Mr Schneider. He held up three fingers. 'There are three simple rules which you must obey,' he continued. He closed two fingers, leaving only the index finger up. 'Rule one … you learn and work hard my way. I will *not* allow sloppiness.'

Chris frowned. He didn't catch the last word, but he let it be. Mr Schneider then raised his middle finger, making it two.

'Rule two … you are *not* allowed to sign here. Always *speak*!' he pointed at his own mouth sternly.

He held up his ring finger: 'Rule three … Failure to obey these two rules … Detention! Do I make myself absolutely clear?'

The maths teacher's head slowly panned from one end of the semicircular formation of desks to the other, taking in each boy's silent nod. Except for Chris, who didn't nod. The man took a few steps towards Chris' desk, which was in the middle of the formation, and looked down imposingly at the boy. 'You did not nod your head to agree with my three rules,' he said. 'What is your name, boy?'

Chris craned his neck, looking up at the towering man. He said nothing. Mr Schneider glanced down at his desk and saw a notebook which bore his handwritten name. 'Chris Matthaus? That surname's German. Where are you from?'

'Highbury, London,' Chris replied, signing at him and smirking in cheekiness. From the corners of his eyes, he saw his form mates sniggering. Mr Schneider remained calm, hiding his displeasure.

'Would you please repeat that …' he asked again, more firmly, pointing at his own lips. '. . . with your mouth, not your hands.'

Ok, fine, Chris thought to himself, *you want me to use my mouth?* He straightened up on his chair, then folded his arms and cleared his throat. 'Highbury, London,' he mouthed silently and daringly.

Mr Schneider heard loud chortles from around the room. He folded his arms, taking in the amusement. He should have told the boy to use his *voice,* not his mouth. He was starting to like the kid already. Probably still had some German blood in him, he mused to himself. He leant down, resting his big hands on the desk, and came face to face with Chris at close proximity. 'Where … are … you … from?' he demanded.

Chris saw that the piercing eyes that stared at him seemed to flame wildly. He knew he was running out of excuses. He didn't even know how to correctly pronounce Highbury, or even London. He wasn't going to give in though. His eyes slid down warily to the pencil case on his desk, which had a sticker of Arsenal Football Club's emblem on it. He pointed at it, smiling with a touch of glee.

The teacher saw what Chris was pointing at and looked back up at him again. 'Arsenal? Is this where you're from?'

Chris nodded.

Mr Schneider straightened up, his eyes still looking down, nodding his head. 'Fine. As you have broken Rule two, I have the pleasure on my first day … Detention!'

Chris groaned inwardly.

Steven caught up with Chris as he strode through the front hall during lunch break. He had not had the chance to have a proper chat with him all morning or at their table. He had gathered from the other boys that the new maths teacher had already made his oppressive intentions very clear to them. 'Bloody hell!' he cried wildly. 'He now has a new name sign: *Hitler Teacher*!'

Steven raised his right arm straight up to indicate the obvious salute and retracted it. He quickly thought about Chris' rarely mentioned background. 'I didn't know you were German!'

'I'm not,' Chris replied. 'My grandfather was. He came here just before the Second World War broke out. That's what my mum said a long time ago.'

'Okay,' Steven decided not to go any further, knowing that Chris would clam up if pressed more about his past. 'Quick kick–about?' he pointed at the field through the entrance doors, kicking his leg.

'No, sorry,' apologised Chris, 'I'm meeting Aaron in the library to chat about his summer. Another time, okay?'

'Okay,' Steven nodded wearily. Chris was *always* with Aaron, he thought to himself. Ever since Aaron first arrived two years back, he and Chris had been inseparable; the best of friends. Steven was already resigned to the fact that he and Chris were no longer best mates, as they had been during their first year. Although he had some good friends in the school, he did not really have a best friend for himself. 'I'll see you.'

'See you later in English,' Chris waved and briskly walked away. Steven sighed. He tucked his hands into his trouser pockets and looked around idly. He saw Michael Hardcastle strolling through from the front hall, carrying a folder. It caught Steven's eye: it had a Liverpool FC sticker on it.

He ran up to Michael, waving at him excitedly. 'I didn't know you supported Liverpool!'

'Yeah, I do,' answered Michael.

Steven placed a friendly arm round his new found Liverpool fan friend.

'Would you like to see my autographed photograph of Emlyn Hughes?'

'You have one?' the Third Former reacted with surprise.

'Yes, come with me to Dorm Four. I'll show you!'

Steven and Michael hurried up the grand staircase.

12

Candid Breasts

"We learn to be racist, therefore we can learn not to be racist. Racism is not genetic. It has everything to do with power".

– JANE ELLIOTT, 1983

Gary dragged David by his tee shirt towards a closed door, marked *Fifth Form Common Room.* Taped below the sign was a sheet of lined paper. The handwritten words screamed *DO NOT ENTER!*

David had been avoiding Basher since Monday. He had managed to stay safe by hiding in numerous places around the school and staying near the duty teacher each evening, thus preventing Basher from touching him. He'd also helped the matrons to sort out the clothes store – and received five good points from them for being helpful – and helped to ferry the daily clothes baskets to each dorm every evening. Whenever he fell under Basher's radar, he would simply turn and run away from him. He realised though that his luck would eventually run out, and it did on that blazing hot Sunday.

After church in the morning, the boys had free time. Unfortunately for David, Mr Bronte was on duty that day; he knew that the useless craftwork teacher would simply grunt and barely lift a finger whenever there was trouble. Eventually, Gary nabbed him.

As they approached the door, Andrew ran past, not taking any interest in them – he was feverish with excitement. He disappeared around the corner just as Gary pushed the door inwards.

David soon found himself kneeling on the lino in front of Basher, who was sitting on a battered armchair in front of an open window. His hands rested on the armrests as he sat like a monarch on a throne. The rest of the prefects stood on either side of the armchair, watching with interest. David quickly sniffed the air, which was permeated by an overwhelming stench of sweaty armpits due to the unexpected heatwave that weekend. He took a quick glance round the common room. It was a square, medium–sized room with light blue painted walls and there was a sofa there. A table with a kettle, dirty mugs, coffee and tea tins and a toaster was propped up against one wall. Ten study desks and chairs faced the two adjacent walls. A few centerfold pin–ups of topless women were taped up. The wooden floor vibrated with a loud stomp and David swung back to face his nemesis.

'Finally!' sneered Basher. 'Now–'

'I won't be your slave!' said David, plucking up courage.

The new head boy clasped his hands and grinned broadly. He left his armchair and approached the still kneeling David. He leaned down, grabbed the back of David's long hair and yanked it, forcing David's head backwards. Basher leaned towards him, their faces almost touching; David's small nose twitched as he smelt the fetor of a recently smoked cigarette. David could see Basher's free hand signing below.

'If you refuse to do what I tell you,' Basher said, 'you will be in really big shit. *Big shit*. Understand?'

'Why me? What have I done?' David whimpered.

'Answer me!'

David hesitated. He screamed when Basher pulled his hair harder. Eventually, he nodded.

'Good,' Basher released his grip and straightened up. He pointed at a table behind David. 'Now, make us all a cup of tea. When you've finished that, wash these mugs, and then you'll clean and polish our football boots, every one of them.'

David hung his head in despair, his hands resting on his thighs. Through his left ear, he could hear the sound of cackling laughter.

'It's so hot!' groaned Dean. He looked up at the radiant sun through his white–rimmed sunglasses and observed again that there was not a single cloud in sight. 'It rained practically the whole of August!' he signed to no one in particular.

Dean looked at Sammy and Ian, who were sitting on the grass close to him. Sammy was shirtless and there was some redness around his milky white shoulders and back. Ian was also shirtless. Dean looked around at several other boys scattered around the grass at the rear of the school. 'Feels like it's still summer,' he commented.

'England's weird,' Sammy said. 'It's pissing down in Belfast right now. The Sunday Mirror said so.'

'It's a late heatwave,' Ian said. 'They can happen, even in spring and autumn.'

'How does it feel to be a negro?' asked Sammy, out of the blue.

Ian shot a look at him, a little incensed by the stupidity of the question. 'How does it feel to be a thick sunburnt paddy?'

'Don't call me a thick paddy,' Sammy snapped back. 'It's okay for you; you can't get sunburnt. It's not my fault I've got white Irish skin–'

'He's black and you're white. So what?' Dean cut in.

'Yeah, but–'

Sammy felt a hard whack on his nose. He fell backwards, his bare back hitting the grass. Something bobbed on his legs and rolled away. He quickly sat up, holding his throbbing nose, checking to make sure if it was not bleeding. His eyes darted to the football that was rolling away from him. Chris kicked it down; it bounced and flew up to his hands. 'What the fuck did you do that for?' Sammy scowled.

'Leave him alone,' replied Chris, pointing at Ian. 'He isn't a negro, a darkie or a jiggaboo.' He fingerspelled the last one. 'He's a black boy. We're white boys. No difference!'

'Jiggaboo?' Dean queried, trying to hide the smirk on his face. 'That's a new one!'

Chris stood and looked down at the still seated Sammy. 'Your lot are blowing up innocent people with parcels and milk bottles. Leave Ian alone, okay?'

'I'm not in the IRA!' Sammy replied angrily. 'Since when did you become a ... what was that word we learnt from Mr Whittle on Friday? Someone with a big brain who's always deep in thought. I can't remember what he wrote on the blackboard, but it was a long word beginning with "P".'

'Philosopher,' Dean said, fingerspelling it.

'Whatever,' said Chris as he slumped lazily on the grass, tugging a bit at his black football shorts for comfort.

Ian smiled, enjoying the banter. He had come to respect the fifteen–year old Fourth Former a great deal, for he was one of the few who did not give a damn about what kind of people they were. He had been the only black boy in the school until Conor Blackwell arrived. There was another new boy, who was Pakistani; Asif Nizamani. For the last two years, he had endured some harassment from a minority of boys, including Basher, and particularly *that* Hendrik Swart.

Hendrik Swart arrived last year; he was a short, scrawny boy with fair hair who came from a part of Cape Town. Ian was told that Hendrik's family had decided to send him to Ewing Hill Park because it was one of the best oral boarding schools in England. They paid the annual tuition fees themselves, as they were wealthy. Ian was initially assigned to look after Hendrik for his first month at the school last year, but when Mr Langston introduced them, a ruckus occurred. Afterwards, Hendrik's parents had a private discussion with the headmaster in his office. Soon after, Ian and Aaron were swapped, Aaron taking Hendrik and Ian, Dermot Jones.

For the last year, Hendrik had taunted Ian with many names associated with his skin colour, "jiggaboo" being his favourite. He had persuaded some boys – mainly from his Form – to join the secret campaign against him. Basher was sometimes part of it in his own way. Ian had been in serious fights with Hendrik, and although he was often provoked, he was always blamed and given more detentions than his tormentor, who was often backed up by his gang. Ian's father told him to stay strong and to stand up against him, but it was difficult. He believed that his father had already reported this problem to Mr Langston, but nothing had been done about it aside from the fact that the headmaster had told Ian to simply ignore Hendrik and that he had to be around his real friends for protection.

Then, earlier that year, in May, Hendrik and five members of his gang had ambushed Ian in the cellar after luring him in. Each boy had a white bed sheet draped over his body. They beat Ian up.

Afterwards, Ian locked himself in a toilet cubicle, crying. Thoughts of revenge or even suicide flooded his bruised head, his hand thumping on the wall in anger and frustration. Ian had been there for a while when the cubicle door suddenly burst open, startling him. Chris flew in, his hand clutching his buttocks. He almost collided with the seated Ian.

'Oh sorry!' I thought it was unlocked!' said Chris.

It *had been locked*. Or had it? Ian couldn't be sure: he was too fraught to remember. Chris stepped back to look for a free cubicle, but stopped when he realised that Ian wasn't using the toilet; he still had his trousers on and was sitting on the closed lid. He saw that Ian had been crying and noticed that he had some bruises on his face.

'What happened to you?' Chris asked.

'Nothing,' Ian shook his head.

Chris wasn't buying that. 'Look, I'm desperate for a shit. Wait outside for me and we'll talk about it when I'm finished. Okay? Out!' Chris yanked Ian from the lavatory seat and slammed the door in Ian's face.

Ian felt a massive weight lifted off his shoulders when he finally told Chris everything a short time later, as they sat under a tree in a private spot outside the forest behind the school. Ian broke down in tears more than once; Chris had had to comfort him in his arms. Chris was shocked and angry; he was already aware of Hendrik's campaign against Ian but had no idea that it had gone too far, or he would have stopped it himself. He said he hated people who hated black people. Ian said it was his own battle, not Chris' or anyone else's, but Chris refused to accept that, although he agreed that Ian's father was right, that he had to make a stand. Chris said he believed that the gang was under Hendrik's influence; they probably did not really understand what they were doing. Calmly,

Chris promised to deal with it with the help of some of his best form mates. After that, he said, Ian was on his own, although he would be there for him if he needed him. A grateful Ian asked Chris why he was helping him. Chris replied simply that he had come from a background where he saw coloured people as equals, but refused to say anything further.

The next thing Ian knew, Chris, Andrew, Dean, Matthew and Sammy had warned off Hendrik, whose gang was quickly disbanded. The crusade finally stopped, and, when Hendrik tried to provoke Ian, he simply ignored him and walked away. Subsequently, Hendrik became a mere shadow to him.

Brushing away the memory, Ian watched Chris bounce the football between his legs on the grass, feeling a sense of gratitude towards his friend. He thought how he was going to have to help Conor and Asif defend themselves against Hendrik, though; he knew the Second Former would pick on them. Fiddling with his new beige hearing aids, he wondered whether he should paint them black or not. He felt quite ridiculous when he looked in the mirror: it was as if he was wearing huge, beige earrings – why couldn't they make them in dark brown or black?

Dean swung round to see someone on his right; Chris, Sammy and Ian all turned, too, to see Andrew running towards them, his hands waving frantically. Urging his friends to stand up and follow him, 'Come on! You'll love this!' he screamed wildly.

Miss Stephenson knelt on a striped blanket, which was laid on the concrete paving slabs. Feeling its hardness, she would have preferred somewhere softer, such as grass, but this was the only place she could find to relax in private on such a hot day, away from the prying eyes of the adolescent boys. Especially *him*, she thought.

Resting her bottom on the backs of her calves, she looked again: she was in a cavity. It was a very small alcove in a concealed part of the school building. It was barely long or wide enough for one person to squeeze in, but it was secluded enough and directly in the sun. In front of her were some large waste disposal bins, which stank a little, but that did not bother her at all. Beyond them were trees and shrubbery. For a moment, she thought she heard something rustling amongst the bushes, but she dismissed it as either being a wild animal or a figment of her imagination. She pulled up her pink top, revealing a bikini top, and dropped it on top of the skirt that she had removed a moment ago. She bent down, resting her palms on the blanket, again feeling the rigidity of the concrete underneath. Her large round breasts bulged inside her bikini top as she lowered herself and rested her front on the blanket.

'What's she doing?' asked Dean, looking bewildered.

Andrew, Sammy, Ian, Chris and Matthew – who had joined them – exchanged glances, wondering who would answer. They were all standing behind the bushes a short distance away from the waste disposal units and the partially visible physics and biology teacher.

'She's sunbathing!' Andrew said incredulously.

'I know that!' Dean said, irked by the insult to his intelligence. 'But–'

'Look!' Matthew pointed, keeping his exclamation silent. Everyone turned and saw, through the branches and leaves, that the teacher was unhooking her bikini strap. Its two ends slid down to the ground.

'Woo!' growled Sammy. 'Wish I could see her tits!'

'I've always *wanted* to see her breasts,' concurred Andrew.

Chris shook his head in profound disbelief. For the last three years, his sex–obsessed form mate had had a crush on the teacher. Physics and biology were one of his best subjects because he was so besotted with her. Whenever he was with her, he would stare at her and her cleavage, lovingly touching her arm and pretending to tumble over in order to lightly swipe his hand on her covered breasts. He even sent her secret Valentine's cards. His name sign was *mad*. Chris was not surprised when Andrew had told him that he had secretly followed her to this secluded location. He saw that Dean was looking up at the building with a knowing grin on his face.

'I have an idea,' Dean announced to the group and turned to Ian. 'Does Shaun Knight still have that cine camera his dad gave him?'

Ian nodded. 'But he won't lend it to anyone.'

'Bring him here!' Dean said. He rounded up the group. 'Here's the plan …'

A short time later, Dean, Matthew and Ian rushed up the narrow emergency stairwell; they used this route to avoid attracting attention. Dean was carrying a metal bucket filled with crushed ice, while Ian had a long rope wound around his right shoulder. Matthew followed behind, carrying Sellotape and a ball of string. They reached the top floor; Dean suddenly came to a halt at the doorway and backtracked a bit. Ian stopped in his tracks just in time, but Matthew lumbered right into their backs, causing Dean to grip the bucket handle firmly to prevent the ice from spilling over. Dean and Ian's eyes darted to their comrade, cursing his typical clumsiness. Matthew smiled apologetically. Dean peered through the doorway to see Miss Turner walking away from them and disappearing into the matron's office at the end of the foyer. He beckoned to his mates to follow him. As the trio dashed towards another closed door next to the washroom, Matthew sniggered as he remembered how they'd got the crushed ice.

He had staggered into the dining room, gasping, with his right hand clasping his throat. The three dinner ladies quickly turned to see him over the counter and moved over to him. Matthew then acted as though he was suffering from the heat, fanning his face with his free hand. When he collapsed dramatically in the middle of the large room, the three ladies hurried round the counter to attend to him. When they left the kitchen, Matthew sat up, pretending to moan and groan, and took a quick glance over the counter at the kitchen beyond. He saw two dark figures sneaking in, silhouetted against the bright sunlight that streamed through a stretch of windows behind. The lanky one with straggly hair was unmistakably Dean and the other, Ian, looked even blacker than he was. Matthew glimpsed Dean carrying the bucket and Ian running across the kitchen, heading for the freezer at one side.

Meanwhile, the three dinner ladies crowded around Matthew, their backs to the kitchen, unaware of what was happening in it. Knowing that they could not sign, he kept them distracted by signing gibberish at them. He took another peek over the counter through the gap between two of the ladies and saw that Dean was frantically scooping crushed ice from the open freezer. Helping Dean, Ian turned to Matthew, indicating that they were almost done. Matthew saw Miss Payne turn away, so grabbed at her skirt to bring her back. Miss Knowles bent down to try to prise her colleague's skirt from his grasp, but he held on. Matthew took another discreet glance at the kitchen and saw that Dean had finished and was on his way out. Ian, following, gave him a thumbs up and they both shot out. Mrs Carr tucked her arm under Matthew's to help him up. Matthew allowed her to do so, releasing his grip on the skirt, and was soon on his feet again. He turned to Miss Knowles; she was the easiest of the three to lipread.

'Would you like a glass of water or something?' she asked him.

'No th–anks, I am … all right nnnow,' Matthew spoke back almost clearly, smiling. He turned and headed towards the doors, leaving the three bewildered dinner ladies behind.

Dean twisted the handle and opened the door. Once they were through, he carefully closed it behind them. They ran down a couple of steps and rushed through a narrow corridor, turning a corner. That part of the building usually went unused, although the boys sometimes used two of the small, narrow lavatories next to a largely vacant bathroom. The trio went for one lavatory; Matthew quickly closed and bolted the door behind him, the boys cramped in the tiny room. Dean handed the bucket to Ian and beckoned to him and Matthew to get on with it. He turned to step on the wooden toilet seat and froze when he saw a mixture of a dark brown substance and toilet paper still floating in the pool of browned water. He groaned and quickly pulled the chain that was hanging from the ceramic cistern above. With his foot, Dean slammed down the wooden lid just as the toilet flushed, and hopped onto it. The lanky boy reached for the small frosted glass window behind the lavatory and pulled up the iron handle. He pushed the window open, thrust his head through and looked down. He smiled when he saw the still–lying Miss Stephenson directly in view three stories down, her bare back to him and right on target. The small lavatory window was one of the cavity's three small windows; the one the boys were using gave them the best chance of achieving their objective. Dean turned to the shrubbery and saw the rest of his comrades still hiding there; he caught sight of Shaun too. He gave them a thumbs up.

Andrew waved back, acknowledging Dean. He turned to Shaun, pointing at the cine camera he was carrying.

'Is it ready?' he asked.

Shaun nodded, gripping the handle of the space gun–like item. Andrew smiled and glanced back up, to see the head at the window popping back inside.

Dean stepped off the closed lid, taking care not to bump into his cramped comrades. Ian had just finished tying one end of the rope to the arched handle while Matthew was busily sticking sellotape to the rim at its base, where the other end of the string was. Dean saw that the ice in the bucket was starting to melt due to the heat, and that there was some water at the top.

'Hurry up!' Dean urged.

Matthew double checked that the string was firmly stuck to the rim; he was satisfied. Bending down to pick up the ball of string from the floor, he suddenly felt a hard whack on his forehead. He swung back up, cupping it with his hand. Dean staggered back a bit, his hand also cupping his forehead, holding the ball of string in his other hand.

'Watch it!' Dean scowled at his friend.

Matthew rubbed his throbbing forehead, cursing his bad eyesight, and straightened his glasses. Dean squeezed through his two friends to get to the door and motioned for them to go ahead. Matthew and Ian carefully stepped onto the closed toilet seat, taking the bucket with them. Matthew popped his head through the window, looked down to get some idea of their target and turned back to Ian. He motioned for Ian to hold the rope while he hoisted the bucket through the window, carefully keeping it level, making sure that no water trickled out. Ian felt the tautness of the rope as Matthew lowered the bucket and Dean began to unwind the ball to allow the string to follow its descent.

The group behind the thicket watched anxiously as the bucket slowly made its way down one of the cavity's brick walls. Chris held his football tightly, smiling. Sammy folded his arms in anticipation. Shaun moved into the leaves for a clearer view, taking care not to snap any twigs. He then positioned the cine camera. Andrew clenched his hands, waiting with great excitement.

'Come on, come on,' Andrew mouthed to himself. He leant over and tapped Shaun's shoulder. Shaun glanced at him behind.

'Film it now!' Andrew commanded.

Shaun turned, switching the camera on, feeling its quiet humming. He held the small viewfinder to his right eye. Through it, he could see the partially visible teacher, in a voyeuristic kind of view, beyond the large bins. It was not a perfect shot as the bins occupied the left third of the frame; the other two–thirds were taken up by the dark brown building, with a small gap in the middle where the teacher was. He wished that the cine camera had a zoom lens like his dad's new JVC video camcorder, but it would have to do. The bucket came into view. It stopped in the middle of the frame, a few feet above the woman's bare back.

'Ready!' announced Mathew as he turned back to his friends inside and beckoned to Dean. 'Pull now!'

However, instead of pulling the string, Dean began to step up onto the already crowded lavatory seat to get to the window. 'I want to see it!'

'No!' screamed Ian silently. He released one of his hands from the taut rope and tried to push Dean back to the floor. He started to lose his grasp on the rope due to the bucket's weight. 'Pull the string now!'

Andrew gritted his teeth when he saw the bucket sway and knock against the wall. Sammy waved his hand furiously, silently urging those in the lavatory high above to pull the string.

Matthew struggled to keep the rope steady while Ian tried to keep his grip on it, but Dean persisted in trying to step onto the seat, even though there was no room for the three of them. Ian silently urged Dean to pull the string as the rope began to slip through his hand.

The bucket swerved slightly down, closer to Miss Stephenson's back. She slowly began to lift her head, sensing something. She looked directly ahead, but could only see the bins and the bushes beyond. Wait a minute, she thought to herself; had she seen something moving in the bushes?

Andrew jumped feverishly, keeping his head low. The bucket was right on target above her back and he could see that she had started to be aware that she wasn't alone.

Puuulllllll! Andrew screamed inside his head.

As though he had heard him, Dean pulled.

The string became taut as it pulled the base rim up, the bucket tipping up with the rope on the handle supporting it. As Miss Stephenson began to rise from the blanket, the bucket turned over and the crushed ice splattered directly onto her bare back. She screamed loudly, feeling its extreme coldness, then shot to her knees, exposing her large, round breasts, which bobbed directly in front of the prying eyes behind the bushes. Waving her arms wildly from the shock, she heard startled exclamations from behind the bushes and immediately recognised one of them.

Andrew screamed wildly; Chris screeched with delight, while Sammy punched the air in triumph.

Miss Stephenson quickly cupped her breasts with her hands, covering her pink nipples. Her head darted up to see the bucket hurriedly being hoisted up to the small window at the top. Embarrassment surged through her; she wished that the ground would swallow her up and she cursed her stupidity – sunbathing half naked at a boys' boarding school? Not such a good idea after all.

Matthew pulled the bucket in, closed the window and stepped off the seat, grinning broadly. Ian's white teeth beamed against his dark skin as he wound up the rope.

'Well?' Dean asked, silently cursing at not having been able to witness the crucial point first hand. 'Splat on her back?'

'Bullseye!' yelled Matthew, gesturing a dart hitting the red circle. 'Saw her tits down there! Woo!'

'Brilliant! Can't wait to see the film!' Dean turned, unbolted the door, and the trio rushed out.

'All on film?' Andrew asked Shaun anxiously.

'Everything!' he replied, backing away from the bushes, brandishing the item in his hand triumphantly. Andrew slapped his back, extremely pleased with their accomplishment.

'Finally saw her tits! Hurrah!' he gloated. He turned to Chris. 'Whaddaya think?'

'It was okay,' Chris, shrugged.

'Okay?!' Andrew stared at his form mate. 'Are you a poof or what? They were beautiful! Like Barbara Windsor's! We're the Magnificent Seven!'

The four boys scooted off, whooping and cheering.

Greg Collinson and his motley crew tentatively ~~walked~~ strutted along on the hard rocky ground of the causeway, hoping that they would not disturb the most fearsome creature of the vicinity.

Suddenly, a huge splash ~~had~~ erupted out of the seemingly still swamp water. A huge prehistoric ~~millopode~~ millipede–like creature called the Mogdaan shot up and it roared loudly. Greg and the rest stopped on their tracks, fearful at the menacing sight of the monster that presided high above them.

"Be very quiet!" whispered Greg as he silently waved down his friends. "It will leave

us alone if we keep very quiet. We must still return to the fourth city of Vaar and rescue our friend, Charles …"

Greg's whispering words were immediately cut short when the fierce creature saw the people and it lurched towards them, exposing its terrifying sharp–toothed jaws. Greg screamed in terror as it came upon him–

Aaron shrieked in fright. Something hard pounded on his forehead, knocking his deep thoughts out of him. He dropped his pen on the desk in shock and looked up to see a football bouncing away from him. Chris left the doorway and crossed the classroom to chase after the straying ball, taking a cheeky glance at his friend, who was rubbing his forehead.

'That hurt!' Aaron moaned. 'What did you do that for?'

'It's Sunday. I'm bored,' Chris answered, kicking the ball to the wall and catching it when it bounced back. He was still smiling about Miss Stephenson as he strode over to Aaron's desk. He noticed the sheets of lined paper and knew Aaron was writing another of his stories. 'What are you writing this time?'

'Well–'

Chris swiped the sheets from the desk. Aaron instinctively slammed his hands down in the direction of the sheets, but was too late. Chris dropped the football and held it down with his foot as he began to read. Aaron rose and slid over the desk to try to get his literature back, but Chris stepped backwards, away from him.

'Warlords of Doom?' Chris scoffed. 'Sounds like our teachers! What's it about?'

'It's part two to that film I saw last year at the cinema. Warlords of Atlantis. It starred Doug McClure, and it was about–'

'Your English's brilliant,' interrupted Chris, amazed. 'How?'

'What do you mean?'

'Being good at English.'

'I dunno,' Aaron shrugged, not out of modesty, but stating a simple fact. 'I just am.'

'I'm shit at English,' Chris said as he handed the sheets back to Aaron. 'I'm always bottom at English in my Form. I try as hard as I can, but it's not easy.'

'Same with most of my Form,' Aaron concurred. 'They always ask me for help during prep.'

'How do you *understand* Mr Whittle in English lessons? I can't lipread him. Even without his beard now!'

'I already know and understand good English. I can't lipread Mr Whittle either, even without his beard like you said, but I understand whatever he writes on the blackboard, and that helps to improve my English.'

'Bighead!' Chris pumped his hands against either side of his head.

'You're hot at football. I'm shit at it,' Aaron hit back, pointing at the football at Chris' feet and returning the same gesture. 'Bighead!'

Chris stared at his close friend for a long moment: he had a good point. He thought about it, then bent down to pick up the football and thrust it at Aaron with a knowing twinkle in his eye.

Aaron placed the ball on the chalked white spot on the grass, then straightened up to look ahead. Chris was positioning himself between the net–less goalposts. Aaron thought for a brief moment about their deal; Chris would help improve his football skills in return for an hour's private English tuition every Sunday afternoon.

'I'm Pat Jennings,' Chris announced as he readied himself in a goalkeeping position, 'and you are ... who?'

'George Best?' Aaron said, from the top of his head; he was always in the newspapers and on television thanks to his extravagant lifestyle.

'He's a drunk!' Chris shook his head. He thought of another name and pointed at Aaron. 'Trevor Francis!'

Aaron knew Chris would say that. The player had scored the winning goal for Brian Clough's Nottingham Forest in their first European Cup Final against the Swedish side, Malmo FF, in Munich last May. Chris had never stopped talking about it since he saw it on television. He thought it was an amazing goal, achieved via a diving header, from a cross by John Robertson. He had been trying to copy the move himself, so far without success. Aaron shrugged. 'Okay!'

'Good!' Chris encouraged him. 'Remember what I told you? Put your foot near the bottom of the ball. Whack!'

Aaron took a few steps back from the penalty spot while Chris widened his legs along the white line, readying himself with outstretched arms. Aaron took a deep breath, his eyes focused on the ball, and ran towards it. He kicked it as hard as he could, slipped backwards and crashed down on the grass, his arms and legs flying wildly. Chris didn't even finch as he watched the ball fly high over him and the bar. He smiled to himself as he looked at his friend on the grass. 'You're George Best!'

Chris encouraged Aaron to try again, explaining once more how to kick and aim at the goal. Aaron practised and improved his shooting, scoring several times.

'You're improving!' Chris said. 'Nine out of twenty. Not bad.'

'You let some in to make me feel better!' Aaron chuckled; he knew that Chris *had* deliberately let a few goals in.

'I didn't!' Chris shook his head. 'You're a good shooter.'

'Liar!'

'OK! I let in two or three!'

'You're a wanker!' Aaron shook a closed hand at him, laughing.

Chris marched towards Aaron, giggling. 'Yeah I'm a wanker. You're a dickhead.'

'*Scrubhead!*' Aaron hit back, grinning, his closed fist rubbing his own head, knowing that Chris hated that name sign. 'Go and scrub inside Hitler Teacher's big nose!'

Chris lunged at Aaron, pushing him backwards; he fell to the ground. Aaron groaned and tried to push Chris off, but Chris was too strong for him. He grabbed both of Chris' wrists in an effort to force him onto his side, but Chris wriggled out of Aaron's grasp and pushed his arms down to the grass. He quickly placed both of his folded legs on top of them, pinning them down. Chris now had the upper hand.

'Don't call me Scrubhead!' Chris said, his smile growing.

'Scrubhead!' Aaron mouthed with exaggeration. 'Scrubhead! Scrubhead!'

Chris released his legs from Aaron's arms and slid down along Aaron's body, resting his bottom on Aaron's denim shorts. He immediately placed his hands on each side of his fallen friend's upper body. He wiggled his fingers hard, tickling him. Aaron protested as he tried to prise Chris' tickling hands away, but Chris held on, laughing. He released his right hand to sign while his other was still at Aaron's right side, like a weapon.

'Say "You're not Scrubhead." Sign it!' ordered Chris.

Aaron refused. He did not even raise a hand to sign. He stared up at his friend in silence instead.

'Sign it!' Chris commanded again, annoyed by Aaron's sudden silence.

Aaron maintained his silence; he kept on staring. Chris began to notice his friend's peculiar mood, as if he had just grown a second head. He began to feel unnerved.

'What are you looking at me like that for?' asked Chris.

'Nothing,' Aaron finally broke his silence, though, he still had that unnerving expression on his face.

'Oh, come on!' Chris said, now feeling awkward. He relaxed his grip on Aaron's abdomen and sat back a little.

'What's up?'

Aaron looked away as though he was feeling some kind of discomfort. Then it dawned on Chris. He hadn't felt it a moment ago, for he was too busy torturing Aaron, but he was feeling it now. Some kind of hardness was protruding under his bottom: it was as though he was sitting on a hard, warm rock that was inside Aaron's shorts. Chris smiled broadly when he realised what it was. He playfully bounced his bottom on it a few times and gyrating around. Aaron flinched, shoved Chris over to the side and sat up, scooped his legs to his chest and rested his forearms on his knees. Chris picked himself up and sat next to him, brushing soil from his bare knees.

'I don't like it,' Aaron said, shaking his head, agitated.

'Then why did you do it?' asked Chris. 'I felt it, honest.'

'Your arse rubbed it,' Aaron replied, pointing down to the closed space between his legs and chest. 'Why?'

'I don't know. We fancy each other!' Chris said, wryly.

'Piss off!' Aaron snapped, a smile growing on his face. 'You're not a girl!'

Chris looked at Aaron for a long moment. He was feeling a strange kind of attraction to him. For the last two years, he had felt something for him; not just a close friendship, but something else. He was never able to understand nor trust his own feelings. Many of the other boys would talk about their tastes and feelings for girls, but he couldn't seem to share the same kind of feelings. He tried to, but felt nothing inside, which confused him. Some of the boys would sometimes drool over Mr Langston's pretty teenage daughter, Shaleen, but he felt nothing for her and he had never thought he fancied her. He had seen some of Andrew's porn mags, but when he looked at the numerous images of naked women, he didn't feel aroused by them, and he couldn't understand why. However, Andrew had once showed him one of his more hardcore magazines, which contained images of half erect penises with splashes of black stars censoring the explicit areas, and Chris secretly felt excited by them, believing that the other boys felt the same because there were vaginas in the images too. On the other hand, when he was in the showers after sports or in the changing room at the swimming pool, he could not help but peek and ogle at the other boys' naked bodies. Aaron was usually the one he looked at most. Every time did so, he felt a strange sensation inside; he couldn't figure out why, but he sometimes needed to release himself in private afterwards. He thought Aaron sometimes looked at him in the showers too, but only to chat with him, just like any other boy would do. Chris *had* been noticing that Dwight Greenland sometimes liked to look at him, though; when he did, he would always turn away, keeping his back to him as he showered. Chris had been trying to fight against these feelings of his, determined not to fancy boys more than girls, but the feeling kept coming back to him. He supposed he would eventually grow to fancy girls at some point.

'Do you think Dwight Greenland's like that?' Aaron said, slapping Chris' arm, bringing him back from his deep thoughts. Chris frowned; he hadn't caught that.

'Fancying boys, I mean.'

'I dunno,' Chris replied, secretly surprised by the link. 'You want him?' he joked.

'No way!' Aaron chortled. 'Yuck!'

Chris rose to his feet, brushing soil from the back of his football shorts. He offered his hand to Aaron, to pull him up. 'Come on, you're in goal. I'll shoot.'

Chris pulled Aaron up to his feet and he, too, brushed the dirt from the back of his shorts. Chris beckoned for him to go the goalposts.

As Aaron went towards the white wooden posts, Chris glanced towards the school building on his right. There was no one around except for a couple of boys, who were sitting on one of the three stone steps at the front, busy signing to each other. The rest were either inside or behind the school, sunbathing under the blazing hot sun.

He saw a face at one of the windows on the first floor above the porch, but it was too far away and too obscured by the reflection of the clear blue sky in the crisscrossed window for him to see who it was.

It was watching him.

13

The Open Day

"[We] felt it was a big step forward, but of course the teachers of the Deaf didn't like it [the signing], it was against the educational policy at that time. They felt that if you allowed children to sign they wouldn't learn to speak; that proved to be quite wrong in the long run."

– PAT KEYSELL (1926–2009); on *See Hear,* looking back at BBC's *Vision On,* an award winning TV programme for deaf and hearing children (1964–1976). It peaked at 6 million viewers a week, making it one of the most popular a children's show ever, 2009

David carefully applied a small red, white and blue ringed flag on top of the grey wing with a pair of tweezers. He slid the moist material into place and gently tapped it with his little finger to cement it. He straightened up, his eyes still on the model. It stood proudly on the worktop and glistened under the light that shone down; the best and only light source in the gloomy interior of the small Hobbies Room. Moonlight shone through the small solitary window, giving the room some silver glow.

He felt so proud of the Avro Lancaster Bomber plane that he'd lovingly and meticulously assembled over the last two weeks: it had taken him longer than he had anticipated because he had had to squeeze it in between his schoolwork, the usual evening and weekend activities and being a slave to Basher. Being in the Hobbies Room was an escape for him and he loved modelling. His mother had given him the Airfix kit of one of his favourite planes as a goodbye present when the new term started three weeks back. Completed, it would be the highlight of one of the many displays for the school's forthcoming Open Day, he thought to himself; his mother would be so proud of him.

'Beautiful!' he said, looking at Aaron who was leaning over the newly finished model on the worktop. 'What do you think?'

'It's brilliant,' replied Aaron, thumbing up. 'You're good with models.'

'This Avro Lancaster Bomber,' David pointed at it, 'what do you know about it?'

'Not much,' Aaron shook his head. 'I saw the film "The Dambusters" on television. Those bouncing balls.'

'It's one of my favourite films,' David exclaimed. 'It was great. Roy Chadwick designed the bombers during the Second World War. Each one has 55,000 separate parts from half a million different manufacturing operations.'

'Wow! Really?' Aaron glanced at the scaled–down version, wondering if this was true.

David noted his form mate's scepticism and waved at him. 'It's true!' he said. 'They built 7,377 of them. 3,922 of them were lost in the war. They dropped a total 680,612 tonnes of bombs.'

He leant over and gently squeezed the fuselage, taking care not to touch the still–moist markings. He turned it over and pointed at the bomb bay. 'The bomb bay stretches to 33 feet.' He fingered the four engines on the underside of the two wings. 'Four Rolls Royce Packard Merlin 224 V–12's. The bombers weigh 36,500 pounds and they can carry up to 33,000 pounds! Bloody hell, it's the ultimate bomber plane!'

'Have you ever been in one?' asked Aaron.

'Not yet, but it's my dream. I've always wanted to fly in one. My dad has promised me that …' David trailed off, his mood suddenly changing, but he quickly restated. 'He's promised.'

Aaron nodded and gazed at the model again, appreciating it. Something caught his eye and he glanced over David's shoulder. The door opened slowly and Basher entered; he was out on the prowl again. His eyes darted to Andy, Johan and Conor, who were standing around another worktop with piles of stamp books on it. He went over, opened one and flicked the pages, causing some stamps to fly out of their little plastic pockets. The three boys stood motionlessly, watching him.

'Boring!' he mocked, slamming down the book, 'Why do you collect that shit?'

He turned his attention to the other worktop where the model was. David quickly slid between his tormentor and his precious hobby, falsely believing that he could hide it.

'What's that?' Basher pointed behind David.

'Nothing,' David feigned.

Basher shook his head. He advanced, pushed his slave to the side and saw the grey plastic item. He smiled with appreciation; he was impressed. 'Very good. Did you do this?' he looked at David menacingly.

David said nothing, but Basher didn't need to know the answer. He carefully picked it up and examined it. Aaron was rooted to the spot, wishing to himself that he could grab it back, but he knew that he couldn't.

'Let's see if it can fly,' Basher suddenly announced.

David sprinted at Basher, screaming at him. Basher slammed the palm of his left hand into David's face, pushing him away. He fell back and crashed down to the wooden floor. Basher lifted the model plane and catapulted it.

'*No!*' David screamed.

The plane flew limply across the small room and crashed against the wall. One of the wings snapped from the fuselage and the two pieces plummeted to the ground. Two sections of the fuselage split open, the tail ends snapping off and the wheels underneath smashing.

'My plane!' whined David. He crawled over to the broken pieces and carefully picked each one up, tears flowing down behind his glasses. 'My plane ...'

Basher watched him, feeling no sympathy at all. He grinned, taking pride in having intimidated the fat boy once more. He took a passing glance at Aaron, who stared at him accusingly, then left the room.

David, sitting on his bed, buttoned up his pyjamas top. His mind was spinning with agitation and frustration about what had happened earlier in the evening; he was still heartbroken. Oh, he really hated Basher for what he had done; for what he was still doing to him. What had he done to deserve it? Was it because he was stupid and fat? Would he be able to endure being harassed and bullied by Basher as well as being his bloody slave until he left next July? Oh, he wished he could stand up to him and beat the hell out of him!

He heard and felt a stomp on the floorboards, but he ignored it, believing it was one of his form mates trying to get another's attention in the dormitory. Another stomp came. David turned to pick up his pyjama bottoms that were resting on the bed beside him; he was about to pull down his underwear when he was suddenly struck by a hard tap to the head. Startled, he looked up to see Spook towering over him, his hands perched on his waist, not bothering to use them, for he could speak well.

'Didn't you bloody hear me stomp?' the prefect said. 'Basher wants you now. In the TV room.'

'Now?' David spoke back, protesting. 'What for?'

'I don't bloody know, do I?' Timothy replied.

David sighed.

Moments later, wearing his dressing gown and slippers, David entered the TV room. Basher probably wanted another cup of tea and some more toast, though David had done just that before he went up to bed. He thought darkly to himself; would he like his tea to be filled with cyanide and toast generously spread with rat poison this time?

The TV room was sparsely occupied with just a few Fourth and Fifth

Formers sitting watching the television. He took a quick glance at the screen and immediately recognised the programme: it was *Tales of the Unexpected,* one of his favourite shows, something he always watched at home. He saw Chris amongst the boys, but no sign of Basher. He took another look around the gloomy room to double check, but he wasn't there.

'Where's Basher?' he asked.

'Don't know, he hasn't been in here this evening,' It was Steven who answered.

Then it hit him. He rushed out of the room, fearing the worst. He dashed back into Dorm Three, puffing and panting, then froze at the doorway when he saw that his form mates were staring at him in silence. He quickly turned his attention to his bed to discover that the mattress had been upturned, the bed sheets and the top blanket pulled apart and crumpled on the floor. The pillow was nowhere to be seen. David bowed his head, his thoughts screaming inside his head; how could he have been so fucking stupid as to fall for this ruse? He slowly crossed the room, taking a quick glance at Aaron, who was watching him with sympathy, and reached his bed. He heaved the mattress back up onto the metal bed frame and then picked up the bed sheets. When he placed the base sheet on the mattress, he discovered that it was stained with orange peel and sticky marmalade. Clutching the sheets tightly, anger erupted inside him.

'*Bastard!*' he screamed loudly.

Mr Arkwright finished writing the last letter on the blackboard, imperiously poked out a full stop with the end of the chalk, and placed the white stick on the wooden groove. He turned round to face the Fourth Formers at their desks, rubbing his hands. He lifted the microphone closer to his beaming grin.

'Right,' he began, 'as you all know, we will have our Open Day on Friday, October the nineteenth, which the last day before half term. Your families will be coming here ...'

Chris' eyes drifted away from the teacher's slowly speaking lips to read the blackboard again; OPEN DAY SPEECH READING. For fear of getting a bad point from the teacher for not paying attention, Chris dared not to move his head to either side, but he managed to strain his eyes both ways to see his form mates at the semicircular formation of desks. They were as terrified as he was, although he knew that Mark, Jamon and Lester would be spared because they had done the last three Open Days. He returned his attention to Mr Arkwright.

'. . . Once again,' he continued, 'there will be a speech reading. I have chosen a boy from each Form to have extra speech lessons over the next four weeks to prepare for ...'

Chris gritted his teeth, praying that it would not be him. Andrew stared at the teacher's mouth, his heart pounding. Steven chewed at a fingernail. Dean clasped his hands tightly over his desk. Matthew knew he was the next one, he could speak fairly well, but he didn't want to do it. The other two stared blankly at the teacher.

' ... I am delighted that it will be ...' Mr Arkwright aimed his outstretched index finger, as though to shoot, at Andrew. 'You, Andrew Brener!' He saw the other boys breathe out with relief, but ignored them as his eyes were still directed at the silent, wide–eyed Andrew. That boy really needed major work on his speech, so it was a good chance for him, he thought to himself. 'I have already rearranged your timetable, Andrew, so that you will have extra speech lessons with me over the next four weeks, starting today. I shall look forward to helping you to improve your speech!'

Andrew crashed face–down on the desk, his headphones thudding loudly onto it.

Later in the afternoon, the Third, Fourth and Fifth Formers loitered by the two silver Ford minibuses that were parked at the front. They had rolled up towels tucked under their arms as they waited for the drivers, Mr Norris and Mr Bronte, to come and unlock the back doors of the vehicles. Chris idly glanced around the waiting boys and saw Steven putting a friendly arm round Michael's shoulder. They're getting on well lately, he thought to himself. Perhaps because they're both Liverpool fans. A soft smack on his head made him turn to see Aaron playfully hitting him with his own rolled up towel.

'All right?' Chris said, staving off the towel with his hand.

'Yeah,' Aaron replied. 'Hey, did you hear what Hitler Teacher did today?'

Chris shook his head.

'He threw the blackboard duster at Derek Ferguson this morning for signing to Andy Farmleigh,' Aaron said, demonstrating by hitting his own head with his closed hand. 'Whack! He got detention too.'

Chris rolled his eyes, not surprised at this. 'He threw a chalk at Matthew Burke yesterday because he couldn't read the small writing on the blackboard so he leaned over to read my notes. He got detention for cheating!'

'Poor him,' Aaron shook his head in sympathy. 'He's got problems with his eyes. Mr Schneider should have ...'

He stopped short when Chris suddenly looked over his shoulder, turning to follow his gaze. Oh, talk of the devil, he mouthed to himself. Mr Schneider emerged through the entrance doors and briskly strolled across the car park to a beige Volkswagen Beetle that was parked next to one of the minibuses. He took his car keys from his pocket as he approached the car. Aaron wondered how that giant could fit into such a small car. If it had been Herbie, it would happily have thrown him into a pile of manure, Aaron was sure. The maths teacher suddenly froze. He'd seen something on the side of the car and leant in to have a closer look, grimacing. He straightened up, darting his eyes across the top to where the boys were.

'Who did this?' Mr Schneider demanded, pointing down at the side which the boys couldn't see.

Within seconds, the boys had streamed around the car to see what the problem was. Chris squeezed through the crowd to find that there was something etched on the driver's door. He squinted to read the scratched lines and smiled discreetly. The writing was small, the marks crude and hasty, apparently made by a sharp tool, but it was clear enough for him to read: *NAZI SCUM!*

Aaron breast stroked idly along through the chlorinated blue water, glancing around the interior of the local swimming pool. It had a high–rise ceiling that consisted of a number of wide, dark grey concrete beams that sloped up from either side towards the centre, each with frosted glass between them. The pool itself was quite long and had three diving boards at the deep end: the springboard, the middle board and the high board. Aaron saw Dean plummeting awkwardly from the high one and a huge splash followed. Aaron looked up to see the waiting boys looking down and fighting over the next turn. At either side of the pool were spectators rows, empty save for Mr Norris, who watched the activity with his beady eyes. Mr Bronte was outside with his pipe as usual. Aaron continued to swim, but slowed down when he saw Basher gleefully dunking David into the water on his right. David splashed desperately as he tried to break free from the bully's grasp. Aaron discreetly swam to his left, away from them. A geyser suddenly erupted directly in his path, frightening him. Chris hopped up, grinning mockingly at his best friend. Aaron floated his feet down to the white titled floor.

'Bastard!' Aaron splashed at Chris, annoyed with him for giving him a fright. Chris quickly countered, his hands splashing water at Aaron, and a fierce splash battle between them ensued. They soon ceased.

'Where's Andrew Brener?' Aaron asked, twisting his daggered hand against the side of his head. He didn't notice at first, but when they got to the changing room, he realised that Andrew was not with them.

'He's at practice,' Chris answered, with a knowing grin.

Goo … llli … aaahhhh.

'Go–li–ath,' Mr Arkwright corrected. 'Very good.'

Andrew exhaled as he looked up from the title page to the teacher beside him. The words *David and Goliath* were printed on the first page of the open ring file that he was holding. He'd spent the last hour in the Speech Room trying to pronounce 'Goliath' – the first and only word he had tackled thus far. His cheeks, mouth, jaw, tongue and nose ached. He lowered his head and flickered through the remaining five pages, all showing double spaced lines of text specially written by the speech teacher for the purpose of teaching speech. Oh, fucking hell, he silently cursed; he was going to have to read the *entire* story in front of over two hundred people at the Open Day. He forced his head up against the sheer weight of the headphones on it and looked warily at the lips of the bespectacled man sitting next to him, expecting the worst.

'You will have to work harder, Andrew,' Mr Arkwright said, his face showing a hint of disappointment. 'I will see if Mr Langston can agree that you'll be excused from all sports sessions so that we can do more work on your speech.'

Andrew slammed the file on his forehead. Oh, why me, he moaned to himself, *why mmmeeeee?*

Friday 12th October 1979.
Dear Mum, Dad and Jamie,
This is a just short letter, as you will all come next week for the Open Day. Half Term Hurrah! I am looking forward to spending a week at Aunt Barbara's in Hove. A lot cats at her house too! Hope her favourite cat, Miscoe, will behave with me!!! She hates me! Hope Aunt Barbara can make an early birthday cake for my 14th birthday!

I am very happy that Jamie can come to the Open Day (lucky him that his school ~~has~~ have allowed him to leave school a day early for half term!). Hope he won't get moody again on the way here! He will meet my best friend, Chris, for the first time since I first came here two years ago and I have told Chris all about Jamie and he is looking forward to meeting him.

Mr Whittle said that he is very pleased that my English is very good now and he will be displaying one of my best stories that I wrote for everyone to read at the Open Day. It is called "Warlords of Doom" (Don't tease me, Jamie, OK?!?).

I best stop now as I am writing this during my lunch hour and I have to post this in the school's post box (my last envelope and last 10p first class stamp!) before 2pm for one of the staff to collect all the letters and post ~~it~~ them at the post office later in the afternoon.

See you next week!
Aaron xxx

Chris briskly strode through the open door into the headmaster's office and saw Mr Langston sitting at his decorative oak desk, writing something on a sheet of paper inside a ring file. He had been summoned to see him. Without even looking up, the principal acknowledged the boy's presence and indicated for him to stand in front of the desk. Chris did as he was told, put his hands behind his back and glanced around the office as he waited; it was a medium sized room with the headmaster's desk positioned directly in front of the door that Chris had come through. Another door on his right led into the secretary's room. Everybody knew she was Mr Langston's wife, Frances. She rarely spoke to the boys, but when she did, she was always cheerful and pleasant. Chris then looked to his left to see shelves mounted on either side of a single window, which overlooked the forest on the west side of the school. The shelves were filled with a variety of books and some ring files.

Chris turned his attention back to the headmaster, who was still writing. He gazed at a framed photograph on the desk, which showed the headmaster himself, his wife Frances and their three children. It had been taken at a wedding; the family were wearing formal suits and dresses. The wedding had taken place in Washington D.C. in April 1976; Chris knew this for a fact, as Mr Langston had told him some time ago. Their eldest, Damien – a young man, now twenty–five – was the groom, marrying an American woman. He was still living in the American capital and they they'd just had a baby. The second, an older teenage boy, Marcus, was now twenty–two and was studying at University of Leeds. Toby Eriswell had told Chris that his eldest brother, James, was also there and that the two had known each other during James' final year at the school. They were now good friends. The third child, Shaleen, was fourteen and was still living in the headmaster's apartment on the first floor, a pupil at the local school. Many of the Ewing Hill Park boys fancied her.

Chris gazed up at the wood panelled wall behind the high–backed leather chair, where a large canvas portrait hung, depicting a prominent and authoritative man in his fifties. The dark suited man was also in the framed picture in the library, albeit a bit younger. He was bald with greying dark hair round the sides, his face prudish and slightly wrinkled, with a small mouth. His austere eyes stared lifelessly at Chris, unnerving him a little. Chris had seen some of the old school films of Mr Benjamin Williams' tenure and had always wondered how the boys had managed to lipread such a small mouth. The Ewing Hill Park School founder and first headmaster sometimes spoke directly, close up, to the camera, but none of the boys who had watched the films could decipher a single word. David had said he was difficult to lipread, and he was one of the best lipreaders in the school. Chris thanked God that the man had retired a year before he'd come to the school, otherwise he felt sure he would have faced the wrath of the former headmaster's infamous black plimsoll spankings on his bare bottom more than once, probably for signing. Chris had been told that the former pupils had a name sign for Mr Williams which mimicked a plimsoll spanking gesture.

He slid his eyes to the right, to a framed black and white photograph next to the painting. It was of Mr Williams and Margaret Thatcher posing together in front of the school. He recalled that the Prime Minister had been Secretary of State for Education during the first half of the decade under Ted Heath's government, and that she had once visited Ewing Hill Park School.

Mr Langston put his pen down and closed the file just as Chris looked back down at him. The principal leaned back against his chair and clasped his hands. Chris saw that the man across the desk had a sober expression on his face. He focused on his lips.

'Christopher,' the headmaster said quietly, 'about the half term. I'm afraid I have bad news for you.'

A short time later, Aaron strolled into the recreation room, which was busy with boys playing table tennis, snooker and darts. Holding the sealed envelope containing the letter he'd written earlier, he found Chris leaning against the wall on his chair. He seemed lost in thought. Aaron went over, waving his envelope, just as Chris sulkily rolled his eyes and saw Aaron approaching.

'Go away!' Chris snapped, abruptly.

'Are you all right?' asked Aaron, taken aback. 'What's wrong?'

'I've got to stay here during half term,' Chris answered, sighing, 'that's what's wrong.'

'No way!' Aaron balked. 'Why?'

'I don't want to talk about it, okay?' Chris said bluntly. 'Are you looking forward to going home next week?'

'Yes, but I'm not going home,' answered Aaron, shaking his head. Chris shot a look at him. Aaron smiled. 'I'm *not* staying here during half term! No way! We're going to my Aunt Barbara's in Hove. It's near Brighton. It's got a pier with a funfair and amusements.'

'Great,' Chris said, hiding his envy. 'Have a nice time.'

Aaron thought for a moment as he looked at his sulking friend. He waved at him again. 'Why don't you come with us?' Aaron said. 'I'm sure Mum and Aunt Barbara won't mind and I think my brother, Jamie, will *love* having you with us!'

Chris raised his eyebrows at Aaron, forcing a half smile. Aaron lifted the back of his last envelope, wondering how he would seal it again after he'd taken out the letter to write in a P.S.

Open Day arrived.

For the last four weeks, the boys had been busy preparing for this occasion; they had created and developed many items to be exhibited around the school.

A range of exhibits of written and artistic school work were mounted on several display boards, as well as examples of hobby work such as models, fishing equipment and stamps; camping equipment; craftwork items; film shows and old school photographs.

During the morning, the boys' parents – and the curious parents of prospective pupils – watched classroom demonstrations where the boys had to respond verbally to the teachers' spoken questions. P.E. demonstrations were also held in the gym, showing parents how sporty – and for some, how un–sporty – these boys were.

Mrs Wheeley hurried through the entrance doors, searching the front hall anxiously, scanning the crowds of boys and their parents.

'Mummy!' She quickly turned to the source of the familiar voice and smiled. David trotted through the crowd towards her, his arms outstretched. She ran to him and they wrapped their arms around each other and hugged tightly.

'Oh, my darling!' she exclaimed. 'You've grown again!'

After a short moment, David finally broke away and glanced eagerly at the entrance doors, hoping to see someone else. 'Where's Daddy?' he looked up at his mother.

'He can't come, darling,' she answered, shaking her head and quietly whispering, 'Look, you already know that he's not living with us anymore.'

'But–'

'Just leave it, all right? Let's not spoil today,' his mother said firmly. She sighed inwardly as she thought briefly about the horrid time she and David had had during the summer. How could Hugo get himself shacked up with that Spar shop trollop? Pixie – what a bloody pathetic name! And she wasn't even any prettier than she, herself, was. Thinner, admittedly, but not prettier. Rumours about their secret hanky–panky had begun to spread around the village and it was Nora from the little post office who had finally brought it to her attention. She didn't believe the gossip at first, but doubt crept in, then eventually, she confronted Hugo about it. He'd initially denied it, but after grilling him and arguing through the night, he had finally admitted it, saying that he was so sorry. Oh, poor David had crept down from his room and listened with his bloody left ear to every word she and his dad had said in that kitchen. Hugo left home that very night, probably headed straight over to that little slut. She put aside those horrid thoughts and looked down at David.

'Now, my darling, show me around those rather exciting displays. Did you make the model plane I gave you?'

David turned away, avoiding the question, and motioned for his mother to follow him through the front hall towards the lobby. He walked past Chris, who was standing beside Aaron, shaking hands firmly with Jamie.

'So, this is the famous Scrubhead I've been hearing about?' Jamie signed with his free hand, with a mocking grin. Chris' eyes darted to Aaron before looking back at Jamie. The two fifteen–year olds broke off their handshake and Jamie turned to his younger brother. 'Are you doing the speech reading today?"

Aaron shook his head hard. 'Bradley Watts is doing it.'

'Pity,' Jamie said impudently, 'I'd have loved to see you on the stage talking like R2–D2! Better luck next year …'

Just then, Aaron and Jamie's parents came upon the boys. John glanced over at a lanky dark–haired boy with smartly dressed parents, and recalled seeing them stepping out of the chauffeur driven Bentley that was now parked outside. Chris followed John's gaze; it was Dean Hopkirk and his parents.

Geraldine turned to Chris. 'Have you got your bag packed?'

Chris nodded in appreciation; she was fairly easy to lipread, he mused to himself.

'Good,' she said. 'We're really looking forward to having you with us down at Aunt Barbara's for a week. Aaron's told us so much about you in his letters.'

Aaron quickly looked away, avoiding his best friend's glare and pointed avidly at the lobby. 'We should go to the Assembly Hall now.'

The hall was filled with masses of people, stretching from near the stage right to the back, near where the canteen was. The partition wall that divided the Assembly Hall and the dining room was fully folded away to one side, giving more space. The boys, their families and the visiting parents of future pupils occupied the many rows of chairs, whilst the staff and the school's governors sat down the right–hand side of the hall. The entire assemblage was watching silently as Bradley Watts, who was standing in the centre of the stage with a microphone hanging on his chest, read aloud from an open ring file.

Je … susssss sssad tha … that Loo rrr … d …

Jamie watched with disbelief. 'This is bloody stupid, he whispered to himself. 'It's like listening to a shitty radio frequency!'

He heard his dad, sitting on his left, stifle a chuckle. Jamie folded his arms and he looked to his right to see Aaron and Chris staring blankly at the stage. Why the hell did they have to do this, he thought; he wouldn't want to do the speech reading either, even though he was hearing! It was so bloody embarrassing. Chris had just told him that Andrew Brener was up after this boy and that he really was absolutely shit at speaking, so how come he'd been chosen to do it for his Form? He thought back a bit; that black boy from Form One – what was his name? Oh, yes, Conor Blackwell. He'd done pretty well with the first reading: his speech wasn't perfect, but it was good enough, apart from the occasional nervousness audible in his voice. The Second Form boy, Jack Aldridge, had been terrible; he'd almost fainted when he started to read and then galloped through without even looking up, in spite of the headmaster repeatedly telling him to do so. Now this boy from Aaron's Form, Bradley Watts … Jesus Christ!

He looked around and saw a myriad of blank eyes staring vacantly at the stage and pondered how this was like the new X–rated film *Invasion of the Body Snatchers* that he and his mates had sneaked into the cinema to see a few months back. He half expected some of them to eerily point and screech emotionlessly, like they did in the film, at each boy on the stage. How the hell could these deaf boys lipread the headmaster at this distance, let alone understand him? Did they have superpowered telescopic eyes that hearing people didn't have? He even tested himself by muffling his own ears with his hands and trying to lipread what was being said; he was quite good at lipreading, he reckoned. All he could see was a tiny, silent black dot. Aaron had told him before that the boys just pretended to understand and that they relied on the phone–goods. Hmmm, Jamie thought to himself; he had a good mind to cross over to the stage and sign for the deaf boys so that they could understand what was being said. Yeah, he would like to do that for deaf people in the future, he mused. Would he be able to make a living out of it?

He winced again when another crackling sound boomed from the speakers around the hall. Earlier, he had told Aaron and Chris that the sound amplification was so bad that it made his own cranky tape recorder at home sound like the Royal Albert Hall. He wondered how the boys could be expected to make anything out of that awful reverberating noise.

He turned his attention back to the stage and saw that Bradley had just finished and was handing the microphone and file over to the principal, who then placed the file on the lectern and held the microphone close to his mouth.

'That was very good, Bradley!' he exclaimed at the Third Former who was descending the steps from the stage. 'Didn't he do well, ladies and gentlemen?'

Polite applause echoed round the hall. Jamie saw that his mother was politely clapping and heard his dad whistling tunelessly. Jamie buried his face in his hands, mumbling through his fingers: 'They should be shot.'

'Now,' the headmaster moved on, 'we move up a Form. Andrew Brener will read *David and Goliath*. He has been working extremely hard on his speech for this occasion. Andrew?' he looked over at the people seated before him, his eyes searching for the boy.

Harry Brener turned to his right to find that his son had dozed off in his chair, his head slumped, snoring gently. Dozy git, Harry thought to himself, slapping Andrew's arm. Andrew shot to his feet, gasping as if he had just come out of a terrible nightmare. He looked down at his sitting dad, annoyed with him.

'It's your turn now,' the stockily–built man with the bald head and deep sideburns said as he pointed his thick, rugged, labour–weary finger at the stage. 'Show 'em what us Northerners can do!'

Andrew forced himself to look at the stage and saw Mr Langston waiting with the microphone in one hand and the file in the other. He cleared his throat. Right, he thought to himself, just get through it and then he'd be done. He left his row and marched towards the stage.

As Harry watched his son, he rolled his eyes. Be proud of the Northerners? Who was he kidding? The boy would be a total embarrassment! He couldn't talk, goddamn it. Irene would have loved to have been here to see her boy on the stage though! Well, she would have been sitting on this chair instead of him if it weren't for that bloody infection. She was so frickin' sick and deathly pale. He'd had to take two days off work at Attercliffe Steel Mill and come all the bloody way down from Sheffield yesterday and stay in a poxy B&B in town for the night, just to come to this circus. He'd also had to arrange with Mike's wife, Deborah, bless her, to help the other three kids get ready for school and cook their dinner for them while Irene lay on her deathbed. Any other Friday and he'd have been out having a few pints with Mike and his mates after work, talking about Sheffield Wednesday and putting the world to rights. What about that new prime minister? A ruddy big–nosed woman running the country? She wouldn't last a term. She and her Conservative puppies were already making spending cuts and planning to upturn the frickin' manufacturing industry. What would she do with the declining steel industry in Sheffield? He couldn't afford to lose his job; he had four kids to feed. They were struggling as it was, on the meagre pay packet Attercliffe paid him each month. The dosh went on the mortgage, bills, food and clothes, with just enough left for a few pints of ale down the boozer. He'd had to ask Mike for a handout to help pay for the train fare and B&B, just to collect Andrew. It would have been cheaper if the boy could have come back up to Sheffield by himself, given the council always paid for his travel. At fifteen, Andrew was old enough to travel alone, but Irene insisted on fetching him home and taking him back to school. She worried too much, bless her, and besides, an escort would prevent him from taking a short detour to a certain shop in a certain part of London to buy – or even steal, for all he knew – those magazines. That dirty little toerag thought he and Irene didn't notice? Ha! He didn't mind Andrew looking at the odd picture of a naked woman. He did that himself at work, what with the pretty Page 3 girls showing off their pert tits in *The Sun*, but he didn't want Andrew to have those hardcore ones. Johnny had found a few hidden in Andrew's room – yeah, he sure had. Oh, the questions that little 'un asked; what was that man doing with that woman and all that! Harry had to make sure that Andrew didn't bring any more of those magazines home, even if it meant searching his clothes trunk and bag. Soft porn, he could keep, as long as his mother didn't know and it was well hidden from his younger siblings. The hardcore stuff would go straight onto the bonfire in the back yard.

Andrew was the oldest and only deaf child in the family. That boy was quite a handful. Communication between him and the rest of the family had always been virtually non–existent. Mumbles and grunts, topped with hand gestures, were the norm with him. Irene tried hard to talk to Andrew, but she always found it very difficult, so they often wrote things down. Understanding his English was a different matter! Oh, it was truly awful. Johnny was far better than Andrew and yet he was half his frickin' age! What sort of English teachers did the school have? Some of his school reports had said that Andrew's English continued to improve steadily. Was that teacher – Mr Whiff or something – on another frickin' planet?! Even Andrew's letters home were like goddamned puzzles; he and Irene would spend hours trying to figure out his indistinguishable words and sometimes had to ask the younger 'uns to help out – more on their level.

When Andrew was diagnosed as profoundly deaf at the age of two, he and Irene were told, in no uncertain terms, not to sign to him. What the hell for and why? Who decided on this so–called unwritten law? They were to use their voices to speak to Andrew. Poor kid, he'd had terrible tantrums when he was younger; he was bloody angry and frustrated at not being able to make himself understood. Well, the feeling was mutual, my boy. He and Irene were as angry and frustrated as he was. Of course, he'd always had more attention from his mother than the other kids, and they were always so jealous of him, fighting for their mother's attention. Johnny was the worst of the lot; he made such big deal out of this, you'd think he hated his big brother. He and Irene had tried to explain to the young lad that Andrew was deaf and that he needed a little bit more attention, but how could they make a seven–year old understand? Since Andrew had been at Ewing Hill Park School, things had been a hell lot easier at home; Irene was able to give more attention to Jenny, Marlene and Johnny. It was one less mouth to feed as well, and that meant one or two extra pints of ale for him! Ha! Still, it was a wrench at first to send the eleven–year old away to a boarding school so far away. It'd been Mrs Rowe, his speech therapist at the partially hearing unit, who'd suggested that he should go to Ewing Hill Park in the hope of receiving a better education and improving his unfathomable speech. She had already resigned herself to the fact that Andrew would never learn to speak properly and she'd implied that he'd never have a normal life in hearing society. What was normal, Harry had replied, the boy sure looked normal enough to him, only his ears weren't working. He also bluntly told her that he was deaf, not frickin' 'partially hearing' or 'hearing impaired' or any of those other daft terms that she liked to label Andrew and other deaf children with. He and Irene had had a lengthy chat about the boarding school though and eventually agreed that Andrew would go, though making that happen had not been without a fight. The bloody idiots in the council's education department had initially refused to agree to fund Andrew, saying that he would be much better off at the new local comprehensive – these new kind of schools were croppin' up all over the country to replace the grammar schools, thanks to that new prime minister lady, who'd been education secretary back then – and being the only deaf kid amongst thousands of hearing kids would help him integrate into the hearing world. A lone deaf pupil in a classroom full of hearing kids, not able to understand a frickin' single word the teachers said? Integration? Huh! Isolation, more like! Not a chance in hell! They'd finally agreed to fund Andrew's place at Ewing Hill Park after Irene had threatened them with legal action. Dunno how she did it, but, the old bird twisted those friggin' idiots' heads round!

If it weren't for Irene catching German Measles when she'd been pregnant with their first, things would have been so different now. God, Harry loved Andrew so much; it didn't really matter if he was deaf or not, he was still his boy. He just wished that he and Andrew could communicate a little better; like a father and son should.

Harry Brener sighed inwardly and scratched an itch on his balding head. He saw that Andrew was already on stage, placing the microphone on his chest. He received the file from the headmaster and positioned himself, ready to speak. Mr Langston sat on a chair at the left side of the stage.

Keeping his eyes down, Andrew felt his back prickle with sweat. His hands trembled and he breathed out heavily. After a brief moment, he finally plucked up the courage to look up.

He froze.

Hundreds of eyes were watching him. Thousands. Millions. Billions. Trillions. Zillions. The large room felt as if it was twisting around him. He felt a sudden heaviness in the air, and began to feel as if he was being sandwiched between two invisible walls. His legs were shaking and he felt as though his feet were melting into the wooden platform. His heart pounded rapidly. His mind became numb with fear at the sight of that sea of faces. He quickly looked down at the file again and forced himself to begin.

Uh … erm … Dddaaafff …

He couldn't do it.

The last four weeks had been *hell*. He'd spent every sports period and most of his free time cooped up in that tiny speech room with Mr Arkwright. He had tried so damned hard to utter the letters and words properly. He felt as though his forehead was full of drill holes trying to even *remember* how to say or pronounce the words correctly. At times, Mr Arkwright had lost both his patience and his temper; this always frightened Andrew into trying even harder. He was ordered to keep on practising the story outside of speech lessons. It soon became an obsession for Andrew: so much so that he had memorised the whole David and Goliath story word for word, yet still he couldn't pronounce most of the words. As the Open Day had drawn nearer, he'd become increasingly anxious and spent much of his free time practising his speech, but he knew without doubt that he would show himself up on the stage. He'd not slept at all in the night before the Open Day, instead he'd been practising his speech in his bed. He was terrified.

Now here he was, in front of everyone. He cleared his mind and scanned his eyes across the hundreds of watching faces. He couldn't do it. Suddenly, he remembered Pat Keysell who'd come to the school earlier that year. *Express yourself in your own way: if you can't use your voice, then use your hands and body,* she told him and the other boys. He saw David, sitting next to his mother, in middle of the fourth row. The penny dropped.

He darted towards the edge of the stage, but the microphone that was still strapped round his neck was attached to the amplification unit backstage by a cord which became taut and pulled him back like an excited dog on a leash. He yanked the strap out and put the microphone on the floor. Standing on the edge of the stage, he waved raucously at anyone sitting on the front row. 'Come over here!' he said, holding out the file. 'Take this file over to David Wheeley! Come on, hurry!'

Toby leapt from his chair and grabbed the file from Andrew. He dashed round and found David in the fourth row.

'Stand up!' Andrew commanded. David slowly rose to his feet as he received the file that had just been ferried along the row, perplexed. 'Speak for me as I act!'

'But–'

'You can have one of my Mayfair mags! The one with Mary Millington! Nice boobs!' Andrew gestured a huge pair of breasts on his chest.

Those in the audience who could understand sign burst into frenzied laughter. Toby returned to his chair, sitting between his Deaf parents who were chuckling.

Jamie was stumped when his dad questioned him. 'Erm …' Jamie paused to think up an excuse. 'He said … that he would give him one of his *Look–in* magazines as a reward. It's got, uh, Mary Poppins in it. You see, Aaron said that David's into flying.'

John frowned, not convinced; he could have sworn he saw the lad on stage gesturing breasts, but he decided to leave it at that.

David glanced down at his mother, who in turn looked up at him with a curious look on her face. He was thankful that she couldn't sign. He thought about the offer for a moment: he'd once briefly glimpsed Mary Millington in one of Andrew's magazines and liked her. Getting the idea of what Andrew was about to do, he gave him a thumbs up. 'All right!'

Andrew melodramatically outstretched his arms to greet the audience. He signed that he was the biblical David character, the youngest of the family. Holding an imaginary staff in his hand, he explained that the imaginary animal in front of him was a sheep, as he fondly stroked its back with his other hand.

'I am David,' David began to read quietly from the file. 'He was a shepherd who looked after the sheep–'

'Speak up!' a voice called out. David turned to see a man standing near at the back. 'We can't hear you, boy!'

Mr Langston strode over to Andrew, placing a firm hand on the boy's shoulder. 'What are you doing? You're supposed to do it, not David Wheatley.'

'Let my son be!' came a voice. Everybody turned to see Harry Brener standing. He raised his voice so that everyone could hear him. 'You know damn well that he can't bloody talk!' A murmur of general agreement echoed through the hall. 'Seems they agree. Go on, let him do what he wants.'

The headmaster slowly released his grip and stepped back, his eyes discreetly glancing over to the right side of the hall where the staff and the governors were seated. Smiling at Rosemary Goldsack, his mind secretly threw a two–fingered salute at the chairwoman of the school governors.

'Very well, go right ahead, Andrew.'

Harry Brener sat down. David cleared his throat and nodded at Andrew for him to start. Andrew held up eight fingers and counted down to his little finger. He gestured that he was the littlest of all. He raised his left hand high to suggest a father figure and fingerspelled the name *Jesse*. He followed this up with the name of a city and he spread his arms around himself as if to demonstrate a large area.

'*David*,' David raised his voice, '*was the youngest of the eight sons of Jesse who lived in Bethlehem. David took care of his father's sheep in the pasture fields around Bethlehem …*'

Andrew cupped his right hand to his forehead, frowning and leaned forwards in a stern and protective pose. He signed the sun and the moon. He whipped his imaginary staff towards the audience and used it like it was a machine gun – *rat, rraatt, rrraaattt* – and signed that they were all dead.

'*David always stayed with the sheep day and night protecting them from the wild animals …*'

Andrew flexed his arms and gestured large biceps on them, then stood sternly to show that he was a strong and sturdy man. Suddenly, he manically whipped his imaginary staff around him, swinging his arms and kicking his legs as though he was doing martial arts. He mimed grabbing several invisible sheep and stroking them.

'David was strong and brave and fought the wild animals to rescue the sheep ...'

RRRRROOOOOAAAAARRRRR!

Those in the audience who could hear jumped from their chairs at the sudden ear–splitting roar. Andrew had character shifted to a roaring lion, holding up an invisible sheep in his gnashing teeth. He quickly shifted back to David, who in turn plunged his imaginary staff into the imaginary lion's body and feverishly waved his hands to show that a good amount of blood was gushing out of the body, before grabbing the imaginary sheep from the lion's jaws.

'Once he killed a lion who was stealing a sheep ...'

Andrew cupped his ears, then indicated that he was very large, curling his hands like they had claws. He growled. Quickly shifting character back to David again, he repeated the killing motion that had dispatched the lion. He then grasped his imaginary staff to make a point for himself.

'Another time he killed a bear that was carrying away a lamb. Living in the fields with the animals in his care had made David strong and fearless ...'

Andrew sat on the stage floor, signed a moon in the air and then a fire in front of him. He smiled broadly at the audience, playing an imaginary harp and sang soundlessly. He raised his arms as if to embrace God. He gestured a heart shape on his chest. He stood up and moved slightly to his left, looking down at the spot where he had sat a moment ago, as though he was now playing God, clasping his hands with great pride.

'During his long nights, playing his harp, singing the songs he made up, he often thought and sang about God. He sang about God's love and protection of the people God had created. These people were to God like the sheep were to David ...'

Andrew darted to the left of the stage. He held up eight fingers again, pointing at the first three and indicating them as taller figures, saying they were his older brothers. He performed them as soldiers by gesturing their body armour, wielding swords and being very strong. Shifting now to a prominent figure with a crown on his head, Andrew fingerspelled that his name was *Saul*. He pointed at the other side of the stage and ran towards it, hopping over an invisible hurdle in the middle where the microphone and the cord rested, suggesting a border. He shifted between several different figures by standing in various positions, indicating them all as being extremely tall. He fingerspelled their name as the *Philistines*. He became one particular character by signing that he was a giant, moving in an exaggerated manner, raising his shoulders high, flexing his muscles and walking in a robotic manner. He pointed to himself and fingerspelled *Goliath.*

'David's three oldest brothers were soldiers in the army of King Saul. The country was in a desperate battle against the great armies of the Philistines. The Philistines lived in the country south of David's country, and they had many giants who lived in their country. One of the tallest and strongest of the giants was named Goliath …'

Andrew ran to the middle of the stage, hopping over the invisible border as if it was between his legs. He pointed to his left, his hands describing armies and tents everywhere. He pointed to his right and signed the hills where King Saul's armies were.

'The Philistine armies were camped across the valley to the hills where King Saul's army were staying …'

Andrew hopped over the invisible border to be in King Saul's territory. He character shifted to *Jesse* and started packing an imaginary sack. He then turned to an imaginary figure on his right, ordering him to take the food sack to the older brothers. Andrew quickly character shifted back to David and stood next to the spot where Jesse was. He nodded his head obediently, heaved the imaginary sack up over his shoulder and lumbered to his left. Once there, he thumped down the sack, turning to his left to view the other end of the stage. He dashed across the stage, again hopping over the invisible wall and became Goliath once more. Marching forcefully towards the front of the stage, he signed and spoke with a shrill, unintelligible voice, directly addressing the audience.

'One day Jesse gathered food in a sack and asked David to take the sack to his three soldier brothers to feed them. When David arrived at King Saul's camp on the hill overlooking the valley below the Philistines' camp on the opposite hill, he heard Goliath yelling across the valley, "Choose a man among you to come fight me. If he can kill me, the Philistines will be your servants. If I kill him, all of you will become servants of the Philistines". . .'

Aaron chuckled, enjoying the performance. Chris grinned broadly. Jamie laughed his head off while Geraldine and John stared in bemusement at the stage, also enjoying it.

Andrew ran back to the other end, again hopping over the invisible hurdle as he became King Saul's soldiers once more. He exaggeratedly wobbled his legs like they were jelly and looked up at the high ceiling.

'This thundering giant of a man who was nine and three–quarters feet tall struck fear into the hearts of King Saul's soldiers. Everyone was terrified of fighting this formidable giant …'

Andrew again became David. He reached up in the air as if to embrace God. He clasped his hands and nodded his head as though to obey a command from above, then walked a few steps to his right and tapped the shoulder of an imaginary person. Switching positions, he indicated the crown on his head to say that he was now King Saul. Turning to his left, he looked down at the imaginary David. Andrew quickly stepped back to become David and signed his line.

'David knew that God would help him, so he went before King Saul and said, "I will go against this heathen man who defies the armies of the living God". . .'

Andrew shifted back to King Saul, who in turn expressed surprise, and signed his response.

'King Saul answered, "You are not able to go against this Philistine, for you are a young man, and this giant has been a trained soldier all of his life". . .'

Andrew shifted back to David. He shook his head and signed back.

'David replied," I used to keep my father's sheep, and when a lion or a bear came and took a lamb from the flock, I went after it and delivered the lamb from its mouth and killed the lion or bear. The Lord who delivered me from the paw of the lion and the bear will deliver me from the hand of this Philistine". . .'

Andrew shifted back to King Saul. He rubbed his chin, thinking about it, then shrugged wearily and nodded in agreement. He took off his imaginary body armour and helmet and fastened them onto the imaginary David, next to him, finally giving David an imaginary sword. Andrew quickly shifted back to David as he received the armour and wielded the invisible sword. He staggered around the stage as if he was under a great deal of weight and dramatically collapsed to the floor. Then Andrew was on his feet again. He heaved the invisible armour off onto the floor and angrily "kicked" it off the stage.

'Since no other soldier was willing to fight the giant Goliath, King Saul decided to allow David to fight the giant. King Saul took off his heavy iron coat and helmet and dressed David in them. But the armour was too heavy for David. He took off the armour …'

Andrew stood silently for a long moment. He quickly raised his index finger, raising his eyebrows and opening his mouth wide as if he had a brilliant idea. He took an imaginary item from his blazer pocket and flexed it like a very large elastic band. He scooted around, looking down, and picked up imagined little objects from the floor.

'He carried with him only his sling and then gathered five smooth brookstones and placed them in his shepherd's pouch …'

Andrew ran across the stage to the enemy's side, but then stopped in his tracks as if he had forgotten something. He ran back to where he had been and addressed the people in front of him by slapping his head, berating himself for his forgetfulness. He then ran back, this time hopping over the invisible hurdle. Raucous laughter from the gathering echoed round the hall. Andrew soon became Goliath again and showed his surprise, barking like a dog and signing his line.

'The giant Goliath cursed David by his heathen gods and shouted, "Am I a dog that you come against with sticks?"...'

Andrew ran back towards the other end, playfully tripping over the invisible low wall in a dramatic way. The hall immediately shook with loud bursts of laughter. Andrew picked himself up and became David again. He knelt and did a short prayer before standing once more. He placed the imaginary stone into the sling and spun himself round as if he was going to throw a discus. He jumped and thrust his right hand hard to sling the invisible stone across the stage. Andrew immediately whizzed across, jumping over the invisible wall, and becoming Goliath again. With his closed hand, Andrew thumped his forehead hard and yelled loudly to signify that the stone had hit its target. He staggered exaggeratedly around for a short moment before collapsing on the floor in a heap. Andrew quickly rose and ran back to the other side and becoming David again. As David, he ran back to where the fallen Goliath was and took out the imaginary sword from the giant's invisible sheath. He performed a Japanese–style Banazi charge on the giant, beheading him. Andrew picked up the imaginary decapitated head. He walked to centre stage to face the audience, triumphantly holding up the head in one hand and the sword in the other.

'Breathing a quick prayer, David placed one of the smooth stones in his sling, drew back his hand and quickly slung the stone straight into the forehead of the giant, denting his brow deeply. The giant fell face down onto the ground. David quickly ran to his form, grasped the giant's sword from its sheath, stabbed the giant with the sword and then cut off the giant's head ...'

Andrew turned once and then threw the severed head into the audience. He thrust out his arms furiously to imply blood splattering all over the people below. He then ran back to the enemy side and became the Philistine soldiers, shaking their legs in fear, before running further away to the end of the stage. He returned to centre stage and patted his shoulders and chest. He put an imaginary crown on his head and outstretched his arms to the audience with great aplomb. He slowly raised his left hand and heralded a Winston Churchill victory sign.

'All the Philistine soldiers ran away in a panic and King Saul's soldiers chased them and robbed their campsites' tents to take their valuables. The people in the towns nearby shouted, danced and sang for joy because of David's victory over Goliath. He later became King David after King Saul had died.'

Andrew bowed.

Jamie shot to his feet, clapping furiously. 'That was bloody brilliant!'

Harry Brener leapt up, clapping hard and beaming with pride. 'Wait till I tell Irene! Oh, she would have *loved* that!'

As one, practically the whole audience rose to their feet, clapping and waving wildly. Andrew watched the standing ovation, overwhelmed. David breathed out, pleased with himself, and closed the file, looking forward to owning his very first sex magazine. Chris and Aaron clapped hard. Toby and his parents waved their hands above them. Toby wished that James were here to see it. Mr McShane, already on his feet, clapped. Hubert, who stood next to him, joined in the chorus. Mrs Munnings slowly rose from her chair and began to clap, unsure of herself at first, although a smile was spreading across her features. Mr Arkwright rested his elbows on his thighs and bowed his head in disappointment and despair; his work had all been for nothing.

David hurried through the front hall, his eyes anxiously searching for someone in the crowd as they were preparing to leave the school. He trotted past Basher, who stood with his parents and Mr McShane at a display board with several paintings and drawings mounted on it. David finally found who he was looking for.

'Good one, mate,' Jamie signed, patting Andrew's back. 'I loved it! You should be an actor.'

'Me, an actor?' Andrew dismissed him, grinning in spite of himself.

Just as Jamie walked away, David rushed up to Andrew. 'Could I have it please?' David asked, his eyes darting warily around him.

'Have what?'

'You know!' David replied.

'I don't have it anymore.'

'But–'

'Mary Millington died two months ago,' Andrew said bullishly. 'Killed herself. Why would I drool over a dead girl?'

'You promised!' David protested, not believing this deceit. 'I did the voice-over for you!'

'Tough. I gotta go. See you after half term.' Andrew turned away.

Mrs Wheeley came over to her son and saw that he was distressed. 'Are you all right, my darling?'

David turned away from his mother, angry with himself, leaving her to wonder.

Basher folded his arms as he waited wearily for Mr McShane to finish talking to his parents. He sniffed again at the stench that was coming from the short, burly man with the wrinkles and the flat cap. Cigarettes and whiskey, Basher thought to himself. That old sod was never without them.

'. . . Brian is such a talented artist,' Mr McShane continued, also signing for Basher's benefit. He pointed at one particularly well executed picture on the display board, which was of Mike Hammer in his heavy metal gear. 'Your son has a great eye for detail. He's one of my star pupils–'

'Aye, aye, aye,' Mr Thompson interrupted, with a touch of an impatient cockney twang, tugging the cap into place. 'He never talks to us at 'ome, so he always draws in his bedroom. 'Ya ought see his bedroom wall – it's like a bloomin' National Gallery!'

Not understanding what his father had said, Basher turned to the art teacher, who in turn conveyed it to him in sign. Basher sighed inwardly; never talked to them? It was more like the other way round!

'We must hurry 'ome now, my dear,' Mr Thompson turned to his wife with dark curly hair, who was taller and looked rather in low spirits. 'I'm off to the dogs tonight, so I canna be late. Come on both of yer.'

Mrs Thompson placed her left arm through the hoop of her handbag while Basher prepared to leave. Mr Thompson had a sudden thought and turned back to the art teacher. 'Mind if I ask ya a question, young man?'

'Certainly, Mr Thompson,' he replied.

'How come yer can talk *and* … sign at the same time?'

Mr McShane conveyed that to Basher, who in turn, rolled his eyes.

14

A New Hope

"Before him, we were nothing; we were pariahs, plunged into chaos and ignorance, marginals, and ignored; now we exist; we have been restored to society."
– A Nineteenth Century banquet toast on the legacy of Abbé de l'Epée (1712–1789)

'Whhheeeee!' a loud voice echoed through the dark, musty auditorium. Jamie swung his clasped hands from one side to the other, almost slipping down from his awkward sitting position, through the legroom between his seat and the row behind him. His right hand quickly grabbed the top of the seat in front of him to control his balance while his other hand held onto the half–eaten ice cream tub that was resting between his folded legs. He looked backwards at the large on–screen projection to see that Darth Vader was examining the brown garment lying on the shiny black floor with his black boot. Jamie soon heard a series of overlapping annoyed voices directed at him: *Hush, hush, hush! Be quiet, boy! Shut the fuck up! Stop waving your hands like a bloody monkey!*

Jamie turned to face Chris and Aaron, who were sitting in the row behind Jamie's seat on the next tier up. Aaron gave a big grin at seeing his older brother sitting awkwardly on his seat, his folded legs resting on it with his back pressing against the hard wooden back of the seat behind him. He was barely visible in the gloomy interior; however, the brightness of the screen behind him was adequate for Aaron and Chris to see him signing what was being said in the film.

Aaron briefly thought back earlier in the day when he, Chris, Jamie, his parents and Aunt Barbara had spent looking around in Brighton. First off, they went to the Palace Pier to check it out. They played some of the penny arcades along both sides of the long wooden structure, ate candy floss and viewed the open sea from the far end. They'd noticed the derelict theatre building on the pier and Aunt Barbara explained, through Jamie, that there'd been a bad storm about six years back and the pier was partially damaged because of this, rendering the theatre building unsafe and in need of demolition. Geraldine's older sister, who was similar in appearance to her, albeit with sad and lonely eyes, recalled how she used to go to watch Dick Emery and other stars there. Other than that, there was not much else to do on the pier, aside from enjoy the cool, sunny morning breeze. Chris loved looking down through the gaps between the wooden planks to the sea below; he said it was only the second time he had ever been on a pier. Jamie mentioned that there was a fairground at Black Rock, east of the town, which could be reached by a short train ride along the beach; however, Geraldine said that they would go there another day. They went to the Aquarium, which was directly across from the entrance to the pier. Passing through the small circular entrance building, they descended steps to go underground and came upon an array of glass tanks with wooden frames filled with sea life. They soon came upon the dolphin pool theatre at the end of the underground facility, where a small school of dolphins demonstrated their skills throughout the day. Chris said the mammals fascinated him and he would love to work with them one day. After lunch, on their way along Kings' Road, which ran parallel to the long stretch of beach, they came upon a huge grey building on the corner of West Road: Odeon Kingswest. Naturally, Aaron wanted to check what they were showing and he was delighted to see that one of the two screens – the smaller one – was screening a rerun of *Star Wars*. Jamie asked Chris if he had seen it and he replied no, which surprised the brothers. Jamie reckoned Chris must be the only kid in the world who hadn't – he and Aaron had already been twice back home. So, he offered to sign the film's dialogue for them, in return for a huge bowl of popcorn with honey, a large milkshake and a bag of Maltesers. Initially, Aaron and Chris had refused to pay such a high price from their meagre pocket money, but Aaron reconsidered, since he had never understood a single line of spoken dialogue from the film, relying instead on reading the tie–in comics. He persuaded a reluctant Chris to accept the deal, knowing he wanted to see it too. Geraldine, John and Barbara agreed to the plan, as it meant they could go to the Royal Pavilion on their own.

Aaron had prayed that there would be no intermission midway through the film, but unfortunately for him, when the Millennium Falcon floated into one of the docking bays in the Death Star, the screen then *Intermission* flashed in big letters, the curtains closed and the house lights went up. He wasn't the least bit surprised when Jamie announced that he would only continue with his job if they bought him two ice cream tubs from the lady who had just strolled down the aisle steps, carrying a tray of iced refreshments. What choice did they have?

Aaron glanced back at the big screen to see a frenzied flurry of laser gunfire in the docking bay between the gunner on the underbelly of the Millennium Falcon and the Stormtroopers, as Luke Skywalker ran up the closing ramp into the ship.

A bright circle of light suddenly beamed onto Jamie. He turned to the source of the light, which came from the aisle and grinned broadly into it.

'This is your final warning!' Jamie heard a disgruntled voice from behind the light. *'One more noise and … you're out, young man!'*

'I told you it was *that* way!'' Aaron sighed inwardly, irritated by his ever–stubborn brother as he pointed up the hill.

'Shaddup!' Jamie snapped at him, looking in the opposite direction, refusing to admit defeat.

Chris tucked his hands into his jeans pockets, distancing himself from the bickering brothers. They were supposed to rendezvous with the adults at the rail station for the short train ride back to Hove after the cinema, but Brighton was like a maze, with sloping wide streets intersected by narrow ones. They all knew the station was on higher ground, but Jamie had insisted on his own route that had clearly taken them further away from their destination. Aaron argued that he knew the way, but Jamie refused to accept that. As the two brothers bickered, Chris observed where they were. They were standing outside The Heart in Hand, a small pub at the corner of North Road and Upper Garden Road. It was just after five o'clock now, and getting dark. The white lined pub walls were clad with dark green tiles, with a red door on the street corner. It was overhung with a dark green sign with white letters bearing its name. It had full windows on both sides.

'Let's go and ask!' Jamie announced, pointing at the pub and heading for the door. Aaron threw up his hands in resignation and followed his brother inside. Chris followed too.

Once inside, they froze.

In the dark, musty, smoke–filled interior, several men, either sitting at their tables or standing, turned their heads to the three teenage boys. Chris quickly glanced at the watching figures, noticing that many of them were wearing shiny black trousers or dark blue jeans, checked shirts or black vests and black leather jackets. Some had moustaches; others had earrings and hand jewellery. There was not a female in sight. Aaron quickly became uncomfortable when he saw two of the men kissing; he realised this was no ordinary pub.

'Oi!' came a voice. Jamie turned to the source, a male bartender standing behind the bar at the left corner. 'You can't come in 'ere!'

'Uh …' Jamie spluttered, now realising what he had just walked into. 'Er, where's … the station?' he asked.

'Up the road,' the bartender pointed to his right, 'then turn right about two hundred yards on and you're there, my lad.'

Chris gazed at one man, who was standing at a high table near the right hand window. He had thick black hair and a moustache, and was sporting a white tee shirt and blue jeans. He was playfully gesturing at Chris to come over to him.

Without thinking, Chris began to move forward, as though hypnotised. Jamie grabbed him and forcibly turned him towards the door before wheeling round to face the man.

'Go fuck yourself, ass–shagger!' he yelled.

The whole room burst into raucous laughter as Jamie turned once more and ushered Chris and Aaron through the door. Chris stopped at the doorway to look back and caught sight of the man again. The man blew a playful kiss at him. Chris felt something inside that he couldn't understand: he felt drawn to this kind of world like a magnet.

Jamie yanked Chris through the door and the three boys ran off up the road.

Jamie kicked the football and it rolled across the flat lawn towards Chris, almost clobbering a sleeping brown cat in its path. Chris stopped the ball with his foot. He looked around at the many and varied felines scattered around the large back garden of the detached house.

'How many cats?' he asked Aaron, his hand swinging around him.

'I dunno,' shrugged Aaron.

'I overheard Aunt Barbara say to Mum last night: Thirty–six.'

'Thirty–six?' balked Chris. He kicked the ball to Aaron, who was standing further away down the flat garden. 'Why does she keep them here?'

'She takes in strays, I think,' Jamie said as he watched the ball roll towards his younger brother.

Aaron stopped the ball with his foot and immediately kicked it to Jamie, before waving at Chris. 'What did you think of Star Wars yesterday?'

'It was okay,' Chris replied, shrugging; it was not his type of film, he thought to himself.

'Okay?' Jamie laughed as he stopped the ball with his foot. 'It was cool! The final battle in the trench was awesome! Boom!'

'That Millennium Falcon's the best ship I've ever seen,' added Aaron, waving his flat right hand to mimic the ship's flight. 'It was beautiful. Can't wait for the next one!'

'It was like a huge squashed tin!' Chris mocked.

'I heard on the radio last month,' Jamie said, 'that they've just finished filming the next one. It's called The Empire Strikes Back, I think.'

'What a shitty title,' Chris said. 'What's wrong with Star Wars 2? It's going to be a bad film!'

'Luke Skywalker will have his revenge on Darth Vader for killing Obi Wan!' Aaron swung an imaginary lightsaber.

'No, I don't think so,' Jamie said, kicking the ball back to Aaron, a mocking grin on his face. 'I think Darth Vader will tell him that he's his dad.'

The ball rolled past Aaron, who stared at his older brother, thinking about what he had just said; surely he was only joking. He always joked. How could that evil lord be Luke's father? That's impossible. No way! Or …? No, no, no, it wasn't possible; Aaron's mind whirled as he turned to run after the stray ball. He kicked it against the brick wall, bouncing it back towards Chris.

'Jamie!' came a voice. Jamie turned to see his dad standing by the back door. 'Dinner's ready!'

Chris, Aaron and Jamie ran in unison towards the house, spreading out their arms and flapping them, mimicking wings. 'Death to the Death Star! Boom!' Jamie yelled.

The family and Chris enjoyed their roast dinner around a redwood table in the dining room. Aunt Barbara rose to her feet, picking up a stack of dirty dinner plates and announced: 'Ice cream anyone?'

'Yeah!' Jamie called back.

Aaron turned to his mother for guidance. As usual, she tapped her index finger beside her lips, speaking clearly. 'She said would you like ice cream?'

Aaron nodded and so did Chris, having just lipread her too. Aunt Barbara took note of their nods and turned towards the door that led to the kitchen.

'Lovely dinner, wasn't it?' John burped, patting his full stomach.

Geraldine turned her attention to Chris, who was sitting opposite her, tapping her fingers on the table to get him to look at her. 'How are your parents?' she asked tentatively. 'You haven't talked about them.'

Chris was thrown by the question. He hesitated for a short moment; this was something that he did not want to talk about. He glanced at Jamie, hoping he would interpret. Jamie nodded for him to go ahead. 'They … er … don't live with each other,' Chris signed.

Upon listening to Jamie's voice–over, Geraldine rested her elbows on the polished wood, frowning with interest. Chris had become Aaron's best friend from the first day they had laid eyes on each other two years back, yet Aaron had said very little about Chris' past in his letters. When he wrote to ask if Chris could come and stay with them during half term, he'd said Chris did not have anywhere to go. She rang Mr Langston the following Monday to enquire about the boy, as she wanted to know what she was taking on. Mr Langston had said that Chris was generally a good and popular lad. He was delighted to know that Aaron had asked her about having Chris during half term, as it would solve a lot of problems. She asked why Chris couldn't go home and the headmaster had replied that he was not at liberty to discuss that at this stage because he had a duty of care, however, he did say that Chris' family situation was difficult and that had no home to go to. He urged her to consider having him and promised that he would discuss the matter further with her once he had the go ahead to do so. She agreed, not because of that, but because Aaron was so fond of Chris – she didn't want to disappoint him. Now, with Chris sitting right opposite her, she had the chance to get to know him a bit better. 'Are they divorced?' she asked him.

'No,' Chris said. 'They never married.'

Geraldine looked at her hearing son who had just finished interpreting, then turned back to Chris. 'Oh, so who do you live with?'

Chris easily understood the question, but fidgeted awkwardly. He didn't really want to answer. He looked at Aaron on his left, then turned back to the woman. 'I … um … don't live with either of them.'

Geraldine and John heard Jamie, surprised at the answer, though it confirmed Mr Langston's claim about the boy having no home. She pressed on. 'Why not?'

'I don't want to talk about it,' Chris shook his head, waving his hand at her to halt the line of questioning.

'But you're my son's best friend,' Geraldine said firmly, 'I feel–'

Incensed by her prying, Chris pushed his chair back, rose to his feet, slammed his hands on the table and shouted at her.

Chu up!

Geraldine shuddered; surprised by Chris's sudden outburst. She figured he'd just told her to shut up. Chris stormed out through the door into the kitchen, almost colliding with Aunt Barbara, who was carrying the ice cream box and bowls on a tray. Aaron glared at his mother with some accusation.

A short time later, Aaron found Chris sitting on the swinging sofa in the garden, his head down and hands clasped between his legs. He walked over to him, carrying the glass of Coca Cola that Chris had not finished at dinner. Standing in front of him, Aaron gently knocked the glass on Chris' forehead to bring him up. Chris had obviously been crying. He took the glass while Aaron sat down on his right. When Chris had finished sipping his drink, Aaron calmly patted Chris' arm.

'Sorry about my mum,' Aaron said. 'She can go on a bit sometimes.'

'It's okay.'

Aaron took a long look at his friend, wondering if he should ask or not. He had asked a few times before, but Chris always clammed up. He decided to try again. 'We've been best friends for over two years now and you've never talked much about your family. You know a lot about me and my family, but I know hardly anything about yours. Why couldn't you go home for half term?'

Chris stared at Aaron for a long moment, thinking hard about it; he had a point. Maybe now was the time to tell him. He sipped his drink again and held the glass with his left hand, freeing his right hand to sign.

'Social Services are looking after me,' he started to explain, 'and have been since I was eight. I don't have my mum or dad anymore.'

'Why?'

'I dunno, but I remember that Mum had a bad drinking problem. I was about seven when she threw my dad out of the flat in Highbury. You know, one of those towers of flats?' Chris gestured a tower block with his hands and waited for Aaron's acknowledgement. 'I don't know why she kicked him out, I remember very little, but I know that she was really pissed off with him. So angry with him over something; I don't know what. She even clawed his face with her fingernails. I still remember seeing the scratches on his left cheek. They bled badly. It happened in my bedroom in the middle of the night, I remember that much. I woke up when I felt a big bang near my bed. Maybe he had another woman and Mum found out, I dunno. I remember that I cried a lot and she cried too. She hugged me hard and spoke words over my head. Of course, I couldn't hear her, but I could *feel* her anger and sadness. She couldn't sign and neither could I–'

'You couldn't talk to each other?' Aaron asked, surprised at this.

'No, we didn't understand each other at all. I could understand Dad a bit, though and I think he understood me sometimes. But not Mum. I didn't know how to sign until I went to Ewing Hill Park School.'

'Really? Is that true?' Aaron gaped. 'But you went to a school before–'

'Schools,' Chris interrupted. 'I went to ... um ... four or five different primary schools, but we weren't allowed to sign. Three of them were PHUs, but still, we weren't allowed to sign. It was all talk, talk, talk. Anyway, when I came to Ewing Hill Park, it was still all talk, but the boys could sign. But that's another story. Going back to my mum–'

'What are your mum and dad's names?'

'Sandra Matthaus and Tom MacDonald,' Chris replied. 'I'm part English, part German and part Scottish. Mum's grandfather came from Germany just before the Second World War broke out. Dad's from Glasgow and they met in London, where I was born. Grandad died when I was about two. I don't know my grandma; I've never met her. I don't even know if she's still alive. I don't know anything about my dad's family. I don't even know if I've got uncles, aunties or cousins.'

Aaron watched Chris with great interest, scratching his nose. Chris took another sip of his Coke. He continued. 'Mum started to drink. Quite a lot. Then she started fucking that shithead, Bob Sullivan. I peeked through her bedroom door many times and saw them doing it. I was eight then. She drank more. She was always drunk, day and night. She couldn't stop. I cried when she was like that. I wanted her back. Bob was a real bastard. He hit her like a fucking punch bag. He sometimes hit me too. But she still loved him and he still fucked her and beat her until she was black and blue. I don't know why. Maybe it was the drink, I don't know. I once tried to stop him by jumping on his back and biting his ear. I just wanted him to stop hitting my mum. He threw me and I crashed against the wall and I broke my right arm. The bone came through my skin. I ended up in hospital for days.'

Chris wiped his hand across his tearstained face; the memories were too painful. Aaron placed a comforting hand on his right shoulder. Chris lifted his right arm and pointed out a small scar near the elbow. 'Social Services found out and they put me into care. I didn't want to leave my mum and she didn't want to leave me either. We both screamed and cried when they took me away. I remember that very well; it was at the estate and there were two people from social services and two policemen. Steve Lewison, my social worker – he's the one you've seen at Ewing Hill Park, picking me up for the holidays and bringing me back – he carried me to his car and drove away. It's been seven years now and I've still not seen or heard from my mum.'

'Where did you stay?'

'In children's homes and foster homes,' Chris answered. 'Five children's homes and eight foster homes. So far!'

'What's the difference between them?' Aaron asked; this was new to him.

'Children's homes are like boarding schools, but without the school bit. There were other children like me: no mums and dads. Care staff looked after us and we went to a local school each day. Foster homes are like staying with a family who care for you like you're part of the family.'

'Which is better?'

'Neither!' Chris half smiled, noting Aaron's surprised look. 'I was always the *only* deaf child in all of them. I couldn't sign or speak and they couldn't understand me and I couldn't understand them. The hearing kids in the children's homes were always making trouble and I always got blamed for everything they did because I was deaf and stupid. I know I'm not stupid, but they always said that. I'd get angry and frustrated for being blamed all the time. I was always being spanked and the kids teased me. I really hated being in children's homes because I was lonely and had no one to talk to. I just used to play football in the back garden, sometimes with other boys, sometimes on my own. It was the only thing I knew and was good at. Some of the children were worse than me; always getting into serious trouble and some staff were just as bad as they were, always hitting them, not only to control their bad behaviour, but sometimes for fun. I once saw one of them throwing a boy – I think he was nine or ten – into a window. Smash! He ended up in hospital for a week and nobody did anything about it.'

'That must have been terrible,' Aaron shuddered, thinking how lucky he was to have a loving family of his own.

'I always ran away,' Chris continued, 'which is why I ended up in five different children's homes. They couldn't cope with me and I couldn't cope with them. Then Steve Lewison got me into a foster home. I was nine or ten then. The family was real nice, but they couldn't cope with me. I think because they didn't know how to deal with a young deaf boy who couldn't speak or sign. They didn't sign either, so it was really hard.'

'Did Steve Lewison find you a deaf family?' Aaron asked.

'I did ask him about that last summer – he can fingerspell now and I've taught him some signs since I came to Ewing Hill Park, so we both understand each other a little better now and he's really brilliant – he said he had tried, but his boss said no. Apparently Deaf people aren't allowed to foster or adopt any children.'

'That's not fair!' Aaron bemoaned. 'Sammy Maguire, Derek Ferguson, Andy Farmleigh, Toby Eriswell and his oldest brother James … they all come from deaf families and it's not a problem. Why can't you?'

'I know!' Chris shrugged. 'Anyway, the first foster family, the Marshalls in Redhill, I was only with them for about three months, I think. I was moved from one foster family to another, I don't know why.'

'Were all of them nice to you?' Aaron asked.

Chris finished his drink and placed the empty glass on the grass. He turned to Aaron. 'No, not all of them: some were okay, some weren't and one family was really horrible. They were all … uh …' He tried to search for words to describe it.

'Different family values?'

'What's that mean?'

'It means each family have their own ways and rules and you have to follow them.'

'Yeah, something like that,' Chris nodded. 'I had lots of problems because I was always … you know … like the only deaf one in the family. No one to talk to?'

'Isolated,' Aaron said, noting Chris's furrowed eyebrows. 'It means you feel lonely and trapped. It's what you just said; you're the only deaf boy in the house and you had no one to talk to. That's isolation.'

'Yeah,' Chris nodded again, appreciating his friend's good knowledge of English. 'We tried to write things down, point and gesture and all that, but I didn't feel comfortable with them. Every day, I would always finish my dinner before everyone else–'

'Same!' Aaron brimmed. 'My mum, dad and Jamie talk over the table, but I always look down, eat my dinner and I finish before them!'

Chris smiled, relating to this. 'I always went straight to the living room to watch television or play football outside. Of course, I couldn't understand what they were saying on television, but it was something to do. I watched football, Match of the Day. I was always bored. It was worse during the school holidays.'

'You said one family was horrible to you. Why?' Aaron asked, moving a little closer to Chris with expectation.

'The Allan family,' Chris grimaced. Even the thought of the name repelled him. 'They were the worst of all. I think they were the reason I ended up at Ewing Hill Park. I was eleven then and they were my fourth foster family. They lived in Ealing in west London. They had two kids; Mike, who was twelve and Rachel, who was nine. They were both alright and their mum was okay, but their dad was really horrible. He was always being cruel to me, blamed me for everything, accusing me of breaking things that I didn't break and so on. He treated me like a dog. Mike would try to secretly help me out of trouble, but his dad sometimes found out and would punish me instead of Mike. I didn't lose my temper or anything like that; I'd already learnt not to from living in children's homes, because I knew that losing my temper would not make anything better. My third foster family was black and they were really good to me. The father was easy to lipread and he told me that it was better to stay cool and not to lose my temper, otherwise I'd get into even more trouble. Staying cool meant the other person would get the blame. I didn't really understand what he meant, but it worked for me. I wanted to be with that family forever, they were really lovely and them being black didn't really bother me at all.'

'Then why did you leave them?'

'I didn't leave them. Those bloody bastards firebombed their house. You know, you see in the news; the National Front? Threw a milk bottle filled with petrol and boom! Luckily, no one was hurt, but Steve Lewison had to remove me for my own safety. I really liked them. That's why I hate those shitheads like Hendrik Swart who bullied Ian Snyman, you know?'

'Yeah, I know. You and your Form stopped Hendrik and his gang last May,' Aaron acknowledged. 'Ian's better now.'

'Yeah, he's a good mate of mine. Anyway, back to the Allans … um … during the summer before I went to Ewing Hill Park, the family decided to go to Wales for the weekend. They had an estate car, you know? One of those big ones with the hatchback. Their dad told me I had to sit in the boot, not on the back seat. There was plenty of room for us three kids in the back, but he told me I had to sit in the boot along with other bags. Like I was a dog. I refused, but he told me that I had to, so in the end I did. We drove all the way to Wales from London and my legs hurt like hell. I had no room to move because of the bags. When we stopped for breaks, I tried to sit on the back seat before we left again, but he refused to allow it and ordered back to the boot. He'd really get cross with me if I didn't obey him, so I sat in the boot. Like a shitty dog!'

'That's awful,' Aaron shook his head in disbelief. 'Did you tell Steve Lewison about it?'

'Yes, later on,' Chris nodded. 'The worst happened on the last day. We were at Mumbles Bay. It's–'

'Near Swansea, I know,' Aaron interrupted. He noted Chris' surprised expression. 'Mum's from Swansea. When we're visiting Grandma and Grandad during the summer, we sometimes go to Mumbles Bay. It's the one with the pier.'

'Oh, right,' Chris nodded. 'Anyway, we went to the beach and they told us to come back to the car by three o'clock to drive back to London. So, I went around the beach and the town by myself. At quarter to three, I went back to the car and sat in the middle of the back seat. The family came back and stood talking outside the car until quarter past three. Then he told me to sit in the boot again. There was no way I could face sitting in there all the way back to London, it was too uncomfortable, so I refused and sat firm. He got really mad with me, pulled me out of the car and dumped me on the tarmac, then drove off without me.'

'Bastard!' Aaron groaned. 'They left an eleven–year old boy behind!'

'Yeah, they did. So, I went back to the beach and walked along the shore. I walked and walked. I didn't really know where I was going and when it got dark, I spent the night in a bus shelter. I didn't know if they had come back for me or not, but I didn't care. The next day, I took the road out of town. I must have walked about fifty miles over the next two or three days. I thought I was walking back to London, but I wasn't and I got lost. I became really cold and hungry and then heavy rain came. I thumbed desperately for a lift until finally a car stopped for me and this nice old couple took me to a town in Wales. I've no idea what it was called. You know, one of those long Welsh names that you can't spell?'

Aaron nodded. Chris sighed as he continued with his story.

'I picked out a house and just knocked on the door and this family took me in, fed me and reported what had happened to the police. We wrote down notes to each other. My English was crap, but I think they understood me. I told them to ring Steve Lewison at Islington Social Services, which they did too. He came over and picked me up and I told him what had happened. I found out later that the Allans did come back for me, but I'd already gone and they panicked. They thought I'd been washed away into the sea or something. Steve Lewison also told me that foster families like the Allans are being paid by social services to look after foster children, so he thought the Allan family were ripping them off by treating me like dirt.'

'And after that?'

'I stayed with Steve Lewison's family for the rest of the summer. I don't think he was really allowed to but it was either that or back to the children's home and he knew how much I hated it there. It was okay at his, really, and they looked after me well. Then I was told that I'd be going to Ewing Hill Park. I didn't really want to go at first, but Steve Lewison said that it was one of the best deaf boarding schools in the country and that I'd be with other deaf boys. He said it would be better than the children's and foster homes.'

'You didn't take the entrance exams?'

'No, I didn't.'

'Lucky you!'

'I think one boy pulled out just before the new term started and I was a last minute replacement. I don't really know how or why, but I was told there was a place for me. I didn't like it at first. I couldn't understand any of the teachers. I was like a wild cat and I ran away on my first day, though I got caught. Mr Langston was really good to me. He's very easy to lipread and he told me to try to make new friends in the school. My form mates liked me because I was good at playing football. That's how I became good friends with Dean Hopkirk, Steven Clarke, Sammy Maguire, Matthew Burke and Andrew Brener. They taught me how to sign and I was fine.'

'What about the school holidays?'

'I go to different foster homes,' Chris answered. 'Not really something I look forward to. This week – half term – Mr Langston told me that Steve Lewison couldn't find me anywhere to go, so I had to stay at school. But you saved me!'

'I see,' Aaron half smiled. It was hard to smile more after all Chris had told him. 'I'm sorry that you've had such a shitty life.'

'No problem,' he shook his head. 'I'm used to it.'

'What about your father?' Aaron asked, changing the subject. 'Have you seen him?'

'No. I don't know where he is,' Chris said. 'I did ask Steve Lewison, but he told me not to worry about him. I think he knows something about him from my mum, but he wouldn't tell me. Maybe when I'm old enough, I'll find out.'

'Hope you will. You said you remember him being a good dad.'

'Yeah.'

'Look,' Aaron paused for a moment, thinking. 'You can tell my mum and dad what you have told me. Not all of it; just tell them enough so that they can understand. Jamie will speak for you when you sign to them.'

'How much will it cost?'

'A Dairy Milk bar. It's his favourite. They're only fourpence.'

Chris and Aaron shared a small laugh; cheap, after what Jamie had charged them for his services at the cinema yesterday. Chris had come to understand from Aaron that his brother would never do what he called "sign language interpreting" for free. Chris nodded in resignation before taking a short look at Aaron. 'You've got a good family. Your mum and dad are great. I like them. Your mum can sometimes understand me.'

'Yeah, she can understand us deaf,' Aaron said, smiling. 'She can fingerspell good. My dad can't, but he tries to talk to me. I can lipread him fine, but sometimes we both write things down.'

'Your brother's good at signing. He looks like he's deaf!'

'We always sign to each other,' Aaron beamed. 'He *loves* it. Mum sometimes gets annoyed when we sign and she wants to know what we're talking about, but Jamie never tells her! Oh, let me tell you a funny story. Last summer, Jamie and I went to Bath for the day just for fun. On the train back, we were sitting with two girls opposite; they were about the same age as us. Jamie and I were signing and he suddenly heard the girls talking about us, saying how sexy and handsome I was and how much *more* sexy and handsome Jamie was. Jamie signed every word the girls said. They must have thought that Jamie was deaf too. They even said they would like to ... have sex with us, and we both laughed. They carried on talking about us until we got to Bristol Temple Meads and when we got off, Jamie shouted thorough the window that he was hearing and that he'd signed every word they'd said. Oh, you *should* have seen their faces!'

Chris laughed out loud, slumping back against the soft foam of the sofa. Suddenly, something landed on Aaron's back, spooking him. He felt sharp points piercing the back of his shirt. He yelled and instinctively reached behind, but whatever it was had already jumped over him and landed on his lap, again digging in its claws, this time through his trousers. Aaron winced and shoved the tabby away from his legs. The dark striped cat landed feet first on the grass, turning to Aaron and hissing fiercely. Aaron responded with a hiss too, clawing his fingers at the cat. It scooted off.

'I hate that cat!' Aaron grumbled. 'It's Miscoe, Aunt Barbara's favourite. He hates me!'

Chris laughed out even more. He felt a great weight lifting from his shoulders, now that he had finally talked to someone about his troubles. He looked at Aaron, who was watching the cat disappear into the bushes, affectionately.

He felt a sense of new hope dawning.

15

Coming Out

"Deafness and gayness are not my problems; they are those of people who do not accept themselves, and therefore do not accept others."
– SAM EDWARDS; in *Eyes of Desire: A Deaf Gay and Lesbian Reader* by Raymond Luczak, 1993

Chris jogged along the hard–packed mud path, the trees and bushes passing him by, feeling slightly chilled by the early November afternoon breeze. He could see some of the Fourth and Fifth Formers running ahead of him. He sighed: he really hated the Monday run, preferring to kick a football around. He couldn't give a toss if he came last, although he very rarely achieved that; some boys *really* wanted to be last; others *really* wanted to be first, either because they liked doing the run, or they wanted it to be over and done with. Many, including him, often cheated quite considerably by taking shortcuts; one of which was through a cricket ground by the small village of Oatlands, across the north road outside the park. He smiled, remembering the detentions he'd been given, along with several other boys, for being caught cheating, even though Mr Norris had been nowhere in sight. They figured that he must have been sitting by the window of a friend's house, overlooking the pitch, secretly snooping on the culprits and taking down their names while having a cup of tea. It was always a risk taking that shortcut, down to pure luck whether the sports teacher would be hiding in one of the houses or not.

Chris thought about the half term he had spent with the Stephens at Aunt Barbara's house in Hove. He'd really enjoyed himself; in fact, it was the best school holiday he had ever had, way better than the ones he had spent in foster homes. He and Jamie had got on famously, all three boys bonded, and, for the first time, he was able to communicate freely in sign during the holidays. Jamie was willing to speak for him when he explained his personal circumstances to Geraldine, John and Aunt Barbara – for a price. They understood, were sympathetic, and were happy enough to accept him into the family. Although it was Barbara's house, not the family home, he really felt at ease for the first time since being separated from his mother. He was now really looking forward to going to the Stephens' house in Bristol for Christmas, if Steve Lewison and Mr Langston agreed to that.

Chris turned to see if there was anyone running behind him, but saw no one. He assumed that he was either the last, or that some of the other boys had ventured deep into the forest. As he turned, something caught his eye. Was that a rustle in the thicket far off to his right? Chris slowed down, then jogged backwards to peer at the bushes in question. The rustling had stopped. It was probably the wind or a wild animal, he told himself. He began to turn, when the rustling started up again. Maintaining his slow backwards run, he caught sight of someone emerging from behind the shrubbery.

Dwight Greenland came out, pulling up his shorts, unaware that Chris was watching him. Another figure popped up from behind the bushes, with his back to Chris. Chris squinted at the tall boy with white hair, who he immediately recognised as the dimwit Tom Quillot. What were they doing behind the bushes, Chris wondered. Were they doing something to each other? Having a smoke? Chatting in private? Just hiding so that they could be last? Why was Dwight pulling up his shorts? Had they had sex? Chris knew that Dwight was a sissy, but Tom? He didn't look like one to him.

Dwight caught sight of Chris watching him and Tom emerging from the bushes, so Chris quickly turned his head and continued running forwards, forcing himself to think he wasn't even aware of what happened.

Later on, Dwight tied his shoelaces, silently looking across the busy changing room at Chris who was finishing knotting his tie. Dwight rose from the bench and put on his blazer, not taking his eyes off the Fourth Former, who, in turn, was putting his own blazer on. The worried prefect waited until Chris had finished signing with some of his form mates, then whipping his damp towel over his shoulder and heading towards the door, before picking up his own towel from the bench, slinging it over his shoulder and following him.

With discretion, Dwight tailed Chris through the covered walkway between the gym building and the rear of the school. He turned to make sure no one was coming out of the double entrance doors behind them, then turned again to look ahead, to make sure no one was coming through the back door of the school. It was slightly dark outside; so far so good, he thought to himself. Then he darted towards Chris, clamping his hands on the surprised boy's sides and forcibly pushing him through an opening in the corrugated iron wall. He then grabbed Chris' right wrist, pulled him hard towards the bicycle shed on the other side and pushed him inside it. Chris crashed back against the cold metal. Once he had recovered from the shock of his enforced detour, Chris stood face to face with an agitated Dwight. It was dark in the bicycle shed, but there was enough light from the darkening sky for the two seniors to see each other's signing.

'Did you see us or not?' Dwight demanded.

'See what?' answered a smirking Chris.

'Liar! You saw us!' said Dwight, angrily.

He had been so careful in the past – he had never been seen or caught until today. For a brief moment, he thought about himself: he had known what he was right from his early childhood. He knew he was a pansy and he was attracted to other boys. He even believed that his parents already knew about him, but were saying nothing about it. Maybe they would when he left school, but right now, he wanted to keep his sexuality a secret. It was too dangerous to be open in this school, for fear of being harassed and bullied by others. He didn't mind the *limp hand* name sign that he'd been given because of being camp, but that was as far as it went. He always claimed he liked girls and often likened himself to a young Mick Jagger, who was dippy like he was; once married to Blanca Perez–Mora Macias, this Nicaraguan woman; now dating that leggy blonde model, Jerry Hall. He knew that his luck had to run out eventually.

'Everybody will know now! Basher will screw me!' he cried.

'No, he won't,' Chris said suddenly. 'I'm not going to tell him or anyone else.'

Dwight stared at Chris in surprise. 'You won't?'

'No.' Why should he give someone like Basher, who he hated, the satisfaction, he thought to himself. Besides, he had always been curious about Dwight. He crossed his heart. 'I promise.'

'Are you sure? Keep it a secret?'

'Yeah. Secret.'

Dwight slumped and exhaled in relief, now knowing that his secret was still safe. Chris gently waved at the sixteen–year old to bring him back.

'Why do you do it? What's wrong with fancying girls?'

'I don't know,' Dwight replied. 'I just … don't. I try to, but I don't seem to be able to.'

'Isn't it wrong?'

'I don't feel wrong. I've done it with boys loads of times. I've seen men do it. Women too. It still doesn't *feel* wrong.'

'Where do you do it?' Chris asked, out of the blue.

'None of your business!'

'Please? I won't tell anyone, I promise.'

'All right,' Dwight said wearily. Might as well humour him since he had promised he wouldn't tell. 'Any secret place. Like in the forest today. In the dorm after lights out if you're very careful. The toilets–'

'With who?'

'Not telling you! One's from your Form though.'

Chris frowned in surprise. Who could that be?

'And the cellar,' Dwight concluded. 'I mostly do it there. It's the safest place to do it.'

'I see,' Chris folded his arms.

Dwight stepped back once, his back touching one of the racer bikes mounted on one of the rails. He folded his arms and thought hard about Chris, who was musing to himself. After a long moment, Dwight broke the silence.

'Why all these questions? Is it because you're the same as me?'

Chris started at this statement. 'No! I'm not!'

'I'm not blind. I've seen how you look at other boys.'

'That's not true–'

'Oh, come on!' Dwight interrupted. 'I've seen you in the showers. Always looking at other boys, especially Aaron Stephens. I don't blame you; he's quite handsome, isn't he? In the swimming pool changing room, you're always peeking at other boys while they're drying themselves, I've seen you. I saw you and Aaron in the front field that time from a first floor window too. You were bumping your bottom on his hard dick, weren't you? Did you like that? I think Aaron liked it. I think he likes you too.'

Chris shuddered. Dwight was the face he'd seen at the window. Everything Dwight had said about him was true, but he refused to believe his claim about Aaron.

'That's rubbish–'

'Yes, I think he does,' Dwight pressed on. 'Did you feel excited when you saw Miss Stephenson's breasts? Yes, I know about that – very funny! Do you feel excited when you look at pictures of naked women in Andrew Brener's sex magazines? You've been very good at keeping your feelings secret–'

'Shut up!' Chris snapped; Dwight was hitting home with hard truth, but he refused to accept it. 'I'm not a poof!'

'You're confused and afraid. I was too, but not anymore. You're very popular here. You'll definitely be head boy next year …' He paused for a moment to let Chris take in the last statement. '. . . yes, you will. You'll do much better than that bloody prat Basher. Being known as a queer here is very dangerous, you know. Do you know Jacques Magnat?'

Chris nodded, pointing at Magnat House on the other side of the corrugated iron wall. 'I know of him.'

'Well, he was Form Five when I was Form One. Everybody knew he was a poof. He was caught many times and Mr Williams wanted to expel him, but they couldn't because his family was very rich and donated loads of money to the school. Paid for Magnat House too. Almost all of the boys bullied him, even me. James Eriswell, who was in his Form and was head boy, didn't – or couldn't – do anything to help him. Some of the staff treated him like he was diseased. Mr Hugentobler, the old art teacher before Mr McShane, was the worst of all: he really treated Jacques like a big shit. No one would touch or even talk to him. He wasn't allowed in the showers with the other boys, so he had to wait until we'd all finished. His life here was absolute hell and I think he was really glad to leave.'

Dwight stepped forward, standing close to Chris, face to face. 'Do you still fancy girls?'

'Yes–'

Dwight promptly thrust his hand between Chris' legs. Chris flinched, but didn't resist. Dwight began to grope him, and with his free hand, signed: 'Tell me you don't like it.'

Chris let Dwight continue feeling about for a short moment. He didn't feel repulsed; he actually quite *liked* it, and soon began to feel the hardness inside his trousers. He quickly pushed Dwight's hand away when he tried to pull the zip down. Dwight stepped back, feeling satisfied.

'Secret,' Dwight said, putting a finger to his mouth. He looked down at his watch in the poor light and pressed the button on its rim. An LED clock lit up, crudely illuminating his face with a dim redness. It was almost five; tea time. He took one last look at Chris and disappeared into the darkness.

Chris laid his head against the cold iron wall. He closed his eyes to mull over things alone in the dark.

Chris could not stop glancing at Aaron over at the Third Form table. He wasn't taking a particular interest in the lively signed discussion that his form mates were having round his own table, though he knew they were talking about their old school teachers.

'My old teacher,' Mark said, 'was crap. He *never* taught me anything! I couldn't understand him–'

'But you're good at lipreading. And speech!' Sammy interrupted, digging his fork into a fish finger.

'I know!' Mark shrugged. 'But he was very difficult to lipread. Some of my friends who are still at my old school told me that he's always leaving the classroom to see that pretty nursery teacher. He must be about fifty years old, and she's only in her early twenties. One of my friends saw him snogging her!'

Everybody at the table tittered.

'Is that true?' asked Andrew, obviously interested.

'It's true,' Mark replied. 'Also, he sometimes sees the headmaster's secretary!'

'So what do your old classmates do while he's with her?' Dean asked, sipping water.

'They chat and play cards.'

Steven tapped the table with the handle of his knife to get Mark's attention. 'There must be something that he *could* teach?'

'No,' Mark replied, 'he'd just hand out those stupid baby books. Like, you know, you write down the missing words in a sentence from a list, do simple sums and things like that. They're really for five to eight year olds, you know? He teaches woodwork too. My old school mates, who are still with him, are the same age as me! I'm fifteen!'

'Lazy fuck!' Sammy shoved the fish finger into his mouth. He chewed it with some scrutiny. 'This is shit. Why can't we have Birds Eye?'

Jamon knocked gently on the table to get everyone's attention. The freckled Suffolk boy had been quiet throughout the discussion – he was the quiet type, but he wanted to follow up what Mark was saying. 'At my old school, we always had the same teacher in the same room. When I told some of my friends back home that we have different teachers in different rooms, teaching different subjects, they were amazed!'

'Same here,' Matthew concurred, waving a buttered knife in one hand and holding a slice of bread in the other. He stuck the knife on the bread, using the butter as glue, leaving his right hand free to sign. 'My friends at my old PHU in Cardiff wish they had the same as us too. Some of the teachers there are really shit – they don't know *how* to teach deaf children!'

'Same,' said Dean, pointing at himself with his knife and fork. The knife joined the fork, to free up his right hand. 'I was in a unit – you know, in like, a portable building–'

'Portakabin,' Mark cut in.

'Yeah, one of those. There were two or three of them outside the hearing school, called Partially Hearing Units. Most of the kids were half–deaf and the teachers were rubbish. No signing. I didn't really understand anything. We sometimes used the big classrooms, along with the hearing children, but that was worse! The teachers tried to use my old hearing aids ...' he gestured an imaginary harness on his chest. '. . . to talk to me, but I'm one hundred percent deaf! I met one of my deaf friends from that school last summer. Roberta Osten. She's seventeen now and she's left school. She said–'

'Girlfriend?' Andrew joked.

'No! She said – she can sign a little bit – that she hated the PHU. Said her English is very poor, her speech's poor and she's ... like, you know, a bit lost? She says her mum blames her for being stupid. I don't know why.'

'They aren't qualified teachers or anything like that,' Steven went back to the main subject. 'Why can't we have deaf teachers who can sign?'

Matthew finished buttering his bread and put his knife on a small plate. He pointed at Dean. 'It's the same with my old PHU.' He turned to Steven. 'Mr McShane told me that deaf teachers aren't allowed to teach deaf children, though he said he knows of two or three – all deaf women – who've just started.'

'That's bullshit!' Andrew said, slamming his hand on the table in annoyance. 'Mr McShane isn't deaf, but he's from a deaf family and he can sign. We understand him better than any of the teachers here, so why can't we have deaf teachers? Hearing teachers should teach the hearing; deaf teachers should teach the deaf. Can a deaf teacher teach hearing people? No, I don't think so!'

Lester waved his hand and everyone at the table turned to the stocky boy with wiry hair. 'We had a deaf teacher at my old school,' he announced.

'Wow!' Steven exclaimed. 'Was he good?'

'She,' Lester corrected. 'She came to my old school after I came here, but I visited it last year and met her. She could sign, but she said she wasn't allowed to sign in classes. She also said she had to spend two years teaching in a hearing school first, before she could qualify as a teacher of the deaf.'

'That's so unfair!' Andrew said, slamming his hand on the table. 'What about hearing teachers? Is she still at your old school?'

'No, not anymore!' Lester replied. 'I'm not sure why, but from what my friends told me, she ignored the school rule not to use sign in classes.'

'That's stupid!' Matthew remarked, shaking his head in disappointment.

Sammy banged hard on the table, causing everyone to turn to him. He smiled with pride. 'At my old school in Belfast, we were allowed to sign in class. Some of the teachers could sign too.'

'Very funny!' Andrew laughed mockingly.

'It's true!' Sammy slammed his flat right hand onto the palm of his left hand in a chopping motion. 'It was great. The school's shaped like a square U and it has two floors; the ground floor's for the full–deaf and upstairs is for the speak–good.'

'Why?' asked Andrew, forming the question with his index finger knocking the left side of his chest, curious.

'If there's a fire alarm, the full–deaf can't hear it, but the upstairs can – it makes it easier to move them outside.'

'Were the Brannigan twins from your school?' Matthew asked, munching his buttered bread.

'Aye,' Sammy replied. 'They were always in trouble. Broke the fire alarm glass! I think the school was happy to see them leave and come here.'

'Same here!' Steven cut in. 'They've left now. I was fed up with them breaking the fire alarm glass here too!'

Lester thumped on the table. 'Do you remember what happened last year when they dialled 999 from the phone in Mr Langston's office and left it off the hook? Police cars, ambulances and fire engines came rushing here, lights flashing everywhere!'

The whole table burst into chuckles, remembering the incident fondly. Sammy returned to the original subject:

'Then I came here, and it's all speaking and listening – rubbish!'

'So why did you come here?' Andrew asked, picking up his knife and fork to scrape his almost empty plate.

Dean waved at Sammy, smirking. 'Maybe you were always blowing people up there, so they sent you here to behave!'

'I'm not in the fucking IRA!' Sammy hit back, his mood changing, incensed by Dean's constant clowning about him and the IRA. He had already told the Liverpudlian many times that he was a Protestant, not Catholic, and Irish Republican Army was a Catholic organisation, but Dean never let go. 'I'm fed up with you saying I'm in the IRA. I'm not. I come from a loving Deaf family–'

'Yeah, yeah, we already know,' Steven interrupted. 'You've told us many times before!'

'Aye,' Sammy turned back to Dean. 'Well, have you ever seen *real* dead people? Bodies blown up? Their chests and heads shot? Splat! Have you?'

'No–'

'Well, I have!' Sammy said bluntly. 'It's horrible! My oldest brother, Kenny, was almost shot down by the RUC because they thought he was in the IRA. He wasn't.'

'What happened?' Chris asked, getting back into the discussion.

'He was riding his motorbike home from the Deaf Club one night. It was raining heavily. He was stopped by the RUC. Said three or four of them had their rifles on him, ready to shoot him down at the slightest hand movement ...' Sammy put his hands up as though to surrender, then continued signing. '. . . He was wearing his helmet and he can't speak well. He couldn't see their faces to lipread them because of the bright headlights behind them. He wanted to tell them he was deaf, but he couldn't because he was too shit–scared. So he slowly – *really slowly* – took his ID out of his jacket pocket and showed it to them. They realised he was deaf and let him pass. Kenny said he had never been so scared in his whole life!'

'It must be hard living in Northern Ireland,' Jamon said, sipping his cup of tea.

'Aye, it is,' Sammy nodded. He turned to Dean sternly. 'Now, stop saying I'm in the IRA, okay?'

Chris forked the last scrap of food into his mouth and glanced over at Aaron at the Third Form table again: he couldn't stop thinking about him.

Another pea hit David, this time one of his glasses lenses. He quietly wiped it away as he tried to eat his supper. Another one ricocheted off the other lens. He'd had enough of his form mates' bombardment and looked up.

'Stop it! Stop!' he pleaded.

More peas flew at him from around the table. He waved his knife and fork, fruitlessly trying to defend himself from the little green bullets. He looked around the table at a multitude of grinning faces; they had been using him as a pea dartboard, catapulting the peas from their spoons.

Suddenly, a small chunk of marmalade landed on his tie. David turned to see that Ian was the culprit.

'What did you do that for?' he asked Ian, starting to feel despondent. 'What have I done to you?'

'It's because this marmalade is crap,' Ian replied, 'and you're crap!'

'Yeah, he is!' Andy added. 'Crap at football! Runs round like a monkey slipping on bananas!'

'P.E. too!' Bradley took his turn. 'He *still* can't jump on the wooden horse. Crash! Bang! Wallop! He can't climb the rope!'

'You're like a Cornish pasty!' Derek mocked him, grinning knowingly at Shaun.

'Naw!' the boy from Cornwall hit back. 'He's like a haggis. It tastes like shit!'

Michael tapped on the table. 'There's one thing he's not crap at.'

'What's that?' Duncan asked.

'Talking!' Michael replied, mimicking David, as if he was a hearing boy. 'He's a big show–off at that! Yap! Yap! Yap!'

A small chunk of butter hit David's mouth. He saw that Derek had slung it. David suddenly lost it.

'WHY DO YOU ALL HATE ME?!'

He slammed his fists down hard, rocking the table and making the items on it bounce. The teacups tumbled, spilling hot liquid spilling. Aaron pushed away from the table as the tea streamed over the edge and into his lap. He slapped David's arm angrily.

'Look what you've done!'

A hand suddenly slapped the back of David's head hard. He whirled round to see Mr Schneider presiding over him, frowning, hands on his hips.

'Be quiet, David!' he snarled. 'Clean up this mess now!'

'I haven't done anything wrong–' David stopped, realising he had just signed to the sign–hater instead of using his voice as usual. He quickly switched on his voice. 'Look, I'm sorry–'

'Detention!' Mr Schneider pulled his trademark invisible trigger.

'It's not fair!' David rose to his feet, starting to weep loudly. He glanced at the Fifth Form table next to him, to see Basher smirking. He addressed the boys who were watching him. 'Why do you all hate me?'

David stormed out of the dining room, crying loudly. Aaron watched him disappear through the doorway, guilt creeping up inside him.

Chris found it difficult to concentrate during the one–hour prep after tea, so found some solace in the lavatory. He had told his form mates that he was feeling a bit sick and needed to go to the toilet. Sitting on the closed lid, he contemplated what Dwight had said earlier. Was he right about everything? Was he the same? A queer? Aaron too? No, he couldn't be; he didn't look like one. He sighed and briefly studied the cubicle walls, amusing himself by reading a series of crude scribbles and doodles. He thought about Aaron again and remembered the pass his friend had made at him on the front field two months back; did he really fancy him? Was he just fooling about?

Chris was beginning to feel sure of himself now that Dwight had suggested the truth to him. He knew that he *had* to be careful. Aaron drifted back into his mind again. Was what Dwight said about Aaron liking him true? He groaned inwardly. He *wanted* him so much, but he was afraid. There was only one way to find out, but was it a risk worth taking? He jumped when a sudden flash illuminated the cubicle. He looked up at the small window above him to see heavy rain in the night outside. Another flash of lightning flared. He glanced at his watch: seven o'clock; prep was over now. He breathed out, making a final decision. He pushed himself up towards the closed cubicle door.

Chris strolled briskly through the front hall, catching sight of Shaun, who seemed anxious.

'Seen Aaron?' Chris asked, tapping his right index finger on his left thumb twice, as per Aaron's name sign.

'I just saw him going to the library,' Shaun replied, pointing in the direction of the library.

Of course, Chris thought, where else would he be? He was the new Library Officer, since Justin Pope had left. As he made his way there, Shaun waved at him. 'Have you seen David Wheeley?' he asked, gesturing the outline of a big stomach. 'He wasn't in prep.'

Chris shook his head, not in the least bothered; he had more important things on his mind. He strode through the corridor, turned through the wood panelled corridor towards the double doors. Once inside the library, he quickly located Aaron, who was sitting by the central oak table with a book.

Chris tapped on the table from the other side to get his attention. 'Come on. Let's go.'

'Go where?' Aaron asked.

Soon enough, Chris and Aaron were making their way through the dim–lit corridor which led to the mainly unused east end of the building that housed storage and a few small, empty rooms. Chris kept glancing back to make sure no one was following them. His heart was pounding rapidly. Aaron tapped Chris' arm with a curious expression on his face.

'Where are we going?' he asked again.

'To the cellar,' answered Chris, keeping his intentions in check.

'Cellar? What for?'

'Wait and see.'

'Okay,' Aaron shrugged. Might as well see what Chris had to show him, he mused; after that, it was back to the library in a hurry. 'Race you!'

Aaron darted off before Chris could even blink. Chris sprang after him. Aaron whooped as he turned a corner into a short, narrow corridor, reaching a closed wooden door at the end. He quickly twisted its iron handle and pushed the door ajar. He stopped briefly at the head of the steep, narrow steps, flanked by damp grey stone walls. At the bottom of the stairs was a small square foyer; it was dark, but Aaron knew the cellar – the boiler room – was on the left through another door. He glanced behind to see Chris turning the corner and heading towards him. Aaron turned and hurried down the stairs, just as Chris shot through the open doorway.

Chris paused on the third step down, turned round and gently closed the door behind him. He made sure it was firmly closed. There was a keyhole, but it had no key in it. Chris turned and squinted down into the darkness to see that Aaron was almost at the bottom. This might be good, he thought to himself; perhaps this kind of play might lead to something more. He descended the stairs, sliding his hands down either side of the narrow walls to stop himself from slipping.

Aaron turned left and fumbled for the handle in the darkness. He found it, pulled it down, swung the door open and shot through the doorway. A moderate light welcomed him and he looked ahead.

He froze.

Chris ran in from behind and collided with his friend, not expecting him to be standing in the doorway. Aaron fell forward, but instinctively managed to keep his balance. Once Chris had recovered from the initial shock, he turned to see what Aaron was gazing at.

He gasped.

16

The Three Musketeers

"No matter how much one shakes off one's deafness, his deafness will pursue him relentlessly."

– On Francis Humberston MacKenzie, later Lord Seaforth (1754–1815); Britain's first Deaf MP for Ross–shire from 1784–90 and 1792–94, who became deaf at age of 12 and used signs and fingerspelling.

David opened his eyes, blinking at the harsh brightness that welcomed him contemptuously. He knew straight away that he was not in his bedroom at home; there was a large window to his right instead of the one that was supposed to be in front of his bed. This room was much larger, the colour of the walls around him different. From what he could ascertain through his blurred vision, they were either a dull white or light grey. That smell, too: it was distinctively sour and starchy. It smelled like the stuff Mummy used to mop the kitchen tiles with, he thought.

He moved his left arm and felt something sticking into the back of his hand. He felt it with his other hand – it was plastic tubing, held down by a plaster. He needed his glasses so that he could see better. With his right hand, he reached out wildly until he touched some kind of metal frame. He wrapped his little fingers around the top of it and tried to pull himself up, but couldn't; he felt so tired and weak. His hand fell back down and he started to feel frightened.

'Mummy …?' he called out quietly.

A largish figure rose behind the metal frame on his right. David could barely see, but he knew it was his mother. She quickly held his hand in a comforting way, fetched something from the side and turned back to him. The metal frames of his glasses soon slid behind his ears and the front arch rested on his small nose. He blinked twice and smiled gratefully when he finally saw his surroundings more clearly.

Mrs Wheeley presided over her son, smiling at him. He turned away from her to see where he was. Soon enough, he recognised that he was in a hospital ward. He gazed back at his mother, who was speaking to him, but nothing was coming out of her mouth.

She turned, hearing someone approach; he looked in the same direction to see Daddy coming in, carrying a bunch of comics and paper bags that he knew contained little sweets. The large man hurried over to the bed and leant over his son, grinning broadly. He spoke, but again, no words came out of his mouth.

'Daddy …' David said quietly, 'why are you whispering?' He turned to his mother, who was speaking to him, but he could hear nothing, only a complete and uneasy silence. 'Mummy … I can't hear you …'

He strained to listen, but nothing came through his ears. He moved his head sideways to try to hear something – anything – but all was silent. He banged the back of his hand on the metal frame and it clattered; he felt the vibrations but he couldn't hear them. Looking at the back of his small hand, he could see that the reddish rash on it was now gone. That was the least of his worries right now, but he was increasingly frightened by the silence.

'Mummy …' he stopped short when he realised that he could not even hear his own voice. He turned to his father, 'Daddy … what's wrong with me? I can't hear anything!'

He saw his mother cup her hand over her mouth, her eyes widening with shock. She said something to her husband, but David couldn't hear the words that flew over his bed. He bawled loudly. Closing his eyes, he tried to remember what had happened to him. He remembered that he'd had bad earache; his head hurt, the back of his neck stiff – so stiff that he couldn't bend it. It had started just after his seventh birthday, two weeks back. His mother took him to see the doctor, who simply told him that it was a bad headache which would go away soon. It didn't though; it got worse and he screamed the house down. He also developed a reddish rash on the back of his right hand and his body began to hurt all over. He vaguely remembered his father driving to the hospital with his mother comforting him, screaming and crying, in the back seat. The next thing he remembered was lying on a trolley, being ferried towards an operating theatre or some other room he couldn't remember … no, wait, that was later. There were doctors and nurses doing things to him; inserting a needle into his arm, which he hated, to take his blood, and performing other medical tasks that he didn't understand. He must have spent two or three days in that bed and his head hurt even more. Then came this … this most horrible thing: he had to lie on his left side and they'd put something into the lower part of his spine, making it numb. His mother was sitting in front of him, holding both his little hands and telling him not to worry and to be very brave. He did not feel anything, but he knew that something was pumping in or out; he had no idea which.

He opened his eyes again and his parents were gone. He listened, but it was all silence. He could see other children in the ward talking and playing, but couldn't hear them at all. He felt as though he was trapped in a sealed glass box. He turned to see a group of five or six young children sitting round a small black and white television, which was perched on a high table in the corner by the window.

He smiled when he recognised the programme on the screen. *Sesame Street!* He wanted to watch it as well, but he couldn't hear it. He should go over there, he thought; perhaps he'd be able to hear it better. He pulled his bedcovers down and crawled towards the end of the bed, as the metal frames on both sides were still up. He soon reached the edge and hopped off. His legs collapsed when his feet touched down and he found himself flat on the white floor. Twisting his head, he looked at the television again; the other children were unaware of him. He smiled when he saw Big Bird flapping around in his usual excited manner, with Curly Bear, Bert and Ernie in tow. He could see the children laughing, but still couldn't hear them. He struggled to get to his feet, but stumbled again; it was as if he had no control of his balance. Deciding to crawl instead, he shuffled across the ward on his hands and knees, like a wounded dog. He passed the still–laughing children, who took no notice of him, and reached the window. Putting his hands on the windowsill, he pushed himself up to his feet, angling them slightly outwards. He took a short, sharp breath and cruised along the window, his right hand sliding across the sill for support, until he came close to the television.

He still couldn't hear it. Maybe the volume was low, he wondered. He rested his hand on the high table where the television was and turned the volume knob to its full. The set suddenly burst into a vibratory blast, but he *still* couldn't hear it. He turned to see the children clasping their ears tight and screaming. A nurse hurried into the ward, excusing herself through the sitting children; she immediately turned the knob back and the vibrations ceased. She turned to him, speaking angrily, but her rapidly moving lips were silent.

'But I want to hear Big Bird!' David said, crying. 'Why can't I?'

With his head slumped, David wiped away the stream of tears that were flowing down his cheeks when he came back from this memory. He tried hard not to think about what was hanging over him, but it was impossible not to. Thinking back to how his life had been since he became deaf was the only escape from thinking about it. He rested his arms on his thighs, looked at his glasses, which he was fiddling with, and thought about the struggles he'd had after returning home from hospital.

Sitting in a wheelchair, wheeled out through the hospital doors by his mother and entering the outside world for the first time in about three weeks, David tried to listen for anything; ambulance sirens, passing cars, people talking, the birds singing, the rustling of litter ... *anything*. But the whole world was in complete silence.

Over time, he had come to accept he had lost his hearing and would never be able to regain it. That was the least of his worries, though. He frequently threw up over the kitchen table, especially after eating eggs, and was constantly ill. He had trouble walking properly and it took him some time to learn to control his balance again. His dad told him to put his toes together because he was walking like a penguin. He had tantrums, frustrated by not being able to fully participate in conversations. His mother always had to attend to him and spoke very slowly to him. Worst of all, though, he had a real struggle learning to read people's lips; he always seemed to misunderstand their lip patterns. "How are you?" his Uncle Bert once asked. "I'm seven and half," David replied. It was very difficult for him to distinguish between *b* and *p*; *thirteen* and *thirty*; *fifteen* and *fifty*; *sweep* and *sleep*; *two days* and *Tuesday*; *I love you* and *elephant shoe*; *married* and *buried*. So frustrating! His mother tried using cued speech, which used certain handshapes to represent pronunciations. However, David found the system too complicated and distracting. Besides, his mother tended to forget which handshapes to use to accompany her speech. His father never bothered learning it and David preferred the straightforward lipreading route best.

Eventually, he began to master lipreading and was able to correctly understand almost every word that was said, although mistakes still occurred. However, what he hated most was the body–worn hearing aids that he had to wear on a harness around his body; the weight of the aids would drag him down. Then there were the hard plastic moulds which hurt his ears, especially when he was chewing food. His mother and the audiologist, Mrs Able, said that the hearing aids would help to him hear something to improve his speech and lipreading. Speech was not a problem, as he was already able to speak and was a compulsive talker, even after he became deaf; he dared not stop for fear of losing his voice. He would sometimes drive his parents up the wall by talking too much, though he wouldn't shut up, no matter how often they told him to shut up. However, he heard absolutely nothing with the aids: he was completely deaf in both ears.

Or so he thought.

At ten, David was already used to his deafness and had started to learn some signs at his primary school in Shrewsbury. Signing was not allowed in the unit, but he picked it up in the playground from some of his deaf friends. He took care not to stray far from them because of the school bullies. They liked to pick on him because he was fat, taunting him about his body aids – they sometimes forced the harness off him, smashing the aids on the tarmac with their feet.

Clink!

He wheeled round to see his mother looking down at the wooden kitchen floor, locating a penny that she had dropped while trying to put it into her purse, unaware of her son's apparent reaction. Did he just hear the penny clink on the floor? Was it just his imagination? He had to be sure.

'Mummy,' he said, walking over to her, 'can you do that again?'

'Do what again?' she asked quizzically, putting the penny back into her purse.

'Drop the penny,' he replied. 'Please?'

Begrudgingly, his mother fingered her purse, took out the penny and dropped it.

Clink!

He heard it again. In his left ear. He stared, dumbstruck, at the penny rolling away from him. He looked back up at his mother, a smile growing on him. 'Mummy, I heard it clink on the floor!'

The series of audiology tests that rapidly followed this revelation revealed that David had developed an unusual form of hearing loss in his left ear. His right ear was as good as profoundly deaf, but his left ear was both deaf *and* hearing. One minute, he could not hear anything, even a loud clatter; the next he could literally hear a pin drop. It was as if his cochlear had a mind of its own. This baffled the medical profession, who cited it as a very rare and unusual phenomenon.

Still holding his spectacles, David rested both elbows on his thighs, his chin on his hands. He stared down at the hard concrete floor, still weeping. His mind drifted back two years, to just before he first arrived at Ewing Hill Park. He hadn't wanted to come here, but his parents felt it was best for him; they believed the school's oral approach would be better for his education than a local school, and thought he would be a fine example to others, thanks to his excellent speech and lipreading skills. That was what his mother told him. He would be popular as well. How wrong she was!

Right from the first day, he was always a target for bullies. That Fifth Former, Kevin Kelvedon, was his first; he'd tormented him throughout his first year. He was once almost electrocuted by a wire hanger that was inserted through the door of the Fifth Form Common Room and hooked up to a plug socket. Kevin had tried to force feed him fishing bait; there were other things Kevin had done to him that he wanted to forget. He was grateful that Kevin had left; good riddance to him!

His second year was relatively okay; not much bullying from a few of the boys, nothing as bad as Kevin. Basher had been the worst, but he was not Basher's only victim. His form mates were alright with him, except for that stupid Scot, Derek, who was always moaning and blaming him for almost everything, from being rubbish at sports to a speech show–off, calling him a farty fat snail and a big useless blob. He even came up with a name sign for David; *huge belly*.

Then there was last summer … it was one of the worst summers he'd ever had; Mummy had kicked Daddy out. He didn't understand it at first, but then he secretly listened, with his left ear, to them arguing in the kitchen one night. His Daddy, the man he'd always looked up to, had found another woman. That young one called Pixie from the Spar, where he always bought little penny sweets. He blamed himself for his parents' split, but his mother told him that it wasn't him.

Then Basher had stepped up his campaign – David had become the head boy's plaything and slave. Everything had deteriorated for him in the last two months. Half term last week was awful; his father wanted to come home, but his mother wouldn't have him back. He had learned that Pixie had dumped him for another, younger, man. Daddy begged for forgiveness, but Mummy wouldn't do it and it was entirely his fault, David blamed himself. Oh, he wished they would get back together and be a happy family again.

Today … today was the last straw. It was the first day back to school after half term and they were already onto him. He'd hated being used as a pea dartboard at teatime today. Even Aaron was angry with him; it was the first time he'd ever done that. *That fucking Hitler Teacher! Not worth living in this fucking world anymore! They'll be so fucking sorry when they find me dead! Fuck the world!*

He raged inside and thought again about the noose hanging down above him. Right, let's get this over and done with, he said to himself. Just get on the chair, neck through the noose, and then jump–

He heard something; a scraping of feet on the hard concrete floor ahead of him. He quickly cocked his head, put on his spectacles and saw Chris and Aaron standing in the doorway.

David hurriedly rose to his feet, stepped on the chair and inserted his head through the noose. With both hands, he pulled back the coil to tighten the noose around his neck. The top, which was tied to a steel pipe on the low ceiling, began to tighten.

Aaron stepped forward, but David raised his hand. 'Don't move!'

Aaron reluctantly took a step back. Chris remained where he was: still staring at the fat boy standing on the chair in the middle of the cellar.

'Go away!' David waved his hand at them. He thrust two fingers at them. 'Fuck off!'

Chris and Aaron exchanged glances, wondering what to do. Aaron returned his attention to David. 'Why … are you doing this?' he asked.

'Everybody hates me!' he snapped back.

'I don't hate you,' Aaron assured him. 'I never did. Honest.'

'Yes, you do!'

'No, I don't.'

Chris discreetly took a step forward, hoping David wouldn't notice. David immediately inched forward; his feet were already half over the edge. Chris forced himself to stop.

'Look, it's not worth it,' Chris said, signing softly. 'Please step down and we'll talk about it, okay?'

'What do you care?' David boomed back. 'You never liked me!'

'You are my friend,' Aaron said, signing calmly. 'Please don't do it.'

'I am not your friend!'

'Yes, I am!' Aaron said back. 'Have I ever said that I hated you? Have I?'

'No ...'

Chris tentatively took another step, but David again clambered forward. He was now balancing on his heels, perilously close to going over the edge, his wobbling steadied by the noose around his neck.

Aaron quickly grabbed Chris' arm, forcing him back as he became worried about his form mate's unevenness on the chair, remembering that David had once told him that he had poor balance; a side effect of meningitis.

'He has poor balance!' he warned Chris.

'What? Like Matthew Burke?'

Aaron nodded.

Chris turned back to David. He quickly assessed the situation in the gloomy, rectangular room, which had stacks of chairs at one end and piles of boxes on either side: David was about twelve, maybe fifteen feet away from him and Aaron. He speculated whether he would be able to run and catch David once he was over the chair. No, that would not work, he said to himself, he was simply too heavy. The second he jumped, his neck would simply snap and it would be too late for Chris to save him. He looked up at the series of metal pipes that came from the boiler room through an opening on the far left of the room. He decided that one of those pipes would be strong enough to take David's weight. So, talking him down was the only option he and Aaron had. Chris bit his lip in frustration.

'Basher's been rotten to me,' David burst into tears, signing and speaking at the same time. 'I've been his slave! He smashed my model plane! I'm no good at sports! My mum and dad have split up and it's my fault! Everybody hates me! Everybody bullies me because I'm fat! It's entirely my fucking fault! I hate you all!'

'It's not your fault,' Chris assured him.

'Yes, it is! I'm better off dead!'

'No,' Aaron said calmly. He thought for a moment, trying to figure out another way of talking him down. 'Look, do you want revenge on Basher?'

Without even looking at him, Aaron sensed Chris' surprised reaction. The rim of his black shoe quickly and discreetly poked Chris' right ankle. Chris winced at the short, sharp pain on his bone, but got the message and turned to David.

'Yeah!' Chris forced a smile. 'Revenge on Basher!'

'He's too big!' David shook his head dismissively.

'Not with three of us,' Aaron said.

Before Chris could even react, he felt another poke on his ankle, this time harder. He winced at the sharp pain and forced himself to smile again. 'Yeah,' he agreed in spite of himself. He pointed to himself, Aaron and David. 'Three of us!'

'Three of us?' David began to relax.

'Yes,' Aaron said. 'Three Musketeers!'

Chris played along, comically impersonating a swashbuckling musketeer, swinging an imaginary sword. David let out a small giggle.

'You're Oliver Reed,' Aaron pointed at David; 'I'm Frank Finlay and he's Richard Chamberlain! Have you seen The Three Musketeers?'

David nodded. Chris shook his head, perplexed: he hadn't seen the film. Aaron ignored his friend's lack of acknowledgement; he would explain to him later. 'Who's the bad guy in that film?' Aaron asked David.

'Christopher Lee!' David answered, signing an exaggerated pair of walrus–style fangs. He was now smiling.

It was working, Aaron thought; David was beginning to calm down. 'Yeah, him! He's Basher. We'll get him!'

'How?'

'I dunno,' Aaron shrugged. 'We'll think of something. We're your friends. Honest.'

'Yeah!' Chris forced himself to agree. It wasn't that he disliked David, just that he had never regarded him as a friend before. 'Friends! Three Musketeers!'

David loosened up and placed his hands on the noose to pull it off his neck.

'Good … good,' Aaron advanced slowly. 'Get down slowly. We'll whump Basher's ass. Promise.'

David took off the noose and stepped down, breaking down in tears again. Aaron quickly went over to the weeping boy and placed a comforting arm round his shoulders. Chris darted forward, passing the two boys, and kicked the chair hard. It flew harmlessly across the length of the room and clattered loudly against a stack of chairs; a vibrating echo resounded through the contained space, causing Aaron and David to jump. The chair hit the floor with a dull thud.

'Just in case he changes his mind, Chris smiled wryly.

Suddenly becoming suspicious, David glared at Chris and Aaron. 'Why did you both come down here? You didn't know I was going to … to …'

David trailed off; he was far too distressed. Chris and Aaron exchanged silent glances; neither of them had an answer. Chris looked away and gazed up at the hangman's rope. He rested his hands on his hips, sighing.

Forks and streaks of white lightning filled the night sky. Thunder roared loudly and rain splattered heavily on the pitch black ground.

He repeatedly pushed down the jack lever and the car slowly rose each time he did so. His wet hands grasped the slippery black tyre, twisting it hard, but he couldn't get it off. He let go and pumped the lever again, rain drenching his arms and hands.

His fingers slipped and slammed hard against the cold metal base of the jack. He screamed in agony, holding his injured hand. Another round of lightning lit up his face, visibly showing its pain and frustration. He tried the jack again, becoming angrier. His brain radiated with red and orange as though it was going to explode. Suddenly, the black iris of his eyes turned white, leaving only the pupils and limbal rings black.

The back of his white shirt began to tear down his spine, revealing a strange green skin. His left shirt sleeve began to rip, again revealing green skin. His face began to turn green, his cheeks expanding, dark green eyebrows growing, his lifeless white irises watching this terrifying transformation in horror. His left biceps and his right forearm bulged as if they were green balloons.

He grabbed the long metal jack with both of his huge green hands, holding it at either end, and easily bent it, as if it was made of liquorice. He slowly rose to his feet. More thunder and lightning flared around the terrifying, fearsome–looking green monster. He outstretched his arms, flexing their huge muscles; his huge muscular chest heaving; his torn trousers tight against his colossal thighs and calves; strips of his shredded white shirt fluttered around him; his face grunting terrifyingly into the night. Lightning flared furiously around him as he roared.

Basher watched, his white sleeves tightly rolled up and his eyes fixed on the television. A flash from the lightning flared through the window next to the television into the darkened room. Unbeknownst to the head boy, some of the boys who were sitting behind him had begun to move away.

Water suddenly gushed down over his face, shirt, tie and trousers. He gasped loudly in shock. Angrily, he looked up to see who had done such a thing and was surprised to see David standing in front of the window holding an empty jug. Lightning flashed furiously, both on the television with the huge green figure still flexing his muscles, and through the window behind David, with almost perfect synchronisation.

Basher raged loudly. He flew from his chair. David threw the glass jug to the carpeted floor and shot off like an overweight cheetah. He darted into the recreation room, whizzing past some boys playing snooker and table tennis, with a demented Basher hot in pursuit.

David shot through another door and turned a corner into a long, dark corridor. He was starting to feel out of breath already, but he knew he had to run as fast as he could to lure the school bully into the trap that Aaron came up with. He prayed hard that it would work.

Chris flicked down one of the four lights switches. A solitary fluorescent light flickered into life on the gym's high ceiling, giving an area of the large hall partial light. Another lightning bolt flashed through the long, narrow windows high up on either side of the wall.

Aaron placed a loaded carrier bag on the varnished floor beside him while Chris bent down to place the rope – the one that David had used in the cellar – across the wide doorway and motioned for his friend to take the other end. They knelt at the doorway, concealing themselves. Aaron leaned forward to peer down the opposite end of the dark foyer, noting that the double entrance doors were still closed, but unlocked. The changing room door on the right and the equipment store door on the left were also closed.

Chris was satisfied with the placing of the rope across the doorway. He reminded himself of the plan: David was to lure Basher into the gym and they'd trip him over the rope on David's signal after he ran into the darkened gym. Then, they'd tie him up and do their work on him using the stuff in the carrier bag. The plan was Aaron's idea – a good one – although Chris had agreed to it with some reluctance. Aaron waved at him.

'What did you want to show me in the cellar?' he asked.

Chris silently cursed to himself; he had forgotten all about that, what with all the business with David. 'Nothing. Forget it.'

'No,' Aaron shook his head. 'If we hadn't gone down there, David would be dead by now!'

Chris knew Aaron was right, but he had no answer for him. He rose to his feet and flicked up the light switch. The gym plunged into darkness. Aaron sighed as he watched Chris fall to his knees in the gloom, resigned. A flash of lightning illuminated the hall for a brief time.

David pushed the back door hard and ran out into the cold, damp air. It was raining heavily and more flashes of lighting followed by. He ran under the covered walkway which led to the gym building. Wheeling round, he saw that Basher had just bolted through the back door, as demented as ever. Promptly, David turned and dashed towards the double entrance doors. With both hands, he pushed them open and darted through the foyer, towards the open doorway into the dark gym. He could barely see the rope on the floor across the doorway and took care not to step on it as he ran through.

Whirling round, David faced the doorway. Without really looking at them, he could sense his two comrades kneeling, holding the rope in the dark. Basher was nowhere to be seen in the foyer, though he had expected him to be there by now. The double entrance doors were still moving; because of him or Basher? David squinted into the obscurity of the foyer, but there was no one there.

'Where did he go?' David muttered, cursing his poor night vision. He cautiously stepped towards the doorway. Chris and Aaron held the rope anxiously, waiting for the signal. David took another step.

A dark figure suddenly pounced through the doorway, his force causing David to stagger backwards.

Basher promptly clamped his arms round his victim. David tried to twist away and the two of them staggered further into the darkness of the gym. Chris and Aaron rose to their feet, cursing themselves for missing the trip. David struggled hard against Basher's vice like grip on his torso, feeling the wetness of the bully's shirt on his back. He could feel Basher's loud chortling; he knew that he'd try to push him down and beat him up. He found it difficult to fight against his opponent's superior strength.

Chris and Aaron quickly came up behind Basher, unsure what to do next. Basher was unaware that he and David weren't alone in the gym. Another lightning bolt or two flashed, briefly showing Basher's squirming body, his back to them. Instinctively, Aaron shouted at David.

Daaavvveeee ... !

David heard this through the hearing aid in his left ear. It was an electronic transmission, but it was Aaron's voice. Suddenly, it gave him a rousing strength that he never imagined he had. He forced himself to put mind over matter and began to wriggle hard until he felt Basher's grasp weakening a little. He tried again, this time with more effort. He placed his hands on Basher's clasped hands in front of him and squeezed the index finger on each of them, then began to pull each of the fingers back to loosen the grip. David felt Basher yell in pain as the two fingers were forced back against the bone. The big boy eventually disengaged his grip, allowing David to shove both of his hands forward and break free. He quickly whirled round to face his nemesis.

'I've had *enough* of you!' David shouted, not signing; instead thrusting his clenched fist directly into Basher's stomach. Basher doubled over. 'I resign as your slave!'

Chris and Aaron could almost see what David was doing in the darkness and saw their opportunity. Aaron ran and slid down behind Basher's legs, crouching. David saw what Aaron was doing and pushed Basher hard. Basher screamed as he stumbled backwards over Aaron, fruitlessly waving his arms and crashing down hard onto the floor with a loud thud. Aaron quickly crawled over and grabbed Basher's legs while Chris knelt. The fallen sixteen–year old found himself rolling over face down. He fumbled for Basher's right hand and held it as he wrapped the rope round the wrist. David hurriedly joined in, found Basher's left hand, still jerking in fury, and held it firmly with his hands, pushing it over. This allowed Chris to hastily wrap the rope round the left wrist and tightened both hands together.

Meanwhile, Basher was struggling hard to free his legs from Aaron's bearlike grasp. Chris slapped one of Aaron's hands and motioned for him to back away a little. Aaron did so, knowing what their next move was. He slid down a bit, then held Basher's ankles as Chris tied them blindly in the dark using the other end of the rope; the lightning that flashed through the windows at the top gave the three perpetrators occasional split–second visibility of their progress. David crawled round in front of the agitated Basher and took an apple from his blazer pocket.

'I love apples, but this one's rotten, just like you!' He pushed the apple hard into Basher's screaming mouth, forcing him to take a bite, and left it there. Next, he whipped some Sellotape from his other pocket, unwound it and bit on it, cutting it. Concentrating, he placed the tape over the apple and Basher's cheeks, applying another piece of tape to further cement the apple in the mouth. Once he was satisfied that the apple was firmly in place, he pulled one of the school's long green and gold coloured football socks from his pocket and stretched it. He quickly wrapped it around Basher's head, covering his eyes and blindfolding him. He tied it at the back, then made sure that it was tight. Chris had finished with the rope and checked the knots at Basher's wrists and ankles, satisfied that they were firmly done.

Aaron flicked down all four switches on the wall and the gym hall flickered into full light. Chris and David joined Aaron at the doorway and they all looked at the pitiful figure on the floor. It was a sorry sight; Basher was rocking back and forth on his front with his arms pulled back and his legs bent over his back, his wrists and ankles held together by the taut rope. He was completely blindfolded by the football sock around his head and silenced by the apple in his mouth.

Aaron bent down and picked up the carrier bag, inserting his hand into it. He took out a pair of scissors, which he passed to Chris, then dug into the bag again, pulling out three small cans of modelling paint and two thick modelling paintbrushes and passing them to David. The trio all looked at Basher, smiling with glee.

A short time later, they had finished with him. Chris tried to wash the red paint off his left shirt sleeve again, but it had already dried; he silently cursed Aaron for his clumsiness with the paintbrush.

Aaron directed the Polaroid he had borrowed from Shaun and squinted through the viewfinder. He clicked the button and the flash went. Almost immediately, a square instant film sheet slid smoothly from the bottom front of the device. Chris took it and held it up. Aaron and David leaned over to witness the picture developing under the light, chuckling at it. Chris held up the other two Polaroid pictures to join the latest one; their third.

With one final look at Basher, the three confederates turned away to exit the gym. Chris flicked up all four switches on the wall, plunging the hall into complete darkness. A flash of lightning flared through the windows near the ceiling.

Chris, Aaron and David danced triumphantly in the middle of the front field in the pouring rain, the flashes radiantly illuminating their bodies and the grass.

Aaron ran round in a short circle, his arms outstretched as though he was a plane, his white shirt and trousers soaking wet. David ran in a straight line with his arms outstretched and then took a spin and ran back the way he had come.

Chris danced on the grass, whooping and cheering as he spun round like a ballet dancer. Aaron and David joined him, spinning around, their arms still outstretched. Chris stopped spinning and jumped into the air, pushing his legs wide apart just as another lightning flash flared furiously overhead.

'We got him!' Chris exclaimed in sign, thumping the air.

17

Prison of Silence

"People put barriers up and the [deaf] children could not communicate. They just didn't know where to go."
– MARGARET KENNEDY, lecturer on child abuse; in *Deaf Victims End 40–Year Silence on Child Sex Abuse,* in *The Observer,* 2005 (explaining how the ban on sign language was a critical factor for the abuse).

How long had it been?

Five minutes? Ten? Thirty? An hour?

It was impossible to tell. Basher scowled to himself. He shook his head hard again; the Sellotape on his left cheek loosened a bit and the half bitten apple dropped down a little further from his mouth. He had had to bite and eat half of the apple, putting his nausea aside and forcing himself to swallow some of the rotten flesh, including the squishy bits, the core and the seeds. He had to do it because his open jaws had become tired, his cheeks and mouth hurting. He had shaken his head violently a few times to try to loosen the Sellotape on his cheeks, but it was proving to be a long, slow process. He had already started to get dizzy and had willed himself not to vomit, for fear of puking directly onto the apple that was still stuffed in his mouth. He'd had to stop for a short break.

He twisted his wrists again, but it was no use: the rope was too tight and his wrists were hurting. He knew that trying to loosen his ankles was no use either, and besides, every time he'd tried to loosen them, his wrists hurt even more because of the taut rope between them. He shook his body violently in desperate frustration. His mind screamed loudly.

Bastards! I will have my revenge! Bastards! Bastards!

He exhaled, the warm air from his mouth bouncing back from the half bitten apple. He thought again about the ambush. David had allies, but whom? He didn't see them because they had come from behind in the dark and he'd had no chance. David was quick enough to blindfold him with the sock. He knew there had been two of them. Chris Matthaus was top of his list: he was the only one who wasn't afraid of him. Yes, it would be him, he thought. Who was the other? Dean

Hopkirk? No. Andrew Brener? Not him. He'd had a strong hold on his legs, so it must have been one of those Third or Fourth Formers. Aaron Stephens? Possibly. Yes, it had to be him. He was Chris' best friend and in David's Form. Yes, most definitely him. That English swot was smart enough to have come up with such a plan. Chris, Aaron and David: yes, it all fitted.

He shivered again, feeling the goose pimples on his arms and a chill on his bare back. He felt a sneeze coming on now and he tried to resist it.

He sneezed, and sneezed again. The wetness bounced back from the apple, back into his face; the snot streaming down from his nostrils.

Oh, fuck!

He shook his head violently to shake the wetness from his face. Another of the tape strips on his left cheek loosened, leaving just one more before the apple would drop and hang from the two strips on his right cheek.

Chris – he knew it had been him – had completely cut up his shirt with scissors, so he was naked down to his waist, save for the collar and school tie that were still round his neck. He sighed, knowing that Miss Hogarth and Miss Turner would be pissed off and give him detention. His Ma would too: she once did in a big way when he was six; he could remember it well.

Ma shook Brian hard on his arm and whirled him round. He felt a hard smack on his bottom, then another came. Brian whirled back to Ma, tears flowing down his cheeks. With her other hand, Ma was holding the beige cotton harness all in shreds, the two aids missing. She swung at Brian's head, but he ducked just in time; her hand brushing over him as she almost lost her balance, managing to steady herself by placing her hand on the kitchen sink.

She screamed hysterically at him, her mouth moving fast.

Naughty boy! You tipped this up and lost the bloody hearing aids again!

Basher winced at this memory. It wasn't difficult to lipread her expressive mouthing when she was angry with him. He hadn't damaged the harness, nor lost the aids. He had strayed away from home, wearing the aids on his chest, because he was bored. He hated wearing them, but Ma made him; if he dared not wear them, she would get really angry with him and sometimes hit him. Five young hearing boys from his neighbourhood had ganged up on him close to a low railway viaduct near his home. He knew who they were; they always picked on him. He tried to fight them off using his fists, but he was hampered by the weight on his chest, and by the cords which ran from the aids to his ears and were always in the way of his hands. Two of the young boys easily held him by the back of his harness while their blonde seven–year old leader used him as a punchbag. Every time Brian tried to fight back, he was pulled backwards, his fists waving helplessly at the jeering ringleader. They soon took off the harness and used their penknives to slash the fabric to shreds. Having done this, they took the two metal boxes out of the pockets, dropped them and stomped on them. One of them then chucked them over the viaduct, directly into the path of an approaching London overground train. Brian watched with a mixture of wide–eyed horror and delight when the dark blue steel carriages with slam doors thundered past.

Basher felt an itch on the tip of his nose and instinctively moved his hand to scratch it, quickly realising that he was still tied from behind. He swung his body towards the floor and rubbed his nose on the floor. He swung back and lay there for a moment, beginning to reflect his childhood.

Bethnal Green was a tough East End neighbourhood. Brian Thompson was born at 176, Vallance Road, a tiny three–bedroomed terraced house, on thirtieth of April 1963. He didn't know why he was born there instead of at the hospital. He was the youngest in his family; there was his Ma and Pa; his older sister, Chloe, who was nine when he was born, and his brother, Adrian, seven.

He did not remember much of his first years until he was about five; he knew, though, that he was the only deaf one in the family. He knew that he could not talk like his brother and sister and frustration caused him to behave badly, throwing things, thumping on tables, slamming doors and screaming at Ma and Pa, just to make himself understood. He could not understand anything his Ma and Pa said to him. He spent much of his time in the bedroom that he shared with Adrian, often drawing on paper and in sketchbooks with pencils and crayons; they were his only sanctuary from the trouble and hardship downstairs. Ma and Pa always rowed; Chloe always moaned and Adrian would argue with anyone in the house, though, very rarely with Brian. Money was tight; Ma worked several jobs; at the launderette, in shops up the road and cleaning in pubs. Pa used to be a shipyard worker at the London Docks until it closed down around the time Brian was born; he was now working as a milkman, doing other odd jobs that brought in money. Half of the income never made it through the front door on Friday evenings, though, as Pa would spend it on drink, fags and the dogs. Ma and Pa rowed over two things: money and Brian. Their house had no bathroom, so they used an outhouse in their backyard for the toilet and bathing in a tub, filled with hot water from the kettle, to bath in.

Basher remembered going to the primary school nearby. There, he wore two brown boxes strapped to his chest by a harness; they each had wires attached to hard plastic moulds and one of them had a microphone clipped to it. He absolutely hated them because they were large, heavy and painful to wear, especially for a five–year old; he'd try his best to dump them at home, but Ma made him wear them and would hit him if he refused. At primary school, he was the only deaf child in his class and he misbehaved because he couldn't understand his fellow classmates or the teachers. He always ended up looking at comics, drawing things and playing with toys, just to keep him quiet, and the teachers, happy.

Basher's bladder was starting to ache. His body was still facing down and the lower part of his naked torso was still pressed against the cold wooden floor. He knew that he would not last long, for he had drunk two cans of Shandy Bass in the TV room earlier that evening.

Oh, where the fuck are they? Come on and find me now!

He rocked to and fro like a rocking chair, the rope holding his wrists and ankles behind his back tightened even more. He scowled at how they rubbed, then heaved himself hard to his right and toppled over, landing on his side. Instantly, he felt the pain and stress in his body easing, though it still ached. He became aware that the half–bitten apple was resting on the floor close to his mouth, so rubbed his right cheek against the floor until the stickiness of the Sellotape began to weaken. He rubbed again and the tape loosened. The last piece of tape on his left cheek finally came away. Finally, he was free of that bloody apple! With his chin, he butted the rotten fruit away as hard as he could. It bobbed away into the blind darkness. He breathed a sigh of relief and lay there for a long moment.

Now, where was he? Oh, yes, the bloody heavy hearing aids. His thoughts projected back to a day or two after his fifth birthday; a day that he could never forget.

Brian ran excitedly down the pavement towards his house on Vallance Road with Ma in tow, carrying two carrier bags of shopping and screaming pointlessly at him to stop. The little boy struggled to run in a straight line because of the sheer weight of the two brown box–like aids he was wearing. For a five–year old, it was like carrying two house bricks on his chest. He fell down once or twice, but was soon back on his feet and running again, even before Ma could stop to help him up. He wanted to get home so that he could watch *Andy Pandy* on their tiny black and white television; he knew that it would be coming on now.

He tripped over a loose slab just before his front door and landed badly. His chest and the two aids crashed hard against the pavement, the palm of his hands scraping the rough concrete, while his knees took a bad knock. Brian bawled loudly, tears pouring down his face. Suddenly, a man's hands clasped him and helped him up. When he was on his feet, he looked up, blinking against the sun that was shining behind the tall figure. Another tall man stood next to him. They both had well groomed dark hair, similar facial features and were wearing similar black suits and ties. Their dark sunglasses also looked alike. One of them bent down, his hand brushing the dirt from Brian's arms. The man smiled at him. Brian wiped away his tears and smiled back. The second man bent his knees so that his head was on level with the boy's and his mouth moved to speak to him, but nothing came out; he took a lollipop out of his jacket pocket and gave it to Brian. The first man ruffled the boy's long dark hair and smiled again. Another hand grabbed Brian's hand; he looked up to see it was Ma, who looked quite frightened by the two men. She quickly spoke to them, nodding her head, and dragged Brian towards their front door. Upon entering the house, he looked back at the two men, smiled and waved the lollipop at them. The two men waved back.

Basher never knew who they were until he came to Ewing Hill Park and stumbled across stacks of old copies of *The Times* that were stored away on a low shelf in the library. Mr Williams used to read them every day in his office and would always put them in boxes in the library afterwards. Basher browsed through them once during his first year, just to pass the time, and came across one, which was dated Thursday ninth of May 1968. Its front page announced the arrest of the Kray Twins the day before – Basher recognised the two men in the accompanying black and white photograph. He told everyone at school that he had once met the Krays, and that one of them had given him a lollipop, but no one believed him. He took the news clipping home at Easter and showed it to Adrian. He believed the story because Ma had told him once that the twins used to live next door in number 178; they'd grown up there during the Second World War. They must have come down to visit their old house; it had been a week before their arrest.

Basher thought about Bell's Primary School for the Deaf in Buckhurst, further east in London, which he'd first attended at the age of seven. It was a weekly boarding school – deaf children stayed there from Monday to Friday and went home at weekends. Basher never knew why he'd been sent there, but he supposed that it was easier for his parents to manage at home without him and that at least he was amongst his own kind, rather than with the hearing children at his old primary school. It was there that he picked up some sign language for the first time, though only on the playground, not in the classroom, as signing was not allowed. It was also there that he was fitted with the new, smaller and slightly lighter Philips Chrome aids. He still could remember the name; they didn't last long though, as they were the ones that were thrown over the viaduct the first weekend home after his starting at Bell's.

The school building was a large detached house, which had dark brown bricks, painted white wooden window frames and a black slate roof with three chimneys. It had three floors. The ground floor had three classrooms, a kitchen and dining room; the second floor four bedrooms and a bathroom for the girls; the top floor three bedrooms and a bathroom for the boys. The headmistress, Miss Marlette Bell, the founder of the school, slept in the large bedroom on the second floor; its window overlooked the front playground. She was in her forties, with curly dark hair and big, round spectacles. She cared for and looked after around thirty deaf children, aged between five and twelve, in the evenings like they were her own. She always smiled pleasantly in the mornings, although she would crossly spank the hands or bottoms of any deaf child who dared to sign in the classroom and always told them to use their voices. Mrs Austen also helped in the mornings and evenings. A garage was on the left of the building, but it was rarely used and the children were told that they were not allowed to go inside.

Basher felt his bladder twinge again; it was aching even more; it was now really filling up and he was starting to feel desperate. He tried to block this by thinking back to his early school days.

For the most part, Brian was happy during his first year at the school; he enjoyed himself in the classroom despite having a great deal of trouble trying to understand his teacher, Mrs Evans. He particularly enjoyed playing with his new friends in the playground.

Until *he* came.

He was someone that Basher would never forget. Not for the rest of his life. He shivered and shuddered, not only because of being half naked in the cold gym, but because in front of his closed eyelids, he could see the image of that man. Tall with black hair, he had a rugged beard and slow–burning eyes.

Standing there. Staring. Smiling at him.

Go away!

He remained in his closed eyelids, as if they were film screens.

Bashed sighed. The bastard would never go away. Never. Every time he saw a man with a beard, he always thought about *him*. Even during English lessons; he'd had trouble even looking at Mr Whittle for the last four years because of his beard. Thankfully, though, he'd shaved it off during the summer and that had made things a lot easier. He still couldn't lipread him, though. Gary Portmore grew his first little beard a month ago, but Basher ordered him to shave it off and banned his form mates from growing their own. They didn't understand why, but accepted it because he has the final say as head boy.

Basher recalled the first day back at school after the summer break when he was eight.

'This is Ray Grimes,' Miss Bell announced to Brian's class. The nine deaf children sitting round a large square table turned to the man who was standing next to the headmistress. He waved at them, smiling through his trim, newly–grown black beard. She turned to the blackboard and wrote his name on it before turning back to the children. 'He's now working here. He will mend things around the school.'

Ray Grimes nodded cheerfully and gestured an imaginary hammer and nail.

Miss Bell chortled and beckoned him to follow her to the next room. Grimes waved goodbye to the children.

Basher coughed twice. He was getting really cold. Would he have to stay here all night, he wondered. He hoped not, or he'd freeze to death. He knew he had to get out of the gym hall, and maybe, just maybe, someone might see him at the entrance from one of the windows in the main building. However, he was still blindfolded. He had tried to prise the football sock up several times by rubbing it against the floor, but it was no use: it was too tight around his head. He had no idea where the door into the foyer was anyway. He also thought that even if he did manage to get outside, he'd freeze even more in the pouring rain than he would inside. It must be bedtime by now, he ascertained, so everyone would be in their dorms by now anyway, except for the Fifth Formers. He cursed Chris for putting him through this ordeal. He should have told one of the prefects where he was by now!

His thoughts drifted back to his old school again. He remembered how Grimes was a well–liked and humorous man. He and several of the other children loved him. Not only did he do maintenance jobs around the school, but also helped with many other things, such as putting the boys to bed; driving the children to the local swimming pool in the minibus; playing some games and reading fairy tales. He was quite easy to lipread, even though he had more of a beard than when he first arrived. Towards Christmas, he dressed up as Father Christmas and gave presents to the children.

Everybody loved Ray Grimes, the handyman.

Then in January, everything changed.

Basher swallowed and thought about it: in hindsight, he knew that they'd all been too young to understand then, but he understood now. He vividly remembered one stormy night in his small dormitory, which had six beds occupied by sleeping boys. Because of the storm outside, he couldn't sleep.

Brian rolled into his left side in bed, trying to get to sleep, but it was difficult because of the lightning that was flashing on the drawn cream curtains; he was scared. Then, he felt a slight gust of wind pass by the end of his bed. Brian opened his eyes and squinted into the darkness; a large, dark figure was approaching the bed opposite his, which belonged to Reginald Adamson, Brian's eight–year old classmate. The figure hunched over him and Brian could just about make out that he was pulling the blanket and bedsheets away. Reginald seemed to struggle against the dark figure, who Brian thought might be Grimes. Who else would it be? The only two adults who lived in the school were Miss Bell and Grimes. Another lightning bolt flashed again, briefly illuminating the room, and Brain saw clearly that it was Grimes; he was holding the boy's body. Maybe Reginald was afraid of the storm like he was and Grimes was calming him down, Brian thought. He began to close his eyes again to sleep when he saw that Grimes was doing something to the boy, but he couldn't see properly in the darkened room. He slowly lifted his head, still keeping his body low; he thought he could almost see Grimes pulling something away from Reginald's still struggling body. Was that his pyjamas bottoms? Had Reg wet his bed again, he wondered. Brian rested his head back on the pillow, turned over to his other side and went to sleep.

Basher's mind circled; that first night, it wasn't obvious to him and he'd thought nothing of it then. However, Grimes came back two nights later and loomed over Joey Mitchell's bed, next to Brian's – he was already wide awake as he had just been to the toilet – and Grimes did the same thing to Joey as he had done to Reginald. Brian was unable to see what he was doing because he was standing between the two beds with his back to him, but there was no storm that night.

Basher thought about Melanie Tully. He smiled, remembering his childhood sweetheart; she was a year younger than Brian and they got along well. She had blond pigtails, rosy cheeks and, always, a mischievous grin. Brian was amazed to learn that she had deaf parents and a sister and brother who were also deaf. It was from her that Brian learned sign language and they both loved playing together in the playground, especially hopscotch. However, on this particular cold day in early February, she was different.

Brian, wearing a thick dark coat, woolly bobble hat and gloves, jumped and hopped across the chalked numeric hopscotch squares, watched by a group of expectant children behind him. His left foot landed on the forbidden square where the stone was, but he quickly moved it to the next square, hoping that no one saw him. When he was finished, he turned to let Helen Holden, who had freckles and ginger hair, take her turn.

'You cheated!' Helen said, chuckling and pointing at the forbidden square.

'No! Never!' Brian responded, shaking his head and smiling.

'Yes, you did!' She countered, nodding and laughing. 'My daddy's a policeman. He'll put you in jail for cheating!'

Brian chuckled. He caught sight of Melanie, sitting alone on a low concrete fence near the school's gates, dressed in winter clothes and a woolly hat. Brian trotted over and stood in front of her.

'Play?' Brian pointed at the hopscotch.

Melanie shook her head and hunched her arms around her body, as if to cradle herself.

'Are you poorly?' Brian asked, noting her mood.

Melanie shook her head again. She took a passing glance to her right. Brian followed her eyes, to see Grimes sweeping the tarmac with a broom further down the playground. Brian shrugged and let her be, returning to the game.

Basher lay idle for a long moment, trying to remember other instances, and suddenly recalled one: the paper plane. He couldn't remember when it was, but knew it was some time during the following spring or summer.

On his own, Brian kicked the football against the wall. He stopped the ball with his foot and looked around the playground, wondering about Leigh Marshall and Reginald Adamson; they were supposed to be playing with him, but they were nowhere to be seen. He spotted Sonia Hill, who he knew was in their class, and waved at her.

'Leigh and Reg? Where?' he asked.

Sonia, a dark haired girl, shook her head, shrugging. 'Molly's not here either. You know where she is?' she asked, signing her name sign.

Brian shook his head. He resumed his kicking. The ball rebounded and bobbed away from him, towards the small iron gates. He ran after it, stopping it just as it crossed the gates, and picked it up. He turned to face the school building and saw something flying out from an open window on the first floor. It was Miss Bell's bedroom window. He quickly glanced around the playground and saw that Miss Bell was there, supervising evening playtime. He glanced back at the window; his gaze followed the object that was gliding away from it; it was heading over the low concrete wall at the front. Was that a paper plane, he asked himself. He dropped the ball and he ran through the open gate, keeping his eye on the plane as it flew. He giggled with excitement as he ran along the pavement, hoping to catch it. Finally, it landed on and Brian picked it up. He looked up at the room where it had come from, squinting, and could see through the half open window that Leigh was looking down at him, his head and shoulders barely visible. He appeared to be bare–chested and looked frightened, but Brian couldn't be sure. He also saw someone else passing behind him. Was it Reg? Suddenly, a man's hand grabbed Leigh's shoulder, his face concealed behind the curtains, and pushed the boy out of sight. The half open window was snapped shut and the curtains drawn. Brian stared at the window, wondering what was going on. He looked down at the paper plane and saw that it had two words written, hastily and in pencil, on top of each wing: *MAN RUDE*.

Basher then remembered another instance. It was during the minibus journey back from the local swimming pool.

Brian was sitting in the row of seats directly behind Grimes, who was driving. He was reading *Dandy* when he glanced up to see that Helen was no longer sitting on the passenger seat next to Grimes and wondered where she was. The children always fought over who got to sit at the front, but on this occasion Grimes said that Helen would be the one, much to their disappointment. Brian leaned forward to peer over the double passenger seat and saw that Helen was slumped across it with her head resting on Grimes' lap. He couldn't see her head from where he was because the driver was obstructing his view. She must be sleepy, Brian thought, and she needed to rest on his lap. However, he also noticed that she was not laying still; her body was slightly moving up and down and Grimes' left hand was resting on her back while his other held the steering wheel. Brian slumped back on his seat to resume reading his comic, thinking nothing of it. He glanced up briefly at the rear view mirror and saw Grimes' eyes staring at him.

Basher buckled. The gym hall was now like one big freezer. Feeling goose pimples on both arms, he shivered. His bladder was now full to bursting. *How much longer?* he groaned to himself. Then, the memory of the day after the minibus drive came back to him: Grimes had finally come for him.

'Come with me, both of you,' Grimes instructed, beckoning at Brian and Melanie to follow him.

Brian and Melanie grudgingly rose to their feet and followed him from the sitting room, which was at the back of the school, towards the door that led to the garage. They went inside; the garage was also Grimes' office, with a desk and a chair; rows of shelves that stored tools; and a worktop.

Basher recalled that it was during the evening, about an hour before bedtime, and he had been playing Snap with Melanie while the other children played other games. Miss Bell was out for the evening. Grimes told him and Melanie that they would be playing a new game and the reward was plenty of sweets. He told them to stamp on some of the school's silvery milk bottle tops which were spread around the floor. The tops had to be flat, Grimes told them, so that they could be given away to charity. Basher remembered stamping them with excitement; Grimes had told them to strip their clothes off while they did it.

Brian, wearing his vest and underpants, knelt and scooped up a batch of newly flattened milk bottle tops to show to Grimes. He rose, turned and froze. The silvery tops slipped through his little fingers, his eyes widened with shock and his mouth opened.

Basher still had that image at the back of his mind; it was the first time he had ever seen one. It was inside Melanie's mouth. Basher could never forget what Grimes had said and gestured to him: *It's like sucking an ice lolly.*

He soon came for him.

Basher felt repulsed. He didn't understand it back then and had let Grimes touch him and do what he wanted to him. Ever since that day though, he'd had bad dreams about it; he was now old enough to know that it was wrong. That was not the only time Grimes had touched him, Basher grimaced. He'd come back for him repeatedly over the next two years. Basher had always tried hard to bury these bad memories, but they still came back to him.

Basher smiled wearily as he thought about Ewing Hill Park's annual Christmas party two years back, when he'd been in Form Three. Some hearing girls from local schools had come to join them; many of the boys tried to woo them, chat to them and snog them. He remembered that the next morning, the Fifth Formers were patting the back of the proud head boy, Theodore Elliott, to congratulate him for something that Basher didn't understand. When he'd asked what was going on, he was told that Theodore had lost his virginity with one of the hearing Sixth Form girls the night before. He didn't understand what that meant until it was explained to him. The older boys said he too would lose his own virginity when he was a little older; *then* he understood.

He had already lost his virginity. At nine, with Melanie, watched by Grimes. He could not say anything to anyone about it for fear of being embarrassed, and no one would have believed him anyway. Just like they didn't with the Kray twins. This was the first time he realised that the things he'd done at his old school were wrong. He did, however, have a private chat with Mr McShane, who was the only adult who could sign, about it in a general way. The art teacher explained that this sort of thing was totally wrong, criminal and evil.

Basher exhaled hard, his nose running from the surrounding coldness. He licked the wet substance that had reached his lips and thought about what Mr McShane had said. At first, he didn't understand why it was wrong; it didn't feel like it at the time. There were times he'd enjoyed it; other times when he hadn't. Melanie wasn't the only girl he'd had sex with; Molly and Helen were two of the others. He didn't like doing it with the boys though, such as Leigh and Reg, but Grimes made him. When he first arrived at Ewing Hill Park, he began to realise why, from the way several boys bullied that Fifth Former, Jacques Magnat. He understood it was filthy and hated it even more, despised queers and poofs big time.

For the past two years, since the art teacher's explanation, he had struggled to even understand *why* he did those things at Bell's. Sometimes, he had felt good about it, but other times, he felt guilty, confused and ashamed. He couldn't tell or talk to anyone about it, for fear of being ridiculed. He had often considered telling Mr McShane about it, but couldn't bring himself to, though he came close at one point. He knew he wasn't a bright boy, but that didn't make anything better. It was a secret that would stay with him for the rest of his life. He wondered about Miss Bell; had she known what Grimes was doing? Why didn't she put a stop to it? What about the other teachers? Surely, they must have *known* something about what Grimes was doing to the children. Perhaps Grimes was too clever for any of them to suspect? Nonetheless, he married her and Miss Bell became Mrs Bell–Grimes.

The worst thing happened to him shortly after the summer, when he was ten, Basher remembered grimly. It was during the journey back from a day out at London Zoo.

Brian was sitting on the passenger seat of the minibus, reading *Beano,* and Grimes was driving while the children yapped and signed noisily at the back. Brian was preoccupied with the comic when, suddenly, it was snatched from his hands. Grimes grabbed Brian's right wrist to pull him over. Brian resisted when he saw Grimes's erect penis protruding through his open fly. He didn't want to do it again. He was more interested in reading the comic, but Grimes pulled him in closer and he resisted again. The black Ford Transit swerved as Grimes tried to control the steering wheel with his other hand. He yelled angrily at him and pointed down, demanding that he play with it. Brian thought about it for a moment, then nodded at the handyman. He moved closer to Grimes, who in turn, smiled broadly and placed his left hand back on the steering wheel to use both hands to drive.

With his fist, Brian suddenly pounded hard on the erection. Grimes screamed wildly, the minibus swerving violently. Brian continued thumping hard. Grimes grabbed the boy's grinning face with his left hand to push him away, but he bit hard on the fingers like a frenzied dog. The minibus rocked again and Brian quickly looked back at the wide–eyed children, laughing at the excitement of the bumpy ride. He grabbed his seat to control his balance, again using his clenched left hand to pound the now limp penis. He bit Grimes' hand hard again to get it away from his face. Grimes lost control of the minibus and he screamed.

Basher could still recall the crash into the lamppost; fortunately, he and the other children were unhurt. Grimes took a bad knock to his forehead, though. Basher thought solemnly about what happened afterwards in Grimes' garage.

Brian, lying face down in her lap, howled loudly as the fuming Mrs Bell–Grimes spanked his bare bottom in a frenzy. She finished with one last hard spank before pushing him to the floor. He wailed loudly, tears flowing freely down his cheeks, and pulled his underpants and trousers up. His bottom ached. He looked up through tear–stained eyes to see Mrs Bell–Grimes sitting on the chair, still red with anger. Grimes, who had a dressing on his forehead, stood behind her, grinning broadly through his black beard.

'You are a *very* naughty boy!' the headmistress scowled at Brian, gesturing an imaginary steering wheel and jerking it hard. 'Grabbing the wheel was very stupid and dangerous! You could have hurt everyone!'

'No, not true!' Brian shook his head, pointing at Grimes behind her and signed.

'He–'

Mrs Bell–Grimes slapped his signing hands hard. 'Don't sign! Use your voice!'

Brian became silent. He knew he could not speak and the headmistress could not understand sign. He glanced over at Grimes, who was still beaming behind his wife's back.

Brian was trapped in his own prison of silence.

Mrs Bell–Grimes rose to her feet, placing her hands on her hips. 'No supper for you tonight, Brian, and it's straight to bed now!'

Brian wailed loudly, still feeling the throbbing of his bottom on the floor. Mrs Bell–Grimes turned to leave the garage, leaving Brian and Grimes alone in the gloomily lit room. When the principal was gone, Grimes closed the door and turned the key to lock it. He turned to the still weeping boy on the floor. Brian could just make out enough through his wet eyes to lipread him.

'You hurt me, you shitty little basher,' Grimes pointed at his groin as he limped towards the boy. He gestured a thumping hand and fingerspelled it. 'B–A–S–H–E–R. Now I'm going to hurt *yours!*'

Brian crawled backwards into a corner, clutching his trousers and cowering. Trapped. He wailed loudly in fear. With the solitary light behind him, Grimes's dark shadow grew and loomed threateningly over the cornered boy.

Basher felt a tear fall from his right eye and roll down through the gap between his eyes and the blindfold. Six years ago, and to this day he could still feel those big hands roughing him up as he tried to fight back, ripping his clothes off and touching him like never before. He could still feel the pain inside him: it was the worst thing Grimes had ever done to him. He had acquired the Basher nickname that became part of him that night, though he never told anyone why. Fortunately, that was the last time Grimes did anything to him, thanks to Adrian and what took place at home the following weekend.

Brian stuck a drawing pin into his bedroom wall to hang a freshly sketched picture on it. He stepped back, sitting on his bed to admire the vast gallery of pencilled and crayoned artwork scattered around the wall; it ranged from drawings of Valance Road, with different scenarios viewed from his bedroom window, to portraits of his family, characters he'd seen on television and some pictures from school. Brian was a naturally talented artist; he spent most of his time at home drawing. The latest was of a menacing looking figure, hunched and monstrous, with sharp claws and crazy long black hair, complemented by a long, ragged black beard and snarling, sharp pointed teeth.

He pulled up his long–sleeved shirt to take another look at a couple of bruises on his chest and another on his left arm. The throbbing pain in his genitals had ceased, but they were still sore. Suddenly, he felt movement to his left; he turned to see his sixteen–year old brother standing in the doorway, wearing his unkempt school uniform. Brian quickly pulled down his top, but Adrian had been there long enough to see the bruises. He sat on the bed next to Brian, dumped his tattered satchel on the floor and chucked a packet of cigarettes and a box of matches onto the small table close by. He turned to his ten–year old brother, concerned.

'Who's been bullying yer at school?' Adrian asked. Brian said nothing. 'Tell me 'is name and I'll sort 'im out. That's what big bruvvers are for.'

Brian shook his head, lowering it, closing his eyes and clasping his hands between his legs. He felt so ashamed of himself; he could not bring himself to tell his brother the truth. After a long moment, Adrian placed his hand on Brian's jaw and gently twisted his head to face him. He leant over slightly and made sure Brian was looking at his lips.

'All right, have it yer way,' Adrian said, speaking slowly and clearly, making sure he was making himself understood. 'I'll teach ya how to fight back. I've fought with some big wankers at my school. It will 'urt, yeah, but you'll be stronger each time. Would yer like that, little bugger?'

Brian stared at Adrian for a long moment, thinking about it.

Adrian had taught him to defend himself; how to fight back hard; how to use different ways to hurt people and, even, how to be a school bully. Every weekend at home, Adrian taught him more.

Every time Grimes came for him, he fought back as hard as he could. Punched him, kicked him, bit him and screamed loudly. The more he fought back, the less Grimes came after him. He tried hard to protect his sweetheart, Melanie, from him, too; sometimes he succeeded and sometimes he failed. Grimes continued his "games" with other children at the school, but quickly left Brian well alone.

Basher then remembered that Grimes had suddenly disappeared towards the end of November one year. He still didn't know why, though he did recall that it happened shortly after Helen Holden had suddenly left the school for no apparent reason. There was not even a goodbye.

The local mayor's visit happened during that time, Basher vaguely remembered. The children happily waved their union jacks at the man, who was bald and had thick grey sideburns and a large paunch, and wore a medallion. A proud Mrs Bell–Grimes accompanied him. The mayor told a story in the classroom that Basher did not think any of the children understood, though he did feel the vibrations on the table caused by his loud voice.

The following March or April, or around that time, Grimes came back; Basher had always wondered where he had been during those months.

He started doing it again.

Basher grimaced as he remembered his twelfth birthday the following year: it was a day he could never forget.

In the school playground, Brian was playing with his yo–yo when Melanie approached him and stood watching. After a brief moment, she waved at him.

'Happy birthday!' she greeted him in sign. She leant forward, pecked Brian's cheek and stepped back, smiling. 'You're twelve now!'

'You'll be eleven next month!' Brian said, already knowing her birthday.

She nodded. 'You'll be leaving for a new school this July.'

'You know?'

'Yes, Miss Austen told my class this morning. A big school. Where?'

Brian shrugged. 'It's on other side of London. Waltbridge. I went there last month for the exams. You pass it and you go there. Mrs Bell–Grimes told me on Monday that I passed!'

'Did you cheat?' Melanie slid a thumb down her cheek, smiling expectantly.

Brian shrugged ambiguously.

'Is it good?'

'Yeah. All boys!'

'No girls?'

'No.'

'Can the teachers sign there?'

'No.'

'Oh,' she said. 'I'll miss you!'

'Me too.' Brian looked at his sweetheart with affection. A shadow loomed over them, interrupting; they turned to see Grimes. He directed his eyes at Melanie.

'Come with me,' he commanded with his finger.

Brian immediately knew what he was going to do with her, so he quickly positioned himself between Grimes and Melanie, sternly guarding her. Grimes chuckled and shook his head.

'Move away, Brian.' He waved him away.

Brian stood firm. Grimes advanced, grabbed his shirt and pushed him away hard. Brian stumbled back and Grimes moved in for the girl. Brian pounced back at Grimes, the force of his now bigger body causing the headmistress' husband to stagger back. Grimes quickly recovered, clamping his hand on Brian's neck and pushing him against the brick wall behind.

'You be quiet, boy,' Grimes warned, locking the boy's neck against the wall. With the other hand, he laid a hushing finger on his lips. 'Stop me again and you'll be in big trouble! Understand?' He slammed Brian against the wall again, to give him a clear message. 'You're a bad boy here. No one will believe you!'

Grimes released him. Brian glared accusingly at the man. With a final mocking smile, Grimes turned to the girl and motioned for her to follow him. Melanie refused, but Grimes grabbed her arm and pulled her across the playground towards the school. The other children watched them in silence. Brian raged and ran towards the entrance door, but Grimes and Melanie had already entered, and the door slammed shut on him. Mrs Evans, supervising playtime, strode over to him and slapped his head to reprimand him.

'Him … hurt her again!' Brian pleaded in sign, pointing at the closed door.

Mrs Evans shook her head, not understanding him. 'I don't understand what–'

'Bad man!' Brian screamed at her, signing feverishly. 'Bad! Hurt her!'

'Stop it!' the bewildered teacher shook the boy's shoulders and slapped his head again. 'Stop signing at me!'

Brian lost it, incensed and frustrated at not making himself understood. He glanced down and found a large chunk of broken concrete lying on the tarmac. He picked it up, aimed it at the frosted corrugated window in the entrance door and threw it before the teacher could stop him. The large glass pane exploded, thousands of shards spraying inwards. Almost immediately, Mrs Bell–Grimes popped into view through the jagged opening, her face twisted red with anger.

Basher thought about what had happened next: he'd been sent home immediately, told not to return until the following Tuesday, after the May Day Bank Holiday weekend. Ma screamed and shouted at him about what he had done and sent him straight to his room without any supper. Basher gritted his teeth at the frustration of not being able to communicate with Ma and Pa; he had tried to write a note to tell them about Grimes, despite his poor command of English, but they didn't believe him. He could not understand *anything* that Ma and Pa said to him. He blamed himself for everything. But at least something positive had come to him the next day; Basher smiled.

Brian stood watching the small black and white television in the living room with keen interest. A female newsreader who he knew was Angela Rippon was on screen; she was new, and was the first woman to present the BBC Six O'Clock News. She was speaking, but no words came to him. He tried to lipread her, but it was impossible. Some news footage appeared, showing the frantic movements of what appeared to be American soldiers and other people trying to board helicopters that were parked inside a large compound. There were masses of panicking, frightened people pushing up against the high metal fences surrounding it. The people inside the compound were rushing around, screaming, the soldiers wielding their rifles and barking instructions. Beyond the fencing and the crowds were buildings that Brian knew were of the Far East. He knew that there was a war going on in Vietnam, but he had never understood why, or why these people were trying to get onto the US Air Force helicopters. The camera jerked furiously, as though the cameraman was being pushed around. A small group of men, women and children, holding paper documentation in their hands, ran for their lives towards the waiting aircraft. The camera swung to follow them. The television switched back to Rippon. Brian was frustrated at not being able to understand anything from the television; he looked at Pa, who was sitting on his usual armchair, watching the news as well. He wanted to ask him about it, but he knew Pa would not bother explaining anything to him, even if he could make himself understood.

A hand ruffled Brian's thick, wavy hair from behind. He smiled and turned, smiling more when he saw Adrian. His tall nineteen–year old brother had undergone a complete transformation. Both sides of Adrian's head had been shaved, leaving a tidy Mohawk with an array of vibrant colours on top; gold earrings hung from both earlobes; a smaller gold ring pierced his right nostril, and he was wearing a black leather jacket, a white tee shirt, blue jeans with rips in them and a pair of tough–looking boots.

'Hey kiddo,' Adrian greeted, grinning at Brian's surprise. He addressed his new appearance. 'What do ya think?'

Brian pointed at his brother, gesturing at his clothing with great curiosity and mouthed: *What's that?* Adrian understood him perfectly.

'It's called punk,' Adrian said.

Bu?

'No, no, not "Bu"!' Adrian shook his head, smiling, understanding his little brother's mucky speech. He wrote the name in the air with his right index finger. 'P–U–N–K.' Brian nodded, understanding him. 'It's a new thing that's just comin' out here in London–'

Adrian turned his head to Pa, who said something to him that Brian obviously didn't hear. He observed the angry exchange of words between them. Adrian finished the brief conversation with a two–fingered gesture at Pa and returned to his curious younger brother.

'Ignore Pa, he can be a bloody turd!'

He glanced over Brian's head at the television, saw Angela Rippon and looked back down at Brian with a mischievous grin. 'Ya still watch her, don't ya?'

Brian shook his head, trying not to grin, but Adrian nodded at him, gesturing breasts. 'Reckon she got nice titties, bruvver?'

Brian chortled and pointed at the television, gesturing about the news footage he had just seen, mimicking the helicopters, American soldiers and the people. Adrian understood.

'The bloody Americans pissed off outta Vietnam yesterday. Do yer know where that is? Near China, yer know,' he paused for Brian to nod. 'The war's over now. Finished! On yer birthday, huh?'

Brian took a quick glance at the television, but the news had moved on to another news item and Harold Wilson, who Brian knew was the British prime minister, was on instead. Taking no particular interest, Brian turned back to Adrian. He noticed that Adrian was holding a carrier bag.

'Sorry I missed yer birthday yesterday, Brian,' Adrian said, making sure that Brian was properly reading his lips. 'I got this for ya.'

Adrian pulled open the carrier bag and took out a pair of boots, similar to his own, and gave them to Brian, who held them by their stout, rugged bases. He read the label: Doctor Marten's. He looked up at Adrian, pleasantly surprised.

'Happy birthday! Twelve now, huh? Yer growin' up real fast! Size seven?'

Brian pressed the boots against his chest with his arms to free up his hands and held up five fingers on his left hand and one on the other.

'Six? Oh, well, ya'll grow into 'em. Stuff some of Pa's newspapers in 'em and ya'll be alright. Feel the front. Go on, mate,' Adrian encouraged him. Brian felt the hardness of the front rims. 'Hard as rock, they are. Kick up the balls.'

Adrian playfully kicked his right boot up to demonstrate, before clutching his own groin and chuckling. 'Ow! Ya know. Painful!'

Brian cradled his birthday present, feeling really pleased. Adrian tapped his head to get his attention.

'I 'ear yer goin' to a new school this September. What was it? Oh yeah, Ewing Hill Park? A boarding school or summat. Yer goin' to a posh school! Clever lad!'

Basher thought about his own hair; what had they done with it? He smelled modelling paint – had they painted it? He had tried to resist by fiercely shaking his head to evade the brushes – two brushes, he figured – but Chris had held his head in a vice-like lock. It had to have been Chris because he was the only one strong enough to do that. He felt some of the longer strands of his hair being pulled up and stuck together with paint. He figured that they were making his hair punky, but with modelling paint? Shit, that'd be hell to wash off, he cursed.

They'd also painted something on his bare back: letters or something. It was impossible to decipher what these letters were, although he thought he'd made out a few of them – *P*, *F* and *N* maybe – there were about eight letters in total, he believed.

I'll have my revenge!

Basher wriggled hard again in anger and frustration, trying to loosen the tight rope behind him, hurting his wrists and ankles, but it was no use. How long had he been here now? It felt like forever.

The Doctor Marten's, he reminisced again.

Brian treasured them like they were part of him. He wore them proudly around the house and outside on the streets. He was an inch or two taller because of the boots' deep, sturdy heels. Once, when he was out on the streets, he met those five hearing boys, now in their early teens, who had tormented him in the past. Robby, the gang's blond ringleader – he knew the name from Adrian – wanted the boots, but Brian gestured that he'd have to fight for them. So, he and Robby fought with their fists, kicked and wrestled. Brian won. He fiercely urged the other four boys to come and fight him too, but they ran away while their thirteen–year old leader lay on the pavement, battered with blood everywhere. Brian kicked Robby hard in the side with his boot, giving him a final message that he was now the king of the street.

Basher guffawed at the memory. Ever since the fight, the five boys had left him alone; he would sometimes encounter them during the school holidays, but they didn't bother him. However, last summer, shortly after Basher finished his third term, Robby, who was now sixteen and a skinhead, found him standing by the black metal fencing outside St John's Church in Bethnal Green.

The two teenage boys were initially hesitant with each other, but Robby broke the ice. He wrote on his pack of Marlboros with his pencil to say how sorry he was to hear about Adrian's death that May, and said that his older brother, Keith, was a mate of Adrian's from school. He offered Brian his first ever cigarette as a peace offering and he gladly accepted it. At first, he had coughed and felt sick from it, but Robby gradually taught him how to smoke properly, like a man, via a series of gestures. Although the communication between them was strained, Brian managed to teach his hearing counterpart to fingerspell the alphabet, so that they could fingerspell words to each other, along with some basic signs.

Basher revelled at his new found friendship with Robby, cemented on that very day, and they remained good mates after he discovered the shocking truth about Adrian's death.

'Oh, I'm sorry, I thought you knew!' Robby said. Brian easily read his lips because of what Robby had written in the remaining space on the torn up cigarette pack, as they puffed away on the last two cigarettes. Robby had muttered something to him about his brother that he was unable to lipread at first. Initially, he thought Robby had said *Aero*, as in the chocolate bar, but the penny dropped when he eventually wrote it down.

Basher rested the side of his head on the cold floor, dispirited. He didn't understand why Adrian had been ill for the two years leading up to his untimely death last May. One minute he seemed fine, the next he was as white as a sheet. Sometimes he behaved well, sometimes he didn't, and he always rowed with Ma and Pa. Adrian sometimes smiled at him, and sometimes he snapped for no reason. He deteriorated over time until he was no longer the older brother he looked up to and loved. He had put this down to Adrian being ill and hoped he would get better. He didn't. Ma eventually wrote down one word to explain it to him: cancer. He believed her. At the funeral, which took place at Stoke Newington Crematorium, he was the only deaf person amongst a small number of people in black and he did not understand anything that was being said. He cried a lot. Everybody chatted at the wake afterwards, but he was the only one who was silent. No one could talk to him; some had patted him on the back to mutter their sympathies, silently nodding, smiling sadly and muttering words that he couldn't understand. Ma, Pa and Chloe never really talked to him about Adrian's death, but how could they? He had been frustrated by this, but it had eventually passed and his return to Ewing Hill Park the next day had made it easier for him to move on. Everybody at school was sympathetic, even Chris and Aaron.

Basher flashed forward to the day that he and Robby became mates;, he could remember seeing Robby's disbelieving look upon realising that his new fifteen–year old friend had not been told the whole truth.

Robby took Brian to see one of his older friends at a squat in Stepney, so that he could see for himself that Adrian had been one of them. He saw it with his own eyes and it sickened him. Brian ran back home, agitated, and lashed out at Ma and Pa in the kitchen. Ma and Pa couldn't understand his aggrieved signing or his slurred speech, so he hastily scribbled it down on the notepad he always used with his parents. He knew that his English wasn't very good, but they understood some of it. Ma tried to dismiss him by writing that they did not want to talk about it. In a fit of rage, Brian tipped the breakfast table over, sending the ceramic plates, cutlery and glass sauce bottles flying. He stormed upstairs into his bedroom and spent the rest of the day and evening alone there, crying for his dead brother.

It was not cancer; it was a heroin overdose, Basher sadly recalled. He hadn't understood it all at first until Robby had explained, writing on the notepad that Adrian had been on drugs since he was seventeen. He had started with marijuana, then cocaine, before moving up to heroin. He overdid it by accident. Basher remembered seeing some track marks on Adrian's arm, but had assumed they were to do with those needles that helped fight his cancer. He was still bitter towards his parents for that. Chloe had known as well; that slut didn't bother telling him either. *Why, why, why?* Adrian was the only one in the family that he looked up to and he knew that Adrian had cared for him, but now he was gone. He missed him terribly.

Basher sighed, wishing someone would hurry up and find him in the gym, as he was now getting really desperate; his full bladder was screaming now, weighing him down on the cold floor. He blocked the desperation with his memory of his last day at Bell's school.

'Promise you'll write?' Melanie asked, looking directly into Brian's eyes expectantly.

'Yes, I will,' answered Brian, crossing his chest. 'You will too?'

Melanie nodded, also crossing her chest and smiling. Brian smiled back, but they were both sad smiles. Brian turned to see the punk Adrian standing, smoking a cigarette, over the road from the school gates where Brian and Melanie were. He had come to collect him. Brian turned back to his sweetheart, who was giggling.

'Your brother looks funny!' she said.

Brian shrugged, not really bothered; he was used to it by now. He glanced across the playground, which was filled with children, their parents and teachers bidding their farewells, to see Grimes leaning against the front doorway, his hands in his trouser pockets and his right leg slightly over his left. Brian thought he saw the handyman sneer, but he couldn't be sure because of his black beard. Brian looked back at Melanie, concerned for her.

'Don't let him hurt you again,' Brian pleaded. 'One more year.'

Melanie bowed her head in helplessness.

Basher remembered writing his first letter to her from Ewing Hill Park to say that he liked his new school; he had made new friends, especially Gary and Timothy, and the teachers were rubbish but he enjoyed the evenings and weekends. He included a portrait of Melanie that he'd drawn from memory, and even drew a love heart next to it.

She never wrote back. He wrote again a month later, but again she did not reply. He wrote again, and still didn't hear from her. Had his letters arrived at his old school – it was the only address he knew to use write to her – or had Grimes taken them? He always collected the post from the postman at the gates each morning. Or, had Melanie lost interest in him? No, she wouldn't have, because they were sweethearts, so it must be Grimes. After a year, he gave up, knowing that Melanie must have left Bell's for another school, though he didn't know where it might be, or where she lived. He thought about her now and then over the next four and half years. Perhaps one day he would meet her again, he thought.

A tiny beam of light suddenly shone through the gap between the blindfold and his nose. Was that the gym lights? He forced his eyes open against the tight fabric and peered down. Yes, the gym lights were on! He then felt the pattering of feet on the floor and he wondered to whom they belonged. He knew there was more than one person, for he could feel their presence around him.

Whoever it was stood in silence for a long moment. They were probably laughing at him, Basher thought, but he had little patience; his bladder was on the verge of bursting and he was desperate to dash to the toilets in the changing room.

Oh come on, help me! Basher mouthed at whoever it was, knowing they could lipread him … assuming they were boys, not staff. But still they stood and did nothing. Frustration sank in.

Fuck it! Come on! he mouthed again, this time expressively loud.

Suddenly, someone pushed him face down the floor, then a pair of hands began to untie the knots on his wrists while another pair of hands did likewise with the blindfold knot at the back of his head.

18

A Moment of Chris–tmas

"Sometimes if you want to see a change for the better, you have to take things into your own hands."

– CLINT EASTWOOD

Chris, Aaron and David turned into the front hall, brimming with pride. They slowed their pace when they saw Basher heading their way from the lobby. His hair was frazzled, cut almost down to his scalp, with some of the red, blue and white modelling paint still visible.

He growled silently at the grinning trio as he began to approach them, but paused when something caught his eye. He turned to the school's noticeboard, pushing his way through a small group of boys who were looking at what he had noticed, and he winced. Pinned to the corkboard, amongst other notices, was a thermal photocopied sheet showing three monochrome Polaroid snapshots of Basher naked to his waist, save for the collar and tie around his neck, blindfolded, wrists and ankles bound behind his back and gagged by an apple stuck to his mouth with Sellotape. His hair stuck out in several spikes, coloured shades of black and grey. The first photograph had him in full view, with part of the gym visible. The second one was a close up of his face with the blindfold and the apple. The third one was of his back, which had painted words on it: *PUNK FUNK*.

Basher pulled down the sheet, smelling its fresh thermal aroma, knowing that the trio must have secretly used the school's large new thermal photocopying machine. He thought briefly about last night's ordeal; his form mates had found him shortly after Chris had tipped them off. Gary figured out that Basher had only spent an hour in the gym, but it had felt so much longer than that. They never stopped winding him up afterwards. As soon as he was free, he bolted to the toilet in the changing room to mercifully relieve himself. He winced at the memory of Tom scrubbing hard on his back with a scrubbing brush to remove the offending painted letters, while Dwight tried his best to remove the paint from his hair, having to cut some out with scissors. Gary and Timothy had taunted him by dancing around performing as punk rockers. Miss Turner further added to his woes by slapping him with a detention when he presented her with his shredded shirt. He didn't know what "funk" meant, so Timothy looked it up in a dictionary and said that one meaning was "coward".

Basher briefly glimpsed another notice that was pinned next to the intimidating sheet. It read: *Tuesday 30th October. £2 REWARD. If you know who vandalised my bedroom door, please see me, Mr Schneider.* Basher ignored it, having no interest; someone had painted a red swastika on Schneider's bedroom door in the staff's quarters last night. Mr Schneider had screamed his head off about it in assembly that morning and Basher couldn't help but secretly laugh when he and his form mates watched Gary mimicking the pissed off maths teacher as he signed the screaming words. Basher turned to the three grinning protagonists, but stopped in his tracks when Mr Langston strolled between him and the trio. The headmaster paused mid–stride and turned to Basher, dismayed at what he was seeing.

'Brian! What happened to your hair?' he asked firmly.

Basher was stuck. David confidently stepped forward and pointed at Basher. 'He painted his hair. He wanted to be a punk funk!'

Basher didn't catch what David had said, cursing at him for speaking. 'What did you say to him?'

'My office, Brian!' Mr Langston ordered him, pointing needlessly in the direction of his office. '*Now!*'

The headmaster marched away. Basher gritted his teeth and followed, but not before turning to the trio: 'I will have my revenge. That's a promise!'

Chris' unlikely friendship with David had blossomed over time. He was initially reluctant about it because he felt he already had enough friends; especially with Aaron. However, he slowly warmed to David, with Aaron's encouragement, and eventually realised that he was not the stupid fat boy he appeared to be.

Chris looked down at the box on the table, containing the smashed Avro Lancaster Bomber model.

'That's the plane Basher smashed two months ago,' Aaron explained. 'It can be repaired, but David didn't want to do it in case Basher wrecked it again.'

'So?' Chris shrugged, folding his arms and glanced around the small Hobbies Room before turning back to Aaron.

'We'll repair it.'

Chris chortled. 'Are you joking? It's … finished!'

'Please?' Aaron pleaded. 'It would mean a lot to him.'

Chris sighed wearily. He looked at the box again, pondering.

They spent all evening painstakingly repairing the model plane piece by piece; Aaron glued a section of the fuselage together; Chris carefully stuck one of the engines on the wing and corrected its position; Aaron returned to the Hobbies Room, carrying two glasses of orange squash and gave one to Chris who happily downed it; Chris carefully placed the second wing onto the fuselage. *Hold it there,* Chris silently commanded, but the wing flopped down. Chris muttered to himself in frustration. Finally, towards bedtime, they did it.

David came in, his eyes and spectacles covered by Aaron's hands, guiding him from behind towards the table. He let go when they got there and David looked down at the newly repaired model in disbelief.

'Did you both ...?' he asked, his eyes widening at his new friends. They both nodded. David quickly moved to Chris and hugged him. Chris felt a little uncomfortable. David turned to Aaron and hugged him as well before returning to the model. Aaron tapped his shoulder just as David was about to touch it.

'Don't touch it,' Aaron warned. 'It's still wet.'

'Thank you, thank you!' David boomed.

The following Sunday, the boys attended church. As usual, they sat, bored; they signed, wrote and drew crude words and pictures on hymnbooks; read comics and glanced around the nave.

'268!'

'261!'

'277!'

Chris, Aaron and David exchanged glances, disagreeing over their supposedly final count of the large decorative arched window's panes. They sighed and looked back, starting their counting again.

Matthew idly glanced around, taking no interest in the proceedings, and thought about half term two weeks back. He had told his parents that the glasses were no good; they had made no difference to his eyesight; in fact, they'd made things worse and given him headaches. He had given up wearing them now and had become increasingly frustrated; it was not only his eyes, but also his walking. Dean teased him for always waddling like a drunken penguin. Matthew brushed it off, though it made him think. He tested himself by walking along the school's car park, realising then that he couldn't walk in a straight line and his feet *were* angled outwards like a penguin's. He already knew he had poor balance – he still couldn't ride a bicycle, couldn't balance on a narrow beam during P.E. lessons, and he struggled to walk properly on uneven paths, particularly in the forest – but he hadn't noticed his meandering gait. He folded his arms, remembering that he had been practising walking straight and keeping his feet together; improving each time. Craning his neck over the heads in front of him just to see what the other boys were doing, he saw a commotion two rows down; two boys on either side of him were teasing Nicolo Perran, one of the First Formers. Matthew recognised the other two First Formers as Warren Southway, a stocky boy with black hair, and Richie Callaghan. Th §ey were taking turns to secretly tap the shoulders of the Italian boy in the middle, while he repeatedly turned, blaming the wrong boy each time. Matthew frowned, recognising this behaviour.

Coming out of the church after the service, Matthew saw Warren tapping Nicolo's shoulder again and ducking when he turned around, not seeing the perpetrator below him, although he should have been able to. Nicolo blamed Richie instead, who angrily protested his innocence. Matthew went over, grabbed Warren by his shirt collar and pulled him up. He also grabbed Richie's and thrust them together. Their heads banged hard and they jolted apart, their hands cupping their heads. Matthew turned to the surprised Nicolo, curious about him.

Nicolo gave Matthew a folded sheet of paper that he had taken from the top drawer of his wardrobe as he sat next to him on his bed in Dorm One.

'That's what my mum wrote down back home during half term when I told her and my dad about problems with my eyes.'

Matthew looked down, unfolding the lined paper and read the simple, handwritten words which were followed by a short list: *You are not able to see on either side or up and down – it is like tunnel vision. You may have poor balance. You may have problems seeing things such as someone waving at you. You may have problems seeing in the dark and in bright light. You may have accidents such as bumping into people, tripping over things and so on.*

Matthew frowned in surprise; this description ticked all the right boxes. Nicolo gently tapped Matthew's arm. 'My mum – she can sign good – she said she got this stuff from this doctor at an eye hospital in London and wrote it down for me. I didn't really understand why they were checking my eyes, but now I think I do.'

'What's the name of the hospital?' Matthew asked.

'Moorfields, I think,' he answered, fingerspelling the name. 'It's in Old Street.'

Matthew looked back at the paper; below the text description was a simplistic penned illustration, supposedly done by Nicolo's mother, showing an oval shape with a smaller circle in the centre. The area between the small circle and the oval's border had several lines to illustrate a dark area.

'Mum said it's like looking through, you know, like, a cone with a hole at the end?' He waited for Matthew to nod. 'Are you the same?'

Matthew hesitated; he wasn't quite sure, but what Nicolo described and what was written on the paper had said made perfect sense to him. He looked down at the sheet again and noticed two long words written below the illustration: *Retinitis Pigmentosa.*

'What's that mean?' Matthew pointed at it.

'I don't know,' the twelve–year old answered. 'I think it's a medical name. Mum said I have some kind of dark spots at the back of my eyes. Like chickenpox!'

Matthew shuddered at this revelation. Did he have those dark spots in his eyes as well? 'Did she … say that you – we – would have this problem for life?'

'She said I was born with it, so I guess, yeah, probably. When I first came here last September, I knew straightaway that I was, like, different to the other boys, you know?'

'Same here!' said the fifteen–year old Fourth Former, glad that he now had something in common with the young Italian boy. This was the first time he had ever met another like him and he felt a sense of relief knowing that he was not alone.

Sunday 25th November 1979.
Dear Terry Neill, Atsenal F.C. Manager,
Hello, my name is Christopher Matthaus, aged 15. I ~~is~~ am from Ewing Hill Park school ~~of~~ for deaf boys in Waltbridge. I am ^a deaf boy. I ~~supoort~~ support ARSENAL!

I ~~am~~ was very, very happy that we won the F.A. Cup Final last May vs Manch~~as~~ester United 3–2. Brilliant last minute goal by Alan Sunderland!

I am interesting to meet you–

'No, no,' Aaron interrupted, tapping Chris' shoulder. 'It's "interested", not "interesting" there.' He pointed at the error.

'But you told me before that a word that ends with "ed" is past tense,' Chris moaned, placing his Biro on the letter on the desk, confused. 'How can it be "interested" if I haven't met him yet? "Interesting" is present tense – you said that!'

'I know I said that, but –'

'Never mind!' Chris grabbed the pen, shaking his head, and begrudgingly crossed out the word. He briefly thought about how, for the last two months, Aaron had been teaching him English for an hour every Sunday afternoon. This was followed by another hour of Chris teaching Aaron footballing skills, as per their agreement. At first, Chris was bewildered by the grammar of the English, but he was learning gradually. Aaron's teaching through sign had made a huge difference, compared the struggle to learn from Mr Whittle. He had learnt more in the last two months than he ever had in the last three years, though he still struggled to understand past and present tense, verbs and their relative participles, and nouns and adjectives, but he was getting there. He hated spelling, especially long words, but Aaron taught him how to break up a long word into groups of two or three letters, memorise them and then write them as one word.

Chris scratched his head with the end of his pen and resumed writing the pretend letter, which was part of his lesson.

Aaron watched his friend in silence, sitting next to him. He reflected on the day they'd agreed to help each other; Chris had said he was desperate to improve his English so that he could read and understand football magazines and newspaper articles, as well as books. He explained how he had been frustrated by his inability to understand even the simplest words, let alone spell them. Aaron was astonished to learn that his friend couldn't spell *kitchen* – *kicten*, he'd fingerspelled – or even understand the grammatical difference between "a" and "the". He put Chris to the test by asking him to write about why he liked football, to see what his English was like. He was shocked, but at the same time, not surprised, when he read what Chris had written:

Football good play me best me like win. Hate lost. Arsenal suport me I love watch on TV. Favrite Alan Sunderland good head kick brillant. Heart phew him score last min goal beat Manutd goalkeeper final May last. Me srcaem love it!!! Play for Arsenal me want. Best deaf footballer in world! My Deraming.

It was as though it was written *exactly* in the order that Chris would sign it, rather than in English order; and then of course there were the spelling errors. Aaron knew several other boys had similar problems. Aaron always came top of his Form in English, followed closely by David, Michael and Derek. The rest were so far behind, even Duncan Nielson who could speak and lipread well, and Aaron had sometimes helped correct their English by letting them borrow his finished prep to read and understand, though he asked them *not* to copy his work, otherwise he'd be in trouble. Sometimes they asked him to explain in sign the aspects of English they did not understand from their English teacher. They would ask him *how* he could possibly understand Mr Whittle's teachings, despite being unable to lipread him properly. Aaron replied that he didn't understand, and put it down to the fact that he already had a good grasp of the English language, which made things easier for him. Brushing away his thoughts, Aaron looked down at Chris' letter again. He spotted another error and tapped Chris' shoulder.

Chris stepped out of the barber shop, sporting a fresh, short haircut, to be welcomed by a grinning Aaron and David outside.

'Scrubhead!' Aaron exclaimed, rubbing his fist on his friend's head.

Chris pushed the hand away. 'Piss off!'

'Mr Langston won't like it,' David reminded him.

'So what?' Chris said. 'It's my hair, not his! I want to look good for the

Christmas party next week.'

Chris and Aaron turned to walk along the High Street, with David following. He put on a voice, impersonating their headmaster:

'Oh no, not again, Christopher Matthaus!'

The eagerly awaited Saturday the eighth of December had finally arrived for the boys.

The Assembly Hall and the dining room, with the partition wall fully folded back, had been transformed into a huge icy cave. Painted white cardboard icicles hung down from the ceiling across the stage; backstage stood a series of cavernous formations, also made from white cardboard, giving the impression of a grotto; the eight floor–to–ceiling side windows were frosted with fake snow that twinkled against the night sky outside, and the fluorescent lighting tubes on the ceiling were covered with brightly coloured crepe paper. Finally, a large brick chimney made of painted paper stuck around a small scaffolding frame rested opposite the windows, and balloons and Christmas decorations graced the walls.

On the stage, a discotheque machine blared out, its multi–coloured lights bedazzling the dance floor. Decagonal and rectangular tables were spread across the area near the canteen at the other end, loaded with soft drinks and nibbles.

The floor was packed with Ewing Hill Park boys, girls from local schools, teachers and school governors mingling and dancing merrily to the music. The boys, who wore smart clothes of their own choice, signed to one another, drank and enjoyed themselves.

Mrs Munnings rocked, clapping her hands merrily to the music. Miss Stephenson and Mr Whittle, holding hands, joined her.

'What's that song?' the physics and biology teacher asked, gazing at the stage where the disc jockey was with a hint of distaste.

'I'll Be Home For Christmas,' Mrs Munnings replied, doing a full turn with excitement. 'The Osmonds!'

Miss Stephenson shook her head. 'Not my taste!'

'Ooh, my dear Penny, The Osmonds are the greatest!' Mrs Munnings grabbed the young woman's hands and forced her to dance to the music. 'I *love* them! If I were any younger, I'd have that *gorgeous* Donny anytime! Come on, dance!'

'You go on ahead, my love,' Mr Whittle encouraged his date, a cheeky twinkle in his eye. 'I'll … er … dance when they put on the Bee Gees.'

'Bee Gees!' Mrs Munnings shook her head mockingly and swung Miss Stephenson's arms.

Andrew pointed at a young teenage girl, who was sitting alone along the wall, and turned to Matthew. 'I like that girl.'

Matthew squinted through the dancing crowd, but he couldn't see her.

'Where?'

Andrew grabbed his form mate's right hand, knowing that his poor eyesight wouldn't help him see the girl, and directed it towards her.

'The one in the pink shirt and blue jeans.'

Matthew finally saw her and turned to his friend. 'She has a flat chest! Plenty of other girls with big boobs!'

'She *does* have breasts,' Andrew pointed at the girl again. 'You just can't see them with your rubbish eyes!'

Matthew shook his head, ignoring him. He touched Andrew's hair, which was neatly groomed to the side, shiny and glistening under the array of multi–coloured lights. He felt a slimy wetness.

'What's that you got on your hair?'

'My dad's Brylcreem,' he replied. He leaned over to Matthew and sniffed his cheek, which had a zingy aroma. 'What's that aftershave? It's nice.'

'Brut 33,' Matthew replied. 'It's new. You know the green bottle with the long neck?'

'In those television adverts,' Andrew nodded. 'The one with Henry Cooper, Barry Sheene and Kevin Keegan?'

'Yeah,' Matthew nodded. 'What's yours?'

'Karate,' Andrew waved daggered hands, demonstrating karate action. He stopped when he looked into the crowd and saw that Sammy and a girl were kissing passionately. Mr Arkwright quickly cut in and prised them apart, shaking his head and muttering at the Fourth Former. Andrew sighed. 'Lucky bastard!'

Leaning against the wall, his hand on the wall and feet crossed, Basher exhaled with exasperation. He thought again about using another approach to talk to the girl standing beside him. She shook her head.

'I … am … sorry … but … I … can … not … understand … your … speech,' said the spotty sixteen–year old girl, showing her wire braces, and each word slow and singular.

Basher barely read her lips, becoming increasingly frustrated by his failed attempts to pull a girl. He looked around, trying to find Gary, but he was nowhere to be seen. Hadn't he seen him leave the hall with that blonde girl with enormous tits? Lucky bugger, that he could speak, he thought. He then spotted David strolling past him and pulled him in. He pointed at the freckled girl.

'Tell her … would she like me to show her our bedroom–' Basher shook his head, indicating to David to forget that last word, and thought of a spot behind the school where he could work on her. 'No, no, no – tell her … would she like to have a look around the school?'

David sized up the girl, shaking his head at her indifferent appearance. He addressed her confidently: 'He said you're an ugly bitch.'

The girl spun round and thrust her clenched fist into Basher's stomach. He doubled up, yelling in pain, as the girl stormed off angrily. David chuckled loudly and walked away.

'*CAN YOU* ... uh ...' a young brunette shouted at Jonah Kaisermann over the blaring music, pointing at her ear then at the discotheque as they danced. '*HEAR IT ... MUSIC?*'

Jonah could easily lipread the girl; she had shouted at him pointlessly. He shook his head, matter of fact; he had been deaf since birth, so had never missed the sound of music.

'*OH ... I AM SO ... SORRY THAT YOU CANNOT HEAR,*' the girl bellowed. '*YOU POOR THING!*'

Jonah ignored her and gazed at Shaun who was mingling through the dancing crowd, filming with his cine camera.

Mr McShane, who stood behind Jonah, had heard what the girl shouted at the boy; he glanced at the stage, thinking about what the girl had said.

Timothy sat on a window ledge outside, facing the car park. His heart was in his boots. He lit a cigarette as he thought again about the girl he'd snogged in the bicycle shed a moment ago. She was lovely, he thought; she was sixteen and had beautiful lips. He thought it was his lucky night as she seemed to be really up for it, but no, she wasn't. When he'd touched her small breasts, she'd decked his balls with her knee and told him in blunt tones that she didn't want to go any further than just kissing. Damn it, he cursed. He thought about Gary; he must be doing it right now. Lucky bastard. He could chat up girls easily. Although he had good speech himself, Gary's was much better – he could talk like a hearing lad, so it made things easier for the hearing girls. He also saw Dean Hopkirk with *two* girls on his arms. He can't bloody speak well, Timothy thought as he drew on his fag before coughing out the smoke. He had to stop doing that as he didn't really like it, but Basher and Gary made him. What had he just been thinking about? Oh yes, Dean. He was rich and was wearing a Lacoste T–shirt and shiny black flares this evening, so Timothy guessed money talked. Well, good luck to him with those two girls, he bemoaned.

Timothy let out a long sigh, looking up at the black sky as he drew in and blew out a mushroom of smoke without inhaling it. Basher had been telling him to breathe it in and blow it out, but he couldn't. His father – the Reverend Sam Hutchinson – would preach to him endlessly about the dangers of smoking if he found out. His mother – the ever–so–good–hard–working church helper and clergy wife, Doris Hutchinson – would probably squeal and fuss over him. He thought about the coming Christmas, which, as always, brought him mixed fortunes. Growing up in the countryside with a vicar for a dad had never been easy, for it meant he led a secluded life. He was a solitary deaf child, living in a vicarage by the church in Hope Valley, a tiny village in the middle of the Peak District and a hour away from the nearest big town, Sheffield. He didn't mind the countryside; in fact, he loved it; it was the sheer loneliness and boredom that he hated, especially during the long summer holidays. Each long day moved at a deathly slow pace with little or nothing to do except watch television, even on a hot summer's day. There was no beach to go to either, just grass everywhere. Don't go too far, Timmy–boy, his mother would tell him if he wanted to go on a long hike to pass the time. Occasionally, his father would drive him and his mother – she couldn't drive – to his favourite town of Derby for a bit of shopping, and to see a movie or watch football at the Baseball Ground. He had no brothers or sisters to play with, nor any hearing friends. He'd been pals with Mackie when they were younger, but they grew apart after Timothy went to Ewing Hill Park. There was no one to talk to except his mother most days. He sometimes got the odd hello, how–are–you, forced smiles and goodbyes from the villagers, but that was about it. No one would talk to him because they didn't know how to talk with a deaf child, even though he had good speech. He had never been away on holiday or abroad during the summer, unlike most of the other boys. Too expensive, Mother always said. He and his parents usually went on a self–catering or camping holiday during the May/June half term because it was cheaper, but he yearned to go on a proper two–week summer holiday. He had, though, spent a week with Gary at his home in Whitby – the little town in the north where the fictional Count Dracula first arrived – last summer and had enjoyed it. He was always envious when the other boys told him where they'd been – Butlins, Majorca and Florida amongst others. His father, being the vicar, wasn't allowed to miss more than six Sundays a year, or go on holiday during Christmas, Easter or any other major religious event.

Christmas was always joyous for his family – well, it would be, wouldn't it, he said to himself; his father had to work through Christmas. On Christmas Eve, he would do the crib service in the afternoon for families; Midnight Mass at night and then the Christmas morning service. Timothy used to go to all three services because no one would look after him at home while his parents were at church. He preferred to watch television; he couldn't understand anything on it in the same way as he couldn't in church, but at least he could switch between three channels, which was better than watching the same old thing over and over again in church. Now, at sixteen, he could choose whether to go to these services or not, although he usually attended Midnight Mass to appease his mother. Mother would then rush home and cook the Christmas dinner while his father slumped, fast asleep, in his favourite armchair after a couple of brandies, knackered in his open dog collar after doing three services in less than twenty–four hours. Timothy would play with his new presents, which were mostly books, wooden toys, board games and clothes that he would rather die than wear outside his home. There was no Action Man, no Dinky toy cars and no Peter Powell kite that he'd long wanted to have – he had the whole bloody open country with plenty of hills to fly the dual–controlled long–tailed kite, but his mother said it was too dangerous because he might fall backwards over a steep slope while flying it and break his neck. No one could shout to warn you, Timothy, because you're deaf, she always told him.

He sighed at that; there would be *no one* around in the open hilly fields anyway! He sucked in and blew out more smoke. He blinked when his eyes became watery and coughed a bit. He really must quit, he thought, as he studied the half smoked cigarette in his hand, feeling the warmth from its glowing red tip. He remembered he had once sung a solo during one of the endless carol services when he was nine or ten – once and only once. He'd sung *Good King Wenceslas* in front of his proud mother, his prouder father and the whole flipping village outside in the dark with a candlelit lectern next to him. Mother had worked tirelessly on his speech for hours most evenings and she wanted to show her efforts off to people. He didn't think much about it at that time, for he was too young to understand then, but now, in hindsight, he detested the memory. He chuckled, remembering how much he hated how she'd sometimes put her hand over her mouth during speech training, then say something for him to "listen" to. Most of the time, he'd get it wrong; when he did get it right, that was because he could read the expressive movements of her cheeks above the hand. She always thought he'd actually *heard* her say it, though.

He did like, though, the summer and Christmas fetes, as they were fun and helped stave off boredom. He sometimes helped with the collection box during the Sunday service, occasionally sneaking a few pennies for himself to buy those one penny sweets from the village shop. He also liked jumble sales as they were a good way of getting rid of the Christmas presents he hated.

He looked up at the night sky again, wondering whether God existed. His father said He did and that He loved every creature on Earth. Timothy sometimes got the wind up from the other boys, especially Basher, about his dad being a vicar, but he always ignored them. In spite of his indifferent upbringing, he loved his parents. Religious studies was one of his best subjects and Mr Arkwright treated him like the son he'd never had. Well, he thought to himself, growing up around the Good Book, hymns and psalms had made him more than well–versed about religion. He was already earmarked to do his Religious Education O Level next June, according to Mr Arkwright, and he was confident he would easily pass.

Would he follow in his father's footsteps and become a vicar, he wondered; a deaf vicar? Yes, that would be good, wouldn't it? A spooky deaf vicar who liked horror films, he chuckled to himself; that would go down well with the parishioners! The question was; did he share the same faith in God as his father? He understood how the boys felt about going to church in Waltbridge every Sunday; Basher had said more than once he was plotting for the boys to boycott it. In his heart, he really wanted to help the deaf feel and understand God's love in their own way. His father once said that he'd had the calling from God when he was a young man, and decided to serve Him, but Timothy never understood that. A calling? Like what?

'Give me a sign or something!' he called out at the night sky in disbelief, drawing in the last of the smoke. At last, he inhaled it, feeling the warmth inside his throat. He blew, the smoke flowing out smoothly as he spoke. 'Like a light–'

He shrieked loudly when a bright light suddenly shone to his left. He shot to his feet, coughing and spluttering, and blinked at the two bright white circles which were growing bigger as they approached him. He quickly discarded the stub, fearing that it might be one of the staff driving up. His fears were soon allayed, however, when he saw the small illuminated yellow sign on top of the car, which told him it was a taxi. The car pulled up in front of the stone steps and the back passenger door opened. Timothy became curious about the woman who was stepping out of the car. He had quickly deducted that she was in her forties and of average height, though what she was wearing did not seem to complement her age; she had on a black mini–skirt that seemed to be too tight for her plump legs, with brown stockings. She also wore a heavily patterned polo neck, covered by a sandy brown jacket. He strolled over to the woman and saw her more clearly, noting the heavy makeup on her face that feebly covered up her wrinkles and baggy eyes, and her dark brown hair, crudely pinned at the back with a plastic hairpin. He smelt some kind of cheap perfume on her.

'Wait here, my love,' the woman leaned into the driver's window, 'I won't be long.'

'Aren't you a bit too old to be partying with young boys, lady?' Timothy said to her with a mischievous grin.

The woman whirled round, wide eyed, at the tall senior boy with the mournful eyes, not amused. 'Gerroff, you cheeky beggar!'

Mr McShane jumped on the stage and consulted with the disc jockey, who in turn put a new vinyl record on the turntable and placed the cartridge into the first groove; new music blared out loudly. Mr McShane turned to face the dancing crowd. The boys cheered and whooped at their favourite teacher, now happy that they were going to follow the music.

'Come on,' Mr McShane commanded the dancing crowd. 'It's by The Stranglers – their new song's called *Something Better Change*. Come on, sign along with me!'

He rocked to the music, his hands flying away. The boys immediately joined in the signed song, their hands also flying out into a crescendo, the hall exploding into a thunderous rustling of hands and loud yelling. Mr McShane stamped his feet as he signed the lyrics.

The boys laughed as they watched and followed the rocking art teacher, his hands moving furiously, his head swinging as he side–stepped to and fro. The girls were puzzled at first by the boys' signing of the song, but they eventually joined in the fun, trying to mimic the boys.

Mrs Munnings, too, gamely joined in by trying to sign some of the lyrics herself. She urged some boys around her to get into the thick of it. She then encouraged Miss Stephenson to do the same, while Mr Whittle swayed to the rhythm. Hubert, wearing a Santa hat, danced away, clapping his hands. He turned to Asif Nizamani, who seemed bewildered by this new form of activity.

'Come on, sign! Yes, you will!' the school gardener encouraged the young Pakistani First Former, who eventually began to follow the masses of fast–moving hands around him. Hubert laughed, nodding at him. 'Yes, yes, yes!'

'What's Miles doing?' Mr Arkwright leaned over to Mr Schneider, sipping his lemonade as he watched the art teacher signing away on the stage across the hall. 'What's this stupid music? Punk?'

'Making a complete ass of himself,' the towering maths teacher nodded, confirming the nature of the music. 'Disgraceful!'

'Absolutely,' Mr Arkwright agreed. Donald Langston had overruled his first choice of candidate for the new art teacher in an interview three and half years back for *that* mimic clown. He was still bitter at being passed over for the position of headmaster in favour of Donald after Benjamin had retired. 'If I was the headmaster, I'd certainly sack *him* without a second thought–'

'Jonathan …' Mr Schneider interrupted, nudging him and directing his attention to Mr Langston, who was approaching them.

'Have you seen Christopher Matthaus?' the headmaster asked, his voice urgent.

'I think I just saw him over there by the stage,' Mr Arkwright said, pointing with the glass in his hand.

Chris danced, signing along to the lyrics and enjoying himself. A hand gently tapped his shoulder, interrupting him; he turned to see the headmaster.

'Can you please come with me?' he asked, beckoning.

The headmaster ushered Chris into his office, closing the door behind him. Chris paused when he saw the woman turning to face him after looking at a picture on the wall. Upon seeing the boy, her eyes widened. Cupping her mouth with her hand, she paled and staggered back a step as though she had seen a ghost. Chris saw Mr Langston utter something to her, concern in his eyes. The woman said something back to him, her behaviour suggesting she was all right.

Chris frowned at the woman, long buried memories spinning back into the fore as he vaguely recognised her. It had had been seven years – almost half of his young life – and she had changed very little, but it was her.

'Is this … your mother?' Mr Langston pointed at her, his eyes doubtful.

Chris nodded.

'Very well,' the headmaster said, turning to the woman. He gestured five fingers for Chris' benefit. 'Five minutes, you said?'

Sandra Matthaus stepped forward, nodding. 'Yes, Mr Langston, five minutes. My taxi's still waiting outside.'

Mr Langston turned to the boy, expressing a hint of reluctance before turning to leave the office, shutting the door behind him. Alone in the room, the mother and son exchanged strained glares for a long moment.

'Hello Christopher,' his mother finally broke the uneasy silence, though anxiety appeared in her eyes. 'Oh my god … you've grown up! You look *so much* like your father.'

She advanced, raising her hand to touch Chris' head, noting his crew cut, but Chris stepped back from her. Sandra halted, taking the hint.

'Can you …' she pointed at her lips, '. . . still lipread me?'

It had been a long time and he'd never been able to lipread her that well when he was younger, but Chris had learned how to lipread people better than he used to. His mother's lips were clear enough for him anyway. He nodded.

'I know I shouldn't have turned up like this tonight,' she began, 'but I had to see you. I haven't seen you for seven years.'

Chris put his hands into his jeans pockets, maintaining his silence. His mother sidestepped, sighing to herself.

'I'm much better now … I've stopped drinking.' she announced. Chris rolled his eyes, nodding and expressing indifference towards her.

'I have! Honest. I've had help in the last year. I've cleaned up.'

'What about that shithead, Bob?' Chris finally broke his silence, signing to her.

'I'm sorry,' his mother said, weakly fanning herself and shaking her head, 'but I don't know signing.'

Chris approached the headmaster's desk, keeping his distance from his mother, and picked up a pen and a notepad that were on the writing board. He wrote down exactly what he had said and held the notepad up for her to read.

'Bob?' she read aloud. 'Oh, he's history! I don't see him anymore.'

I don't believe you.

Sandra easily lipread her son's silent comments. 'I'm never going back to him again, I promise you that.'

Chris lowered the notepad, still glaring hard at her. Even after seven years, the memory of seeing his mother drunk all the time, being lied to all the time, and Bob hitting them both still haunted him. All those broken promises that she would leave the man he hated and the pain of being separated from her at the age of eight was still with him, as well as the memories of spending the few next years growing up in places he did not call home. Yet, his mother never bothered to come and take him home. Over those years, his love for his mother gradually left him. So, in his eyes, this woman standing in front of him was a complete stranger to him.

Sandra bowed her head and sighed heavily. She lifted her head, gingerly stepping towards Chris.

'Look, Mr Lewison, the social worker, knows I'm here to see you tonight. I told your headmaster that and he said he'd ring him on Monday morning to check. They've given me the go–ahead for you to spend the New Year with me, as you're old enough now. I know you're staying with your friend ... what was his name again? Oh yes, Aaron Stephens ... over Christmas in Bristol, but that's perfectly fine with me. We'll make a fresh start in 1980! What do you think?'

Chris thought about the offer, unsure, but he knew she was right. They had to start over at some point, though he was still apprehensive about it. He nodded with a half smile to indicate that he liked the idea, though he secretly remained dubious. His mother smiled back, nodding to show her gratitude, although the air of tension was still around them.

'Okay,' she said, 'I'd best go now. My taxi's waiting outside. The trains between here and London are rubbish. Besides, you're having a Christmas party here, so I won't keep you.'

She tentatively inched forward to peck Chris' cheek, but he shook his head to tell her not to.

'Oh, my dear son,' she said wearily. 'Can't I at least kiss my boy goodbye? Please?'

Chris paused for a short moment, then nodded. She lifted her head, placing her hand round Chris' neck to pull him down, and pecked his left cheek. Stepping back, she rubbed the red lipstick smudge from his cheek with her thumb.

'Goodbye, Christopher.'

A flurry of hands shot up into the air, waving and clapping. Mr McShane finished his signed song performance, waving back at the appreciative crowd and thanking them. Aaron lowered his hands, searched around and wondering where

Chris was; he'd been there a moment ago. The crowd began to diminish with the boys and girls moving away in different directions. Aaron caught sight of Steven sitting next to Michael, his arm over his shoulders, pally. He went over to them.

'You two in love?' Aaron joked, noting the friendly arm.

'Ha, ha!' Steven chuckled, withdrawing his arm. 'We're just good friends. Where's *your* boyfriend?'

'Piss off! He's not my boyfriend!' Aaron hit back, chuckling. 'Have you seen him?'

'He's probably snogging a girl somewhere!' Michael said.

Aaron turned away to leave the hall to look for his best friend.

Standing on the stone steps at the front entrance, Chris watched his mother hop into the back of the waiting taxi, closing the door after her. She wound down the window to give her son one last look before the car drove away towards the winding driveway.

Aaron joined his friend, having just briefly glimpsed the woman on the back seat of the cab. Chris acknowledged him, his eyes still fixed on the departing cab as it disappeared into the pitch black darkness, the headlights and the red taillights shrinking into the void.

'Who was that?' asked Aaron, pointing at the departing taxi.

'My mum,' Chris replied with a sad smile.

Aaron turned to the darkened driveway, surprised.

19

The Secret Young Interpreter

"One who is capable of interpreting the meaning of 'secret–speech' becomes the first to come across the 'source of knowledge'."
– ATHARVAVEDA

John switched off the engine of his Austin Maxi. He exhaled wearily, resting his tired hands on the steering wheel, then looked at his watch: almost five o'clock. He then gazed through the windscreen at the cold night and turned to Aaron on the passenger seat.

'Home sweet home!' he announced. He briefly thought about the long drive back, silently cursing again at the typically horrendous Christmas bottleneck on the M4. They had left Ewing Hill Park at ten o'clock that morning, having spent the night in a poxy B&B in Waltbridge; he had expected to arrive home some time in the early afternoon. 'Bloody traffic! Go on inside, boys. Your mum must be worried. I'll bring in your trunks.'

Aaron glanced at Chris on the back passenger seat, smiling nervously at him. Chris smiled back, opened the car door and stepped out. Aaron followed suit, and Chris joined him as they faced the house. Chris saw that it was a typical three–bedroomed Edwardian semi, located in a suburb north of Bristol called Westbury–on–Trym. The large living room window had multi–coloured fairy lights around its edges, while a Christmas holly wreath hung on the front door, which was dark blue with six small, frosted panes. Looking around in the dark, Chris saw that the quiet street had rows of semi–detached houses on either side, along with rows of parked cars. The lampposts shed a partial orangey light along the stretch. Aaron opened the small white iron gate that led to a short concrete path which ran up to the front door and went through it. Chris followed him.

Geraldine leaned over to open the oven door and checked the shepherd's pie inside. She heard the front door opening, straightened and looked through the kitchen doorway to see Aaron and Chris coming down the hallway. She smiled and hurried over to them, her arms outstretched.

'About time you got here!' Geraldine bellowed, wrapping her arms around her son and kissing his cheek. She stepped back to size him up. 'Oh, you've grown again … you're now a little taller than me!'

'Hello Christopher,' Geraldine turned to Chris, quickly observing that he was an inch or so taller than Aaron. 'You've grown as well – you're now as tall as Jamie. Or have I shrunk?' She laughed weakly at her own joke. Placing her hand on Chris' neck, she pulled him in and gave him a kiss on the cheek.

Excusing herself, Geraldine made for the front door, to see her husband outside. Aaron glanced up and saw Jamie descending the stairs, smiling at him.

'Hi butthead!' Jamie said, knocking his own forehead with his fist. He reached the bottom and knocked Aaron's head in turn, before hugging him fondly and pecking his forehead. He turned to Chris. 'Hi mate. Good to see you again. Hope you've been looking after my baby butthead!'

Chris and Jamie shook hands firmly, their arm muscles rigid as they pulled back. Aaron watched with interest as they tested their strength against each other, remembering that they had often arm–wrestled at Aunt Barbara's during half term, and that they had been equals in strength. Chris quickly released his grip, hoping that his challenger would stumble back, but Jamie managed to control his balance.

Geraldine came back inside, grabbing Aaron's hand and motioning for him and Chris to come into the living room. She tapped her lips with her index finger for the deaf boys to read them. 'Come, I want to show you something.'

'Guess what Mummy's got for Mummy's boy!' Jamie grinned broadly at Aaron. As he followed him and Chris into the next room, a voice called out through the open front door.

'Jamie!' his dad bellowed. Jamie went out and saw his dad struggling to pull a large trunk out of the car's boot.

'Come and help me with this bloody thing! What has Aaron got in there? Dumbbells or what?'

Aaron's mother directed him and his friend towards their new Philips colour television which was in the corner by the front window. A Christmas tree, complete with decorations and fairy lights, stood proudly next to it; underneath it were some presents. She tapped proudly on a small, dark grey box, which was about the size of a paperback and had a rotary volume knob on top. A small microphone was attached to the television's black speaker grate. A long, thin black cable was plugged into the jack at the back. Aaron glimpsed the *Sarabec* logo on the front of the television; his eyes followed the cable which ran from the back of the box towards the top of the skirting boards.

'Aaron,' his mother tugged his shirt sleeve to bring him round, again tapping her lips. 'You remember the audiologist, Miss Graham? She said that this might help you to listen to the television and understand what's being said. This is called a loop.'

Lub?

'No, no, Aaron, not lub!' Geraldine shook her head. She fingerspelled slowly; 'L–O–O–P. Now, switch your hearing aids to "T" please. You too, Christopher.' She beckoned to him.

Aaron and Chris exchanged blank looks. Aaron flicked the tiny switches on each of his aids, making sure that they were in the middle between the on/off and volume controls. Chris did the same. Geraldine turned to the television and switched it on. After a short moment, the *Newsround* title graphics appeared on the screen and a familiar face with neatly parted black hair appeared, speaking to the camera. Geraldine twisted the box's rotary volume knob and turned to the two deaf boys, smiling hopefully.

'Well? Can you hear John Craven now?'

Aaron and Chris listened.

Nothing. Complete silence.

They shook their heads. Geraldine's hand flew to her chin, perplexed. 'You can't hear the television? How strange! She said it would work.'

Jamie entered, chuckling loudly, followed by his dad. 'Mum, I *told* you so. This thing won't work for them – they're too deaf!'

'John,' Geraldine turned to her husband, ignoring Jamie. 'Can you check if it's working properly?'

Begrudgingly, John crossed the room to the television, took the device and examined it. 'It seems to be working fine.'

Signing, Jamie relayed what his father said to Aaron and Chris, trying hard not to collapse with laughter.

'I can't understand it,' Aaron's mother said, turning to him. 'Never mind. We'll tell Mrs Moreliver about it tomorrow.'

Oh no, not her again, Aaron groaned to himself, not that woman with the gold tooth!

'Aaron,' Geraldine said, noting her son's aversion to the woman, 'she is *very* interested in you and she likes to know how you're getting on at Ewing Hill Park, especially regarding your speech. Right, supper's in fifteen minutes.'

Geraldine trotted to the door with her husband following. When they were gone and out of earshot, Jamie slowly turned to his younger brother, making himself quite obvious.

'*Aaron* ...' Jamie put on a snobbish and patronising voice, his mouth deliberately expressive, '. . . *your speech is IMPROVING! But NOT good enough! Work hard! Talk! Talk! Work harder!*'

'No, you're not having *that* card!' Aaron shook his head in despair.

'We agreed last time–'

'No!'

'Okay, fine,' Jamie said, incredulously. 'I'll go out tomorrow–'

'Don't!' Aaron sighed resignedly. 'All right, you win.'

Jamie folded his arms, grinning. Chris frowned at the brothers, wondering what they were on about.

'Aaron ...' the woman said slowly, '. . . your speech is IMPROVING! But NOT good enough! Work hard! Talk! Talk! Work harder!'

Aaron rested his elbows on the breakfast table, clasping his hands together and nodding, not in response to the woman sitting across the table, but to indulge her.

He really disliked Mrs Moreliver. Even her appearance repulsed him: in her fifties, she had thick, curly grey hair, wrinkles and huge, thickly rimmed pointed spectacles. She would wear a grossly old–fashioned dress and a patterned woollen overcoat that seemed to have come from the last war, or was perhaps bought at a jumble sale. She resembled Margaret Thatcher, only with a shorter nose. When she smiled, she loved to flash her gold front tooth. Worst of all, she was *impossible* to lipread. No matter how hard she tried to speak slowly and clearly to him, he couldn't understand a word she said. And she'd always get a bit annoyed when Aaron failed to understand her. Who was she anyway, he wondered, and why was she so interested in him? He glanced at his mother, who was sitting next to Mrs Moreliver, and remembered her saying that the woman was from the education department at the council and that she'd helped to get them to agree to pay for him to go to Ewing Hill Park. He supposed she wanted to be nosey about how he was doing there to please herself or, perhaps, to report to her boss. He didn't really care; he wanted the meeting to be over so that he could get on with his holiday. He discreetly glanced between his mother and Mrs Moreliver; behind them, across the length of the kitchen, Jamie popped into view behind the glass kitchen door. He tapped on the right muff of the headphones he was wearing and gestured a thumbs up at Aaron. As his mother and the woman from the council chatted, Aaron discreetly slid his hand underneath the table to feel the metal cylinder that was stuck on the underside with Sellotape, making sure the microphone was still there. He immediately withdrew his hand when his mother turned to him, smiling. He smiled back innocently, his eyes drifting away to the thin black microphone cable which was trailing discreetly along the corner of the worktop and the chequered floor, towards the back door. It trailed under the door, ending up outside, camouflaged by a snake–shaped draught excluder. The cable was plugged into a small battery–powered amplification box with a volume control knob outside. Jamie's headphones were hooked to it.

Aaron recalled that they had done this a few times in the past; whenever Mrs Moreliver came to visit. Her first visit, when he was about ten, was when she was new to her job. She'd glowered at him like a cackling witch, speaking into his body worn hearing aids like they were megaphones. Worse, she'd positioned her face quite close to his, her breath like a dustbin, sometimes accidentally spitting on his face. Every time he tried to lean away from her, she leaned forward. She was impossible to understand and always got narky if he didn't respond to her questions or comments. So, Jamie offered to help by signing for him the next time she came round, but she refused to allow it, saying that signing was forbidden and that it was more important for Aaron to continue learning to speak and lipread. She also said she did not want to feel upstaged by an eleven–year old boy like Jamie, "speaking" for his younger brother. Jamie refused to accept this, so came up with a cunning plan; he would secretly sign for Aaron every time she came, in return for payment – the pickings from Aaron's favourite Top Trumps cards. Aaron refused at first, but eventually accepted; he had no choice.

Aaron had always insisted on having their meetings in the kitchen, not the living room, which puzzled his mother. The back door had the only window in the house that didn't have a net curtain. He also insisted on his mother and the woman sitting with their backs to the back door, which again puzzled his mother, because it meant the light was facing him, instead of the other way round. Whenever Mrs Moreliver spoke, Jamie would pop into view and sign what she was saying, listening through the concealed microphone, then disappear. This secret plan had worked without fail for him and Jamie for the last four years. So far, so good.

Aaron cautiously looked over the two women to see Jamie pulling a card from his top pocket, giving him a thumbs up in glee. Aaron cursed silently; he'd been forced to "pay" Jamie his most coveted Top Trumps card: the red Ferrari 308 GTS. It was his ultimate dream car and he had always refused to give it to Jamie, but Jamie had told him that it was to be *that* card the next time she came to visit, or he wouldn't do it. Aaron had reluctantly agreed, with a heavy heart. Chris' head popped into view; peering at Aaron through the glass. Jamie gently pushed him out of the way. He pointed at the woman and signed hurriedly:

Are you doing well at school?

Aaron quickly turned to the woman who was leaning over, close to his right ear, as though he had heard her speak.

'Yeeesss,' Aaron responded. It was easy to say that.

Mrs Moreliver leaned back, exclaiming and clapping once. She muttered something to Geraldine in excitement. Aaron's eyes darted to the back door to see Jamie grinning, mimicking the council lady and signing:

She said your speech is WONDERFUL and your hearing aids are MARVELLOUS! WOW! WOW!

Aaron glared at his brother, knowing he was exaggerating the wow factor. He felt a tap on the table and turned back to the woman, who was saying something close to his face. He politely leaned back a bit, secretly peering through the gap between the two women to see Jamie at the back, frantically slapping one hand on top of the other, pointing at Aaron, then elaborately slapping his own bottom. Jamie signed:

She said have you been in any trouble at school?

Aaron turned to Mrs Moreliver, smiling innocently, and shook his head. 'Nnnooo.'

Again, it was easy to say that, Aaron thought to himself. Of course, he was telling a white lie, but if he told the truth, what would she say? Perish the thought. He rolled his eyes, seeing through the glass window that Jamie was sliding his index finger across his chin repeatedly.

Liar! Liar! Liar!

Aaron's mind screamed at him, silently telling him to shut up. His mother tapped her mouth for Aaron to watch it. 'You are doing very, very well in English and English Literature, aren't you?'

She turned and muttered something to the lady, who was sipping her cup of tea, holding the saucer in her other hand. Mrs Moreliver muttered something in response, the rim of the cup hovering below her lower lip. Aaron rested his elbows on the table and casually directed his eyes to the back, to see Jamie signing:

She said you are such a CLEVER BOY!

Jamie slid a thumb across his forehead in an exaggerated manner and gestured wildly with both hands on either side of his head, as though pumping it:

Bighead!

Aaron felt riled by his brother's antics: he had never done this before. He must be showing off to Chris. He stuck up two fingers at Jamie, quickly turning them round when his mother turned to him.

'Yes, Aaron,' his mother said, noting her son's two numeric fingers. 'You got two As in your English and English Literature mock exams last week. I was just going to tell Mrs Moreliver about that.'

Aaron sighed wearily, resting his hands on the table. Behind the two unsuspecting women, he saw that Jamie was merrily sticking up two fingers back at him, repeatedly. Suddenly, Jamie's body jolted violently; he yelled and clasped the headphones as if he were receiving an electric shock. He flew out of sight just as Geraldine and Mrs Moreliver turned around, having heard something, but they saw no one there.

Mum!

Geraldine and Mrs Moreliver whirled back to Aaron, distracted. He motioned that he was running, gestured a big thumbs up and produced his index finger.

'Yes,' Aaron's mother said, understanding him. 'I was also going to tell Mrs Moreliver that you're very good at cross–country running. You came first in your school's House Cross Country race.'

Aaron nodded, beaming. He quietly breathed a sigh of relief, but wondered what had happened. He glanced at the window by the sink to see Chris discreetly coming into view, grinning cheekily. He signed through the glass:

Turned up the volume! Full! BOOM!

Aaron spluttered loudly, giggling. Geraldine and Mrs Moreliver turned to him, wondering why he was laughing. Aaron quickly stopped himself and saw, from the corner of his eye, that Chris had already disappeared from view. Jamie reappeared at the back door, the headphones askew on his head, screwing his right ear with his little finger to relieve the ringing. He soon repositioned the headphones. Chris' head popped back into view next to Jamie, grinning at his school friend.

The mother turned to Aaron, again tapping her mouth with her index finger. 'I'll show her your excellent school report.'

She rose from the table and turned. Jamie panicked, comically bumping his chest on Chris' leaning head, and pushed himself and Chris out of view just in time. Geraldine headed towards the end of the kitchen, where the back door was, and picked up a stapled document from the worktop. A pen that was resting on the document rolled over and plummeted to the floor. She bent to pick it up and froze suddenly when she saw the black wiring winding along the corner of the worktop and across the floor. She picked it up curiously and straightened back up. Aaron shuddered at the discovery while Mrs Moreliver slowly lowered her cup and saucer, watching Geraldine inquisitively.

The bemused mother pulled the wire. Aaron quickly put his hand under the table, grabbing the microphone as it became unstuck by the tautness of the wire. Geraldine's eyes followed the cable, seeing that it led underneath the breakfast table; she turned to see that the other end was poking through the gap at the bottom of the door. She bent down, moved the draught excluder, straightened back up and opened the door.

Jamie quickly took off the headphones and swung them behind his back, although he knew that his attempt at deception would be useless. His mother stepped outside and saw Jamie and Chris standing, their behaviour innocent.

'What are you both doing out there?' she demanded. She saw that the wire she was holding led to the amplification box, and another wire from it led behind Jamie's back. 'What's this?'

John entered the front door, carrying a rolled up newspaper under his arm and a lunchbox in his hand. He yawned, glad to be home from another mediocre day at the Rolls Royce plant. He looked at his watch: now six o'clock. Closing the door behind him, he took off his navy blue scarf and turned to go through into the living room.

He walked in, greeting his wife, who was sitting in silence in an armchair on his right; the three boys were sitting silently on the sofa adjacent to it. 'Evening all,' he addressed. 'How was your day?'

Geraldine rose to her feet, her manner ambiguous. She stood beside her husband, folding her arms and frowning at the three boys on the sofa. John quickly sensed that something had happened.

'What's wrong, Geraldine?' he asked, starting to get worried.

'The boys …' Geraldine broke the silence, her voice harsh. 'They have been *naughty* today.'

'Oh, no,' he said quietly. He directed his eyes at Jamie accusingly, knowing only too well the fifteen–year old boy's influence on Aaron. Now he had dragged Chris in as well. 'What have they done?'

Geraldine suddenly burst into a fit of laughter, her head rocking back and forth, her right hand clutching her chest and her left hand slapping her husband's right arm. John was alarmed at his wife's raucous outburst. He grasped his lunchbox tightly.

'You should have *seen* her face!' Geraldine managed to say through her ear–splitting giggles. 'It was so funny!'

'What?' John said, bemused. 'What happened?'

Geraldine burst into another peal of laughter. 'Oh, her face when they told her what they did today!'

She turned away, heading towards the hallway, still giggling loudly. John turned to the boys, bewildered. 'What have you boys done?' he demanded.

Chris, Aaron and Jamie burst into laughter, rolling around on the sofa.

20

A Mother's Love

"Sign language! … It seems such an obvious – the obvious – response to an absence of hearing. If you can't go in via the ears, use the eyes instead."
– LORRAINE FLETCHER; *Language For Ben: A Deaf Child's Right To Sign*, 1987

Geraldine trotted through the hallway towards the kitchen, still giggling. She heard the boys bursting into laughter in the living room and chortled loudly, knowing that John had just asked them about what had happened.

Oh, the poor woman, she thought; she believed she'd made herself understood to Aaron for the past four years! That sneaky toerag, Jamie! Secretly interpreting for Aaron behind their backs! Now she understood why her son had always insisted on sitting in that position at the breakfast table. Couldn't blame him for that; he could never really lipread the Senior Teacher of the Deaf. Hell, how on earth did her deaf pupils manage to understand her? Granted, a few of them could probably hear through their hearing aids, but what about the majority of them, profoundly deaf like Aaron, who couldn't? What kind of an education system did they have for deaf children?! In his letters, Aaron sometimes complained about a few of the Ewing Hill Park teachers who couldn't make themselves understood. On the other hand, he also mentioned how there were others who could. Like that Mr McShane, the charming art teacher, who could sign. And Mrs Munnings, too, who was starting to make herself better understood because she had just started signing. Aaron's latest school report noted a marked improvement in his geography and history work, so that must be working, she thought.

Geraldine walked into the kitchen and moved a large steel kettle from one of the four iron hob rings on the gas cooker. She shook it, checking for water inside: it was almost empty. She turned to the sink next to the cooker and looked out into the cold night beyond the window.

She thought about the day she first met John at Casewell Bay; a day she would never forget. It was a hot Saturday in July 1960. She was twenty–two then and was feeling down after being dumped by that selfish twat, Daffyd. Mam had encouraged her to go to the beach just outside Swansea to relax and enjoy herself. At first, Geraldine didn't feel like going, but Mam insisted on it, saying that she had a "good feeling" about it. She had never understood her Mam's uncanny "feelings" when she was growing up in her Welsh hometown; she didn't understand them even now. Mam always *knew* when things were about to happen or were already happening somewhere, and was *always* right. There were too many incidents to mention, though, the one that had always spooked her the most was the day Aaron was born. He was about two weeks late and it was a long and painful labour. When he finally came out, the umbilical cord was round his little neck, almost choking him. Fortunately, for him and his mother, the paediatrician was quick to deal with it and the baby was perfectly healthy. Shortly afterwards, John rang up Mam to tell her the good news, but somehow she already knew; even that the baby almost suffocated during birth. She also correctly guessed the exact time he was born. She didn't predict his name though – Aaron Joseph Stephens.

Geraldine stared blankly out into the darkness, seeing her own reflection in the window as her memory rolled back to Casewell Bay again.

The large sandy beach was packed; the sea filled with masses of excited people, splashing through the waves; the sun shining down blisteringly; the air still and humid. She was lying on a blanket on her own when, suddenly, a beach ball bounced off her. She picked it up and saw a little girl in a swimsuit running towards her, her arms outstretched, giggling. The young Geraldine threw the ball back at her, but she failed to grasp the large plastic ball with her tiny arms and it bounced away. The ball strayed past Geraldine and she rose to fetch it, but when she got to it, another pair of hands had already grabbed it.

She looked up to see a young, tall and rather handsome man with black hair. He was quite well built, with a bit of hair on his bare chest and a pleasant smile. He reminded her of her favourite Hollywood heartthrob, Gregory Peck, only slightly thinner. She'd seen his latest film, *On The Beach,* recently at the pictures with Daffyd, who was a science fiction nut. She had imagined herself as Ava Gardener in the film, being romantic with Gregory Peck.

'Hi,' the man greeted her, with an accent that sounded Bristolian, before leaning down to give the beach ball to the little girl. She took it happily, muttering something oddly incoherent at the man, used her hands to gesture some kind of a sign saying thanks, before trotting away. Geraldine and the man exchanged quiet glances, recognising that the girl may be deaf.

'Oh, poor thing!' she said as she watched the departing girl, before turning to him. 'She must be suffering from being deaf and dumb.'

The man nodded, smiling broadly at her. 'Lovely day, isn't it?'

Her heart fluttered at hearing him speak. He introduced himself as John

Stephens; in turn, she introduced herself as Geraldine Taylor. John told her he had just come back from serving three years with the National Service in Malta and Cyprus; he'd been offered a new job at the Rolls Royce plant in his home town of Bristol and would be starting there the following Monday. He was in Swansea for the weekend with his two brothers, Neil and Mark, to celebrate his new job.

Geraldine bowed her head, turning the tap with her left hand. With her right thumb, she pressed down the kettle's latch and positioned the spout under the steadily flowing cold water, filling the kettle. She thought back to that hot day again.

Mam was right, as usual; something *did* happen. Geraldine and John got chatting and she met his two brothers; they had to return to Bristol the next day, so she and John exchanged phone numbers.

Checking the amount of water in the kettle, Geraldine thought happily about the three years of courtship that had followed before they got married in Swansea. They'd then bought the house where they were living now. Geraldine became pregnant and John bought an Alsatian puppy to keep her company; she called him Bram. Jamie was born on the seventh of March 1964. Oh, he was a beautiful baby and was always so quiet; she smiled to herself as she turned the tap off. She placed the kettle on the hob, picked up a box of Swan matches and lit a ring. Blowing out the match, she placed the burnt matchstick back into the box, still reflecting.

Then Aaron was born on Sunday the fourteenth of November, 1965. Aside from the scare with the umbilical cord, the paediatrician had counted ten fingers and ten toes and declared that he was a perfectly normal, healthy boy.

Geraldine smiled sadly, thinking about how she and John couldn't have predicted how this beautiful blonde baby would change their lives forever.

Mam had had another of her "feelings" when she saw her new grandson and said that this baby was "special". Geraldine assumed that she meant it in a figurative sense, but Mam insisted there was something different about him. Despite Mam's statement, Geraldine and John had no reason to suspect their youngest son was any different to twenty month–old Jamie. Aaron chuckled when he was tickled, wriggled his toes and kicked when he was talked to, appreciated having new and different things to look at, cried when he was hungry or upset and said *a–goo* to his granddad, just as Jamie had done. He also "talked" to the toys hanging over his cot.

Geraldine turned, resting her bottom against the front of the cooker and folding her arms. She gazed at her corkboard – or *The Board of Life,* as the family jokingly called it – on the wall above the breakfast table. It had a series of handwritten notes, black and white and colour family photographs taken since the boys were born, article clippings, fingerspelling and basic sign cards, leaflets, Green Shield stamps and coupons pinned to it. She smiled proudly at one of the black and white photographs, which was of Aaron as a baby lying on a baby mattress with Jamie, as a toddler sitting next to him, smiling cheerfully. Aaron must have been about six months old and Jamie twenty–six months old when that photograph was taken, she thought. That was around the time when she and her husband had begun to suspect that there was something not right about Aaron.

Although they believed that all babies did not develop at the same time, they soon began to realise that Aaron's development was significantly slower than Jamie's had been when he was the same age. Even Suzanne, the baby girl from next door who was born about two weeks after Aaron, was rapidly overtaking him. Another suspicion Geraldine had was that he wasn't paying attention to what was happening around him. One of the first things she noticed was when she was hoovering Aaron's room whilst he sat playing with his toys in his playpen, his back to her; he did not turn around immediately. Another time, Geraldine remembered, she had accidentally dropped an empty saucepan on the kitchen floor, close to where Aaron was sitting, yet he hadn't reacted to the loud clang. Jamie did, though; he came running into the kitchen having heard the noise. Aaron seemed unlikely to notice anything unless he saw it with his own eyes. She also wondered why some people often distracted him when they came in, while the other babies didn't. Jamie once threw a plastic toy at his little brother, annoyed at him. Geraldine comforted the crying Aaron and told off the two–year old Jamie, asking him why he had done that. He said he was fed up with Aaron always ignoring his chatter and shouts.

Geraldine looked at another photograph on the corkboard, which was of another couple with three young children – the Maidsons from next door – along with the young Aaron and Jamie, all posing. Geraldine remembered a particular incident one September morning when Aaron was about ten months old, which had further confirmed her suspicions about him.

She had gone out into the back garden with Aaron riding on her hip, and started talking to Simon Maidson over the fence. Little Suzanne was similarly perched on his hip.

'Hello, Suzanne!' Geraldine greeted the ten–month old. She turned and giggled at her.

'Hello Aaron!' Simon called out.

Aaron didn't turn to the neighbour; his eyes were fixated on the washing blowing on the line. Geraldine told him softly to look at Simon and Suzanne, but he ignored her. She turned a bit, so that Aaron could see them over the fence; he bounced happily once he saw them.

'He must have a problem with his hearing,' Simon said.

Simon was a local GP, who happened to have deaf parents, so he immediately recognised the problem. He checked Aaron's ears with his auriscope, discovering some gluey stuff inside them. He said that it might explain why the boy was not hearing anything, though Geraldine felt that it might be more than just glue ear.

Geraldine sighed, hearing the kettle behind her starting to boil. She moved away from the cooker, looking down at the breakfast table, and picked up the latest Habitat catalogue. She idly flicked through the pages, not taking any interest in the items pictured. She closed the book and put it down, thinking about the operation Aaron had had to clear the gluey stuff; she remembered weeping over her precious, sleeping little baby in his hospital cot, praying that he would be all right. The doctor had told her and John that Aaron was fine; however, he would be referring him to the audiology department for a hearing test. Geraldine worried that he might be deaf, but John had reassured her that he was a perfectly normal hearing child, like Jamie. He said the hearing test was only to check and confirm that the gluey stuff had been fully cleared, but she still had her doubts.

Geraldine half smiled when she saw the little card from the audiology department still pinned to the top right hand corner of the corkboard. She'd never got round to throwing away the old card, which had several handwritten appointment dates listed on it. Perhaps, she thought, it was a sentimental reminder of the difficult time she and John had been through in the process of establishing Aaron's deafness.

Aaron didn't respond well to the hearing tests, which involved banging metal instruments together behind him, but the doctors couldn't be certain whether he was deaf or not, saying he was still young. They agreed to try again with a second appointment in a few weeks' time. Geraldine was, by now, convinced that her boy was deaf, so she and John set out to conduct their own hearing tests at home, to establish if Aaron was indeed deaf, and if so, *how* deaf. They slammed doors; dropped pans behind him; called him; squeaked toys behind him; rattled things; banged lids together; shouted at him; whistled at him and whispered to him. Even Jamie, bless him, got into the act too, clapping his hands and whooping hard behind his little brother, and Bram barked at him in such happiness. Sometimes Aaron turned; sometimes he didn't. The second hearing test appointment came; Aaron had an electrocochleograph test, which involved having several surface electrodes stuck on his small head while a tiny microphone and earphone were inserted into the canal of each ear. At first, Aaron was uncomfortable with the wires around his head, but Geraldine managed to calm him down, as she was told it was very important that he relaxed in order to fulfil the test. Mrs Wilson, the audiologist, measured his hearing by transmitting some clicking sounds.

Geraldine didn't really understand the terminology or how it all worked, just that the lady used an electrograph to collect graphical data. The test took about forty minutes, then it was confirmed that Aaron had very severe hearing loss in both ears: in other words, he was profoundly deaf.

Geraldine looked away from the hospital card on the corkboard, thinking about the bus ride home from the hospital with Aaron and Jamie. For her, it was a long ride because she was still numb with shock and emotion, her head spinning with thousands of thoughts, anxieties and fears. When John walked through the front door after work, she wrapped her arms around him and cried her eyes out.

'Aaron's deaf,' she finally said through her tears. 'Oh, John, what will we do?'

Geraldine still didn't know whether this distressing news had hit her or John hardest; John never really opened up and talked about his feelings, although they shared similar concerns and fears about Aaron's future. Questions flew; how was he born deaf? Why was he deaf? Had something gone wrong during pregnancy? Had she eaten or drunk something she shouldn't have? Had she had an accident, no matter how small? Had she been ill? Was it the umbilical cord round his neck during the birth that caused it? Was it simply down to some form of genetic disorder that other parents of disabled children had?

Then they wondered whether Aaron would grow up as a normal child. Would he be a vegetable? Would he need looking after for the rest of his life? Would he have low intelligence? Would he be able to talk like a normal hearing child? How would he feel about being deaf? Would he be able to learn how to write English? Would he be able to communicate with them? Would they be able to communicate with him? Would he get a good specialist education? Would he be able to get a job? Would he ever meet a girl? Would he have children? Would he ever be able to hear anything? How would he survive in this big, complicated world? There were so many questions and so few answers.

'Look, darling,' John had said softly one morning, resting his arms on the breakfast table and looking into the eyes of his still weeping wife. 'He's still our son, whether he's handicapped or not, and we'll always love him. I know it's going to be very difficult but we will just have to adjust to something that's totally new to us.'

Geraldine turned back to the cooker; the kettle was still boiling. She crossed the kitchen towards another worktop. As she picked up a white ceramic teapot, she saw a ball of blue wool and some knitting needles propped up against the wall. She chuckled, as the sight of it sparked another memory.

Aaron had powerful hearing aids fitted by Mrs Wilson on the advice of Professor Sanderson, the ear specialist, who'd also confirmed to Geraldine and John at their next appointment that Aaron was profoundly deaf for sure. The hearing aids were a heavy, cumbersome Amplivox model with hard plastic earmoulds. The audiologist said they would help him talk and become a normal child. Geraldine and John were delighted with them, believing the aids would help them all, but their twelve–month old baby constantly yanked the moulds from his ears and cried, trying to pull the aids from his chest. Every time Geraldine tried to put the moulds back into his ears, he pulled them out. John brought home a large pair of headphones that he was given by a work colleague whose brother worked for the RAF, in the hope that they would work better for Aaron. Unfortunately, the headphones were too big and swamped his head. Exasperated by her failure to keep the moulds in, Geraldine had decided to knit Aaron a hood with earflaps that tied under his chin, trapping the moulds inside, so that he couldn't take them out.

Geraldine opened the lid of the teapot and peered into it. Cold tea and a few old tea bags were still inside. She thought back about the number of hearing aids that Aaron had worn since then. The moulds were hard plastic, which made it painful for him to eat. He had refused to wear body worn aids at home all his life, but seemed to be more content with the recently introduced behind the ear hearing aids, although she knew that *any* hearing aids were of little or no benefit to him. Geraldine went back to the sink, replacing the lid on the teapot and leaving a little gap. She turned the teapot upside down and the cold tea spilled down through the small opening, the tea bags thudding onto the underside of the lid she was holding. As she watched the brown liquid stream away, her mind flitted back to things had been before the eventual discovery of Aaron's deafness.

Aaron was always screaming and crying. He liked to be held and every time Geraldine left him alone in his cot, he cried. When she held him, he stopped crying. Every time she tried to make him sleep on his side, he cried, but when he lay on his back, he would gaze up and coo happily at his mother. No matter how many times she fed him to try and make him sleep, he always cried every time she left him alone. Even on car journeys to and from Swansea, visiting Mam and Father, Aaron would refuse to sleep while Jamie always slept. Aaron was always *very* attentive to everything that was happening around him, even during feeding. Professor Sanderson said that Aaron's reactions to some of the home hearing tests that she and John had conducted on him may have been due to his quick eye perception, sensitivity to vibration and simply feeling their presence around him. He also explained that the hair cells in both of Aaron's ears were dead and that there was no cure or treatment for this type of hearing loss.

The flow of the cold tea trickled down to a drip. Geraldine carefully separated the upside down lid with the old tea bags on it from the teapot. She turned and walked towards the back door where the pedal bin was. She placed her foot on the pedal, making the flap on the top of the bin swing open, then bent slightly, turning the lid, allowing the tea bags to plummet into the white plastic liner. She straightened, releasing her foot from the pedal, and looked through the glass in the back door into the blackness beyond. She thought about the times that followed the diagnosis.

At first, Geraldine felt that she could not even talk to her little baby, but she soon became fiercely protective of him and loved him more than ever. She and John agreed that they would do everything in their power to give him the best upbringing possible. They would give him plenty of love and care, find out as much about deafness as possible, help him to hear things through his hearing aids, help him to learn to talk, help him to fit into the hearing world, find out about the best education he could have, and get support for the family.

Geraldine silently chuckled to herself as she turned away from the back door towards the worktop, holding the teapot in one hand and the lid in the other. She placed the lid on the worktop and reached for the chrome teabag tin that was next to the blue wool and knitting needles. She opened the lid and took out three fresh teabags. She thought back to all those years of Aaron growing up: it had had not been easy bringing up a profoundly deaf child, especially during the first few years of his life.

Simon from next door came and gave Geraldine some information from the National Deaf Children's Society, which was about deaf children and how to talk to them. Simon had got it through his deaf parents who knew someone who worked for the organisation. To her astonishment, the leaflet was dated 1934. She telephoned the organisation to ask for the updated version, but was told that what she had was the latest they had. She and John were not impressed.

A few weeks later, John brought home an address for the John Tracy Clinic based in Los Angeles, USA. He was given it by a work colleague whose wife was an education officer. Apparently the clinic gave free monthly distance learning lessons to parents of deaf children under the age of five, all over the world. Geraldine immediately wrote to ask for lessons, and a month later, their introductory letter came through the post. For Geraldine and John, it was like a breath of fresh air. The letter firstly reminded them that their baby was still the same baby they had had before s/he was diagnosed as deaf, and s/he shouldn't be treated any differently now. It encouraged parents to talk to their babies in exactly the same way as they had done before they knew they were deaf. It also said their baby would watch the mother's face a lot, picking up clues, and that they would learn to lipread from watching the mother's face. Parents were also encouraged to sing to their babies.

Month after month for a year, a new lesson came through the post. They gave parents ideas about how to communicate with their babies orally, showing them things and putting a hand or finger by their mouths when they talked, as a deaf baby would follow hands rather than lips, to encourage the idea that hearing people used their lips to talk. They were also encouraged to go for walks, stop their pushchairs and point to things, such as hedges, and talk about them. They were reminded to face their babies when talking – not something that came naturally – and to make sure that their faces were in good light, and to be aware of their facial expressions.

One day, there was a knock on the door. Carrying a fourteen–month old Aaron, Geraldine answered it. A young woman, who'd introduced herself as Miss Shields, said she was a teacher of the deaf at the Partially Hearing Unit at Henbury Court Infants, Juniors and Seniors School. Mrs Wilson, the audiologist, had asked her to visit to offer support and advice. Geraldine and Miss Shields talked a great deal about Aaron in the living room; although Geraldine suspected the woman did not have much experience with deaf babies, some of her advice was invaluable. Geraldine asked about learning sign language to communicate with Aaron after discovering it amongst the vast amount of information she had collated.

'Don't use sign language!' the teacher of the deaf said bluntly. 'It's banned. You must talk to him and he must learn how to talk. That is the way it is, so that he can be normalised into hearing society.'

Geraldine popped the three teabags into the pot and closed the lid. Banned, my foot, she thought. Why on earth was sign language not allowed? She sighed as she walked back to the cooker, placing the teapot on the worktop next to it. She thought again about what the woman said about normalising Aaron into society. To her and John, Aaron was as normal as anyone else in the world. So much so, they no longer considered him "handicapped" – a nasty word to describe anyone disabled, she believed – as they had first perceived him at the time of the diagnosis. They also saw that deafness was *not* a learning disability. They simply saw Aaron as a beautiful deaf boy. She remembered that she had had another visitor; a senior teacher of the deaf named Mr Lloyd, a grey–haired man who was responsible for the education of the deaf in the area. He had said exactly the same thing, stressing that the oral/aural approach was the best and only way to educate deaf children. Professor Sanderson and Mrs Wilson advocated along similar lines, suggesting that sign language often distracted deaf children from learning written and spoken English. Geraldine turned to face the corkboard again, thinking about everything those professionals had told her and John at the time; they had believed every word. She smiled when she glanced at a small printed card pinned to the corkboard, which showed the two–handed fingerspelling alphabet, remembering that it was given to her shortly after Aaron had moved to Elmfield School for the Deaf near their home at the age of seven. She folded her arms, hearing the kettle still boiling behind her, and thought back to the six years that followed Aaron's diagnosis.

It was a very difficult time for her and John to begin with; they had to learn how to raise their deaf child fast. This was something totally new to them; they tried to talk slowly and clearly to him, they tried to make him talk too, but with little or no success. They tried to make him understand simple things by using gestures, but it was always a struggle and they tried to make him try to listen to sounds through his powerful hearing aids – when he had them on – but this literally fell on deaf ears. When he tried to say something to them, they couldn't understand him, so he had tantrums and threw his toys in frustration, sometimes crying. He generally refused point blank to wear his body worn hearing aids; every time he was told to wear them, he would get angry and point at the hard plastic moulds, using gestures that they hurt his ears.

Aaron was not the only problem Geraldine and John had; Jamie became jealous of all the attention they gave to his three–year–old brother.

'You *always talk* to Aaron, not me!' the five–year old complained.

'Jamie,' his mother tried to explain, 'you can hear what we say. Aaron's ears aren't working properly, so he has to *see* what we say.'

Sometimes Jamie understood, sometimes he didn't. He was too young to understand Aaron's deafness. Then Aaron began to invent some of his own signs, which were mostly for simple things, such as *eat, drink, plate, swimming, drive, wee–wee, poo–poo, fell down* and *dog*. Geraldine and John began to learn and understand what their deaf son was saying, which made things a little bit easier for everyone in the family. Even Jamie became interested in what Geraldine called *home signs*. Aaron and Jamie, being very young boys, were able to communicate with each other about a variety of things by pointing and gesturing.

When Mr Lloyd suggested that Aaron should start pre–school at the Partially Hearing Unit at Henbury Court School, where Jamie also attended, Geraldine and John were reluctant at first. The unit was for partially deaf children and was housed in a hearing school environment, but they had no other option. Geraldine thought Aaron disliked the school because he had some problems fitting into the completely oral classroom environment, but she had hoped he would mature over time. But he could not settle; he often came home from school upset, frustrated and disoriented.

It was also around then, that at the age of three, Aaron began to realise written letters meant something. The unit had suggested to Geraldine and John that they could create flash cards to help Aaron to identify things. She had firstly made a card which bore Aaron's name, and placed it on his dressing gown in his bedroom one evening, knowing he would see it upon waking. He was delighted to see his own name on it, and dragged the whole family to his bedroom, pointing at the card and then at himself. Geraldine and John then made more name cards for Aaron, and placed them on things: "Chair" on the chair, "Table" on the table, "Door" against the door, "Cooker" on the cooker, "Car" on the bonnet of their car, "Grass" on the lawn ... They wrote down almost every word they could think of for things in the house for Aaron to learn. He absolutely *loved* it and he wanted *more*.

When Aaron was about five, writing fascinated him; he practically *never* stopped writing about anything that he could think of. In fact, he had the hunger to read and write anything that came his way, demanding to know what this and that was or what things meant. Geraldine had already learned how to talk to him properly, using clear and expressive speech, and he was able to understand almost every word she said by lipreading; he also sometimes placed his hand on her throat to feel the vocal vibrations. He wanted *more* all the time, which sometimes exhausted his parents.

The unit also made an excellent suggestion that Aaron should learn different names for generic things, and not say, for instance, *bag* for every kind of bag; they should be identified as different things – handbags, carrier bags, rubbish bags, paper bags and luggage. Aaron loved learning and Geraldine soon came to realise that it was most important for him to learn as much vocabulary as possible, although the school had told her that he should learn to speak first to help him understand English better. She disagreed about this; it was her view that if a deaf child was able to learn as much vocabulary as possible, this would help him or her to better understand the meaning and context of written English grammar. She also discovered that some other parents tended to talk in "shorthand" to their deaf children, leaving out the connecting words and proper names for things. Geraldine was determined not to let this happen to her son; she felt that this kind of rather lazy approach limited the deaf child's development.

Geraldine turned back to the cooker and saw that steam was beginning to rise from the kettle's sealed nozzle. Not long to go, she thought, and returned her attention to *The Board of Life*, gazing at a glossy sheet of paper pinned to it, featuring a full–page article and a photograph of the family posing happily. Geraldine chuckled at the photograph, which had been taken about nine years earlier when Aaron was five; she'd had blond curly hair then (she thanked God that hairdo was only a one–off), John had thick, parted black hair and deep sideburns, Jamie had straggly dark brown hair, while Aaron's blond hair ran down to his neck. Geraldine had always been so proud of the article she had written for a national magazine for families of deaf children. It was always a good talking point for visitors, particularly the mothers of newly diagnosed deaf children who came to visit Geraldine for a cuppa and a chat. She pulled out the drawing pin and took the sheet from the board. Even though she had read her own article countless times over the years, it was still an absorbing read. She began to read it again:

THE SHADOW CHILD

By Geraldine Stephens

In all the stories and reports one reads of the struggles and successes of deaf children, there always seems to be one glaring omission, in my opinion. That is the part played by the other child or children in the family – they are mere shadows, sometimes mentioned, sometimes not.

Jamie was 20 months old when Aaron (our profoundly deaf son, now 5) was born. We made all the usual efforts most parents make to prevent jealousy in the first–born before the second arrival, and in this we succeeded to such an extent that jealousy plays a very small part in our family lives today. We were careful to include Jamie in everything we did for the baby; it was always "Mummy and Jamie will do so–and–so" and I became adept at feeding Aaron on the couch with one hand while reading to Jamie with the other! As they got older there was always room on my lap for both of them, one knee for each – and this still applies, though it's a bit crowded now that one is 7 ½ and the other 5.

Aaron was 10 months old when we discovered he was deaf. He was a very independent baby, determined to do everything for himself, even feeding himself before he could properly hold the spoon, and more of his dinner went on the walls and floor than into his mouth! By contrast, Jamie much preferred someone (usually myself) to do things for him, although he fed himself well and easily when he was 10 months. Nowadays they do most things together, and there is little to choose between them in independence and behaviour. When they bath together, for instance, they wash themselves (doing each other's backs) and even wash their own hair. Their favourite game is "seals", which involves much rolling and splashing, and more water ends up on the floor than in the bath very often!

When we knew Aaron was deaf, we tried to make Jamie understand that we had to teach Aaron to talk – of course, he was too young to know what deafness is, but it became a case of "Mummy and Jamie will have to teach Aaron to talk" and he always joined in our after–dinner sessions – Aaron' best time of day – when Aaron sat in his high chair and Jamie and I sat opposite, holding various objects by our faces and naming them. Then we progressed to picking up objects as we named them, both boys taking it in turn, and by the time Jamie was 2 ½ he would get into Aaron's cot in the mornings and "read" to him. Of course he couldn't read, but he would show Aaron pictures and say "horse" and "cow" and so on. As they got older, Aaron would copy Jamie in everything – and still does; for example, whatever Jamie draws Aaron will draw, and in this way has learnt what castles, flags, helicopters, etc. are – adding immeasurably to his development and knowledge. He has learnt to play imaginary games with Jamie (and is rarely himself – he's usually a snowman, or a duck, or a kangaroo or something), to do somersaults, to draw and paint, to hold his breath under water (which I feel is quite an achievement for a small deaf child). Jamie has just learnt to swim – mainly under water – and neither of them has the slightest fear of water.

Because of Aaron's handicap, Jamie has had to learn a high degree of tolerance and patience, and Aaron has learnt to take turns from an early age, after weathering many storms and tantrums!

As any parent knows, the hardest part of having a hearing child and deaf child in the family is maintaining a balance between the two. The deaf child needs so much attention, both physically and in speech, to a point where the hearing child often gets neglected and overlooked. Visitors always ask about the deaf child and show little interest in the achievements of the hearing one – and they give sweets to one and not the other, although this is not much of a problem to us, as Aaron doesn't like sweets. Where punishment is concerned, a mother has to play it craftily in order that the hearing child feels justice has been done. Many times when Aaron has unknowingly misbehaved I have scolded him quietly and out of his sight, so that Jamie feels he has been punished for something that he (Jamie) would be punished for. As far as jealousy goes, it seems to be more apparent now that Aaron is older and more competition than he used to be, but most of it is natural jealousy between two brothers of a close age, and we make great efforts to treat them both as equally as possible, and if it is not possible, to give Jamie an adequate explanation as to why the treatment is different. Aaron so obviously adores him – flies to him with hugs and kisses whenever he comes home from school, and hero–worships him so much, that Jamie feels himself to be bigger and better in most respects.

Jamie has grown up with a very protective attitude to Aaron as he was always expected to keep an eye on him whenever they were out playing, to prevent him getting into danger, and he has become very good at finding him whenever he is out of sight. He can't bear Aaron to cry, and will often give in to him to prevent it (which is very bad for Aaron really).

On the other side of the coin, he has always been a far more clinging child than Aaron, even before Aaron was born, and runs to me at the slightest provocation. He has less confidence, and always needs my support and backing in any new venture, whereas to Aaron the entire world is his friend! He finds communication with Aaron inadequate sometimes and gets frustrated because he can't make him understand what he wants and then sparks fly.

Jamie is just beginning to realise what deafness means – after a wrestling game which turned into a quarrel when Aaron pulled his hair, he dissolved into floods of tears and said "I wish Aaron could hear and talk like other boys, and I could play proper games with him, but he will talk one day, won't he?" Aaron does talk now of course, in his own way, and this is entirely due to his own efforts and those of everyone around him, including Jamie himself.

Geraldine smiled proudly at the article once more. She pinned it back to the board, then folded her arms and thought again about Aaron's education at the Henbury Court PHU.

In spite of Aaron gaining a fair amount of vocabulary at home, he still struggled at the PHU. Geraldine and John were told that Aaron tended to feel a bit isolated in the classroom and that the teachers always struggled to teach him to speak. Geraldine went into the unit early one afternoon, only to discover to her shock that Aaron was sitting in the corner reading comics instead of taking part in the class with the partially deaf pupils. The teachers admitted that they could not contend with Aaron's demands as a profoundly deaf child and that his intelligence was far superior to the others' despite his profound deafness, which, in their opinion, was quite unusual. Aaron had achieved easily in many subjects, while the others had struggled. They also said that her seven year old deaf child was not suitable to continue in a mainstream environment, though Geraldine had always believed that Aaron was in fact far *too good* for the unit because he had developed a lot more at home than he did at school. Mr Lloyd then suggested that Aaron would be better off in a specialist school, Elmfield School for the Deaf; Geraldine and John already knew about the school, as they had found out later that it was in their local area, Westbury–on–Trym. Geraldine had always wondered why Mr Lloyd had not suggested the school in the first place. He'd implied that the profoundly deaf children there were "less clever" than those at the PHU, and he was doubtful that Aaron would achieve anything there. Geraldine refused to believe this until she saw it for herself.

Geraldine turned her attention back to the fingerspelling card on the corkboard, chuckling at the memory of seven year–old Aaron's very first day at Elmfield after the Easter break of 1973; a day that she would never forget.

Geraldine and nine–year old Jamie arrived at Elmfield School to pick up Aaron at the end of his first day. The playground was filled with deaf children scurrying to meet their parents. The children were happily waving their hands, wiggling their fingers and gesturing hand shapes at one another.

'Mum,' Jamie tugged his mother's long skirt as he looked up, 'what are they doing with their hands?' he pointed at them, expressing curiosity.

'It is called sign language,' his mother answered. 'That is how the deaf talk to each other.'

Jamie looked back at the playground, totally fascinated by what he was seeing. Aaron trotted briskly through the small crowd towards his mother and older brother, bubbling and whooping. Geraldine knelt to give him a loving hug and he immediately signed happily to her.

'My name is A–A–R–O–N!' he signed then fingerspelled.

This was the first time that Geraldine had ever seen Aaron fingerspell his own name, even though she didn't know the fingerspelling alphabet. Aaron gave her the fingerspelling card; Jamie leaned over to look at the illustrations and immediately placed his right index finger on his left thumb, signing the first letter of the alphabet, becoming even more fascinated by the new language.

When they got home, Aaron didn't stop talking in his own way about his first day at Elmfield. He was a completely different child and a huge breath of fresh air, Geraldine proclaimed, because he had realised he was not the only deaf child in the world and he was able to communicate easily in sign with his own kind outside classes. Even Jamie got excited, mastering the entire fingerspelling alphabet within thirty minutes or so and Aaron was thrilled to bits that he could finally communicate properly with his older hearing brother. Jamie demanded to know more of the signs he had picked up at school; Aaron was more than happy to teach him and Jamie became quite fluent in sign language over the years. Jamie returned the favour by helping Aaron with his homework, helping him to improve his English and interpreting their favourite television programmes and family gatherings for him. Because of this, the brothers were very close; Geraldine had always believed that the help had enhanced Aaron's intelligence even further.

Geraldine looked away from the fingerspelling card on the board, smiling as she remembered trying to learn and finally mastering it after two or three weeks, although Aaron had always preferred to lipread her because he was so used to it. John never really bothered to learn any signs, let alone to fingerspell; he preferred to speak slowly and clearly or to write things down. Sign language was not the only thing she had to learn though, as Elmfield used Cued Speech as a method of communication in the classroom. Elmfield was one of the first schools for the deaf to use this method, although sign language was allowed outside the classroom. She thought the synching of symbolic handshapes and speech was difficult to learn and quite complicated to grasp. Aaron tried it and hated it, preferring sign language which was much easier to do; she agreed with this view.

Geraldine turned back to the cooker, remembering the hotpot in the oven. She crouched, opening the oven door, and checked inside. The gravy inside the glass casserole dish was bubbling and the sliced potatoes on top were browning nicely, so it was almost ready. She closed the door, deciding to give it ten more minutes. She straightened, taking another glance at the kettle; the steam was rising more rapidly now through the gap in the nozzle. Nearly boiling, she mused and smiled proudly to herself when she thought about the four years that had followed at

Elmfield.

Aaron was happy at Elmfield, despite the difficulty he had understanding the complex Cued Speech approach during lessons. His education progressed exceptionally well; so well that he was top in many subjects, including English. He always did his homework; he usually did it first in pencil and then checked it with his parents or Jamie, so that they could help and make corrections or suggestions. Once this was done, he rubbed out his pencil writings and redid them in pen. He handed in his homework every day; something that some of the other deaf pupils rarely did. The school was pleased with his education and called him a perfect role model for other deaf children, although Geraldine knew that some of the older deaf pupils were quite jealous of him and sometimes bullied him. She mused on the fact that his English literacy skills were so far ahead of the other deaf pupils'; something which had always puzzled her. He seemed to have a better ability to understand the written language than many others. Geraldine thought again about what Professor Sanderson and Mrs Wilson had warned her about shortly after Aaron's diagnosis – sign language detracted from deaf children's ability to learn written language. Now, she saw absolutely *no evidence* of that. She now firmly believed that sign language *actually enhanced* deaf children's understanding of written English.

Bilingualism, she called it.

Aaron mixed well with the other deaf children at the school, made some friends, played games, and had sleepovers; either at his home or at his friends'. His deaf friends loved Jamie, for he also could sign and he always came in handy when it came to interpreting television programmes for them, and especially for signing the songs from his Elvis record collection.

When Aaron was about ten, Mr Lloyd retired and Mrs Moreliver took his place as the Senior Teacher of the Deaf. Geraldine had always thought Aaron disliked her because she would glower over him and he complained that she was difficult to lipread. Mrs Moreliver had been impressed with Aaron's education at Elmfield, but it was she who had suggested that he should go to Ewing Hill Park to further his education the following year, as she felt he would not properly fulfil his potential at Elmfield. She did, however, acknowledge that the school was a very good one; they were already considering moving away from Cued Speech to the new Total Communication in class. She went on to say that Ewing Hill Park, a boarding school, was one of the best oral technical schools for the deaf in the country. She had recently learnt that Mr Donald Langston, who she knew well, had been appointed as headmaster a year before; he was a very good man. She also revealed that although the school was oral, the deaf boys were now allowed to sign in their own time, as Mr Langston had just relaxed the strict rules imposed by his predecessor, so Aaron would be fine there.

Geraldine crossed the kitchen, still thinking about the wrench she and John had felt at the time. She opened one of the top cupboard doors, took out two mugs, placed them on the worktop and closed the door. She thought about the year that followed.

Geraldine and John had had much discussion about whether to agree to send Aaron to a boarding school two hundred miles away. They were quite conflicted over this because they didn't want to send him away, however, at the same time, they knew he would get a better education there. They visited Ewing Hill Park on its Open Day the following October and met Mr Langston for the first time. There, they were impressed with the way the school was run and the way the deaf boys were educated in different subjects by different teachers in different classrooms, despite the oral approach. They also briefly met Chris, who was a First Former then, in passing, and the new art teacher, Mr McShane, who they discovered was fluent in sign language because of his deaf family. They liked the fact that the school was one of the very few schools for the deaf where pupils took the CSE, O Level and, if possible, A Level examinations, which they wanted Aaron to do. They were also impressed with the exhibition displays developed by the boys themselves and felt that their son's practical and social skills would benefit even further outside the classroom; it was an ideal environment. So, the decision was made; he would go there.

The following December, Aaron took the preliminary entrance exams at Elmfield. He was confused about it all at first, but he took them anyway. Then, the following March, he took – and passed – the main entrance exams at Ewing Hill Park. Aaron said that he liked it there and wanted to go in September, which pleased Geraldine and John, though it was still heartbreaking for them. In August that year, their dog Bram had to be put to sleep; the fourteen–year old Alsatian had eaten something toxic, they didn't know what, but it made him sick. This was on the same day that Jamie's idol, Elvis, died. Poor lad, it had hit him hard. He had been stroppy for quite a while after that, even on the car journey to the school on Aaron's first day a month later. All told, it was a distressing time for all of them.

Geraldine picked up the two mugs and thought about the fight she had had with the education department at the council to get them to agree to fund Aaron's place at Ewing Hill Park. They had initially refused, saying that it was their policy to fund deaf children only for schools within their area. Fortunately for her and John, Mrs Moreliver fought tooth and nail for them, finally convincing her superiors that Ewing Hill Park was the best place for Aaron; she pointed out that he was not the first, nor the last, deaf child in the area who went to a boarding school out of the area. She also promised them that she would report on Aaron's progress regularly; hence the visits to see him during school holidays.

Geraldine walked over to the table and put the mugs on it. The kettle behind her began to hiss, but her mind was still preoccupied with Aaron and his education at Ewing Hill Park.

Aaron had shown remarkable achievements in his education there, particularly in English. His English teacher, Mr Whittle, always commented in Aaron's school reports that he was pleased with his progress. Geraldine already knew he had improved; she could see this for herself from his letters; his written English had showed a gradual improvement over the last two years and three months and was now excellent. She was also pleased with his progress in the other subjects he was taking, although he did often struggled with maths, which had never been his strong point. As for his speech; it was alright. He still couldn't speak well, but it was much better than it was before he went to Ewing Hill Park. Geraldine appreciated Aaron's honesty in his letters about how some of the teachers were difficult to understand. She also enjoyed reading about other things that Aaron wrote about school life, though she knew there were other aspects that he only shared with Jamie in his letters to him; he always made sure that all of those envelopes were sealed tight with Sellotape. Cheeky beggar, Geraldine smiled, but she supposed they were simply being brothers who loved to tell each other everything.

Geraldine suddenly heard Chris yelling and laughing in the living room, followed by the sound of Aaron laughing. She thought about Chris. Poor lad, what a terrible life he'd had. When Chris explained his situation through Jamie at Barbara's last October, Geraldine and John's hearts had gone out to him. They saw how close Aaron was to Chris and that Chris had got on extremely well with Jamie, so they agreed to have him over Christmas. Mr Langston got them to contact Chris' social worker, Mr Lewison, who was good enough to drive over to Bristol last month to meet them and discuss Chris. Steve Lewison had given them the lowdown on his personal circumstances, though he remained tight-lipped about the boy's father. Steve Lewison said Chris was really a good and extremely mature boy, albeit a little hot tempered. He thought Ewing Hill Park had done wonders for Chris' education, development and discipline, so he and his superiors were quite pleased. Steve Lewison mentioned that he was learning sign language through a deaf friend of his wife's, which really helped him to communicate with Chris, as well as with his other deaf clients. John asked why sign language was banned.

'I don't really know why,' Steve Lewison replied. 'Apparently, from what I've been told, it's been banned for about a hundred years now.'

'Surely,' Geraldine said, 'we've seen for ourselves that it's very effective.'

'I agree,' John added. 'But *why* is it banned?'

Leaving the question unanswered, their discussion soon moved to the idea of the Stephens fostering Chris over the school holidays for his remaining years in education; Islington Social Services would be happy to provide funding to support the fostering. Geraldine told Steve Lewison she and John had already discussed this and agreed to have Chris.

Hiss.

Geraldine folded her arms as she thought about Chris' mother, who had apparently sobered up. She and John reluctantly agreed that Chris should return to London on New Year's Eve to be with her, on the advice of Steve Lewison, though the option of fostering still remained should things not work out for him and his mother. She gazed back at the corkboard, still pensive. She saw a photograph of a group of seven women, including herself, and some young children. She smiled, remembering how the photograph had been taken at the first Mothers of Deaf Children meeting she had organised shortly after Aaron went to Elmfield.

Upon discovering that there was little or no support for parents of deaf children in the area, she decided to do something about it. Through word of mouth and telephone calls, she got some mothers of deaf children at Elmfield and Henbury Court to meet at a playground in Westbury-on-Trym. They shared various experiences about bringing up their children and were united in agreement that there was a need for a family support group for them. One mother, Michelle, said she knew another woman who lived in the Yorkshire Ridings. She'd been to her first meeting for parents of deaf children in a village hall back in January 1970, which was organised by two mothers who each had a very young deaf boy. There was absolutely no support for parents of deaf children in the area, so they wanted to do something about it, starting off in a small way. Their first meeting attracted about a hundred parents and deaf children. As a result, the Yorkshire branch of the National Deaf Children's Society was formed, with about fifty members from the meeting, and it was still running to this day. Geraldine thought this was an excellent example of how important it was to have family support groups and she wanted one, like a family centre, in Westbury-on-Trym. Perhaps, one day–

'*Geraldine!*' a voice boomed, snapping her out of her deep thoughts. She whirled round to see John standing in the doorway, pointing at the cooker. 'The kettle!'

Geraldine turned to the cooker and saw a huge cloud of steam billowing furiously from the kettle, filling the kitchen with a damp mist. John hurried over to the cooker, grabbing the tea towel and wrapping it round the hot handle. He carefully picked it up and moved it to an unused ring. He turned off the flame, then shook his head and sighed.

'What's taking you so long?' John turned to his wife with a wry smile on his face. 'I'm bloody gasping for a cuppa!'

21

1980

"Just a thought … it is interesting to see that DEAF people can function in the hearing world very well while hearing people cannot function well in the DEAF world."
– Gil Eastman, Professor on Theatre & Drama Studies at Gallaudet (1934–2006)

Chris sat on his bed on the floor, tucking his legs between the sheets and blanket and pulling his pyjama bottoms into a more comfortable position. He reached for his dark blue pyjama top and began to put it on. He glanced at the half open door expectantly, but the black haired man in blue tights still greeted him; he had a red and yellow S–shaped emblem on his chest and wore a red cape. His clenched hands stretched forward, he was flying towards Chris. The top of the poster on the back of the door screamed his name.

He smiled, remembering the film they had seen a few days before at the ABC on Frogmore Street. It was a rerun and Aaron and Jamie had already seen it three times, but they wanted to see it again anyway and Chris hadn't yet seen it. He'd thoroughly enjoyed it. He chuckled at the memory of Jamie, who had signed the film's sound for them again – extorting the usual high price of extra confectionary, of course – jumping on his seat, his right arm outstretched, screaming *Suuupppeeerrrmmmaaannn, go, go!* as the superhero flew furiously up the Daily Planet tower to rescue Lois Lane, who was hanging perilously from the undercarriage of the helicopter stranded at the top.

Chris began to button up his pyjama top as he looked around Aaron's bedroom, which was nothing more than a haven for toys, games, models, posters, books and other merchandise, most of which were related to film and television. The first time Chris had been into the bedroom, two weeks before, he'd been quite astounded by the sight and spent some considerable time browsing: it was like being in a museum. He picked up some from an array of toys and models he recognised, the X–wing fighter; The Saint's white Jaguar XJS, and the Aston Martin from Goldfinger with a pop–up bulletproof shield at the back and a passenger ejector seat. There was much more – Dinky cars and little action figures from Star Trek, Star Wars and Planet of the Apes. An Action Man and Steve Austin dolls also rested idly on a shelf along with several others that Chris didn't recognise. He also saw some board games stacked up on top of the wardrobe and he read some of their names along the sides; Mission: Impossible; Kerplunk and Subbuteo. Aaron said that there were more board games in Jamie's bedroom and in the living room. Chris then browsed the bookshelf, which had a collection of movie novelisations, science fiction novels written by Arthur C. Clarke, Ray Bradbury and Douglas Adams. He picked out an extremely thick paperback called The Stand by Stephen King and flicked through it, astonished to discover that it had over 1,300 pages. Aaron said he'd got the latest novel from his dad last Christmas, and it had a deaf character in it. Chris came across a collection of hardback annuals and idly read some of the names along their spines: The Wombles, The Sweeny, Logan's Run, Battlestar Galatica and Space 1999. Chris turned to Aaron's bed, which was by the wall opposite the door; his own bed was on the floor adjacent to it, by the window. He saw the Star Wars cinema poster on the wall by Aaron's bed and shook his head, hinting to Aaron that he was definitely a sci–fi freak. Aaron smiled back and told him he'd got the poster through a school friend of Jamie's whose father worked at the Odeon in Union Street.

Chris was equally amazed when he walked into Jamie's bedroom shortly afterwards to see that Jamie was just as bad as his brother; his bed was positioned in the centre of the room with a Scalextric track running round it, there was a shelf holding a full collection of Elvis LPs and posters of The King all around the room. Aaron commented that Jamie's name sign was *Elvis–style microphone,* although Aaron sometimes changed the gesture slightly to look more like *sucking a dick* to tease Jamie. There were posters of other pop groups; Chris later learned their names from Jamie: The Jam, The Police, the Bay City Rollers, Blondie and the Boomtown Rats. Like Aaron, Jamie had a collection of hardback annuals that included Top of the Pops, Charlie's Angels and The Muppets, which surprised Chris, but Jamie said he absolutely loved the show.

Chris finished buttoning up his pyjama top. He looked at the door again, wondering how soon Aaron would be up with their hot chocolate. He rested his forearms on his covered thighs, thinking about the Christmas he had spent with the family.

It was the best Christmas he had ever had. He still vaguely remembered some of the Christmases he had with his parents when he was younger, before their split. The last seven years of Christmases in children's and foster homes were an experience that he would rather forget, especially the one with the Allan family, who had treated him with contempt and did not give him any Christmas presents.

Chris looked down to the end of his bed at a football with red and white pentagons on, with the Arsenal FC emblem printed on some of them. It was from Aaron. He smiled broadly, remembering Aaron's face when he'd opened Chris' present, to find he had been given *all* of the Top Trumps cards he had used to "pay" his brother for his signing jobs. Chris explained that he couldn't afford to buy Aaron a Christmas present, so while Aaron and his mother were out Christmas shopping, he had challenged Jamie to a bout of arm wrestling; best of five, and they'd agreed that Jamie would relinquish all of Aaron's Top Trumps cards if he lost. They were even at two–all, with the fifth and final match the most strenuous, but Chris won. Aaron whooped and hugged Chris while Jamie bit the bullet.

Chris slumped back on the pillows and thought about the wonderful Christmas dinner Aaron's mother had cooked: it was the best he had ever eaten. He also chuckled as he remembered how Jamie had reluctantly agreed to sign a repeat of the Morecambe and Wise 1977 Christmas Special for free, in the spirit of Christmas. He had never laughed so much at their jokes, especially that sketch with them and Penelope Keith dancing down the half–finished staircase. Jamie did a really good impression of Eric Morecambe, even borrowing his dad's glasses for added effect. Chris also enjoyed playing with the new Atari ST console that Aaron and Jamie got from their parents for Christmas. The wood–finished box with a slot on the top hooked up to the television and they played Pac Man and Ping Pong on it. He also enjoyed riding Jamie's Raleigh Chopper on the quiet roads outside and playing some of the board games, especially Subbuteo; he loved beating Jamie, which he did most of the time.

The door slowly opened, alerting Chris. Aaron walked in, carrying two mugs of hot chocolate. He crossed the room and handed one to Chris, who then placed it on the low table next to him. Aaron put his on the bedside table next to his bed. He turned, pulling up his jumper and looking at Chris.

'Are you looking forward to tomorrow?' Aaron asked.

'I don't know,' Chris shrugged. 'My mum's meeting me at Paddington station.'

Aaron pulled up his tee shirt, revealing his bare upper body, and picked up his pyjama top. 'I wish you could be here for our New Year's Eve party tomorrow.'

'Same here,' Chris concurred as he watched Aaron put on his top, 'but I also want to be with my mum. A fresh start, you know?'

'I understand,' Aaron nodded, finishing buttoning up his top. 'I'll see you back at school next week anyway.'

Chris nodded, flopping his hands on the bed. He watched Aaron unzip, pull down and take off his trousers before turning to put them on a chair by the bedside table. Chris' eyes drifted away, wondering about tomorrow. How would things be with his mother, who he hadn't seen for seven years? Would they get along? Would she keep her promise not to drink again? Was she still seeing that bastard, Bob Sullivan? Would he and his mother be able to make a fresh start? Would he no longer have to live in children's or foster homes? Would he *go home* for the holidays at long last?

Chris brushed the questions from his mind. He turned to see Aaron's bare bottom as he pulled down his underwear and reached for his pyjama bottoms from the bed. Chris stared at Aaron, not able to take his eyes off him, as he turned and, with his left leg supporting his weight, put his other leg into the right trouser leg. Chris glimpsed part of his dangling member, partially shadowed beneath the pyjama top.

Aaron saw Chris watching him from the corner of his eye, so he quickly finished putting his pyjama bottoms on. He whirled round just as Chris looked away. Aaron stamped on the carpet to get his friend's attention.

'You looked!' he chuckled, pointing at his groin.

'No, I didn't!' Chris shook his head, feigning innocence.

'Yes, you did!' Aaron approached his floor bed, laughing. 'I saw you!'

'I didn't, honest!' Chris crossed his heart.

'Liar!'

Aaron pounced playfully on Chris, pushing him back and getting on top of him. Chris was at a disadvantage as his legs were still inside the bed, meaning he was restricted to using only his arms and hands to defend himself. Aaron continued to clamber on Chris, trying to reach his upper body, to tickle him. Chris grabbed Aaron's hand to prise him away as he tried to pull his legs out from between the sheets, but Aaron's weight and legs were pressing on the bed, making things difficult for him. He winced when he felt a hard pressure on his groin; he looked down to see that Aaron's left knee was unintentionally resting on it. Or was it intentional? Chris couldn't tell, but it was hurting his testicles. He thrust his free hand towards Aaron.

Aaron yelped, feeling that something had groped him down below. His eyes darted down to see that Chris' hand was through the slit of his pyjama trousers. Aaron grabbed his wrist and forcibly pushed it away. He backed away, crossing his legs, and sat at Chris' feet.

'You … touched it!' Aaron snapped at him.

'It was an accident. I didn't mean to do it,' Chris said, again feigning innocence.

'No,' Aaron shook his head, not believing him. 'It wasn't an accident. Tell the truth!'

Chris knew that he was cornered; he had no believable answer for it. 'No–'

'You fancy me, don't you?'

'I … I …' Chris tried to explain. 'Look, I'm sorry–'

'You're a poof!' Aaron rose to his feet, keeping his balance on the floor mattress and looking down at his friend. 'Forget it. Goodnight.'

Aaron hopped off and jumped onto his own bed, then got in. Chris slumped back, his head resting on the pillows.

Aaron started to read his latest copy of 2000AD, but stopped short on page two as he began to wonder about his best friend.

The long hand struck midnight.

A chorus of *Happy New Year!* echoed around the living room. Aaron looked away from the familiar white clock face on the television and knocked on Jamie's head with his fist.

'Happy New Year, butthead!' he exclaimed.

Jamie responded with the same gesture. 'Happy New Year, butthead!'

Geraldine pulled Aaron round and kissed his cheek, before doing the same to Jamie. 'Happy New Year, you two! It's 1980 now!'

Aaron glanced around the crowded living room; the family had invited some of the neighbours to the party. He had counted about twenty of them, including himself, in the house. Suzanne Madison, a fourteen–year old hearing girl from next door who Aaron knew fancied him, came over and deliberately kissed his lips for a long moment. The pretty brunette stepped back, her heart pounding.

'Happy New Year, sunshine!' she said loudly and headed away with a big grin on her face. Aaron blushed and soon felt a hard slap on his back, but he ignored his brother.

A hand clutched his right shoulder; he turned to see his dad standing drunkenly between him and Jamie. His other hand was on Jamie's arm. He pulled them close to him and hugged them fondly. Aaron craned his neck at his dad's rambling mouth. 'Happy New Year, my wonderful boys!'

When their dad staggered away, Jamie pointed at the empty wine glass that Aaron was holding. 'More red wine?' he asked, swallowing the last bit from his own glass.

'Mum said we were only allowed one glass,' Aaron pointed out. He was feeling tipsy. 'We've already had three!'

'Don't be a wimp!' Jamie snatched the empty glass from Aaron's hand and headed for the door into the hallway.

Aaron's mother turned back to Aaron. 'Where has Jamie gone?' she wondered.

Aaron gestured an imaginary glass and pointed in the direction of the kitchen.

Rib–eeennna.

'Ribena, good,' she nodded, knowing what her son meant. 'As long as both of you don't drink any more of the wine. Anyway, I hope Chris is enjoying himself with his mother right now.'

Aaron wondered the same thing. He thought about that morning when he, Jamie and their dad had taken Chris to the station for him to catch the train to London. Chris and Aaron had barely conversed since the night before. They were still feeling a bit awkward about what had happened and it was difficult to talk about it with the family around, particularly Jamie. When Jamie went to the toilet at the station, taking advantage of John's lack of knowledge of sign, Chris told Aaron he was sorry for what happened and he hoped they would still be best friends. Aaron agreed with a broad smile and said that it was best forgotten. They hugged fondly.

Something clinked on his forehead, causing him to break off his thoughts. He saw that Jamie was holding up an almost full glass of red wine and smiling widely.

The small colour television was still showing scenes of celebrations by masses of revellers crowded around Trafalgar Square and the Big Ben. An array of fireworks dominated the night sky with colourful explosions, streaks and rains.

Chris took another sip from a bottle of Budweiser, staring blankly at the television from a battered sofa. He looked around the small living room, which had a wall mirror above a small, half lit gas fireplace. A mantelpiece stretched between them; a handful of Christmas cards rested across it, along with other little ornamental items. He looked at the window and the glass door which led to the small eighth floor balcony. He could almost make out some distant explosions in the night sky. He then glanced at another door, which was ajar, next to the window; it led to the small kitchen. He scanned in the other direction, seeing another closed door on the wall opposite the window and balcony. A small round table was in the corner, next to that door. He took another sip of alcohol. How many of these had he had this evening, he wondered, four or five? He wasn't even drunk.

He was still too angry to be drunk.

He brushed his hand across the dark brown weave of the sofa fabric and thought how it was the same old sofa that he remembered. The living room had not changed much either, except for the small colour television which had replaced the old black and white one. Even the cream paint on the walls was the same, after seven years. He knew this because there were still some doodles crayoned on part of the wall. she had given him a rollocking for doing that when he was little, but she'd never bothered to wash it off. Perhaps, he thought, she'd wanted to leave it there as a reminder of her absent son. He looked up at the pink lightshade hanging down from a solitary light; it was the same one as he remembered. The patterned carpet, already worn and smelling stale, was the same one too. A dog wouldn't want to lie on it, he mused to himself.

The closed door on Chris' right suddenly opened and he turned to see his mother stagger in, carrying a bottle of gin in her hand.

'Christopher!' she exclaimed drunkenly, almost falling over when her knee banged against the sofa's armrest, but she managed to keep her balance. 'Happy New Year!'

Chris glared hard at her, saying nothing.

'Oh come on, it's New Year!' Sandra Matthaus leaned close to Chris. The stench of her breath recoiled him, but he kept his eyes on her lips. 'I'm allowed to have a drink to celebrate!'

Chris glanced behind her at a figure emerging through the door. He was a tall and stocky man with a dark brown ponytail and a crooked moustache that reached his jawline. He had a brutal face that seemed to have been hardened by punches; a black panther tattoo adorned his right forearm and he had a cobra on the other. Chris' eyes threw fire at him. He thought about how that bastard had got out of prison yesterday – he'd been inside for some crime, Chris didn't know what – and he'd turned up suddenly this evening with a bagful of booze, including the gin his mother was now holding. Instead of slamming the door on him, she had *welcomed* him in. It was supposed to have been a quiet evening for him and his mother and things were looking good until Bob Sullivan arrived and she started drinking again with his encouragement. They'd just been in the bedroom and Chris didn't want to know what they'd been doing in there.

'Look,' Sandra began to explain, noting her son's anger. 'I know you're a bit upset about Bob being here, but please do try to understand–'

Chris suddenly flew from the sofa and threw the glass bottle at the wall mirror. Both the mirror and the glass exploded on impact with a thunderous shatter, several dozen glass shards showering the mantelpiece and the carpet, leaving a large jagged hole with a web of cracked lines on the mirror.

'I hate you!' Chris screamed at his mother, signing feverishly. 'I fucking hate you! You fucking promised!'

Sandra stepped forward to try to calm her agitated son. 'I don't understand what you're saying–'

Chris lunged at her, pushing her hard. She stumbled backwards, crashing on the sofa behind her and the liquid from the bottle spilling onto her unkempt blouse. Bob advanced towards Chris, grabbing his neck and forcing the boy to stagger back. His back slammed against the window, pinned by the stocky man's strong grip. Chris managed to twist his neck slightly free from the choking grip and squinted underneath Bob's thick crooked moustache to partially see his angrily moving lips.

'You fucking shit–'

Fuuucccooofff!

Bob slammed Chris' head against the window, which held, having guessed what the boy had just tried to say. He squeezed Chris' neck tighter with his large, rough hands. Chris began to suffocate; he quickly grabbed Bob's wrist with both hands to prise it away, but the grip was still too strong. He ground his teeth, glaring hard at the face of a man he hated. They were now almost the same height, though Chris remembered well that he had once been less than half his size. Every time Bob had given him a beating, he could never fight back. He wasn't even his father, but a fuck buddy for his mother, yet he liked to throw fists at them both. But now, he had grown up; he was now stronger and wiser. And, he no longer feared him. His head screamed.

No more! No fucking more! No more!

Chris spat a large amount of saliva on Bob's face. The brute was momentarily distracted, his grip loosening slightly. Chris seized his chance and drove his right knee between the man's legs as hard as he could, feeling the bobbing of his testicles inside his blue jeans. Bob doubled up, finally releasing his hold on Chris, stumbled back a bit and clutched his aching groin with his hands. Chris advanced, driving a clenched fist directly at Bob's nose with all his might. He felt a sharp crack in the nose; blood suddenly sprayed down from his nostrils, turning his dark brown moustache crimson. Bob's head jerked back with such violence. Then, Chris threw a hard punch at the exposed laryngeal prominence, forcing the Adam's apple inwards. Bob collapsed to the floor, clutching his neck and gasping for breath. Chris, in a state of blind rage, was not finished with him yet and not giving the man the chance to fight back; he stamped on the man's groin as hard as he could, feeling the crushing of his crotch. He stamped again, this time harder. Bob screamed loudly, his legs jerking spastically and his torso bending forwards. Chris swung his right leg, his foot hitting the underside of Bob's jaw hard. The man's head tossed back, taking his body with him to the floor. In a rage, Chris blindly and relentlessly kicked his ribs hard several times, feeling some break. Then, he turned to the rubbish bin next to the fallen man, which was full of empty Budweiser bottles, and took one out. Holding the top stout, Chris slammed the bottle hard on Bob's head, shattering the glass and splitting open his forehead. Blood seeped down from the wound, his face quickly turning red. Tiny glass shards wedged themselves into Bob's skin; some into his eyes and some into his hair. Bob convulsed, screaming in agony and slumped back, unconscious.

Chris stood back, holding the half broken glass bottle in his blood stained hand, looking down at the motionless Bob Sullivan. He couldn't believe what he had just done. *He* began to cry.

He closed his eyes and thought about all those beatings he'd suffered at the hands of that bastard when he was eight. He'd beaten up his mother too. He felt a sense of retribution; although he hated himself for what he'd just done, he'd never felt that good. He opened his eyes and stared down at the man again: he saw nothing but a bloodied piece of filth. He didn't even feel any sympathy towards him.

He turned to his mother, who was still lying on the sofa, motionless and numb with shock. Her mouth was wide open and she was clutching the gin bottle for some kind of comfort. Chris and his mother stared at each other for a long moment: Chris pitied her and wondered how she was feeling about him at that very moment.

Chris dropped the jagged bottle on the carpet, wiping his tears with the back of his other hand. He made for the open doorway that led to the small hallway and grabbed his coat from the peg on the wall next to the front door. He turned to see his mother slowly rising to her feet, still clutching the bottle. Bob lay still behind her. Chris had never felt so disappointed in his mother and hoped that he would never see her again. Not ever.

'Christopher …' she pleaded, crying. 'Please don't go …'

Chris turned, opened the front door and walked outside into the cold night.

He slammed the door behind him.

Friday 11th January 1980.
Dear Mum, Dad and Jamie,
My first week back at school gone already!!!

Chris did not have a good New Year with his mother. He said she'd started drinking again and Bob turned up that evening. Chris and Bob had a really bad fight and Chris ran away. He spent the night somewhere in a bus shelter or something and then he went to see his social worker, Mr Lewison, the next day. He stayed with him until he came back to school last Sunday. Can he come and spend half term with us next month, and also the Easter holiday at the end of March? (We can talk about the summer holiday later). Can you please telephone Mr Lewison and Mr Langston to talk about it? Chris really enjoyed himself with us at Christmas and he wants to come again. I know Jamie would love to have him back too!!!

I told my Form that we got the Atari ST for Christmas and they were very jealous! Chris told me that Dean Hopkirk got a new moped from his parents for Christmas. Lucky him, his family's rich! I wish we were rich!

It is really, really cold outside. We had to play football on the front field on Tuesday and I froze to death! My toes turned white, like big white balloons! It was impossible to run around. Mr Norris wore lots of clothes, a woolly hat and gloves, while we all only wore our football shirts and shorts. I had to wear my tracksuit bottoms, but my legs still froze! Afterwards, we all ran to the hot showers. Our feet felt like they were made of ice and the hot water was a big relief! No, Jamie, I'm not a wimp!!

Last Wednesday, Mr Whittle told me that because of my top marks in the English mock exams last December, he thinks I should take the C.S.E. English exams this summer! Form Five normally take C.S.E. and O Level exams, but he thinks I should go for it this year and perhaps do O Level English next year when I'm in Form Four. Gulp! Do you think I should do it or not?!?

Jamie – do you still have the £2 Woolworths voucher that Uncle Neil gave you for Christmas? Buy a Rubik's Cube! It's a new coloured puzzle cube; you sort of shuffle it and then you have to work out how to turn it back and get the same colour on each side of the cube. Shaun Knight, who's in my Form, got one for Christmas and it's really brilliant. All of the boys here want to play with it! I'm going to buy one at Woolworths with my voucher when I go shopping tomorrow afternoon. Buy one!!!

I'd best go now as lunch break is almost over now and I have to post this letter in the school postbox.

Love,

Aaron xxx

Friday 8th February 1980.

Dear Mum, Dad and Jamie,

One week to go before half term!!! I can't wait to come home for a week! Chris is also looking forward to staying with us. Thank you so much, Mum, for helping to arrange with Mr Lewison for Chris to stay with us for a week, and for the Easter holiday!

Please do not worry too much about me and Chris going to Bristol by train for the first time. I know you are very worried, Mum, but please don't! We'll both be all right and we won't miss the 16.05 from Paddington. I know Jamie will say that Chris will look after me like a big baby. No way! I'm not a big baby, I'm 14!!! Chris wants to write something for you below (he's sitting next to me, watching me write this letter. I'm helping him to improve his English, you see!).

Last week, there was a senior football match between Weyton Comprehensive, a local hearing school, and us. Chris played and it was a very rough game, but we won 3–2. There was a big fight after the match though. Lots of boys fought, including Chris!!! We really HATE each other and we always fight every time we play them. It was like World War 3! After half term, the school will play both junior (I'll be playing as a defender) and senior football matches against Boyd Hill Grammar School. They also have girls there. Why can't we have girls at Ewing Hill Park as well?!?

I'd best stop now because Chris is waiting to write his letter and is telling me to shut up!!!

Love,

Aaron xxx

Dear Mr and Mrs Stephens and Jamie,

I am ~~write~~ writing to say thank you very much for ~~agreed~~ agreeing to have me for the half term next week. It ~~was~~ is much appreciated (Aaron fingerspelt that for me, Jamie, okay?) and I am very grateful.

I am really looking forward to seeing you all again. I know Jamie is very excited to see me again. I am too! Do not worry about Aaron, I ^will look after him like a BIG BABY on the train next week! He just thumped me on my arm!!!

See you next week.

Chris.

Friday 7th March 1980

Hey Jamie,

HAPPY BIRTHDAY BUTTHEAD!!! SIXTEEN NOW!!!

Chris says HAPPY BIRTHDAY SHITHEAD! You always call him Scrubhead, so he's calling you Shithead now!

Did you run back home from school because you couldn't wait to read this letter that was waiting for you (you know I always write to you on your birthday!)? Don't show this to your new girlfriend, Tracey, please!!!

We both can't wait to come home for Easter on the 28th! Three weeks' holiday, hip, hip hooray! Plenty of Easter eggs to eat!

Do you remember that I told you about the mysterious Phantom of Ewing Hill Park who's been terrorising our mad German maths teacher, Mr Schneider? Well, he (or she?) has struck again! I told you at half term, in January, he found a parcel in his desk drawer during a maths lesson with Chris' Form and it was filled with real shit. Mr Schneider was very lucky not to put his hand in (Chris said his Form had wished he had done!).

Anyway, two nights ago, the Phantom set fire to most of his clothes, which were taken from his bedroom. Mr Schneider was out at the time. At first, we all thought that Hubert, the school gardener, was having a bonfire and burning leaves at the back of the school, but we found out the next morning that they were his clothes!!! No one knows who the Phantom is. Mr Schneider's tried to blame all of us, even Chris and me, but we haven't done anything. Mr Langston is very cross about this and wants to know who's been doing this to him. We all hate him because he's a bloody crazy Hitler Teacher. So far, I've had 9 detentions from him for signing! Chris has had 17! Everyone's counting their detentions from him and there is a prize at the end of next term (before the summer holidays) for whoever's had the most! We've all put in 50p to buy whatever the winning boy wants! At the moment, Andrew Brener from Chris' Form is in the lead with 25 so far!!! If he wins, we all know what he wants – more sex magazines!

Did you watch that film called "SCUM" on BBC last Saturday night on the small black and white TV in your bedroom? Many of us did! We sneaked down to the TV room late at night (we had to tiptoe down the side of the grand staircase because the wooden steps always creak). WOW, what a brilliant film! It's about a boys' prison called Borstal. It's like our school! They were always swearing. Gary Portmore and David Wheeley listened to the TV and signed what they said. We all tried not to laugh at the swear words because we might have been heard! The ending, when the boys rioted in the dining room, was brilliant. We didn't get caught, but we were very tired the next morning. We didn't go to church! (See my letter to Mum and Dad).

I'd best stop now. Have to write the letter to Mum and Dad now. See you on the 28th, Butthead!

Aaron xxx

Friday 7th March 1980.
Dear Mum and Dad,
I've written my birthday letter to Jamie. It has Sellotape on the back, so don't try to open the envelope and read it, Mum!!!

Last Sunday, none of us boys went to church. We all refused to go and Mr Arkwright was very upset about it, but Mr Langston wasn't! I don't know why. The vicar came to school for Assembly on Monday morning and he preached on for about 10 minutes – none of us even understood a word he said! David Wheeley said (he can hear very well) he talked about God and about God loving us. He encouraged us to go to the church every Sunday (I don't think we will) and he also talked about the hymn books, saying that they were books of prayer, not sketchbooks for writing and drawing rude things in! (No, I haven't done that, but lots of the other boys have). Yesterday, Mr Langston said that we would not be going to church every Sunday, but once every month!

On Thursday last week, a boy from Form Four, Jamon Cranley, was suspended from school for one week (he's back on Sunday). We were all shocked by that because he's always a good boy who rarely gets into trouble. Chris said Jamon had an argument with our maths teacher, Mr Schneider, over something … I don't know what, but Mr Schneider lost his temper and punched Jamon's nose and Jamon punched his big nose back in revenge. He was reported to Mr Langston and then suspended for a week! Not fair!

I am still working very hard some evenings, doing my work as Assistant Editor of The Stag Press. I know you receive the newsletter every week. The Editor, Mark Cameron, told me that I'll be Editor when I'm in Form Four this September. I am enjoying it very much, as it is helping me to improve my English. It is always very interesting reading the articles while typing on the typewriter, but my fingers sometimes slip through between the keys and get stuck! I am still helping Chris with his English and he is doing very well. His English is now much better. He still helps me with my football, and I am much better now too! I am still nervous about the C.S.E. English exams this June, but Mr Whittle said not to worry. I am the youngest boy in the school's history to take C.S.E. English!

Must stop now, lunch break is almost over. Have to post this now. We've got swimming later this afternoon, hurrah!

Love,

Aaron xxx

Friday 18th April 1980.

Dear Mum, Dad and Jamie,

Thank you Mum!!! Thank you for agreeing!!! I love you very much!!! Chris is looking forward to coming to Aunt Barbara's in Hove with me for the May Day Bank Holiday weekend. I am so happy that Jamie will be coming too! Please let me know what time his train will arrive in London and meet us at Victoria Rail Station. Please give Jamie £5 or £10 to give to me, so that I have some spending money in Brighton. (Jamie – don't steal it!!!)

The Physics Room has some new "listening" equipment to replace those horrible, big and heavy headphones. I don't know what it is called, but Miss Stephenson wears a microphone round her neck and our hearing aids hear what she says. It's a bit like that loop box we had at home last Christmas (you returned it). But I can't hear anything! In fact, no one in my Form can hear with it, except David Wheeley. Chris says only Mark Cameron from his Form can hear it. I am not bothered though, because it is better than wearing those heavy headphones!!! I hope the other classrooms will have the same thing!

Last Saturday, me, David Wheeley, Andy Farmleigh and Shaun Knight went into the Radio Rentals shop in Waltbridge and saw a new colour television called Philips on display. It had a small box with buttons on it. The lady in the shop (David helped us to communicate) said that it was called a "remote control", and you press the buttons to change between the three channels! She also showed us something we had not seen before: she pressed a button and the screen changed to CEEFAX (on BBC1 and BBC2) and ORACLE (on ATV or LWT). It is like seeing a newspaper on television, but with coloured letters on a black background. The lady said it was called Teletext and that it was new. She thinks we might have those text boxes (called sub–titles) to help us to follow what is being said on television very soon! Can we get one of those TVs at home please?!? (And, can I please have the old TV in my room? Jamie has one in his room).

Yes, Mum, I will be very nice to Aunt Barbara in two weeks' time and I will say how sorry I was to hear about the death of her favourite cat, Miscoe. Poor cat, getting run over by a car.

Must stop now. Will write again next week.

Love,

Aaron xxx

Sunday 20th April 1980.
Hi Jamie,
The Phantom of Ewing Hill Park has struck again!!! Mr Schneider found a baby doll hanging by its neck from the light in his bedroom. It was wearing black and white striped clothes – like prison clothes – that a little child would wear. Chris recognised the doll, as he found it lying on the road near the school last week. It was badly damaged. He brought it over and Mr Langston teased him for being like a girl! Chris threw it in the school's big bin afterwards. Then, it was in Mr Schneider's room! Mr Langston is very angry about it. We still don't know who the Phantom is!

Mr Schneider is getting worse! You know he has been giving almost everyone detention for signing, but now he has started hitting some boys during maths lessons. He does things like slapping their heads for poor speech; he's always throwing the blackboard rubber at us for not paying attention or not listening to what he's saying in his microphone (he should know we can't hear!!!) and he is always losing his temper. We are all getting FED UP with him!

Last Wednesday, some of the boys (won't say who they were!) stole the detention book that was locked in Mr Langston's desk and threw it in the lake at the back of the school! I was told it was floating, so the boys had to throw stones at it to sink it. It had almost everyone's names in (including mine). All written by the mad German, but he was very clever: he had his own little black book (his own detention book) with all of our names in it! I think about 40 of us had to take detention last night. We had to use the Assembly Hall instead of one of the classrooms because there were too many of us doing detention! It's a school record now! I do not think Mr Langston was very happy with that, though I am not sure if he was not very happy because we were not behaving well or because Mr Schneider's gone bonkers. David Wheeley did speak to Mr Langston last month, I think, to complain about him, but nothing happened!

Last night, most of us sneaked down to the TV room to watch a Hammer Horror film called "The Ghoul". It was good, but it got a bit boring later on. But we got caught! Mr Bronte, who was on duty yesterday, came in (we all thought he had already gone home!) and we all ran out through the only door. Poor Mr Bronte got knocked down like a rag doll during the stampede! He was not hurt, and he did not give anyone detention (don't think he was able to see who we were, as the TV room was dark).

Chris and I are really looking forward to the May Day Bank Holiday weekend at Aunt Barbara's. Don't steal the money that Mum will give to you for me. I know you!!! I am also happy that Aunt Barbara's Miscoe is dead! I HATED that cat! I'll now get some peace and quiet at her house!

See you soon!
Aaron xxx

PART III

RESOLUTIONS

22

Leap of Faith

"Do you see how I feel like I'm on the fence, like I'm pretending to fit into both worlds and not feeling that I fit into anything?"
– SHANE SPURLOCK, who committed suicide because of being not able to deal with isolation during his mainstreamed years as a deaf child, 2005

Monday May 5, 1980.

Chris and Aaron, sports bags full of weekend clothes slung over their shoulders, walked through the school's entrance doors. Aaron looked around the front hall, which was bustling with several boys. He noted that most of them were signing excitedly about the May Day Bank Holiday weekend; and also about how the SAS had stormed into the Iranian Embassy in London earlier that afternoon.

Aaron thought briefly about the weekend he, Chris and Jamie had spent at Aunt Barbara's, which they had enjoyed tremendously. Then, the news came on Jamie's radio on the train back to London, and he'd given a signed commentary of the dramatic moment; the SAS had leapt through the windows after abseiling from the top of the building, and sounds of gunfire followed. Jamie said that five of the six terrorists who had besieged the building since Wednesday had been killed and nineteen hostages had been rescued. Aaron hoped to catch the six o'clock news on television once he and Chris were back at school.

'Good weekend?' Andrew greeted them.

'Yeah! It was brilliant!' Aaron turned to Chris, to see him nod in agreement.

'You?' Chris asked his form mate. 'Good weekend up in Sheffield?'

'Not really,' Andrew replied grimly. 'My dad's just lost his job at the steel works. Same with many others too!'

'Oh no,' Chris put down his bag, showing concern towards his friend. 'Why?'

'Mrs Thatcher!' Andrew replied, gesturing a long, pointed nose. 'My dad said – he wrote down – that she was closing down lots of the steel works around the country ... '

Aaron's eyes drifted away, uninterested, and he caught sight of Mr Langston shaking hands with a man in dark blue overalls. Aaron recognised him as one of the maintenance men who had been coming to the school lately to deal with an ongoing heating problem. Aaron briefly watched them talking, but did not understand what they were saying. He checked his watch: half past four: thirty minutes until teatime, he thought. He turned back to Chris.

'I'm going up to Dorm Three,' Aaron said, gesturing at his bag. 'I'll see you later.'

Chris nodded in acknowledgement before turning back to Andrew. Aaron walked past the headmaster and the maintenance man as they conversed.

'The heating should hold out for the moment,' the maintenance man was explaining. 'We'll have a look at the pipes in the cellar again next week.'

'Thank you for coming, especially on a Bank Holiday,' Mr Langston said. 'That boiler has always been a problem.'

'Well, as I've said before,' the man pointed at a large cast iron radiator by the wall, 'this building needs a complete overhaul, with a new heating system.'

'That'll be the day!' Mr Langston half smiled. He waved his hand around to illustrate the ominous size of the building. 'Our school budget is always tight and we can't afford it.'

'I quite understand, sir,' the workman nodded. 'Well, I'll be seeing you next week then. Good day.'

The maintenance man turned away, heading towards the entrance doors, passing Chris and Andrew who were still conversing in sign. Putting his hands into his trousers pockets, Mr Langston sighed when he saw that Chris had had another crew cut. The boy must have had it done in Brighton over the weekend, he thought. The headmaster turned away, mumbling to himself.

Dean groaned as he walked into the corridor that led to the dining room and saw that there was a queue of about twenty boys, and Mr Arkwright standing in the doorway. The religious studies teacher was fiddling behind Carl Dunn's right ear, checking his hearing aid.

Dean turned to Matthew, who had tagged along, and pointed at the teacher. 'Is he on duty today?'

Matthew nodded.

'Shit!' Dean moaned, sliding two crooked fingers down his cheek. He immediately placed both hands behind his ears, which were covered by his medium length dark hair, to confirm to himself that he was not wearing his hearing aids. He must have left them in his bag when he returned to school. No, they were in the top drawer of his wardrobe in the dorm, he remembered suddenly. He looked back at the doorway and saw that Carl was reciting something to Mr Arkwright. Dean rolled his eyes, knowing what. He knew he would be punished with three Bad Points if he was caught not wearing his hearing aids. He really hated wearing them because he felt they were of no benefit to him; even when he reluctantly wore them in compliance with the school rules, they would always be switched off.

He turned to his best friend. 'Hold my place. I'll be back!'

Dean was gone before Matthew could say anything. He put his hands on his own ears to check his aids and whistled. He felt a short, sharp vibratory burst through both of his moulds, which confirmed that the batteries were working.

Dean ran frantically through the connecting passageway, passing Chris and Aaron, who were on their way to the dining room. His mind began to spin with memory flashes of his mum: she *always* checked that he was wearing his aids; she had an endless supply of little round batteries and would check and change them even if the old ones were still working; she also constantly cleaned his moulds and made sure that the aids were sitting comfortably on his ears.

Are they comfortable? Yes, Mum. Are you sure? Yes, Mum. Are the batteries working fine? Yes, Mum. Can you hear me? N–Yes, Mum. Both of them? Yes, Mum.

Always worrying about everything, Dean mused as he turned into another, wider, corridor that led to the lobby. Mum worried. She always asked and he always answered Yes, Mum or No, Mum. She'd been no different back when he'd had those old body aids. She would take the two aids out of his harness and speak loudly into the grated microphone of each one, as if they were megaphones. Oh, he *hated* her doing that. Now, with his new behind the ear aids, it was worse. She liked to shout loudly – *really loudly* – around their big house to make sure he heard her properly, but he never could; he just felt the loud vibrations of her voice on his moulds and sometimes on the furniture.

Dean reached out, pushed the panelled wooden door open and ran through the doorway into the lobby. He made his way towards the grand staircase, looking up at the crucifix that was mounted high up on a wall.

Dean immediately thought about his devout Catholic parents. Mum prayed every morning and night at a small shrine in their hallway. It consisted of Christ on a crucifix that was similar to the one above him but much smaller, some candles on a small table, and a Bible. His dad sometimes used the shrine, too. The family attended church every Sunday morning. Dean believed that his mum often prayed for a miracle cure for his deafness.

Dean arrived at the foot of the grand staircase, chuckling to himself as he remembered the faith healer and the audiologist he had met during Easter break the previous month. He ran up the stairs, his lanky legs taking two or three steps at a time.

Mum had met the faith healer through the church. What was her name? Mrs Bran? No, Mrs Bray. She was a small, pleasant old lady. He and his mum went to see her for something he didn't understand at first, but when they arrived at her tiny bungalow, he soon realised who she was and that she was going attempt to cure his deafness. The old lady had a little room with only a chair in the middle. The walls were covered with framed newspaper clippings about her faith healing and how she had helped many people, including some television stars, by healing their pains and injuries. He recognised Syd Little and Eddie Large, who were north–westerners like him, in one clipping. He was told to sit on the chair, relax and close his eyes. Mum had to leave the room, leaving Mrs Bray alone to do her work. He still remembered feeling some kind of strange vibrations seeming to flow directly from her hands onto his ears. It lasted for about fifteen minutes, he figured. When she was finished, Mum hurried into the room, clutching her rosary bead necklace and asking … Can you hear anything now, Dean? Er, no, Mum. Nothing at all? No, Mum. Are you sure? Yes, Mum. Put on your hearing aids now, Dean. Do you hear better through them now? No, Mum. It probably will take time for your deafness – your hearing – to adjust. We'll go and see the audiologist tomorrow to test your hearing. All right, Dean? Yes, Mum. Are you sure you're all right? That Mrs Bray hasn't done any damage to your head? No, Mum.

Dean reached a landing, stopping for a moment to take a short breather. He turned to look up at the next flight of stairs that led to the first floor. He inhaled, then ran up them, thinking about the idiotic audiologist he had met the following day.

Dean sat on a chair in a small internal room, with a small table and a glass window that covered half of the wall in front of him. Through the glass, he watched the balding audiologist, Mr Onslow, preparing the audiology equipment on his desk. Mum sat next to him, again clutching her crucifix, watching the proceedings expectantly. Mr Onslow began to fiddle with the control knobs on a dark brown unit that was concealed from Dean's view. The man then nodded, motioning for Dean to get ready. Dean picked up a trigger button that was resting on the small table; it had a cord attached, which ran through a small hole to the control unit on the other side. Dean put his elbow on the small table and leaned forward a bit. Wanting to feel the vibrations, he gingerly touched the base of the small headpiece that was resting on his left ear. The audiologist shook his head, gesturing for Dean to move his finger away from the headpiece. Dean sighed reluctantly, lowering his hand and grasping the trigger button harder. He really hated coming to the hospital during school holidays, for he could never really hear any of the beeps that the audiologist made. He sometimes managed to correctly "listen" to a beep if it was quite loud, but it was more to do with the headpiece vibrating than him actually hearing it. He sometimes felt sudden sharp echoic bursts. Every time the audiologist lowered it a decibel rate, Dean tried to discreetly touch the headpiece to feel the low vibrations, but the ever–watchful Mr Onslow always caught him cheating. After every test, Dean read the audiologist's report; it would be 150dbs, never quieter, every time. Like most of the other boys at his school, he was profoundly deaf, full stop.

Dean reached the first floor, still sniggering at the memory. He ran past a huge wall mirror with a decorative gold frame, heading for the double doors.

Dean pressed the button with his thumb again, unsure whether the audiologist had beeped him or not. It was always down to guesswork, pure luck and a battle of wits as he closely watched the man's actions through the glass, trying to observe his behaviour, his facial expressions and his next move. Dean sometimes succeeded, sometimes failed.

Then, suddenly, Dean saw something behind the audiologist; he knew it had always been there, but he had never really thought about it before. He sat properly, smiling gleefully at the man behind the glass and beckoned for him to carry on. *Beep*. Dean pressed the button *Beep*. Dean pressed it again. *Beep*. Again, Dean pressed it. Mr Onslow frowned, staring blankly at Dean. He looked down at the controls, adjusted the knob and pressed it again. *Beep*. Dean pressed the button. *Beep*. Dean pressed it again, trying hard to suppress his growing smile. The man was beginning to look bewildered. He adjusted the knobs again and Dean presumed he was lowering the decibel rate. *Beep*. Dean pressed the button. Mr Onslow shook his head, scratching his scalp with his fingers. Mum leaned over to query, but he warded her off and directed his attention to the boy. *Beep*. Dean pressed the button, discreetly gazing behind the audiologist at the reflection in a small mirror that was on the wall near the desk. The angle was awkward, but Dean could clearly see the audiologist's right forearm, which moved every time he pressed the button on the control unit. *Beep*. Dean pressed the button. Mr Onslow sighed, shaking his head again, perplexed. He stood, leaning over the control unit to check the wires at the back, but they all seemed to be in order. He sat back, checked the controls again and adjusted the knobs. Dean guessed that the man was lowering the decibel rate even more. The audiologist then stared coldly at Dean through the glass, ready to pounce as though he was a cowboy preparing to draw his gun. Dean grasped the trigger button tightly, also ready. He grinned at the audiologist, thinking of himself as Clint Eastwood and rubbing his thumb on the button. Their eyes met intensely for a long moment. Dean carefully gazed at the reflection behind his enemy and held his breath. The man's brows furrowed. His right forearm swiftly moved in the reflection. *Beep*. Dean pressed the button. Mr Onslow staggered back as though shot, raising his hands in defeat.

He folded his arms as Dean bounced on his chair, exclaiming. He clenched his left hand triumphantly while swinging the trigger button by the cord in his other hand, before grabbing it and coolly blowing on the top, as though smoke was rising from it. Through the glass, he watched his confused–looking foe lean over to Mum, muttering and pointing at the equipment and Dean. Mum slowly turned in the direction of her son, cupping her cheeks and exclaiming to herself.

Dean pushed the double doors open and ran into the gloomily lit foyer, still grinning at the memory of her words, lipread through the glass; *It's a miracle!* He turned into Dorm Four and briefly thought about his family.

Life in their seven bedroomed detached house in the exclusive Calderstones area of Liverpool had never been easy for Dean, with him being the only deaf child in the family. Mum tended to fuss over him and worried about him more than anything else in the world. His stockbroker Dad, meanwhile, worried more about the stock trade and the world's finances than about his deaf son. Dean believed his parents had never accepted his profound deafness and that they tended to pretend he was hearing. He got on well with his older brother, Max, though he spent most of his schooldays at a private boarding school, so he didn't really know him that well. Cherry, his younger sister, however, was the opposite; she was very much like Mum and spoke too fast for Dean to lipread. He didn't know whether she did it on purpose to annoy him, or if it was her natural way of speaking. Signing was not allowed in the house, as his devout Catholic parents believed that he should have faith in God through hearing, not through his hands. He absolutely hated going to church every Sunday with his family; he was bored stiff, unable to follow the proceedings. They also tried to improve his fuzzy speech by paying for private speech lessons, but he could only manage to say a few words at a time, not full sentences, never mind take part in conversations. Yes, Mum and No, Mum were the only things he ever seemed to say to her. Dad rarely spoke to him, though he did sometimes manage to point and gesture. He bought him anything he wanted though, like the moped he got for Christmas.

Family dinners, especially big family gatherings, were the worst for him. He felt isolated, with spoken conversation flying over his head. He always finished his dinner first before everyone else; Dad told him not to do that as it was rude to finish eating before the women had finished theirs. Dean ignored him, though; how could he wait for a long time with a few scraps left on his plate while the women finished chattering? His food would be cold by then. After each dinner, he went up to his room to play games and read comics or had a kick about in their big back garden.

He knew that he was one of the very few boys at Ewing Hill Park who came from a wealthy family and that his parents had paid privately for him to get the best education and, they hoped, to improve his speech. And improve it did – not dramatically, as he still struggled to say some words – it was slightly better than when he had first arrived at the school. Dean's name sign, *rich*, was given to him by his best friend, Matthew. Dean had invited Matthew to his home for the May Day weekend and his parents had paid for their first class train fares. Fortunately, Matthew had good speech and was able to communicate with Dean's parents; he struggled to read their lips in poorly lit conditions, but got on well with them nevertheless. It had been a great weekend, despite the terrible news that a seventeen–year old deaf girl, Roberta Osten, who he knew from his old PHU, had killed herself. Dean didn't understand why she had hanged herself in her bedroom, but he remembered mentioning to his form mates at a dinner some time ago that she looked quite lost within herself.

Mum had worried and fussed about Dean and Matthew's return trip to school today, Dean recalled as he approached the wardrobe next to his bed. Are you sure that you can manage to get back to London by train? Yes, Mum. You don't want Jameson to drive you down … ? No, Mum. Have you got your tickets in your coat pockets? Yes, Mum. Don't lose them! No, Mum. Have you packed your lunches in your bags? Yes, Mum. You will ask the school to telephone us immediately when you arrive, won't you? Yes, Mum. Are your hearing aids working? Yes, Mum.

Dean yanked open the top drawer and grabbed both of the aids. He frowned when he noticed something amiss in the drawer. He took out his Striker football magazine, opened it and grimaced. Someone had stolen his Penthouse. It had been hidden inside the centre pages. Oh, fuck! Who'd taken it? Not Andrew Brener, definitely; he had more than enough of them stashed under the floorboards next to his bed. Miss Turner? Wouldn't be surprised if it was her, as that nosey assistant matron sometimes did random drawer checks. Probably for herself and Miss Hogarth. Dean shook his head, not too worried at the moment. He threw the football magazine back into the drawer, then looked at the pair of aids in his hand and thought about them.

Matthew took another step; he was now next in line for Mr Arkwright's checkpoint and Lester Morrison was just finishing reciting something to the teacher. Matthew turned to glance back into the corridor again, wondering what was keeping Dean. He suddenly felt a gust of wind passing by his face, but thought nothing of it. He leaned further out from the line of boys to get a better view, but saw that Dean still had not returned yet. He turned back to take his turn, but shrieked when he bumped into the back of Dean, who was standing in front of him; Dean wobbled forward slightly. Matthew cursed to himself, quickly realising that the sudden gust that he had just felt was Dean running past him, but because of his tunnel vision, he hadn't seen him.

Dean stood in front of Mr Arkwright, smiling broadly.

'Good evening, Dean,' the religious studies teacher greeted him.

Oooood efeennn

'Very good,' Mr Arkwright nodded, smiling at the boy. 'Are your hearing aids working fine?'

Yes, Mum.

'Pardon me?'

Dean shut his eyes and imaging a wooden mallet marked '*Stupid*' hitting his head. He opened his eyes again.

Yes Sssir.

Mr Arkwright placed his hand on Dean's left ear and felt under his long dark hair, checking that he was wearing the hearing aid. Dean turned his head to his left to show the teacher his right ear, which also had a hearing aid in it.

'Very good,' the teacher nodded, putting his hand into the breast pocket of his brown wool jacket and taking out a small piece of paper. He held it up for Dean to read. 'I know you can never remember the words.'

Dean read the note, which comprised of the words of a Grace prayer:

For what we are about to receive, may the Lord make us truly thankful. And may we always be mindful of the needs of the others, for Jesus' sake. Amen.

Dean cleared his throat, preparing to say the words that were in front of him. He already knew every word by heart, thanks to his family and the school; he just couldn't say them correctly.

Fuuur w–waT wee aaarrr pouT To ree–cee–fffeee, Baa Thee looorrrD mmmaKeee USSS Truuuleee TaaannnKvuuul. AnnnD Baa wee aaal–waaaeeesss pee mmminnnD–vuuul ooov Thee nnneeeDsss ooov Thee oooTheeesss fuuur Jeeesss–uuusss sssaaaKeee. AaaMeeennn.

'Very good!' Mt. Arkwright smiled, nodding again, pleased as punch. He put the note back in his breast pocket and patted Dean's shoulder. 'You speak like a normal hearing boy and your hearing aids are helping. Keep it up, Dean. Now, go on, have your tea.'

Dean gave the teacher a complementary bow before turning to go into the dining room. He waited for Matthew to finish his turn and then joined him. They walked along the counter, sliding their trays along. Dean looked back to check Mr Arkwright was busy with another boy in the doorway, then tapped Matthew's shoulder.

'Ha, ha!' Dean pointed at the teacher. He took both of his aids off and flicked open their small battery compartments to reveal their emptiness. 'Stupid fool!'

Aaron strolled into the library, carrying a book. He turned to a small lectern where an open record book was, picked up the pen, looked at the list to find *Hunchback of Notre Dame – Victor Hugo,* and ticked the checkbox next to it to confirm its safe return. He looked at his digital watch, which read 18:52, then wrote down the date – Monday 05/05/1980 – and the time. He felt a tap on his right shoulder and turned to see Sammy.

'Where's Chris?' Sammy asked, scrubbing his own head with a clenched fist, signing his name sign. 'I can't find him anywhere.'

'I don't know,' Aaron answered. 'I haven't seen him since teatime.'

Sammy turned away, exasperated. Aaron turned in the opposite direction and went over to one of the shelves to put the book back.

Chris pulled up his jeans, tucked in his tee shirt, then fastened, zipped up and buckled his belt. He brushed the dry mud from the back of his trousers and made sure that he was decent. He looked around the small clearing amidst the enclosing undergrowth, with trees and shrubbery around him. Through a gap, he glimpsed the rear of the school, which was barely visible in the distance. He returned his attention to the secluded area and watched Dwight Greenland finish zipping up his jeans, brushing away the dirt from his own back. Chris thought briefly about him; he had finally succumbed to Dwight's secret, but persistent, advances last March; the same night that the Phantom of Ewing Hill Park had struck again, with Mr Schneider's clothes burning nearby; he'd never forget that! Like everyone else, he and Dwight thought it was Hubert burning some leaves, only to discover later that it was not the case. He wished he could have caught whoever it was and reported the culprit to the school, but then again, he would have been asked what he was doing in the woods at that time of night. Ever since Dwight found out about Chris last November, he had pestered the Fourth Former. Chris had tried to resist the older boy's advances, but he became more and more drawn towards him. He didn't understand why at first, but the pull was simply too strong for him to fight so he gave in. Chris had become Dwight's new regular for the past two months and they often did it in that secluded part of the forest in the evenings.

Dwight was now all clothed. He took a step towards Chris but then he suddenly shuddered, his eyes darting behind Chris. Chris promptly whirled round, but there was nothing there apart from a slight movement of twigs in the bush. He turned back to Dwight, easing his nerves.

'A wild animal,' Chris assured Dwight, though not convinced himself.

'Probably,' Dwight shrugged, not convinced either; all the same, he was probably right. 'So you and Aaron went to Brighton over the weekend?'

'Yes, we had a great time. His older brother, Jamie, came too.'

'Aaron,' Dwight paused for a moment, 'Have you done it with him yet?'

Chris shook his head, knowing what he meant. 'I don't think he's like … us, you know?'

'Gay?' Dwight placed his closed right hand, with his thumb up, on the palm of his left hand and swayed it back and forth.

Chris frowned, shaking his head: this was a sign he had not seen before.

'It's a new sign I learnt from Geoffrey recently. He's from a group that has people like us. G–A–Y,' Dwight explained, fingerspelling the last word. 'All of them are deaf. It was set up in London about two years ago, I think.'

Chris placed his right hand on the palm of his left hand, trying to mimic what Dwight had showed him. Taking his hands, Dwight closed Chris' right hand, pulled up his thumb and swayed the hand slightly. Chris stared blankly at his hands, fascinated by the new sign. Dwight tapped Chris' head, bringing it up. 'For women, it's … ' he fingerspelled it. '. . . L–E–S–B–I–A–N. Like Miss Hogarth and Miss Turner.'

Dwight pulled out Chris' right index finger, keeping the protruding thumb visible, to form an L handshape, and waved it back and forth. 'That's the sign for lesbian.'

Chris dropped his arms and pondered for a short moment. 'I just don't think Aaron is that.'

'Have you tried?'

'Two or three times, yes, but–'

'He won't do it,' Dwight said, reminding Chris about himself. 'Like you wouldn't do it with me before.'

Chris stared at his secret lover, taking his point. He was probably right; Aaron might have really wanted him, but was too afraid. Chris knew that feeling well.

'I'm probably wrong about him though, but it's up to you,' Dwight concluded, putting an end to the topic.

Chris looked up to the darkening sky before looking back at Dwight. 'It's getting dark, we'd better get back. You go first.'

Dwight nodded at their usual arrangement; they always separated before and after to avoid the suspicions of anyone at the school. Dwight turned and squeezed through a small opening between two overgrown bushes. Chris remained where he was, putting his hands into his flared jeans pockets.

He thought about Aaron again.

23

Blind Kiss

"Falling in love with your best friend is a lot more easier than being in love with your best friend."

– ANON

'Good morning, boys,' Miss Stephenson greeted the Fifth Formers as she walked into the Physics Room. 'Lovely day, isn't it? Hope you all had a good Bank Holiday weekend.'

The ten Fifth Formers acknowledged their physics and biology teacher. She picked up a microphone with a short black wire hanging from it and placed the strap over her neck. She flipped its small on/off switch.

'Everybody hear me?' she asked.

Gary, Timothy and Carl nodded. Basher nodded, pretending, and gave her an indirect thumb up. The rest did not respond.

'Right,' Miss Stephenson said, fingerspelling and using some basic signs that she had recently learnt from Mrs Munnings and Mr McShane, 'as you know, all of you will be taking your CSE Physics exams next month, and Timothy and Tom will also be doing the O Level. We should be starting to revise now and … '

Basher yawned, not bothered. He was more interested in thinking about the coming Saturday's FA Cup Final match between Arsenal and West Ham, hopeful that the latter would be the victor. He gazed at the calendar on the wall and noted that it was the sixth of May. *Hurry up, Saturday the tenth,* he silently muttered to himself. He was very much looking forward to renewing his rivalry with Chris that week; Saturday would be the big one; he was anticipating another of their famous fist fights during the live screening of the match in the TV room. He returned his attention to the teacher.

'All right, everyone?' she concluded and pointed at a shelf at the back of the room, picking up some photocopied thermal papers 'I have typed a list of what I think you might need to revise. Use the books over there to help you. All right?'

As the boys began to move to do what they were told, Miss Stephenson flicked the microphone switch again.

'Excuse me; I have to go out for a moment. I won't be too long.'

Miss Stephenson turned and left the room, closing the door behind her. Dwight went over to the teacher's desk and picked up the sheets. Gary turned and spoke to Timothy.

'Spooky, is the careers officer coming tomorrow or Friday?'

'Thursday,' he replied. 'You're last on the list. I'm third.'

'Is it the same dumb blonde as before?' Gary asked. 'What was her name? The ugly one with the big boobs?' He gestured exaggeratedly big breasts.

'Mrs Teale,' Timothy replied, half smiling to himself. 'I thought she was alright.'

Gary shook his head, disagreeing with his friend, and rose to make his way towards the shelves when, suddenly, he began to hear something through his hearing aids. He listened. It sounded like a hurried pattering of feet. He looked around the room, but no one was hurrying around. He listened again. He worked out that someone's feet were definitely hoofing away on a hard wooden floor. He also heard what sounded like an echoing against the walls, possibly in a narrow corridor. He looked at his form mates and saw that Timothy and Carl were also listening.

'You can hear it too?' Gary asked Timothy, grinning knowingly at him.

'A little bit. Your hearing's better than mine and Carl's.' he replied. 'Echoing sounds. I can't identify them.'

'What's happening?' Basher asked, rising to his feet, curious.

'She's got the on/off switch the wrong way,' Gary explained. 'It's on instead of off. I can still hear her.'

'I thought you told her you could hear her through the microphone?' Basher queried.

'Yes, I can hear her fine, with or without the microphone,' Gary answered. He placed a finger on his lips. 'Hush!'

The entire room fell into silence as they watched Gary, Timothy and Carl. Gary listened. It sounded like the door being opened and shut. Then came what sounded like feet clambering on a tiled floor, followed by what sounded like a cupboard door opening and slamming. Gary winced at the slamming sound. Basher folded his arms, watching the trio standing motionlessly and staring into space. Dwight placed his hand on his BTE aid, but he was hearing nothing. Gary sniggered. *Was that a zipper being unzipped?* he pondered. Then came the rustling of what sounded like a form of clothing; *that must be her trousers*, he thought.

'What are you hearing?' Basher demanded.

'Hold on!' Gary told the head boy. 'Here it comes ... '

Next came what sounded like water squirting into a pool. The distinct, but distorted, humming of Miss Stephenson's voice soon muffled it.

Gary burst into loud laughter. Timothy sniggered. Carl yanked both of his aids from his ears, disgusted. Basher glanced quizzically at the bemused Dwight, who in turn, shrugged.

Chris emerged from the English Room carrying his Arsenal pencil case and a ring binder. The rest of his Form followed, also having finished their lesson. Steven caught up with him and patted his shoulder.

'Looking forward to this Saturday?' Steven asked. 'Arsenal to win again?'

'Yes!' Chris exclaimed. 'Two FA Cups in a row!'

'You'll get into a fight with Basher again!'

'He's welcome. He's scared of me!'

Chris turned his head, alerted by a waving hand in the corner of his eye. It was Mr Langston approaching him from the lobby. Chris quickly went over to the headmaster.

'Christopher,' the headmaster said, 'you have a letter.'

Chris frowned in surprise.

'I know,' Mr Langston said, noting the boy's reaction. 'You don't often get letters, but it's waiting for you on the post shelf.' He pointed in the direction of the shelf.

Without a second look, Chris dashed off, leaving the headmaster standing.

Duncan threw the fork down onto his empty plate, disgruntled. 'Rubbish lunch again! That mince's awful!'

'You English always make shit food,' Derek chuckled, pointing his knife at his form mate and then at the bowl in front of him, which had a slice of apple pie with custard in it. 'The apple pie's horrible too!'

Shaun hammered on the table to get the young Scot's attention. 'You love blackberry pie and that's even worse!'

Ian waved at Aaron, who was finishing his lunch. 'We're going to play Killer Darts in the recreation room after lunch,' he announced. 'You in?'

'No thanks,' Aaron shook his head, placing his cutlery on his plate to free up his hands. 'I'm writing my letter home.'

'I thought you normally do that on Fridays?' Ian asked.

'Yes, I do, but I wanted to do it today,' Aaron explained. 'To write about our weekend at my aunt's.'

Ian turned to ask Jonah if he would be interested instead. Aaron picked up his cutlery, his gaze drifting idly around the dining room; he saw Chris sitting quietly at his table.

Later on, Dwight strolled through the wide corridor leading from the lobby, going nowhere in particular. He stopped when he saw Aaron sitting at a desk, writing, in the Geography and History Room. An idea started to form; if Chris couldn't get Aaron to do it with him, then perhaps he could help them. He turned and entered the classroom, stamping on the carpeted floor and waving at Aaron, who looked up from the desk.

'Where's Spooky?' Dwight asked, holding up clawed hands. 'Timothy Hutchinson.'

'I don't know,' Aaron shrugged. 'Haven't seen him since lunch.'

'Never mind. He'll reappear again like a ghost!'

Aaron bowed his head to resume his letter writing, but felt another stamp on the floor. He looked back up at the Fifth Former.

'Chris,' Dwight scrubbed his closed hand on his own head, 'tells me that you're into films?'

Aaron nodded. 'Why?'

'There's a new film that I saw recently,' Dwight began. 'It's a foreign film. It had subtitles. You know, like, reading the English words in foreign films? Anyway, there was a funny scene where someone wrote something on the wall.'

Dwight turned and headed for the blackboard, picked up the chalk and began to write in large letters. Aaron folded his arms, watching the prefect writing across the entire length of the blackboard. When he was finished; Aaron laughed heartily at what he saw.

SEX IS BEAUTIFUL!

Dwight turned, smiling at Aaron. 'You're not alone.'

'I'm not alone?' Aaron shook his head, not understanding. 'What do you mean?'

'It means … ' Dwight paused, trying to find the words to explain without making himself too obvious. 'Chris … he likes you and you like him.'

'Of course, I like him,' Aaron said. 'He's my best friend.'

'No, no, no, that's not what I meant,' Dwight sighed, now beginning to realise that he wasn't making himself clear. Time to get to the point, he thought. He rounded the teacher's desk, heading towards Aaron. 'He … *loves* you!'

Aaron stared at Dwight for a long moment before shaking his head dismissively and laughing. 'Don't be silly!'

Dwight turned to see that the door was still open and decided he wanted to close it, so that he could have some privacy with Aaron to talk further. He trotted over to close the door, then saw something in the corridor. He hurried back, waving frantically at Aaron, telling him to get out of the room right away. Aaron quickly rose to his feet, grabbing his leather letter case and folding it up, unsure why he was following Dwight's instructions. Dwight grabbed the two dusters that were on the chalk shelf and dashed towards the door, urging Aaron to follow him. Dwight ushered Aaron away from the door towards a narrow corridor opposite; they hid there with the classroom still visible to them through the door. Dwight peered around the corner, followed by Aaron, and saw that Mrs Munnings had just finished reading something that was pinned on the wall at the entrance to the wide corridor. She began to trot through towards her classroom, carrying a stack of books and papers.

Dwight leaned back, pushing Aaron back too, hiding them from the approaching woman. Mrs Munnings strode into the classroom, hurrying towards the teacher's desk and heaved the pile onto it. Aaron and Dwight discreetly watched the geography and history teacher through the open door. She took a short, deep, breath and exhaled. She turned to face the blackboard, absently read the words on it and turned back to her desk. Realising what the words said, she shrieked loudly, then whirled back to the blackboard, slapping her hands on her cheeks, her eyes wide with shock. Her fake eyelids fluttered rapidly as she read the incriminating words again. She frantically looked down at the narrow shelf, desperately searching for the duster, but she could not find it.

Aaron tried hard not to laugh as he witnessed the comical sight. He glanced at Dwight, who was sniggering. He looked back at the panicking lady, who was ferociously wiping the blackboard with the palms of her hands, bosom heaving, the chalk dust smearing everywhere. The boys quickly headed away, knowing that she might see them. As they made off, Dwight dropped the two dusters on the floor.

Aaron peered through the door of the changing room, finding Chris sitting alone on a bench, bouncing his football against the wall in front of him. Aaron approached, waving at him. He thought back briefly to the last ten minutes of lunch break that he'd spent searching for him. Matthew had told him that he'd seen Chris heading to the gym hall.

'I've been looking for you.'

Chris did not answer him as he looked broodingly at the wall. He threw the football; it bounced against the wall and came back to his hands. Aaron sensed that his best friend was in a mood. He moved closer to Chris, gently tapping his head. Chris looked up at him.

'Are you all right?' Aaron asked.

Chris shrugged.

'What's wrong?' Aaron pressed, gingerly.

Chris reached for his back pocket, took out an envelope and gave it to Aaron. 'It's from my mum. Read it.'

With the letter in his hand, Aaron sat down next to Chris. He glanced at the door behind them; had he seen something move in the foyer? There was nothing there. It was probably a trick of the light, he thought. He looked down at Chris' name and the school address handwritten on the envelope. He turned it over, pulled the letter out and unfolded it. He read:

Saturday 3rd May 1980.
Dear Christopher,
This is your mum. I know you're probably still upset and angry with me, but please read this letter. I want to explain.

First of all, I know I haven't been a perfect mother to you and I'm truly and deeply sorry about that. I know that you have had a very difficult time since you were separated from me when you were only eight years old. Everything went wrong because of your father. I know that you might say I shouldn't blame him, but I do. I don't want to talk about him and I never will.

Please believe me, there has never been a single day that I did not think about you. I love you and always have. I've tried countless times to get you back, but the social services would not let me. I finally sobered up as soon as Bob went into prison, and last December I was given the chance to have you over the New Year. I blew it, though. It's my fault for letting Bob into our flat and I'm very, very sorry about that.

What you did to him made me realise how grown up you are now. You're no longer my little boy, but a proper son. I was so proud of you, to be honest with you. God, you beat him! After you walked out, I threw him out. I didn't care that he was injured and I told him never ever to come back again. He still hasn't.

I've been going to a support group every week that helps people with drinking problems and I think I'm doing really well. I'm determined to get my life back together and I want you to be part of that.

I know you're doing very well at school (Steve Lewison posts me copies of your school reports), especially in English, and I'm very, very proud of you, Christopher.

Look, I'm thinking of moving out of this country. My distant cousin, Eleanor, lives in Australia and we've been writing to each other for some time now. I'm thinking of moving to Australia for good, living with Eleanor for a bit, then we'll see what happens. I've had enough of it here. I want to make a fresh start and I'd really like for you to come with me after you finish school next year. Think about it.

I'll telephone Mr Lewison soon to see if I can see you sometime this summer (I know you'll probably go to your friend Aaron Stephens' again) so that we can talk about it, alright? I know you don't have good speech and I can't sign, but we can always write things down. If you don't want to see me, though, I will understand.

My address is at the top of this letter, so if you want to write back, that would be absolutely brilliant. Perhaps we could start to get to know each other better by writing to each other?

I hope to hear from you soon. I'll post this letter today, so I hope you'll receive it soon.

Much love,

Mum x

Aaron slowly folded the letter with a lump in his throat and put it back into the envelope. He handed it back to Chris, who pocketed it. He tossed the football; it bounced back from the wall and he caught it. He glanced at Aaron, who was still gazing at him with genuine sympathy.

'How do you feel about that?' Aaron asked.

'I dunno,' Chris shrugged. He threw the football at the wall; it bounced back to the tiled floor and into Chris' hands again.

'Do … you want to go with her to Australia?' Aaron asked, secretly hoping that he didn't.

'No.'

'Why not?'

'I just don't. I'll miss England. Arsenal too,' Chris threw the football again and it bounced back to him. Catching it, he looked at Aaron affectionately, freeing his right hand to sign. 'And you too. You're my dearest, best friend.'

Aaron's eyes met Chris' for a long moment, touched. Chris turned away, breaking off the gaze, but Aaron gently patted Chris' left arm to bring him round.

'Do you … ' Aaron paused as he thought about what Dwight had told him a moment ago, '. . . love me?'

Chris frowned, surprised by the question. He wrestled within himself whether to admit it or not; he was still unsure about him. *Has Dwight talked to him or something?* he wondered. His heart began to pound, his emotions swirling and his mind spinning with thoughts of desire. He threw the football hard at the floor, taking out some of his inner frustration. The ball bounced and hit the wall hard, bouncing high up and hitting the ceiling. It spun aimlessly down at the two sitting boys. Both Chris and Aaron instinctively pushed themselves from the bench, reaching out for the red and white sphere. They both grasped it, then fell back to the bench, playfully tugging the ball from each other. Aaron leaned back hard, pulling the ball with him, giggling loudly as Chris lumbered forward. With his right leg supporting his weight, Chris rose over the ball and Aaron, his left knee resting on the bench. Aaron twisted forward to pull the ball from his opponent's hands, making Chris slip and lose his balance for a second – he stumbled forward. His face banged against Aaron's, their noses and lips touching. Chris quickly drew his head back, apologetic, but saw that Aaron did not seem to be reacting badly to the accidental kiss. Chris suddenly felt an overwhelming rush inside; he felt that he could no longer contain himself. It was now or never.

Chris leaned forward, his lips gently touching Aaron's. Aaron's eyes widened, astonished, but he closed them as he allowed Chris to kiss him passionately. Aaron felt his own mixed emotions rushing up inside, though he wasn't quite sure whether it was the surprise of the kiss itself, or if he was actually enjoying it. He felt Chris' fingers wrapping round his, stroking them. Their hands, which were still resting on the ball between them, clasped tightly. Chris tilted his head slightly so that his warm moist lips pressed harder against Aaron's. Aaron felt Chris' throat pounding and realised it was coming from his heart. His own heart was pounding too.

Aaron opened his eyes. His head jolted back and he pushed Chris away, his wide eyes looking behind Chris. Chris spun round, but saw no one in the doorway. He turned back to Aaron, who was now trembling like a leaf.

'What did you see?' Chris asked, his signing urgent.

'I thought I saw someone standing there!' Aaron cried out, panicking. 'He saw us!'

'Who?' Chris began to worry.

Aaron closed his eyes to think. The image in his mind was vague. It was only for a split second. Someone seemed to have been moving away from the door; from his brief glimpse of it from behind. Aaron wasn't sure. Had whoever – or whatever – it was had been standing there long enough to see them kissing, or had they passed without even seeing them? Or, was it a figment of his imagination? Was it a trick of the light? A trick of the eye? His mind was too muddled by the shock of the kiss.

'I don't know!' Aaron said, opening his eyes.

Chris leapt to his feet, throwing his football to the floor, and dashed towards the doorway. He ran into the foyer and then to the entrance. When he went outside, he saw no one under the covered way. He put his hands on his head, unsure of himself.

Basher leaned against the wall in the lobby, holding up *The Mirror,* beginning to read the sports page. Chris marched up purposefully and stood in front of the head boy. Basher peeked over the top of the newspaper.

'Yes?' Basher mouthed at him, raising his eyebrows.

Chris stared at him for a moment, thinking hard. If Aaron had seen someone in the doorway, Basher would be his prime suspect. He knew he could be wrong, but he had to at least try and find out.

'Did you see it?' Chris asked, trying not to be too obvious.

'See what?' Basher mouthed again, still clutching the newspaper, not bothering to use either of his hands to sign.

Chris glared at Basher again, trying to figure out whether he was telling the truth or not. The Basher he knew would have pounced in, catching them in the act; he would also have spread the news about them around the school by now, like wildfire. Yet no one had said anything: it was now evening. Perhaps, Chris thought, it was only Aaron's imagination. He glanced at the newspaper; the front page covering the Iranian Embassy siege.

Basher went back to reading his newspaper, taking no further interest in his adversary. Chris took another look at him, before leaving, satisfied.

'Are you sure no one saw us?' asked Aaron, tentatively touching the door that led down to the cellar, his heart pounding with excitement and fear.

'It was only your imagination,' Chris reassured him. 'Come on.'

'I still don't know if we should do this,' Aaron hesitated, not convinced. He looked through the dark corridor on his right again to make sure that there was no one there. For a moment, he thought he saw something dark moving in the night, behind the window at the end of the corridor, but realised he was just being jittery. He turned, looking at the cellar door again, now realising why Chris had wanted him down there last November, when they had stopped David from killing himself. He was still confused and uncomfortable about what they were going to do.

'I think it's wrong.'

'Come on,' Chris urged, impatiently. 'It'll be fine, I promise.'

Aaron nodded, took a breath and pushed the door open. He stepped inside and began to descend the narrow, gloomy staircase. Chris took one more look into the dark corridor and then turned and followed Aaron.

He closed the door behind them.

24

Turning the Tide

"Every deaf mute in the United States has it in his power to climb to a higher grade of attainment, and in the College at Washington the studious and earnest youth receives all encouragement. I never had the honour of mingling with such intelligent mutes until I entered this College."
– FRANCIS MAGINN (1861–1918), founder of British Deaf and Dumb Association in 1890 ('dumb' was dropped in 1971), upon his return from Gallaudet College.

Mr Langston sighed.

He drummed his fingers on his desk, lost in his own thoughts. His mind was still buzzing and he was trying hard to block it out.

He leaned against his high–backed leather chair, resting his elbows on the armrests, and clasped his hands. He thought fleetingly about what had happened earlier that evening.

When he was told there was a problem with the heating again, he'd gone down to the cellar to investigate the boiler and give it a good whack. When he'd turned into the boiler room next to the cellar room, he'd *seen* them.

The headmaster looked across his desk at Chris and Aaron standing in front of him, their heads bowed, shoulders slumped and their hands behind their backs. He winced as he thought about them again in the cellar; they hadn't even done anything – not at that point, anyway – and it was only his intervention that had stopped them from going any further. They were cuddling each other, fully clothed, and that was about it. He *knew* what they were going to do next though; he had been warned by his predecessor, Benjamin Williams, that the school had a history of boys practising what he regarded as "improper and intolerable sexual activities". Saying that the school would not tolerate it, he'd singled out Jacques Magnat as a prime example, but he couldn't expel him because his wealthy family had made generous donations to the school, including the Magnat House building. Mr Langston then thought about Dwight Greenland, who he believed may also be one, but Dwight had always been careful not to get caught. That was the least of his worries at the moment, though.

He slammed his hand hard on the desk, loud enough for Chris and Aaron to flinch. Their eyes met the headmaster's.

'Why did you do it?' he demanded.

The two boys said nothing, shamefaced.

'It is disgusting, very unethical and intolerable … ' He paused, reminding himself that deaf children could not easily lipread long spoken words. 'It's bad, it's wrong and it's not normal!'

Chris and Aaron briefly exchanged silent glances before looking back at the principal.

'I will *not* have this kind of … filth in this school,' the headmaster continued. 'What do you both have to say?'

'Sorry,' Aaron said, knowing he had said the word clearly.

Sor.

Mr Langston heard Chris speak, shaking his head. He put his index finger by his mouth for Chris to see, and spoke slowly to correct his problematic speech. 'Sor–ry.'

Sorreee.

Mr Langston heard Chris' slightly improved pronunciation; it wasn't perfect, but he decided to leave it at that.

'Now, don't ever do that again, Christopher and Aaron. Understand?'

Chris and Aaron shook and nodded their heads in agreement.

'Aaron,' the headmaster directed his attention at the Third Former, 'please leave us. I want to talk to Christopher alone.'

Aaron hesitated, glancing at his best friend, but eventually turned and headed for the door. He went through it and closed the door behind him.

'Christopher, can you still lipread me clearly?' Mr Langston asked. He knew the boy could, but he wanted to make sure Chris understood what he was about to say.

Chris nodded.

'I am very disappointed in you,' the headmaster leaned forward, resting his arms on the desk. 'Why did you do it?'

Chris shrugged, not out of apathy, but apology.

'You don't know why?' the headmaster asked.

Chris frowned, shaking his head; that wasn't what he had meant, but he decided not to bother correcting him, for he couldn't speak well enough to make himself understood.

Mr Langston took his answer as a curt no. He sighed, rose to his feet and walked round the desk. Chris stepped back a bit to make room for the principal to stand between the desk and him. The man rested his bottom on the edge of the desk, his eyes level with the boy's.

'You're a good boy,' he began to say calmly. 'One of the best pupils I've ever had. You're a natural leader. The boys look up to you. Your education here is very satisfactory; especially your written English, which has improved remarkably in the last seven or eight months. That pleases me a great deal.'

Chris could not help but smile, recollecting Aaron's private hour–long English tutorials each week for the past eight months, which had helped him immensely. Mr Whittle, suspicious at the sudden improvement, had sometimes accused him of cheating or copying other boys' work. Once, a few weeks back, the English teacher put him to the test by making him write an essay about football in front of him, so that he could witness the boy using the good command of English that he had remarkably developed. Chris would never forget the teacher's astonished face as he wrote. His English was not perfect, but it was good enough to convince Mr Whittle that no cheating was involved.

'I will tell you something, Christopher,' Mr Langston continued. Chris focused on the man's lips. 'You're in line for head boy next term.' He paused as Chris' eyes widened, then placed his hand on his shoulder affectionately. 'Don't throw away this chance. Oh, and don't tell anyone about this yet.'

Chris nodded in appreciation. Mr Langston patted his shoulder, slightly disappointed with himself that his conversations with the boy had been a one–way street for the last four years.

'I know you don't have good speech, which is a shame really because I would have liked you to talk to me. At least you can write to me in good English now and that's good enough for me.'

Chris nodded, silently mouthing *thanks*.

'One more thing before you go, though,' the headmaster smiled, 'for your own sake, please be careful, my boy. I don't want Mr Lewison to find out about what you did this evening. I'm trying to help you. All right?'

Chris nodded again; smiling gracefully at the man he had a high regard for. He turned and headed towards the door. Mr Langston watched him leave. He stood there, staring at the closed panelled wood door for along moment. He placed his thumb and index finger under the arch of his spectacles and rubbed the bridge of his nose, then looked at his watch: twenty–two minutes past eight. He folded his arms and crossed his lower legs, balancing on the desk with his bottom.

He thought about Chris, remembering about how he'd arrived at Ewing Hill Park. He was unable to enrol at the school in the first instance, but a vacancy came up just before the new term started because the original boy – Lee McCarthy from Stirling – was forced to withdraw. Though Lee had successfully completed his entrance exams, his local education authority had refused to fund his place at the school. Feelers were immediately sent out to local education authorities around the country to advise them of the vacancy, hoping to make up the required number of ten boys per Form. A couple of days later, Mr Langston received a telephone call from Mr Lewison, a social worker from Islington Council, who told him about a troubled eleven–year old deaf boy called Christopher Matthaus. Mr Lewison had visited the school that very afternoon and they had discussed the boy. The headmaster was initially reluctant to take the boy in after the social worker had briefed him on his background, but he eventually agreed when Mr Lewison confirmed that the education department at Islington Council had agreed to fund his place. Mr Langston believed that they were quite desperate to have the boy settled down, disciplined and properly educated in an environment that was ideal for him, rather than going from one children's home or foster home to another (and therefore, from one school to another, too). Besides, Mr Langston thought; like most boarding and grammar schools, Ewing Hill Park relied one hundred percent on fees from local education authorities and donations from wealthy families, so, in the absence of other applicants, he had no option but to accept Chris. When Chris arrived on the first day, he was like a wild cat; he had no sign, speech, written language or social skills; his discipline was practically non–existent and his behaviour highly erratic during the first week. Football was the thing he knew best, from what the headmaster could see. Nevertheless, the boy settled in quickly once he made new friends in his Form. Mr Langston also saw that Chris picked up sign language very quickly, which pleased him. Mr Arkwright had said that he had been trying to teach him to speak, but he could tell the boy was one of those deaf children who would never acquire good speech.

Mr Langston turned and walked around the desk, still thinking about Chris: he had demonstrated a remarkable maturity during his years at the school. Mr Lewison himself had recently begun to learn basic sign language, so that he was better able to communicate with Chris; he encouraged the headmaster to consider doing the same. Aside from his rusty fingerspelling skills and his own name sign, he knew *nothing* about sign language. For many years, he had wondered whether deaf children would be better educated through sign rather than the oral approach. He thought about Chris' remarkable improvement in written English. Surely, he thought, this could not have been as a result of Mr Whittle's teaching through the oral method. Chris had shown very little improvement until last September or October, according to Mr Whittle's reports. Someone must be privately tutoring him. Aaron Stephens? That would be obvious, wouldn't it? Aaron was extremely good at English – one of the best in the school – and he and Chris were very close. So, he must be teaching him English through sign and that was paying off, Mr Langston ascertained.

He sat down on his chair and took off his glasses. With his other hand, he took a handkerchief from his trouser pocket and began to rub the lens with it. He reminisced about how he'd become a teacher of the deaf. It was that film, *Mandy*, that had inspired him.

He was twenty–five when the film came out in the summer of 1952. He had just completed his two years' National Service in Malta and was at a crossroads about his future; he knew that he wanted to teach French, history or art, but did not want to be just an ordinary teacher. He was courting Frances Rodgers at the time; they decided to go and see the film, for Jack Hawkins was in it and Frances was a big fan. Besides, he adored Phyllis Calvert who played the mother of the title character. It was also filmed in his hometown of Manchester. The story was about Mandy, a young deaf and dumb girl whose parents were uncertain about her future because she could not hear or speak. Then, they met an enigmatic speech therapist, played by Jack Hawkins, who finally taught Mandy to speak in a Manchester school for the deaf. At the end of the film, Mandy cried happily when she finally was able to talk, after being made to say the letter "*b*" repeatedly, holding a balloon close to her mouth. Mr Langston and his date cried at the tear–jerking finale, which had made him believe that the deaf and dumb *wanted* to talk and could be taught to do so, to achieve better education. That was the deciding factor for him.

Mr Langston leaned back against his chair, still rubbing his spectacles. He knew by now that it was all a false belief, but how was he to know then? A year or so back, he asked Mr McShane, a fellow Mancunian, whether he had seen the film. He said he had, on television.

'On the whole,' he said, 'it is a good film from a production standpoint, but it's also a pretentious, paternalistic and a propaganda film that's much favoured by strong oral advocates, I'm afraid.'

Mr McShane was not in the least bit surprised when he learned that the headmaster had been inspired by it, telling him that he was not the only teacher of the deaf who had been. He'd grown up in a Deaf environment, he added, where many Deaf people did not speak, yet they possessed good work related skills and communicated in sign language without any problems. He believed that the film painted a false picture that deaf children *wanted* to learn to talk and if they could not, they had no future. Mr Langston took that as a valid point, knowing deep down that it was true.

He finished rubbing his spectacles and checked the lenses, seeing that they were spotlessly clean. He put them back on and idly folded his handkerchief as he thought back to his early years again.

After marrying Frances a year later, Mr Langston had enrolled on a teaching degree course at Manchester University, studying there for three years. Their first son, Damien, was born during the first year, and their second son, Marcus, three years later. Mr Langston took a gap year after graduating with a first class honours, working in various part time jobs to help to support his young family. He then returned to Manchester University, enrolling on a year–long teacher of the deaf course. His main lecturer was Professor Alexander Ewing, who was close to retiring. He and his colleagues had taught him and about seventy other students how to instruct the deaf orally. They were taught about the use of acoustic equipment such as headphones and microphones to enable deaf pupils to listen to their teachers and isolate their voices from background noise. They had lessons in how to speak slowly and carefully, how to repeat things in other ways, such as by writing on a blackboard. They learned how to understand deaf people's sometimes abstruse speech, and how to ensure that their acoustic equipment was working properly (if it was not, getting it repaired was a high priority). The course had led him to understand that speech and lipreading were much more important than the curriculum; the deaf would not be able to understand his teachings if they did not possess adequate speech and lipreading skills. To that end, it was very important that he kept *talking* to them. Finally, it was strongly stressed to him and his fellow students that the deaf were not to use sign language in the classroom.

The seventy or so students were split into groups of ten, each assigned a senior tutor specialising in five–eleven and eleven–sixteen year olds. One group consisted of overseas students who came from places such as Hong Kong, Jamaica, South America and Australia; all of whom were already experienced teachers in their home countries.

Mr Langston leaned forward, resting his elbows on the desk and clasping his hands. He thought about some of the other students; he had become good friends with one, Muriel Constable, who became Muriel Moreliver when he and Frances attended her wedding in Bristol two years after the course finished. He also knew Mr Arkwright, but they never really became well acquainted then, and still had not; he knew that Mr Arkwright had always resented him for taking the principal's job. He once met Benjamin Williams during the course when he had given a talk about Ewing Hill Park, which was then in its ninth year of existence; as a student, Mr Langston had found the boarding school most fascinating and decided that he wanted to work there one day. He thought his year–long course was interesting, fun and productive, preparing him for the new challenge ahead.

It wasn't long before Mr Langston got his first teaching job at St. Andrew's Primary School in Levenshulme, Manchester. It had a small unit for deaf children; he taught them basic history and art using the oral method. He enjoyed working with the young deaf children there and stayed for two years, his heart touched by how happy their faces were despite their deafness, so keen to learn and their willing to participate in activities. On the other hand, though, he soon discovered that communication between the young pupils and their teachers was strained. He couldn't understand why at first; he believed the children could lipread their teachers easily and that their Brownie hearing aids – each wore two big, heavy brown boxes and a headset – should have helped them, but they did not seem to. He found the job difficult at first, but gradually settled in once he got over his frustration and impatience; he preferred teaching children aged from eleven to sixteen.

Over the next fourteen years, Mr Langston and his family moved from one oral school for the deaf to another. His third child, Shaleen, was born during this period. Mr Langston was ambitious; he wanted to be a headmaster of a deaf school. He organised many school activities, led deaf children on field trips, took them on exchange visits around the country and Europe, and participated in conferences on education, meetings, administrative work and budget planning. He also undertook a two–year modular course in school administration. One of his best qualities was the excellent lipspeaking skill he had developed, meaning many deaf children understood him well, although not always. He had to give up teaching French, one of his best subjects, because he found it impossible to teach deaf children a foreign language via spoken English. History therefore became his main subject and he had a brief spell at Ewing Hill Park teaching history before he moved on to become deputy head at another oral school for the deaf in Plymouth.

Then the position of headmaster at Ewing Hill Park came up; a successor for Benjamin Williams who was retiring from his twenty–five years as the headmaster. He applied for the job, was shortlisted and interviewed. He didn't think he would get it, but to his surprise, he did.

Mr Langston smiled, fondly remembering the shock of getting the job over a number of candidates, including Mr Arkwright. Benjamin Williams had told him it was his sixteen years of experience in teaching deaf children, his leadership and administrative skills, his desire to head a boarding school and his earnestness and care for deaf children that got him the job. The former headmaster also explained the vision he had had upon forming the school:

Ewing Hill Park was founded as the Britain's first ever dedicated grammar or technical school for deaf boys, to educate them at the highest standard through the oral method and to help them to prepare for the future. The boys should aim to do better than their hearing counterparts. When they leave school and go out into the world, they should be smarter, better behaved and harder workers than hearing people, because if an employer has to choose between a deaf boy and a hearing one, it is easier for him to choose the hearing one. The school's pupils should be able to show that they are better than their hearing competitors.

Mr Langston nodded, agreeing with the vision, although he had since changed his views about the oral philosophy. He looked at the framed photograph of his family on the desk, thinking about Damien in Washington DC. Six years back, at the age of twenty, he had moved across the big pond to study for a degree in economics at George Washington University after winning a scholarship there. He really never understood why his eldest had chosen an American university over those in Britain, but that was the decision he had made. As a child, Damien was always fascinated with America; his father guessed that he simply wanted to go there and, with any luck, live there. Mr Langston chuckled as he remembered the shock the family had had when Damien came home for Christmas a year later and announced he was getting married. He had met a girl called Annette, and their wedding was to be on the seventeenth of April the following year, which fell on Easter weekend. At first, Mr Langston and his wife were concerned for their twenty–two year old son, getting married so soon after meeting the girl; especially as he was still studying. However, they gave him their blessing after Frances pointed out that *they* had got married while he was still in university. Mr Langston rested his elbows on the armrests, clasped his hands together and rested his chin on them, reminiscing about his family's trip to Washington DC that year, shortly after school broke up for Easter.

He had never ever imagined the trip would change his life forever.

The low–key wedding took place at the small, contemporary United Church of Christ in downtown DC, next to St Patrick's Cathederal. There, Mr Langston and his wife had met Annette's parents, Hoke and Yvette Blackman, for the first time; they got along, although he sensed some tension between them. He supposed it was probably natural, since both families had been thrown together so quickly and hadn't had a chance to get more acquainted; he hoped he would get used to the idea of them as in–laws in time. Annette was a beautiful, intelligent young brunette and he couldn't blame his son for falling in love with her. During the wedding ceremony, Mr Langston couldn't help noticing a smartly dressed woman with immaculate blond hair standing at the end of the platform, her hands moving; she was mostly using her right hand to wriggle her fingers in a structural way. He knew she was using sign language and fingerspelling with one hand, but it looked so different to what he'd seen back home, where the deaf used both hands to fingerspell. He leaned forward on his pew to see a young woman sitting with her eyes fixed on the signing woman, seeming content with the proceedings of the wedding. It was the first time he had ever seen anything like that. He wondered if it was possible to do such a thing as translate from the spoken word to sign.

At the reception afterwards, Mr Langston went over to the woman, curious to know about her.

'Hello,' he greeted her, 'I was watching you in the church. Were you, er, signing the proceedings?'

'Yes sir, I was,' the woman replied. Then she recognised him. 'You must be Donald Langston, Damien's father?'

'Yes, that's right. How did you know that?'

'Why, of course, your son told me,' she replied, beaming.

'So, are you, uh, a volunteer for the church, helping the deaf or something?' he asked.

'Oh, no!' the woman laughed heartily. 'I'm a professional sign language interpreter.'

'Oh really?' Mr Langston frowned in surprise. A *professional sign language interpreter*, he thought; that was new to him.

'My name's Tasha.' She took a business card from her handbag and gave it to him. He looked down at the card, which had the *RID* seal – Registry of Interpreters for the Deaf, Inc. She continued, bursting with pride. 'It was formed twelve years ago – 1964. Since our profession was recognised by the government, our numbers basically mushroomed.'

Annette, her white wedding dress flowing, strolled over with the young woman he had seen watching the interpreter earlier. She introduced her to him, signing as she spoke.

'This is Donald, my new father–in–law. This is Kristen, my best friend. She's deaf.'

Mr Langston had already figured that one out for himself, shaking Kristen's hand. He turned to Tasha.

'Tell her that I'm very pleased–'

'Tell her that yourself,' Tasha raised her hand, interrupting him and directed him to the young woman next to her. She stood beside Mr Langston, beaming at him. 'I'm only here to facilitate communication!'

'Oh.' He turned to face Kristen, slightly embarrassed by his own ignorance. As he spoke, he saw that Tasha was signing every word he said. 'Pleased to meet you, Kristen.'

'Pleased to meet you too!' Kristen's hands flew while he listened to Tasha's voice–over.

'So, uh, what do you do?' he asked.

'I'm studying for a BA degree in English at Gallaudet College,' she replied.

A young deaf woman studying for *a BA in English?* Mr Langston, being polite, managed to contain his reaction. It was not just because she was deaf; it was simply the first time he had ever met a deaf person who was studying the English language at such a high level. How had she managed to get that far? He knew about Gallaudet College from Damien, but he hadn't gone into much detail. He was very curious about how Kristen managed in the classroom, considering how he knew the boys at his school often struggled with English.

'That's most interesting, Kristen. So, how do you understand your English teacher?'

Kristen stared long and hard at him. 'Have you been to Gallaudet College?' she asked.

Mr Langston glanced at the Gallaudet College visitors' leaflet again, reading that Thomas Hopkins Gallaudet and Alice Cogswell were embodied together in a bronze statue standing before him. He presumed the man was the founder of the college, and, judging by his clothes, it had happened in the early nineteenth century. He had no idea who the woman was, though. He looked over to his left to see the security kiosk, the way he had come in. Behind him, there was an imposing chapel–like building; the two statues were looking at it. Built with brown sandstone, it had tall, arched windows across the side, and a tower. The building had a deep triangular roof. He glanced down to his right and saw a man wearing a rather smart suit watching him, but he was too far away for the headmaster to see him properly. The man disappeared around the corner, taking no further interest in the stranger.

He headed into the campus. He thought again about what Kristen had explained to him, through Tasha, about Gallaudet; what it offered, the sheer size of the campus, the students, the classes, the teachers and much more. He found it impossible to imagine, so she encouraged him to visit the campus to see for himself. So, here he was, while the rest of his family had gone shopping in town. It was the last day of their stay in the American capital before they returned to England. He strolled along, appreciating how well designed the landscape was; a mixture of concrete slab paths, lawns, several trees and bushes. He saw that the buildings were an assortment of old and new; the west side, where he had come in (as per the map in the leaflet), consisted mainly of old buildings from the early twentieth century. As he walked along the straight, wide road – the Lincoln Circle, a kind of square route around the campus – towards the east side, he could see some box–like buildings rising above the old buildings, one being eight stories high. He saw they were the halls of residence – or dorms, as the leaflet told him they were called Clerc, Cogswell and Krug Halls. There were several large buildings on either side of the road, some old and some modern, including an auditorium. He passed several young college students along the way, observing, but not taking any particular interest, in their signing. He looked at the leaflet again and saw that there was a playing field up ahead, so he thought he would check it out first and then walk round the campus in an anti–clockwise direction, back to the entrance, then that would be it.

He arrived at the playing field, which also had an athletics track and bleachers. American football was being played on the field and he decided to stick around for a bit to watch the game; he was into rugby, though he knew there were certain differences, most notably the players' padded wear and helmets. He stood close to the line and folded his arms as he watched. The game moved, with both teams lining up for the snap. The quarterback raised his hand to show three fingers. A thunderously deafening *boom* from behind made him jump out of his skin – he whirled round to discover that he was standing close to a huge bass drum. *Boom!* The drummer whacked it again with a large drumstick. The stunned Englishman quickly cupped his now ringing ears with his hands, stunned. The drummer whacked the third and final *boom*. With his hands still covering his ears, Mr Langston turned back to see that the opposing lines of players had snapped together, crashing against one other in their padded uniforms, their arms and hands tangled. The quarterback received the oval shaped ball kicked from the snap, ran backwards a bit and threw the ball across the field. A wide receiver ran towards the touchdown, aiming to catch the approaching ball. he realised why they were using the bass drum; the one of the teams – or both teams, he couldn't tell – was deaf and they could not hear the snap call. If it they didn't have a drum, they'd have to line up in a curve instead of a straight line, so that they could see the snap count. They needed the bass drum to *feel* it. Ingenious, he thought. He moved away to a quieter area and watched the game for a short while.

He decided to have coffee before continuing his tour of the campus. He walked up to the Student Union Building, where the cafeteria was. Needing to relieve himself first, he went straight to the restroom inside without taking much notice of his surroundings. When he was finished, he went over to the cafeteria, looked around the four food counters and found one that sold beverages. He went over to it, ordered coffee and paid at a till. He then turned into an area with square tables and chairs, noticing that the man he'd seen at Chapel Hall earlier was watching him from one of the tables.

He froze, holding his warm paper cup tightly as the noise gradually hit him: he'd seen and heard the people around him when he entered a moment ago but was too preoccupied with the need to relieve himself. He looked, his eyes and mouth wide open, at the *hundreds* of people seated at tables around the vast open space, their hands flying and their heads turning, making a bewildering array of vocalisations. He turned full circle to the sound of high–pitched laughter that reverberated around him. He winced at the deafening sound of a door being slammed somewhere. He squirmed at the sound of breaking wind. He shuddered at the loud thumping on tables. He felt disgusted at the sound of noisy eating and burping. He grimaced at lips smacking together. He frowned at the sound of clunky dangling bracelets on some women's moving wrists as they banged them on the tables. He heard more hands. He began to feel nauseous, his head spinning and his eardrums pounding. He had heard these noises before at Ewing Hall Park and in the dining rooms at his former schools, but *never at this magnitude.* He had to get the hell out, now.

He rushed out, and then breathed out a sigh of relief.

'It's a different world out here, isn't it?' a voice came from behind.

Startled, Mr Langston whirled round, the hot liquid from the paper cup splashing his right hand. He quickly grabbed the cup with his other hand, wiping the hot wetness on his brown velvet jacket. The same man he'd seen at Chapel Hall and in the cafeteria a moment ago stood at the entrance, hands in the trouser pockets of his dark blue pin striped suit. Mr Langston took a better look at him; he was in his mid–fifties with back combed wavy hair and a distinctively chiselled chin. His dark eyes seemed to radiate warmth. He was about the same height as Mr Langston, though a little stockier. He could sense sincerity and graciousness from the smiling man.

'It's a bit noisy in there, isn't it?' the man indicated to the building behind him. 'I've seen so many hearing people react like you did when they experience something like that for the first time. You get used to it.'

'Well, I suppose so,' Mr Langston said, half–smiling. He sipped his coffee.

'I'm Edward Merrill.' He stepped forward, extending his hand. Mr Langston returned the handshake, which was firm. 'I'm the president of this college.'

'Donald Langston,' he returned.

'You're from England, aren't you?' Merrill said, picking up the accent. 'Whereabouts?'

'Manchester, but I'm now based in Waltbridge, just outside London,' Mr Langston replied. 'I'm the principal of a boarding school for deaf boys there.'

'Oral?'

'Yes.'

'And what brings you here, Mr Langston?' Merrill asked with a smile.

Sitting on the bench, He gave Merrill a brief background to his new tenure at Ewing Hill Park, about the school itself and the trials and tribulations of teaching deaf boys orally. He also told him how much he loved his job and cared for the boys, and finally, he explained about his eldest son's wedding, where he met Tasha the interpreter for the first time and Kristen told him about Gallaudet. In exchange, Merrill explained how he was from North Carolina, had a PhD in Educational Administration and was the fourth president of the college, at which he had begun his tenure seven years earlier. He explained his role, which was mainly administrative. Contrary to Mr Langston's assumption, he didn't have to wear a medallion – he didn't even have one. He also explained that he was a strong advocate for the deaf, had written and published several articles about the deaf and sought funding for research work. He had overseen the development of the Model Secondary School for the Deaf, housed on the same campus, to which he promised to take Mr Langston later.

Mr Langston finished his coffee and they went for a walk through the campus, with Merrill introducing each building as they passed. They stopped by an ominous looking building, which Merrill said was the Edward Miner Gallaudet Memorial Library, containing a wealth of literature on deaf history. Mr Langston asked who Edward was and whether he was a descendent of Thomas Hopkins Gallaudet.

'He was the youngest of his eight children,' Merrill replied. 'The eldest was Reverend Thomas Gallaudet. Like their father, they were hearing, but they were actively involved in the field of deafness and sign language. Their mother was deaf and they grew up being bilingual in sign language and English. Edward was the college's first president, for a rather magnificent forty–six years from 1864. Formerly known as the Columbia Institution for the Deaf and Dumb, under Edward Miner Gallaudet's leadership the institution applied for college status. When Abraham Lincoln signed a bill authorising the new status, Gallaudet College became the world's first college for the deaf.'

Mr Langston said he had assumed that Thomas Hopkins Gallaudet was the college's founder, and asked about Alice Cogswell. Merrill explained further.

'It was named after the Gallaudet family. As for Thomas Hopkins Gallaudet; in 1816, Alice's father, Dr Mason Cogswell, asked Gallaudet to sail to England to learn about the education of the deaf, but by pure chance he met Abbé Sicard, Laurent Clerc and Jean Massieu – the latter two being deaf – who were educators from France. They just happened to be in London too. Abbé Sicard succeeded Abbé de l'Epée. Have you heard of him, Donald?'

'I can't say I have, I'm afraid.' he replied, pushing his hands into his pockets as he and Merrill walked on.

'He was a mid–eighteenth century priest in France, not deaf, but discovered sign language,' Merrill said. 'Anyway, Gallaudet was fascinated by Clerc and changed his plans to travel to France with him to learn more about their education methods for the deaf. That's how he came across the one handed manual alphabet, which was developed by Abbé de l'Epée. Gallaudet invited Clerc over to America and that was how ASL – American Sign Language – was introduced and the rest is, as they say, history.'

'So,' Mr Langston turned to Merrill, 'this college teaches students through sign language, not orally?'

'Absolutely!' Merrill replied. He pointed wildly into the distance. 'Come, I'll show you.'

Merrill took Mr Langston to Hall Memorial building; they entered a large classroom where a professor was signing to about twelve students, who were sitting in a semi circle. The professor paused momentarily when he saw Merrill and his guest stray towards the back of the room. Merrill's hands flew as he signed to the professor, presumably telling him to carry on; Mr Langston watched in astonishment.

When Merrill was finished, Mr Langston whispered to him: 'You can sign?'

'Of course I can,' Merrill replied with a smile. 'And there's no need to whisper. We're the only ones in this room who can hear!'

Mr Langston's attention turned to the professor, surprised. It was the first time he had ever seen a deaf teacher. 'You mean he's deaf?'

'Yes, he is,' Merrill folded his arms. 'He's a professor of English. He's teaching English here. He's one of the five teaching English.' Merrill pointed at the professor.

Still watching the professor, Mr Langston asked, 'Are there other deaf professors teaching other subjects?'

'Of course, let me see,' Merrill folded his arms as he recollected. 'Biology, Chemistry, Business Administration, Economics, Mathematics, History … ' Merrill continued as Mr Langston slowly turned his head from the professor to the president, his mouth opening. '. . . Drama, Physical Education, Psychology and Socialogy. I think I've got most of them.' There was no hint of sarcasm in his voice.

'All deaf?'

'Yes, all deaf. There are hearing professors, but they can all sign. There are absolutely no communication barriers on this campus.'

'I'm afraid I've always believed that signing detracted the deaf from learning, as well as impairing their speech development … ' Mr Langston stumbled.

'What did you teach before you became headmaster?' Merrill asked with a hint of curiosity.

'Art, History and French.'

'Ah, French!'

'What?'

'You taught French through English, didn't you?' Merrill asked. 'To help them understand the language.' He paused for a moment. 'Let's suppose you're a pupil learning French. Would you want your teacher to instruct you full in spoken French, or in English?'

'Definitely English; I wouldn't be able to learn French without it. That's what I did at school.' Mr Langston replied.

'Exactly,' Merrill said. 'You teach in *their* language, not yours.'

'I'm not sure I quite understand.'

'Look at them,' Merrill nodded at the deaf students. 'They're being taught through their own language – sign language. Oralism is like trying to learn French through spoken French alone ... you've already said that you needed to use spoken English to help you learn the language. Effectively; it's the same for the deaf, trying to learn English by only being taught it orally. No wonder the boys at your school are struggling.'

'So, are you saying my boys would be better taught through sign language?' he asked. 'It's not even a proper language, is it?'

'It is a proper language,' Merrill said firmly. 'ASL was recently recognised as a language in its own right, after William Stokoe, our linguist here, proved that ASL is a *bona fide* language with its own grammar, vocabulary, structure and syntax. I'm sure other countries, including yours, will follow suit.'

Mr Langston wanted to check out the Model Secondary School for the Deaf – or MSSD as it was better known – that Merrill had mentioned earlier, so they walked to the north of the campus. Along the way, Merrill explained the application process. Prospective students would undertake entrance exams; most were successful; those who failed tended to be those who did not have a good command of written English for a variety of reasons, including being taught in oral schools. So, they studied in the campus for a year to polish up their written English through sign language. They would then retake their entrance exams, and many passed. Most of them went on to achieve at higher levels after graduating. Mr Langston asked about non–signing deaf students who passed the entrance exams; how would they cope? Merrill told him they had to go to the college's summer school to learn sign language – fast – by the time they started their first semester, they'd be reasonably versed in sign language. A curious Mr Langston then asked whether hearing teachers were expected to possess signing skills when they applied for jobs at Gallaudet. Merrill explained that this was strongly encouraged, but not required; those who had the requisite teaching qualities but did not know signs were able to learn the language on free courses.

Their conversation moved to another subject; this time, Deaf schools in general. The headmaster wondered about the state of them in America, so Merrill explained that a century ago, most Deaf schools used signing, but many had gradually shifted to the oral approach, believing it was better. However, in the last fifty years or so, they had realised oralism was not working, thus most had reverted back to using sign. He also said that there was controversy three years back – in 1973 – when a law that allowed American deaf children to be mainstreamed into their local hearing schools, in the same way as disabled children were, was passed. The argument was that the disabled children could hear and speak, while the majority of deaf children could not, and would struggle in mainstream education. Mr Langston said the same problem was emerging in England, though no policy on mainstreaming had yet been formalised. Not yet anyway, he told Merrill. He briefly explained that, from what he understood, the Warnock Committee of Inquiry had been set up two years back to look into the special educational needs of disabled children in Britain, with a report due to be published in two years' time. Despite Mr Langston and Merrill's differing views on educating the deaf, they agreed that the mainstream approach was a fundamentally wrong, fallible and cheap option. Turning the situation around, Mr Langston pointed out that if a hearing child were in a classroom full of signing deaf children and a signing teacher, he would struggle.

They crossed the road that divided the college from MSSD, arriving at the school, which was on higher ground. It was a large, three storey modern building, light brown with a flat roof, surrounded by several trees. Merrill told his guest how President Johnson had signed the Model Secondary School for the Deaf Act ten years back, designed to be a model school for all deaf schools in America to follow. Merrill and the Secretary of Health, Education and Welfare signed an agreement seven years ago, shortly after he became president of Gallaudet, authorising the development of MSSD on the campus. The aim, he explained, was to educate deaf pupils aged between eleven and sixteen in all subjects via sign language, and to prepare them for their next step; higher education at Gallaudet College. The school was first opened a year later and made a huge impact. Several hundred deaf children from all over the United States came to this school, which currently had about two hundred pupils. Mr Langston was most eager to have a look inside.

In the hallway, Merrill stopped to converse with a staff member, while Mr Langston gazed around the modern surroundings. Merrill returned to him, shaking his head in slight disappointment.

'Merv Garretson, the principal, is out of office today,' Merrill said, heading for a classroom door. 'You would have liked to have met him. I'd have been happy to interpret for you both.'

'You mean he's deaf?!' he followed Merrill, his jaw dropping. 'A deaf principal?'

Merrill opened the door and poked his head inside; Mr Langston heard him ask someone inside if he and his guest could come in. Merrill leaned back, opening the door wide to let him through. 'Yes, a deaf principal. Half of the teachers here are deaf too.'

The men walked to the back of the large classroom, which, like most of the other classrooms, had about twelve pupils sitting in a semicircular formation with a young female teacher signing at the helm. Mr Langston observed that the boys and girls were between thirteen and fourteen, so they must be in Form Two or Three, he ascertained. He knew the teacher was teaching history, as he could see some scribbles on the blackboard about the American Civil War. Wait a minute, he thought; the teacher wasn't wearing the microphone on her chest. She must be deaf as she wasn't using her voice to speak to the pupils, but hadn't Merrill spoken to her at the door just now?

'Is she deaf?' he asked, pointing at her.

'Oh, no, she's hearing,' Merrill replied.

The headmaster turned to the teacher, confused. 'But she isn't speaking to them. Why isn't she using the group hearing system?'

'Why should she?' Merrill asked. 'Look at the kids, are they using any?'

Mr Langston moved the end of the semicircular formation of desks, and took a better look. He saw that *none* of the twelve kids were wearing the group headphones; nor was any form of equipment attached to their desks. Whilst three children were wearing body–worn hearing aids, he noted, the rest were not.

Amused by his guest's reaction, Merrill said, 'Oh yes, we used to have them in the 1960s but it was proved to be very ineffective. Oh, don't tell me you still use them in England?'

Mr Langston nodded with embarrassment. He thought of the cumbersome things that the boys at his school had to wear; he knew for a fact that they *hated* them because they hurt their heads and ears, and replacing them with the FM system, funds permitting, was high on his to–do list. Perplexed, he turned to Merrill.

'This is a fully operational school for the deaf,' Merrill explained. 'All of the students here are taught in signs by deaf and hearing teachers. Some of the hearing teachers may speak sometimes, but not often, because, uh, speaking and signing at the same time makes their signing choppy. It's a visual language, so why the need for the FM systems?'

'But what about those kids wearing hearing aids?' he pointed at the three pupils in question. 'Surely they *need* something to help them hear the teacher?'

Merrill shook his head gently. 'Some of them may hear better than others, or speak well, or it could just be the parents insisting on their kids wearing them. As for the rest … hearing aids just don't work for them. I would say, perhaps, ten percent of the kids here wear them. They have the freedom to choose whether they wish to wear hearing aids or not here.'

They have the freedom to choose to wear their hearing aids or not? Mr Langston thought to himself, astonished at this revelation. Back home, it was a strict hearing aids wear rule for deaf children.

'Most of them,' he heard Merrill continue explaining, 'have said that they can only *feel* the rhythmic vibrations in their ears, nothing more, and often nothing at all. They can't hear any sounds, never mind words, no matter how powerful their aids are. And anyway, even those who can hear words would still struggle in the classroom. They're *all* deaf, you see. They're using their eyes to learn, not their ears, just like how blind kids learn using their ears, not their eyes. Even our oral schools don't use that kind of equipment in their classrooms. Their teachers may have strong views on oralism, but they're also realists; they *know* that the whole point of oralism is for the deaf use their eyes to lipread. They tend to speak, write and gesture while they're teaching, and headphones and microphones simply get in the way. So, they only use the equipment to instruct kids in speech rooms, not classrooms.'

Mr Langston slowly turned his attention to the class, unsure whether to believe Merrill's explanation or not, though he knew many deaf schools in England wouldn't agree with the Americans' view. He carefully observed the children's receptiveness to their teacher; although he could not understand a single thing they were signing, he could see that they were extremely receptive and seemed to understand almost everything that their teacher was saying. She occasionally wrote on the blackboard, but only to help the pupils refer back to things, rather than repeating herself. The pupils conversed in sign to one another and actually seemed to be *enjoying* the lesson. Merrill remained silent; the headmaster presumed the president wanted him to observe.

A boy with long black hair looked up at the stranger with big, round eyes and signed briefly to him. Mr Langston turned to Merrill, who had been watching.

'He asked what your name is.' Merrill said. He fingerspelled to the boy, answering on his guest's behalf. The boy responded with another signed query. Merrill shook his head, signed something and pointed at the man with white hair and glasses. 'Now he's asking if you have a name sign. Do you have one?'

'Well, yes,' the humble man answered, remembering he'd been given by James Eriswell, who told him that of all the boys and staff had their own name signs, which tended to be based on their appearances, characters, names, habits, or just something that had been made up. They helped the boys to identify who they were referring to; James said this was very commonplace amongst Deaf people. His name sign consisted of an "L" handshape, the index finger pointing upwards and the thumb touching the top of the signer's cheek, indicating the first letter of his surname and the fact that he wore spectacles. He signed it to the boy, who mimicked it with appreciation. 'What's your name, boy?' he asked.

The boy glanced at Merrill for a signed translation, then swiftly zigzagged out the first letter with his index finger, following up with three more letters that Mr Langston couldn't follow.

'Zane,' Merrill said.

'Hello Zane,' the headmaster greeted him. He looked expectantly at Merrill, who nodded for him to go ahead. As he spoke, Merrill translated. 'So, um, do you like this school?'

Zane watched Merrill, and then nodded at Mr Langston. He signed a question and Merrill translated. 'He asked if you're a teacher.' Mr Langston nodded, he knew it wasn't the correct answer, but close enough.

Zane asked another question; 'Can you sign?' translated Merrill.

Before he could answer, Merrill started signing something to the boy; he presumed that the president was telling the boy who the man really was, where he came from and what he did. Everyone in the classroom, including the teacher, was watching him. Zane waved at him and pointed at his eyes with two fingers, telling him to watch him. Mr Langston carefully observed his signing.

He pointed at himself, sombrely shook his head, then circled his mouth with a crooked index and middle finger …

He stared at Zane, fascinated and mesmerised by his signing, that seemed so smooth and flawless. It was the way he moved his arms, demonstrated with his hands and wriggled his fingers; not forgetting his bodily movements and facial expressions. Even though he couldn't understand a word he said, he could *see* that there was a logical structure to his signing; it had beauty and purity. He had seen some deaf children signing back home, particularly at Ewing Hill Park (sometimes secretly), but he never really paid much attention, believing they were simply signing in broken English as a way of making themselves understood. He realised now that he was wrong; those boys were using British Sign Language, yet they were suppressed from doing so by his own kind. Merrill must be right: it was a *real* language. After when Zane had finished, Mr Langston turned to Merrill expectantly, hoping for a translation.

'Zane,' Merrill began, 'said "I don't like oralism because it's bad. I was very unhappy at my old school, right from first grade, because everyone spoke. Everyone here uses signing and I'm very happy here. My mom and dad are very happy too because I'm doing so well here".'

That summed it all up, Mr Langston mused. A girl at another desk waved at him and signed something. He turned to Merrill, who translated.

'She's asking if you can sign.'

'Um, I don't sign … ' Mr Langston muttered, starting to feel a bit embarrassed. He saw Merrill respond to the girl, who followed up with another question:

'She asked why not.' said Merrill.

The headmaster was rooted to the spot, stuck for words.

'Mr Langston?' came the teacher's voice. Mr Langston turned to her, thankful for the rescue. She spoke and signed at the same time for everyone's benefit; 'Why don't you come over here and tell them all about England and its history? I'd be happy to interpret for you.'

'I'm not sure I–'

'Go on, Donald,' Merrill encouraged him. 'It's not every day these kids get the chance to see an Englishman.' he smiled wryly.

Mr Langston saw that the children were watching him enthusiastically, wide eyed with anticipation. He nodded graciously, took off his jacket and went over to the front. With the teacher interpreting for him; signing and voicing over for the young teenagers; and occasionally writing on the blackboard, he talked about England. His impromptu history lesson covered the Romans' invasion, civil wars, some of England's most famous kings and queens such as Henry VIII and his six wives, Queens Elizabeth I and Victoria, famous London landmarks such as Buckingham Palace, the Tower Bridge, the Tower of London, the Houses of Parliament and the Big Ben, the London Underground and the lights at Piccadilly Circus. He talked about the First and Second World Wars, disputing one pupil's claim that America won the second war by pointing out to her that it was an allied effort, led by Britain, that had won the war. He talked about Queen Elizabeth II, her 1953 coronation and the Silver Jubilee that was being organised for the following year. He mentioned the royal family and the new prime minister, James Callaghan, who had succeeded Harold Wilson after his shock resignation earlier that month; the headmaster believed that Margaret Thatcher would become the country's first female prime minister if her opposing party won the next general election. He mentioned how she had visited his school a few years back, answering another pupil's question that he was not headmaster then. He then moved on to sports, admitting that he was much more of a fan of rugby and cricket than football – or soccer to the Americans – the pupils were surprised to learn that rugby players did not wear pads or helmets. At that, he joked that rugby players were much braver than American footballers, chuckling as he heard echoes of disagreement around him. The session finished off with a flurry of questions from the children; he answered every one of them.

The teacher thanked him for his time and the entire room burst into loud clapping and hand waving. Even Merrill, who had been watching at the back throughout, clapped loudly. he felt very humbled and overwhelmed. He had never enjoyed teaching so much; the realisation now sinking in that it was the *first time* he had ever made himself understood the first time round, rather than having to repeatedly explain the same thing over and over again. He had covered several different historical topics in just a short time instead of a month, or even a year, as he'd used to do during his teaching years. He had also understood the pupils' questions and comments through the teacher interpreting, which was, again, something new to him. How could he have been so *blind* in believing that the oral approach was the best and only way to instruct deaf children? He thought Merrill was right: if he wanted to help the deaf, he had to be *part* of their world, not outside it. He couldn't force them into *his,* hearing, world either. For many years as a teacher of the deaf, when he had finished a class, his pupils would take off their headphones and sign to each other; he would not intrude because they were in their own world. Now he understood. He had glimpsed a part of their world at Gallaudet and it worked. He wanted the same for Ewing Hill Park. That way, he thought, the deaf boys – and deaf children at other deaf schools – would be better educated into the hearing world, rather than being pushed into integration.

Class finished, Mr Langston and Merrill walked back to the main campus. Something was bothering him.

'What happened?' he asked Merrill. 'Why's there so much oralism in deaf schools back home?'

Merrill stopped walking, making Mr Langston stop too. His eyes met his new friend's, which unnerved him slightly. 'I take it that you don't know what happened almost a century ago?'

Mr Langston spun his chair to the side and stared blankly at the night sky through the window as he thought about what Merrill had explained to him. The president admitted that he didn't know much detail about what happened a century ago, only what he had read of the literature written by Edward Miner Gallaudet who was there with his older brother, Reverend Thomas, when it happened. However, what Merrill knew was more than enough for the headmaster to understand the scale of it all. It made sense to him.

It made a lot of sense with regard to what was happening in the education of the deaf. How could those fools have done that? He had long believed the truth that was created by so many lies. How many deaf children had suffered and were still suffering due to that egomaniacal absurdity? The damage was already done and it would take many years to be reversed, if that were even possible. he wanted no part in that any longer – he cared deeply for deaf children and promised himself that he would try to make changes, however small; even if they wouldn't change the world, at least he would gain some level of satisfaction.

Mr Langston leaned back, his chair tipping slightly as he thought about Merrill, who had been good enough to send him copies of the homework the MSSD pupils had done about his session. Apart from some grammatical, spelling and punctuation errors, he was surprised to learn that their written English was generally excellent. In fact, it was *far better* than what his pupils had at his school.

He clasped his hands and twiddled his thumbs, reflecting on his first day back at school after the Easter break.

Still slightly jet–lagged from the trip, Mr Langston observed the dining room activity in silence as he ate his lunch at the staff table. Many of the boys were speaking – or trying to, from what he could see – to each other, their faces strained, trying their damndest not to use their hands, fearful of being caught by the ever–watchful staff members. Although the hall was filled with bright sunlight from the large floor–to–ceiling windows at the other end, he felt a sense of sobering darkness and overwhelming mediocrity around him. It was as if he was seeing through a black veil. His thoughts flashed back a few days, to the sight of hundreds of flying hands in the dining hall at Gallaudet. His mind snapped back to harsh reality and he pondered: was this school still stuck in the Dark Ages? Scooping up a lump of mashed potato with his fork, he looked up again as he put the fork in his mouth. He saw the head boy, James Eriswell, sitting at the Fifth Form table at the other end, and thought about him.

'You wanted to see me, sir?' James Eriswell said almost perfectly, upon entering the headmaster's office after lunch.

Mr Langston studied the tall seventeen–year old for a short moment. Fair haired with hazel eyes, the lad came from an extremely large clan who had been deaf for generations, yet by some fluke, he had excellent speech and lipreading skills as well as being fluent in sign language. He was one of the most popular boys in the school, so it was no surprise that Mr Williams had selected him as head boy just before he retired. He wished he could have known the lad longer. When he had started his new job as headmaster the previous September, James was the first boy to walk into the office to introduce himself and they had hit it off. Even his son, Marcus, who was the same age, became good friends with him. A born leader, he thought, the boy would be sorely missed when he left school in two months' time, though he believed the lad would do extremely well in the future.

'I want you to tell the boys,' the headmaster finally said, 'that signing will be allowed outside the classrooms.'

'Excuse me?' the head boy stared at him in surprise.

'You heard me, James.' Mr Langston clapped once. 'I'm now lifting the ban on signing that's been in place since this school opened. All boys are free to sign anywhere, anytime; even in the dining room. Just not during lessons.'

For now, he told himself.

'But why?' James asked, still in disbelief.

'Let's just ... say that I want to make some changes here.'

'What about the staff–?'

'Leave them to me,' the headmaster replied. 'Now, go and make the announcement.'

The head boy hesitated for a moment, still unsure, then nodded and left.

Half an hour later, he returned, in a state of disbelief. 'They don't believe me, sir. They think I'm making trouble to get them punished!'

Mr Langston chuckled as he looked away from the window, remembering his own reaction. He'd eventually had to go to the Assembly Hall, where the boys had already gathered to receive the head boy's news. Once there, he asked James to convey the announcement again, in sign. For the first time since he had been at the school, the headmaster saw the entire congregation of fifty boys burst into ecstatic cheering and whooping, clapping and waving their hands high in the air. He felt as though an enormous weight had been lifted off their shoulders as well as his own.

Mr Langston quietly drummed his fingers on his desk, remembering the severe opposition he had received from some of his staff once they'd heard the news.

Mr Arkwright was the most vocal, speaking out vehemently against his decision, saying that signing would impair the boys' moral development. Mr Langston disagreed and pointed out that James Eriswell came from a strong Deaf family whose first language was sign language; yet, he was one of the most intelligent boys and maintained excellent speech and lipreading skills. He also noted how he had seen almost every boy signing secretly when members of staff were not looking; there was no evidence of this affecting their speech. Besides, he said, many of them weren't good at speaking anyway. Mr Langston chose not to share his experiences at Gallaudet for the time being, to avoid fuelling another heated debate.

Mr Langston rose to his feet and walked over to a framed canvas painting of the school, which was on the wall next to the door. He stood in front of it and once more admired the beautifully detailed oil painting of the brown Georgian building. A pair of white pillars stood on either side of the entrance doors, the car park and the field in front, trees in the distance at the rear of the school and a clear blue sky with some patchy white clouds. The headmaster had never known who painted it, for he had never bothered to read the tiny artist's signature at the bottom. He now decided to kill his curiosity, so leaned over and squinted at the tiny faint grey handwriting. He sighed when he recognised the name: Franco Hugentobler. Him, of all the people in the world, he cursed; painting something so incredibly beautiful, yet he was someone that he wanted to forget. Now the atrocity had come back from the deep recesses of his memory; he relived it all over again.

The short, stocky fifty–year old French art teacher, balding with a double chin, had been aggravated by the decision to lift the ban on signing. He felt the staff should have had a vote on this first, but Mr Langston rejected his view, knowing he would have been outvoted. A few weeks later, into the following May, Mr Langston walked into the Art Room to discover a weeping First Former, Tom Quillot, standing in a corner with a stack of books balancing on the palms of each of his outstretched hands. Franco Hugentobler was smacking his wrists with a steel ruler if he dared to lower them under the strain. The headmaster put a stop to this, immediately suspending the art teacher pending investigation. As it turned out, Franco Hugentobler had been emotionally and physically abusing a number of boys for several years. He was still using the cane and plimsoll punishments, already outlawed by Mr Langston, who had always believed that there were more effective methods of discipline than a hard smack on the bottom and had ordered all staff *not* to lay their hands on the boys unless it was absolutely necessary. However, he discovered the art teacher had ignored the order, particularly relating to the juniors who were too scared to report him. From what he had seen, Franco Hugentobler didn't seem to know how to interact with the boys or how to communicate with them properly, and often took out his frustrations on them. A good, enlightened, emotionally intelligent teacher of the deaf, who is able to tune in to deaf children, would never abuse them. The headmaster had no option but to sack him.

Mr Langston looked away from the painting, thinking he should replace it with a new painting of the school, to get rid of all the bad memories associated with the former art teacher. He thought about asking Mr McShane if he could do one; he may even suggest a competition for the boys to enter, aiming to paint the best picture of the school. Hmmm, he mused; that would be an excellent idea, and would mean that the winning boy's painting would be kind of immortalised in the school's history. Mr Langston then remembered the interviews for a new art teacher.

Mr Langston was one of the five panel members, alongside Mr Arkwright, Mrs Munnings and two governors; the chairwoman, Rosemary Goldsack, and Robert Denham, whose deaf son, Patrick, was a former pupil. The headmaster wanted each candidate to undertake an art lesson after their interview for the boys to judge, but Rosemary Goldsack objected to this idea and insisted that the candidates' responses would be sufficient. One candidate after another was interviewed, and when Mr McShane, the last candidate, walked in, Mr Langston immediately *knew* that the young man was the one; he was a breath of fresh air and came from his hometown of Manchester. Mr McShane had a vibrant personality and excellent communication skills, though he kept his knowledge of sign secret during the interview. Mrs Munnings and Robert Denham liked him while Mr Arkwright and Rosemary Goldsack preferred Mrs Gainsborough, who was excellent at art, but did not possess any qualifications in or have any experience of teaching the deaf. When the panel took a short recess for Mr Langston to consider his deciding vote, he ventured out into the front hall and saw Mr McShane signing to James Eriswell as though they knew each other. The surprised headmaster confronted him about it.

'I'm very sorry, sir,' Mr McShane said, embarrassed. 'James and I know each other. We both are from deaf families and know each other; the deaf world's very small, you see, and, I'm the only hearing person in my family. I'm what you call "Me Hearing, Mother Father Deaf". I can sign fluently. I didn't want to say anything about that at the interview because, er, I've had interviews at lots of schools for the deaf in the past few years and every time I've told them about my background, I haven't got the job. They always seem to choose people who teach using the oral method. So, I decided, just this once, not to say anything about my fluency in sign language. Now that you know, I guess I've cocked up again–'

'Miles McShane,' the smiling headmaster made up his mind, shaking his fellow Mancunian's hand. 'You've got the job.'

Mr Langston smiled, remembering the shock and delight on Mr McShane's face. His final vote came up against some resistance from Mr Arkwright and Rosemary Goldsack, but they eventually accepted it. He had decided on Mr McShane not out of sympathy, but because he was an excellent art teacher who could communicate with the deaf. And, yes, as he had admitted to himself then, it was because of what he had seen at Gallaudet; he wanted to start making changes to drive the school forward, instead of dwelling in the past. Mr McShane was the perfect first seed of the many he would sow. However, progress in the last four years had been painfully slow, held back by those who dragged their heels and insisted on following the oralist philosophy endorsed by Benjamin Williams. Williams' vision, was absolutely spot–on, Mr Langston had always believed. It was the *philosophy* he wanted to change, but the school's board of governors refused to do so.

Mr Langston put his hands in his pockets, glancing at a thick ring binder, labelled *Board of Governors' Meeting Minutes*. He thought about the board meeting that had been held on the eleventh of September of that same year, which was the Saturday after the new school year began, after his full first year as headmaster.

Most of the eight members of the board were quite dismayed when they learned that Mr McShane, who had started his new job earlier that week, was fluent in sign language and that Mr Langston had deliberately withheld this "vital information" from them. Upon being asked to explain why, he told them all about his experiences at Gallaudet and explained that he had also visited some schools for the deaf around Britain that used sign, or sign and speech combined. He also gave out copies of the MSSD pupils' homework Merrill had sent him, as evidence of their excellent written English skills.

'That was very interesting, Donald,' Rosemary Goldsack said, resting her hands on the table. 'Do you believe that the deaf would be better educated through signing?'

'I'm beginning to.' Mr Langston replied, sitting down and feeling quite exhausted, albeit satisfied, after his lengthy presentation on his ideas and future plans for the school for the board's consideration. He looked expectantly to the chairwoman, who was sitting at the other end of the long table in the library. Six board members were round the table, three on either side. Mr Langston observed the middle–aged woman's bony face, dead eyes and permanently miserable smile. Her hair was scraped back into a bun, held by a gold–tinted hairpin. Her body was scrawny; so scrawny that Mr Langston had often wondered if she was anorexic. She had a deaf daughter, Alexandria, who was now in her final year at the sister school, Boyd Hill Grammar School. Rosemary Goldsack had always talked a great deal about how proud she was of her daughter's excellent speech and lipreading skills, and how she was doing magnificently well at school. She even boasted that Alexandria was the "perfect role model" for every deaf child, as she "talks beautifully" and "does not use signing". Mr Langston had met the girl a few times over the past year when she had visited the school with her mother. Though not unintelligible by any means, Alexandria's speech was not nearly as good as her mother had led him to believe. She could sign too; when her mother wasn't looking. He once spotted her signing to Jacques Magnat and from what he could see, she was quite fluent. Also, according to what he'd been told by some of the Boyd Hill teachers, she struggled in most subjects.

'Does anyone agree with Donald?' Rosemary Goldsack asked, looking around the table. She directed her attention to the short, burly middle–aged man with a heavy moustache on her left. 'Tony?'

Tony Booth leaned forward, clasping his hands. Formerly a headmaster at another oral school, he shook his head, looking at the headmaster and waving his index finger as if to admonish him. 'I've said this before and I'll say it again: sign language is simply broken English grammar with signs for English words. You say it's a proven *bona fide* language, Donald? I find that very hard to believe.'

'I agree with Tony,' a woman's voice piped up. Mr Langston turned to see Jenny Moog, a young woman who was representing an organisation that advocated the listening and talking approach to deaf education. 'It's always been my strong belief that deaf children can learn different subjects, including English, better through lipreading.'

'Absolutely,' Rosemary Goldsack nodded.

'I don't agree,' Robert Denham said, his voice verging on irritation. Mr Langston smiled discreetly to himself, grateful for his secret ally. The well–proportioned private financer, unlike the rest of the board members, had always kept an open mind on various issues, including sign language. Like Mr Langston, Robert Denham used to believe in the oral approach. 'My son, Patrick, who you all know was a pupil here, is now twenty years old, but his literacy skills are far below that; perhaps equal to someone half his age. His English is *terrible*.' He picked up the copies of the MSSD pupils' homework to express his annoyance. 'How can it be that their English is better than that of most of the boys here, let alone most of the deaf kids in this country?'

'Patrick,' Robert Denham went on; 'he's just got a job doing manual labour. My wife and I aren't too happy about that, but what can we do? I wanted him to work at my private finance company and perhaps take over when I retire. But he can't. Patrick came here to get a *better* education, but he didn't get one. Even those school reports we received … to be quite frank, I strongly believe they were more than a little exaggerated. So, Donald's experiences at Gallaudet, I think, make a lot of sense. Deaf teachers teaching deaf kids English – that's quite incredible, isn't it? Deaf professors too; I'd have loved for my son to be one! These people were educated through sign language, not orally. I'm not saying we should have the same here … well, we don't know of *any* deaf teachers around here, anyway. I mean, there must be a few, but where are they? Anyway, my point is, I feel we should explore the possibility of introducing signing into the classrooms–'

'Perhaps … ' everyone turned to Daniel Lish, a former teacher of the deaf for whom Mr Langston had scant regard because of his misleading opinions that were rarely relevant to the matters discussed. 'Your son did not pay much attention to the teachers?'

'Quite the contrary, Daniel;' Robert Denham said, glaring at his fellow board member, barely disguising his anger, 'he *did* pay attention. But he found all of the teachers here difficult to understand. Surely, this is a school for the deaf, so teachers who are trained to instruct the deaf should at least be able to make themselves understood. Patrick told us that the other boys had the same problem too. That's why I joined this board last year; to try and do something about it, but so far I've only met resistance from all of you. We're way behind the Americans, so I *urge* all of you to support Donald's ideas for changes to this school. They'll help us to move forward and get this school on the map.'

Robert Denham sat back, folding his arms, satisfied with his lecture, although he knew it would fall on deaf ears as usual.

'This school is *already* on the map!' Professor Herbert Quigley, a bearded retired ear specialist from the Ear Foundation, leaned forward, spreading his hands. 'It's one of the best in the country.'

'Absolutely!' Tony Booth concurred. 'And we pride ourselves in that, so what's the point of mending what isn't broken?'

'I agree. My daughter hasn't had any problems with her education,' Rosemary Goldsack cut in.

'Not *every* deaf child can manage.' Mr Langston spoke out, his voice firm. 'I've now come to realise that the oral approach *does not* work for *every* deaf child. Some, yes, but not all. That is why I want to start making changes here. I have a responsibility to ensure that all of the boys here get the best possible education and I believe that's best achieved through *their language*, not ours. They should be leaving school with the highest possible achievements. I'm not saying we should abandon the oral method altogether: it can still be used. Our boys will continue getting speech training. But, we should include sign language in addition to what we already do, so there'll be no communication barriers. If the board is at all concerned about making sure that these boys do well, then I urge you to give your full support for my ideas. There's no point in dragging out the past; we must move forward and keep up with the changing times.'

'Hear, hear!' Robert Denham exclaimed.

'Very well,' Rosemary Goldsack said, her voice reserved. 'You've made your point, Donald. I think this calls for a vote.' She addressed the board members. 'You've listened to Donald's presentation and you've made your arguments. I'd like to propose a motion that the oral method should be favoured in the classroom over signing. Anyone second that?'

'I second it!' Isabelle Hall put her hand up. Mr Langston rolled his eyes, not surprised at the peculiar, bespectacled speech therapist. From what he had heard, she had a bit of a fetish; she liked the deaf and deafblind to touch her mouth with their fingers … and their feet. She *always* agreed with everything Rosemary Goldsack said.

'Thank you, Isabelle,' the chairwoman nodded, smiling. 'Anyone in favour?'

Five of the eight board members raised their hands. Mr Langston and Robert

Denham exchanged awkward glances, keeping their hands down.

'Five votes to two,' Rosemary Goldsack said mockingly, 'I don't think I need to ask for those against.' she said sharply. She looked across the length of the table, her expression triumphant, at the silent headmaster. 'The vote has been carried, Donald. To recap: the oral method must continue within classrooms, and sign language, or whatever it's called, is not to be used. The boys can do what they like elsewhere. You were appointed last year to uphold and continue philosophy and Benjamin William's vision. Your ideas to transform the school, however interesting they may seem, would be like … let's say, ignoring fact and pursuing fiction. This school prides itself on being a prestigious establishment, providing its boys with the best education. You are not to turn it into a circus. I strongly suggest that you concentrate on that and do not make any radical changes based on your own subjective views. Do I make myself clear?'

Subjective views? Mr Langston shook his head in disgust. Didn't she bloody know the meaning of hypocrisy? Ignoring fact and pursuing fiction? Oh, come on, Rosemary, wake up to what's *really* happening around you!

He had always thought that the chairwoman had pulled out the motion as if it was a rabbit from a magician's hat, out of sheer arrogance. She *knew* she'd gain the majority vote anyway. She'd even had the bloody nerve to say that the school had a higher examination success rate than most other deaf schools. Had she actually *seen* the statistical records that the school had kept for the last twenty–nine years? Less than a quarter of the boys achieved the top three grades. Hardly an achievement – or was it that the education system for the deaf was really *that bad*? So bad that the school had actually achieved higher grades than other deaf schools? Jesus Christ, he cursed; those people on the board were so institutionalised! Except for Robert Denham, of course; he had had been supportive. The Kent man had often disagreed with decisions made at the quarterly board meetings, especially on issues relating to educating the deaf. It was no surprise to the headmaster that Robert Denham had increasingly become disillusioned; after the last board meeting a couple of months back, he had said he was seriously considering resigning from the board, but Mr Langston had begged him not to, otherwise he would be fighting these people alone. He had hinted that it was only a matter of time before things would turn around, and Robert Denham had agreed to stay on for the time being.

Ever since that meeting almost four years back, Mr Langston had struggled to move the school forward on what was always a tight budget. The continued technical problems and the repair of the obsolete acoustics equipment were costing the school a fortune. The school needed more money to fund a complete equipment overhaul, although he had managed to purchase a new FM system for the Physics Room, which worked with the new behind–the–ear hearing aids. Still, it wouldn't make much difference to many of the boys, as they had to rely on lipreading alone, although he had noticed that Mrs Munnings was already using some signing in her lessons. Miss Stephenson had just started doing that too. Mr McShane was the most popular teacher, which didn't surprise the headmaster. He should at least try to learn some more sign himself, he mused. One day, when there was time, perhaps. He chuckled to himself as he remembered Andrew Brener's signed performance of David and Goliath at the Open Day last October, which he had secretly enjoyed. He also knew about what the boys called the "phone–goods", who secretly interpreted during morning assembly. He wasn't blind! It was something he had always wanted to address; ensuring full access to communication; but the governors' continued refusal held him back.

Mr Langston brushed away his thoughts, turned away from the shelves and stopped to glance at one particular dossier that was slightly askew. He took it out so that he could put it back in properly. He sighed when he realised what he was holding: the *Warnock Report of the Committee of Enquiry into the Education of Handicapped Children and Young People (1978).* He thought he had thrown it away and couldn't understand why it had ended up on the shelf. He was certain he had chucked it into the bin, so one of the staff – Mr Arkwright? – must have found it and put it there without him knowing.

He walked back towards his desk, idly flipping through the pages. He had thrown the report away two years back because he had found its findings to be shocking and quite disastrous; so much so that he was very worried about the future of deaf education in Britain. He thought about how this state of affairs had come about, knowledge gleaned from what he had read in the report. Commissioned by the government, Lady Warnock chaired a committee of inquiry in 1974, looking at children with special educational needs – SEN – in the education system. They concluded that 20% of children in the school population could have SEN, but only 2% might need support over and above what a mainstream school could provide. The Warnock Report recommended that there should be specialist provision for children with SEN, which could protect the 2% – he had never really understood the reasoning behind these figures or where they came from – and ensure that they received appropriate provision. In other words, the report recommended that deaf and disabled children should be integrated into mainstream schools and support provision made available. The idea behind this was that the child should fit into the school, rather than the school fitting the child.

Like him, many other heads of Deaf schools he knew disagreed with these recommendations. They meant that there was a danger of local education authorities wrongly assessing deaf children as having learning disabilities because of their communication difficulties. He knew this only too well, from his experience of working in a few PHUs. For the last five years, as headmaster of Ewing Hill Park, Mr Langston had come to realise the enormous benefits of educating the deaf in their own environment, like at this school, over placing them in mainstream settings. Did the Warnock committee know and understand the huge differences between deaf and disabled children in terms of education, communication and social aspects? Did they think they could simply throw a deaf child into a hearing school to "help" them into the hearing world? Did they expect the deaf child to easily follow in a hearing classroom environment, even with support? Had they explored the potentially extortionate costs of support provision? No, they damn well hadn't, he muttered, slamming the dossier shut.

He sighed, becoming concerned. If the recommendations became policy – and he wouldn't be surprised if they did, given Margaret Thatcher's strong policy–making measures – that would have a disastrous impact on the future of the deaf schools, including Ewing Hill Park. Deaf schools around the country were already in decline, but if it became policy, local education authorities would opt for the cheaper option of mainstreaming, sounding the death knell for specialist schools over the next twenty years or so, he predicted. He was also worried about the wellbeing of deaf children in mainstream schools, knowing that many would struggle.

'One day,' Mr Langston told the dossier, as though speaking to it, 'you'll look back and realise that you were wrong, Lady Warnock. But it'll be too late then, won't it?'

Frustrated, he threw the dossier into the bin, hiding it under crumpled pieces of waste paper so that it would not magically end up back on the shelf again. As he straightened up, he spotted his top right hand desk drawer. He took out a small keyring, fumbled through the keys and unlocked the drawer's padlock with one. Mr Langston had had to have the padlock fitted after the drawer was broken into a couple of months back. He opened the drawer and took out a new black book labelled *Detention Book*. He opened it and flicked through the pages to the latest entries, sighing when he saw two pages full of the names of boys who would be undertaking detention that coming weekend. Mr Schneider had signed off almost all of them.

Mr Langston was becoming increasingly concerned about the maths teacher; he had received complaints from some boys about his alleged improper conduct in the classroom, and about how he was what they called "trigger happy", dishing out detentions for signing and trivial misbehaviour. Also, he had a volatile temper and a penchant for inflicting fear.

Mr Langston had discussed these complaints with Mr Schneider a number of times, but he denied them and believed the boys hated him, which, according to him, may have been the reason that they had come up with these slanderous lies. He did, however, acknowledge that he had been issuing frequent detentions, protesting that was because the boys always misbehaved with him and challenged his authority. Mr Langston didn't buy any of the maths teacher's claims, homing in on his past experience with Franco Hugentobler. However, there was no evidence from either side and the headmaster had been quite frustrated by that. He thought about the end of last summer when William Parsons had suddenly died of a heart attack two weeks before the new school term. The board of governors had held an emergency meeting to discuss his replacement, at which Daniel Lish mentioned he knew of a very good maths teacher of the deaf called Heinrich Schneider from West Germany, who had long wanted to teach in England. He said that Schneider was one of the best teachers in Germany, trained in the oralist tradition. He got his Master's in Mathematics. Following this, he got a Diploma in Pedagogy and Hearing Impairment from Heidelberg Institute of Education that trained oral teachers of the deaf in Germany. The former teacher of the deaf believed that Ewing Hill Park would greatly benefit from Mr Schneider. Mr Langston had reservations about him, as did Robert Denham, but they had no choice but to accept him, for there was insufficient time to advertise for a new maths teacher; he and Robert Denham would be outvoted by the board anyway. Mr Schneider immediately handed in his notice at an oral school for the deaf in Berlin, flew over and became Ewing Hill Park's newest teacher. Mr Langston remembered how he knew that the towering German was trouble as soon as he met him. He had been right; he may have to appraise the maths teacher in July after the school broke up for the summer. He believed that the majority of the board of governors would be most keen to keep him at the school, so if he did decide to dismiss him, he would be facing the wrath of Rosemary Goldsack, who might then decide to look for a new headmaster. She hadn't said anything about that, though she had dropped some hints, and he knew he had to be careful because he cared a lot about the deaf boys and their education.

Mr Langston threw the detention book back into the drawer and closed it, deciding not to padlock it for now. He slumped in his chair, disgruntled. His mind strayed to the issue of the mysterious "Phantom of Ewing Hill Park", as the boys called him – or her – that had been terrorising Mr Schneider ever since he'd arrived. Although he had little regard for the maths teacher, he thought the hate campaign against him was criminal. He hadn't brought the police in yet because there was no evidence whether it had been done by one of the boys, a member of staff or someone from outside. The board were made aware of it; they demanded that the culprit was caught by any means necessary and expelled with immediate effect. Then, the case would be hushed up to avoid any bad publicity. However, the headmaster had been unable to find a way to catch the Phantom.

He recapped the thoughts he had had that evening. A single thought hovered high above the myriad: something major needed to happen at this school to fuel radical changes; turn the tide. *But what, when and how?* he wondered.

Mr Langston looked at his watch: almost ten o'clock. Oh, he mumbled, time had flown. He sighed wearily. He was on duty tonight: it was his responsibility to ensure all of the boys were in their dorms with the lights out and that every window and door was locked – a task he had always hated. Employing additional staff such as houseparents or care officers, as well as a full–time caretaker, were part of his plans for radical changes. These houseparents or care officers would take the burden off the two matrons who both already had enough to do, maintaining the clothes of fifty boys, and other things. Having just one duty teacher for fifty boys each evening and weekend was beyond preposterous, he thought – goodness knows what those teenage boys did when the duty teacher's back was turned? What Chris and Aaron had just done, for example. He also wanted to appoint a new speech therapist to work solely with the boys. Mr Arkwright would probably object to that, though. Covering these things would mean increasing the school's fees; most local education authorities would be very reluctant to pay and the board of governors would be unwilling to sanction it. Besides, he thought, there wasn't yet a statutory requirement for the necessary additional support staff.

When he had completed his checks, he would go up to his family's apartment on the first floor. Frances would be waiting for him with a cuppa ready. She'd probably nag at him again to get round to looking for a house in Waltbridge for them instead of the apartment that they'd been living in for the past five years. He'd then watch World in Action on television after the news and then he'd be off to bed. He realised the next day was Wednesday, so the weekly staff meeting was in the morning. He was already dreading it.

Mr Langston rose to his feet and walked around his desk towards the door. He flicked off the lights.

24

Educating Sex

"Sign language is the equal of speech, lending itself equally to the rigorous and the poetic, to philosophical analysis to making love."
– DR OLIVER SACKS; *Seeing Voices*, 1991

'Oh, for god's sake, this is 1980, not bloody 1880!'

The staff room descended into an uneasy silence.

Mr McShane sat back, folding his arms and crossing his legs. His anger began to settle as he looked round the circle of sitting figures who were staring blankly in his direction. His eyes directed an invisible ray of fire at Mr Arkwright, incensed by the pompous man.

Mr Langston sighed, resting a small stack of papers on his lap. He rubbed his nose as he briefly thought about the fighting between Mr McShane and Mr Arkwright, which had sometimes dominated staff meetings. It reignited last March when the headmaster had decided that the boys could stop going to church after their continued boycott. Mr Arkwright vehemently objected to this, arguing that it went against the school's tradition; he felt it would seriously affect their faith in God. However, Mr McShane disagreed, saying it should be their choice whether they went to church or not. He pointed out to Mr Arkwright, a devout Christian and regular churchgoer, that he should know that the Church would never condone forcing people to attend, or prevent them from attending, and questioned why the school forced boys to go against their will, irrespective of tradition. Mrs Munnings agreed with Mr McShane, noting how the boys tended to misbehave in church because they were bored and had trouble following what was being said at the services. She had put herself to the test by muffling her own ears to see if she could follow anything, but she couldn't, which had made her realise what the problem was. She explained how she had once tried to interpret, using basic signs that she had learnt, but had had to stop because *everyone* was watching her instead of the vicar and she felt quite embarrassed. Mr Langston agreed, saying there were other, more productive, activities for the boys to do on Sunday mornings, but Mr Arkwright refused to accept this, so a compromise was reached: the boys would go to church once a month. However, the boys maintained their boycott, despite their being threatened with detention by Mr Arkwright, which the headmaster often overruled.

Finally, he decided that the boys could stop going to church altogether, which had once again sparked a row between Mr McShane and Mr Arkwright during the meeting. Mr Arkwright was quite livid and preached on about the same old things, while Mr McShane put his foot in it, accusing him of living in the past.

Mr Langston was already tired of the ongoing saga between the two at loggerheads: he really wanted to bang their heads, though he had always secretly sided with Mr McShane. The headmaster directed his attention to the cranky teacher.

'My decision is absolutely *final*, Jonathan. Is that crystal clear?'

Mr Arkwright said nothing, but his silence was enough for the headmaster. He read the next item from the agenda on his lap. He cleared his throat and looked around the circle, hesitating as he knew what he was going to say next would spark another round of debate.

'I want to discuss … sex education for the boys.'

The staff room fell into a stunned silence.

'Are you saying that the boys should have sex education?!' Miss Stephenson finally broke the silence.

'That's what I'm saying,' he replied.

'I don't agree!' the physics and biology teacher shook her head.

'Why not?'

'Because … because it's embarrassing!' she looked around. 'I mean … how do we teach *deaf* boys about sex?'

'I'd have thought you'd know all about that, seeing as you teach biology, Penny!' Mr Schneider said with a mischievous grin. 'Or is that you're too embarrassed to teach boys about sex because you're a woman?'

'That's beside the point!' she hit back.

'They already know enough about sex,' Mr Bronte waved his empty pipe. 'So, there's no point in educating them about the birds and the bees.'

'How do you know that, Harold?' asked Mr Norris, frowning at the craftwork teacher.

'Cause they just do, Joe,' he replied to the sports teacher. 'I didn't get any sex education at school before the last war and I was quite a ladies' man. All I had to do was court those lovely ladies, dance with them and–'

'Let's suppose,' Mrs Munnings cut in, raising her voice over the old man's, taking no interest in more of his bygone time rants; 'we agree to this suggestion, how do we go about it?'

'I must point out that the boys, although deaf, are not stupid.' Mr Langston said.

'I absolutely agree,' Mr Whittle nodded. 'They're no idiots, though they might need some guidance to ensure they know the facts in good faith. So, may I suggest taking a direct, but sensitive, approach? Be as frank as possible without over–sexualising it.'

'He's right,' Mr Langston nodded at the English teacher and addressed his colleagues. 'Don't insult their intelligence–'

'Some boy wrote "sex is beautiful" on my blackboard yesterday!' Everyone turned to Mrs Munnings, a mixture of groans and titters amongst them.

'I'd *love* to have seen your face!' Mr Schneider chortled, his grin now wider.

'It's not funny!' Mrs Munnings gave the maths teacher a hard stare. She turned to the headmaster, becoming curious. 'What's brought this on, Donald?'

Mr Langston rested his forearms on the stack of papers on his lap and clasped his hands. He thought for a moment, knowing that this was delicate.

'Well, the most important thing is that we must educate them to take interest in girls, explain how to interact with them, take precautions, make them understand about having babies and–'

'Wait a minute,' Mr Arkwright interrupted, 'you just said "educate them to take interest in girls". Are you saying that an act of … sodomy has been committed here?'

Mr Langston did not reply, silently cursing his mistake, but his silence confirmed it.

'Oh my god! That's disgusting!' screamed Miss Stephenson. 'Who?'

'I'm afraid I can't answer that, Penny.' Mr Langston shook his head.

'Criminals!' Mr Bronte bellowed, pointing the mouth end of his pipe at the headmaster. 'It's illegal! I do hope that you, Donald, will expel those sick–'

'It's not illegal anymore!' Mr McShane cut through; his voice heightened with irritation. 'It's bigots like you, Harold, who have a problem with not accepting homosexuals as equals. We've no business in what they do in the bedroom, just as they've no business in what anyone else does in *their* bedrooms. They're human beings, not lepers! I'm not surprised about homosexuality here, anyway; it's a contained boys' boarding school, for Christ's sake! It happens at boarding schools; the boys here are bound to go through phases and experiment with their sexuality, just like any other curious teenagers – boys and girls, both. It's a natural part of growing up. Do you all expect them to wear chastity belts? Like for me–'

Mr McShane clammed up as he realised that everyone was watching him silently, their eyes wide with astonishment. *Oh Jesus*, he thought; he had gone on a bit and *almost* exposed himself. He had been so incensed with Mr Arkwright that he was still boiling inside. He quickly calmed down, glancing at Mr Langston, afraid for himself. He had always been so careful to keep his sexuality a secret, for fear of losing his job, keeping his personal life private from the boys and his colleagues alike. The boys' parents would scream blue murder if they knew there was a gay teacher at their sons' school. He had come here to teach art, nothing more. He knew his responsibilities as a teacher, though. He glanced at Miss Stephenson, remembering her failed attempts to woo him; he was thankful that she'd turned to Mr Whittle. He told her he had a partner, Kerry, back home; she had always assumed Kerry was a woman because of "her" unisex name; he was always careful not to say *he, she, him* or *her*. It was always just *Kerry*. He knew if they found out they wouldn't believe that he had no interest in the boys, as there was always that misconception, and they'd show him the door. Donald had already made him aware that the governors were watching him like hawks because of him using the forbidden signing in his art lessons; apparently, they had "spies" who would report to them. Mr McShane knew that Mr Arkwright was one. He glanced across the room at him, imagining that if he were sacked, Mr Arkwright would happily hold the front door open for him, playfully pointing outside and grinning. He might even spit at him, just like some people did at gay men down in Brighton. No, he thought, he was not going to give him the satisfaction. Not by a million miles. Kerry would be really livid at him for losing his job. Being a deaf gay man, was tough enough; his local deaf community tormented and ridiculed him. Because of this, he and Kerry had had to move to Brighton. Finding a job was already tough; Kerry reminded him that he was most fortunate to be working at Ewing Hill Park and that he was making a great impression on the boys because of his fluency in sign language; something Kerry had never had at his oral deaf school. He said school had been a traumatic experience: he was physically and emotionally abused by some teachers who forced him to speak and punished him severely if he dared to sign. Because of his experiences, Kerry dreamed of becoming a sigh language tutor, teaching teachers of the deaf so that they and their pupils could communicate better with each other as he didn't want them to suffer as he had. Sadly, he was generally met with indifference at the deaf schools he approached. So, Kerry felt Mr McShane should keep his sexuality a secret for the time being, for the sake of his job. He felt that he had a crucial part to play in the deaf rights campaign to change people's attitudes towards educating the deaf through sign language. Mr McShane had to agree with him.

'Miles?'

It was normal, as he grew up, to have deaf people around him and hear deaf voices. When he was learning to talk, he just learned how to communicate with deaf people. He couldn't remember when he realised his parents and siblings were deaf – he just knew that if he wanted to talk to them, he had to make sure they were looking at him, whereas with other people, hearing people, he could just talk when they weren't looking. It was completely natural to him.

He excelled in art and decided he wanted to be a teacher of the deaf, so after graduating with a degree in general art and design, he enrolled on the year–long course at Manchester University, like most of his colleagues. Unlike many of his fellow students, however, he refused to allow himself to be brainwashed by the biased oral teachings there. Some of the other students were quite amazed that he could communicate in sign; only a few were genuinely interested, while the rest scrutinised him with suspicion.

'Miles!'

The first and last school he taught at before Ewing Hill Park was strictly oral. He saw that the deaf children there, though happy, struggled to follow some of their teachers and, in turn, the teachers struggled to understand their pupils. He knew and understood deaf people, their thoughts and feelings. He perceived some of his colleagues as bad teachers because they weren't very interested in the children and teaching in general, not just because they didn't sign. They just wanted an easy life. He was once told that when a young deaf teacher was appointed as a teacher at a deaf school, two oralist teachers there handed in their notices in protest. Their loss; her gain, he thought. He was thankful to Donald Langston, not only for giving him the job four years back, but also for allowing him to sign in his art lessons–

'*Miles!*' Mr Langston called out again, this time louder, and with a hint of exasperation in the tone. Mr McShane snapped out of his private thoughts. 'You were saying about yourself … ?'

'I – I'm just saying that I feel that, uh, the boys should understand that there are other avenues in life … that it doesn't necessarily just have to be boys and girls coming together.' That was lame, he thought, but it should do it.

'All right,' Mr Langston addressed everyone. 'It seems we all have our opinions about this issue. Miles is right that we can't expect the boys to wear chastity belts or prevent them from ever doing this … kind of thing, which is why I feel it's important for them to understand what's right and what's wrong. As their headmaster, I have the responsibility to ensure good conduct amongst the boys and I don't want this coming to the public eye. It'll be quite easy for the press to make a big deal out of it just because they're deaf. So, who's going to do it?'

'Not me!' blurted Miss Stephenson.

'Nor me,' added Mrs Munnings.

'Definitely not me,' Mr Schneider sat back. 'I'm not popular with them anyway.'

Mr Bronte and Mr Norris both shook their heads. Mr Whittle fiddled with his fingernails, his eyes downcast, not acknowledging the headmaster's gaze. Mr Langston turned to Mr Arkwright, but he already knew his answer. He turned to Mr McShane.

'No thanks,' Mr McShane said.

'But you can sign–'

'I teach art, nothing more. I'm sorry.'

'But it has to be someone like you who can convey such a delicate subject that they could understand.' said Mrs Munnings.

'They can understand you well enough now, Elizabeth,' Mr McShane pointed out. 'You've been learning quite a lot from me.'

Mr Schneider raised his hand. 'Why do we need signing to help educate the boys about sex? It's no different from any other subject we teach them. They'd benefit much more if they were taught about sex ... orally. No pun intended, of course.'

'I agree with Heinrich,' Mr Arkwright nodded.

'I don't.' said Mrs Munnings. She sat up in her chair, addressing her colleagues. 'Look, I was trained to be a teacher of the deaf, using the oral method. It's a highly challenging job, but I love it. I always found it extremely difficult to make myself understood. I used to have to keep repeating the same things over and over till I was blue in the face. I had to write *everything* on the blackboard. I couldn't understand what most of the boys were saying to me because of their speech were ... like Greek to me. In most instances, their prep work didn't match what I'd taught them; I'd have to explain it all over again and go through the same old process. I had nothing else to turn to.

'Then one Saturday last May, I was on duty and some of the boys wanted to watch a programme on the television here because most of the others were watching the FA Cup final in the television room. Their programme was just half an hour long, but it was on BBC2 at the same time as the kick off. As the boys were in the staff room, I had to stay with them, so I watched it as well. It was called *Signs of Life* on the BBC. It actually had deaf presenters who signed, but there was a voice over, and they talked about education, employment and telecommunications. There was this deaf lady – Dorothy, I think – who did a beautiful signed poem called *Language For The Eye,* which really touched me. Anyway, one of them, a deaf man, talked about education for the deaf. At first I doubted him, but he made me start to realise that the oral approach isn't always the best way of educating deaf children. The following month, I attended the launch of a book called *The Deaf School Child* by Ruben Conrad; I read it from cover to cover during the summer break. I don't need to explain about the book; you already know I've raved about it, however, it further confirmed that oralism's a failure–'

'It is not a failure!' Mr Schneider butted in.

'Let her finish, Heinrich,' Mr Langston said, keeping his enjoyment secret.

'Thank you, Donald,' said Mrs Munnings. 'Anyway, I went to a seminar by the National Union for the Deaf, which talked about the rights of deaf people. I was surprised to discover that those speakers – signers – were the same people from that programme–'

'Bloody activists!' Mr Bronte boomed.

'Be quiet, Harold!' Mr Langston called out before turning back to Mrs Munnings. 'Please continue.'

'They're not activists,' she went on. 'They're campaigning for the rights of deaf people. One of the presentations was about Total Communication. It's a combination of sign, speech and sound, to cater for *all* deaf children. It influenced me a great deal, so I asked Miles if he could help teach me sign language. He was more than willing to. I have to admit, it was quite difficult to learn at first, but I slowly improved and started to use it in my lessons. It worked! The more I signed, the less I had to repeat or write on the blackboard. Also, I was able to understand the boys much better, as I let them sign to me too. Their prep work improved quite considerably as well. Penny's just started doing the same, isn't that right?' She turned to her.

Miss Stephenson nodded in agreement. 'It's still early days for me, but, yes, it's starting to work for me now too.'

'Another interesting thing,' the geography and history teacher said, 'is that a couple of weeks ago, when I took the Fourth Formers to the Natural History Museum in London, we came upon a group of Jewish people. You know the kind; wearing those black clothes, hats and all that. I saw some of the boys making some risqué jokes about them – they forgot I can sign now – and I was so angry with them. They didn't really understand their history, so I talked about the Holocaust in their next history lesson. I suppose I was still angry with them … I sort of *signed* my way through the entire lesson; I don't actually remember if I *spoke* as well, but the boys were very receptive to what I told them. Even their prep work – I asked them to write about the Holocaust – was really excellent. They all had their own versions, but they were all correctly based on what I'd said to them, rather than the other way round and based on what I *didn't* say!'

'Thank you, Elizabeth,' Mr Langston said. He turned to the sound of loud clapping. Mr McShane was applauding vigorously with a huge smile on his face, his eyes darting sternly at Mr Arkwright and Mr Schneider. Oh, if only he could join in, Mr Langston mused silently as he addressed his colleagues. 'Anyone like to comment on what Elizabeth's just said?'

No one did. Mr Langston wasn't sure if it was because of Mrs Munnings' groundbreaking speech, or because they were anxious to know who would be unlucky enough to have to take on the task of educating the boys on sex. He pulled a sheet of paper from his lap and began to tear away a thin strand of paper. It was brutal, he thought, but it was the only solution he could think of at that point, since no one was willing to do it.

'Very well ... Before we move to the next item on the agenda, this weekend's teachers of the deaf conference, which Elizabeth, Jonathan and I will be attending, we do need to address the issue of who's going to be doing sex education. I still feel it's important, but no one seems to be willing to do it. So, to resolve this; we'll draw straws.'

'Right,' Mr Whittle said nervously as he glanced around the semicircular desk formation of Third Formers, headphones on ready. 'We won't be doing English today.'

The English teacher forced a beaming smile, clasping his hands in an exaggerated manner and sandwiching the microphone between them. He silently cursed himself again for drawing the short straw earlier that morning. *Oh, why me?* he mused. He'd had to skip lunch to read some basic literature on sex. Even Penny, bless her, had had the cheek to try to give him a "quick lesson" during lunchtime, but he'd declined and told her he'd prefer to save it for Paris this weekend. He read as much as he could to refresh his knowledge on the subject, and now, it was the moment of truth. He lifted the microphone closer to his mouth.

'I'd like to talk about ... sex.'

The entire classroom became muted. He wasn't sure if he'd failed to make himself understood or if his announcement had silenced them. Suddenly, David Wheeley, who was sitting at the far left of the desk formation, burst out laughing. His form mates turned to him, wondering why. Mr Whittle knew that David was the only one who could understand every word he said. The chubby boy quickly signed something to his friends that Mr Whittle couldn't understand. Suddenly, the entire room burst into laughter.

'David!' Mr Whittle called out. He was now even more nervous than before. 'Don't use sign in this classroom ... what did you tell them?'

'I simply told them what you just said: you were going to talk about sex.' David replied.

'Oh ... ' Mr Whittle muttered. He waved at the boys to tell them to quiet down. He glanced at David, raising the microphone closer to his mouth. 'Right, thank you very much, David.'

The teacher turned to face the blackboard. He picked up the chalk and wrote

SEX on it. He soon heard muffled chortling from behind and paused for a long moment.

He turned to face the boys, who were now wide–eyed. 'So … man … ' He pointed at himself to indicate his gender, then pointed to the space on his right and gestured an imaginary figure, his hands swiftly sliding down in a curved outline. He finished off by gesturing crude bumps on his chest. '. . . and woman. Have you got that?'

He observed the boys' reactions; they seemed to be either interested or perplexed; he couldn't tell which.

'Good! Now, when they fall in … love, they marry and they have sex – children – um, do you know how they do it?'

He waited for a response, but received none. He nervously glanced at David, waiting for him to say something, but he remained silent. Either he was doing it on purpose to conform to his form mates' behaviour, or he didn't know the answer. He looked at Aaron, who he knew could lipread him well because of his good command of English, but he, too, remained silent. Frustration began to sink in.

'This is serious!' he told them. He pointed at the word on the blackboard. 'Sex.'

The boys nodded in acknowledgement. Ah, he thought; that's more like it. 'That's how they do it.'

David's hand shot up. 'How?'

'A very good question, David!' The teacher pointed his microphone at David, praising him. He then saw the rest of the boys' heads turning in the direction of David, frowning. Had they missed the question, he wondered. He turned to the blackboard and wrote *How?* on it. He turned back to the boys, who were now watching him. 'Man and woman come together and they have sex. Do you understand that?'

Once again, a muted response welcomed him. He sighed inwardly. He thought for a moment to try to find another way to explain to them. He remembered the comment he had made at the staff meeting earlier that morning about taking a direct, frank but sensitive approach. He raised his microphone and cleared his throat, his tongue clicking the back of his teeth nervously.

'Men firstly must have an erect … penis. I'm sure you know what that is. Penis.'

All of the boys were picking up their pens in unison, holding them up as if preparing to write something down. Mr Whittle groaned, again raising his microphone.

'No, no, no, that's not what I said! P–E–N–I–S.'

He turned to the blackboard, the chalk in his hand hovering by the black slate, hesitant. He eventually began to draw a crude white shape; kind of a long, slanted

U, and finished it with two more shapes beside it that resembled some kind of balls. He wrote *PENIS* in large letters next to it. He soon heard more muffled tittering behind him. Christ, he said to himself, this was *embarrassing*.

'An erect penis,' he said, turning slowly. 'When they – man and woman – have sex, the erect penis will go into the vagina. Do you know what that is, boys?'

He waited for a response, but no boy put his hand up. Only David tittered. He sighed, knowing he would have to repeat that word again. 'Vag–ina. V–A–G–I–N–A.'

He turned to the blackboard, dreading his next course of action. He drew a crude downward oval shape and wrote *VAGINA* next to it in large letters. Once again, he heard muffled screams of laughter behind him. He sighed. Either they already know all about sex, he thought, or they were deliberately winding him up? Or was it that the boys really had not understood a word he was saying all along? Maybe he was doing it wrong? Other than lovemaking, there were other aspects of sex education that he believed the boys were unaware of, such as the anatomy of genital organs, boys' and girls' puberty, masturbation, the dangers of sexually transmitted diseases, protective measures, pregnancy, menstruation, sexual relationships and sexual health. Okay, he said to himself, the boys already knew about masturbation, but it was still part of sex education anyway. They need to be taught these important things, but not in the way he was trying hopelessly to do it.

He recalled how, when he was training as a teacher of the deaf at Manchester University ten years back, sign language was never on the agenda. He remembered how some teachers who worked in boarding schools for the deaf had been exposed to sign language; they brought it up sometimes, but it was never followed up. The rest, himself included, had come from jobs in hearing schools, or were teaching graduates who had not been exposed to sign language. He thought the concept behind the course seemed to focus on helping deaf children to think in words, express themselves through the English language, develop good command of English and learn to speak. He began to think that the tutors did not believe that using sign language would aid deaf children in becoming literate. He was told that sign language had no grammar and that it would disturb deaf children's capacity to learn English.

He arrived at Ewing Hill Park straight after Manchester University, taking over his predecessor, Mrs Hull, who had moved to Boyd Hill Grammar School. For the last nine years, he had taught English at Ewing Hill Park and had always found it a challenge to teach the boys through English however minimal it was. Upon arrival at the school, most of them had little or no vocabulary; even at the ages of eleven or twelve they were four or five years behind in all subjects and didn't appear to realise that it mattered. Why didn't their former schools identify this and do something about it, he wondered, or was it that their teachers had similar problems in trying to instruct their deaf pupils? Why was this issue so prevalent in so many deaf schools? What about their parents? Why hadn't they – mainly hearing parents – done something to improve their deaf kids' literacy skills at home? Perhaps they had been trying to, but had found it difficult because their kids couldn't perceive things orally. He thought about Aaron and wondered how he was way ahead of everyone else in his Form in English; ahead of most of the other boys at the school, for that matter. There were a few – only a few – other boys like him. Chris Matthaus sprang to mind; how the flipping heck had he improved his English so quickly in the last eight months? It was almost as if he improved on a weekly basis. The boy had always languished at the bottom of his Form for English, but now he was hovering near the top.

He thought about the boys' English in general. They didn't even know the simple difference between "a" and "the". He'd had to tell most of the boys that they could not say "a sun ... " instead of "the sun ... "; that often confused them. Teaching them grammar was another thing they had problems understanding; on average, there would be two or three mistakes in each line they wrote and they had no idea that that wasn't very good, or that they could do anything about it.

Frequently during his lessons, he recalled, the boys had that *too hard, not fair!* attitude when he gave them a task. He thought the boys believed they couldn't be expected to do it because they were deaf. He refused to believe that.

He also knew now that they'd had problems lipreading him for a number of years, before he finally realised his beard was in the way. Brian Thompson sprang to mind; the lad *hated* his beard for some unknown reason, so he decided to shave it off last summer to see if that helped, but it didn't Brian, or many of the others either, and he couldn't begin to understand why. Still, his new appearance had won Penny over, so he couldn't complain. Perhaps Elizabeth was right after all; the oral approach wasn't working and they needed to be taught in their own language.

He'd always considered sign language as a bastardisation of spoken language, – a necessary evil – but now, he wasn't so sure. Bill Stainer, an oral teacher he knew, once told him that signing made the deaf inferior. "They cannot achieve on a level playing field in the hearing world," he told him. He pointed out to Bill that his statement made it easy to disempower a specific group like the deaf, and that "cannot" was a dangerous word that easily became a self-fulfilling prophecy. He still believed that the deaf could learn successfully; it was simply a case of doing it in the right way. So, different syntax or not, *understanding* what was being said was more important than trying to make them understand through a method that they effectively couldn't use. He wondered if speech and sign language shared the same component of the brain. Donald had briefly told him about what he'd witnessed at Gallaudet, and especially at MSSD, four years back, and it had intrigued him a great deal. He already knew for a fact that the boys' headphones and the microphone he was holding were completely useless, but he was bound by the school policy to use them. He knew nothing about signing, though; perhaps he should have heeded Penny's encouragement to start learning it. That might help him to teach English better, he thought. He supposed he'd have to wait and see if Donald could change things at the school; if so, then who knows?

He picked up the duster and rubbed the blackboard. He turned to face the boys, lowering the microphone.

'Look, I'm trying to … oh, forget it. It's obvious you already know something about sex, so there's no point in me trying to explain it. We'll leave it at that for now. So, let's get back to English: we'll talk about collective nouns, all right? Anyone know what they are?'

After tea, Aaron trudged along the corridor from the dining room with some of his form mates. He glanced back and saw Chris hurrying up to him. Aaron turned and increased his walking pace.

Chris, too, picked up speed. He had been quite frustrated by not having been able to catch his best friend all day. He could understand why, but he really wanted to talk to him. The events of the night before had not left his mind all day. He found it hard to concentrate on his lessons, was quite moody at mealtimes as he couldn't take his eyes off Aaron at the other table, and was off form when playing cricket that afternoon. He couldn't get Aaron out of his mind and was desperate to talk to him, but Aaron had avoided him all day. He glanced around the corridor, making sure not to attract attention, and saw that the boys filing out of the dining room were either too busy signing to each other or minding their own business. He ran up to Aaron from behind just as he turned a corner.

'Please, one minute?' Chris begged Aaron. 'In the toilets, now?'

Chris pretended to urinate into a urinal while Aaron pretended to wash his hands as they waited for Toby Eriswell to finish at another urinal. When he left the small room and the boys were alone, Chris turned to Aaron, despair in his eyes.

'About last night–'

'I don't want to talk about it,' Aaron raised his hand.

'But–'

'I don't want to talk about it, all right?' Aaron snapped.

Chris stepped forward, his despair turning to anger. Aaron turned towards the door, but Chris pulled him by the arm. 'I'm sorry about last night, all right?'

'All right,' Aaron nodded weakly; he was still reeling. When they were in the cellar, he had still felt nervous and awkward. He'd gone over and over it in his head; he wasn't sure if he wanted to do it, or even if he felt the same way as Chris felt about him. He and Chris had then talked about other things for about ten or fifteen minutes to ease the tension. At that point, however, Aaron had decided that he didn't want to do it. He saw the disappointment on Chris' face, and told him he'd think about it, so they hugged – just a friendly hug, like they'd always done – and Mr Langston suddenly walked in. They tried to explain that they hadn't done anything, but the headmaster refused to listen and ordered them into his office.

Aaron shook his head and looked at his watch: almost six o'clock. He didn't really want to talk to Chris until he had cooled down.

'I've got to go to prep.'

Aaron turned and left the room. Chris tilted his head back, closing his eyes and biting his lip.

Chris sat back on a chair, tilting it backwards so that the top of the chair's back was resting against the wall, balancing on the back legs. He opened a red and yellow book he had just found lying on the chair. It was all about wild boars. He glanced up at the boys playing table tennis, darts and snooker in the recreation room, not taking any particular interest in their activities. He glanced at his watch: five past seven. He quickly thought back to the hour's prep he had just finished, which had helped to take his mind off things, but once finished, he started thinking about Aaron again. So, he'd come to the recreation room, found this book and decided to read it, to try to occupy himself for the rest of the evening.

Suddenly, he felt a loud stomping on the floor; he turned to see Gary Portmore standing in the doorway. He made a surprise announcement.

'Everybody to the Assembly Hall!' he pointed in the direction of Magnat House. 'Now!'

The boys hesitated, but the prefect stomped his foot again. *'Now!'*

The boys reluctantly stopped whatever they were doing and begrudgingly made their way to the doorway. Gary saw that Chris was still sitting reading the book. He stomped again to get Chris' attention.

'Are you bloody deaf or what?'

'Yes, I'm deaf, you dickhead.' Chris replied broodily.

Gary marched over, not impressed with him. He grabbed the book from Chris' hands and chucked it behind him. The book flew across the entire length of the large room, crashed against the wall and plummeted to the floor. Hands on his hips, Gary stared hard at Chris, telling him that he had no choice.

The usual set up had formed in the Assembly Hall, with four straight lines of ten standing boys, each about six feet apart, with the shortest boy at the front and the tallest at the back. They were all facing the stage, where the Fifth Formers loitered as they waited for Basher to arrive. Chris was second from the back of his line, with Dean behind and Steven in front of him. He glanced at the line on his left to see Aaron standing third from the back, with Michael behind and David in front of him, lost in his own thoughts. Chris glanced around at the boys signing and asking questions about what was happening and what Basher had to say this time. He looked out of the floor–to–ceiling windows beyond the line of First Formers to see that the sun was beginning to set, the dark orange haze shimmering above the darkening trees outside. In the distance, dark clouds were slowly gathering.

More stomping on the wooden floor interrupted his idle gaze; he turned to see that Basher had just entered. The head boy slowly marched in, passing the Fourth Form line, stony–faced, eyes fixed upon the stage ahead. His arms and legs swung rhythmically, as though he was a marching soldier. He soon reached the steps and climbed them. He marched towards the centre and stood there in silence for a short moment. He eventually addressed the gathering before him.

'Two of you have been having ... ' Basher paused, preparing for the big moment, '. . . filthy sex!'

Chris' eyes widened in shock. He slowly looked over at Aaron, to see he was already looking at him, also shocked. He gazed back at the stage and saw that Dwight was looking pointedly at him, also anxious. He gazed back at Aaron, who was still looking at him, his expression even more worried. *Oh shit*, Chris thought, *how the fuck* had Basher found out about him and Aaron? Or even him and Dwight? Had someone been hiding in the bushes behind them; he'd thought it was a wild animal? Or, had Mr Langston told Basher? No, there was no way he would have done; the headmaster was far too good for that. So, someone *must* have found out and told Basher. He saw that the other boys were glancing at each other, wondering who the two boys were.

Basher waved his hands, stamping his feet. All heads swung back to the stage.

'I'll come down now and pick out these two poofs!'

Aaron almost choked; his heart beginning to pound. He swung his head round to see that Chris was rubbing his anxious face. He jumped as he felt a loud thud, and swung back to see that Basher was on the floor. He watched Basher turn towards the First Form line.

Like a soldier, Basher marched. He stopped between the first and Second Form lines and turned to his left, facing the juniors. He stood there for a short moment then turned again to his left. He marched, arms swinging in a theatrical manner, passing the second and third lines on his right.

Chris' heart was pounding rapidly, his throat dry, perspiration trickling down his back. He watched Basher arrive between the Third Form line and his own. The head boy stood there for a short moment, and then turned; now facing the seniors. He began to march between the two lines.

Aaron watched Basher, wide–eyed in crushing horror, his head shaking with extreme fear and his teeth clattering violently. He felt urine beginning to trickle from his bladder. He clasped his hands tightly as he watched Basher pass the second boy on either side.

Chris desperately tried hard to remain standing; he felt like his legs would collapse. His heart pounded even louder and his back was like a waterfall.

Basher swung his arms as he marched past the third boy on either side, staring blankly at the partition wall ahead of him. He marched past the fourth boy on either side.

Fifth.

Sixth.

Aaron's heart pounded ferociously as the beefy Fifth Former marched past David; he was upon him now.

Chris gritted his teeth, now frightened. He had never been so frightened before. Not as far as he could remember, though his mind flashed back to the memory of Bob hitting him when he was eight. But he'd never been this frightened of anything … until now. He felt his stomach churning as he watched, terrified, as Basher walked past Aaron.

And he stopped.

Right in front of Chris and just behind Aaron.

The head boy slowly raised both his arms simultaneously, forming a perfect horizontal line, as though he was on a crucifix, his hands reaching out like tentacles. With his stony face still directed at the partition wall, his eyes moved from side to side, seemingly at Chris and Aaron.

He pounced, grabbing a shirt collar on his right.

Aaron closed his eyes and began to scream.

Then Basher leaned to his left, grabbing another shirt collar.

Chris closed his eyes and he, too, began to scream.

26

Fists

"You can no more abstain from signing when instructing a deaf person than you can abstain from speaking when instructing a blind person."
– LAURENT CLERC (1785–1869)

Basher held onto Steven Clarke and Michael Hardcastle's shirt collars firmly. Chris slowly opened his eyes, his silent scream easing down. Upon seeing Steven and Michael, he gasped in shock. Aaron, too, slowly opened his eyes, panting heavily, and his jaw dropped open.

Basher swiftly turned, taking his catch with him, as they struggled to break free. He dragged them towards the stage, watched by the stunned gathering. Chris exhaled hard, shock and relief sinking in. He began to hyperventilate, his chest heaving hard and his legs almost giving way, but managed to control himself. His shirt was stuck to his soaked back as he wiped sweat from his forehead. Aaron calmed his heavy breathing, also wiping perspiration from his forehead. His bladder ached and he was desperate to pee. He steeled himself not to look at Chris: he didn't want to see his relieved face.

Basher positioned Steven and Michael in front of the stage, facing the boys. He released his grasp and hopped up on the stage behind them. He stood and thrust his arms wide, embraced the gathering as if he were the messiah.

'They,' he pointed down at the two boys, 'were caught having sex in the upstairs bathroom just after prep–'

Hendrik, at the front of the Second Form line, waved excitedly to get everybody's attention. 'It was me! I caught them!'

Basher stamped on the stage to bring everyone's attention back to him. 'They're fucking queers! Poofs! Filth! Come on, say they're queers!'

Queers! Basher made the limp–wristed gesture repeatedly, signing the insult. Almost every boy in the hall collectively followed suit, joining in a chorus of chanting that reverberated around the large room: *Queers! Queers!* Steven bowed his head in shame while Michael burst into tears. Chris and Aaron stood silently and watched the pandemonium of flapping hands.

Chris looked at his watch again: just after half past eight. He glanced around the darkened black and green seclusion that surrounded him and looked up between the branches and leaves above to see that the darkening sky was filled with clouds, pensive. After the episode in the Assembly Hall, Aaron had demanded to talk to him, but it had to be somewhere private outside the school. The walls, he said, had eyes for the deaf. Chris suggested that they met in the secluded spot in the forest at the rear of the school – which he and Dwight used for their own purposes – and gave him specific directions to find it. He did not tell him how he knew about the spot, though.

He looked down sharply, spotting something white rustling amongst the shrubbery ahead of him. Aaron ducked under a low tree branch as he stepped over a raised root, pushing away twigs and leaves, his white sleeves rolled up. Once he was through, he stopped to assess the small clearing, awestruck at the almost perfect hiding place. He turned to his friend, hesitant for a moment.

'We were almost found out,' Aaron finally said, taking a step forward.

'But we weren't,' Chris said, also stepping forward. 'That means no one saw us kissing in the changing room yesterday. You imagined it. Only Mr Langston knows. He wouldn't tell Basher about us.'

'How do you know that? Basher can be a bastard, you know.' Aaron said, but deep down inside, he knew that Chris was probably right.

'Doesn't matter now,' Chris shook his head. 'Our secret's still safe.'

Aaron looked into Chris' eyes, thinking: *but for how long?* He put his hands into his pockets, turning away from Chris. He felt a drip on his head and looked up at the dark clouds, a few more rain drops splashing on his face. He turned back to Chris, shaking his head.

'I don't want to do it again.'

'What?' Chris stepped forward, feeling his heart sink.

'No more!' Aaron's hand swept from left to right. 'No more!'

'But,' Chris protested, 'you *wanted* it last night!'

'You wanted it!' Aaron snapped back. He slammed his hands on his head, agitated with himself. He began to weep, heavier raindrops splattering on his face, mixing with his tears. 'I'm confused!'

'I'm not ... confused,' Chris said, honestly.

Aaron lowered his hands, meeting Chris' eyes for a long moment. He began to realise something else. He closed his eyes to recollect. The way Chris always looked at him. In the showers too – he wasn't that blind. Tried it on him once before only to stop David from killing himself. Groped him once. Then ... Dwight told him Chris loved him. The kiss. The cellar. Got caught before they had even started.

Opening his eyes, he contemplated the secluded area he and Chris were in right now; he became suspicious. 'You did it here with Dwight, didn't you?' Aaron asked. 'You told him you … wanted me. He told me yesterday. Is that true?'

Chris put his hands into his pockets, bowing his head and thinking; it was true, though he didn't know that Dwight had told Aaron about his feelings for him.

Aaron watched Chris in astonishment; his silence said it all. He was now torn between affection and repulsion towards his best friend. He knew he had to ask another question. He waved hard at Chris, who looked up.

'Why do … you do it? I mean, why do you fancy boys not girls?'

'I don't know,' Chris shrugged, taking his hands out of his pockets to sign. 'I do like girls, but … I don't feel the same way as other boys do. Maybe we're both like that–?'

'No!' Aaron shouted back, swinging his clenched right hand. His hair and shirt were now wetter than ever from the rain. 'Not me! It's wrong! Mr Langston said so!'

'Well, I don't feel wrong!' Chris snapped back.

Aaron took a step forward, confused emotions building up inside; lashing out at Chris. 'Well, I think it is! It's not normal. I didn't like what we did yesterday–'

'That's not fair–!'

'Shut the fuck up!' Aaron screamed threateningly, his emotions raging. He now *knew* what he was feeling. 'I'll meet a girl, marry her and have children. That's *normal*. I don't want … filth like you.'

'Please!' Chris advanced, reaching out to console him.

'No!' Aaron backed away. 'Get away from me! Don't fucking touch me!'

Chris, incensed by Aaron's defiance, lunged at him, grabbing his arm. 'Wait–'

Aaron twisted his body, trying to break free from Chris' grasp, but it was too firm. Chris attempted to hold his other arm with his other hand, but Aaron pushed it away. Chris grabbed Aaron's school tie in an attempt to stabilise himself, but Aaron pushed him away. Chris almost slipped in the wet mud, but managed to keep his balance by tightening his grip on Aaron's arm. Aaron felt his biceps hurting, and without a second thought, he swung his fist squarely at Chris' chin. Chris' head jerked back to the side, he released his grip on Aaron's arm and fell backwards. He crashed down into the mud, legs flailing, the hearing aid in his right ear flopping over. He lay there, stunned. Aaron looked in horror and disbelief at his distorted friend, then at his throbbing knuckles. He thought to himself in disbelief that this was the first time he'd ever hit Chris during the close friendship they had shared for almost three years. He and Chris had had a few trivial arguments or minor scuffles, but they always made up straight afterwards because of their strong bond. They had *never* fought until now. And, he *hated* it. But right now, he felt nothing but loathing and pity towards Chris.

Chris slowly lifted himself up and sat on the wet ground, nursing his throbbing jaw and looking up at Aaron, who was now crying. He couldn't believe that Aaron had punched him. And that hurt; it was not just the pain on his chin.

'*Fuck you!*' Aaron angrily thrust a two–fingered gesture and pointed a stern finger at Chris, tears flowing down his cheeks. 'You're … filth! We're finished as best friends! I *hate* you!'

Aaron turned and stormed off the way he had come, soon disappearing into the darkness beyond the overgrowth. Chris folded his legs, resting his forearms on his knees. His shoulders slumped as he began to cry, the heavy rain drenching him.

Steven felt a cold hand shake his left shoulder. He refused to acknowledge it, or even turn his head, for fear of another hateful remark, a punch or even more spit on his face. He cursed himself for getting caught with Michael in the bathroom. He and Michael had been so careful over the last two years, but he knew his luck would run out eventually. How the fuck had Hendrik found them in there? No one ever ventured into that bathroom on the top floor at that time of night. The lock was broken, but still no one came in. Or, had that shithead suspected him and Michael and secretly followed them? Now everyone knew about them. That year and the one after it were going to be living hell for him; it had already started, in fact. He was now dreading lights out in his dorm tonight – he'd rather die than face it. He huddled in the corner of the recreation room, scooping his legs up, but the cold hand still shook his shoulder, this time harder. He thought he might as well turn to see whoever it was: what was one more hateful word, punch or spit? He tentatively turned his head and saw Chris bending over him, his face sorrowful. Steven gasped at his form mate's dishevelled state.

Chris was dismayed to see that Steven had a bruise below his right eye, and his lower lip was cut. 'Are you okay?' he asked, bending and stroking Steven's long, frizzy, sandy hair gently.

'Are you talking to me?' Steven said, weakly. 'No one else will.'

'You're still my friend,' Chris said. He sighed, looking at Steven with regret. 'Why didn't you tell me?'

Steven chuckled at the absurdity of the question. He looked away for a short moment and then returned his gaze to Chris.

'Would *you* have told me the same thing? That you're a poof?'

He had a point, Chris thought.

'But you're not a poof,' Steven went on. 'You wouldn't understand.'

Chris stopped himself from putting the record straight. He really wished he could tell him, but knew he couldn't. Then it dawned on him. Dwight had once mentioned that he had done it with one of Chris' form mates, but would not reveal who. *Was it Steven?* Chris wondered.

'We used to be good friends,' Steven tapped Chris' arm to bring him back from his private thoughts. 'You're always with Aaron. You're his best friend and Michael is – was – my best friend. Best friends always tell each other everything. We don't really talk like proper friends any more, you know? We only talk about football and stuff like that; we don't talk like *real* friends.'

Chris nodded, though Steven's unwitting comment about his friendship with Aaron had hurt him even more. He promised himself that when he became the next head boy, he'd do everything in his power to protect Steven and Michael from the hate campaign against them. He would have ultimate authority over every boy in the school; they just had to get through the next two months before the summer break.

'Look at me, you've got to–'

A foot gently kicked his bottom, interrupting him; he looked up and saw that Andrew and Matthew were presiding over him.

'Are you talking to him?' Matthew pointed at Steven. 'He's filth!'

'You'll get VD from him!' Andrew mocked. 'Yuck!'

'Fuck off!' Chris threw a two–fingered gesture at them.

'He needs a good scrub down to wash away the dirt!' Andrew said to Matthew before turning to Chris again, pointing at his crew cut. 'Use your scrubhead!'

Andrew and Matthew burst into laughter. Anger boiled inside Chris; he really hated being called Scrubhead, and this time, he felt Andrew had gone too far. He lost it. He sprang from the floor, grabbing at Andrew. Andrew staggered back from the sudden force, losing his balance and collapsing flat on his back. Chris immediately got on top of him, not giving him a chance to manoeuvre; the next thing Andrew knew was a hard punch on his nose and he groaned in pain. He shut his eyes, clamping his hand on Chris' face to push him away, but with Chris being the strongest boy in his Form; he knew it was useless. Again, he felt a punch on his nose and then something burst through his nostrils. He finally opened his eyes when he felt the weight easing off him, and saw that some of the other boys were pulling Chris away from him. He breathed a sigh of relief and touched his aching nose, seeing that his fingers were smeared with blood.

Chris wrestled from the grasp of those around him, telling them he had calmed down. He looked down at his fallen and bloodied friend, now beginning to regret what he had done. Suddenly, the lino vibrated to a stomp; everyone whirled round to see Mr Langston standing in the doorway, his face red.

'What is going on?' the headmaster screamed, his hands on his hips.

Chris had been summoned to the headmaster's office for the second night in a row.

'What's wrong with you, Christopher?' Mr Langston demanded. He sat fuming in his leather chair, ignoring the filthy state that Chris was in. 'You were in here last night and now here you are again! What have you got to say for yourself?'

He me be los by tember.

Mr Langston thought hard about what Chris had just said, trying to decipher his words: he had over twenty years of experience of figuring out the incomprehensible speech of deaf children.

'He made you lose your temper?'

Chris nodded.

'Why?' he asked. He waited for Chris to reply, but could see that he was reluctant. He knew, too, that he would only get another round of intangible speech from the boy and he was too tired to work it out again. Writing things down was a better method of communication, but it was almost half past nine now; bedtime for Chris' form.

'Forget it, Christopher. Can you write a short report about what happened and give it to me tomorrow?'

Chris nodded, mouthing an *okay*.

'Good,' the headmaster rose to his feet and waved a cautioning finger, 'but I'm warning you; I won't have this kind of behaviour from you again. Once more and you're in big trouble. Understand?'

Chris nodded, turned and briskly walked towards the door.

27

Careers

"Relying on lip–reading is inadequate as lip–readers understand only part of a conversation and use guesswork to fill the gaps. Written notes are unsatisfactory too, as many deaf people have often had poor quality education and may have a lower than average literacy. A qualified interpreter should always be present in a consultation between a clinician and a deaf patient who uses BSL to enable better two–way communication."
– DR ANDREW ALEXANDER; *Deafness Might Damage Your Health,* in *The Lancet* (about lack of BSL/English interpreters in the NHS), 2012

The lights flicked on, stomping feet vibrated the wooden floorboards and the beds were banged at. Aaron awoke to the sight of Miss Turner marching noisily across the room, shouting and clapping. He watched her reach the window to draw open the curtains, and saw that Michael's bed next to it was nothing but a tangled mess of sheets. He thought briefly about the attacks on him after lights out; the culprits were some of his form mates and some of the younger boys from the other two dorms. Derek had led the crusade and encouraged the others to torment Michael, but Aaron refused to participate. Aaron pulled the sheets over his face, wishing he could sleep more: he'd barely slept all night because he couldn't stop thinking about what had happened the previous evening. His right knuckle was still hurting a bit from the punch.

Chris opened his eyes, blinking at the hard light above him. He ignored Miss Hogarth as she clumped across the room. He turned to Steven's bed next to his; a crumpled mountain of sheets and blankets, bare feet exposed at the end. He groaned, still wishing he could have stopped all the attacks on Steven the night before, but he knew he *had* to do nothing but watch in desperation. He yawned loudly; it had been a rough night for him.

Aaron sat, placing his breakfast tray on the table. He glanced over to the next table to see that Chris was quietly eating his breakfast; he seemed to be deep in thought. Aaron turned as he felt a tap on his upper arm.

'I hate Thursdays,' Ian moaned. 'They're always so boring!'

Aaron nodded weakly, not really bothered about the boy's grumpiness. He tucked in, his eyes straying back to the other table, to see that Chris was waving at someone.

Andrew, who was sporting a plaster on his nose, looked up from his breakfast at Chris.

'Look, I'm sorry for what I did to you,' Chris said.

'That's all right,' Andrew, shrugged, pointing at his nose. 'Nothing's broken.'

'Friends?' Chris asked tentatively, extending his hand.

'Yeah, friends.' Andrew smiled, leaning over the decagonal table. Chris did likewise and they shook hands. He sat back, feeling a little bit better now. He glanced over to the Third Form table to see Aaron busily eating his breakfast.

The boys swarmed around the front hall, signing to each other and preparing for their first lesson of the day. Chris trudged through towards the lobby, carrying his ring binder and Arsenal pen case. He saw Aaron picking up an envelope from the post shelf. He slowly went over to him and gently tapped his shoulder. Aaron turned to him.

'Letter from home?' Chris asked nervously, trying to be pleasant. Aaron met his eyes coldly. Chris felt as though the room had suddenly frozen and there was an air of tension around them.

'Yes, a letter from home,' Aaron answered, putting the envelope into his blazer pocket. 'I gotta go. I don't want to be late.'

Aaron turned away. Chris bowed his head, frustrated. He soon felt a tap on his shoulder; he turned to see that David had a concerned look in his face.

'Are you two alright?' asked David, pointing at the departing Aaron. 'You seem a bit, er, *quiet* with each other.'

'We're fine,' Chris lied. 'See you later.'

Chris walked away before David could even lift a hand to sign. He watched his friend walk down the corridor, suspicion creeping into him. He thought back to the evening before, when he'd seen Aaron crying alone on his bed in Dorm Three; he'd noticed that his school clothes seemed to be soaking wet. He wanted to comfort him, but decided not to, believing he wanted to be left alone. Later, he saw Chris entering Mr Langston's office, and also noticed his dishevelled state. He had wondered why they had been outside in the rain; had they had an argument, or even a fight? David shook his head, deciding not to worry about it for now. He supposed Aaron would tell him eventually. Perhaps he'd try to cheer him up a bit today. He passed Gary as he walked.

Gary folded his arms, nudged Timothy with his elbow and pointed at the entrance doors. 'Here she is.'

A woman entered, carrying a large briefcase. She glanced around the bustle of boys, expecting to see someone, gently ruffling her thick blonde perm to tidy it a bit. Her eyes widened when Mrs Munnings weaved through the young crowd towards her.

'Hello, Mrs Teale,' she greeted her. 'Good to see you again.'

'And you too, Mrs … ' Mrs Teale struggled to remember the teacher's name. It had been a year since her last visit.

'Munnings,' the teacher reminded her.

'Oh yes, sorry,' she beamed, apologetically.

'Come with me, I'll take you to your room,' Mrs Munnings beckoned. 'I'll bring you a cup of tea.'

Gary and Timothy watched Mrs Munnings lead Mrs Teale past them, towards the lobby. Discreetly, they eyed up the woman, who was in her thirties. She was wearing a cream keyhole top, which flaunted her large cleavage. The top was quite tight, which added to the faultiness of her appearance. She also wore dark brown skirt which flowed from her wide hips; it had square frills around the hem and complemented her black high heeled boots.

Gary was tempted to wolf–whistle, but decided not to.

'Have her breasts grown bigger since last year?' Timothy said, gesturing them exaggeratedly. 'Or has her waist become thinner?'

'Or maybe she's got those new silicone implants!' Gary twinkled and slapped his friend's back. 'Come on. Maths with Hitler Teacher now.'

The two seniors marched away.

Mr McShane gently closed Conor's right hand, leaving only his thumb visible. He directed the hand at a small display of plants on a little table in the centre of the Art Room.

'Use your thumb to measure the plants over there. Start from the top and then count down with your thumb. Think of it as a ruler, then do the same on your drawing. Okay, Conor?'

The First Former nodded. He squinted at the plants, using his thumb to measure them, as instructed. Mr McShane turned to the rest of the First Formers, sitting at their easels around the plant display, drawing busily. He glanced at the wall clock: eleven o'clock. He checked his watch and it was five minutes early. He sighed to himself. Those little toerags had done it again: they'd turned the clock five minutes forward so that they could have an extra five minutes' break after the second lesson at ten past eleven. He went over to the wall, plucked the clock from it and turned the big hand back to the correct time. He chuckled upon hearing some groans behind him and put the clock back on the wall.

'Miles?' a voice called out from behind.

Mr McShane turned to the doorway see Frances Langston, the school secretary, leaning through the half open door. 'I'm sorry to interrupt, but you have an urgent telephone call. It's in my office.'

Mr McShane waved at his pupils and signed to them that he had to go out for a minute. He also warned them to leave the damn clock well alone.

Gary trotted along the corridor, hands in pockets, lost in thought. He went past Mr McShane and Mrs Langston, who were walking briskly. He took no notice of them as he turned to open a door.

He entered, closed the door behind him and walked over to the chair in front of the table that Mrs Teale was sitting behind, her head down, writing something on a sheet that was inside a ring binder. He sat, folded his arms and legs and waited for the careers advisor to finish. His eyes were drawn towards the exposed oval area on her top, appreciating her cleavage. He observed the size of her large breasts as they bulged down; 42D, he guessed. He had learned about breasts sizes from Lindy, with whom he'd lost his virginity at the Christmas party. He revelled in the memory of caressing her breasts, which were huge for a sixteen–year old. Mrs Teale finished and tilted her head at the boy.

'Hello,' she greeted him, looking down at her list of names before returning to the young lad. 'Gary Portmore. You're the last one in. I'm, eh … ' She held up a note with her name written in black marker pen. 'Mrs Teale.'

Gary nodded in acknowledgement.

'Good boy!' The careers advisor put down the note. Then, she pointed at a biro and a refill pad with half of its lined sheets already rolled back. She spoke slowly and patchily to Gary. 'Please … write … about … what … you … would … like … to … do … in … the … future … Do … you … understand … me?'

Gary stared at the pad for a long moment, thinking about it. His form mates who'd been in before him had told him all about the careers advisor's patronising attitude. She knew absolutely *nothing* about deaf people; most of them had struggled to communicate with her, writing everything down on the pad, and had received some rather dubious advice about their future careers. Gary gazed into her eyes.

'Thanks,' he spoke perfectly and clearly: 'but no thanks. I'll use my voice. And please do speak a little bit faster.'

Mrs Teale stiffened, clasping her hands on the table, a weak smile growing on her face. 'Alright, Gary. So, what would you like to do in the future?'

'I'd like to be a solicitor,' he answered bluntly, clasping his hands and resting them on his lap.

The careers advisor stared blankly at the lad. Gary waited in expectation, already knowing what her answer would be, from what his form mates had told him.

'A solicitor?' she said, finally. 'Why would you want to pursue that as a career?'

'Because it's what I want to do,' he replied. 'I'd like to study law and then work for deaf people in specific legal areas. I don't know what they are just yet, but it's the career I want to pursue.'

'Well,' the woman shook her head, 'to be perfectly honest; I don't think it's the kind of career that you should pursue–'

'Why not?'

'Well, um, I don't think you really understand the nature of that particular job. It's not something that deaf people can do, I have to tell you this, because–'

'Because we're too stupid?'

'I didn't say that!'

'No, but you implied it,' Gary leaned forward, resting his arms on the table, his face close to the careers advisor's. He briefly thought about his father, who was a lowly office clerk working for a small law firm in the northern town of Whitby. 'Listen, did you know that my dad's a barrister? He works for a big law firm in the north east of England and he's one of the best. He's won high profile legal cases. He's my hero. I told him I wanted to be a solicitor and he's very happy with that idea. You'll know by now that I'm not exactly unintelligent and I'm confident that I'll do very well in my eight CSE's and six O Level exams, including English and English Literature, next month. Now, imagine, my dear lady, if I told my dad that you were advising me against becoming a solicitor, I'm sure he'd advise *you* to pack in your stupid job and work as a buxom cleaning lady. Just like you told my form mates to go for crummy jobs instead of their chosen careers.'

'Look–'

'I'm not finished yet!' Gary snapped. He waited for the woman to nod for him to continue: 'Thank you. Right; let's see – Tom Quillot said he wanted to run his own business, but you told him he'd be better off working in a shop. Dwight Greenland wants to be a hairdresser, but you told him he can't do that because he wouldn't be able to communicate with the customers, and you advised him to consider a sweeping job or something like that. Carl Dunn wants to work in television, but you suggested he works as a computer programmer using those punched cards. Basher – Brian Thompson – wants to be a professional graphic artist, but you told him he'd be better off as a painter and decorator or a hospital porter. He's really good at art, did you know that?'

'I'm sure he is–'

'Timothy Hutchinson said he wanted to be a vicar ... ' Gary stopped short, thinking about that again for a moment; was Spooky just joking, or was he serious?

He brushed the thought aside. 'But you told him that vicars communicate with people for a living and you didn't think he could do that, and suggested he could become a scientist instead. Well, let me tell you, there are quite a few deaf vicars around; did you know that? I know of one, and he communicates with *deaf* people.'

Mrs Teale sat back, folding her arms below her breasts, which made them look even bigger. Gary glared at her; he could see that her face had become strained and that she resented being upstaged by a deaf sixteen–year old. He briefly thought about his upcoming exams – four CSE's and three O Levels; okay, he'd exaggerated a little about them, he thought, but it was quite effective. He looked down at the pad for a moment, flicking through the pages of handwritten conversations between his form mates and the careers advisor. He glanced through them; some of them confirmed what he had just told the woman. He chuckled when he spotted that someone had written that they wanted to be a landscape architect, but other writing – Mrs Teale's – said he should think about taking up a gardening job instead.

'Do you remember James Eriswell?' Gary looked up at the silent careers advisor. Her eyes widened as she fiddled with her varnished red nails. 'Yes, you do, don't you? Tall and blonde. He was the head boy here when I was in the First Form. He told me you had the hots for him – you even unbuttoned your blouse a little for him. I know this because he's my older sister's boyfriend, you see. She's deaf too. Anyway, he said he wanted to be a journalist, but you told him he couldn't and advised him to work in a low paid warehouse job or something. You seem to believe that it's easier for hearing people to get the deaf to do shitty labouring work, so that they don't need to communicate with them. Well, James achieved straight As and Bs in his O Level exams here. He also got an A in his A Level English and he's now studying for a degree in journalism at Leeds University. He's got a work placement as a junior staff writer for the local paper, and I think he'll do really well in the future. Not bad for someone who's from a completely deaf family, eh? His kid brother, Toby, is a First Former here, by the way.'

'Well, I'm very pleased for James,' the careers advisor leaned forward, seemingly lost within herself.

'The whole point, Mrs Teale, is that deaf people *can do anything* but hear,' Gary concluded. He pointed at the large closed file next to the careers advisor 'Now, I'd like you to take a look in that lovely big file and "advise" me on my first step towards becoming a solicitor.'

Mrs Teale sighed to herself; Gary could see that she was wishing she could strangle him. She begrudgingly heaved the big file over in front of her, opened it and bowed her head.

mar ar

'Aye, I'm a smart arse!' The careers officer's head jolted up in surprise. Gary was grinning broadly. 'I've a very moderate hearing loss. I can hear sounds without my hearing aids – they just give me extra volume. That's how I heard you call me smart arse. I can hear most words, apart from sounds such as "s", "sh", "t" or "ed"; only in the middle or at the end of each word, not at the start. So I always have to figure them out, though, lipreading does help. Anyhow, please carry on.'

The careers advisor went back to the file and opened one of the dividers. Gary folded his arms in triumph.

David picked a book from the shelf, opened it and headed towards his desk, stopping by Aaron's on the way. He saw that he was still brooding and playing with the triangular prism; earlier, he'd noticed that Aaron wasn't paying attention to Miss Stephenson's lesson on the visible light spectrum. He now knew for sure that something was up between him and Chris; the curiosity was killing him. He decided to try to get something out of Aaron.

'Are you okay?' David asked carefully.

'I'm fine,' Aaron shrugged.

David knew that he wasn't telling the truth. Perhaps, he thought, he could help him with the prism and get Aaron talking, then he might eventually open up about what had happened. So, he inched closer to his friend, pointing at the triangular glass on the desk. 'Do you want me to help you with that?' he asked.

'Not really,' Aaron answered.

'But you weren't really watching Miss Stephenson when she was talking about–'

'Leave me alone!' Aaron snapped. 'I'll be fine. Now, go away.'

David nodded silently, a little hurt by his friend's outburst. He decided to leave him alone and turned away. Aaron watched him go, feeling a little regretful, but he knew it was not the right time or place to talk to David about what had happened. Perhaps later, or tomorrow, or over the weekend, he thought. He still couldn't stop thinking about Chris and he was aching badly inside.

Chris yawned as he walked through the corridor to the dining room with some of his form mates. He was very tired after a bad night's sleep, so he hoped that lunch would refresh him. He looked at the menu on the wall to see what was for lunch; it was liver, mashed potatoes and runner beans. He sighed; he *hated* liver. He went over to the counter, picked up a tray and joined Mr McShane, who was conversing with Mr Langston.

'Donald,' Mr McShane said as he scooped some mashed potato from a large bowl and dumped it on his plate, 'I had a telephone call this morning from a neighbour of my parents'. It's my mother; she's had a bad fall and she's in hospital.'

'I'm sorry to hear that,' Mr Langston said. He tucked a pair of tongs into a bowl of runner beans, shook away the loose bits and placed the rest on his plate. 'I do hope it's nothing too serious.'

'That's the problem,' Mr McShane explained. 'You see, my parents are deaf and the neighbour said they're having difficulties with communication at the hospital. I'm the only one who can help them communication with the hospital staff.'

'That's quite a burden for you, Miles,' the headmaster said, passing the tongs to him. 'Have you been interpreting for them all your life?'

'Most of the time, yes,' Mr McShane answered, waving the tongs like a conductor's baton, as a means of expressing himself. 'I can't say I blame them. We've got no professional sign language interpreters here, not like the ones in America that you told me about. We've got social workers for the deaf, who are mostly useless at interpreting between deaf and hearing people; the missioners for the deaf are helpful, but they're always too busy to help interpret ... there's also some hearing friends they can call on and the odd nurse who know some basic signs. But it's not the same as having a professional sign language interpreter. Worse still, they tend to take over and start discussing deaf patients' private details with the doctors, leaving the patients, and their deaf relatives with no clue as to what's going on. They often just get told sporadic information afterwards. This kind of thing peeves me off. My mother wants me to go up to Manchester for the weekend tomorrow to help out, but I'm on duty–'

'You go and see your mother. Family is more important.'

'But what about the duty roster?' Mr McShane frowned, though a small smile was growing on his face. 'That'd leave just–'

'I'm sure he'll volunteer to take your place,' Mr Langston interrupted, knowing to whom they were referring. He patted the art teacher's shoulder and then lifted his tray, smiling. 'Besides, what can possibly go wrong tomorrow evening?'

A hard poke in Mr McShane's back startled him; he turned to see Chris, who was pointing impatiently at the pair of tongs.

'Hurry up with that!' Chris complained.

28

The Long Bad Friday

"Education makes people easy to lead, but difficult to drive, easy to govern, but impossible to enslave."
– HENRY BROUGHAM (1778–1868)

The early morning sun shone brightly as four rows of ten boys lined up in the car park for their daily roll call. The Fifth Formers loitered in front of them, checking that everybody was present and correct.

Chris yawned weakly; it had been another rough night, although not as bad as the night before. He gazed idly at Steven, who stood in front of him, his back to him, thinking about the poor lad – they had done it to him again last night and he'd been powerless to stop them. He wondered what Steven was thinking. When his eyes drifted to Aaron on the next row, his heart still wrenched. Apart from their brief exchange in the toilets yesterday morning, they had not said a word to each other all day. He knew David was suspicious about their falling out, but neither of them had said anything to him yet. He closed his eyes for a brief moment, thanking God it was Friday; he was looking forward to the next day's FA Cup Final, hopeful that Arsenal would repeat last year's success against West Ham. He'd cheer up if – *when* – they won, and maybe, just maybe, he and Aaron *could* make up. After his anticipated fight with Basher, of course. But if Arsenal lost, Aaron would probably come and offer him sympathy, and then … who knows? He really wanted to tell him how sorry he was, from the bottom of his heart, and he wished the day would fly by quickly. He sighed, then gazed into the distance to see Hubert pushing a wheelbarrow filled with long gardening tools along the winding driveway. The school gardener briefly glanced back at the roll call and continued his way. Chris watched him disappear behind the trees and shrubbery. Turning away, he saw the boys disbanding and heading towards the school for their breakfast.

Chris sat on his usual chair, placing his breakfast tray on the table. He looked at Steven, who was on his left, head down and eating his cereal. He sighed when he noticed that Dean, who was sitting next to Steven, had again moved away from him. Chris defiantly moved his chair a little closer to Steven's and began to eat. A jolt on the table alerted him; he looked up to see Sammy, who was sitting next to Andrew, thumping on the table.

'Why have you moved closer to him?' he asked, pointing at Steven.

'So what if I have?' Chris replied, digging his spoon into his bowl.

'He shouldn't be sitting at *this* table!' Sammy pointed hard at Steven. 'Why are you siding with this filth?'

Chris plopped his spoon down in the milk, the anger inside him surging. The entire table had given Steven a lot of shit at teatime yesterday and he'd had to put a stop to it, telling them to leave him alone because he was in a bad mood and he wanted to eat in peace. It was a lame excuse, he thought, but at least they'd stopped. Chris had privately told Steven afterwards that he was still his friend, telling him to bear with it until the summer break; he promised to protect him when they were in Form Five. He saw that he'd given Steven a glimmer of hope; the boy burst into uncontrollable tears, getting it out of his system. Chris had comforted him with his arms. He really wanted to say something to those idiots round the table; it was burning inside him and he wanted to get it off his chest. He banged loudly on the table for attention.

'When I'm head boy this September–'

'Wait,' Andrew interrupted. 'You said *when* you're head boy. Do you know something we don't?'

Chris cursed himself for letting it slip. 'I mean *if*–'

'No, no, no, you said *when*!' Mark boomed, waving his spoon at him. 'Has Mr Langston said something to you?'

'Come on, tell us!' Matthew, next to him, slapped Chris arm.

Chris surveyed the nine boys, who were watching him expectantly. His shoulders sank; he might as well tell them. 'Yes, he did say that I'll be the next head boy.'

The table burst into cheers and groans; Chris frowned at their mixed reactions. 'What?' he waved his index finger. 'What's going on?'

Lester, a triumphant smile on his face, said, 'We've been betting on who's going to be the next head boy. It was either you or Dean, and I bet on you. Those who lost are gonna have to give up something they love!' He turned to Andrew, gleefully.

Dean and Sammy patted Andrew's head, gloating and giggling. Andrew fought them off, aghast. Matthew thumped on the table, also happy.

'Remember, you promised; the hardcore ones!'

Chris looked round the table, still perplexed. Sammy turned to Chris, noting his puzzled look. 'Andrew bet on Dean. He lost, so he's giving us half his sex magazines!'

Mark waved at Chris. 'We all knew you'd be the next head boy anyway, but we wanted to do a little bet, just for fun!'

'*Vee*!' Chris flicked his index and middle fingers on his chest, rolling his eyes.

'What were you saying before?' Sammy reminded Chris.

Chris thought about that briefly and decided not to bother: he would tell them when he became head boy. He shook his head, picking up his spoon.

'Nothing.'

Matthew waved his fork at everyone. 'I've just found out that Mr McShane's not on duty tonight!'

The nine heads around the table exchanged surprised glances.

'Why not?' Andrew queried.

'Family reasons.' Mark said. 'He told me he has to go back up to Manchester this evening.'

'Then who's on duty tonight?' Dean asked.

'I know Mr Langston, Mrs Munnings and Mr Arkwright are going away for the weekend tonight. A conference or something,' Steven plucked up the courage to join in. 'Mrs Munnings told me yesterday.'

'And Mr Whittle and Miss Stephenson are going to Paris for the weekend,' Sammy turned to Andrew, grinning. 'How romantic!'

'Shut up!' Andrew thumped Sammy's arm, feeling jealous once more.

'Mr Bronte was on duty last night, so he can't do it again tonight,' Chris said.

'Mr Norris is *never* on duty on Friday evenings,' Matthew said. 'Dunno why!'

The entire table fell silent: there was only one possibility left.

With the exception of Chris', all of their right hands shot up in unison, gesturing a *Heil Hitler* salute. Chris sighed, tucking into his now spongy Weetabix.

'It's going to be fun tonight.' Sammy remarked with a hint of sarcasm in his signing.

Aaron smoothed down the part of his bed sheet that was folded over the blanket and tucked it between the mattress and the metal frame. Then, he ruffled his pillow and placed it against the wooden headrest. There, he said to himself; that's done. He thought about last night; he had slept a little better than the night before, but the noisy footsteps in the dark had sometimes interrupted his attempts to sleep and he knew that some of the boys were still having a go at Michael. Once, a pillow fell on his face and he'd thrown it back wherever it had come from, out of frustration rather than pleasure. Then there was a loud crash which shook the floorboards. The melee finally stopped when Miss Turner burst into the dorm, turning the lights on and threatening everyone with detention if they did not stay in bed. Aaron looked over at Michael's bed, which was upturned, with the metal frame visible atop. Michael was standing by it, naked, bawling his eyes out. David found his pyjamas lying on the floor, near his own bed, picked them up and gave them to Michael. Aaron knew that David wasn't involved in the attack. Miss Turner helped them to get Michael's bed sorted and warned the boys again to leave him alone. After she was gone, though, it started again; quieter this time. Aaron had turned away, buried his head under his pillow and tried to sleep again.

Aaron sighed wearily and walked around to his wardrobe on the other side of his bed. He opened the top drawer and picked up his favourite Paper Mate pen, which Chris had recently stolen for him from W.H.Smith & Sons. He put it in his inside blazer pocket, pausing as he thought about Chris once more. Deep down, he missed him terribly. He was still angry with himself for punching Chris two nights before; he'd never meant to do that; and hated himself for breaking up their friendship – his heart was still in anguish. He yearned to make up with him, but he still held back. Perhaps, he thought, he'd give it one more day; maybe he'd wait until that evening, or tomorrow. He thought Chris was right that their secret was still safe – *it had to be* – otherwise they would be suffering the same fate as Steven and Michael. He was now convinced that whatever he'd seen in the changing room was down to his imagination, nothing more, so he told himself to stop worrying and relax. He thought Chris was probably queer, which was fine with him, but he was still confused about his *own* feelings – *was he a queer like him or not?* He knew Chris would come to him before or after the following day's Cup Final; when he did, Aaron knew he would embrace him without a moment's thought. And then they'd forget about what had happened and be best friends again. Aaron half smiled to himself, liking that idea. He pushed the pen down, its clip tightly locked onto his pocket. He glanced at his watch: almost nine o'clock. Assembly now, he mused and headed away.

Basher panted heavily as he pushed himself up, his hands flat and toes balancing on the floor. He crashed back down again; arms spread wide. Looking up, he saw Mr Norris waving his finger and speaking rapid–fire at him as usual.

'You'veonlydoneeightpushupssofaryouslob!' the sports teacher said without stopping for a breath. 'EveryoneelsehasalreadydonetwentysohurryupBrian!'

Basher glanced around the gym hall to see the rest of his Form watching him with broad smiles on their faces. Basher really *hated* PE lessons; he'd never been good at PE. He quickly glanced at his watch – it was almost ten past ten – only fifteen minutes left of the first lesson of the day, he thought. He suddenly felt a hard, painful rap on his head. Twisting back, he saw the short teacher bending over him, knocking on his head with his knuckles.

'Comeonwehaven'tgotallday!' he yapped. 'Servesyarightforsmokinginsecret.' He gestured an imaginary cigarette. 'Nowhurryupanddotwelvemore!'

Basher groaned.

Hendrik fiddled idly with his headphones' mouthpiece, watching Mr Arkwright write on the blackboard as he spoke into the microphone in his other hand, his back to the Second Form boys. Hendrik knew the religious studies teacher was speaking; he could feel little vibrations on his ears. He sighed inwardly as he glanced at his watch: quarter to eleven. Twenty–five more minutes to go before the twenty–minute break, and he was desperate for a pee. He glanced at the blackboard, on which were several long extracts from the Bible: this time from The Gospel According to Luke. Hendrik really hated religious studies lessons; he always struggled to understand the Good Book, as the teacher liked to call it, because of its dry, dense text. He'd never been able to understand a word Mr Arkwright said; he tried his damnedest to lipread him, but it was no use. He wasn't the only one, though; all of the other teachers were the same, except for Mr McShane and Mrs Munnings, who signed her classes now.

He turned to Rowan, tapping his arm to bring him out of his deep thoughts. 'Can you hear what he's saying?' he pointed at Mr Arkwright, who was still facing the blackboard and speaking into the microphone. He took care to sign quietly for fear of the teacher hearing his hands chafing together.

'Nope!' Rowan replied quietly in sign.

'But you have better hearing than the rest of us.' Hendrik queried.

'Yes, I can hear,' the bespectacled boy with dark hair explained, 'but not *words*. Only sounds. I need to lipread him to help me, but he's facing the bloody blackboard!'

'Ah. Anyway,' Hendrik changed the subject, 'who do you think will win the FA Cup tomorrow?'

'Doesn't bother me; I don't support Arsenal or West Ham.' Rowan said. 'I support West Brom.'

'Why them?'

'That's where I come from.'

'But they have three black players!'

'So? They're brilliant. I've got ... ' Rowan stopped short, remembering how his form mate had a strong dislike for black people. He was going to tell him about the football programme he had in the drawer of his wardrobe in Dorm Two, which was signed by Cyrille Regis, Laurie Cunningham and Brendon Batson. His dad wasn't too happy with it; he said having one black playing for an English football club was bad enough, but *three*? Rowan didn't care, though, because he liked to watch them, despite how some of the other fans, especially the opposing ones, chanted hate stuff at them. He was worried that if Hendrik saw his programme, he would take it and rip it up, or even use it to wipe his bottom with.

'Nothing.' He shook his head.

Mr Arkwright turned to face the boys. Hendrik and Rowan quickly stopped signing, folded their arms and watched the teacher silently.

Hammering hard with a wooden mallet, Toby tried to smooth the curves in a copper plate atop a domed iron mount, held in place by a vice on the worktop, but he wasn't doing a very good job. The twelve–year old sighed loudly in frustration as he looked around at the rest of the First Formers. Suddenly, someone snatched the mallet from his hand; he turned to see Mr Bronte shaking his head, muttering something. Toby tried to lipread him, could only see the old man's lips moving unintelligibly. He remembered his older brother, James, telling him that the teacher was an old fool and absolutely impossible to lipread. Just nod, pretend to understand and watch how he does it, he'd told him once. Toby stepped back a bit to allow the teacher take over the hammering. He mumbled a few words, brandishing the mallet and gently banging on the copper plate, turning it around as he did so. Mr Bronte muttered something to Toby, laughing at a joke Toby obviously hadn't caught; Toby responded by nodding and forcing out a pretentious laugh. He glanced up at the wall clock: five minutes left of the third lesson before lunch, he muttered to himself; it was fish, chips today, and those yucky mushy peas.

Andy, Bradley, Duncan, Jonah, Ian, Derek and Shaun gathered round, looking down at the grass. A medium–sized bird lay there, its black body and bright yellow chest twitching. One of its black wings was askew and it struggled to move.

'Must have broken its wing,' Duncan straightened up.

'Poor bird!' Jonah remarked, gazing down at it with sympathy.

'What's it called?' Ian asked Andy, given his knowledge of birds.

'It's a golden oriole,' Andy replied. 'It's from abroad, I think.'

'It's good as dead,' Derek said, raising his foot to mercilessly stamp on the bird.

Bradley held Derek back, angry with him. 'Don't!'

'I was only teasing!' Derek laughed.

The group turned to see Ian waving at someone across the front field, then all turned again to see Hubert walking over to them. The school gardener broke through the circle of Third Formers and saw the injured bird.

'Oh goodness me!' Hubert clasped his hands, making sure the boys were watching his lips. 'Poor little bird.' He bent down, carefully picked up the bird with both hands and stroked its head. It flapped weakly, but Hubert held onto it. He stood up, nodding. 'Wing broken ... yes, broken.'

Kannn yooouuu help himmm?

Hubert heard Duncan's request. He nodded, stroking the bird with his index finger. 'Yes, yes, I can help him. Make him better.'

Shaun glanced at his watch: almost two o'clock; time to get back for the afternoon lessons. He waved at everyone. 'It's nearly two – art now!'

With a final look at Hubert and the bird, the boys ran off towards the school. Hubert watched them as he stroked the bird again. 'Poor little bird; Hubert will make you better.'

Chris quietly drummed his fingers on his desk, deep in thought and not paying any attention to Mr Schneider, who was drawing a white circle on the blackboard with a large wooden compass. Chris put his finger under the muff on his right ear to scratch an itch and adjusted the muff a bit to make its weight more comfortable on his head. He was still thinking about Aaron; how he was missing him. He was feeling a bit depressed again and wished tomorrow would hurry up–

He shrieked as a sudden burst of sound shot through his eardrums. Swinging to his right, he saw that Dean had just cranked the volume up to full, on the control panel on his desk.

'Wake up!' Dean mocked.

Chris angrily punched Dean's arm and turned the volume down. A piece of chalk whacked his forehead. He swung round, cupping his forehead with his hand, to see the towering maths teacher leaning over the front desk, one arm outstretched, holding the compass in the other.

'Pay attention, Christopher!' he demanded. He straightened and turned back to the blackboard.

Dean picked up the chalk from the floor. Chris quickly turned to him, knowing what he was about to do, but was too late. Dean threw it back at Mr Schneider; it bounced off the back of his groomed blond hair. The teacher whirled round, his face red.

'Detention!' he shot at Chris.

'It wasn't me!' Chris protested in sign. 'It was him!' *Oh, shit,* he cursed.

'Another detention for signing!'

'I didn't do it!' Chris silently mouthed back, keeping his hands in check.

Mr Schneider rounded his desk and was at Chris' a split second later. He thumped the wooden compass down hard on it, the sharp metal point close to

Chris. Chris looked at it, stunned, and slowly looked up at the tall man towering over him; his face was even redder and his eyes on fire.

'Another detention!'

Chris lost it. He shot to his feet, his two–fingered gesture instinctively thrusting directly underneath the maths teacher's long beaky nose; a finger grazing either side of it.

'Fuck off!' he screamed loudly. Mr Schneider stumbled back, dropping the compass and cupping his nose. Chris stood there for a second, shocked at what he had just done. It was an accident, he told himself, but right now, he didn't care. He panned from side to side to see his dumbstruck form mates watching him, his anger still boiling inside: he knew he had to get out now to calm down. He stormed out of the classroom.

Chris dumped his blazer on his bed, collected his Arsenal football from his wardrobe and went downstairs, deciding to go through the east side of the building en route to the small field behind Magnat House, to have a kick–about on his own. Holding the ball, he quickly glanced at his watch: half past two. He turned a corner and strode briskly down a long, narrow wood panelled corridor towards the set of double swing doors at the other end. He knew there was a tiny foyer behind the doors which led to the exit. He slowed his pace when the double doors opened inwards and Basher emerged.

Chris stopped. Basher stopped too, the doors swinging behind him. Their eyes met. Chris wondered if Basher's presence was an accident or not, but he didn't care; he wanted to get outside. He resumed his approach. Basher began to walk towards him. When they were a few feet from each other, Chris moved to his left so that he could pass through. But Basher moved to his right, blocking the way. Chris sighed inwardly and moved to his right; again Basher blocked his path.

'Get out of my way,' Chris mouthed at his adversary, who smiled back menacingly. Chris glared hard into Basher's eyes, thinking about all the battles he'd had with him in the time he'd been at the school. He had never really understood *why* they hated each other, though. Basher had started it, with an assault on him in the showers in his very first week, for no apparent reason, and their intense rivalry had gone on from there.

'I don't like people like you,' Basher said.

'Fine,' Chris mouthed back. The feeling was mutual. But, he thought to himself, *why*? He knew he wouldn't get an answer from the head boy, but he asked anyway, pressing the ball against his stomach with his left hand to free up his right hand to sign. 'Why? Why do you hate me?'

Basher stared into Chris' eyes, contempt on his face. Finally, he said, 'Because you remind me of someone I hate.'

I remind him of someone he hates; Chris pondered. That wasn't the answer he had expected. He shook his head and advanced forward to push his way through the little gap between Basher and the wall. Basher stood firm. Annoyed, Chris grabbed the lapel of Basher's blazer while Basher grabbed Chris' shirt. Chris tried to wrestle himself free by pushing Basher away, but he couldn't, so let go of the ball, grabbed the other lapel and pushed the Fifth Former square on. Basher crashed against the wall. He grabbed Chris' shirt with his other hand and twisted round, forcing Chris to swing round; his back thudded hard against the other wall. Chris yelped at the sudden pain and swung a clenched fist at Basher's face. Basher jerked his head away and it didn't stun him; still clutching Chris, Basher headbutted him. Chris responded with another punch in the face, this time harder. Basher yelled and rammed him hard against the wall behind, then tried to get behind Chris, to get him into a headlock, but Chris had already anticipated this action, turning to prevent Basher from rounding him. Basher decked Chris' left cheek hard and Chris responded with another punch, this time on the nose. Basher screamed, blood bursting through his nostrils. Anger erupted inside him; Basher lashed out at Chris, grabbing his neck and pushing him against the wall. The back of Chris' head hit the wall hard and he scowled. Basher began to squeeze Chris' neck and he started to choke. Squinting at Basher, he saw that his face was completely twisted; his forehead wrinkled, his teeth gnarled and his eyes showing a kind of repulsion; something he had never seen in him before. It was like they were … murderous. He felt the oxygen drain from him and knew he had to break free. He cocked his knee up hard between Basher's legs, feeling his testicles bob. Basher doubled up, loosening his grip, but still he held on. With great effort, Chris pushed up Basher's jaw, forcing Basher away. Basher finally released his grip and Chris' right fist flew hard at Basher's mouth, hitting teeth. Basher crashed backwards, arms flailing violently, and slammed to the wooden floor with a loud thud. Chris rubbed his neck, gasping for air. Basher slowly turned over, his right elbow resting on the floor, his left hand touching his lips, blood streaming through his fingers. Chris looked scornfully at his fallen foe for a moment before picking up his football.

'You're gonna be very sorry,' Basher said, using his bloodied left hand to make the warning.

Chris turned and headed towards the swinging doors.

Chris tried to concentrate on keeping the ball in the air, using his feet and his thighs, but it kept rolling to the grass after only a few bobs. Again and again he tried, but his mind wasn't on it; still spinning with all the incidents happened this week. He was still hurting from his fallout with Aaron. He tried to control the ball again, but it bounced back to the grass. He sighed, bowed his head and closed his eyes for a moment. Opening them again, he glanced at Magnat House, its eight white framed floor–to–ceiling windows spread across the dark grey concrete wall, the east side of the school partially visible above its flat roof.

Frustration sank in; he whirled round and kicked the ball hard, not caring where it went. He watched as it flew over the small field, then bounced twice on the grass and into the hands of Hubert. The school gardener, who was standing at the edge of the field with the trees behind him, looked silently across the field at Chris.

29

Repercussions

"Incredible as it may seem, it took only a small clique of hearing educators and businessmen, late in the last [19th] century, to release a tidal wave of oralism that swept over Western Europe, drowning all its signing communities. In America, the submersion of sign language was nearly as complete, for although the European wave reached our [America] shores attenuated, Alexander Graham Bell and his speech association had cleared the way for its progress from east to west."
– DR HARLAN LANE: *When The Mind Hears: A History of the Deaf*, 1984

Chris looked around, still awestruck by the small room; it bore little resemblance to a typical living room. He was sitting on a cream high–backed armchair in the middle of the room with a low coffee table in front of him. A similar armchair sat opposite him, but at a slight angle. Apart from the furniture, which stood on a dark patterned rug over polished wooden floorboards (there was a floor lamp behind the other armchair, a small dressing table on one side and a landscape picture on the wall above it), everything else in the room was different to anything he had ever seen before. Floor–to–ceiling dark wooden shelves full of books covered almost all four sides of the room. He saw that these were mainly old publications, judging by the design and age of their spines and their overwhelming musty odour. They filled every single space on the shelves; Chris couldn't see any gaps. There were even more books, piled waist high, in one corner. He glanced up at the low white ceiling, which had dark wooden beams, and wondered if this room had more books in it than the school's library.

He turned to the window on his left, which had white net curtains on it and overlooked a small garden surrounded by trees; he could almost see the rear of the school in the distance. There was a long trestle table by the window; it was occupied by five cages with little pets in them, mostly gerbils, hamsters and mice. Next to one was a metal tray filled with hay, on which a yellow chested bird, a fresh–looking splint on one of its wings, was sleeping soundly. Chris saw that more books were stacked up underneath the table. He looked behind the armchair for something, but it was not there. He looked around the room again, but couldn't see it. There was no television set. His attention was drawn towards the door when Hubert entered, carrying a tray laden with a ceramic teapot, a pair of cups and saucers and a plate of Rich Tea biscuits. As he watched the gardener walk towards the coffee table, Chris thought about how Hubert had invited him over to his tiny cottage.

As far as he knew, none of the boys had ever set foot in the house, and hadn't done so in all the years Hubert had been there. Hubert always kept all of his doors and windows locked, had net curtains at all of the windows so no one could see inside, drew all of his curtains tightly at night, and refused to let anyone in. He never talked about his life or his past, although it was believed he came from Eastern Europe. That at least, he thought, must be something he had in common with the gardener. Hubert very rarely talked to the boys, except when occasionally helping them out in the grounds; in which case, he would say a few words, but he never signed. He was well known for having a kind heart but always kept himself to himself. It was said that there were only three things he loved and cared about: his gardening job, animals and the boys. They'd obviously forgotten about the books. From what Aaron had told him after reading *The White Stag*, the school's annual magazine, way back when Hubert was eighteen and drifting from one place to another, he'd walked past the school. This was shortly after it had first opened in 1950, and Hubert could see that the grounds needed a lot of work; he'd offered to help, as he had some gardening experience, although he never said where this was gained. Mr Williams had given Hubert the job on the spot and he'd moved straight into the cottage, which belonged to the school; it had been a gamekeeper's cottage and was the second oldest building on the estate. Hubert was the longest serving member of staff at the school.

The bespectacled man with long black hair placed the tray on the coffee table then sat in the other armchair. He smiled at Chris, pointing at the plate of biscuits and nodding for him to take one. Chris leant over, took one and sat back. As he nibbled on his biscuit, Chris watched Hubert pour hot tea into both cups, and then milk from a small jug. He declined the offer of sugar cubes, finished his biscuit and picked up his cup and saucer, sipping just as Hubert did. Chris wondered what he would do now; just sit there, drink tea and say nothing all afternoon? He took another sip.

'Lovely tea, hmm?' With his free hand, Hubert slid his thumb across his chin and fingerspelled a "T" before gesturing drinking from a cup.

Chris spluttered. Had Hubert just signed? He wiped the wetness from his chin with the back of his hand, staring blankly at the gardener opposite. Hubert chuckled and sipped his tea.

'Yes, I can sign,' Hubert nodded, signing with his free hand. 'Not as well as you, but good enough.'

'But how?' Chris frowned at Hubert quizzically, pointing at the school through the window for reference. 'You ... you *never* sign!'

'No, no, no,' the gardener shook his head. 'Not there. *Here*, yes. You are my first.' He pointed down, referring to his house. 'I have learned very, very well, from watching you boys over the last thirty years.'

Chris sipped his tea, a smile growing on him.

'Trouble, eh?' Hubert nodded, slapping his hand and pointing at Chris.

Chris told Hubert what had happened in the maths lesson. Hubert shook his head; not out of disappointment, but in unsurprised acknowledgement. He leaned over for a biscuit, nibbled it and placed the half–eaten biscuit on his saucer.

'A bad teacher,' Hubert said, shaking his head. 'I do not like him.'

Nor do any of the boys, Chris thought. 'He's so cruel.'

'Cruel, yes,' he screwed his index finger against the side of his neck. 'Tell me more?'

Chris told Hubert all about Mr Schneider; his improper conduct during maths lessons; how he hated sign language and gave boys detentions all the time, even for signing outside lessons; how he forced some boys to speak – he sometimes stuck a small screwdriver, instead of a lollipop stick, into boys' mouths to make them utter a letter – and gave them detentions if they failed to satisfy him. He also told how the boys loved to dare each other: "Sign to Hitler Teacher or we'll fire you!" (Chris explained that *we'll fire you* was their way of saying with fingers pointing *we'll bully you*) and they always chose to sign to him. Worst of all though, from the boys' point of view, he was a rubbish maths teacher.

Hubert sighed, finished his tea and placed the cup and saucer back on the coffee table. He pointed at Chris' cup. 'More?' Chris nodded and finished off his tea. Hubert poured fresh hot tea into both cups and placed the teapot back on the table, gazing up at Chris. 'Do you ... know why?'

'Know why what?' Chris leaned over to pick up his cup and saucer and take another biscuit.

Hubert leaned back, cup of tea in hand. 'It is ... wrong. In my thirty years here, I have seen it all. Signing is good, but I have seen many boys ... punished. For talking with their hands, not their mouths. It is just wrong!'

'What do you mean?' Chris asked.

'Look,' Hubert waved his hand around the room, indicating the books. Chris looked around and then at him. 'I read a lot. Know a lot. I have been all over the world; I have collected books, visited libraries and old bookshops, you see? I know your history.'

'My history?' Chris shot a puzzled look at the gardener. Did he know about his past?

Hubert chuckled at his wrong choice of words. 'Deaf history, I mean. I have plenty of books here about your deaf history. It is wonderful ... very rich, yes. I have learned so much. Someone will write a big, fat book about it soon, take my word for it. That will open everyone's eyes. But me,' he tapped his head and winked. 'It is all in here.'

'But what has this got to do with Mr Schneider?' Chris queried, sipping his tea.

'Everything,' was Hubert's reply.

'I don't understand.' Chris shook his head, perplexed.

'You will,' Hubert said, waving his hand. 'Sit back and I will tell you. Sit back.'

Chris did as instructed; his head resting against the soft fabric of the chair's high back. He watched with great interest in what Hubert had to say.

'For centuries,' Hubert started to sign, 'it was believed that the deaf could not be educated or instructed in religion. In the 1750s,' Hubert went on, 'a hearing hearing priest in France, Charles–Michel Abbé de l'Epée, noticed two deaf girls communicating with each other using their own form of signs. These deaf two girls were once under the care of Father Vanin, who also taught them. Father Vanin passed away in 1759, leaving the two girls in loneliness and despair. He watched them carefully. After a short time, he learned their language and found that he could explain religious ideas to them.'

'I wish Mr Arkwright could do the same!' Chris joked, interrupting Hubert, who laughed, nodding in agreement.

Hubert continued by explaining that Abbé de l'Epée began to seek out other deaf children on the streets of Paris: many were poorly fed, lonely, uneducated and living roughly. He established a shelter for these deaf children. The number of children grew and In 1763, Abbé de l'Epée started a school for poor deaf children in Paris and almost immediately, he was overwhelmed with so many deaf children coming. Abbé de l'Epée soon came to the conclusion that teaching through sign language was proving to be effective. He developed a well–structured education system for deaf children, and invented new signs to show grammatical features of the French language, known as the French Method.

'It became sign language,' Hubert announced, 'like you use now. It is a bit different now, yes, but it started there. From this humble beginning, deaf students became educators of the deaf, writers and even professors. More followed, and became poets, lawyers, artists and politicians – all deaf. Education through sign language was considered normalover the next century.'

'What happened after that?' Chris asked, finishing his tea.

'I will come back to that later, yes,' Hubert nodded. He took a two pence coin from his pocket and showed it to Chris. 'Every coin has two sides.' He placed it on the table, heads up. 'Sign language.' He turned the coin over; tails. 'Oralism.'

Hubert explained how in 1770, a Swiss doctor called Johann Conrad Amman published a book called *The Speaking Deaf*, strongly stating that the oral method was the best approach. Samuel Heinicke, a teacher who was already developing his own oral approach in Germany, subscribed to Amman's ideas about the importance of speech and speech reading. Heinicke took in his first deaf pupil around 1754; his success in teaching this pupil was so great that he vowed to devote himself entirely to this work. He believed a spoken language to be indispensable to a proper education, and that it formed the basis for reasoning and intellectual thought. Heinicke's oral approach became so popular that it continued after his death; it became known as the German Method, or Oralism as it was known now.

'That's why Mr Schneider's always so proud of it,' Chris said, putting his cup and saucer back on the table and sitting back. 'He always goes on about how important it is to hear and speak. But I can't do either!'

'I know you cannot, but he cannot sign either,' Hubert said, pointing at the coin. 'Two different sides.'

Hubert then told Chris how Heinicke was not the only one who'd advocated oralism. 'Abbé de l'Epée had a French rival in Jacob Rodrigues Pereire, who often challenged his work. He developed secret methods in instructing the deaf orally. One time, Abbé de l'Epée invited Pereire to his school to prove that the deaf could be educated through sign; Abbé de l'Epée seemed to have made his point, but Pereire was to have the last laugh from his grave a century later.

That again, Chris thought, what did happen a century later?

'Patience,' Hubert raised his hand, sensing Chris' silent reaction. 'One more thing, okay?' He picked up the coin and fingered its rugged edge. 'If you cannot please one or the other, then why not both?'

Hubert noted the puzzled look on Chris' face. 'Thomas Braidwood opened Britain's first deaf school in 1760 in Edinburgh; this, and other early deaf schools that followed, used what was called the combined system: sign and speech. The deaf pupils who used this system excelled in their education and went on to achieve great things.'

Hubert suddenly went silent, resting his hands on his lap. Chris shuddered; the room had somehow suddenly become more cold and gloomy. Clutching the armrests, Chris waited for Hubert with bated breath.

'Then in 1880, everything changed,' the gardener finally said grimly. 'In 1878, in Paris, two French businessmen, Isaac and Eugene Pereire – they were Jacob's son and grandson – joined up with a French teacher, Marius Magnat. He was running a small oral school in Geneva, and they showed him Jacob's manuscripts, detailing his secret oral methods. You see, they were disillusioned by the supremacy of signs and the combined system and they wanted to swing the pendulum to oralism. Magnat was inspired by a number of different congresses that were happening in Paris, so along with two educators, Adolphe Franck and Leon Vaïsse, they converted to oralism. Vaïsse was ousted as the director of the Paris Institution for the Deaf because of his conversion. So, they all hastily organised the first so–called "international" Congress of Teachers of Deaf–Mutes in Paris that year, in an effort to swing the support round to their favoured method. That backfired because the combined system was still favoured, although they did win some support for oralism.

'Shortly after,' Hubert took a moment to think; 'a new organisation called the Pereire Society was formed and an organising committee was set up. This included influential French and Italian oralist advocates.' He raised his eyebrows. 'It was recommended that the second international congress should take place in Milan, Italy, because their two deaf schools had recently converted from the combined system to oralism, so it was an ideal venue.'

'Can I ask ... ?' Chris put his hand up. Hubert nodded for him to go ahead. 'Did they have, like, support from the education people or the government? I mean, did anyone like, pay for it?'

'No,' Hubert said bluntly. 'They did not. It was the rich who paid for it.'

'But,' Chris shook his head, confused, 'you said it was an international congress for the education of the deaf, so they *must* have been part of it.'

'No,' Hubert shook his head again. 'It was ... what's the word? Oh, yes, *unrepresentative*. You understand?'

Chris nodded, thankful for his better command of English. 'That means, like, they were only a small group who had nothing to do with the education system. Right?'

Hubert nodded. 'Now, let's see ... ' He put his index finger on his lip, thinking about something, then scanned the vast collection of books. 'Where did I put it?'

He rose and walked over to the shelves behind Chris, found the shelf he was looking for and slid his finger across the books' spines. He stopped at one, took it out, gave it to Chris and sat again.

Seeing he was holding an old hardback of average size, entitled *Report of the Proceedings of the International Congress on the Education of Deaf–Mutes, Milan, Italy, 6th–11th September 1880 by Mr A. Kinsey, Secretary for the English–speaking section,* Chris looked up at Hubert quizzically.

'I found it in a small downstairs library at a very small deaf organisation in Gower Street in London.' Hubert explained. 'It is very rare. Everything in it will ... make sense.'

'So, what happened?' Chris held up the book as a matter of reference. 'How did it change everything?'

Hubert sat up properly, rubbing his hands as he prepared to tell the story; Chris watched in anticipation.

'The congress took place at Regio Instituto Tecnico di Santa Marta,' – Hubert managed to fingerspell the name expertly – 'and about one hundred and sixty–four delegates attended. There were eighty–seven Italians, fifty–three French, eight British, five Americans, three Swedish, one Belgian, one German and I am not sure about the rest.'

'Only *one* German?' Chris queried. 'You said Germany invented the oral system.'

'Yes, it was odd, but these people were invited by the committee.'

'Were there any deaf ones?' Chris asked.

'Only two,' Hubert replied. 'Claudius Forestier from France and James Denison from America. The other two from America were the brothers Reverend Thomas and Edward Miner Gallaudet. They were hearing, but their mother was deaf and they grew up using sign language. Have you heard of Gallaudet College?' he asked Chris.

Chris shook his head.

'You should go there one day,' Hubert said with a smile; his manner making it obvious to Chris that he'd been. 'It is a big college. Signing everywhere! They have a good, big library. Edward Miner Gallaudet wrote about the congress too ... very interesting reading.'

Chris sat back and watched Hubert continue.

'The first day, which was, um, Monday the sixth of September, started with the introductions, the seating arrangements of the language–speaking groups, the reading of the week's programme and the eight resolutions. The next day, Tuesday, they jumped to the third item on the programme: methods of educating the deaf. Papers and debates on the sign, oral and combined systems dominated the whole day. Someone called Mrs St. John Ackers from England, who had a deaf daughter with her husband, Benjamin, gave a paper attacking signs. She said they were "mimic" and believed that the oral method was more successful for her daughter; she was fully convinced by the "immense superiority of the German System over all others". That was well received by most of the delegates present. Edward Miner Gallaudet defended the combined system in his paper, maintaining that signs were the natural language of the deaf. Mr Elliott, of Margate Asylum for the Deaf and Dumb, also here in Britain, supported that view ... his school used the combined system, which he thought was workable.

'But two other people, one who claimed to have had over twenty years' experience, responded by saying that the oral method helped the deaf to develop ideas, language and to express themselves in speech, which had "enormous gain" over sign. Reverend Thomas Gallaudet rebuffed that, though; he said he'd used sign language for fifty years and it was important for the deaf to be "lifted from ignorance to ideas". He accompanied his speech with sign, and signed the Lord's Prayer. He was booed and jeered.' Hubert waved his hand dismissively. 'They were not interested. Worse still, Abbate Balestra, a powerful Italian oralist – Milan was his idea – said signs were like pantomime. Told everyone to vote for oralism.'

'Vote?' Chris queried.

'Page nineteen,' Hubert pointed at the book. 'Resolution 1. Read it.'

Chris opened the book, flicked through and found the page. He read: *Considering the incontestable superiority of speech over signs in restoring the deaf–mute to society, and in giving him a more perfect knowledge of language, the Congress declares that the Oral method ought to be preferred to that of signs for the education and instruction of the deaf and dumb.*

'They voted 160 to 4 in favour,' Chris read out in sign and looked up at Hubert. 'What does that mean?'

'It means … they said the deaf must be taught orally, not in sign, in classes,' Hubert explained. 'Like at our school. The four who voted against were the Gallaudet brothers, Denison and Elliott. The rest … applauded!'

'That's not fair!' blurted Chris.

'No,' Hubert said grimly. 'Not fair. But worse came, sadly.' He continued; 'Wednesday's proceedings, which started in the afternoon, were, again, dominated by a series of attacks against sign language from everyone. They called for it to be abolished! They believed signs gave crude descriptions of objects and actions. It was also stated that sign language reversed the progress of language.

'Dr Peet, of New York School for the Deaf, disagreed, saying that sign language developed naturally in the deaf child and compared it to how an artist paints a picture to express himself visually. Abbate Balestra hit back, saying that signs formed only a crude language of mime and could *not* be developed into a proper language. Another, called Miss Hull, a teacher of the deaf, gave a paper venomously criticising the different deaf education systems, except for the pure oral method, saying she'd given up signs because they injured speech; she'd given up the combined system because it injured the voice and language, and she'd given up Manual Coded Speech because it reversed the process of nature and hindered ready command of speech. Her talk was interrupted several times by loud applause.'

Lost in his history lesson, Hubert went on to explain how Signor Fornari of Milan gave a talk, firstly saying that he had once favoured signs and that teachers needed to use them so that their pupils could understand them. However, he was concerned that once deaf pupils had learned signs, they could not be forgotten; he felt they seriously damaged spoken language development. So, he called for sign language to be abolished. Abbate Giulio Tarra, the congress president, concluded the day in a powerful address, saying that the pure oral method *must* be used and urging that the deaf pupil be taught to move his lips, not his hands. According to Abbate Tarra, the oral method was possible and the combined system impossible. It was illogical in turning a deaf baby into a speaking adult, because if one moved their hands, head and body at the same time as their lips, the pupil's attention would be distracted, he said. He strongly believed that the oral method was a wonderful instrument. His address was received with enthusiastic applause from most delegates.

'More tea?' Hubert offered, shaking the now empty teapot. Chris nodded and asked to go to the toilet.

Emerging from the little bathroom, after relieving himself, Chris looked across the small hallway at Hubert in the kitchen, back to him, busily brewing another pot of tea. He instinctively glanced over at what appeared to be a tiny room, two full–length dark blue curtains in its doorway. He assumed it was a broom cupboard or something, but then something caught his eye through the small opening between the curtains and he decided to have a look …

A short time later, when Chris and Hubert each had tea in their hands, Hubert resumed the story. 'The next morning began with further onslaughts against sign language, and Tarra followed up his address, repeating his support for the pure oral method and its "great advantage" over signs. He quoted one of the delegates: "When God gave a soul to man, He gave him the faculty to form ideas, and to express them He gave them speech". He added that he had taught through sign for many years but converted to the oral method because he was satisfied that the pupils at one of the Milan schools of which he was Director of understood religious ideas better orally than through signs, which he called "abstract and grossly material images". Speeches against signs and the combined system dominated the whole morning and again echoed the superiority of the pure oral method.

Many of those who gave speeches, Hubert said, had converted to the oral method from signs – he believed that, judging by what was written in the book, they had simply "jumped on the bandwagon like lemmings" even though they probably doubted the validity of the oral method.

The president then called for resolution number two.

Chris flicked through the book and found the page: *Considering that the simultaneous use of speech and signs has the disadvantage of injuring speech, lip–reading and precision of ideas, the Congress declares that the Pure Oral method ought to be preferred.*

'150 to 16 in favour,' Chris read out as he looked up at Hubert, dismayed. 'Does this mean that sign language was ... banned?'

'In schools, yes,' replied Hubert, grimly. He elaborately gestured a big *X*: 'Banned!'

'In the afternoon,' Hubert moved on, 'the delegates were invited to one of the two Milan schools for the deaf in order that they could show off their oral successes. It was said that most of the delegates were hoodwinked by their rather elaborate show, where the pupils were paraded, and answered questions asked *only* by the school's Italian teachers, who were also delegates. Elliott's request for an Italian stranger to read out a passage for the children to lipread and recite was rejected.' Hubert raised his eyebrows theatrically. 'Sometimes the pupils, even those who could speak, failed to understand a question, so a teacher would use elaborate mouth movements ... ' Hubert moved his mouth around as wide as he could and wriggled his tongue. '. . . to try to disguise their failure. It has also been said that information about the pupils' histories, how deaf they were, their speech and lipreading skills and intelligence would have helped the delegates to assess each pupil, but was deliberately withheld. And, well, the demonstrations did not convince some of the observers, even those favouring oralism. One said there was evidence of long preparations, involving intense drilling and personal management, to produce the most striking effect. It was also said that many of the pupils on show were not born deaf but became deaf later, having already mastered speech from an early age.'

'Like David Wheeley?' Chris interrupted.

'Yes, like David Wheeley,' Hubert replied. 'He was not born deaf?'

Chris shook his head. 'So it was a fake show then?'

Hubert nodded, leaning forward, resting his now empty cup on his lap. 'A *big fake*.' He smiled incredulously. 'The amusing thing was that it was so carefully rehearsed and so perfect that there were *no* mistakes, not one! Some of the pupils even correctly answered questions *before* they had been asked!'

Hubert continued, telling Chris how Denison, who was a deaf ASL user, saw some of the Italian pupils signing while they were waiting outside. They stopped abruptly when they saw the American watching them; when he asked them, in sign, if they had just signed, they shook their heads blankly. However, when he told them he was deaf and used sign, they pleaded guilty, with sorry smiles, as though they had eaten the forbidden fruit. Edward Miner Gallaudet also said he saw quite a number of signing deaf pupils hidden away.

The following evening, a lavish theatre show was thrown at the La Scala, with deaf pupils from the Milan schools performing in spoken Italian; the audience had copies of the script to help them follow the proceedings.

Chris and Hubert shared a chuckle as they remembered Andrew Brener's performance at the previous October's Open Day. Noting how Hubert had had to listen to many embarrassing readings by the boys at each Open Day, they both shuddered to even think about the pupils at the theatre.

Hubert followed on with the Friday of the congress, which began with an address on higher education from Edward Miner Gallaudet. He reiterated his view that the deaf would be better educated through sign and then talked about Gallaudet College, at which he was the first President. He said that most, if not all, of the deaf students there – who were educated through sign – graduated with excellence. He also said he wanted to see more special deaf schools and colleges in Europe. The rest of the day was dominated by discussions about higher education, governments' provision of deaf education, funding and some debates about sign and oralism. Resolution number three was passed unanimously, calling on governments to take responsibility for providing education for the deaf.

'That week,' Hubert rambled on, 'they had twenty–eight points to talk about, but they only talked about oralism versus sign. The last five resolutions were passed in a hurry on the Saturday morning, without even being discussed.' He gestured as if flipping paper. 'Resolution four was passed to create guidelines on instructing deaf pupils without sign language; resolution five called for the need for instructional books for teachers; resolution six wanted oral instruction to continue for the pupils after leaving school; resolution seven allowed the for an extended length of oral education with a maximum class size of ten; and finally, resolution eight was passed, agreeing to phase out pupils' use of sign language and to the segregation of signing and oral pupils if necessary.

'And then, they were all done!' Hubert exclaimed, though his expression was sombre rather than excited. 'There were other papers that were not delivered during the week, yet were accepted. Oh, that silly one by Dr Symes–Thompson; read it to me.' Hubert pointed at the book.

Chris found an extract and signed it; 'The deaf children who were taught to speak lived healthier lives than those of signing deaf children. The passage of air through the mouth which accompanies speech reduces the risk of epilepsy, odour from the ears and chilblains … what does that mean?' he asked Hubert.

'They are a kind of skin ulcer,' Hubert said. 'Blisters, itchiness and sores.'

'He's saying that signing gives you a bad rash!' Chris laughed at the absurdity.

Hubert rested his elbows on the armrests and used his hands to tell the final stage of the story. He told how the congress finished that afternoon with speeches from delegates exclaiming on the "incontestable superiority" of the pure oral method, "praising and congratulating" the congress and the "highly constructive" discussions on the best and most natural way of educating the deaf. Benjamin St. John Ackers gave a long, powerful and eloquent closing address about the universal supremacy of the pure oral method, finishing with the Italian words, "Viva la parole pura!"

'The pure word lives!' Hubert translated. 'And so, it began on … September the eleventh, 1880 … ' He stopped abruptly as though the room was suddenly turning dark and cold. Chris became momentarily still, feeling the same, although he couldn't be sure of it. 'That date … changed everything.'

Suddenly, Hubert bounced in his armchair, his hands shooting up wildly, as though they were a water geyser. Chris jumped back in fright. Methodically, Hubert thrust both hands at his young friend.

'A tidal wave! It swept all over Europe; here and the rest of the world!'

'What?' Chris leaned forward, shaking his head. 'What are you talking about? What tidal wave?'

'The tidal wave of oralism,' Hubert said calmly.

'But you said it was only a *small* congress that had nothing to do with the education system,' Chris queried. 'How could it become … so big?'

'What's that phrase?' Hubert tried to think, then raised a finger, remembering it. 'The creation of a thousand forests is in one acorn.'

'From little acorns mighty oaks do grow,' Chris said, remembering it from a number of quotes that Aaron liked to tease him with to test his understanding of their meanings.

'Yes, yes,' Hubert nodded.

Hubert concluded that the congress location, organising committee, schedule and demonstrations, membership and the officers of the meeting had been artfully orchestrated to produce the desired effect; a single aim was achieved.

'It was basically a quest for a vote,' Hubert summed up.

'Everything was fixed?' Chris leaned forward.

'Yes, it was,' Hubert nodded. 'They called it *The Treaty of Milan*. Many called it a victory, a few were angry at the fix. But still, it had a powerful impact. Then came the Dark Age … I have heard stories … Terrible stories.'

Counting off his fingers, Hubert outlined the devastating impact of the congress; deaf schools that used sign or combined systems quickly adopted the oral method; sign language in Britain was gradually forced underground as the oralist movement strengthened; hundreds of oral schools were set up while more and more signing deaf schools were forced to reform to the oral method or were closed down; Deaf teachers and professors were sacked from their jobs and replaced by hearing teachers who couldn't sign; class sizes were reduced to a maximum of ten per class, so that the pupils could lipread their teachers more closely; the cost of deaf education rose rapidly, due to the costs of the training and provision of hearing oralist teachers, post–school training for students and acoustic equipment. In some oral schools, deaf children who dared to sign were severely punished, and rewards were given to those who used speech; some even forced deaf children with poor sight (including those who were nearly blind) to lipread rather than using tactile methods of communication.

Hubert continued, explaining that the decline in deaf education was long and steady and reached its lowest point in the 1950s when Professor Alexander Ewing – no relation to the Ewing–Boyd Hill family, Hubert said – started a new training course for hearing teachers of the deaf at Manchester University. He taught them how to teach deaf children through the oral method using headphones and microphones. He and his wife Irene became a huge influence on oral education around Britain, and across the world.

'But they're rubbish!' Chris cried out. 'And painful to wear too.'

'Yes,' Hubert nodded. 'No use at all. It is very stupid. Your hearing aids do not help, do they?' he pointed at Chris' aids.

Chris shook his head, pointing at one. 'Most of the other boys say the same.'

'I know. I have been here since the school first opened,' Hubert pointed in the direction of the school outside. 'I have seen many different hearing aids of all shapes and sizes … they have never made much difference. They only work for a few deaf children, not all of them.'

Hubert raised a finger, remembering something else. 'Oh, yes, I must not forget that one. The Lewis Report!'

Despite the widespread availability of hearing aids, Hubert expanded, the government became concerned about the dropping standards in deaf education. So, in the mid–Sixties, it commissioned a committee – under the chairmanship of Professor Michael Lewis – to investigate if there was a role for fingerspelling in the education of the deaf. The Lewis report was based, rather carelessly, on the results of questionnaires sent to all the schools and PHUs in Britain.

'Mr Williams received that questionnaire; I remember seeing it on his desk one time when I was bringing in a plant,' Hubert said. 'When the report was published in 1968, I managed to get a copy for myself. It is here somewhere.' Hubert looked around the living room, wondering where it was, but shook his head. 'It does not matter. I have a good memory. The eight main points made in the report were,' Hubert counted on his fingers as he explained; 'One: sign language and oral/aural methods were conflicted. Two: oralism must be used. Three: there must be no return to silent education. Four: there were differing views over the timing of the return of signing. Five: signing should be used for multi–handicapped pupils. Six: there were conflicting views about signing for older deaf children. Seven:

there were differences in views about the combined system. And eight: they said sign language was non–linguistic. So, the Lewis committee decided to leave deaf education as it was.

'They just did … nothing!' Hubert said grimly. 'You continue to suffer, my boy. Another thing … have you seen an old film called *Mandy*?'

Chris shook his head. After when Hubert had explained briefly about the film he had seen at the cinema twenty–eight years back then caught it again on television and that how much he *hated* it because of its very pro–oralism message, he said, 'It was written by Professor Lewis' wife, Hilda, based on her own novel called *The Day Is Ours*. I do … wonder *why* the government wanted her husband to do this report!'

Chris shook his head in disbelief. All those years of being told to try to listen through his hearing aids and they *still* didn't understand they were of no benefit to him.

'But they are now starting to open their eyes,' Hubert said.

Some oral schools began to realise that their methods weren't working and started to introduce signing to support speech.

'A few schools started to use the Paget Gorman Sign System,' Hubert fingerspelled the name, noting Chris' puzzled look. 'I do not know much about it, but an Oxford–Brookes student teacher came here for a month just before you came … what was his name? Oh yes, Mr Ackmar. A lovely young man, he was. He could sign a bit. He showed me it. Very cumbersome; not the same as Signed English. You sign the same simple things in time with speech, but anything more often forces speech to slow down. It was the opposite of what the oralists said was needed for deaf children to benefit from their hearing aids. The poor boys here were so confused by it. Mr Ackmar ended up *training* them instead of educating them!'

Chris shook his head, sighing.

'There is a new system called Total Communication,' Hubert said before shaking his head. 'No, no, not new. It is very similar to the combined system, like how I am signing and speaking to you. You do understand me, yes?'

'Everything.'

'Good, good,' Hubert smiled broadly, pleased with himself. 'This improved things. Not just here, but also in other countries. Many schools there switched back to the combined system. Even two of the French key organisers of the congress, er, Adolphe Franck, who was responsible for the sign language–killing resolution number two, and Leon Vaïsse … later, they realised the failings of the pure oral method and publicly reverted back to their original views on the combined system. All too little, too late!' Hubert sat back, his face sorrowful. 'The oral method was too … uh, what is the word?'

'Deep rooted?' Chris pressed his right index finger hard against his left index finger to signify it.

'Fixed, yes,' Hubert nodded. 'Like glue.'

Chris reclined, his hands resting on his stomach, thinking about the story. He felt as if he had just woken up from a bad dream. Although he didn't fully understand some of the things that Hubert had talked about, he was now beginning to see it all, kind of like seeing a painting as a whole but not the details when viewed closer, and he could feel an anger growing inside him. All those terrible years he'd had growing up in care, being moved from one home to another and one oral school to another, not making himself understood and getting into trouble for it. And now, at this school, although he had become a much better and more mature boy, it was still tough not understanding why he couldn't understand his teachers. He'd believed it was his fault for being so stupid, but now knew for sure that he wasn't. Now, it was all clear to him.

'The oral teachers were wrong,' Chris said calmly. 'They were all wrong!'

'No,' Hubert leaned forward, rocking his head to and fro. 'Not wrong, really. They simply did not … understand. Some are good, some are bad, but they all believed in, um, a truth that was formed by too many lies.'

Chris sighed and looked at his watch; twenty to five now. He'd spent the whole afternoon with Hubert and missed four lessons. A detention for each miss, he mused to himself, but he didn't care about that. He stared at Hubert, who was now meditating. Chris knew he had to ask him about something that had been bothering him since the mid–afternoon recess. He gently waved at the gardener, causing him to break off from his deep reverie.

'You're Jewish, right?'

Behind the round spectacles, Hubert's eyes widened.

'I saw the Star of David in that little room behind the curtains,' Chris pointed in its direction. He knew its name from Mrs Munnings; she'd talked – signed – about the Holocaust a couple of weeks back. Hubert's room had a small table with two long candles on it, a Jewish skull cap, a Hebrew prayer book and few other things that Chris couldn't identify. 'I'm sorry I peeked into your little room, I couldn't help it.'

Hubert sighed wearily, knowing the game was up. He had never told anyone this. 'Yes, I am Jewish. A Hungarian Jew.'

Chris raised his eyebrows. The long standing rumour that Hubert came from Eastern Europe was finally confirmed. He was now even more curious, however.

'Why did you come here many years ago?' Chris asked. 'Do you have a family?'

'No family, no,' Hubert shook his head, his expression sombre. 'Only me left.'

'Only you left?'

'The Holocaust,' Hubert said with a sinking heart, 'you know what that is?'

Chris nodded silently.

'My family all died in the concentration camps. Only I survived. I moved around the camps – Strasshof in Hungary, Auschwitz and, lastly, Bergen Belsen.' He fingerspelled them all for Chris. 'For labouring work. I was a boy then; alive because I was a good gardener. The last camp, I stayed there until 1947 – two years after the war had ended. We did not know it was over. A few deaf Jews were there too. I came here two years later to escape from the bad memories. Every night, I would pray for my family. The pain inside me … it is too much. I like working here because I understand you deaf, how you feel and your deafness … it is peaceful, yes, a wonderful kind of peace for me. That's how I became so interested in your deaf history. I have learned a lot.' He tapped his forehead.

'I have a big memory. Not like a *normal* memory, but … whatever I see or read, it stays in there and I remember everything. You and I, we share the same things in life; history, community, language, identity and culture. Those who do not understand try to take these things away from us, but the more they try, the stronger we become.'

Chris was silent for a long moment, thinking about what Hubert had just said. He felt a strange sense of affinity with his new found friend. He also understood better why Mr Schneider was–

Then it hit him.

Chris stared hard at Hubert, studying him. No, it couldn't be, he thought, shaking his head; it was impossible. But the answer was right in front of him – it seemed logical. He hoped he was wrong, but there was no other explanation for the mystery now that he knew. He *had* to ask. He leaned forward, resting his elbows on his lap, and waved at Hubert.

'*You're* the Phantom … '

30

Matron's Truth

"I am, indeed, deeply thankful to think that there should be such a desire that this [Oral] system should be universal, and I hope and believe that such will be to a great extent the result of this Congress, throughout the countries of the civilised world. Let me conclude by saying Viva la parola!"
– BENJAMIN ST. JOHN ACKERS, giving his closing address at the Second International Congress of Teachers of Deaf–Mutes in Milan, 1880

Aaron sat, silently watching the commotion in the front hall. Boys scurried to and fro, some happy and excited that it was the end of the week and they had the weekend to look forward to. He glanced at his watch: just after quarter to five. He sighed to himself; it had had been a mixed day for him. One minute he was fine, the next he was moody. He still couldn't stop thinking about Chris, and about his own confused feelings and regret. He knew he needed to see Chris that night, but who would make the first move? He was told that Chris had been absent all afternoon after a bust up with Mr Schneider and wondered where he had been.

He watched Mr McShane hurrying towards the entrance doors from the lobby, a weekend bag in tow. He joined Mr Whittle and Miss Stephenson at the door; both had their own weekend bags. Aaron watched them exchange a few words before leaving together. Aaron thought they were probably going to Waltbridge railway station for the London train, and then heading their separate ways. Mr Bronte and Mr Norris had already left, for they had no late afternoon lessons. Aaron scented a sudden whiff of perfume; he looked over at Mrs Munnings who was walking through, looking radiant with a tidy black hairstyle, fresh red lipstick and freshly applied scent. She regarded Aaron as she trotted past carrying a large black leather weekend bag. Aaron watched her as she made for the entrance doors and walked down the short stone steps, towards a waiting Rover which was parked at the front, where Mr Langston and Mr Arkwright were waiting. Its boot was open; the large female teacher put her bag into it just as Mr Arkwright got into the back seat. Mrs Munnings went for the front passenger seat, then the headmaster slammed down the boot and got into the driver's side. A moment later, the car reversed to the right and then advanced towards the driveway. Aaron watched the car disappear from view through the glass in the doors.

Miss Hogarth walked up the steps, her attention directed at the departing car, waving farewell. She entered, wearing a dark brown overcoat and carrying a plastic carrier bag. She trotted through, passing Aaron, who watched her go into the lobby towards the grand staircase. He thought about her, and suddenly recalled seeing her and Miss Turner hugging and kissing passionately in the clothes store a few years back. He thought about that.

Aaron entered the matron's office. Miss Hogarth was starting to unbutton her overcoat while Miss Turner was finishing sewing a button on a boy's school shirt at the central work table. Both matrons acknowledged Aaron at the door.

'Hello Aaron,' greeted Miss Hogarth. She glanced at her watch. 'You should be at the dining room by now for tea.'

'Can I talk to you please?' Aaron asked the matron.

'Yes, of course you can,' she replied. 'What is it?'

Aaron glanced at the assistant matron, who was snapping away a thread from the button, finished with it. She looked at Aaron and took the hint.

'I'll go down to help with the tea,' Miss Turner rose to her feet, leaving the shirt on the table and headed towards the door. Aaron stepped aside to let her pass. Miss Hogarth motioned to two chairs propped up against the wall next to the clothes store. Aaron sat on the one closest to him while the matron sat on the other.

'What is it, Aaron?' Miss Hogarth asked.

Aaron hunched forward, his forearms resting on his lap, thinking. Finally, he turned to the matron. He signed slowly, knowing she only knew basic signs.

'What's it like … to be in love with her?' He pointed at the door, indicating the assistant matron.

'I beg your pardon?!' Miss Hogarth balked.

'I saw both of you in the clothes store when I was in Form One,' Aaron pointed at the door behind her. 'Kissing … and touching. The button, remember?' He pointed at his collar button.

Miss Hogarth's head slumped. She rested her hands on her lap, the back of her mind screaming *I knew it!* She quickly turned to the boy with a concerned look.

'Did you tell anyone?'

Aaron thought about that for a long moment, deciding whether to tell her the truth or not. He knew he would get into trouble either way, so he decided: 'No.' He shook his head.

The big matron stared down at the boy, wondering whether she could trust him. She recalled that particular evening when they were almost caught by him. She'd told Colleen that she was convinced he'd seen them in the clothes store, but she said he'd only got as far as tripping over the iron cord, which saved them. But shortly afterwards, the boys ... looked at her and Colleen in a strange way, smirking knowingly, in an unpleasant manner. It was as if they knew, but they said nothing, just dropped a few cheeky hints. Some boy drew a heart with an arrow through it, bearing their initials *EH* and *CT,* and pinned it to their office door. There was also a page torn from a pornographic magazine – presumably Andrew Brener's – which showed two young naked lesbians caressing each other; that was pinned to the clothes store door. Although the matrons were not amused by it, they couldn't help but chuckle at their names written on each of the beautiful woman, and considered it a compliment. They also both received Valentine's cards, tucked under their bedroom doors, the following February; both claimed they hadn't sent them. She was convinced that Aaron had seen them and told everyone, but she had no proof. She looked at him, sensing he was in some sort of distress and he wanted to talk about something, so decided to leave it at that.

'Why do you prefer women, not men?' Aaron broke the brief silence.

'I just do,' she replied honestly. 'I've always been like this, ever since I was a young girl.'

'Is it wrong?'

'No, I don't feel it's wrong. Not at all.' She paused, now understanding his line of questioning. 'Are you in love with a boy here?' she asked calmly.

Aaron cringed at that question. 'I don't know.' He shrugged. 'He says he loves me, but I don't ... feel the same way. I mean, I love him as my friend, but ... oh, I don't know!'

'Do you *feel* that you like boys, not girls?' Miss Hogarth levelled eyes with Aaron's. She was now beginning to understand it all. The boy was going through an adolescent phase like most of the boys she had seen during her sixteen years at the school, firstly as assistant matron, then as matron. It was all in their hormones; they tended to have mixed emotions that sometimes confused them about their sexuality, and eventually they grew out of it. Then again, though, some were already aware of their sexual orientation, as she had been when she was a young girl. Jacques Magnat, for one, she remembered, and Dwight Greenland too. But Aaron? She couldn't be sure – he didn't really look the type, but then again, no one ever did.

Aaron shook his head.

'Have you been caught together?' she asked.

Aaron nodded grimly. 'Mr Langston caught us, on Tuesday night in the cellar. But we didn't ... you know? I mean, I told him I didn't want to do it, but said I'd still think about it. So we just hugged, and that's when Mr Langston found us. We tried to tell him we didn't do anything, but he didn't believe us.'

'Who is he?'

Aaron shook his head: he didn't want to tell her now. Miss Hogarth sighed, thinking about it for a moment. She had already decided not to press for the identity of the other boy; it was not important right now. He had come to her to seek guidance and she would give him that.

'Were you caught too?' Aaron suddenly asked her.

Miss Hogarth looked into Aaron's blue eyes for a long moment. She saw the intelligence in him and wondered; would this boy understand what she could tell him? It was something she had never talked about except to Colleen. It was a painful, but long forgotten, memory. She decided she could trust him, in the hope of making him understand himself better.

'Yes, I was,' she said, finally. 'It was a long time ago.'

'What happened?'

'I was sixteen at the time,' she said. 'I don't suppose you've heard of the Magdalene Laundries?' She fingerspelled the name. Aaron shook his head. 'Not many people have. They're still around, but I don't think there are as many as there used to be. Anyway, they were all over Ireland, where I come from. They were institutions where what you call "fallen women" were sent.'

'Like who?' Aaron straightened up, folding his arms and becoming interested in the story.

'Like, you know,' the matron explained, 'women who had family problems, or perhaps misbehaved in society, or became pregnant before marriage or had mental problems. But some of them – or many, for all I know – were sent in for no real reason at all. That happened to me, unfortunately. There was this boy who tried to … force himself on me.'

'He tried to rape you?' Aaron said, his signing quiet.

Miss Hogarth nodded hard, her large glasses slipping down her small nose. She pushed them back with her finger. 'Yes, he tried to. But I fought back; I even crushed his balls, but I was accused of attacking him and they sent me to the convent in Waterford.'

'But that's not fair,' Aaron shook his head in disbelief. 'He tried to hurt you!'

'Aaron, in those days, women in Ireland *had* to be respectable,' the matron said. 'Those who were very beautiful were considered flirtatious, you know, like trying to woo boys for sex, but they weren't; they were simply beautiful by nature. But they were sent to the laundries anyway, to make them … less beautiful. Anyway, me and the other girls there had to do labouring work, mostly doing laundry for people.'

'Did you get paid?'

'No, nothing at all,' Miss Hogarth saw Aaron's shocked reaction. 'The laundry was run by the nuns. The conditions were terrible. We slept on hard beds, got up at five o'clock every morning, said long prayers, scrubbed floors, washed and sewed all day long. We were not allowed to speak to one another; if we did, we were severely punished.' The former Magdalene noted how Aaron was frowning at the irony. 'Yes, that's right, Aaron, it was a bit like how the deaf were punished for signing. Thank goodness Mr Langston allowed it here four years ago. Anyway, we were also beaten, had our clothes stripped off just for fun and other awful things were done to us that I don't want to talk about.'

'That's awful!' Aaron grimaced. 'Couldn't you get out?'

'It was like a prison,' she replied. 'Then one day, I met a young girl the same age as me,' Miss Hogarth went on. 'Her name was Isa. At first, we all thought she was backward ... ' She circled her index finger next to her temple. '. . . but she wasn't. She was deaf. She couldn't speak, but she could use some signs. I think because of her deafness, they thought Isa had mental problems. But when I got to know her after a while, I could see she wasn't backward at all. In fact, she was quite bright ... she was beautiful too. People just couldn't understand her, that's all. She had it worse than most of us at the laundry, though, because it was so easy for them to do terrible things to her. So, all us women stuck together to help her, but I was always the one closest to her. I learnt some signs from her, which helped her a little bit.'

'You couldn't speak, but you could sign?' Aaron asked wryly.

'Yes, something like that,' Miss Hogarth smiled sadly. 'It was a lovely, silent language. Other women learned it as well, so that we could get secret messages to each other by hand instead of whispering. Isa became part of the group. She and I became very close and realised that we were in love with each other. We sometimes kissed and cuddled in secret ... I knew what I felt, and I think she did too. A few of the other women knew too, but they kept it a secret. I promised her that when we got out, we'd go to England and start a new life there. She liked that idea very much. We eventually found a secret hiding place in the convent and sometimes at night, we'd go there for ... you know?' Aaron nodded, knowing what she meant. The matron fell silent for a long moment; the memory was painful.

She finally turned to him. 'After a few months, we got caught in that secret place. I think someone told them, I don't know. They took Isa away, to a mental institution, I was told. Oh, how we screamed and cried for each other as they dragged her away and held me back. My heart was shattered to pieces! It took me a very long time to get over that. I cried for her every day and night, but the worst thing of all was how they treated me like filth, for what I am. They called me names, spat on me, beat me even more than the others and made me work more too. After two years, I finally got out and took a boat from Waterford to Wales, and then travelled to England. I was a maid for a few people before getting the assistant matron's job here. Mrs Walton was the matron then, and then I became matron six years later when she retired.'

'Do you still think about Isa?' Aaron asked.

'All the time, yes,' she replied, her face sunken. 'I've no idea where she is now.'

'I'm sorry,' Aaron signed, rubbing his chest with his fist.

'Thank you, Aaron. Please don't tell anyone about this, okay?' she said.

'Okay,' Aaron nodded, crossing his heart. 'Mr Langston said it was wrong.'

'He has his own views,' the matron said. 'Of course, I don't agree, but we're all entitled to have our opinions, whether we agree with each other or not. He has a responsibility for every one of you boys here; you need to understand that. The important thing is that only he knows about you and that boy, and no one else. Because, if they find out, your life here will be very difficult ... like it is for Steven Clarke and Michael Hardcastle right now.'

'You know about them?'

'We're not blind,' she replied, pointing to herself and then the worktable in front of them. Aaron knew what she meant.

She sighed, glancing at her watch: just after five. 'Look, Aaron, whatever you're feeling right now, you must keep it within yourself. If you still like girls, then you'll be alright; just tell that boy how you feel and he'll understand. But if you *do* like him, then you both must be very careful. Don't let what happened to me happen to you. Alright?'

Aaron nodded, smiling for the first time since Tuesday. He felt as if a great weight had been lifted off his shoulders, relieved to have talked to someone about it.

Miss Hogarth gently brushed Aaron's blond hair before clasping both hands on her lap, smiling radiantly at him.

31

Storm in a Teacup

"The Oral Method benefits the few; the Combined System benefits all the deaf – anyone who upholds the oral method as an exclusive method is their enemy."
– REACTION FROM THE MILAN 1880 CONGRESS.

Rushing through the connecting corridor towards the dining room, Aaron saw something rather peculiar. He slowed his pace upon reaching the doorway and saw that everyone was standing up, their attention directed at the staff table, instead of sitting and eating their tea. Aaron looked over to see Mr Schneider, who was the only staff member present, holding something up. He squinted at it, recognising the wooden blackboard compass; one of its two legs was hanging limply. Aaron caught sight of David waving hurriedly at him from the Third Form table and briskly walked over to his usual chair, next to David's.

'What's going on?' he asked David.

'Someone broke it,' David pointed at the item the teacher was holding. 'He got everyone to stand up and won't let us eat until one of us owns up.'

Aaron looked around the room, guessing that no one had done so yet. He caught sight of Chris at his table, secretly feeling pleased that he was alright. He turned to Mr Schneider who was speaking again; he barely managed to lipread him from the distance.

'I say again,' the big man demanded, 'who did this?' He heard a muted response. 'No? Unless one of you comes forward, everyone will get detention.'

Mark secretly conveyed the threat to his form mates in sign; a general shaking of heads in protest ensued.

'He broke it himself!' Matthew said, his eyes directed at Chris.

Chris nodded; he and his form mates knew that, but none of them would put their hand up and say so, for fear of being mistaken for owning up; besides, they knew Mr Schneider wouldn't take the blame. Either he'd forgotten he'd broken it, or he was a nutter, Chris decided. He knew he had to tell Basher, but they weren't on good speaking – signing – terms at the moment. He discreetly glanced at Gary at the next table and quietly waved at him, keeping his hand low. Gary spotted him and nodded for him to go ahead.

'He did it himself,' Chris pointed at the staff table. 'This afternoon, he whacked it on my desk!'

He saw Gary's shocked, but silent, reaction. *What? Is this true?* he mouthed back. Chris nodded. He saw Gary turning to tell Basher, who was next to him. Basher, whose lower lip was cut and swollen, leaned back to glance at Chris, shaking his head in apparent disgust. Chris felt a discreet tap on his thigh, which was resting against the edge of the table; he turned to see Mark tapping him.

'He's going to count down from five and if no one owns up, we'll all get detention!' Mark conveyed.

Chris turned to the staff table to see that Mr Schneider had just put his other hand up, showing five fingers. Chris kept his eye on Mark, who was watching the teacher, conveying.

'OK, this is your last chance!' Mr Schneider bellowed. 'Five!' Then, he folded his thumb.

'Four!' David conveyed. Aaron glanced around his table at the worried faces of his form mates. He turned back to the teacher, who was folding his little finger.

'Three ... ' Toby mouthed to himself. His table was closest to the staff table and he could see the teacher clearly. He eyed his form mates anxiously, thinking to himself; he'd had more than enough detentions from that mad German in the last eight months – more than James had had in his entire five years here; he wasn't too pleased with his little brother. He saw the man folding his ring finger.

Hendrik looked around his Second Form table, wishing he could point at a form mate, to escape another detention, but he was too scared to do so in case he got the blame. He saw that the teacher was slowly folding his middle finger. *Oh come on*, he mused; someone put his bloody hand up now!

Mr Schneider held up his index finger for a long moment, challenging everyone. There was no response, so he began to fold it. He stopped midway, when his attention was suddenly directed to the other end of the room. Every head in the room whipped round to see who he was looking at.

Basher had his hand up.

He walked round the table and slowly crossed the room, walking towards the staff table. Everybody watched him, either with curiosity or in awe. He stopped in front of the rectangular table, facing the maths teacher, then turned round, raising his arm and pointing in the direction of the Fourth Form table. It didn't take long for Mr Schneider to figure out who the head boy was pointing at.

'Christopher Matthaus?' he said. 'I should have known.'

Mark whirled round to Chris, frantically waving at him. 'He's pointing at you!'

Chris shook his head violently, protesting. He left his table and marched up to them. 'You did it, not me!' he screamed in sign, pointing at the teacher. 'He's lying!'

'Double detention!' Mr Schneider screamed, putting up two fingers and shooting an imaginary trigger at the approaching boy.

'Bastard!' Chris swore at Basher, now even more incensed. 'I didn't do anything! Tell him the truth!'

Basher promptly stepped forward, stopping Chris. 'Shut up!' he snapped.

Anger erupted inside Chris; he threw a fist at Basher's chest, but Basher grabbed his arm at the second swing, restraining him. Soon enough, some of the prefects surrounded him. Gary's arm was wrapped round his neck, pulling him away, while another two prefects held his arms. Basher jerked his head in the direction of the door; Aaron watched in disbelief as the prefects dragged Chris towards the door and he disappeared from view. Some of the others stood guard in the doorway, keeping him out. Aaron looked at David, who was also dumbstruck.

'Thank you,' Mr Schneider said. 'Everyone may now sit and eat.'

Slowly, everybody sat, still stunned by the incident. Andrew angrily thumped on the table.

'That Hitler bastard did it!' he bemoaned, slamming the table again. 'We all saw him. Is his memory fucked or what?'

'Basher lied!' Matthew angrily pointed at the head boy behind him as he returned to his table.

'We have to tell Mr Langston!' Dean said.

'He won't believe us!' Sammy pointed out.

'We've got to do something!' Andrew declared, his loud voice reverberating. 'We all hate Mr Schneider. He's a mad German!'

'I've had twenty–seven detentions from him so far!' Sammy announced, trying to lighten things up a bit. 'Mostly for signing!'

'I've had thirty–one! Beat you. All for signing!' Andrew said back.

Steven warily thumped on the table and everyone turned to him. 'I've had an unlucky thirteen.'

'My total's ... fifteen, I think,' Dean joined in the count.

'I've only had two from him!' Mark boasted. Everybody groaned. 'Well, I *can* speak well, so it's been easy for me!'

'I've had ten,' Jamon Cranley added. 'And I was suspended for a week because of him!'

'He's the worst maths teacher ever!' Lester said. 'I've had seventeen detentions from him, by the way!'

'Twenty–one for me,' Matthew took his turn. "Some for trying to get to the blackboard because I couldn't bloody read his small handwriting!' He pointed at Lester. 'I agree with him.'

The last two gave their counts and all nine boys around the table nodded in agreement.

'So, what do we do?' Andrew looked at everyone; they all exchanged blank glances. Suddenly, a clatter on the table alerted them. They turned to see Steven sternly banging his empty plastic teacup against it.

'Shut up!' Dean tried to grab the cup from Steven, who was next to him, but he stubbornly held on it and continued banging, this time louder. If Chris was secretly supporting him, Steven thought, he should return the favour. Dean tried to grab it again, but Andrew stopped him.

'Come on, let's all do it!' Andrew encouraged everyone, now getting the idea. He grabbed his own teacup and banged it. 'Come on!'

They all picked up their teacups, some pouring their fresh hot tea back into the metal teapot in the centre of the decagonal table, while others either gulped down theirs or filled their saucers with it. Soon enough, all of the Fourth Formers were banging their teacups on the table.

Mr Schneider rose to his feet; his eyes directed at the clattering. He waved his hand. 'Be quiet, you lot! Stop that!'

The clattering continued.

The German giant stormed towards the table; the other boys stopped eating as they watched him. Soon, he presided over the unruly boys and tried, unsuccessfully, to grab Andrew's teacup.

'Stop it!' Mr Schneider screamed down at him.

'Or you'll give us detention?' Andrew signed, intentionally, at him. Elaborately, he held up his hands, expressing pretentious guilt. 'Oops, I signed to you!'

'Detention!'

'Oh, thank you! Thirty–two!' Andrew grabbed the man's huge hand and kissed it. Mr Schneider pulled his hand back, recoiled.

Suddenly, a new clattering sound echoed around the room. Mr Schneider whirled round to see that the entire First Form table had joined in the chorus, with Toby, the only one standing, banging his teacup and staring sternly at him. Then came another clattering sound, this time from the Second Form table. Hendrik was banging his teacup, along with the rest of his form mates, displaying the back of his middle finger at the maths teacher.

Aaron watched the commotion, his mouth wide open. He jumped when his table vibrated and saw that Derek was the first to bang his cup. Immediately, everybody around the table followed suit; Aaron saw Mr Schneider turning his attention to them. Finally, Aaron grabbed his own teacup, turned it over to spill the contents on the table and banged it.

The dinner ladies could only stand behind the counter and watch in horror while Miss Turner paced behind the counter, trying to figure out what to do.

Basher rose to his feet and marched to the centre of the dining room, waving at everyone to simmer down before joining the maths teacher.

'Stop it!' Basher waved everyone down again. 'Stop–'

He flinched as something struck his chest, then looked down to see a squishy boiled tomato dropping to the floor, leaving a red blob on his white shirt. He looked up to see who had thrown it and saw that Andrew was standing, poised.

'Lying bastard!' Andrew screamed at Basher.

Mr Schneider, now even more incensed, pushed Basher aside, screaming. *'Stop it! Detention for everyone!'*

Basher shot a look at the maths teacher, then tapped his arm and pointed at himself.

Mmmeee?

'Yes, you too!' he replied dementedly. *'Detention!'*

The room descended into a deathly silence. Feeling betrayed, Basher took one last look at the towering man. He coolly marched back towards his table, walked round it, sat and grabbed his teacup. He banged it, the brown liquid splashing out. The prefects quickly followed suit.

The entire dining room erupted into a thunderously deafening, clattering crescendo as each and every boy banged their teacup. Mr Schneider whirled round, his eardrums bursting.

Out! Ooouuut! Ou! Ooow! Out! Ooouuut! Ou! Ooow!

The teacher's head jolted around, squirming at the high–pitched chanting that followed. All of the boys' mouths were moving exaggeratedly, as if blowing at him, seeming to synchronise with the banging. Mr Schneider cupped his ears, trying to protect his ringing eardrums.

Miss Hogarth ran into the dining room, having heard the din from the corridor, and gasped at what she was seeing. *'What's going on?'* she yelled out above the noise. She saw Mr Schneider in the centre of the room, his hands on his ears, advancing towards the Fourth Form table. 'Heinrich!'

The maths teacher grabbed Sammy's wrist with his huge hand and tried to prise his teacup away, but Sammy stubbornly held on, shaking his hand violently to break free from the grip. He jumped to his feet, pushing his chair back, and wrestled with the big man as he tried to break free. Sammy spat a mouthful of saliva up at the teacher's face, distracting him for a second; the boy finally wriggled free.

'You fucking paddy!' Mr Schneider wiped the saliva from his face and promptly slapped Sammy in anger. Sammy screamed as he whirled aside, his legs giving away. He stumbled, his head hit the edge of the table and he yelped before hitting the floor hard.

The clattering quietened down once again. Mr Schneider quivered at the eerie silence, his heart pounding at the mass of silent staring eyes and his anger still escalating within.

Basher rose to his feet, chucking his teacup away. Despite knowing that he was disliked by everyone – not that he liked them either – he was not impressed by what the teacher had done to Sammy. Like the other boys, he hated the teacher. He'd had more detentions in the past eight months than he'd ever had in the four years previous – mostly for signing, both in and out of the classroom. This time, he said to himself, Mr Schneider has gone too far. He wanted him out. He stomped both of his feet and waved his hands. Each and every head turned to him.

'Come on, everybody out!' he commanded, pointing at the door. 'Move it!'

Almost immediately, all of the boys simultaneously rose to their feet. Chairs were pushed back or crashed to the floor, teacups flew towards the tables and the boys surged towards the door. Aaron hesitated for a second before joining his form mates. Andrew and Dean helped the dazed Sammy up to his feet. Matthew put his hand in Sammy's trouser pocket and took out a handkerchief, placing it in Sammy's hand, then guided it up to the gash on his forehead to stem the blood that was trickling down. Dean put Sammy's other arm round his shoulders and, with Andrew's support, helped him towards the door. Miss Hogarth stepped aside from the doorway, her back against the wall, as the boys swarmed through it like ants. Mr Schneider desperately tried to grab each passing boy, but they easily evaded him. He finally managed to catch hold of Ian's thick Afro hair and the black boy screamed in agony. He grabbed the teacher's big hand with both of his, trying to prise it away, but the grip was too firm. Suddenly, Mr Schneider screamed as something hot splashed onto his face, quickly releasing the boy. He wiped his stinging eyes and saw Jonah holding a teacup, the remaining liquid dripping from it. He tossed it aside, grabbed Ian's arm and pulled him away to join the exodus.

Chris stalked irritably through the wood panelled corridor towards the double doors, hands in his pockets. He had already decided to go to the library to read a book or something to help him calm down, swearing to save all his anger towards Basher for the football tomorrow. Suddenly, a jolt came from behind; he spun round to see the boys streaming through the corridor towards the library.

'Hitler Teacher's gone mad!' exclaimed Conor as he passed him.

'He hit Sammy Maguire!' said another.

Chris spotted Sammy amongst the oncoming horde, with Dean and Andrew helping him. Chris was shocked to see the state he was in. He pushed through the advancing bodies.

'Is he okay?' Chris asked Dean.

'He did that!' Dean pointed behind him; Chris knew who he meant.

'We're having a protest,' Andrew announced. 'We want him out!'

'Who–?' Chris stopped short when he saw Basher turning into the corridor, followed by the prefects, and said no more.

Once everyone was in the library, the double doors were slammed shut. On Basher's orders, every one of the twelve heavy oak chairs from around the central table and some black cushioned metal chairs were piled up against the doors, creating a mountainous barricade that almost reached the top of the high ceiling. A few lighter plastic chairs were added for good measure. The three large double framed windows were locked. Then, the long dark green curtains were drawn, blocking out the twilight outside. The chandeliers above flickered to life, bringing light to the room.

Basher climbed onto the table and waved at everyone, addressing them like a general giving his soldiers a pep talk, ready for battle. The boys gathered round.

'We all know that Mr Schneider is a bad and cruel teacher … ' the boys cheered in agreement. '. . . and we want him out! Am I right?'

A chorus of nodding heads and waving hands answered that.

Miss Hogarth and Miss Turner burst into the headmaster's office, heading for the desk. The matron took a piece of paper from the pocket of her brown attire, reading the phone number written on it, thankful that Mr Langston had given it to her in case of emergency. He told her that he trusted her more than he did Mr Schneider, although he had hoped it would not be necessary to call. She looked at her watch – quarter to six; she knew that Mr Langston, Mr Arkwright and Mrs Munnings would not have arrived at their hotel yet, but she had to try anyway. She picked up the receiver and dialled, reading the number as she did so.

Basher jumped from the table, pleased with himself. Chris pushed through the crowd towards him, angry.

'Why did you lie to Mr Schneider about me?' Chris demanded.

'I had to!' Basher replied bluntly. 'We all would have had detention!'

'What's your problem? You're leaving after your exams next month,' Chris pointed out. 'There's no need for this–'

'Shut up!' Basher snapped. 'I'm still the head boy, so fuck off!'

Chris backed away, knowing there was no point in arguing with that dimwit. He'd have nothing to do with Basher's plans, for fear of jeopardising his chances of becoming the next head boy; he was on a last warning from the headmaster, as it was. So, he decided to just sit back and hope that their self–enforced internment would end amicably.

Aaron watched Chris walk away from Basher, secretly pleased that his friend had stood up to that idiot. He decided now was the time to patch things up with him, so went over.

'Are you okay?' Aaron asked Chris.

'Yeah,' Chris replied, expressing surprise and delight at seeing Aaron. 'You?'

'I'm OK,' Aaron smiled back, his eyes meeting Chris' affectionately.

Chris sensed his best friend's composure and knew for sure that they were going to make up. He had already accepted that he and Aaron would never go beyond their close friendship. He still felt a strong bond towards him though, but accepted it could be nothing more. He had promised himself that he would never try to force Aaron into anything like what they'd done last Tuesday, as Aaron was not like him. There was only one question he really wanted to ask: 'Are ... we friends again?'

Aaron stared at Chris for a long moment, thinking. He almost said yes straight away, but hesitated. He wanted to tease him for a bit first, so that they could, perhaps, become even closer once they'd laughed off his answer.

'Maybe,' he replied, trying to sustain his growing smile.

Chris's smile disappeared, disappointed at the answer.

Aaron shook his head to tell him that he was only joking, but he was rudely interrupted by the stomping of feet behind Chris. Matthew, his head sticking through an opening in one of the three curtains, was stomping his feet and waving. He pulled his head away and pointed.

'He's here!' He swung back and pulled the curtains wide open.

Mr Schneider was standing outside on the ledge, his hands resting on the glass panes, peering through. His contorted features, silhouetted by the setting sun behind him, were the picture of demented aggression. His huge, thick lips sneered, baring his white teeth in an intimidating manner through the glass. His huge body almost covered two thirds of the locked windows.

Scores of boys rushed towards the window, thrusting their index fingers at him and shouting: *Out! Out! Out!* The maths teacher growled back, slamming the window with the palms of his hands; he said something to the boys, but they continued pointing and chanting. The curtains were drawn back again.

Miss Hogarth replaced the receiver, sighing inwardly, and turned to her assistant. 'They haven't arrived yet. The receptionist said it may be that they're stuck in the London traffic – it's Friday evening, after all. She'll tell Mr Langston as soon as he checks in and tell him to ring back immediately. I have to stay here for the call.'

Miss Turner turned towards the door. 'I'm going to see what's happening.'

Miss Hogarth watched her leave and closed the door behind her. She sat on the high–backed leather chair, cursing at the timing of the incident, though she couldn't blame the boys for aggravating Mr Schneider. He had it coming to him sooner or later, she thought; he had been a real bastard from what she'd gauged from some of the boys. She had no regard for him either.

Dear God; she glanced up at the ceiling as she prayed: let's hope no harm would come to the boys.

32

The Darkest Hour

"The problem is not that the (deaf) students do not hear. The problem is that the hearing world does not listen."
– Rev Jesse L. Jackson, an American civil rights activist (commenting on the *Deaf President Now!* campaign, 1988).

Sitting on the carpeted floor, Aaron glanced at his watch again: now almost quarter to nine. It'll be pitch dark outside, he thought, wondering why it was taking so long for anyone outside to do something about their self–imposed siege. The double doors had rattled twice in the last three hours; they knew Mr Schneider had tried to break in. The second time he did it, David and Gary heard what sounded like loud ramming on the other side of the doors; their mountain of chairs threatened to collapse, but held fast. Aaron also wondered whether Basher would do something to end it all, for there was no way any of the boys would be willing to stay cooped up in the library all night. Some, particularly the younger ones, were becoming restless, but Basher and the prefects – under the head boy's orders – told them to stay quiet and stay put. Some of the boys, including him, were forced to open one of the windows and urinate into the flowerbeds below it, while on the lookout for the mad teacher who might have been lurking outside.

He half laughed to himself as he recalled the joke he had told Duncan whilst they were at the window – he thought Hubert's flowers, which they were peeing on, might turn into triffids like the ones in that film, The Day of the Triffids, that they'd seen recently in their Saturday evening film show. He and Duncan chuckled at the memory of Mr Arkwright, who was on duty that evening, using a portable blackboard next to the screen to write the "subtitles" on. He also sometimes held a torch below his face so that he could convey the dialogue to the boys in spoken English, but they couldn't follow him anyway and joked that they were more terrified by the grotesqueness of his illuminated face than the triffids themselves. They both preferred Mr McShane's strategy; he could sign almost every line of dialogue and all of the boys could follow everything. Duncan finished peeing and told Aaron that he preferred the new subtitles, which had just started to be used in projected films, especially for the deaf. Aaron zipped up and told him that he still relished seeing Jaws with subtitles for the first time last March.

Aaron looked around the library. His stomach rumbled again. He was hungry and so were most of the others; they'd had to skip most of their tea because of what happened in the dining room. And they also missed the weekly Friday evening tuck shop, which Mr Schneider, as duty teacher, was supposed to coordinate. He'd just have to wait and see what happened.

He thought back to the last three hours – they had flown by so quickly; the boys had made the library into their playground. He watched Shaun sliding across the length of the polished oak table on his front, then coming off at the end and crashing down to the floor. Derek climbed on the other end of the table to take his turn, also lying on his front. Michael and Andy held his arms as they prepared to launch him forward, but Derek slammed Michael's hand away and told him he didn't want his poofy hands touching him. Michael reluctantly backed away and Bradley took his place; he and Andy pushed Derek and he slid, shrieking and whooping as he fast approached the other end. Aaron saw a queue had formed for this impromptu slide. He chuckled weakly as he saw Asif and Johan racing against each other as they climbed up some bookshelves. On his left, he saw three boys building a high–rise tower, using hardbacks as building blocks. Opposite him, Andrew was showing Ian a copy of the National Geogr*aphic* – from their delighted grins, Aaron knew it wasn't pictorial landscapes they were looking at. He glanced at Basher and some of the prefects playing poker on the floor in the other corner, observing that the others in the room were either signing to each other or reading books. He spotted Chris, who was busy chatting to some of his form mates, and chuckled at how Chris was talking again about the human–conducted electricity chain that Spook had masterminded a few months back. He'd made all of the boys, including Aaron, hold hands in a circular formation in the front hall. At one end, Spook touched a wall mounted timer switch, which was for the exterior lights in the front porch. There was a narrow gap around the unit's sides that seemed to emit an electric shock if one's other hand was touching the cast iron radiator next to it, which had given Spook the idea for his experiment. Basher stood at the other end of the human chain and put his free hand on the radiator. The conducted electricity swept from one boy in the human chain to another; each jumping with mild shock and giggles. Aaron brushed away the memory and saw Dean leaning over to Sammy.

'Are you okay?' Dean asked Sammy.

'I'm okay,' he replied, patting the cut on his forehead with his hankie. 'It's only a small cut.'

Suddenly, heads turned to the barricaded doors as the high piled chairs wobbled slightly. Some boys rushed over, pushing against the stack to steady it. A plastic chair tumbled to the side.

Timothy rose to his feet, pointing at the door. 'He's trying to push his way in again!'

On the other side of the doors, Miss Turner let go of the handles, cursing to herself. 'Shit! They're still barricaded in!' She had already reported this to Miss Hogarth over two and half hours ago, and was now becoming even more concerned. Miss Hogarth had rung the hotel again about an hour ago, but Mr Langston and company had still not arrived; she suspected the London traffic was at its worst.

She turned and shrieked, cupping her mouth with her hands. A partially shadowed figure had just appeared at the other end of the gloomily–lit corridor. His imposing form seemed to melt into the darkness around him, as though he was part of it. He stood there for a long moment, regarding the assistant matron. Miss Turner was frozen, staring at him wide eyed and quivering. Despite the distance between them and the dim light that surrounded them, she could see that his face was demented; grinning deliriously with his cold eyes sparkling in the darkness. Then, she saw something glistening. It was something long and silvery, partially concealed from view at his side.

'What are you doing, Heinrich?' Miss Turner finally spoke up, her voice trembling. 'What's that you're holding?'

He did not answer her, but gave her a quick nod instead and disappeared from view; Miss Turner knew he was heading for the emergency exit door. She hurried down the corridor in a state of fear and panic.

Chris glanced at Aaron who was sitting chatting with David and some of his other form mates at the far end of the library, wondering whether he should go over to them or not. He was still feeling a bit miffed by Aaron's assertion about them "maybe" being friends again. Was he joking, or did he want some more time? He returned his attention to the small group of seated boys, who were talking about Mr Arkwright.

' … and he waved his finger at me. He said, "You don't talk to me, I *talk* to you!" And I told him, "Sorry, but I don't understand you," and he couldn't understand what I said!' Lester said, laughing at his own joke.

Toby waved at the group, cutting in. 'My older brother, James, told me this really funny story about when he was here. He was Form Two, I think, and there was this physics teacher, before Miss Stephenson. What was his name … ?'

'Mr Kellen,' Carl said. 'He left before I came here. The one with the moustache who always waved his finger. I've heard he was a real mean bastard and he was impossible to understand – no one could lipread him at all.'

'Yeah, him. James said everyone in his Form, and others, failed both CSE and O Level Physics because of him. Anyway, he told James' Form that they had to use their voices, not their hands. He always said the same thing to everyone in almost every lesson. You know, James can speak well – he's the only one who can in my family, I dunno why – and he got really fed up with Mr Kellen saying the same bloody thing. So when Mr Kellen turned to write on the blackboard, James yelled "Fuck off!" … '

Playing the teacher himself, Toby raised his right hand as though writing on the blackboard, then froze and slowly turned. He then turned back to the group to continue; '. . . and he marched over to James and told him off and asked him why he'd said that. James replied that he'd been told to use his voice, not his hands, so he wanted to express his annoyance at the teacher for saying the same thing over and over again! Mr Kellen clammed up!'

The group laughed at this story.

'No one's perfect!' Carl commented. 'Remember that big science place last year?' Everyone nodded. 'Mr Arkwright and Miss Stephenson took us there. We were with hearing pupils from other schools and there was a man on the stage that talked about science stuff. I didn't understand a word!'

'Me neither!' Dean agreed. 'And we were sat at the front and Mr Arkwright thought, like, we could easily lipread him. But I couldn't!'

'I can easily lipread some people,' Timothy said. 'But I couldn't do that. So I fell asleep!'

'Me too!' Ian nodded, laughing.

'I got detention from him for talking!' Andrew grimaced. 'I was bored shitless.'

'Worst of all,' Steven joined in, wary of the reception he might get. He saw Chris nodding discreetly at him to go ahead. 'Miss Stephenson asked us to write what the man had said in prep!'

'And she was, like, confused.' Chris added. 'We couldn't write *anything*. Why do we have to go to that stupid place every year?'

'We're going there again in three weeks' time!' Sammy reminded the gathering. 'I'm going to pretend I'm poorly.'

'I tried that last year,' Timothy said. 'But Miss Turner put a thermometer in my mouth and said I was fine!'

Miss Hogarth was still staring at the telephone in front of her, twiddling her thumbs impatiently. She jumped in fright when Miss Turner stormed into the office, her hands all over the place.

'I think Heinrich's gone crazy!' she screamed. 'He's going to do something stupid!'

Miss Hogarth rose to her feet. 'What? What's happened–?'

The telephone rang.

Aaron looked at his watch again; this time it was five past nine. He watched David as he signed away to a small circle of boys.

'Mrs Bonnington told me to stop pretending to be deaf because I can talk very well!' David said.

'But you can hear!' Conor pointed out.

'I'm stone deaf in my right ear,' David replied, pointing at it, then flapping his hand carelessly at his left one. 'But this one … sometimes, I'm deaf as a post, sometimes I've got super hearing!'

'Like the Bionic Woman!' Shaun mimicked running in slow motion.

'She told me the same thing,' Mark joined in.

'Did you really have music lessons last year?' Conor enquired.

Aaron nodded.

Conor shook his head, shocked. 'But we're all deaf. Why do we need to learn music?'

David shrugged. 'It was Mr Arkwright's idea, I think–' Suddenly hearing a loud scraping noise, he turned, his left ear scanning. 'What's that noise?' The entire room was already noisy enough with a flurry of moving hands, squealing voices and some banging, but no one was doing anything that involved scraping.

He listened again; this time, the scraping was even louder. He quickly rose to his feet, waving at everyone to hush. The room fell into silence and the boys watched David, who was scanning his head around like a radar dish. The scraping was still going on. He turned to Gary, who was sitting next to Basher, knowing he was the only other boy who could hear as well. 'Listen!'

Gary joined David at the centre of the room, listening internally through his hearing aids. He heard it too. He was so used to hearing and deciphering a lifetime of different noises that he immediately recognised that particular sound. It was one of the most common – and annoying – things he tended to hear at school: the scraping and screeching that a wooden frame made when a window was pushed up or down. He gasped as he took in the three curtained windows on two adjoining walls. 'The windows!' he yelled, gesturing a rectangle and frantically pointing at each of them.

All eyes whizzed in different directions to the three windows, but which one?

Toby and Mark jumped to their feet, ran to the closest one and quickly pulled open the curtains, but were met by their own reflections in the black glass.

All attention turned to the next one; Hendrik and Jonah were already on it. They drew open the curtains: nothing there either.

Almost immediately, all heads swung to the third and final window, the solitary one on the wall adjacent to the barricaded doors. Warren and Richie cautiously approached the dark green curtains, which were now swaying slightly; the two First Form boys pulled them open. Warren jumped back in fright, arms outstretched, and crashed to the floor.

Mr Schneider had just hopped in, the lower window behind him open. The long forked iron bar that the German was holding had smashed one of the small panes at the bottom of the upper frame in; he had then put his hand through to unlock the latch. He stepped forward, taking care not to step on the shards of glass on the floor.

The boys began to huddle together, staring in shock and pointing fearfully at the unwelcome intruder. Mr Schneider saw their reactions and believed they were about to start panicking.

'Calm down!' the teacher commanded loudly, waving them down as he moved towards the centre of the large open space between the central table and the wall with the two windows. 'Stop this nonsense! Please calm down!'

'He's gone mad!' Johan screamed in sign.

'He's going to hit us with it!' added Andy, pointing at the iron bar.

Some of the younger boys began to scramble, shaking their heads and pointing at the danger, their expressions fearful.

Noting their fear, Dwight turned to Basher and Gary, 'Do something! He's frightening them!'

Gary saw that Timothy and two of the prefects were discreetly circling behind the maths teacher; he quickly decided to tell him to drop the bar, to prevent a potential affray and allow the protest to end amicably. As he scrambled through the crowd, waving at his three form mates to try and stop them, they lunged at their gargantuan target from behind. Timothy got the man into a headlock as he climbed on his back, while the other two held him on either side and attempted to floor him. Gary rushed forward, angry at being ignored by his friends.

'Mister, drop it!' Gary commanded, reaching out for the bar.

Mr Schneider whirled round as he tried to dislodge the weight around him, swinging the bar in an upright position, inadvertently forgetting that he was still holding it. It hit Gary's forehead hard, knocking the living daylights out of him. He screamed loudly as his head jolted, then flew, arms flailing, and tumbled towards the two cushioned metal chairs close by. His jaw struck the edge of one and his head jerked as he slipped between the chairs, pushing them apart. He crashed on the floor, then lay there, dazed, a gash on his forehead seeping with blood.

'He's flipped!' Chris said, to no one in particular.

Mr Schneider turned away from the dazed prefect, shocked at what he had just done, and saw the stunned, but accusing, eyes around him. Some were signing aggressively at him and, although it was incomprehensible to him, he could sense their fear and alarm.

'It was an accident!' he shouted as he tried to wrestle himself free from his three attackers. 'Get off me!'

One of the three prefects grabbed the iron bar and tried to twist it from the man's big hand, but he held onto it. The giant teacher wheeled round like a lion trying to throw off attacking hyenas. The boy who tried to take the bar lost his grip and flew backwards, hitting his back on the shelves. The other two held on, though; Timothy tried to grab the bar with his free hand, but it was well out of his reach. He wrapped the same arm around the man's forehead instead, while his other arm tightened around his neck and his legs locked around his waist. The teacher swung the bar over his own shoulder as he tried, again, to wrestle free, but the fork end of the bar struck Timothy below his right eye. He yelled in shock and pain, but still held on, even more determined to bring down the aggressor.

Chris turned to Basher, shoving him in the chest. 'You're the fucking head boy! You brought us here! Do something, coward!'

'I'm not a coward!' Basher snapped back, pushing Chris away. He surveyed the frozen semicircle of boys and then the scuffle, trying to decide whether to help his comrades or not. Finally, he pushed his way through the frightened boys and lunged at the man, but despite his beefiness, instead of forcing the teacher to stumble backwards, Basher comically bounced back like a ball upon impact and crashed to the floor with a loud thud. Some boys chortled, amused by the comic relief amid the escalating tension.

Chris advanced through the increasingly restless boys, shaking his head in disappointment at his adversary, and began to lunge at the teacher, aiming his outstretched right foot at his stomach. Aaron stepped forward, agape, as he watched Chris advance towards the still fighting man, briefly glimpsing the wall clock at the same time. The big hand had just reached eleven past.

The whole library suddenly plunged into darkness.

Miss Hogarth and Miss Turner gasped in fright, stopping dead on their feet as they looked up at the now black high ceiling of the front hall. They looked around in the pitch–black darkness; all lights and power had gone. Miss Hogarth turned to look through the glass of the entrance doors; there was nothing but impenetrable blackness.

'It must be a power cut!' She heard her assistant say. 'Stay here. I'll go and get us torches.'

Chris had already stopped a few feet away from his target. He wheeled round, but all he could see was dark figures scampering around; he knew that the boys were now in a state of hysteria and that they had to get out. He felt a bump on his left and squinted to see who it was, but it was difficult to identify him. He squinted again in the faint silvery light that was coming from the open window and saw the white plaster on his nose. Andrew.

'Get them out!' Chris commanded his friend, pointing at the barricaded doors. Andrew hesitated; he could barely see Chris' signing in the dark. Chris pulled him in the direction of the doors to give him the message.

He felt Andrew whisk by him towards the large table and hoped he had got the message. He thought he saw that some dark forms had already reached the mountain of chairs at the doors, but he couldn't be sure. Andrew slid across the table towards the barricade.

David was dead on his feet, his body on auto–pilot, reaching out wildly with his hands. He could see nothing. He tried to grab someone; anyone; to help guide him, but he was being jostled by those running around him. He called out to Aaron for help as he always had done, but knew shouting was pointless. Suddenly, a body crashed against him and they both stumbled to the floor. His glasses flew off. Lying flat on his back, David heaved the lean body away from the wrangle, but he couldn't see who it was. He scrambled around on the floor on his hands and knees, searching for his glasses.

Mr Schneider swung the bar round as he tried to prise off a final fifth form boy who had climbed on his back shortly after he'd finally thrown Timothy off, instead viciously hitting a passing boy with the bar; he screamed in agony and the teacher heard him fall to the floor. He was becoming increasingly aggravated by what was happening around him, and discarded the bar, belatedly realising it was becoming a danger to everyone.

Toby got up onto his knees, clutching the back of his throbbing head and feeling the bump that was now growing. He howled in agony. Looking up, through the dark he could see the moving form of Mr Schneider. From his point of view, he was huge: the tallest in the school; Toby was the shortest and barely came to the man's waist. He shot to his feet, enraged, and threw a revenge punch directly at the man's stomach, as hard as he could.

Mr Schneider arched forward, feeling the sudden sharp blow, bringing the still clinging boy on his back with him. In a blind rage, he threw a fist in response to whoever it was in front of him.

Despite the darkness, Toby saw it coming; although he knew the fist would fly over his head by a foot or two, he still ducked out of instinct. His eyes wildly followed the thrusting hand above him; he felt someone next to him jolt and fall limply on top of him. Toby couldn't see who it was, although he knew it was a senior, judging by his size and weight. He held the stunned boy up with all his strength, wrapped his arm around his waist and ferried him away from the danger. He briefly glanced back and thought he saw what he now perceived as a monster haul the other prefect from his back and throw him to the floor with a loud thud.

'Stop this madness!' Mr Schneider screamed out, angry with himself for making the situation so much worse. He cursed how the boys had misunderstood his original intent to get the situation under control. He heard a kind of rumbling, then clattering and crashing, and swung to the source, his eyes searching the black void. He could half–see a huge abstract mountain against the wall that seemed to be tearing itself apart. He realised what was about to happen. '*Watch out!*' he screamed.

The topmost heavy wooden chairs tumbled down, along with some of the plastic and cushioned metal chairs, which bounced down the makeshift hill and fell hard onto some of the boys. The deafening series of crashes from the stack rocked the whole library. A couple of chairs landed on the oak table, while others crashed or bounced around the floor. Shouts and screams penetrated the blackness, then sounds of panic and the hurried pattering of feet echoed. Bradley screamed as the top end of the heavy chair struck his head, sending him down. Andrew stumbled backwards to the ground, crashing onto a couple of boys behind him, their arms and legs tangled. He groaned when one of the cushioned metal chairs crashed on his stomach. Sammy quickly tumbled forward and lifted one of the heavy chairs from on top of the fallen Jamon, who was clutching his chest in agony. Aaron picked himself up, after having narrowly escaped the avalanche; he could make out that a boy was pinned underneath a couple of heavy chairs. He went over and pulled one away while Ian took the other. Aaron quickly bent to pull the boy away and he felt him sobbing loudly; his left hand pointing at his right arm. Touching his hair and feeling that it was curly and rigid, Aaron recognised him as Conor. He and Ian carefully helped him up, then he suddenly remembered David and knew that he needed help in the dark. He turned and tried to find him against the dark figures that were scrambling in his direction, but he couldn't see him. Some boys had hopped onto the table while others went round or crawled under it. He also spotted some boys jumping through the open window.

David crawled, his hands combing the carpet. Something – or someone – hit his side and he stumbled, but quickly got back on his knees and continued the desperate search for his lost glasses.

Matthew desperately tried to move around, his hands reaching out wildly. All he could see were fast moving, dark abstract shapes that seemed to form part of the darkness. He felt alone and frightened. He thought he saw a menacing, imposing shape in the centre. Was it moving towards him? Or was he wrong?

He couldn't tell. He cursed himself for having absolutely no sense of visual perception in the dark; he felt completely disconnected, like a broken light bulb. Something suddenly grabbed the front of his shirt and he shrieked in fright. He grabbed it with both hands; it was a huge hand, so it must be Mr Schneider; he felt vibrations flowing through his violently shaking hand. He tried to wrestle himself free, screaming out at his apparent attacker.

'Ge–t off meee!' Matthew shouted.

'Matthew! Tell them to stop!' Mr Schneider called out, but he knew it was meaningless, for the boy had some form of night blindness. He was desperate for someone who could sign, so that he could get the atrocity under control, but so far, he was getting nowhere.

In the dark, Dean vaguely saw that the monstrous shape was attacking someone. He squinted harder and could almost make out the shape of a boy. Was that Matthew? *Oh shit, Matthew!* He yelled silently, kicking himself for forgetting about him, knowing about his night blindness. He grabbed one of the fallen cushioned metal chairs and swung it onto the big man's back with all his might.

Matthew felt a sudden thud and a scream from the man. The big hand pushed him away. He lost his balance and fell backwards, hitting the back of his head hard against the wall. Feeling a thunderous crash at his feet, he knew immediately that Mr Schneider had been struck down. The next thing Matthew knew was a hand grabbing his left arm; he resisted it at first, but then a hand slid quickly under Matthew's and guided it to sign a name sign: *rich*. Matthew instinctively touched the boy's head with his other hand, feeling his medium length hair; it was Dean. Dean pulled him up and grabbed his arm. Another hand suddenly grabbed Matthew's other arm; he fumbled to feel the boy's small face. Was that Nicolo? Yes, it was him! Like Matthew, the Italian boy had night blindness. Matthew could feel the boy trembling: he was scared stiff. He grabbed the lapel of Nicolo's blazer as Dean pulled both of them towards the doors.

Mr Schneider slowly rose to his feet, then wheeled round, clawing like an enraged monster. He stomped towards his prey, demented. Some of the boys at the back of the panicky, pushing crowd had already seen the ominous dark shape coming towards them from the other side of the table. They shoved the crowd forward, frightened, in an effort to hurry the others up. Someone thudded against Mr Schneider, attempting to stop him, but Mr Schneider thrust the palm of his hand hard into the lad's face and pushed him out of the way, no longer feeling any remorse: he was too far gone.

Basher thudded to the floor hard. He was trying to get to the boy who was crawling on the floor a few feet away; he couldn't be sure who it was, but he wanted to help him. But, that monster was standing between them. He glanced under the table, seeing dimly that several legs were finally moving towards the double doors.

Chris threw aside the last chair that was securely propped up against the handles and someone yanked them. The doors swung open.

Miss Hogarth and Miss Turner hurried down the corridor towards the library doors, their bright torch beams wavering wildly. They both gasped when the doors burst open and directed their beams straight ahead. The boys spilled through the doorway, like a pack of huge frightened rats, running away from an inferno.

As the river of boys flowed past the matrons, jostling them as they ran past, Miss Hogarth directed her torch at some of them, making out snatches of their feverish signing.

' ... Mr Schneider's gone mad ... '

' ... hurt us ... '

' ... hit everyone with the bar ... '

' ... thumped me ... '

' ... fought with us ... '

Miss Hogarth swung her circle of light from one boy to another as they passed, noting their excited and terrified faces. Bradley came into view, his nose bleeding heavily, followed by a limping Timothy who was nursing a badly cut eye. The second circle of light shone on Dwight and Tom, who were carrying a semi–conscious Gary over their shoulders, his head slumped, blood flowing from his forehead, his white shirt heavily stained. The matron's torch shone on Conor, who was sobbing loudly, his right arm resting on his chest, held there by his other hand. Rowan and Ian were helping him along. She noticed that Conor's arm looked awkward and caught him mouthing *Broken!*

Her assistant's circle of light moved to Dean, who was leading Matthew and Nicolo through, as if he were a train engine pulling two carriages. Matthew raised his hand, shielding his eyes from the hard light while Nicolo turned his head away from it. Miss Hogarth shone her torch on Toby, who was helping a bigger boy who was wobbly on his feet; she tilted the torch up to see that it was Carl, sporting a huge bruise on his left cheek.

Aaron scanned the fleeing boys, now that he could see slightly better in the light from the two moving torches. He couldn't find David amongst them; he must still be in the library, he thought. He turned back into the darkened hell. Chris instinctively yelled after him, then cursed himself for it and ran after him.

David had finally found his glasses; they were bent, but wearable. He rubbed both lenses to check them and discovered a crack on one of them. He put the glasses on, pushing the lopsided frames behind his ears. Suddenly, a hand grabbed his shirt and he was yanked up like a rag doll. David immediately knew it was the mad teacher; he heard him growl something at him, but was too frightened to listen.

'David,' the raging maths teacher roared, 'you've got to–'

David sent out a shrill, high–pitched scream.

The scream echoed through the corridor. Both Miss Hogarth and Miss Turner gasped loudly at it, swinging their torch beams into the darkness beyond the open doorway.

'Oh, my God!' Miss Hogarth shrieked. She turned to her assistant. 'Call the police!'

The beam from the assistant's torch took a 180–degree turn. Miss Hogarth heard her running away, with several other pairs of pattering feet behind her. She headed towards the library.

Helped by the torchlight that was coming from the corridor, Aaron was able to spot the iron bar on the floor. He picked it up, turned and advanced towards the huge shape, wielding the bar. He wanted to rescue his friend. Chris jumped onto the oak table to get across and saw that Mr Schneider was still holding the screaming David. He could only watch in disbelief as Aaron swung the bar at the man's back.

'Stop screaming!' the teacher shook David violently in an effort to make him stop, but it was in vain. Suddenly, he felt a hard whack on the top of his back. He exclaimed loudly, releasing David, and whirled round to see Aaron holding the bar. Enraged, he pounced at Aaron, grabbing him by the neck with his colossal right hand and snatching the bar with the other. Aaron released his grip on the bar and grabbed the teacher's strangling hand with both of his hands. He choked as he felt his neck being squeezed.

Everything seemed to move in slow motion. Chris darted across the width of the table, sprang and flew high towards his huge target. Mr Schneider turned to his right, having just heard something and, for the briefest of moments, saw a flying figure chillingly silhouetted against the bright, wavering torchlight from behind. Chris's left leg rose, the base of his foot directed at the man's face, while his other leg struck the side of his upper body. The sudden double blow sent the maths teacher screaming, twisting and flying back, releasing his grip on both Aaron and the bar, his outstretched arms swinging wildly. He spun once, his legs giving way, and tumbled towards the floor. Aaron sagged back, almost losing his own balance and gasping for breath. David stumbled away from the dark falling figure. The ground shook thunderously as the German crashed to it awkwardly. Chris somersaulted sideways, his arms waving aimlessly, then crash–landed on the soft floor and rolled over once to cushion his fall.

Chris quickly picked himself up and grabbed the iron bar to move it away from the fallen giant.

A bright circle of light suddenly shone onto him and he impulsively raised his hand, the iron bar in it, to shield his eyes from the blinding light. The torchlight wobbled, then swerved round and the beam shone up under Miss Hogarth's frumpy face so that Chris could see her, the upward beam giving her a chillingly grotesque look.

'Put it down, Christopher!' she ordered, pointing at the bar. 'Now!'

Chris threw away the bar; he was going to do that anyway. The beam of light then panned to Mr Schneider, who still lay dazed on the floor, and then moved to Aaron and David, who both blinked in the harsh light. She heard a rustling sound in another part of the room and moved the beam to the source. Basher suddenly popped up into view.

Aaron still couldn't believe that what had happened in the library had only lasted a matter of minutes; it had felt much longer. He watched as two police officers led a handcuffed Mr Schneider, his head bowed in shame, towards a waiting police car, its solitary domed blue light flashing atop. Aaron glanced around the commotion–filled car park; there were three ambulances, four police cars and a couple of cars that he assumed belonged to the detectives. The array of flashing blue lights and headlights were the only source of light outside the still–darkened school. Most of the boys had converged to one side of the car park, watching the proceedings with excited interest. Through the back door of one of the ambulances, Aaron saw Gary being tended to by one of the paramedics; he knew Gary would have to go to hospital, as the cut on his forehead looked really bad. Bradley was sitting opposite him, pressing a swab on his potentially broken nose. Other boys with minor injuries were in the other ambulances. One had already taken Conor and Mrs Munnings to hospital, as Conor had a broken right forearm. One of the paramedics had checked Aaron's neck, but declared there was no serious damage. It still ached a bit, though.

Mr Schneider got into the back seat of the police car, helped by one of the officers while the other walked round to the driver's seat. They drove off, the car's blue light still flashing.

Mr Langston watched the car go as he walked towards to a plain clothes detective sergeant, whose name he had already forgotten. 'I'll find out what happened.'

'Of course, sir,' the detective said. 'We will be informing the authorities about this though.'

'I'm aware of that,' Mr Langston nodded, knowing what he meant. He sighed and looked at darkened school as he reflected back on the evening's events. The London traffic had been nothing but a complete nightmare; he regretted having insisted on driving to the hotel on the other side of the city instead of taking the train. He, Mrs Munnings and Mr Arkwright had had to stop somewhere for a bite to eat, knowing it would be too late to have supper once they arrived at the hotel. When they got there, the receptionist told him he had to call the school urgently and he was dumbstruck when Miss Hogarth told him what was happening. He and Mrs Munnings immediately returned to school, first taking the underground and then the train to Waltbridge, which only took them an hour. Mr Arkwright was to tell the conference organisers of their withdrawal and drive his car back the next morning. The police and ambulances were already there when they arrived. He'd been upset and totally speechless when he was told what had happened and seen some of the injured boys. According to the police, they'd found Mr Schneider cowering on the library floor, crying. He didn't resist arrest. They described the library as a "battle zone". It wouldn't just be the authorities who would have to be informed, as the detective had warned, but also the boys' parents – some were already oversensitive as it was – and the governors, who would be demanding answers. The media, too; they would have a field day with this, particularly with the boys being deaf. He almost could see the elaborate descriptions of the incident, coupled with the tragedy of the boys' deafness. What a good excuse for them to conjure up some misconceptions and misinterpretations of what happened. Lurid headlines flashed into his mind and he quickly shook them away. He promised himself that if – a big if – any journalists wanted a story, he would make sure he was the one to give the official version, no one else. He'd tell them not to use the term 'dumb', which he felt was quite offensive, although he knew they'd ignore his request anyway – negativity sells. He was also worried that local education authorities around the country, which were always reluctant to fund deaf children's places at specialist schools, might decide not to send any more boys to Ewing Hill Park, thus threatening it with closure. So, he had to get answers fast, he told himself.

Suddenly the lights inside the building and the external porch light burst into life, illuminating the car park. The boys cheered and whooped at the welcome return of electricity. The headmaster glanced at his watch: eleven minutes past ten. He turned to the gathered boys.

'Everybody, go to bed!' he waved them on, pointing up at the top two floors. 'Go on, now! Move it!' The boys obeyed and streamed towards the entrance doors. Mr Langston then waved at Basher, stopping him from following the others. He turned to face the headmaster. 'Brian, my office, *now*.'

Basher nodded obediently. As the headmaster matched past him, expecting him to follow, Basher glanced at Chris, who was heading towards the school with everyone else.

He grinned.

33

The Rise and Fall of Christopher Matthaus

"After being wrongly diagnosed as a schizophrenic he spent 46 years incarcerated in Britain's mental health system – longer, longer than the Guildford Four (a mere 14 years) and Birmingham Six (17 years) rolled into one."

– LUKE HARDING and DAVID BRINDL; *46 Years Locked Up For Being Deaf,* in *The Guardian,* 1998 (on the case of Leslie Brown, a deaf man who was sent to a mental hospital in 1950 for arguing with a work colleague).

It was a strange morning for everyone.

The boys carried on with their usual morning routine, as if nothing had happened the previous night, although there was only one topic of conversation to start off their day with. They all talked about what happened in the library. Some commented that it was terrible, while some others thought it had been good fun. They also told each other their own versions; some accurate and some elaborated; and they were all united in their belief that Mr Schneider had gone berserk and had hurt some of the boys on purpose. They hoped he would never return.

The boys were told to skip their hour of morning prep; instead, they played their Saturday morning football on the two front pitches earlier than usual. After almost two hours, they then showered and dressed in their school wear (they could change into their own clothes that afternoon if they wished to). They had an hour and a half to spare before lunch.

Chris strolled into the front hall, looking for Aaron; he hadn't talked to him since they were in the library. Aaron's last words to him was still echoing inside his head – he would "maybe" be friends with him again – and he really wanted to get it cleared up. Besides, he thought, they'd helped each other to bring down the maths teacher, so they must still be friends. Once that was out of the way, he would ask Aaron to go into town with him after lunch, for a quick bit of shopping to buy stuff like Shandy Bass cans, some crisps and his favourite weekly *Match* magazine, which would have a preview of the afternoon's cup final. He was really looking forward to the match, though he wasn't sure if he and Basher would get into a fight after what had happened last night; he believed the boys had seen enough violence for now, so promised himself that he would not start anything. If Basher wanted a fight, that idiot would have to make the first move.

His thoughts were interrupted by a hand waving in the corner of his eye; he turned to see Mr Langston waving at him.

'Christopher,' the headmaster said, 'please come with me.'

Chris sat in front of the headmaster's desk, surprised to see Miss Hogarth already sitting next to Mr Langston. The headmaster closed the door, went over to his seat and sat down. He rustled some papers that were in front of him. Chris noticed that they were mostly scribbled notes, but he couldn't read them, as they were upside down to him. Mr Langston looked solemnly at the boy opposite him for a short moment then pointed at the matron.

'Christopher,' he began, 'I've asked Miss Hogarth to be here to help us understand each other. I know you can lipread me well, but I want to understand you.' He pointed at the scribbled notes on his desk and waved his hand at them. He'd had enough of that for now and had decided to ask Miss Hogarth to help facilitate communication; she was the only staff member present who could understand sign language. She had pointed out that she only knew basic signs, but that was good enough for him. Mr McShane had called earlier that morning and was surprised to find that the headmaster was still at the school instead of at the teachers of the deaf conference. Mr McShane said his mother was very ill in hospital and would be spending some time there, so had requested a week off work, which the headmaster granted. He decided not to tell Mr McShane about what had happened for now. Mrs Munnings was still at the hospital, looking after Gary Portmore, who had spent the night there under observation as he had bad concussion; he was due to be discharged in the early afternoon, along with Conor Blackwell. Both Mrs Munnings and Gary Portmore would have been useful in helping with communication, but he'd have to make do with Miss Hogarth for now. The police were still keeping Mr Schneider in custody and wanted some more information from the boys as soon as possible, so that they could question him then either charge or release him on bail pending further investigation.

'I don't want you to write things down. I want you to talk to me with your hands. She will tell me what you're signing. Do you understand?'

'Yes, I understand.' Chris slid his index finger across his forehead.

'He says he understands,' Miss Hogarth conveyed.

'Good,' Mr Langston nodded. He leaned forward, placing his clasped hands on the desk. 'Christopher, um, from what I've been told, it seems you started the trouble yesterday. Is that correct?'

Chris got what the headmaster said, but looked at the matron, who was conveying in sign, for confirmation.

'*Me?*' Chris nodded a few times in surprise, pointing at himself; his eyebrows and jaw dropping at this accusation.

'He said ... ' Miss Hogarth paused and pondered what he had just said. Did he say "it was me", or was he shocked at being accused? His facial expression and body language seemed to suggest the former, but then again, maybe not. Signs were one thing; their facial expressions and body language were another. That had always confused her, as she only knew some signs, but not everything else. Mr McShane had explained that this was a natural part of their rich language that not many hearing people understood.

'Elaine?' the headmaster's voice gently broke in. Miss Hogarth turned to him, still deciding. Then she looked at Chris, who was watching her, unaware of her private dilemma. After a short deliberation, she finally decided.

'He said ... it was him.' She said quietly.

Mr Langston closed his eyes; that was not the answer he wanted to hear. He opened them again and paused for a moment, finding his words. He knew Miss Hogarth was probably wrong, since he, too, had seen Chris' surprised reaction and knew that it could not have been him that started the trouble. However, there were other things that he couldn't ignore. One way or another, he wanted answers from the boy. 'So ... you did start it then?'

Chris frowned, puzzled at the question. He ignored the matron's signed translation and cut in, signing fast to the headmaster. 'I didn't! Mr Schneider did. He broke the blackboard compass himself but he blamed me for breaking it. I was thrown out of the dining room and we all went into the library–'

He stopped when he felt a pounding on the desk and turned to see Miss Hogarth thumping on it and waving at him.

'Slow down!' the matron yelled at him. 'Stop! I can't follow you. Hold on while I try to explain to Mr Langston what you have just said.' She silently cursed herself for having agreed to do this. Had she managed to digest what Chris had said, or should she ask him to repeat it? Her confidence was already sinking and she really wanted to get out now, but knew she couldn't. The sooner the interview was over, the better, she thought. Her brain worked rapidly as she tried to piece together what Chris had said. 'He said Mr Schneider believed Christopher broke the ... the ... '

'The blackboard compass,' Mr Langston said. 'I know about it.'

'Yes, the blackboard compass,' she nodded. 'Christopher said he lost his temper and stormed out of the dining room in protest. He said he led the boys into the library ... '

Chris watched Miss Hogarth explaining to the headmaster, not understanding any of it, but assuming she was voicing over correctly for the headmaster, who in turn nodded quietly at every word. Then he turned to Chris.

'Why did you all go to the library?' he asked.

'I don't know,' Chris replied, shaking his head. 'Ask Basher – Brian Thompson.'

'He says he doesn't know,' Miss Hogarth interpreted correctly. 'He said to ask Brian Thompson.'

'I already have,' Mr Langston replied. He looked down at the scribbled notes in front of him, re–reading some of the written conversation he'd had with Brian the previous night. He griped at the lad's level of English, which was nothing short of awful: a hearing seven year old could write far better than that. *Libarry?* Jesus Christ, he mused, a seventeen–year old boy like Brian Thompson couldn't even bloody spell library. He would have to have a word with Mr Whittle about this, but right now, it was the least of his worries. He looked up at Chris. 'He said you made everyone go into the library. You made everyone barricade themselves in with the chairs against the doors. You made everyone stay in there all evening.'

Chris understood what the headmaster was telling him, but looked at the matron, who was conveying it to him in choppy sign. He shook his head hard, not believing it. He pointed at himself: '*I* made everyone do that?'

'He said he made everyone do it,' Miss Hogarth conveyed quickly, believing she had done so correctly.

Ignoring Chris' shaking head, believing he was denying it all, Mr Langston pressed on: 'Why?'

Chris started to become suspicious about the way they were communicating with each other. 'I don't understand. We all only wanted Mr Schneider out.'

'He wanted Mr Schneider out,' Miss Hogarth said. 'Understand.'

'You most certainly achieved that, Christopher,' Mr Langston said. He leaned back and waved his hand across. 'He's not coming back.'

Chris frowned, open mouthed, shaking his head in disbelief. There was something amiss about the whole thing, he thought; Basher was lying out of his fat arse. He began to move his hands to sign.

'Be quiet, Christopher!' Mr Langston raised his hand at him. 'Your recent behaviour has been unacceptable. First, there was your dirty incident with Aaron on Tuesday night–'

'Aaron?' Miss Hogarth's head swung at him, secretly shocked. She should have known it was Chris whom Aaron had refused to name yesterday.

'And then there was your fight with Andrew Brener on Wednesday night,' Mr Langston continued, ignoring the matron's reaction. 'I didn't receive your written report yesterday morning; the one that I asked you to write about the fight.'

Chris kicked himself; he had completely forgotten about it; far too preoccupied with his falling out with Aaron, his secret support for Steven and everything else. He sat up properly to explain.

'And now, last night's trouble, that *you* started.' Mr Langston thumped on the desk to halt Chris. 'You almost seriously injured Mr Schneider with the bar.'

'What?' Chris' eyes moved to the matron who conveyed what the headmaster just said in sign, confirming what he had lipread. 'What are you talking about?'

Upon hearing Miss Hogarth's voice over, he said, 'You were going to strike him down again with that iron bar.'

'I never hit him!' Chris protested.

'He said he never hit him.' Miss Hogarth said, correctly.

'That's not what Brian Thompson said.' Mr Langston said sternly. 'He said you lost your temper, jumped from the table and kicked Mr Schneider in the face, and also on his side. Then you hit his back with the bar! The police said there were bruises on his back that they believe were caused by the bar. Brian claims he tried to stop you from hitting Mr Schneider again, but you hit him in the mouth with the bar instead. He's got a swollen lip to show for it! You were about to hit Mr Schneider again when Miss Hogarth stopped you.'

Chris could only sit there in stunned silence, watching Miss Hogarth finish her basic interpreting. He was boiling with anger at all of the lies that were directed at him.

'You saw me in the library!' Chris snapped at Miss Hogarth. 'I didn't hit him! Tell him that!' he pointed at the headmaster.

'I didn't!' Miss Hogarth said back. 'I only saw you *holding* the bar when I came in!'

'I picked it up to move it away from him! He was hurting everyone with it! I only kicked his face to stop him from hurting Aaron!' Chris mimicked a strangling gesture.

'He said he kicked him–' Miss Hogarth clammed up when Mr Langston raised his hand at her.

The headmaster exhaled deeply, trying to calm himself down. He was hurting a lot inside. He had always loved and respected Chris like he was his own son. He had helped him out of his personal doldrums, to become an incredibly mature and well–liked boy who had a potentially great future ahead of him. But now, he felt betrayed. Especially with what he was about to say to him; he didn't believe it himself, but he knew he *had* to tell him.

'Christopher ... ' the headmaster leaned forward, his manner sombre. ' ... I believe you're what the boys call the Phantom of Ewing Hill Park.' He stopped as he waited for Chris' reaction.

Chris had already got what Mr Langston said, but still gazed at the matron to make sure he hadn't misunderstood. She confirmed what the headmaster said. Chris felt his body turning into lead, the sudden heaviness of the air coming down on him. His mind became numb.

'No, it wasn't me,' he said calmly, shaking his head. 'It was … '

He stopped as he remembered the promise he'd made to Hubert the previous day, reflecting on what had happened.

Hubert had denied Chris' accusation at first. Chris pressed on, however, saying that he had worked out that some of the Phantom's actions were reminiscent of the Holocaust. The *Nazi scum* scribbles on Mr Schneider's Beetle, for example; the swastika – in red paint, representing blood – on his bedroom door; the packet of manure in the classroom that represented the Jews' distress; the burning of most of Mr Schneider's clothes on the bonfire, which represented the burning of the Jews and; finally, the doll in striped pyjamas hanging in his room, which represented the clothes the Jews wore during their time at concentration camps.

The fact that these actions were linked to the Holocaust had never crossed anyone's mind until Hubert revealed he was a survivor and Chris put two and two together, based on what Mrs Munnings had taught them about the Holocaust. He also pointed out that Hubert had full access to the whole school; he could have done it without anyone noticing because he was probably the last person to be suspected.

Hubert suddenly broke down in tears. Chris left his chair, took the tray away from the low coffee table and put it on the floor. He then sat on the table and touched the gardener's hand comfortingly. After Hubert had wiped away his tears with his handkerchief, he explained why he did it.

When Mr Schneider first arrived at the school the previous September, Hubert saw him outside the Maths Room. When Schneider had tried to introduce himself to the gardener, Hubert had almost had a heart attack. It was as if he had seen a ghost or someone had returned from beyond the grave, though he said he knew it was not actually him in the flesh.

'He was a different man, yes,' Hubert said. 'But they looked alike.'

'I don't understand,' Chris said, resting his elbows on his lap.

Hubert explained how he'd broken into Mr Schneider's bedroom a few weeks later – he had keys for all of the doors – while he was downstairs teaching maths. He knew he shouldn't have done it, but he *had* to find out. He found a small wooden box under the bed; inside it was old stuff from the Second World War – medals, an old diary and a few letters written in German, a few other items that were of no interest to him and a small framed black and white photograph. It confirmed Hubert's fears; in the photograph was a big, tall man in an SS uniform, holding a little boy of about three years old in his arms. A woman – presumably his wife – stood next to him. The man bore an uncanny likeness to Heinrich Schneider; so much so that Hubert believed the little boy must be the maths teacher. The SS officer Hubert recognised without doubt – Herr Klaus Schneider, was one of those responsible for the burning of several thousand Jews in the chambers, including Hubert's family, at Auschwitz. He would never be able to forget the man's face. He believed Herr Schneider had either killed himself or been executed shortly after the war and assumed the mother had raised her son herself.

'But he was only a little boy at that time,' Chris pointed out despite himself; he had no regard for the German either, but he thought what Hubert had done was totally wrong. 'So why do you blame him?'

'I know, but he still behaves like his father here. Like father, like son, you know, eh?' Hubert replied. Chris nodded, knowing what the gardener meant. He was also surprised at how small the world was.

Hubert told Chris he wanted to make the man suffer, so he did those terrible things to remind him of what his father and others had done. Regret had crept in though, and Hubert had already decided to stop terrorising him. He made Chris promise not to tell anyone, ever. And Chris had promised.

Chris flinched when Mr Langston banged on the desk. He stared at the headmaster for a long moment. He couldn't understand why he was being accused. 'Why do you think it was me?' he asked.

Mr Langston looked down at the sheet of papers and found what he was looking for. 'After what happened last night,' he began, 'I started thinking. You see, it all started to come together. First of all, the markings on Mr Schneider's car, do you remember that? You were around the car park at the time, weren't you?'

'Yes, I was, but–'

'And the swastika on his bedroom door last November was done in red paint. According to Miss Hogarth, you had some of that on your shirt at the time, didn't you?'

Chris thought hard about the accusation and realised that Aaron had accidentally splattered some red modelling paint on his shirt while painting Basher's hair in the gym. 'No, you're wrong–'

Mr Langston held his hand up, his face like stone. He glanced down at his notes as though he was a court judge reading out the charges. He looked up at Chris again. 'The package in the Maths Room, you were there, weren't you? And that night last March, there was a bonfire which burned his clothes. This morning,

I asked Mr Bronte, who was on duty that evening according to the old rota, and he remembered seeing you coming out from the forest that night; what were you doing there?'

Chris already knew the answer; it was his first time with Dwight. But he could hardly tell the headmaster that, so he chose not to answer the question. Mr Langston sighed and Chris could see that the man he had always respected was on the verge of breaking down.

'And the doll,' Mr Langston said grimly. 'You found it, didn't you? I remember teasing you about being a girl. You threw it away.'

'Yes, but–'

'How did you get into his bedroom to hang it up?'

'I didn't!'

Upon hearing Miss Hogarth's voiceover, Mr Langston slammed his hand on the desk. 'Stop lying! And now yesterday … you had a fight with Mr Schneider during the maths lesson, broke the blackboard compass, started the trouble in the dining room and then the library. You have a personal vendetta against him!'

'I didn't fucking do anything!' Chris screamed at the headmaster. 'Basher totally lied about me!'

'Stop lying!'

'I'M NOT LYING!' Chris shot to his feet, slamming his hands on the desk. He suddenly realised that Miss Hogarth may have inadvertently misunderstood most of what he had told the headmaster. 'What have you told him, you bitch?!'

'SHUT UP!' Mr Langston snapped, rising to his feet and pointing angrily at Chris.

'NO!' Chris screamed loudly, erupting into a blind, uncontrollable fury. He grabbed his chair and swung it towards the desk with a thunderous crash. The papers, telephone, framed family photograph and some other items flew off. Miss Hogarth jumped to her feet, pushing her chair back and cupping her mouth in shock.

'CALM DOWN!' the headmaster commanded; his loud voice echoing around the room.

'NO, I FUCKING WON'T!' Chris crashed the chair on the desk once more.

'You've had your last chance!' Mr Langston bellowed. 'You're out of Ewing Hill Park. Expelled!'

Chris froze, still clutching the chair. He shook his head, feeling his world collapsing around him. 'No, you can't do that to me.' He mouthed, silently and pleadingly.

Frances Langston burst in from the secretary's room next door, anxious after having heard the noise. Mr Langston raised his hand at her, his eyes still on Chris.

'It's all right, dear. Get me his social worker, Mr Lewison, on the phone now. He'll be at home.'

The secretary paused for a moment, glancing at the boy, but a firm nod from her husband made her turn and hurry back to her office.

'I'm very sorry, Christopher,' Mr Langston said sombrely. He took off his glasses and bowed his head. 'So sorry.'

Chris collapsed to the floor. He sat and bent over to his right, his forehead touching the carpet for a moment. He placed his hands over his grief–stricken face, tears flowing through his fingers. He looked up at the headmaster, who was looking down at him with dismay.

'I haven't done anything wrong,' he pleaded in sign, tears pouring down his cheeks.

34

Basher's Revenge

"Revenge is a dish best served cold."
– OLD CHINESE PROVERB

Andrew lined up his cue on the white ball, aiming it at the red, and whacked it across the green felt surface. The white ball hit the red ball, which rolled towards the corner pocket. Andrew straightened up, pleased with himself, and glanced at his opponent, Sammy. He walked round the snooker table, deciding which colour to go for next. He decided on the pink and bent over the snooker table to take his aim.

The door to the recreation room suddenly burst open and Matthew burst in. He crashed against Shaun, who was on his way out. Matthew ignored the stumbling Third Former's moans and directed his attention at Andrew and Sammy, waving at them excitedly.

'Chris has been expelled!' he announced.

'*What?!*' Andrew straightened up. 'What for?'

'He's being blamed for the trouble last night!' Matthew replied.

Andrew threw the cue to the snooker table, anger surging within him, and stormed towards the door. 'That lying bastard!' he screamed out in sign.

Matthew and Sammy exchanged glances; they both knew what the neurotic boy was going to do. They ran after him, leaving the other boys in the room to exchange shocked glances.

Toby ran into the TV room, waved agitatedly at some boys who were watching Saturday Swap Shop, then blurted out the shocking news.

Some of the Fifth Formers watched with feigned interest and amusement as Basher, who was sitting on his battered "throne" armchair, boasted once again about his heroics the previous night.

'I held onto him,' he ranted on, 'we struggled, but I held on. We were equal in strength–'

Dwight burst into the common room, his expression shocked. Everyone turned to him. 'Mr Langston's expelled Chris Matthaus!' he announced.

The prefects exchanged surprised glances, but Basher smiled at the news. He quickly left his armchair, heading purposefully towards the door.

David ran down the corridor, puffing and panting. At the back of his mind, one question screamed; *where the hell is Aaron?!* He couldn't find him anywhere. He turned a corner and almost bumped onto the very person he was looking for, who was coming out of the toilets. Aaron staggered back a bit at the sudden impact; he was about to tell David to watch it, but David slapped down his hand to tell him to shut up.

'I've been trying to find you,' David said, in between pants. 'Chris has been expelled!'

'What?' Aaron shook his head, shocked. 'Why?'

'He's been blamed for starting the trouble last night,' David answered.

'That's bullshit!' Aaron shrieked, shocked and angry at the news. He began to march on. 'We have to tell Mr Langston!'

David grabbed Aaron's blazer sleeve to stop him; he had one more thing to say. 'And ... I just saw Miss Hogarth telling Miss Turner that he's been found out as the Phantom of Ewing Hill Park!'

Aaron felt his whole world spin round him. He shook his head in utter disbelief. He knew for a fact that Chris was not the culprit – there was absolutely no fucking way he would do that kind of thing. He knew him far too well. Someone – probably Basher for all he knew – had lied to the headmaster.

'I'll come with you and help speak for you,' David urged Aaron on.

They darted off towards the front hall, only to be met there by Basher, who had just marched through from the lobby. He grabbed their school ties as if they were horses' reins, and dragged both boys back to where they had come from. They struggled hard to break free from the choking grip.

Basher took them along the corridor to another corridor midway down and slammed both of them against the wall; they groaned at the dull thump. Basher scanned in both directions, making sure they were alone before returning his attention to them.

'You'll both say nothing,' Basher said, pointing at Aaron and David.

'I have to!' Aaron said angrily. 'Chris hasn't done anything wrong!'

'Too late,' Basher grinned. 'Mr Langston believed me.'

'You lying bastard!' David screamed at Basher.

'We'll tell him the truth!' Aaron stepped forward, not afraid of the bully any more. 'He'll believe us and everyone else. They know *you* started it!'

Basher pushed Aaron back to the wall. He shook his head, still grinning evilly. 'No, you won't. I know about you and Chris.'

Aaron's eyes widened.

Basher took a step forward. 'I saw you in the changing room on Tuesday.' He opened his mouth wide, wiggling his tongue wildly as though he was kissing exaggeratedly. 'Yes, I saw you!'

Aaron screamed inwardly; he *knew it!* He'd been right all along; he *had* seen someone standing in the doorway. He wondered what Basher had been doing in the gym building, but decided not to ask him.

'Rubbish!' Aaron shook his head violently. 'We didn't–'

'The cellar.' Basher cut in like a sharp blade, leaning forward. 'Both of you went down there later that evening. Guess who told Mr Langston to go down there?'

Basher told Aaron what had happened. That night, Basher was having a smoke on his own in the dark outside, standing around at the far east of the building. It was always a very quiet spot, he said. Glancing through a small window he had seen Chris and Aaron hurrying along the darkened corridor that led to the cellar door. He'd seen Aaron telling Chris he thought it was wrong, and Chris dismissing his concerns. Aaron had turned and looked at the window, but Basher quickly hid away, then looked back and seen them going into the cellar. Basher had taken a last puff on his cigarette, discarded it and gone back inside. He'd found Mr Langston nearby, correcting a crooked picture frame.

'Hello Brian,' the headmaster greeted him. 'How's your revision going?'

Fiiinnneee

'Good, good,' Mr Langston nodded. 'Keep it up, boy. Mr McShane said he believes you'll do splendidly with your art O Level.'

Basher nodded, muttering thanks to him. Then he pointed at a cast iron radiator on the wall, shook his head and hugged himself as if he was feeling the cold. He pointed at something and gestured five fingers.

'The heating's gone down again?' Mr Langston worked out what the head boy had said. 'There's no heating in the fifth form common room?'

Basher nodded, trying to conceal his smile from the headmaster.

'. . . and he caught you both, right?' Basher told Aaron.

'We didn't do any–'

'Oh, come on! Do you think I'm a fool?' Basher knocked his fist on his shaking head.

David looked from Basher to Aaron and then back at Basher again, bewildered. 'What are you talking about?'

'They're queers,' Basher said bluntly, coldly flapping his hand.

David slowly turned to Aaron. He now understood why they'd had a falling out, but still found it hard to believe. Aaron looked at David.

'Is this true?'

Aaron didn't answer him.

Basher waved at them to get their attention. He eyed Aaron first. 'You say nothing and I say nothing.' He slid his finger across his mouth, then directed his eyes at David. 'You too. You say anything, I'll tell everyone you're a poof too.'

'But I'm not!' David protested.

'Oh, I know that!' Basher said. 'But you three are always together, so would anyone believe you aren't?'

David became silent at the threat. 'Why are you doing this to us?'

'Revenge,' Basher answered. 'Punk funk, remember? I swore to myself that night in the gym last November that I'd get revenge on you three. I was waiting for the right time and it came yesterday. Yes, I made everyone go to the library, so Chris could be blamed for it. It worked perfectly!'

'Why did you lie to Mr Langston about Chris being the Phantom of Ewing Hill Park?' Aaron demanded to know. 'You–'

'What?' Basher cut in, waving his index finger in genuine surprise. 'What do you mean, he's the Phantom?'

'Don't lie!' David snapped at him.

'No, I didn't know that.' Basher crossed his chest. 'Honest.'

Aaron and David exchanged surprised glances. Basher stepped back, his smile growing in delight; his revenge had just got even better.

'So, it was him!' Basher exclaimed. He couldn't wait to tell his form mates about that. 'Wow.'

Aaron felt his body sinking through the ground. Basher took one last look at Aaron and David, then placed a finger on his lips and nodded at them. He turned and headed away, thrilled with himself. Aaron slid his back down the wall, sat and slumped, his head between his bent legs. David stood there, lost and bewildered.

35

Goodbye Scrubhead

"As long as we have deaf people on earth, we will have signs. And as long as we have our films, we can preserve signs in their old purity. It is my hope that we will all love and guard our beautiful sign language as the noblest gift God has given to deaf people."
– George Veditz, President of National Association of the Deaf, USA, 1913

Holding his Arsenal football and wearing his favourite red Adidas tee shirt; white collared with three white stripes on each of the sleeves; dark blue jeans and white trainers, Chris reached the landing of the grand staircase.

He looked down at the lobby and hesitated. Two rows of boys stood wide apart in perfectly straight lines, stretching from the foot of the stairs to the front hall. They were all wearing their full school uniforms – buttoned dark green blazers, black trousers, white shirts, black, green and gold striped ties and black shoes. They were facing each other motionlessly; their arms by their sides and their feet close together. It was as if they were soldiers ready for inspection.

Chris felt nauseous, his emotions jangling and his legs turning to jelly. Who arranged this, he wondered; he wouldn't be surprised if it was his form. It was almost three o'clock and he had expected most – if not all – of the boys to be in the TV room for the football by now, assuming he'd leave quietly. He began to descend the wide polished wood steps, thinking about the last few hours.

Chris had repeatedly and tearfully pleaded with Mr Langston to reconsider his decision, but the headmaster was adamant that he had to go. Chris saw in his eyes that this was not what he wanted, but he had made his decision. Chris also pleaded innocence against all charges, including being wrongly accused as the Phantom of Ewing Hill Park. He told Mr Langston to ask Aaron about the red paint on his shirt, but he still couldn't answer the headmaster's repeated question about why he was in the woods during the burning of the clothes. Chris was finally told to be quiet and pack some of his things; the rest would follow later.

With a heavy heart, Chris eventually packed a few of his clothes and personal belongings into his bag in Dorm Four. Some of the prefects had guarded the door, preventing the other boys from entering. He had caught sight of Aaron desperately trying to get through and begging the guards to let him, but he was denied access. He had to wait in the dorm until Mr Lewison arrived, so he spent the next hour or so sitting alone on his bed, brooding and crying for much of the time. His thoughts whirled, confused and dejected by what was happening to him. Why did everything seem to fall so perfectly into place against him, he asked himself. Why hadn't Aaron and David tried to tell the headmaster the truth? Or had they been prevented from doing so? Did Basher have something to do with that? What about the others? They were his witnesses, but they were saying nothing! Had they all turned their backs on him now? No, they wouldn't, he told himself, but *why? Why me? Oh fuck, why me? Why me?!* Chris howled silently, resting his head in his hands.

The prefects let the headmaster through and he sat on the bed opposite Chris. After a short moment of silence between them, Mr Langston said he was still so sorry, but he had no choice but to expel him. He wished him the very best of luck with his future; perhaps one day, he said, Chris could write to tell him how he was doing or even better, come and see him. He also said he hoped Chris would understand and forgive him for his difficult decision, one day. Chris said nothing throughout the conversation, for he knew anything he tried to say would not change the headmaster's mind. Besides, he did not know sign language, so there was no point in Chris even trying. Mr Langston rose to his feet, telling him that Mr Lewison was here and it was time to go.

Chris reached the foot of the stairs, staring ahead. The corridor of boys stretched all the way through the front hall towards the entrance doors, which were fully open, and outside to the dark blue Fiat saloon that he recognised as belonging to Mr Lewison. He took a couple of steps forward, then stopped directly in between the first boys on either side of him. He had already observed that the first five boys on either side were the First Formers; the shortest first and the tallest last. Then, five Second Form boys followed on either side; again, the shortest first and the tallest last; this formation was repeated with the Third, Fourth and Fifth Formers, all the way along.

Chris slowly turned his head to his left to see Toby Eriswell. Toby maintained his neutral face, still gazing at the boy opposite him. He slowly raised his right hand towards his head, while his left remained straight down; he closed his hand, placed it on top of his head and slowly moved it in a perfectly clockwise motion, before slowly and automatically lowering it again. Chris then turned slowly to Nicolo Perran, who was doing exactly the same thing. Chris felt a tear trickling down his cheek as he looked ahead at the corridor of boys: they were giving him the grand honour guard's salute, using his name sign instead of rifles.

Chris slowly advanced another couple of steps, briefly stopping between Richie Callaghan and Conor Blackwell; Richie did exactly the same as Toby and Nicolo. Conor, however, had a plaster cast on his right arm, which was held against his chest in a sling, covered by his blazer. Chris was secretly pleased to see that the black First Former was all right. With his left hand, Conor repeated the same farewell gesture. Chris tightly clasped his football as he resumed his slow walk, passing Johan Broadwater and Warren Southway on either side, who both repeated the same process. He passed the last four First Form boys, not looking at either side, although he glimpsed Asif Nizamani[1] repeating the gesture. He reached the shortest two Second Formers: Hendrik Swart and Rowan Ince. Chris briefly glanced at the white South African, who met his eyes briefly before signing the *scrubhead* name sign. Chris gave him a quiet nod and moved on.

He slowly passed Dermot Jones and Jack Aldridge on either side, then the rest of the Second Form boys, their heights rising as each one of them signed the same farewell gesture. He fought back tears, choking and bowing his head once or twice. He slowed down his pace upon reaching the Third Form section; half of whom were inside by the entrance and the other half outside, down the three wide stone steps. Andy Farmleigh and Shaun Knight were the first to give him the signed farewell. He then passed the next two – Derek Ferguson and Jonah Kasiermann – who followed with the same goodbye. Biting his lip and clasping the ball tightly, Chris slowly walked through the open doorway, knowing that this was the point of no return. He stopped on the top step for a long moment, still looking ahead. His mind whirled with a thousand memories of his time at the school, as if blurred split–second images were being played in front of his eyes.

From the corners of his eyes, he saw Duncan Nielson and Bradley Watts, who had a large plaster on his nose, slowly signing his name sign. Chris then descended the next step. He stopped and turned to his left to see David Wheeley, who was desperately trying to stem the heavy flow of tears behind his slightly crooked and cracked spectacles. He had a cardboard box in his hands. Chris stepped towards him, gazing down at the open box. Inside was the Avro Lancaster model plane that Chris and Aaron had helped repair: it was still in good condition. Chris looked back up at his friend, his heart wrenching.

'This is for you,' David said, pressing the box against his stomach with his left hand so that he could sign with his other. 'To remember our friendship.'

'I can't–'

'Please.' David wiped tears from both cheeks. He then placed his closed hand on top of his head and circled it once in a proud and dignified manner before resting his right arm back at his side.

1

Chris quietly nodded a few times to show his gratitude and acknowledge his friend. He turned to his left, expecting to see Aaron at the other end of the step, since he was the third tallest boy in his Form, but saw Michael Hardcastle there instead. Confused, he looked at the final step, next to David; Ian Snyman, the tallest boy in his Form, was standing there. He saw that Lester Morrison was standing at the other end of the step. Chris felt his heart constrict. Michael Hardcastle did what he had to do and Chris stepped down to the final step. He saw tears trickling down Ian's dark cheeks; with great effort, he managed to sign Chris his farewell. Chris did not need to see Lester; he knew that he bade him farewell.

His feet touched the tarmac, his gaze directed at the car at the end of the corridor of boys, and there he saw Aaron, at the end of the line, next to Gary Portmore. Chris exhaled, swallowing and sniffed hard. He moved on, passing Jamon Cranley on his left and Mark Cameron on his right; *scrubhead,* they both signed. He walked past two others who followed suit, then stopped at the next two; Andrew Brener was on his left, a fresh bandage on his nose, a shiner on his left eye and a swollen lower lip. Chris guessed Andrew had been in another fight with someone; Basher, he assumed. Andrew was sniffing; his teeth clattered and a tear rolled down his right cheek. He closed his eyes, slowly placing his right fist on top of his head and circling it before bowing his head. Chris really wanted to hug him to thank him for their good friendship, but resisted the urge. He slowly panned to his right; Matthew Burke immediately signed his farewell. Chris moved forward to the next two, seeing Sammy Maguire bravely signing. Chris then turned to the next boy, dreading what he was about to see. Steven Clarke was quivering like a leaf and he knew why; he was going to have a year of hell without him there and Chris hated himself for that. He decided he wanted to say goodbye to Steven properly, so walked over to him, placed his hand behind his head, pulled him forward and kissed his forehead.

'Take good care of yourself,' Chris silently mouthed to him. 'Be brave.'

Steven nodded weakly, wiping his tears. He then managed to straighten up a bit and signed the name sign in a dignified manner. With a final nod, Chris turned to the next two boys. The lanky Dean Hopkirk was the last one in his Form; Chris stood in front of him, face to face. He discreetly rolled his eyes, indicating Steven, and mouthed to Dean, whom he knew would be the next head boy instead of him, compelling him to promise to help protect Steven. Dean hesitated, his eyes darting to Steven, not wanting to honour the promise. Eventually, after seeing Chris' urging look, he nodded and mouthed his promise. He straightened up, placed his right hand on top of his head in a smooth motion, circled it and gave a final nod.

Chris then saw Dwight Greenland; the Fifth Former immediately blew a discreet kiss to Chris before doing what everyone else had done. Chris nodded, secretly thanking Dwight for his part in discovering himself. He moved on, passing the rest of the prefects, including the white–haired Tom Quillot, as they in turn signed the name sign as he passed. He noted Carl Dunn had a huge bruise on the left side of his face and Timothy "Spook" Hutchinson had a swollen gash across under his right eye. Chris then turned to Gary Portmore, who had a huge plaster taped across the length of his forehead and a small cut down the top of his right cheek. Despite his minor injuries, he stood proudly and performed the farewell gesture.

Chris slowly walked over to Aaron, who was standing next to Gary.

Their eyes met lingeringly. Chris wanted to say something but couldn't bring himself to do it. Aaron wanted to say something but didn't know what to say or how to say it, in spite of his heart urging him otherwise. He glanced behind Chris at Basher, who was standing last in his line. Basher looked back at Aaron, zipped his index finger across his lips and gave him the evil eye. Chris knew who Aaron was looking at. He knew Basher had something to do with Aaron's apparently forced silence. It suddenly dawned on him that Basher might have blackmailed him into keeping his silence … he *knew* about their secret. Chris closed his eyes in despair; Aaron had been right all along that it was Basher he saw in the changing room. He could not understand, though, why Basher had gone to such extremes to stitch him up. He opened his eyes again and saw that Aaron was fighting hard to hold back tears. Tears began to flow down Chris' cheeks again, his facial expression urging Aaron to say something, but Aaron quietly shook his head. He stepped forward and placed his arms round Chris. Chris tucked his football underneath his left arm so that he could wrap the other around Aaron. It started as a feeble hug then became a long, tight embrace.

I'll love you always, as a friend Chris sent a telepathic message to his friend.

I'll miss you so much Aaron replied in his mind, as though he'd received the message.

Aaron slowly leaned back, releasing himself from the hug, and stepped back. With his left arm straight down, slowly and with a great deal of effort, he raised his right fist towards his head and feebly circled with it. Having done this, he let his arm drop back down. Chris took a final look at his best friend, studying his face once more. He turned towards the parked car, stopping at Basher on his right.

Basher stood there, like a committed soldier ready for inspection. Chris threw accusing eyes at the head boy. He had an overwhelming desire to lunge at him, beat the shit out of him, or, worse still, kill him. He felt nothing but extreme hatred for the boy. But he knew it would not do anyone any good, so he decided to leave it there, with great reluctance. Perhaps one day, he thought, he would avenge. In a pretentious way, Basher signed *scrubhead* without even meeting Chris' eyes. Chris turned to the car, ignoring the small smirk on Basher's face.

He looked across the top of the car to see Hubert standing next to his motorised wheel–driven lawnmower in the centre of the playing field, watching him. He, too, signed Chris' name sign.

Chris turned to face the school and saw that the corridor of boys had already dismantled; the boys from inside were streaming outside and many of them gathered around him. Chris knew he had one last thing to say to them. Holding the ball underneath his left arm, he slowly placed his closed right hand on the top of his head, circled it and let it drop back down. He turned, opened the back passenger seat and hopped in, closing the door. Mr Langston and Mr Lewison shook hands while David put the box into the boot and closed it. Mr Lewison then hopped into the driver's seat, shut the door and started the engine.

The car slowly moved off towards the winding driveway and a small mob of boys ran after it, like frenzied fans chasing after a famous star. Aaron slowly turned to watch the car pass him, while some of the boys flowed past him towards the departing car.

Chriiisss! Aaron screamed silently, a cascade of tears flowing.

A dark shadow loomed over him. He whirled round to see a large, towering figure silhouetted against the sun. She stood over him sorrowfully, her face sympathetic and her big heart touching him.

'It was him, wasn't it?' Miss Hogarth pointed at the departing car.

Aaron burst into uncontrollable tears. He buried his head in the matron's cleavage, muffling his loud wailing. Miss Hogarth slowly wrapped her arms round the boy, rested her chin on top of his head and cradled him hard.

She understood.

With tears flowing down his cheeks, Chris twisted his head round to look through the back window and saw that some of the boys were still running after the car as it reached the end of the driveway. A cluster of trees began to sweep past on either side, the dark brown building that he had spent the last three, almost four, years in now rapidly shrinking from view. The few remaining determined boys still ran after the car, but eventually gave up when it picked up speed. Chris slowly sat back and started to breathe heavily. Tears began to flood from his eyes. The agony inside him became too much for him to handle. He crossed his forearms over his anguished face and slumped, lying on the back seat.

He cried and cried.

PART IV

LEGACY

36

The Return

"... I found myself and others coining a new label of 'Deafhood.' Deafhood is not, however, a 'static' medical condition like 'deafness.' Instead, it represents a process – the struggle by each Deaf child, Deaf family and Deaf adult to explain to themselves and each other their own existence in the world. In sharing their lives with each other as a community, and enacting those explanations rather than writing books about them, Deaf people are engaged in a daily praxis, a continuing internal and external dialogue."
– DR PADDY LADD; *Understanding Deaf Culture: in search of Deafhood,* 2003

Chris slowly opened his eyes, a tear trickling down his cheek.

Swallowing, he wiped away the wetness with the back of his hand, the image of the cluster of passing trees becoming a distant memory.

He looked around and saw that the service had finished. The pews were now emptying as people streamed down the aisles on either side of him, towards the exit. Some remained in their pews; either musing alone or signing to one another, while others loitered, standing.

Chris emitted a short, sharp sigh and then rose to his feet.

Coming out through the doors, he saw several people in the churchyard, their hands moving, chattering. He looked around to see if he recognised anyone, but did not, for the younger faces of his old school friends were still etched in his memory.

He took a few steps towards the gravel path, his hands in his pockets. Suddenly, a hand tapped his shoulder. He turned to see a bespectacled middle aged man, balding with a large paunch and rugged hands; he had a look about him that was labour–weary. The man studied Chris for a long moment, trying to place him.

'I know you ... ' the man pointed at him. Then, the penny dropped. 'You're ... Chris Matthaus, right?'

Chris frowned at the man, trying to place him, but the child behind his adult features eluded him. The man's face lit up, beaming broadly.

'It *is* you!' the man exclaimed, brushing Chris' head. 'I still remember that scrubhead!' He noted Chris' perplexed look and twisted a flat hand on the side of his head, signing his name sign; *mad*. 'It's me, Andrew Brener!'

Chris and Andrew wrapped their arms round each other, hugging tight. Andrew broke off the hug, shaking his head in astonishment.

'Where the hell have you been?! We've been trying to find you for years!' said Andrew.

'Well, I–'

Andrew suddenly raised his hand, cutting Chris short, and waved excitedly at a man behind Chris, telling him to come over. Chris turned to see a tall black man in a long black overcoat walking briskly over to them. Chris easily recognised him despite the wrinkles on his face; he had short Afro hair and resembled his father. Ian Snyman regarded Chris curiously. In the corner of his eye, Chris saw Andrew telling him who he was; Ian's mouth dropped open then he grinned, flashing his white teeth. Within a second, Chris and Ian's arms were around each other, hugging hard.

Soon enough, a small crowd had formed around Chris, curious about the commotion. A tall, slim man with lanky legs, slightly taller than Chris, stepped forward. Chris furrowed his brows at the man, who had short, parted dark hair, tinted with grey at the sides.

'Dean Hopkirk?' Chris guessed.

Dean nodded, a smile growing on his face. 'Is that really you, Chris?'

He didn't need an answer from him; his long arms were already around Chris and they hugged. Suddenly, a hand pulled Chris away from the hug and he saw another man; bespectacled with milky white skin and thinning chestnut hair; his upper body shaped like a barrel.

'Sammy Maguire!' Chris greeted him, recognising him in spite of his huge waistline. They shared a quick hug.

A man with a beard soon came over and introduced himself as Mark Cameron.

'I can't believe it!' Mark shook his head in disbelief before hugging his old form mate.

Next, a large, plump man joined the crowd and slapped Chris' shoulder. Chris turned and greeted David Wheeley.

'Still remember the way here?' David pointed in the direction of the school and then at the church.

'I'll never forget!' Chris said back, smiling. 'I visited the school this morning, then went to see Hubert at the nursing home.'

'How is he?' asked David.

Chris thought briefly about the visit. The nursing home was in a secluded location near Weyton, the next town. He'd driven past Weyton Comprehensive, revelling in the memory of the intense rivalry between them during football matches. Upon arrival, a care nurse who knew basic sign language took him to a day room in the Mary Rose Owens Wing where Hubert was. The nurse told him that the recently built extension was named after the world's oldest woman who had died nine years before, and that she had been deaf too.

The nurse explained that because of his Alzheimer's, Chris would find it difficult to communicate with Hubert. Chris' heart sank when he saw a frail old man sitting silently in a wheelchair. He was heavily wrinkled, with sparse white hair, a straggly white beard and almost lifeless eyes. Chris sat next to him then held Hubert's clasped bony hands that were resting on his lap, covered by a blanket. Hubert did not respond to the touch. Chris sat there for a long time, thinking about the day he'd been inside Hubert's tiny cottage; the stories the reclusive genius had told him about the dark, transgressional episode in Deaf history, his experiences at concentration camps and the disturbing truth about the identity of the Phantom. All of these memories felt like yesterday to him. Looking at the old man, Chris wondered if Hubert could have chosen a different path in life; he could have exploited his intellect, used his extraordinary memory for good causes and helped many people. As he had helped Chris. Yet, he'd found peace from the horrors of the Holocaust by working as a gardener at the school, right until the end. Chris prayed Hubert would soon find even greater peace, and that he would finally rejoin his family, in another life.

He'd been told that all of Hubert's books had been given away to good homes and libraries. The more valuable ones were sold; the money donated to charities and Jewish organisations.

Chris tried to tell his old friend who he was, even placing his closed hand on his head to signify his name sign, in the hope of making Hubert remember, but it was in vain. Hubert didn't even seem to register that there was a visitor sitting in front of him. Looking at the wall clock and seeing it was now quarter to two, Chris knew he had to leave for the service, so grasped both of Hubert's hands to bid him a final farewell. He rose and walked over to the doorway, stopped there and turned to take one last look at the former school gardener.

Hubert's closed hand was on his head, shaking as though he was struggling to keep it there. There was a hint of smile on his frail face and his eyes seemed to gaze at Chris. Chris smiled and then laughed.

'You two met up again before today?' Andrew asked curiously.

Chris brushed away the brief memory of the visit, nodding. 'He found me,' he said, pointing at David.

All eyes turned expectantly to David.

'You're not going to believe this!' David began, his hands moving confidently.

'You know, it's like what you see in the news about people trying to find their long–lost family members or friends for years, then all of a sudden they're, like, you know, living round the corner, or they bump into them in the street. A billion to one chance thing, you know? Like if you're searching for something, like a lost wedding ring; you can't find it and then it just turns up by itself. That happened to us.' He pointed at Chris and then to himself. 'He wasn't exactly round the corner, though! Last week, my company wanted me to fly over to Perth in Australia – of all the places in the world – to broker a deal. I really didn't want to go, but a job's a job. The deal had been agreed and I was to go down there for a few days to meet the client, sign on the dotted line and all that. The day before I left, the news of Mr Langston's passing came, which was sad, but to be expected; as you all know, his health was failing. I knew I'd be back in time for the funeral, so, I flew thousands of miles down under, but when I got to the hotel, I received an email saying that the client had changed his mind and cancelled the deal! Bugger it; I'd come all that bloody way for nothing! It was one of those things, I suppose. As my flight back home wasn't for a few days, I decided to do a bit of sightseeing. It was warm down there, you see, so I went to the tourist information centre and picked up some leaflets. Quite a few of them were about swimming with dolphins, and I've always wanted to do that, so I asked the lady which one she recommended. She saw that I was deaf and recommended me one that was run by a deaf guy; she said it was really good … '

Chris smiled as he watched David continue telling the story, his mind rolling back to the previous week.

' … I thought, great! So I went over to the place to book myself in. This young lad behind the desk saw that I was deaf and waved at that other man – the deaf guy – and we signed to each other. You know, we Deaf like to have a little chat. I had the strangest feeling that I'd seen or met him before – his face was so familiar – but I couldn't pinpoint it. Then I spotted those framed business commendation certificates hanging on the wall and most of them had his name on … '

37

The Aftermath

"Proficiency in a first language would correlate to competence in a second language because a single cognitive process underlies language acquisition for both languages." – JAMES Cummins (on his model of Linguistic Interdependence that formed a basis for bilingual–bicultural education), 1976

'Chris Matthaus?!' David shrieked, his chunky arms swinging open.

Before Chris could react, he found himself inside a mighty bear hug, his feet almost lifted from the floor, shaken helplessly like a rag doll as David hopped around. Chris struggled to break free from the burly man's grip until David eventually released him.

'Oh my God!' David held Chris' upper arms, studying him once more, making doubly sure that it was definitely him. Broody eyes? Check. Facial features? Older with a few wrinkles here and there, but definitely him. Hair? The same crew cut, now dark with a hint of grey. About six foot tall, an inch or so taller than David? Yep. Good, strong physique, even for a forty–seven year old (apart from a slight beer belly)? Check. Yes, it was definitely Chris Matthaus. Clasping his hands, David whooped again with delight.

'I'm sorry, but–'

'It's me! David Wheeley!' he pointed at himself, cutting Chris short. 'Bigger and more fat. Shorter hair – look I'm almost bald! Got rid of the glasses – contact lenses now. Moustache here … ' he pointed at the thick, greying dark hair between his nose and mouth, and then at his left ear. ' … and cochlear implant there. But it's me, David! Remember me?!'

Chris gaped, not so much from the shock at seeing his old school friend after so many years, but because of his complete transformation. He was totally unrecognisable from the fourteen–year old boy that Chris remembered. He grinned broadly and wrapped his arms round David's plump body, returning the gesture.

Breaking off the embrace, David whipped a mobile phone from his breast pocket, excited and trembling. 'I've got to text Aaron–'

'No!' Chris hastily placed his hand over the mobile. He wanted to wait and chat with David first.

'But I've got to tell him! He's been searching for you for years!' David protested.

'No. Please!'

Reluctantly, David put his mobile away again.

Walking down the road towards the wharf where they had agreed to have lunch in a bar, Chris told David what had happened to him after his expulsion from Ewing Hill Park.

Steve Lewison had placed a despondent Chris in a children's home for the weekend until he could deal with his situation the following Monday. Chris ran away the next morning and went to his mother's flat. She was shocked, but delighted, to see him. Still hurting badly, Chris wrote notes to explain what had happened. Sandra told him that she wanted to go to Australia straight away; not because of what had happened, but because Bob Sullivan – who had scars on his forehead – had made death threats to her; he wanted revenge on Chris, to kill him even. After a period of soul–searching, Chris agreed to go with her. Sandra had some savings, so two one–way plane tickets to Perth were booked, their new passports fast–tracked and their visas approved. Chris wrote to Steve Lewison (who had found him at the flat and agreed that he could stay there for the time being, although as he was almost at the legal age of sixteen, there was not much he could do), thanking him for all the help he'd given him over the years and wishing him the very best of luck.

Before long, they were in Perth. They stayed with Sandra's distant cousin, Eleanor, for a short while until they found a place of their own. Sandra worked as a waitress, and in several other jobs, and kept herself sober while Chris finished his education at a school for the deaf. When he left school the following year, Chris did some odd jobs to help support himself and his mother, then after a couple of years, he decided to travel around the continent. At the time, Sandra had a full time job working for a tour company. When Chris returned after travelling for a year, he finally came out as gay to her. Sandra was upset at first, but Chris explained how his travels had opened his eyes; particularly his time in Sydney which had a strong gay and lesbian community; and told her that he'd had brief relationships with men. After a while, Sandra accepted this. However, Chris soon discovered that she had been drinking again: she admitted that it had always been a struggle for her not to touch a drop. This time, Chris supported her as best as he could, although they'd had some difficult times. After a year or two, Chris decided to go off to university to study business management. He successfully applied for a scholarship to Gallaudet, which had acquired university status by then, enrolling for four years, majoring with a master's degree in business management and a minor in English.

'Hang on,' David stopped in his tracks just outside the entrance to the bar, his mind latching onto something he'd read about on the internet some years ago. 'Were you at that, um, Deaf President Now thing?'

Chris nodded, grinning. 'That happened in March 1988. It was totally wild!' He held the door open for David, and then described what happened as they sat on stools at a high table by the window, overlooking the sea.

Deaf students at Gallaudet had been campaigning for a deaf president to succeed Jerry C. Lee, a hearing man, who had resigned after three years in the role. Deaf President Now rallies were held while the Gallaudet's Board of Trustees considered three candidates; Elisabeth Zinser, Irving King Jordan and Harvey Corson. The latter two were deaf, but Elisabeth Zinser won the presidency, sparking a mass protest because she was hearing. The students, supported by the university's administrators, barricaded the campus gates using heavy duty bicycle locks and hot–wired school buses, moving them in front of the gates and letting the air out of their tyres.

'Just like what we did in the school library! Only with chairs, though.' David couldn't help but comment, munching some peanuts from a nibble bowl. The bartender brought them two bottles of beer.

'Anyway, we made four demands,' Chris continued, swigging his beer; 'firstly, for Zinser's resignation and the selection of a deaf person as president. We also wanted the immediate resignation of Jane Bassett Spilman, who was the chair of the board of trustees – she allegedly said "the deaf were not yet ready to function in the hearing world" when the board made the choice. Finally, we wanted to restructure the board of trustees so there'd be a fifty–one percent majority of deaf members, because at the time, there were seventeen hearing members but only four deaf ones … '

Chris went on to explain how the mass protests and marches grew stronger by the day and the campaign for the deaf president went on for almost a week, attracting a huge amount of media attention from all over America. The campaign was in the main news headlines, both in the newspapers and on television, over all states for a whole week. They received messages of support from famous political and media figures. They also received donations, food and supplies from businesses, friends and anonymous people in aid of the protest, as well as outside help from the Deaf community and workers' unions. After a long stand–off, Zinser eventually resigned, all four demands were agreed to and Irving King Jordan became Gallaudet's first ever deaf president.

'That day changed everything,' Chris concluded. 'To them, it was the second greatest moment in American Deaf history, after the visit of Laurent Clerc, who introduced ASL about two hundred years ago.'

A sandwich lunch was then served and Chris went back to his time there. 'Gallaudet is, in contrast to Ewing Hill Park, a completely different world. Sign language is everywhere! All lessons are in sign language. I had to learn ASL fast and it's so different from BSL and Auslan. It's true that deaf people *can* be taught well through sign language – I graduated with a master's and my written English is near perfect now. During my time there, I got together with a man called Kiefer and we toured America together for a year or so until we broke up. Um, and then I returned to Perth to look after my mother. I set up my own tour business, initially to take tourists round Perth and the western regions, then I expanded into swimming with dolphins. I've wanted to work with them ever since I saw them at the underground aquarium in Brighton. Anyway, my business did well and it's won a few awards: you've seen them.' He sighed a little, and then continued. 'Eleven years ago, my mother was diagnosed with liver cancer, partly because of the drink … she died a few months later with me at her bedside. Erm, I've had a few relationships, but I've never really committed to anyone in a long term thing. But I'm pretty content with my life here.'

Chris finished off his beer and motioned for the bartender to bring them two more. David clasped his hands over the table, taking in what Chris had just said. He knew he had to share the news.

'The day before I flew down here,' David began, 'Donald Langston passed away.' He watched Chris' head bow for a moment. The men shared a moment, remembering their old headmaster. Then, breaking the silence, David said, 'I'm not quite sure whether it's a sense of irony or pure coincidence that we found each other just after his death, but in a strange way, I'm glad it happened. He'd been in poor health for some time now, so it's one door closed, another opened, I guess.'

Just then, the bartender delivered the new bottles and took away the empty ones and their plates.

Taking a quick sip, Chris gazed at his friend across the table. 'So, what happened?' he asked, the question obvious to David.

'Chris … you *changed* the school,' David said after a moment, clasping his hands together as he tried to piece together the long–forgotten memories. 'Basher blackmailed Aaron and me into silence about you and him. Yes, I know all about it. He told me. You only kissed him and you didn't do anything in the cellar, I know that. But Basher saw you on both occasions. It was him who told Mr Langston to go down into the cellar to check on the boiler. We knew he'd lied about you, but who would believe us? Basher even threatened me, saying I was part of this … thing. Then you were exposed as the Phantom of Ewing Hill Park. I know you weren't, but most of the boys believed you were expelled because of it – Basher made sure of that. Aaron and I thought Basher must have lied to the headmaster about that too–'

'No,' Chris interrupted. 'Mr Langston came to that conclusion all by himself.'

'Yes, we know that now,' David nodded. 'We discovered that many years later when Aaron was researching for his book about Ewing Hill Park; he interviewed Mr Langston, who quite candid about his seventeen–year tenure. He admitted that he'd made a grave error of judgement about you and he regretted it. To this day, no one knows who the Phantom was.'

Chris closed his eyes briefly, wondering whether he should tell David the truth. He quickly decided that it was best to take the secret to his grave. 'Aaron wrote a book about the school?' Chris opened his eyes, taking a short detour from the subject.

'Yes, he did,' David replied with a smile. 'He's a full time writer. The book's called *Ewing Hill Park: A Staggering 59–Year History*. It was published two years ago on the school's sixtieth anniversary. You can download it as an ebook from the internet, if you like. It's got everything in it – the good, the bad and the ugly times, personal accounts and experiences from the boys, and later, the girls, and members of staff. It's also got the uprising against Mr Schneider, different perspectives on what happened in the library, and the aftermath. It's a truly honest history of the school.'

Chris half smiled at the aptness of the title. 'Anyway, please carry on.'

'Okay, right, back to what happened,' David took another sip of beer first while his mind whirled. He put down the bottle. 'Mr Schneider was charged with assault, GBH and causing serious disturbance. He was released on bail, but they ordered him never to return to school. For a couple of weeks after the trouble, no–one knew what was going to happen. Aaron was sent home for a week the day after you left. He was so distressed. He couldn't stop crying … he was missing you badly. When he came back he was OK, but still hurting. So was I. We became closer than we were before.'

David paused when he saw the glum look on Chris' face, sensing his regret and guilt, even though he knew it wasn't his fault. He quickly moved on.

'Then they brought in a temporary maths teacher – Mr Thirwell – and he had a massive beard!' David gestured the beard exaggeratedly to lighten things up a bit. 'He was absolutely *impossible* to understand! Even by me! He always talked loudly into the microphone, expecting us to hear him as if we were hearing boys! Worse than Mr Bronte, he was, but thankfully, it was only for two months before the summer break.'

David took another sip, then continued. 'Thirdly, you remember that boring science place that we always had to go to every year?' Chris nodded, remembering it. 'Well, we were supposed to go, the week before the end of May half term I think it was. We didn't go there. Instead, we went on a long field trip to a steam railway museum of some sort in Cambridgeshire. All of us went, on a coach, and Mr Bronte and Mr Norris came with us. We didn't think much of it really; at least it was better than going to that science place. What we didn't know at the time, though, was that the school held a secret parents' meeting that same day. All of the parents were there, all gathered in the Assembly Hall. Mr Langston and Rosemary Goldsack, she was the chair of the governors as you may remember, had written to all the parents shortly after the incident to inform them about it. Well, then the parents demanded a meeting. Oh, let me tell you something. Rosemary Goldsack didn't want the letters to be sent to Deaf parents, nor did she want them at the meeting, but Mr Langston refused to accept that and still wrote to them. Then he said Mr McShane and someone else he knew would be at the meeting to interpret for Deaf parents, but Rosemary Goldsack refused to allow it. They clashed fiercely over it, but despite her strong objections, he still went ahead with it. And so, the meeting began … '

It was a turbulent meeting, David explained, and Mr Langston gave a carefully prepared speech – he later revealed in the book that Rosemary Goldsack had written it – to explain what happened, putting sole blame on Chris as the main perpetrator because of a personal vendetta against Mr Schneider. They said he led the revolution, which resulted in his expulsion. There was no mention of the Phantom. The headmaster then said that everything was back to normal and under control, although he also gave the parents the option of pulling their sons out of the school, saying he would not stand in their way. He concluded his speech by thanking them for coming and asked for questions.

'You expelled an innocent boy!' came a loud and angry voice from the seated congregation. All eyes turned to see Geraldine Stephens standing up angrily. 'Christopher Matthaus didn't do anything wrong! Aaron told me everything. It was Brian Thompson who started it!'

'How dare you accuse my son!' Mrs Thompson stood up behind her and pointed at the headmaster on the stage. 'He said it was Chris–'

'That's a goddamn lie!' Geraldine snapped back. She turned to the stage, her voice louder. 'And what about the Phantom of Ewing Hill Park? Yes, he told me about that too!'

Rosemary Goldsack rose from her seat at the end of the stage and hurried over to stand beside the headmaster. She checked the woman's name with him before turning to her, her voice unsteady. 'Mrs Stephens, I think that, perhaps, er, you may have misunderstood your son–'

'Oh, I certainly didn't!' Geraldine cut in, her voice like a sharp blade. 'My eldest, Jamie, is a fluent signer and he interpreted *every word* Aaron said! My husband, John … ' she pointed at John who was sitting next to her. '. . . and I know that Christopher is actually a good lad. There is absolutely no way he would have done it!'

'What the blazes are you talking about – this Phantom thing?' came another voice, this time from Irene Brener, now standing.

Geraldine explained it all to everyone. When she was finished, a rapid flurry of questions flew at the stage. Mr McShane, who was interpreting on the stage, became resigned to the cascade of angry, overlapping voices and simply relayed as best he could.

Why is my son not getting a good enough education here? Why hasn't his speech improved? His English is terrible and he's fifteen – his younger brother is only eight and his English is a friggin' whole lot better! Why are some of your teachers so difficult for the boys to understand? Why aren't the hearing aids helping my son to improve his English? Speech too! Why doesn't this school ever have enough batteries for my son's hearing aids? Why is there only one responsible adult looking after fifty boys each evening and weekend? My son has always complains about the headphones in the classroom – they hurt his ears. They don't work for my son either! The school reports are fabricated! That art teacher on the stage with moving hands – is that sign language? But he's hearing! Look at the Deaf parents; they understand what's being said here because of him, so why can't my son have the same in the classroom? No, I don't agree with you on that – my son must be taught orally! Bullshit! My son can't bloody lipread the teachers! Those reading sessions at the Open Days are pointless and embarrassing – I loved that lad … what was his name? My son, Andrew Brener! Oh yes, thanks Mr Brener – marvellous, he was! Thank you, Mr … ? Reverend Hutchinson – my son's Timothy, by the way, and God bless you! Signing is better than oralism! I agree! I disagree! My son, Gary speaks beautifully! So does my David! My Mark too! My son signs beautifully! My son, Jamon, was suspended for a week because of that bloody German son–of–a–bitch! He threw chalk at my son, he told me! A blackboard duster too! He hit my son! My son, Toby, had more detentions from him in eight months than his older brother, James had in five years here! For signing! My son can't speak or lipread, so why isn't signing allowed in classrooms …

Mr Langston carefully listened as much as he could to those assembled, finally shouting at them to stop and sit down. They did. Resting his hands on the lectern, he sighed, his mind deep in consideration. Finally, he set out to explain how he had struggled for the last five years to move the school away from the old traditions into modern times–

'Donald!' Rosemary Goldsack jumped from her seat anxiously and made her way towards him. 'I don't–'

'*Be quiet,* Rosemary!' he snapped hard at the chairwoman, his voice loud enough to be heard by everyone, not caring what he said to her. *Enough was enough!* 'I've had *enough* of being put down by you and your goddamned institutionalised governors! Now, *sit down* and shut the fuck up!'

Reluctantly, the scrawny woman sat. Mr Langston then addressed those gathered before him vigorously and passionately. He told them all about his long battles with the governors over his efforts to move the school forward, and about what he'd witnessed on his visit to Gallaudet. He said they had Deaf teachers, Deaf professors, sign language interpreters, happy deaf kids who had the freedom to choose to wear their hearing aids or not, their high academic scores – all because of sign language. It had completely changed him. He'd visited a few signing Deaf schools in Britain and now believed that the oral method was nothing but a failure. Sign language was the key to Deaf education; that was not his opinion, he said, but an absolute fact. He believed pursuing oralism to be as pointless as flogging a long dead horse; like many other oral teachers of the deaf, he suspected, he'd been blinded into believing in something that hadn't worked for so long – it was based on a truth formed by too many lies, he said. He cared deeply for deaf children and wanted the best from them, but this could only be achieved through their *own natural language.*

He then outlined his plans for the future; the introduction of Total Communication would work for every deaf child, he thought, although sign language would be their primary method of communication. He promised the parents they'd see dramatic improvements in their sons' education. He said he would scrap all of the obsolete headphones, and the new FM system that the Physics Room already had would be installed in all classrooms. It would only work for those few with residual hearing, and so would not be used as a main tool for aural instruction. He explained how he wanted to appoint a dedicated speech therapist as part of the boys' personal development, not as part of their education. Funds permitting, he wanted to establish a new sixth form college for students to be taught through sign language. He wanted to appoint new Deaf teachers, and give hearing teachers the opportunity to learn sign language – he was prepared to do so, personally. Finally, He admitted that it may be too late to improve the seniors' education, but not too late for the juniors and future pupils.

He allowed Mrs Munnings to come on stage to share her experiences as a sign convert. Mr McShane joined in, speaking and signing simultaneously about himself, his experiences and how the boys loved him. Miss Stephenson, too, joined in and concurred with her colleagues. She encouraged a reluctant Mr Whittle to join them; he told them that although he was still on the oral side, he acknowledged the importance of educating the deaf through sign language. Mr Arkwright remained seated, silent. Lastly, Robert Denham confirmed Mr Langston's claims of his struggles with the governors and told everyone about his son, Patrick.

Mr Langston finished off his address by saying that he no longer wanted Ewing Hill Park School to be primarily oral; he wanted it to be the best Deaf school in Britain and that could only be achieved with everyone's support. He thanked his colleagues for their contributions and then everyone for listening.

And then, he announced his resignation.

'It sent shock waves through the Assembly Hall,' David said, his hands spreading out to illustrate the effect. 'There was a long, stunned silence. According to Aaron's mother in the book, nobody was quite sure whether he was serious or not. He probably said it to force the issue – we don't know – but then someone from the audience called for the chair and the governors to resign instead. Of course, Rosemary Goldsack refused. Aaron's mother reiterated the call. Then all of sudden, many others followed it up. They practically chanted for them to go. Some even threatened to remove their sons from the school. A few others threatened to go to the press about the incident and suchlike. Hell, it was a farce – they were worse than us boys!'

'And then what happened?' Chris asked before taking a look at his watch: almost three o'clock.

'Well, they had an emergency board meeting afterwards. We know very little of what happened, but apparently, there were massive rows. Rosemary Goldsack finally agreed to resign; so did the rest of the board, except for Robert Denham, who became the new chair. His first task was to reject Mr Langston's resignation and it didn't take much persuasion for him to stay on! Excuse me, I need to go for a piss.'

David left the table, heading for the gents. Chris fiddled with his empty beer bottle, mulling over their chat. He hadn't realised it before, but a long–suppressed anger was now beginning to creep up inside him. David soon returned to the table and called out to the bartender for two more beers.

'The school,' David resumed, '. . . changed. A lot. Mr Langston was well ahead of his time. The board of governors increased from eight to twelve. Four of the new board members were Deaf; one of whom was Toby Eriswell's mother. Geraldine Stephens also joined. Because of his private finance company, Robert Denham had good contacts, so he got one or two investors onboard to help fulfil the vision. Some educationalists who were strong advocates of sign language and total communication also joined – no medical professionals – they weren't needed as it was all about education, not medicine. Out with the old, in with the new. Mr McShane couldn't be involved in the interpreting, as it was a conflict of interest, so he got a few good signers that he knew in – remember we didn't have proper qualified BSL interpreters then – to help with the communication between the Deaf and hearing members.'

Chris gripped his bottle with both hands, mesmerised by the story. David took another sip.

'The next thing Mr Langston did,' David said, 'was to summon Basher into his office, with Mr McShane interpreting. He demanded the truth from the lad. At first, Basher stuck to his story, but when pressed, he finally admitted that he'd lied about almost everything about you. Mr Langston went mad. Really fucking mad! He immediately stripped him of his head boy status and appointed Gary Portmore until the end of the term. He told him that as soon as he put down his paintbrush at the end of his O Level art exam – that was his only exam, see – he was out of the school, pronto. He did that, in shame. A lot of boys told him to fuck off and they were glad to see the back of him. Finally, Aaron and I were able to tell everyone the truth; that you were *not* the Phantom, nor did you start the revolution. Of course, questions were asked about the Phantom's identity, but, like I said before, it's still a mystery.'

Chris almost let it slip, but quickly retracted, hiding his knowing expression. 'Yes, I wonder who it was.'

'So, anyway, Mr Langston then set about reinstating you, but your social worker … what was his name again?' David furrowed his eyebrows.

'Steve Lewison,' Chris reminded him.

'Yeah, him,' David nodded. 'He said that his superiors weren't impressed and wouldn't agree to fund your place at the school again. Besides, you'd already left the country with your mother.'

Chris sighed inwardly; even though it was more than thirty years ago, the soul–searching wrench of leaving England was still with him, though he had no real regrets. He wondered how different his life would have been if he'd stayed on. There were too many "what ifs" that could never be answered; what had happened, happened and he had to live with it, although he had sometimes felt a twinge or two of regret. The niggling grudge against Basher still lurked at the back of his mind; a good punch on his face might finally help to exorcise that ghost for once and all.

'Chris?' David waved his hand in front of Chris', who was staring blankly into space, breaking him out of his private thoughts. 'You okay?'

'Sorry, yeah, I'm okay,' Chris smiled. 'I was just thinking, that's all. Anyway, about the school … ?'

David leaned forward, resting his elbows on the table, and allowed himself to rack his brains for a moment, piecing together his own memories and the events that followed after he had left school. 'The changes started slowly at first but progressed quickly after the summer break … '

First off, David said, all of the old wooden desks with the control panels and headphones were replaced with new ordinary desks with angled sides, so that they could be arranged in a semicircular formation. The teachers' desks had FM systems attached to them; it had never worked for the majority of the boys, but at least they didn't have to wear those headphones any more, much to their relief.

Mr Bronte had been "retired", while Mr Norris left to teach sports at a hearing school. Mal Walker, who was Deaf – the school's first ever Deaf teacher – took his place. He was an energetic but tough young man and the boys respected him. The new craftwork teacher, Dominic Ash, didn't know any sign language when he arrived, but picked it up pretty quickly: Mr McShane's Deaf partner, Kerry Durham, taught the staff sign language every week.

'In a way,' said David, 'he was the first ever Deaf sign language tutor, though nobody thought of it like that at the time–'

'Wait a minute,' Chris interrupted. 'Are you saying Mr McShane's gay?'

'Yep!' David smiled back. 'He and Kerry became civil partners the first day that same sex civil partnerships became legal in Britain … that was about seven years ago. Aaron was there and so were Mr Langston and his wife, Frances.' Chris raised his eyebrows. 'Yes, his attitude's changed. Well, you see, Chris, er, you remember their daughter, Shaleen? That pretty girl that a lot of the boys fancied?'

Chris grinned, picking up the obvious. 'She's a lesbian, right?'

'Right! She married a Deaf woman and they have two kids.'

Chris laughed at the irony. The memory of being caught in the cellar, then summoned to the headmaster's office for his lecture about the rights and wrongs of it all came flashing back to him. He shook away the long forgotten memories and beckoned for David to go back to the story.

'Because of what happened with Mr Schneider, we had four new houseparents to look after us during the evenings and at weekends. No more duty teachers. Elaine Hogarth and Colleen Turner continued with their duties until the mid–nineties, I think, when the use of school matrons was phased out. They're now seeing out their lives together in Ireland, by the way.'

'Looking back, it's hard to believe we only had *one* duty teacher looking after fifty boys!'

'I know,' David agreed. 'But back then, it wasn't statutory for children's residential places to have a certain number of responsible adults, or even have them vetted. The mind boggles, doesn't it? I think it was Children's Act in, um, 1989, I think, that made it compulsory.'

'What happened to Mr Schneider?' Chris asked, folding his arms over the table.

'Well, the following October, he stood trial at the Crown Court. He still pleaded not guilty to all of the charges. Some of the boys and their parents were there, including me and my parents, and Aaron and his folks. I remember us waiting outside the courtroom on the first day very well – it was a four day trial. The parents were going to act as our "interpreters" – there were no BSL interpreters back then – although Mr McShane and that other one, I can't remember her name, were also there for the Deaf parents, I think. Well, we didn't even get called in as witnesses because Mr Schneider suddenly changed his plea to guilty. Waste of time and money, but that's the justice system.' David shrugged. 'Apparently, he was fined and didn't go to prison. Rumour has it he was ordered to never work with children again and he went back to Germany – God knows what became of him. According to Mr McShane, who was in the courtroom, Schneider claimed the boys attacked him first, but we know that wasn't true. It was his extreme oralist beliefs and his loathing for sign language that were his ... ' David paused, trying to attach a term.

'Achilles heel?' Chris suggested.

'Yeah, Achilles heel, yeah,' David nodded. 'In a way, the language and communication problem he put up became his own worst enemy. Anyway, back to the school ... '

Mr Arkwright was the only staff member to refuse to attend the school's weekly sign language lessons, and he continued teaching speech and religious studies orally for another year, before deciding to leave to teach at Weyton Comprehensive. He later said he no longer felt part of Mr Langston's vision and wanted to move on. Mr Ackmar, who once had a spell as a student teacher at Ewing Hill Park, returned to teach religious education after gaining a degree in theology from Cambridge University. He had already disregarded what he called the "useless" Paget Gorman method, in favour of sign language. The school then appointed a part–time speech therapist to instruct the boys' in speech as part of their personal development. Mr Whittle continued teaching English, but struggled to acquire a reasonable level of sign language, although there was a marked improvement in the boys' English learning. He married Miss Stephenson – now Mrs Whittle – and they decided to leave Ewing Hill Park at the same time as Aaron and David finished school. Mrs Whittle was pregnant, so they moved up to her native Yorkshire to raise their new family and Charles took up a teaching post there.

Much to the surprise of everyone, James Eriswell returned to Ewing Hill Park, this time as the new English teacher. It was later revealed in the book that Mr Langston had headhunted James and persuaded him to take up the post after he'd finished his degree at University of Leeds. The educationalists asked questions about the appointment of an inexperienced Deaf English teacher, but it was pointed out to them that the school – and other oral schools for the deaf – had always employed hearing teachers who weren't qualified to teach deaf children, let alone make themselves understood. Mr Langston deemed it necessary for a peer to teach that subject; James Eriswell was the ideal choice, he said, because of his fluency in sign and written English as well as his strong Deaf background. With Mr Langston as his mentor, James became an instant success with the boys. He arrived when Toby was in the Fourth Form, and his younger brother, Casey, followed him a year later. The other boys liked to wind them up about it, often nicknaming them *brother teacher* and *brother pupil.*

More new Deaf and hearing teachers who could sign, or were prepared to learn, came to teach and new subjects were introduced, such as technical drawing, woodwork, computer science and drama. When GCSEs replaced CSEs and O Levels in the mid–Eighties, the school adopted the new National Curriculum with subjects such as science of all three subjects, Information Technology and humanities. A Sixth Form College was built on the west side of the school; opening in 1983, named Langston House after the headmaster who pioneered its development. For the first time ever girls were allowed in; many of whom received an education sign language for the first time in their lives. Disillusioned by the pro–oral stance taken by the only two teacher of the deaf training courses, Mr Langston set up a new pro–sign training course for aspiring Deaf and hearing teachers. This brought in some much needed extra revenue in addition to the increased tuition fees paid by the boys' local education authorities, although increasing numbers of deaf children going to their local mainstream schools. Until Mr Langston's retirement in 1992, the school's academic scores saw a marked improvement on a yearly basis, all because of instruction through sign language, mirroring what he had witnessed at Gallaudet and MSSD several years before. Just before he retired, Mr Langston invited Edward Merrill and his wife to the school to showcase his achievements and to thank him for his inspiration. Three years later, Merrill died.

James Eriswell, who'd been trained by his former mentor over ten years, succeeded Mr Langston as the third (and the first Deaf) headmaster of Ewing Hill Park at the age of only thirty–two. A year later, he attended the first ever seminar on sign bilingualism in Deaf education in Sheffield. There, he learned how the concept of bilingual–bicultural – BiBi – education was that deaf children, irrespective of how deaf they were, used sign as their natural first language. Spoken or written language came as their second language; either acquired after or at the same time as the native language. So, in bilingualism, sign language was the primary method of instruction, while the bicultural aspect emphasised Deaf culture and created confidence in deaf children by exposing them to the Deaf community. James Eriswell strongly believed that there was a correlation between BSL and English literacy skills because the former could predict and enable the acquisition of the latter. The Deaf teacher had proved this by successfully teaching English in sign language for ten years prior to his promotion. In addition, other research studies he had come across had proved that bilingual deaf children showed more development in cognitive, linguistic, and meta–linguistic processes than their monolingual peers. This approach was already successful in Leeds, as well as in America and Scandinavia. He thought that since oralism had failed. Cued Speech was too abstract and limited. Total Communication, although workable to a certain degree, had its drawbacks, sign bilingual education was the ultimate key.

Eventually, David went on, the school and college adopted the sign bilingual approach over Total Communication – it did not take too much, since all the teachers used British Sign Language now anyway; the hearing staff members only needing to stop using ftheir microphones. In addition, he introduced a new policy that gave the pupils and students the choice of wearing their hearing aids or not – he'd always said that were never been any evidence of the benefits of wearing them in schools and he questioned the compliance in rules by other oral schools. Individual speech therapy remained as an option while hearing aids and, later, cochlear implant support, were still provided.

Ewing Hill Park's sister school, Boyd Hill Grammar School, closed down in 1996. David explained that the school, which had remained strictly oral, closed because of its low pupil numbers. Tuition fees were paid by local education authorities, and increasingly they preferred the cheaper option of mainstreaming. Year upon year, the declining numbers had serious implications on the school's budgeting. Like Ewing Hill Park, Boyd Hill's main building was a Grade 2 listed building, so modernisation, improvements and access requirements couldn't be carried out. The surrounding land was also listed and was too small to build additional buildings on. Like Ewing Hill Park, Boyd Hill was obliged to admit deaf children with additional needs and behavioural issues (the standard entrance exams having been phased out), causing further funding constraints to accommodate their needs. Finally, the school's heartbroken governors decided to close it down.

Noting the closure of Boyd Hill and several other specialist Deaf schools around the country for similar reasons (as well as political moves to integrate deaf children into mainstream schools by calling it inclusive education), James Eriswell knew his school would be under threat, too, and was determined not to let that happen.

The school acquired most of Boyd Hill's pupils, and Ewing Hill Park became a mixed school and college. With Robert Denham's backing, Ewing Hill Park acquired funding to build a new specialist centre for deaf pupils with additional needs next to Langston House, naming it the Denham Centre after the chairperson. Three new dormitories were built around the school to accommodate the extra boarders; they were named the McShane, Munnings and Matthaus Halls – or the MMM Halls, as they were called.

Chris raised his eyebrows, grinning in surprise.

David chuckled. 'James Eriswell decided to name one after you. You may not know this, but you're a legend. Your departure ignited the change, so it was a natural choice. Aaron cut the ribbon on your behalf and gave a great speech about his friendship with you. I was there too. Shed a tear, I can tell you!'

Chris was lost for words, but appreciated the gesture. 'McShane and Munnings?'

'Oh, er, Mr McShane left in 1995, I think, to work as a freelance interpreter, although he came back to interpret in meetings and suchlike. He and Kerry are still living in Brighton, so travel wasn't a problem. He was Mr Langston's first seed in his efforts to change the school, so, again, he was an obvious choice for the name. He cut the ribbon. As for Mrs Munnings, well, it was named in her memory. She was diagnosed with breast cancer early in the nineties and had to retire early from teaching. She was a very successful sign convert, you know, she was inspired by that programme, *Signs of Life* back in 1979. Do you remember that?'

Chris shook his head: it had escaped him.

'It was shown at the same time as the kick–off of the FA Cup Final between Arsenal and Manchester United–'

'Oh yeah, I remember now,' Chris interrupted him. 'You, Aaron and a few others watched it in the staff room, didn't you? Arsenal won 3–2! I'll never forget that!'

'Yeah, well, interestingly, it was a pilot for *See Hear!* which was first broadcast in ... October 1981, I think, and is still going now; it's actually one of the BBC's longest running shows ever. Anyway, back to Mrs Munnings; she had a mastectomy – breast removal – but unfortunately, the cancer had already spread and she died shortly after. Her grown–up daughter, Elise, cut the ribbon in her honour.'

Chris and David became silent, praying for their former geography and history teacher.

'James Eriswell didn't stop there,' David finally broke the silence. 'He had a rather extraordinary vision for revolutionising the school and the estate. You know it's kind of like an island, surrounded by five roads?' With his hands, David drew an invisible pentagonal map in the air, a slightly angled vertical line through it and pinpointing the school in the centre. Chris nodded.

'Well, he knew the school wouldn't survive long because of the mainstreaming policies and changing times, so other avenues had to be explored. He wanted to expand Langston House into Britain's first ever dedicated Deaf university, build a big new learning centre for classes, demolish the eyesore that was Magnat House and build a big cafeteria with facilities for cookery courses, an arts and media centre, a sports complex with indoor and outdoor pitches and courts, oh, and a conference centre, including a theatre. Pretty impressive, eh? There were also houses and flats for the students in the plans; surrounded by landscaped gardens and trees that would be maintained by students studying horticulture. The school itself was to become the administrative hub. It was also handily close to London, remember. Even Waltbridge District Council was excited by the plans because it would boost the local economy, provide jobs and, most importantly, put the town on the map. So they agreed to support the development. They were all up for it.'

'Like Gallaudet?' Chris remarked, fascinated.

'Yeah, like Gallaudet,' David nodded. 'Not just for Britain, but Europe too. Funding could be sought from the European Union, as well as Deaf associations, to get money for courses and projects for Deaf students from all over Europe to study there. It didn't really matter what their native sign languages were; they could still acquire BSL or English, or even both, under the bilingual model; they could easily become multilingual, in fact. So, money would be coming in all the time. Of course, it would take years to develop – Rome wasn't built in a day – but it was all on the plate. The mind boggles, Chris, but it was viable.'

David took a short, sharp breath to ease his excitement, and then continued. 'James Eriswell wanted to drop the name Ewing Hill Park because Ewing signifies oralism; he wanted to call the whole place Surdania Academy Park.' David noted Chris' puzzled look. 'Surdus is Latin for deaf and Surdania means "land of the deaf". So ... ' David left this hanging, the answer already in the air.

Chris' eyes darted to David with a hint of scrutiny. An unusual name; one that people would probably either love or hate, though it had some kind of merit, he thought to himself.

'Everyone was excited by it,' David said, 'the fully–fledged sign bilingualism environment that we've long yearned for. The school was already at its peak with high achieving scores. It was also well organised and had an outstanding OFSTED Grade One mark. So, there was no reason not to build on its success. Buying the school and its estate from the next generation of the Ewing–Boyd Hill family was the first step in the developmental process. Robert Denham, even though he was in his seventies, set about striking a deal with them, with financial backing from Jacques Magnat. Remember him? He inherited a vast fortune from his parents. Dean Hopkirk, Hendrik Swart – ironically, he married a black woman, by the way – and a few other wealthy former pupils were also going to chip in. Unfortunately, it dragged on and on because the Ewing–Boyd Hill family were reluctant to sell. In 2004, a deal was finally struck. A pre–contractual agreement was signed to secure the deal while the proper legal paperwork was compiled by both sets of lawyers. Gary Portmore was one of them, on our side – yes, he became a lawyer as well as a MP; tell you about him later. Everything was going well … '

'But it didn't end well, did it?' Chris chipped in, having already sensed the inevitable.

'No, it didn't,' David shook his head grimly. He glanced at his watch – it was just after half past six. He was surprised at how the time had gone by so quickly. He felt a loud rumble in his stomach. Talking about the past had made him hungry. 'Can we go somewhere to eat?' he asked.

38

End of an Era

"It is the greatest obstacle to good provision … There are far more children statemented than we ever envisaged. It has ceased to be about what the child needs and has just become a battle for resources."
– BARONESS MARY WARNOCK, upon realising the failure of her 1978 *Warnock Report on Special Education* Needs, calling it "invented" and "disastrous", 2003

After Chris had invited David over to his house for the evening, they'd first stopped at a supermarket to buy beer and nibbles, and then a Chinese take–away, before arriving at Chris' bungalow in the suburbs.

While Chris was in the kitchen putting the food on plates, David browsed around his spacious open–plan living and dining room. A framed photograph on the wall caught his eye and he went over to it, gasping in surprise as he saw that it was a photo of Chris' Arsenal football and his Avro Lancaster model plane, placed against a wall that had childlike doodles crayoned on it. Chris came in with the plates and smiled as he saw David staring at the picture with his mouth wide open. David turned to Chris, pointing at it with a question mark in his face.

Putting the plates on the table, Chris said, 'When we came here, I couldn't take the football that Aaron gave me for Christmas, or the model that you gave me. My mother and I only took what we could fit in our cases, and left everything we didn't need back at the flat. So, I took a photograph of them against that wall – I did those drawings when I was little – using my mother's new camera. You know those old rectangular things?' He gestured a small camera with a viewfinder at the end. 'I had that photograph enlarged and framed it to remember our friendship.'

David nodded and walked over to the table, still speechless, then sat and picked up his cutlery. Chris sat too and took a large prawn cracker from a bowl.

'Tell me about Aaron,' Chris said, nibbling it.

'Aaron … after you left … ' David paused as he recollected.

Despite still being distressed, Aaron took his CSE English exam and managed a Grade 3. (The following year, he took it again and achieved Grade 1.) He also took O Levels in English and English Literature in the Fourth Form, and got an

A and a B, respectively. In Form Five, he took A Level English – the first ever Ewing Hill Park boy to have done so and he studied it at the local college with full communication support provided by the school – and got a B.

'Who was the head boy in his Form?' Chris interrupted, scooping up some rice with his fork.

'Ian Snyman,' David answered, then returning to the subject of Aaron.

After school, Aaron had studied English at University of Bristol. Despite struggling for three years with little or no communication support, remarkably, he achieved a first class degree. He had some help from another student, Suzanne Maidson; the girl from next door who he'd known since they were babies. They courted, got married and had three children – all deaf – who were educated at Elmfield during their primary years. Their eldest, Joseph, then went to Ewing Hill Park; he was in the sixth form when James Eriswell departed. Their daughter, Isabelle, went to Ewing Hill Park two years after her older brother and was unfortunate enough to fall foul of the change during her last two years there. According to Aaron, her schoolwork suffered badly. Instead of staying on in sixth form, she went to a deaf college that used BSL. Their youngest, Christian, who was born three years after his sister, stayed in Bristol throughout his education.

Aaron took on various jobs to support his family over the years, but writing was always his passion; he wrote both fiction and non–fiction books, including the one about Ewing Hill Park, and, recently, he helped to write his mother's book, *Raising Aaron*, about her experiences of raising her deaf child. He also wrote short made–for–television film scripts that were produced by Deaf people and shown at Deaf film festivals around the world. Suzanne became a registered qualified sign language interpreter, so money wasn't short for the family. Both were strong advocates for sign bilingual education; recently, they were involved in a massive campaign against Bristol City Council's decision to close Elmfield School.

'Why?' Chris asked, taking another prawn cracker.

David sighed. He ate more of his dinner and sipped his beer. 'Well, to cut a very long story short,' David said, putting down his bottle, 'Apparently, there was a review to find a way of improving the education system in Bristol. They decided to close Elmfield and place deaf children in Hearing Impaired Resource Bases – HIRBs as they're now called – for inclusion rather than to save money. Well, this sparked outrage and a huge and highly vociferous campaign started to save the school ... that lasted for almost two years. They set up a Facebook campaign group and an e–petition, which collected nearly five thousand signatures from all over the world. Parents of deaf children wrote to their MPs and councillors to express their anger and concerns about the decision. Erm, the media got involved as well, and there were regular reports about it; a local TV company did a "day in the life" of a pupil at Elmfield, to show what it was like being at a signing Deaf school. Even some celebrities such as Derren Brown and Barbara Windsor got involved in supporting it and helping to spread the message ... there was also support from the NDCS, BDA, WFD and, um, the Equalities Commission. MPs and councillors were invited to the school and the kids told them how important it was to them and why the HIRBs would not work for them. They were moved to tears and pledged their support. The kids also made a few engaging BSL videos and uploaded them to the internet.'

'But Bristol City Council wouldn't budge?' Chris asked, guessing their stance.

'No.' David shook his head. 'They even changed their excuse and said money was the issue, even though Elmfield was mostly funded by authorities *outside* the area. That was silly, I mean, the school presented their financial reports, so anyone could see that. Also, it had high academic ratings; it even had an OFSTED Grade One performance rating as being outstanding! Eventually, they set up a working party to review the decision, and towards the end of last year, it was recommended that the school should stay open. They had to make some changes, though, such as slightly reducing the number of pupils, including more with additional needs, and there was to be a new sixth–form college and rebranding. In March, these recommendations were agreed. They won!'

Chris smiled, sipping his beer, pleased with the good fortune. 'And, how about you?' he asked him.

'Not much, really, I'm afraid,' David scoffed at his own wit. 'My parents got back together after that parents' meeting that I told you about. Mummy, bless her, is enjoying her retirement. Daddy's dead though. I'm married to my third wife, Catherine, who's hearing but has Deaf parents. You don't want to know about my first two! We've got a beautiful daughter, Cassandra, who's thirteen – she's deaf. And as for me, well, I'm a partner in a private charter and freight airline business that my friend Scott and I set up. We've got a few staff and some pilots, and although I can fly planes and helicopters, I mostly do the wheeling and dealing. That's why I'm here; to broker a deal, but it got shelved. It's probably a good thing that happened – I found you, didn't I?'

They shared a chuckle.

'So, how's your daughter doing at school?' Chris wondered, finishing his beer.

'There's only one word for it: terrible!' David said bluntly. 'She's in a mainstream school. Catherine didn't want to send her away to boarding school. Of course, I disagreed, but I had to accept defeat. Cassandra's my precious girl, you see. Anyway, she isn't doing well at school. She did alright at primary, but secondary's a different ball game. No BSL support, zilch, even though she has a statement of SEN – Special Educational Needs. My wife and I have been fighting for support for her for some time now, but those bloody idiots at the local education authority still refuse to pay!'

'In America,' Chris offered, 'although I don't know much about their education system, I do know there're hundreds of signing Deaf schools, each with hundreds of deaf children. There are also mainstream – or public – schools, and the law there says they have to accommodate deaf kids' needs, including sign interpreting support. That law was passed back in 1973.'

'That's almost forty years ago now!' David exclaimed. 'And we still don't have one in Britain! Yes, we've got the Equalities Commission, but it's usually down to individual tribunals and that can take time ... it's costly, too. She does, though, have a peripatetic teacher of the deaf, but she only gets one hour of that each week. The teacher of the deaf can't even sign and my daughter struggles to understand her.'

'Are you saying that teachers of the deaf travel to different mainstream schools in your area, just to spend an hour a week with each kid?'

'That's how it works, unfortunately,' David shrugged. 'On average, there's one teacher for every thirty deaf pupils; sometimes they only get half an hour a week! Insane, isn't it?! It's not the only problem, though. She's also being bullied by some of the hearing children. She won't admit it, but I know – I went through the same thing, remember? And she gets so tired after school because she has to use her eyes all the time, trying to understand the teacher and the other kids, as well as reading what's on the board. We've complained so many times, but it's difficult. One teacher even had the bloody nerve to suggest she should have a cochlear implant like I have ... ' He pointed at a tiny circular device above his left ear. '. . . Remember my "super–hearing"? Well I lost it, so I opted for the implant so I could regain some hearing, but my wife and I don't want to force one on Cassandra. Plenty of these "medical professionals" have said she should have one too; according to them, it's the best and only way to help her, but we know that's not true, so we've refused. It has to be *her* decision, not ours. If she wants one, then we'll support her, but she hasn't said anything about it yet. I've heard from many, many other parents of deaf kids, some with Usher, that pen–pushers like medical professionals and pro–oral educationalists often bang on about cochlear implants as "must haves" and sign language as a "no–no", and it's causing a helluva lot of confusion and distress. Really, there needs to be some kind of guidance to help parents make informed choices!'

David exhaled, letting out his anger and frustration. 'Anyway, back to that teacher ... he believed that having a cochlear implant would help her follow her classes better. I told him that cochlear implants might help deaf kids to develop good speech, but they aren't "magic bullets", and kids with cochlear implants or hearing aids are just as deaf as the rest of them. It's their language development – and I mean *BSL* development, not their hearing, that helps them.' He sighed. 'Making the deaf listen is like making the blind read, I told him. I even said that he and some of the other teachers need deaf awareness training. They always say it's inclusion, but for Cassandra, it's *isolation*.'

'Does she have any deaf friends?' asked Chris, clasping his hands.

'Some, yeah,' David said, 'but most of them don't sign. We once took her to a local deaf children's society, but it was all very oral. They ignored Cassandra's signing, like it was some kind of taboo, and even told her not to sign to the other deaf kids, who'd been fascinated by it. She didn't like that; us neither. They actually told us that learning sign language stops them speaking!' David paused to allow that thought to sink in, then resumed signing. 'Look at me, I've been signing since I went deaf at seven and I still haven't lost my voice. Hell, you should've *seen* those poor deaf kids – they seemed so lost. Couldn't sign, didn't speak well and as for their written English? Forget it! Wait till they grow up – they'll be shocked when they go to university or meet other Deaf young people.'

'Yeah, I know the feeling,' Chris agreed. 'I've had many Deaf friends like that. Culture shock, you know. It can actually cause psychological distress and depression ... I've seen people blame their parents for not introducing them to Deaf people and sign language in the first place.'

'Darned right!' David nodded. 'We never went back to that place again.'

'Is Deaf education in Britain really that bad?' asked Chris.

From what he knew, due to problems with his daughter's education, David gave Chris the lowdown on the state of Deaf education in Britain. Firstly, he explained about the 1978 Warnock Report and that the then Prime Minster, Margaret Thatcher, had implemented the 1982 Education Act based on the report's recommendations, thus giving local education authorities greater powers to mainstream more deaf children. It quickly became a battleground for parents, schools and councils; it was estimated that three quarters of deaf children did not have statements of SEN. Almost nine in every ten deaf children now attended mainstream schools, David said. The mainstream education system was too dependent on the oral/aural approach and there was a false belief that hearing aids or cochlear implants (it was estimated that seventy percent of deaf children who started school already had them) would help, when in fact sign bilingualism or Total Communication were the key tools of effective instruction. Inevitably, the latest government statistics showed that six in ten deaf children failed to achieve five A*–C GCSE grades, whereas seven in ten hearing children did.

'That's a very poor record,' Chris said, picking up their dirty plates.

'And it's going to get worse now that local authorities are making such huge cuts to deaf education services,' said David, picking up the empty prawn cracker bowl and placing it on the top of the plates that Chris was holding. 'There's another thing, Chris. Aaron recently told me a shocking thing about the Warnock Report. Apparently, a *very* reliable source told him, many years after the inquiry, that a member of the Warnock Inquiry Committee had told them that during the inquiry, they'd interviewed several people, including disabled people, for their views on integration. One "well known" Deaf person was interviewed through a highly skilled sign language interpreter friend. This Deaf person told them about how important it was for Deaf children to be educated through sign language in Deaf schools, and that they were against integration. Afterwards, the committee debated it and decided that the interpreter had made a mistake in voicing over what the Deaf person had said, instead, they believed that Deaf people actually wanted integration! Also, it's been reported that Margaret Thatcher has publicly acknowledged, years later, that she had "serious reservations" about the Education Act. Too little, too late!'

Chris rose to his feet, shaking his head in dismay. 'Coffee?'

Sipping their coffee, welcoming the change from the beer they'd been supping for the last nine hours, Chris and David spent the next couple of hours chatting about world affairs, football and films, debating a number of topics. Chris suddenly changed the subject to a more personal one.

'You said that Donald Langston's funeral will be next week?' he asked.

David nodded. 'The date hasn't been fixed yet, but from the texts I've had from home, it seems like there'll be a memorial service at the church in Waltbridge – the one we used to go to – towards the end of next week. I think quite a lot of people are going.'

'I'll come back to England with you and go to that, if that's okay with you?' said Chris, sipping his second coffee, gazing at David expectantly. He'd been thinking about it since early afternoon, deliberating over whether to go or not.

'Of course you can!' David smiled, delighted at the news. 'I'm sure the others'll *love* to see you. Especially Aaron.'

'Don't tell anyone I'm coming, alright? I just want to, you know, surprise them!' Chris put his mug down on the table. David nodded in agreement. 'I'd need a place to stay though, so would you mind ... ?'

Moments later, Chris had booked his one–way flight – he'd worry about the return later; he had a dual British/Australian passport – and upgraded David's ticket to business class using the details David had in his mobile. He also bought Aaron's book on Ewing Hill Park's history and his mother's book, in eBook format, to read on the long flight and at David's family home in Shropshire. It was after midnight by the time he was finished, and it was then that he asked about Jamie

Stephens.

'Jamie,' David said, 'as you would expect, is a sign language interpreter; has been for over twenty–five years now. Er, he's divorced now and has two daughters who're at university. In the Eighties, when he was fresh out of college and the girls were young, he did part time jobs to keep his family afloat; he'd do things like interpreting at Ewing Hill Park and at weddings, meetings and stuff. We didn't have registered qualified interpreters then, but the profession eventually started to grow towards the end of that decade. Jamie was one of the first generation of sign language interpreters; there was a bit of politics about BSL versus Sign Supported English but Jamie stuck to BSL. Then, in 1990, the BDA had their Centenary Congress in Brighton. You heard about it?'

'Yeah, I've read about it,' Chris nodded. 'I'd just graduated from Gallaudet and saw on the news that Princess Diana was there and she signed!'

'I was there and so was Aaron,' David grinned, revelling fondly in the memory of one of the biggest Deaf events in British history. 'There were over three thousand Deaf people there for a week! Jamie was one of the group of new BSL and SSE interpreters – there was a BSL interpreter at one end of the stage and an SSE one at the other. Princess Diana was the patron of the BDA, of course; she'd been learning BSL and apparently *loved* it. The media went crazy when she signed her short address; there were camera flashes everywhere and it was splashed all over the front pages the next day, with full centre spreads too. They even showed close up photos of her signing hands and everything. It even hit the national television news for a while. It was amazing! I think she boosted Deaf people's image, and must have inspired thousands of people to learn BSL. Sign language became kind of "normal" after that.'

'It was tragic that she died though.' Chris commented. 'And what about Aaron and Jamie's parents?'

'They've retired to Wales now,' said David.

He then talked about what had become of their closest form mates, beginning with the news that Steven Clarke and Jamon Cranley were both dead. Steven died of AIDS related illnesses in 1986; when there was international panic over the "gay plague". He was one of several Deaf gay men who died of that because they didn't fully understand the information that was circulated on sexual protection and sexual health, it wasn't accessible to them. Jamon was killed in a motorcycle accident in Suffolk two years later. Lester Morrison, David added, was in prison for the third time; this time for drug dealing and burglary.

Dean Hopkirk, old *Rich*, as expected, became head boy, keeping the promise he'd made to Chris; he and his form mates protected Steven from homophobic bullying, although nothing could be done about Michael Hardcastle. The day he left Ewing Hill Park, he took his parents and Mr Arkwright out into the car park, removed both of his hearing aids, showed them their empty battery compartments and joyfully threw them up into the air, much to the three adults' shock. He told them he was deaf, full stop, and didn't need them, and hasn't worn them since. He went on to live a life of luxury for some years, then got married, had four hearing children and used his own capital to set up a production company to make films and television programmes.

Andrew Brener left school with few qualifications, although he did well in physics. After doing a Youth Training Scheme, he worked for years as a plasterer and decorator until he was recently forced to retire due to tennis elbow. With a rather colourful domestic background, David said, Andrew had been married and divorced three times and was now seeing a woman half his age. He had five children and was now also a grandfather, twice over! He was also a well–known actor in the Deaf community, having acted in films, on television and in theatre. Sometime during the last decade, he went to college in Sheffield to study English; he'd been frustrated by his inability to write and understand a reasonable level of English, especially when it came to reading scripts. Throughout his year there, he had full BSL support and achieved a C in his GCSE English exam, which he was happy with, telling David that he'd learnt a lot more about English through BSL in that one year than he ever had in his five years at Ewing Hill Park.

Matthew Burke went to college in Cardiff to study mathematics before taking up a job in a factory, but he'd had to give it up after only a few years because of his vision.

'Usher syndrome, right?' Chris remarked, shuttering his hands inwards on either side of his head. 'I know all about it. It's a combination of deafness and RP; I've friends who have it and I sometimes volunteer as their guide.'

David nodded, going on to say that the term had become widely known during the mid–Eighties. Matthew had had to stop working at his second job in an office at the age of thirty because of his deteriorating sight, and although he still had some residual sight, he was now almost deafblind and needed full mobility and communication support outside his home. Matthew struggled to meet a woman for years, until he finally met Delia, who was Deaf, and they had a son, Corey, also Deaf. He was now fifteen and attending mainstream school, David said. Matthew and Delia had had problems with the school because of the inadequate education Corey was receiving; he was the only signing deaf pupil in an oral–only class. The other parents had refused to allow their deaf children to use BSL. Corey struggled to follow his part–time communication support worker – Matthew said she had terrible BSL skills; more like very patchy SSE. Sometimes Corey's own BSL even got mixed up with her SSE and his parents often had had to "correct" his signing. The school had also sent Matthew and Delia warning letters about Corey's continued refusal to wear his hearing aids, suggesting that not wearing them would impede his speech development (he didn't have any speech) and English skills from improving, which the parents thought was ridiculous. Corey already had an excellent command of written English as his parents had encouraged him to write a lot and read as many books as he could; they sometimes explained what things meant through BSL at home. He was the best in his class at both English and Maths, which had always impressed and confounded his teachers. Other orally taught deaf pupils tended to struggle, even with their cochlear implants and hearing aids.

Sammy Maguire returned to Belfast, got married and had six children; three of them deaf. David said that Sammy didn't have much contact with his ex–form mates for a number of years, only appearing at the school's grand reunions; it was only when Facebook started a few years back that they all got back in touch properly. A dedicated family man, Sammy had worked in many different jobs and was currently a lorry driver.

Mark Cameron, said David, had worked in mental health for over twenty–five years. Married with three kids, he was also a counsellor for Deaf people with mental health problems; David mentioned that quite a number of Mark's clients had suffered the effects of poor education in oral or mainstream schools, as well as problems at home. Many had been deprived of the chance of developing language before the age of five because their parents couldn't sign, resulting in delayed language acquisition. Deaf children then weren't able to adequately communicate their feelings, which led to frustration, behavioural problems and, consequently, affected their mental wellbeing.

After a short toilet break, they regrouped outside in Chris' large back garden, complete with swimming pool. Standing on the patio, David breathed in the cool air and looked up at the clear night sky. Chris glanced at his watch: one o'clock.

'You tired?' David asked, noting Chris' glance. 'Shall I go back to my hotel ... ?'

'No, no, I'm fine, honest,' Chris shook his head, smiling. 'Oh, it's so good to see you again. I don't know why I never bothered to keep in touch for all those years. I guess I was probably too afraid, you know? Even after all this time, I still feel, um, a bit hurt, I think. I suppose I wanted to put my past behind me. But now ... now that you're here, it's kind of, like, a big slap on my face and I'm beginning to regret it now. The worst thing is, I loved Aaron. Not the romantic kind of love – unrequited – that I once had for him, but love for a friend. That bastard destroyed it, and that *really* hurt.'

Chris' shoulders slumped. He put his hands in his pockets and sighed. David patted his shoulder comfortingly.

'Do you want me to tell you about Brian Thompson?' he asked. Chris nodded silently. 'I don't know much about what happened to him after school. What I do know, though, is that Gary Portmore and Timothy Hutchinson – who's now a vicar – no longer have anything to do with him. I know he had a good job as a comic book artist for a few years. Hand drawn stuff, like. But when computers came along, he got sidelined; many others did too. I think he was unemployed for quite a long time until, I think about ten years ago, when he got a job as a community support worker for Deaf people with mental health issues. It wasn't the sort of job he wanted, but it paid the bills. I know all this because he was in a newspaper article back in, um, around 2005, I think. It was a long one, but I'll try to remember as much as I can. You see, Chris, Brian was sexually abused at his old school before he came to Ewing Hill Park.'

'What?!' Chris gasped, shaking his head. It was hard to imagine that his fiercest old adversary; a bullying, ignorant bastard like Basher could have been a vulnerable victim of one of life's ultimate betrayals. 'How come?' He folded his arms, interested.

'Well, he was about eight when this man called … um … Ray Grimes came to his school in east London as a handyman. St Bell's Primary School for the Deaf, it was called. Long since closed and razed down. Grimes soon started systemically sexually abusing the boys and girls there. Several of them for several years, Brian said. Grimes also married the headmistress, Marlette Bell. Chris, you remember we tied him up in the gym to help me get revenge on him?' Chris nodded; how could he ever forget that? 'Well, he relived the nightmare of his ordeal. He swore revenge on us … ' he trailed off.

After a moment to collect his thoughts, David resumed his story. One day, he said, Brian was escorting a client to Old Church in South London, a facility for Deaf people with mental health issues, and he met a woman who was a patient there. To his surprise, it was Melanie Tully, his childhood sweetheart, who he hadn't seen since leaving St Bell's. She had post–traumatic stress disorder because of the frequent sexual abuse she'd suffered from Grimes. She told him that their classmate, Reginald Adamson, had killed himself; not only because of the abuse, but also because of the terrible secondary mainstream education he'd had. Another of their old friends, Leigh Marshall, had also tried to commit suicide, but was saved and was now married with two kids that he was fiercely protective of. Others, like Brian and Melanie, were still trapped in their own psychological prisons of silence. They soon became a couple and made a difficult decision.

'To his credit,' David said, gazing into nowhere in the night, 'he and Melanie pushed for an investigation into the abuse with the hope of bringing Ray Grimes to justice. They managed to round up twenty–two of his survivors; there were many more, but they were either too frightened or didn't want to relive their ordeals all over again. There was a court hearing in London and the newspaper article I read came out shortly after that. Sadly, it didn't go well … '

The judge, David recalled, had decided that the case could not proceed. He ruled that bringing a prosecution against Ray Grimes was an "abuse of process", because the events happened so long ago. He noted that some of the key witnesses had died; the school was demolished and there was no surviving documentary evidence to support their claims. He felt that their memories alone could not be relied upon and that Grimes, who was in his eighties and had Parkinson's, would not be fit enough to stand trial. He also pointed out that the survivors had waited too long to bring this to the attention of the authorities.

The judge's comments angered Brian and the other survivors. Grimes had rights, they said, but so did Deaf people; they felt like they were at the bottom of the pile because of their deafness and the fact that they couldn't speak. They pointed out that it was difficult enough for hearing survivors of abuse to open up; even more so for Deaf survivors, who weren't allowed to use sign language at school. Brian claimed he had tried to tell a teacher on one occasion, when Grimes had taken Melanie off for his own pleasure, only to be slapped for signing, and subsequently suspended. He also claimed that when he was nine or ten, Grimes had savagely raped him, describing the black–bearded handyman as an evil, vicious paedophile who preyed on vulnerable deaf children, taking advantage of their inability to communicate. However, Marlette Bell–Grimes, who had retired to the countryside with Ray, accused them of telling slanderous lies about her sick, frail husband, saying how deeply hurt she was; she had devoted years to working with deaf children, after all.

'What's even more disturbing though,' David continued, 'is that during the investigation, they uncovered information about Grimes being arrested in late 1973, I think, for indecently assaulting two girls at the school. One of them had a dad who was a policeman. He made the arrest himself. Grimes pleaded guilty and asked for other, similar, offences to be taken into consideration. He blamed overwork and said none of the children were alarmed or upset. And … the local mayor had visited the school, and he spoke up for Ray Grimes! He said he'd visited the school a number of times and was always struck by how extremely happy the deaf children there seemed to be. So, in the end, Ray Grimes was just fined fifty pounds and was never jailed. He was ordered to stay away from the school for two years after the case, but he went back the next day. And, yes, he started it again.' David sighed. 'Marlette Bell–Grimes denied all knowledge of the case. Of course, this pissed the survivors off and I've heard they were considering taking legal action against the authorities for their failed duty of care. I don't know what's been happening since then, though. We've recently heard that Ray Grimes has died, but obviously, the survivors' suffering goes on.'

Chris bowed his head in disbelief. Although he still felt no warmth for Brian Thompson, he did feel sorry for him and the others. 'It's still happening around the world. Deaf children are very easy prey for abusers,' he said after a while.

'Yes, it is,' David agreed, becoming silent as he tried to remember something else. It escaped his mind, however, and he shrugged it off. 'Never mind. Anyway, things have improved a lot now. We're more vigilant, have better awareness and criminal record checks. Oh, that reminds me. Do you remember Justin Pope?' he gestured the outline of a cross and Chris nodded. 'Well, he and his wife – she's Deaf – were trying for children for years but they couldn't conceive. So, they applied to adopt or foster a deaf or hearing child, but they were turned down because they were Deaf. Luckily though, as you probably know, there was a successful campaign in the mid–nineties, I remember it well, and Deaf people are now allowed to adopt and foster. Aaron said you grew up in children's homes and foster homes. That must have been tough.'

'Yes, it was,' Chris said. He jerked his head in the direction of the kitchen. 'I'll make another coffee.'

They spent the next hour in the kitchen, reminiscing about their schooldays, laughing and cringing as they went along. David smiled as he remembered something.

'Do you remember Shaun Knight's video of Miss Stephenson's breasts?' he asked Chris, sniggering.

'Yeah, I was there, but I only saw the film a few times,' Chris grinned, revelling in the memory of the boys cramming into the tiny Hobbies Room to secretly watch the cine film projected on the wall over and over again, to much whooping and delight.

'You can see it again on YouTube,' David said, resting his bottom on the worktop. 'Shaun Knight converted it digitally and even cropped the image for a closer look. It's a bit blurry though, but still funny. It's had thousands of views!'

'How is he? Still making films?' Chris asked.

'He's still living in Cornwall with his wife; she's Deaf too. Two kids: one deaf and one hearing. He's made some great short films.' One sprang into mind, having seen it recently at a Deaf film festival. 'One was a really powerful documentary about deaf education in Cornwall. He made it because he's had serious problems with them over his deaf son's education. He and his wife wanted the boy to go to a signing Deaf school outside the county, because Cornwall's among the worst for Deaf education. The film showed parents who were worried sick about their deaf children's education. One even accused them of being like Nazis because they didn't care. There was a court case against them a few years ago … it was potentially a landmark test case that would have paved the way for other parents to sue their local education authorities for failing in their duty of care. But, it collapsed the day before the end of the trial because the key witness, who used to be a senior teacher of the deaf, and who'd agreed to testify for the prosecution, suddenly changed her statement to say they didn't fail in their duty of care. Apparently, she'd been threatened several times before and during the trial and they finally "got to her". The film also showed a really distressing account of a deaf boy who'd killed himself because he couldn't cope in his mainstream school. He had no support, wasn't allowed to sign, he was bullied and he was, you know, just so lost. Blamed his parents and the school for it. His death hit the national news and the Deaf community was really angry, of course, but nothing further came of it.'

'That sounds terrible,' Chris remarked solemnly.

'Yes, it was,' David shrugged. 'The issues are pretty much the same around the country. Only a few kids do well in mainstream. Like Penny and Charles Whittle's son.'

'Their son's deaf?' Chris took a packet of biscuits out of a cupboard and waved it at his friend. 'Still hungry?'

Walking over to Chris, David nodded. He took a biscuit from the pack and nibbled it. 'Penny Whittle wrote a book about it. I've read it. When Dan was diagnosed as deaf, the audiologists, ENT specialists, teachers of the deaf, the lot of them, gave Penny and Charles biased pro–oral information. Same old story, but, as teachers themselves, they had more sense. They knew oralism wouldn't work for Dan, so they were determined that he acquired BSL early and got a sign bilingual education. Leeds had good provision then, so Dan had to travel to a mainstream school there from his home somewhere in Yorkshire every day. He had Deaf teaching assistants who used BSL throughout his education – that's something that we're missing out on, you know. I've heard that so many mainstream schools prefer hearing CSWs over Deaf teaching assistants, even though somebody Deaf would be far more fluent in BSL, do a better job, *and* be a good Deaf role model! Anyway, Dan's never used hearing aids or his voice. He's got excellent qualifications; he got a first class degree in maths and was headhunted by a big technology firm! And well, he got two or three promotions in quick succession and now has a shit hot job.'

'All because he had sign bilingual education,' Chris munched his second biscuit as David took another from the pack. 'The sad thing is, parents often just believe what those professionals tell them, and stick to that belief, no matter what.

Why isn't the government doing something about this? Like, recognising BSL as a legitimate language? What's their problem?'

David finished his biscuit, declined the offer of another one, and thought about that for a moment. He took a quick glance at his watch: five to four. He was beginning to feel drained, but not too tired.

'You remember Gary Portmore?'

Chris nodded, putting the biscuits back in the cupboard and turning to David.

'Well, in case you didn't know, he's now James Eriswell's brother–in–law,' David said. 'He became a solicitor and then an MP. He gave a really interesting talk at a Deaf conference last year; Aaron and I went to it. He talked generally about his long battles with government over a few issues, including legal recognition of BSL. The sticking point is that BSL isn't a spoken language, so the government doesn't feel that they *can* recognise it legally, just acknowledge it simply as a language in its own right, which they did back in 2003. We had BSL marches with thousands of people before that, but they wouldn't listen. Another issue is the cost of implementing and financing the legal obligations that would come with formal recognition.'

'I've read somewhere that there's a European Charter for Regional or Minority Languages that includes sign language?' Chris queried.

'Yes, I believe so,' David answered, 'but if we wanted to use it on our government to force them to legally recognise BSL, we'd need to raise a lot of money first to cover the campaign and all the legal stuff. That's not the only problem, though; it's the attitude and, well, the mindset of the MPs and peers that needs changing. According to Gary, they seem to see spending thirty thousand pounds on a cochlear implant for each deaf baby or child as an one–off payment that solves the problem once and for all – after that, they think there's no need for communication support, replacement hearing aids and so on.'

Chris rolled his eyes. 'That's not always the case. Deaf children with cochlear implants still need support in schools!'

'I agree. Gary mentioned that;' David said, 'he's a cochlear implant user too; he went to a cochlear implant conference where a professor said there's *no* evidence that cochlear implants actually help deaf children to hear and speak and there's *no* difference between their outcomes and those of deaf children who wore hearing aids thirty or forty years ago. The research that claims cochlear implants improve their users' speech and the quality of their lives is all focused on carefully selected deaf children – a low percentage of the whole cochlear implant population – to help them to win more funding and support, and influence parents and politicians.'

'I've a friend in Sydney,' Chris latched on, 'who's recently broken up with his girlfriend. They're Deaf and they have a baby, also deaf. The girlfriend's hearing grandparents – her parents live in Cairns, so she's staying with her grandparents in Sydney – are demanding that the baby has a cochlear implant. The father refuses to allow it. Really, it's wrong to push for it.'

'They always read too much into it,' David agreed. He pointed at his own implant. 'Even with that, I still can't understand people when they speak to me from behind or on the phone; I just hear sounds. This doctor guy on television recently said that with a cochlear implant, a deaf person who previously couldn't hear a chainsaw going off next to them could go on to speak to a stranger on the phone! What crap!' He laughed incredulously.

Glancing at the kitchen clock, Chris saw that it was almost half past four; he was surprised at how quickly the night had passed. He sighed, shaking his head at David's "doctor guy"; that was overstating things a bit, he thought; this kind of controversy wasn't just in Britain, but also in Australia and the rest of the world. He didn't have a problem with cochlear implants as such – to him, they were simply enhanced hearing aids – he had Deaf friends who had them and they frequently used sign language. In America, he knew there were some Deaf parents with cochlear–implanted children, which had always been a controversy, yet they still used ASL as their first and natural language. As he and David had discussed earlier, it was the medical profession and pro–oral educationalists he had a problem with, because of their biased and misinformed influence.

Pushing away his thoughts, Chris beckoned for David to sit on the sofa in the living room.

'Tell me what happened to Ewing Hill Park,' Chris asked. 'You said earlier that James Eriswell left. Why?'

'Everything collapsed,' David said grimly. 'While the legal paperwork to buy the school and its land from the Ewing–Boyd Hill family was still being drawn up, Robert Denham suffered a heart attack during a board meeting towards the end of, um, 2004. He survived, though he had to step down as chairperson. You see, he'd already had two heart bypasses. Rumour has it that he had the heart attack during an argument with one of the board members, Del Talaro. He has a deaf daughter who went to Boyd Hill Grammar School years before it closed. We're not sure what the argument was about, but apparently it was linked to the sale. Del Talaro elected himself as acting chairman. When he came on board as a governor a few years before, he was all smiles and went along with everything that the school had in progress.'

'But let me guess, he wasn't?' Chris cut in, sensing the obvious. 'He was a secret oralist, right?'

'Yeah, correct,' David nodded, despondently. 'I think he strongly objected to the sale. By all accounts he was a clever and calculating man. We think he deliberately tried to provoke the heart attack, knowing Robert had a weak heart, but we've no proof, of course. After that, he ousted all governors who were either Deaf or supported James Eriswell, and brought in his own people – all oralists and medical professionals. Inevitably, a few months later, James Eriswell resigned. There was no way he could achieve his vision under Del Talaro. That shocked everyone! He maintained a vow of silence about it for four years, and then spilled the beans on his blog, with more in Aaron's book on the school's history. Have a read! Chapter thirty–eight: End of an Era.' David pointed at the iPad on the coffee table in front of them. 'I'll make us one last coffee.'

Lounging on the sofa, Chris read sections of the eBook that he'd downloaded earlier.

After James Eriswell's departure, Del Talaro appointed a hearing friend of his, Violet Hubbard; the former head teacher of a girl's college who had no prior experience with deaf children. She immediately banned signing throughout the school and ordered the hearing teachers to use their voices. The Deaf teachers either left in disgust, or were dismissed and replaced by hearing teachers of the deaf who couldn't sign. She also brought the FM system back to the classrooms and all students were made to wear their hearing aids at all times; they were punished if this rule was broken.

The Sixth Formers protested against these sudden yet oppressive changes, but were quashed and the ringleaders expelled. Most of the first year students didn't return to college for their second years as planned, and the student numbers dropped rapidly. The annual tuition fees for both the school and college tripled in order to meet the increased costs of employing extra staff, the technological aids and the higher cost of running everything. The school's numbers continued to decline year on year; not only because of the stronghold of mainstream education, but because of the financial and publicity woes that soon followed. The financial backing that was promised by wealthy former pupils who supported James Eriswell's vision was withdrawn. Lawsuits and tribunals flowed in against the school for unfair dismissals and unlawful discrimination, which contributed to an even bigger hole in the pot. The school's reputation was repeatedly tarnished by a series of negative articles, both printed and on the internet, in addition to its now terrible reputation in the Deaf community because of its return to oralism; as a result, parents and local education authorities were reluctant to send their pupils to the school. Its academic ratings dropped; its OFSTED performance grading too. Ultimately, like its sister school thirteen years earlier, Ewing Hill Park could no longer function, announcing its closure in January 2009. The doors closed for the last time the following March.

James Eriswell created a blog called *Surdania* on the day of the closure. Chris read a copy of his first post in the eBook.

DREAM SHATTERED BUT NOT GONE

So, the inevitable has happened.

For the last four years, I've kept a vow of silence.

Until now.

After 59 years, Ewing Hill Park School and College close their doors today. Del Talaro has destroyed everything that Donald Langston and I built over the years to make the school one of the best and most successful Deaf schools in Britain, because of his (hearing) arrogance, selfishness and blindness in trying to fix what wasn't broken.

When Del Talaro – questionably – became Chair of the governing board, it soon became clear that he was not all he seemed to be. I tried to reach a diplomatic compromise with him and his new oralist board, but it was clear that he would not help fulfil my dream.

I didn't resign. I was ousted.

The school and college were already on their knees financially because of steadily declining pupil numbers and increasing costs. Essentially, it was imperative that our ultimate dream of Britain's most prominent and highly–organised Deaf education establishment was achieved, in order not only to survive, but also for the future of Deaf people.

It is no surprise that this cruel twist of fate has ended this dream and, inevitably, Ewing Hill Park; in a spectacular fashion.

I'm no longer angry or bitter. Just sad.

Looking back to my five years as a pupil, ten years as a teacher and thirteen years as the headmaster of Ewing Hill Park, I'm immensely proud of what I have achieved for myself and everyone else.

But the British Deaf education system, as a whole, continues to be in crisis and is too fragmented. It's dominated by hearing educationalists, who stubbornly refuse to change or even acknowledge the problem. If they are concerned about its current state, then they need to work together with Deaf people, who are the real experts.

It is quite ironic that education and vulnerable children are among the key areas under the government's protection, but this does not seem to always apply to Deaf children and young people.

I think there is an urgent need for government to commission extensive, independent national research to explore the impact that the poor Deaf education system is having on deaf children's attainment; not just in terms of their educational achievements but also their social well–being and inclusion.

Also, it is crucial that the government legally recognises British Sign Language (BSL) as a true and natural language of the Deaf, so that it is protected from abuse, and to pave the way to better Deaf education, and thus to a better quality of life for Deaf people.

Many people may not realise this, but BSL is actually the second most used minority language in Britain after Gaelic, Welsh and even the hardly–spoken Cornish language – all already recognised by the government. Many other countries, even some in the Third World, have legally recognised their sign languages, so why not here?

"It is the fear of failure that drives you, but it is visualizing success that gives you the positive mindset and confidence to feel like you can accomplish anything".

– The above quote reminds me that Deaf people will not be disregarded and the immense power of sign language is not to be underestimated.

It may be the end of an era for us, but the dream and the legacy live on.

Posted by James Eriswell, Wednesday March 18, 2009

Chris silently put the device on the table and sat back on the sofa. Drinking the last of his coffee, David gazed at him expectantly.

'It's like that–'

'Yes, I know,' Chris interrupted. 'Milan 1880 all over again.'

'You know about that?'

'Only too well,' Chris half smiled. 'Those hearing people never listen and learn.'

David shook his head in weary agreement. 'It seems that history's always repeating itself.'

Chris sighed. He thought for a moment about how his old school had made him the person he was now. Something was bothering him, though. He turned to David.

'How many Deaf schools are left now?' he asked him.

'Um,' David looked up at the ceiling as if to collect the answer from it, then looked back at Chris. 'About twenty, I think. Only one each for Scotland and Northern Ireland. None in Wales. Two are boarding schools in England; both still oral – and still using headphones and microphones in classrooms. Others are day schools, some with boarding departments. Most of them use Total Communication; the rest use the sign bilingualism or are oral. Some had to be closed due to the age of their buildings and moved to new, modern schools. Generally, though, Deaf schools are few and far between now.'

David glanced at his watch: almost six o'clock. He yawned, exhausted by their marathon eighteen–hour chat. They both agreed to call it a night so that David could return to his hotel to get some sleep before they met up again later in the day. David called a cab, and when it came, they hugged once more.

Chris opened the front door to let David push open the screen door. They saw the cab waiting at the end of the short driveway, the sun rising in the distance behind it. As David began to walk down the steps, he turned to his old friend; a final thought coming to him.

'Oh, yes, now I know what I was trying to remember before.' David said, his tired brain igniting its last awake cell. 'You know that sicko, Ray Grimes? His name was really an alias, you know, like a second name?'

Chris leaned against the doorway, his body screaming for bed. 'Yeah, that can happen.'

'Yeah, well, he used his middle name and his mother's maiden name, Grimes. That only came to light in court; even his wife didn't know.'

'What was his real name then?'

'Thomas Raymond MacDonald,' David answered, failing to notice Chris' stunned look. 'Rumour has it he had a deaf son, but nobody knows who he was.' David shrugged. 'See you later.'

David turned and staggered down the driveway. Chris let the screen door swing back into his frozen face.

39

Final Resolution

"Behold, I am coming soon, bringing my recompense with me, to repay each one for what he has done. I am the Alpha and the Omega, the first and the last, the beginning and the end."
– REVELATIONS 22: 12–13

Chris retched, the bitter substance flowing fiercely from his mouth. Grasping the toilet basin, he heaved hard, trying to control his breathing. Perspiration streamed down his face and his head throbbed. He threw up again; he hoped this time would be the last; his stomach was easing down again.

Sitting on the bathroom floor, his back against the wall, he took short, sharp breaths. Closing his eyes, *Oh, Jesus fucking Christ,* he cursed to himself. He was divided about whether his sickness was a result of the food and drink he'd consumed, or the mind–numbing shock. Perhaps both, he thought. Resting his head against the wall, his hands on his lap, he thought about his past life. It was as if jigsaw pieces were coming together fast, finally forming the full picture for the first time in his life. The first thing that came into mind was the question Aaron had asked him while they were discussing Chris' troubled life at Aunt Barbara's house.

What are your mum and dad's names?

Sandra Matthaus and Tom MacDonald.

He never knew his father's middle name or his Scottish family – he was too young at the time. After all, he thought, communication with his parents had always been virtually non–existent. Wait a minute … does Aaron still remember the name? Did he make the connection when he found out Grimes' real name? David didn't seem to know that, so Aaron either must have forgotten or … kept quiet?

His mind flashed further back … vague and distorted projections of long forgotten memories swirled … his parents' atrocious fight in his bedroom. His mother went crazy over something, didn't she? Oh God, she must have caught him doing something. Molesting him. What else could it have been? And … she clawed his cheek with her sharp nails, didn't she? Blood spurted out from the wound. After he ran out – the last time he ever saw his father – his mother came running to her crying little boy and cuddled him; he could feel her crying too.

Chris scooped up his legs, rested his arms on his knees and bowed his head between them, beginning to weep. He was seven years old when his father left ... was that in 1971? Yes, it was around then. Wait a minute ... didn't David say Ray Grimes started to work at Brian's old school around that time? He couldn't remember exactly when his father left, but ... it must have been around that time. The black beard ... he must have grown it to cover his scars! Oh fuck, that sick and evil motherfucker! He had all those young, vulnerable deaf children at his mercy. He *knew* they couldn't communicate with hearing adults. Took advantage of the sign language ban. That made it pretty easy for him to do what he wanted with them. Chris knew that paedophilia was a sick psychological disease, but it still repulsed him. Especially when it was his very own flesh and blood.

Chris exhaled heavily, his mind still swimming with thousands of thoughts ... his mother's drinking ... did she start drinking because of what happened? Had one drink led to another and another and another until she couldn't fucking stop? Oh, Jesus, that was why! And drink had led her legs to open to Bob Sullivan. The beatings too. Everything went from bad to worse. Separated from his mother. Grew up in homes he never called home. All because of his father. He fucking destroyed the family. He suddenly remembered the only letter from his mother. When ... ? Oh yes, in the changing room where he'd kissed Aaron. He tried hard to remember what she'd written.

Everything went wrong because of your father. I know you might say I shouldn't blame him, but I do. I don't want to talk about him and I never will.

She never had talked to him about his father; she'd taken the horrible secret to her grave. Did Steve Lewison know? He must have: he'd been very protective of Chris, hadn't he? Chris closed his eyes, sighing inwardly. It was a kind of final resolution – the jigsaw pieces of his life, once lost, were now found and finally in place.

Chris splashed water on his face and scooped more water into his mouth. He washed away the sour taste of bile and spat into the porcelain sink. Bending over, he let the water drip from his face. After a short moment, he turned off the cold water tap and looked up into the large mirror in front of him. In the reflection, he saw himself and the bathroom behind him. He blinked at the hard light that was coming from the strip above the mirror.

His memory suddenly flashed back to the night of the school's Christmas party when his mother had turned up unexpectedly. She'd looked shocked when she saw him in the headmaster's office. He'd always assumed it was because he'd grown up so much and she hadn't seen him for almost half of his young life. But …

Oh my god … you've grown up! You look so much like your father.

Chris stared blankly at his own reflection, pensive. Then he remembered the violent fight he'd had with Basher in the corridor before the uprising against Mr Schneider.

Why do you hate me?

Because you remind me of someone I hate.

Had Basher seen some kind of resemblance between his adversary and his abuser? He had tried to strangle him, hadn't he? Basher had had murder in his eyes while he was doing it … and that had frightened him. Oh God, he'd *seen* Ray Grimes in him, only he didn't know they were father and son.

Resting his hands on the edge of the sink, his mind seemed to cloud over darkly; the image in front of him strangely obscured and he shivered suddenly. Cold perspiration broke out on his forehead, numbing coldness creeping down his spine. The air around him wasn't at all cold, but he felt like he was inside a cold meat store. Blinking, he tried to rid himself of the numbing coldness. Was it his eyes, or was the bathroom going dark behind him in the reflection? An unsettling oppressiveness seemed to form around him. His heart pounded hard; his breathing became laboured.

The figure in the reflection was smiling hauntingly at him. His white teeth beamed broadly through some kind of black mass and his eyes … cold and perverted eyes … stared back chillingly. The darkened bathroom in the reflection seemed to melt around this obscurity: it was laughing deliriously.

But Chris wasn't smiling. Or laughing.

'*Nooooo!*' Chris' anger exploded and he screamed loudly. He swung his fist hard at the mirror, which shattered into masses of cracks. The reflection became nothing but an array of streaky white lines. No more of whoever … that was. Gone.

Chris grimaced in pain as blood flowed from his knuckles and splattered into the sink.

He almost screamed when a hand suddenly touched his shoulder.

40

Grand Reunion

"[We] reject all resolutions passed at the ICED Milan Congress in 1880 that denied the inclusion of sign languages in educational programmes for the Deaf children / students … [We] acknowledge and sincerely regret the detrimental effects of the Milan conference, and … [we] call upon all Nations of the world to remember history and ensure that educational programmes accept and respect all languages and all forms of communication."

– CLAIRE ANDERSEN, Chair of the 21st International Congress on Deaf Education in Vancouver, Canada, 2010; 130 years after the 2nd such Congress, in Milan in 1880. This was a result of 30 years of campaigning for an apology and rejection of all the Eight Resolutions passed.

He whirled round.

David retracted his hand, startled by Chris' sudden reaction to the touch. 'Whoa, easy, man!'

Chris blinked, the haunting memory spinning away into the recesses of his mind. Closing his eyes briefly, he sighed in relief, although still trembled slightly.

'Are you okay?' David asked, concern on his face. 'You seemed … a little lost there for a minute.'

Chris nodded, although his heart was still racing. He took in his surroundings, aware that more people had gathered around him, studying and commenting on him in disbelief. He felt awkward at being the centre of attention. Studying their faces, he realised didn't know most of them, although he thought he recognised Shaun Knight, Derek Ferguson, Duncan Nielson and, unmistakably, Tom Quillot, because of his white hair. Suddenly, a short man pushed his way through, followed by a taller man. Chris thought the smaller one with brown hair must have been a few years younger than him; the taller one with thinning blond hair was much older. Despite their height differences, they shared similar facial features. The short man gazed up at Chris, obviously now believing what he'd just been told, and beamed broadly. Chris recognised him instantly: that infectious, impish grin was hard to forget.

'Toby Eriswell?' Chris asked.

Toby nodded then pounced on him and they hugged. Toby broke away, looking up at Chris in delight, and turned to the other man. 'That's him! Chris Matthaus!'

The man turned to Chris, his face bursting into a pleasant smile; he extended his hand. Shaking it, Chris frowned; he'd never seen this man before.

'This is my brother, James,' Toby introduced.

'The boy who changed the school!' The former Ewing Hill Park headmaster exclaimed in sign with his free hand, his other hand still shaking Chris'. 'It's a great honour to have finally met the legend. We must meet up again very soon as I'd *love* us to have a chat and perhaps persuade you to do an interview for my Surdania blog!'

Dean turned, having just seen someone further down the churchyard. Chris' eyes followed his old school friend, who was hurrying over to a rotund man who was almost bald and wearing sunglasses. His left hand was tucked around another man's arm, while a white cane hung down from a strap on his right wrist. As they walked on, Dean rudely grabbed the man's arm from the other man, quickly put his right hand under the man's left hand, signed his name sign and told the man to come with him.

As he watched Dean playfully drag Matthew Burke across the gravel path towards him, his white cane swinging to and fro from its strap, Chris remembered an interesting, but tragic, fact in Geraldine Stephens' book, which he'd read while staying at David's house. After his diagnosis, Geraldine had tried to find out as much as possible about deafness and how to communicate with deaf babies. She came across the John Tracy Clinic in America, which was an oralist organisation, and subscribed to its monthly distance learning courses. It turned out that John was the son of the Hollywood legend, Spencer Tracy, and he had Usher syndrome. In spite of his parents' efforts, John was never good at lipreading or speech, and his lipreading skills became worse as he began to lose his sight. So the oralist approach was a complete failure for him, but that didn't change his parents' views. After they'd died, John was kept sequestered at home under the care of his sisters. Many years later, the sisters finally agreed to hire an ASL teacher to teach John tactile ASL. Unfortunately, John died before he could finally expand his social life and get to know other people like himself. Reading that had really brought it home to Chris how important it was for Usher and deafblind people to have sign language or some other form of tactile communication, rather than relying solely on lipreading and speaking.

Dean positioned a confused Matthew in front of Chris and began to explain to his best friend in hands-on BSL, but Chris stopped him. He put his own right hand under Matthew's left, slowly lifting it as if to hold hands. Chris stared into the sunglasses. Matthew registered the man, but his facial expression told Chris that his remaining sight couldn't decipher his face. Chris remembered he had to tell him his name as many Usher and deafblind people had trouble identifying people's faces. Looking at Matthew briefly, he felt a sense of sadness and sympathy towards him even though he knew he shouldn't.

'It's me, Chris,' Chris finally fingerspelled his name into Matthew's left hand, meaning conveyed by touch, then he lifted their hands towards his head. With his hand closed, he circled both of their hands around his head. '*Scrubhead*. You invented it, remember?' he signed.

With his other hand, Matthew slowly pushed up his sunglasses, blinking a few times as his eyes slowly adjusted to the brightness before finally registered his long–lost form mate. He shrieked loudly, opening his arms, and crashed his body against Chris'. Chris returned the embrace tightly.

David suddenly raised his hand and waved at someone above the heads of the crowd. Chris broke away from Matthew and turned to see who he was waving at.

Chatting into a mobile phone, a man stepped out of the church, swung his head in the direction of David's call and walked briskly over, still talking.

Chris recognised him as the sign language interpreter who had interpreted the service. As he approached, Chris was able to take a good look at him; he hadn't earlier on. He was the same age as Chris, with tidy brown hair and a goatee beard. Though quite lean, he had a small paunch that was visible through his open suit jacket. He still had that brassy, no–nonsense attitude about him, a feature that Chris had never forgotten. Chris smiled widely in anticipation. The man hung up, put his mobile in his inside pocket and greeted David.

'Hello David,' the interpreter said, 'how was your trip down–'

David cut him short, pointing at Chris next to him. The man turned to Chris and stared at him. Chris grinned even more, anticipating the moment with relish. The man shook his head, perplexed, as he tried to put a name to the man in front of him.

'Don't I know you ... ?' he muttered.

'Chris Matthaus!' came David's impatient voice.

Hearing this, Jamie Stephens' mouth dropped.

'Hi Jamie,' Chris signed his *Elvis microphone* name sign.

'Fu–!' Jamie clammed up, quickly turning back to the church, apologising silently before turning back to Chris. Their arms were around each other within a second. After a long and emotional embrace, Jamie broke away. 'I'm so pleased to see you! Aaron's been trying to find you for years ... ' he paused, glancing around the watching crowd before returning to him. ' ... you haven't seen him yet, have you?'

Chris shook his head.

'I think I just saw him and his wife Suzanne inside,' announced David, pushing his way through the crowd.

'We're going to have a big piss–up at The Boars, that pub down the road, later,' Dean pointed in its direction excitedly and slapped Chris' back. 'We're gonna have one fucking big grand reunion!'

'Wish Steven Clarke could be with us today,' Sammy bemoaned. 'Jamon Cranley too. Bet they're looking down at us, so happy that we're all reunited!'

'And Lester Morrison's looking through the bars,' Mark said sarcastically, gesturing an invisible pair of bars.

Chris glanced at the people around the churchyard, squinting when he saw someone in particular. 'Excuse me.' He headed away.

Striding down the long, wide gravel path towards the far end of the churchyard, Chris passed some people he thought he recognised; Miles McShane talking to Penny and Charles Whittle, who were all in their mid–sixties. He glanced at two men standing signing to one another over a headstone and recognised one of them – those arched eyebrows and mournful eyes could only belong to the Reverend Timothy Hutchinson. Although much older, he'd hardly changed; the other man was Gary Portmore. Chris turned right, passing three men standing on an intersecting path between some graves, signing to each other. One of them, a bald man in his early fifties with a small beard around his mouth, looked like Dwight Greenland, but Chris couldn't be so sure, deciding that he'd go over to him later and say hello. He had no idea who the other two were, although one of them was black. Conor Blackwell? He looked to be in his forties, so that must be him, he thought.

Chris arrived at the end of the path and stood in front of a man who was standing by a low concrete wall near some shrubbery. The black jacket he was wearing seemed to be a size or two too small for his flabby body. Holding a cigarette between yellow–stained fingers, he drew on it; staring into nowhere. He'd not changed that much, even after thirty–two years, though he was now bald, plump and wrinkled.

Sensing his presence, Brian Thompson turned to face Chris, who was standing a few feet away.

He froze.

Chris stared down hard at his old adversary, who was now a good few inches shorter than him. Brian stared back, his mouth slowly dropping open and his face turning white. He shuddered, quietly shaking his head in apparent fear and disbelief. Chris wondered if Brian was seeing his old foe or the ghost of Ray Grimes from beyond the grave – without the black beard.

Before Brian could react, he found himself flying backwards, his stout arms flailing, and crashing against the low wall behind him. Then, his body slid down, slumping on the ground. Blood began to trickle from his nostrils and he lay there, dazed.

Chris rubbed his slightly–scarred knuckles to soothe their throbbing. He breathed out heavily, almost crying. Closing his eyes, his mind swirled back to the pain and animosity that had tormented him for years. Now ... he felt a sense of retribution; an enormous weight was lifting off his shoulders and the heaviness on his chest was gradually slipping away. He knew what he'd just done was unnecessary, but he'd never felt so good.

With one last look at the still stunned former head boy, he turned round.

And he stopped.

A man in a black suit stood midway down the long gravel path; his arms hanging loosely at his sides, his legs wide apart and his head slightly turned, staring silently at Chris. The whole crowd outside the church stood in distant silence, watching the two men.

As though in slow motion, Aaron walked towards Chris just as Chris walked towards him. As they came closer together, Chris saw that although older, taller and seasoned, Aaron had hardly changed; he still had blond hair, albeit much shorter; still had those celestial blue eyes behind his oval spectacles; still had those kissable lips; he was still an inch or so shorter than him, and still had that intelligent and amenable personality about him.

They stopped a few feet away from each other, their gaze still lingering on each other. Feeling as though the whole world was watching them and holding its breath, Aaron struggled to find his first words. He lowered his head and closed his eyes to reflect. How could this be possible? All those years of searching for him; it had almost become an obsession. He'd searched high and low around the world through various sources, following the rumour mills and trawling the internet. But each time, he'd come to a dead end. He had almost given him up for dead. Now, out of the blue, of all times and places in the world, the only best friend he'd ever had was now standing right there. He opened his eyes and looked up at Chris.

'It's been a long time,' Aaron said, finally.

'Too long,' Chris said solemnly.

'But how? I mean ... how ... ' Aaron trailed off, shaking his head, as he couldn't find the words. He glanced behind Chris to see that Brian was now coming round on his knees, nursing his bloody nose. Aaron gazed back at Chris quizzically.

'It's okay,' Chris said, sensing Aaron's inquisitiveness. 'David told me everything.'

'What? He did?' Aaron frowned in surprise. He glanced behind to see David standing next to Suzanne amongst the crowd in the distance. David quickly waved back, indicating that he would explain later. Aaron turned back to Chris, still bewildered.

Suppressing his escalating emotions, Chris took a step forward, his mind racing with a thousand thoughts; but only one thought hovered high above them. Not a thought, really, but an unanswered question that had stayed with him ever since he'd stepped out through the doors of Ewing Hill Park School.

'I've been waiting for thirty–two years to ask you this again,' Chris slowly extended his right hand. 'Are we … friends again?'

Aaron's eyes slowly rolled down to the waiting hand as he thought about it. He still remembered, too. He slowly lifted his right hand, his palm gently touching Chris', their fingers slowly wrapping in a feeble grip. Their gazes met.

Then, Aaron slowly lifted his other hand, closing his middle three fingers; leaving only his thumb and little finger visible.

'Maybe,' Aaron repeated the same answer, slowly shaking that hand.

He smirked.

Grasping hands tightly, Chris and Aaron pulled themselves into a firm embrace, their chests crushing together. Chris slammed both arms around Aaron; Aaron followed suit. The sides of their faces pressed tight together, their bodies rocking as they hugged tightly, not wanting to let go of each other again.

Tears flowed down Chris' cheeks. Aaron, too, burst into a flood of tears and sobbed loudly; his long suppressed emotions finally out. He held Chris even tighter.

Chris opened his eyes, tears still flowing, feeling as though the world was spinning fast around them. And then, he stared up at the sky, laughing with joy.

A Note from the Author

Although *Innocents of Oppression* is a work of fiction, much of it is based on fact and our people's real–life experiences in Deaf schools and mainstream settings.

Opinions on this book will differ. However, I believe many Deaf people will relate to aspects of the story. What cannot be ignored is the fact that the deaf education in Britain hasn't changed much over the past two centuries.

Descriptions of the Milan Congress (more on this later), the Rueben, Lewis and Warnock Reports and many other things associated with deaf education are all true events.

Ewing Hill Park School, its Waltbridge location and the entire timeline are fictional. Elmfield, Gallaudet and the Model Secondary School for the Deaf do exist, however. The latter two actually used ASL in classrooms during the 1970s and still do so today – something that never happened in Britain back then, and in many cases, still does not happen at all to this day.

Many of the incidents relating to oralism throughout the story may seem absurd, ridiculous and parodic. Unfortunately, however, they were inspired by real–life experiences of the many people that I interviewed; some of my own included, too. I was once asked whether this book is anti–oralism. It isn't: it simply highlights the issue, from both Deaf and hearing perspectives, as you'll have already read.

In *End of an Era,* David Wheeley's accounts of the state of deaf education in Britain are based on recent anecdotal evidence. The figures included, such as those relating to deaf children's GCSE standards, are available at the time of writing. I could have written a lot more about this, but time and space did not allow.

I would also like to stress that the comments about cochlear implants in the above chapter do not reflect my own personal or political views; they are based on some of the views and experiences that some parents of deaf children have shared with me.

Although much of the story is based on fact, some aspects are purely fictional and used for dramatic effect, such as the Phantom, which serves as a basis for Chris' expulsion. However, the boys' revolt in *The Darkest Hour* is based on a true–life incident: I experienced something similar at my old school, albeit with a different, yet equally disturbing conclusion.

Basher's sexual abuse story in *Prison of Silence* is based on a 2005 newspaper article which was written about systematic sexual abuse that went on at a primary school for the Deaf in East London between the late 1950s and early 1970s. Writing that story was very tough, but importantly, it highlights one of the book's strongest themes: the language and communication barriers faced by many deaf children who aren't allowed to use their natural language; sign language. Although there is better awareness and vigilance when it comes to child abuse now, this issue still remains.

With the exception of people from history, all characters in the story are fictional; based on people's real–life experiences and backgrounds.

The Milan 1880 Congress proceedings described by Hubert in *Repercussions* are real. The (extremely rare) book by Kinsey exists. The arrogant and eloquent nature of the congress is an accurate reflection: I simply summarised parts of the book (The full version is at milan1880.com).

The success on sign bilingualism described in *The Aftermath,* when Ewing Hill Park converts to sign bilingualism, is based on some successful sign bilingual Deaf schools in England, America and Scandinavia. Even though there is proven success in sign bilingualism, as evidenced by research, I was unable to give statistics in this book because there is no national system put in place that compares deaf children's' attainment levels in different educational settings.

The school's conversion and ascension, post–Schneider, is, in a way, an allegory of the deaf education in United Kingdom, which is in a desperate need of a change for the better.

Shortly after I had finished writing this book, the Government announced changes to its provision for children with special educational needs, thus giving parents of deaf and disabled children the option of controlling their own allocated budgets, using them to pay for their chosen support rather than battling with their local education authorities. Statements of special educational needs will be scrapped in 2014 and replaced with individual Education, Health and Care Plans. In principle, this may be of some benefits, but it doesn't solve many of the long–standing wider issues described in this book.

Finally, going back to the Conrad Report, let's talk about this. In *Chris' New Haircut,* Mrs Munnings explained about *The Deaf School Child.* If this four–year research was commissioned by the government that exposed the failure of oralism and the lies by the oralists, then why has nothing been done about it? The observation is that this report was published at the time when there was a trend for mainstreaming as a result of the Warnock Report, and upon realising that they couldn't win the sign vs speech war and that their lies would be laid bare, the oralists seized the opportunity to advocate the right for a deaf child to be integrated into hearing schools and to break up the Deaf schools to maintain their stronghold on the soul–destroying philosophy that deaf children must be denied access to sign language, deaf adults and the deaf community. *The Deaf School Child,* however powerful and groundbreaking, sadly had the opposite effect and, because of this, deaf children in education will always be the innocents of oppression.

I do hope you enjoyed reading it.

Nick Sturley
25th June 2012

Acknowledgements

I would like to express my eternal gratitude and appreciation to everyone who has helped with the book, in one way or other. They have given me confidence, hope and encouragement with their support, contributions and consent. Without them, it would not have been possible to write this book.

This book was proofread and edited by TeamHado.com with the help of a grant from The Author Welton Foundation, which is administrated by the Society of Authors in conjunction with the Authors' Foundation. I would like to take the opportunity to give my heartfelt thanks to Shane Gilchrist for his services for ensuring that there are no historical and cultural inaccuracies in the book.

actionDEAFNESSBooks

Innovative and progressive, Action Deafness Books is the UK's leading publisher and online retailer of books on D/deafness and D/deaf issues. By D/deaf people, for D/deaf and hearing alike, Action Deafness Books works to deliver a publishing platform that enables people to put their experiences and writing into the public domain. To empower D/deaf people to write, to record and use language – at the same time, allowing hearing people to learn of the D/deaf experience through the works we publish.

But what is more, we work to promote and foster integration between D/deaf and Hearing publishers, distributors and booksellers; to bring the two worlds together in a unique association of interests and one that facilitates learning, the development of new ideas and the sharing of best practice.

We're hugely excited with our success to date - we've worked with the likes of Jacqueline Wilson, Julia Donaldson and Joyce Dunbar; we've published new writing by authors such as Nick Sturley, Tamsin Coates, Ken Carter and Dr. Harold Silver. Our U Sign brand has become an instant hit and we've commissioned a range of children's adventure books – all of which feature D/deaf children as heroes!

From the London Book Fair to the Leicester Literary Festival, the Library Show to the DocWoof Film Festival, we've engendered D/deaf awareness and allowed D/deaf people to be full and participant members of the literary world!

It's an exciting journey we're on and we want you to be part of it! If you are a D/deaf, hard of hearing, deafened or deafblind author with existing work in print or if you aspire to be a published author, then do get in touch – we want to hear from you!

Contact us at: adbooks@actiondeafness.org.uk

Visit: www.actiondeafnessbooks.org.uk

Follow us on Twitter @ActionDeafBooks